The Golden Lotus

JIN PING MEI

金 瓶 梅

VOLUME 2

Lanling Xiaoxiaosheng (Pseudonym)

A translation from the Chinese by Clement Egerton,
with the assistance of Shu Qingchun (Lao She)
With a new introduction by Robert Hegel

TUTTLE Publishing

Tokyo | Rutland, Vermont | Singapore

Published by Tuttle Publishing, an imprint of Periplus Editions (HK) Ltd.

www.tuttlepublishing.com

Copyright © 2011 by Periplus Editions (HK) Ltd.

Based on the edition first published in 1939 by Routledge & Kegan Paul Ltd.
Pinyinized and corrected for this first Tuttle edition.

Library of Congress Cataloging-in-Publication Data

Xiaoxiaosheng.
 [Jin ping mei ci hua. English]
 The golden lotus = Jin ping mei / Lanling Xiaoxiaosheng (pseudonym) ;
a translation from the Chinese by Clement Egerton, with the assistance
of Shu Qingchun (Lao She). —1st Tuttle ed.
      p. cm.
 ISBN 978-0-8048-4170-2 (v. 1 : pbk.)—ISBN 978-0-8048-4171-9 (v. 2 : pbk.)
 1. China—Social life and customs—960–1644—Fiction. 2. Domestic
fiction. I. Egerton, F. Clement C. (Frederick Clement Christie)
II. Lao, She, 1899–1966. III. Title. IV. Title: Jin ping mei.
 PL2698.H73C513 2011
 895.1'346—dc22   2010049040

ISBN 978-0-8048-4171-9

Distributed by

North America, Latin America & Europe
Tuttle Publishing
364 Innovation Drive
North Clarendon, VT 05759-9436 U.S.A.
Tel: 1 (802) 773-8930; Fax: 1 (802) 773-6993
info@tuttlepublishing.com
www.tuttlepublishing.com

Asia Pacific
Berkeley Books Pte. Ltd.
61 Tai Seng Avenue #02-12, Singapore 534167
Tel: (65) 6280-1330; Fax: (65) 6280-6290
inquiries@periplus.com.sg
www.periplus.com

First Tuttle edition
15 14 13 12 11   6 5 4 3 2 1   0611TP

Printed in Singapore

Contents

List of Principal Characters

LI GUIJIE (Cassia) or **GUIJIE**, a singing girl, niece of Ximen's Second Lady, sister of Li Guiqing

LI JIAO'ER (Picture of Grace), Ximen's Second Lady; later wife of Zhang the Second

LI MING, a young musician, brother of Li Guijie

LI PING'ER (Lady of the Vase), wife of Hua Zixu, later Sixth Lady of Ximen

LIN, LADY, a lady of quality, mother of Wang the Third and mistress of Ximen

LIU, "Old Woman," a procuress

MENG YULOU (Tower of Jade) or **YULOU**, Third Lady of Ximen; later, wife of Li Gongbi

PING'AN, boy of Ximen

PAN JINLIAN (Golden Lotus) or **JINLIAN**, originally a singing girl, later wife of Wu Da, and afterwards Fifth Lady of Ximen

PAN, "Old Woman," mother of Jinlian

PANG CHUNMEI (Plum Blossom) or **CHUNMEI**, maid to Wu Yueniang and later to Pan Jinlian; afterwards wife of Major Zhou

QITONG, boy of Ximen

QINTONG, boy of Meng Yulou; later lover of Pan Jinlian

QIUJU (Chrysanthemum), kitchen maid of Pan Jinlian

RUYI'ER (Heart's Delight), or Zhang the Fourth, nurse of Guan'ge

SHUTONG, Zhang Song, secretary to Ximen

SONG HUILIAN (Wistaria), wife of Laiwang and mistress of Ximen

SUN GUAZUI or **SUN TIANHUA**, or Crooked-headed Sun, associate of Ximen and member of his brotherhood

SUN XUE'E (Beauty of the Snow) or **XUE'E**, originally a maid in Ximen's household; afterwards Ximen's fourth wife; also known as the Kitchen Lady

WANG, a Buddhist nun

WANG, "Old Woman," a procuress

WANG CAI (Wang the Third), a young nobleman; son of Lady Lin

WANG JING, brother of Wang Liu'er, later servant of Ximen

WANG LIU'ER (Porphyry), wife of Han Daoguo and mistress of Ximen

WEN BIGU, a dissolute scholar, secretary of Ximen

WEN, "Old Woman," a procuress

WU "THE IMMORTAL," a fortune-teller

WU, "Uncle," or Wu the Elder, brother of Wu Yueniang

WU DA, brother of Wu Song and first husband of Jinlian

WU DIAN'EN, friend of Ximen and member of his brotherhood

WU SONG, brother of Wu Da, and avenger of his murder

WU YIN'ER (Silver Maid), mistress of Hua Zixu, adopted as ward by Li Ping'er

WU YUENIANG (Moon Lady), or the Great Lady, Ximen's principal wife

WU ZONGJIA, abbot of the Temple of the Jade Emperor

XIA YANLING, a magistrate, friend of Ximen

XIAOGE, posthumous son of Ximen by Wu Yueniang

XIAOYU (Tiny Jade), maid of Wu Yueniang; later, wife of Daian

XIE XIDA, friend of Ximen and member of his brotherhood

XIMEN QING, the central figure of this book, the owner of a considerable estate at Qinghe, and later a magistrate

XIMEN DAJIE (Orchid), daughter of Ximen and wife of Chen Jingji

XIUCHUN (Hibiscus), maid to Li Ping'er and later to the Second Lady

XUE, a eunuch of the Imperial Household, friend of Ximen

XUE, "Old Woman," a procuress

YANG GUANGYAN, also Yang the Elder or Iron Fingernails, manager of one of Ximen's shops

YING BAO, eldest son of Ying Bojue

YING BOJUE, friend of Ximen and member of his brotherhood; known as Beggar Ying

YINGCHUN (Welcome Spring), maid of the Sixth Lady, later of Wu Yueniang

YING'ER (Jasmine), daughter of Wu Da by his first wife and stepdaughter of Pan Jinlian

YUN LISHOU, friend of Ximen and member of his brotherhood

YUXIAO (Autumn), maid of Wu Yueniang.

ZHANGJIE, Qiao Zhangjie, infant daughter of Madam Qiao, betrothed to Guan'ge

ZHANG SHENG, servant of Major Zhou

ZHENG AIXIANG (Perfume) or **AIXIANG**, a singing girl, sister of Zheng Feng and Zheng Aiyue

ZHENG AIYUE (Moonbeam) or **AIYUE**, a singing girl

ZHENG FENG, a young actor

ZHINGQIU, maid of Wu Yueniang

ZHOU, Major, later General Zhou, neighbor of Ximen

ZHU SHINIAN, friend of Ximen and member of his brotherhood;

THE GOLDEN LOTUS

CHAPTER 54

Ying Bojue Gives a Party

Precious wine is worth a fortune
Let not the wine cups, then, stay idle in the hand
In the presence of the flowers.
Rise and dance and drink with the flowers.
The flowers are silent
They know men love them.

Let us not say farewell till we have drunk our fill.
Look at the flowers
Already one is faded.
Yet, though the flowers fade
Next year they will be as beautiful again.
So much cannot be said of these fair maidens.

It was arranged between Nun Wang, Li Ping'er and Wu Yueniang that the religious ceremony should be performed next day. Yueniang sent all the necessary things to the temple. She said to Chen Jingji: "Tomorrow the Sixth Lady is making intercession for a blessing on her child, and you must go to the service." But Jingji said:

"Father is going to the gardens outside the city, and I shall have to look after the shop. It would be better to ask someone else to go to the ceremony." As a matter of fact, Jingji, hearing that Ximen Qing was going to a party with Ying Bojue, thought it would be an excellent opportunity for him to amuse himself with Pan Jinlian. Yueniang believed that he really was going to look after the shop, so she did not press him any further. She told Shutong to go to the service.

While Ximen Qing, Ying Bojue and Chang Zhijie were still talking, Qintong came back. "I have been for the two singing girls," he said. "Wu Yin'er is not well. She will not be able to go tomorrow, and Han Jinchuan will take her place."

"You had better go and tell Dong Jiao'er," Ximen Qing said. Chang declared that as they were going outside the city they did not need a second girl. The two men went away.

The next day, Ximen Qing got up before dawn. Yueniang had arranged breakfast for him and, as soon as he had eaten it, he got into a sedan chair and went to the temple of Guanyin for the beginning of the service. Nun Wang came to the temple gate to meet him.

The nun read the prayers, and afterwards Ximen Qing went to change his clothes. Tea, cakes and fruits were brought for him, but he took only a mouthful of tea. Then he went back to his chair, bidding Shutong stay for the remainder of the service. When he reached home, the sun had only just risen, but Ying Bojue and Chang Zhijie had already arrived.

Ximen Qing laughed at them. "Who ever heard of invitations for breakfast?" he said. "It is true I am not busy today, but we can't go till afternoon."

"You don't understand, Brother," Ying Bojue said. "Twenty *li* outside the city there is a park belonging to a eunuch. It is beautiful and it is quiet. But it is so big that it would take two days at least to appreciate all its beauties. We must go early and spend all day there."

"Brother," Chang Zhijie said, "you have nothing particular to do today. That is why we came so early. Let us start at once."

"If you will have it so," said Ximen, "you go first and I will join you there."

The two men set out, but, sending the attendants in advance, they themselves went to the bawdy house and waited for Han Jinchuan to go with them. Ying Bojue had arranged for refreshments and engaged two actors.

Some time after Bojue had gone, Ximen Qing got into his sedan chair and went out of the city.

A thousand trees cast a deep shadow
And a brook meanders through them.
White walls enclose the ever-blooming flowers
And pleasant houses screen the quiet landscape.
Peach flowers blossoming at Wuling
Make the fisherman lose his way.
Plum blossoms flowering on the Yu Mountains
And the poets exchange verses in the sunshine.
It is paradise on earth.

Ximen Qing could not help exclaiming at the beauty of the scenery. He got out of his sedan chair and went into the gardens. Ying Bojue and Chang Zhijie came to welcome him, and they went together to an arbor. Han Jinchuan and the actors kowtowed to him. Tea was served.

Bojue would have had wine, but Ximen said: "There is no hurry. Let us take a stroll together." He took Han Jinchuan's hand and Ying Bojue led the way. They went to a verandah, then, following the vermilion railings, came to a place where there were many willow trees and an arbor of roses. They passed the Taihu stone and the Pavilion of the Pine Winds. So they came to the Pavilion of Unusual Characters. Behind this were about thirty plum trees, and among them a small high building called the Tower of the Plums. In this were many poems written by famous men. Ximen Qing studied them attentively. They went to the peony bed, where there were many different kinds of rare peonies. Then they turned to the north, and here was the bamboo grove with a small pavilion with the sign "Listen to the rustling of the bamboos," and a small arbor called the Coming of the Phœnix. The signs were all written by men of great renown for their skill with the brush. On the right was a goldfish pond and, on the bank, a small arbor with a sign: "Here you may enjoy the water." They leaned on the red railings for a while and watched the goldfish swimming about in the water. They made the pond seem like an embroidered coverlet. Ximen Qing was especially pleased with this. But Ying Bojue led him to another high building. This was the "Tower for Listening to the Moon." There were many poems by famous men here also, and panels of carved wood painted in characters of green. They went down from the building and turned towards the east. There they saw a great artificial mound with a cave in it called the Cave of the Eight Immortals. In the cave was a marble chess table. Iron flutes and brass long flutes hung upon the walls. It was a place where immortals might have dwelled. When they came out of it, they climbed the mound and from its summit could see the whole extent of the garden.

They had walked for some time, and Chang Zhijie said to Ximen Qing: "Brother, you must be tired. Let us rest in the arbor before we start out again."

"But we haven't been around one-tenth of the garden," Ximen Qing said. "How can we say that we are tired? Don't you know that sedan chair men walk a hundred *li* day?"

They laughed but went to the arbor. Ximen Qing took the place of honor with Chang Zhijie on one side of him and Ying Bojue on the other. Han Jinchuan sat beside Ximen "I must offer you my most sincere thanks for all your trouble," Ximen said to his hosts.

"Brother, it is not worth mentioning," said Bojue. "This is but a poor cup of wine that I am able to offer you."

They drank together, then the two actors came before them. They took their instruments and sang a new song: "Every Word Is Exquisite, Like a Pattern of Flowers." They sang very sweetly, and their voices lingered. Ximen Qing praised them. "It is a pity they are boys," Chang Zhijie said. "If they were girls, no price would be too high for them."

"If they were girls," Ximen Qing said, "we should have asked them to sit down before this. We should not have allowed them to stand and sing."

"Brother," Bojue said, "you are an officer to the manner born, and what you say always bears the stamp of authority."

Everybody laughed. They drank their wine, and Bojue, taking a large cup, suggested that they should play the game of giving orders. Ximen was not anxious to begin, but Bojue pressed him, and at last he agreed. "I will take the words 'Wind,' 'Flower,' 'Snow' and 'Moon.' I will begin; Brother Chang shall be next; then our host, and, lastly, Han Jinchuan. Each must make a verse and bring into it one of my four words. When he begins, he must drink a cup; and, if he fails, he must drink a second cup and tell a story. If the story is a poor one, he must tell another. I will begin." He took his cup and drank it. "'The clouds are few, the wind gentle. It is nearly noon.' Now, Brother Chang, it is your turn."

Chang drank his cup and said: "Chasing the flowers and following the willows, I crossed the stream." Then it was the turn of the host. Ying Bojue drank his cup of wine, but he seemed dazed and could not get out a word.

"Brother Ying," Ximen Qing said, "you must pay your forfeit and drink another cup."

"Let me think a moment," Bojue said. He racked his brains, and Ximen asked him again. "Of the glory of Spring," he began, "a few degrees have been revealed."

Ximen Qing roared with laughter. "That doesn't include a single one of my words," he cried. "That verse won't do. You'll have to drink two cups."

They called for Bojue's story.

"Once there was a scholar on his way to the Capital," Bojue began. "His boat was anchored in the Yangzi. At nightfall he asked the boatman to go and anchor somewhere else, for, he said, 'There are bandits in this place.' 'Where?' said the boatman. 'Don't you see that inscription on the stone tablet there, "Bandits on the river"?' The boatman laughed and said: 'That isn't "bandits on the river." How could you make such a mistake? It is not "bandit" but "poem".' 'Well,' said the scholar, 'they both look alike to me.' "

"I don't believe any scholar would make such a mistake," Ximen Qing said, laughing.

"Brother Ying," said Chang Zhijie, "you must drink ten big cups."

"Why?" said Ying Bojue, astonished.

"Think for yourself," Chang Zhijie said.

Ximen Qing was reputed to be the wealthiest man in all Shandong, and, when Bojue had spoken in his story of the scholar's confusing the word "poem" for "bandit," he might have been taken to refer to Ximen Qing, for the word for a very wealthy man has the same sound.

Ximen Qing himself had not at once seen the point, but now he understood. Bojue realized that he had made a slip. He drank two cups of wine and asked to be forgiven.

"If you did not deserve to be punished, I would not punish you," Ximen Qing said, "but you do deserve it, and I cannot let you off."

Bojue felt uncomfortable, but he drank a few cups more. "You have too much to say," he said to Chang Zhijie.

"Now you must tell us another story," Ximen said. But Bojue was afraid to commit himself again. "Never mind," Ximen said, "it is only fun, come along." Bojue felt more at ease.

"When Confucius was traveling in the west," he began, "someone caught a unicorn. For some reason Confucius did not see it, and, day and night, he wept and cried bitterly in his house. His disciples were afraid that he would fall ill, so they got a bull, dressed it up in copper coins and tried to persuade him that this was the animal. But the moment Confucius set eyes on it, he saw through their trick. 'Obviously,' he said, 'this is a very wealthy bull, but why do you try to make out that it is a unicorn?'"

When he had finished his story, Bojue fell upon his knees before Ximen Qing. "I know I am not fit to live," he said, "but I really didn't mean any harm."

Ximen Qing laughed and told him to stand up. Han Jinchuan laughed too. "Beggar Ying," she said, "you are always trying to be smart at other people's expense. Now you've put your foot in it. Father, don't pay any heed to him."

Bojue was annoyed at this. He went to Han Jinchuan and struck her on the head. "That rascal Chang," he said, "is bad enough. There was no need for you, you little whore, to say anything more." He had hit her hard and hurt her. She dared not cry, but it was clear that she was very much put out.

"You dog," Ximen Qing said, laughing, "first you make rude jokes about me and then you begin hitting people. What punishment do you really want?"

Bojue laughed and put his arm around Han Jinchuan. "My daughter," he said, "where were you brought up with such tender care that you are ready to cry at a little tap like that? It surprises me that you are able to put up with things as big as a donkey's."

Han Jinchuan turned her head and looked scornfully at him. "Beggar," she said, "pray when were you there to see? You are talking nonsense. It is your wife who has to endure a thing as big as a donkey's."

"Why, of course I've seen," Bojue said, laughing. "The gentleman is famous for his beauty, his asininity, wealth, youth and idleness. He is just the sort of man you like. And that reminds me of another story. There was once a young lady whose thing was getting rather the worse for wear. Somebody told her that if she put a piece of alum into it, it would recover its former tightness. This the young lady did, but she found that it tightened her up so much that it hurt. This made her very sorrowful. She was standing outside her gate when a passerby said: 'That little whore is trying to look like Ba Wang.' The young lady heard him. 'What!' she said, 'Ba Wang indeed! Why, I can't even manage Fan Kuai!'"

They all laughed at this, even Han Jinchuan. Ying Bojue finished his wine and offered another cup to Ximen Qing, asking him to take the last turn in the game. "It is Han Jinchuan's turn," Ximen said. Jinchuan would not play, and Chang urged Ximen. Ximen drank a cup of wine and said: "Up the staircase of the clouds, let us go to the cavern of the immortals in the palace of the moon." So the game was finished.

Ximen Qing changed his clothes and went for a stroll. Bojue was still calling for more refreshment. Suddenly he noticed that Jinchuan had disappeared. He looked about and found that she had gone around the artificial mound and was relieving herself behind the arbor of roses. He picked a branch from a flowering shrub and quietly went over to her. Squatting down behind her, he touched the heart of her flower. Jinchuan was startled, jumped up before she had finished what she was about, and wet her drawers. At that moment Chang Zhijie crept up behind Bojue and pushed him so violently that he fell forward and caught all the piss in his face. He sprang to his feet, laughingly cursed Chang Zhijie, and ran after him to beat him. Ximen Qing stood beside a pine tree and roared with laughter. Even Han Jinchuan laughed and skipped with delight. "Beggar Ying," she said, "now you've got what you deserved." They went back to the table.

"Now, you dog," Ximen Qing said, "you have had your joke at our expense. What about telling us a story against yourself?"

"I don't mind in the least," Bojue said. "One day a rich man let out a fart. A man standing by, one who always lived by sponging on the rich man, said: 'I smell nothing.' This alarmed the rich man. 'That's bad,' he said. 'If there is no smell to my farts there must be something wrong with me. I must see a doctor.' 'Wait a moment,' said the sponger, 'I will make sure.' He put out his nose and pretended to sniff again. Then he smacked his lips. 'Ah,' said he, 'there is a splendid aftertaste. You have nothing to worry about.' "

They all laughed. Chang Zhijie said: "You have made rude remarks about our brother, but why should you draw a picture of me?" They all laughed again. Ying Bojue asked Chang Zhijie to guess fingers with Ximen Qing, and Han Jinchuan sang songs for them.

Chen Jingji, when he was sure that Ximen Qing had gone out, dressed himself and waited for an opportunity to approach Pan Jinlian. He dared not go to her openly, but went to the Snow Cavern hoping that she might be there. He waited for a long time but she did not come. At last he lost patience and went to her room. Fortunately, no one saw him. When he came to the door he could hear her singing in a low sweet voice: "Why did you love me and then forget me?" This seemed a proof that she really loved him. He rushed into the room and threw his arms about her. "How could I ever forget you?" he said. "Yesterday, my darling, the Great Lady told me to go to the temple of Guanyin, but I would not go. I was think-ing of you all the time. Today, Father has gone to drink wine, and I went to the Snow Cavern to find you, but though I waited and watched until the eyes nearly came out of my head, your dainty shadow never appeared. Now I have thrown discretion to the winds and come to you here."

"Don't speak so loud," Jinlian said, "there will be trouble if you are heard."

Suddenly, through the window, she saw Xiaoyu coming with a roll of white silk. The girl turned and went away again. "That maid must have forgotten something," Jinlian said. "Did you see how she turned and went back?" She thought it probable that the girl would return. "You must go at once," she said. "We can do nothing now." Chen Jingji was made to vanish like a whiff of smoke. Jinlian was right. Yueniang had told Xiaoyu to take the silk to her so that she could draw the pattern of a skirt, but the girl had forgotten to bring the pattern and went back for it. Luckily, the maid did not catch Jinlian with Jingji. When she returned with the pattern, he had slipped away. But when Jinlian took the silk, her hands were trembling.

Ximen Qing and his friends were becoming tipsy, and he was anxious to go home. Bojue urged him to stay. He knelt down and said: "Brother, is it because you are angry with me on account of that joke I made about you that I can't persuade you to stay?"

Ximen laughed. "You dog," he said, "nobody bothers about what you say."

Bojue took a large cup and filled it for Ximen Qing. Chang Zhijie offered him some fruits. Ximen thanked his host and prepared to leave. He gave Han Jinchuan a tael of silver and told Daian to give the young actors three *qian* each. "I am drunk," he said as he got into his sedan chair. The two boys followed him. Bojue told the servants to clear away and dismissed the young actors. He rode back to the city beside Han Jinchuan's sedan chair.

When Ximen Qing reached home, the sun had set. He went to sleep with Li Ping'er. The next day she said to him: "Ever since the baby was born, there has been something wrong with me. When I look in the mirror, I see how pale my face is. I never want to eat or drink, and, when I try to walk, my legs seem to give way beneath me. If it is anything serious, what will become of my baby?"

Ximen saw that she was crying. "I will send for Doctor Ren," he said. "I am sure you will be all right when you have had some medicine." He told Shutong to write a letter and ask Dr. Ren to come. Shutong went on the errand, and Ximen Qing went to the hall. Ying Bojue came to thank him for coming to the party the day before, and Ximen, in return, thanked him. They sat and talked. Then Shutong came and said: "Doctor Ren is here." Ximen Qing at once went to receive him, introduced him to Ying Bojue, and the three men sat down together. Shutong brought tea.

"Kindly tell me who is ill," Dr. Ren said.

"My sixth wife is not feeling very well. I shall be grateful if you will make a careful examination."

"Is that the lady who had a baby?" Dr. Ren said.

"Yes," said Ximen, "but I don't know why she should not be well."

"Let me go and see her," the doctor said. Ximen Qing took him to Li Ping'er's room. The doctor sat by the bedside, and one of the maids opened the curtains very slightly. Li Ping'er put out her right hand and rested it upon a case of books wrapped in a handkerchief.

"First, I will try the pulse," Dr. Ren said. When he had found the place, he put three fingers on the pulse. He bent his head and examined it carefully for some time. Then he removed his hand, and Li Ping'er slowly withdrew hers. She stretched out her left hand, and laid it on the books. Dr. Ren examined it. Then he said to Ximen Qing: "I have now examined the lady's pulse and—I am very sorry— I must see her face."

"We are good friends," Ximen Qing said, "there need be no difficulty about that." He told the maids to pull the curtains aside. Dr. Ren looked at his patient. Her face was like a peach blossom, her eyebrows dark like willow leaves. He looked at her for a minute, then said to Ximen Qing: "I have seen your lady's face, but I have not come upon any sign of anything serious. I must have more details about her illness. We doctors have to find things out from our patients themselves."

Ximen Qing sent for Ruyi'er. She came in, dressed in her best clothes, made a reverence to the doctor and told him about her mistress's illness: how her mouth was always parched, and how she suffered from sleeplessness. Dr.. Ren stood up and bowed. He said to Ximen Qing: "I don't believe it is anything serious. In people of the common sort, their bodies are so tough that their blood can stand anything, and we can give them almost any kind of medicine. If we make a slight mistake, no great harm is done. But a lady like yours is more delicate. We must not allow the slightest possibility of error, for, if we give her anything that is not exactly what we should give, there may be serious danger. That is why I have to ask questions and find out what she has to say. It is essential. The other day, I went to see his Lordship Wang's wife. Her illness was very similar to your lady's. I asked a few questions, investigated the symptoms and examined her, and so got an excellent idea of the trouble. I went home, read some of the prescriptions of the ancients and compared them with my own ideas upon the subject. I gave her some medicine to get rid of her fever and something to strengthen her at the source of her weakness. The treatment was most effective. The lady took only three or four doses, and then she was completely recovered. His Lordship was most grateful. He sent me silks and money, and his lady sent me something too. He also sent me a special signboard and, when he gave it to me, the musicians played so loud that the sound reached the heavens. There was inscribed upon it: 'The Learned Doctor with Miraculous Powers.' A few days ago, a friend of mine came to see me, and he says the characters are done in the *Yan* style. Every character seems to stand out. When I was young, I did a great deal of reading. It was only because my family had come down in the world that I began to practice the art of medicine. I think I can prove that the title of learned doctor was not altogether undeserved."

"I feel more satisfied now that you tell me there is nothing serious," Ximen Qing said. "I may say, Doctor, that, though I have more than one wife, this is the only one for whom I really care. She has borne me a son and I look to her to rear him. We must not have any trouble. I have confidence in your remarkable skill. She shall be carefully looked after, and, when she gets well, you shall have a handsome fee. I am only a soldier and cannot attempt to rival his Lordship, but I know what is right and proper."

"Since you are so kind," Dr. Ren said, "I will not take any payment from you. Indeed I would rather that you should not even pay for the medicine."

Ximen Qing laughed heartily. "I am not the sort of man to take medicine for nothing," he said. "And that reminds me of a very interesting story. I once heard of a man who said that a cat with the mange can be cured by a certain black powder. Somebody asked him what would cure a mangy dog. 'Give it some white medicine,'* the other said. So, Doctor, you see white medicine is fit only for dogs."

Dr. Ren clapped his hands and laughed. "Then I don't know what you will do to me if my prescription happens to be for white medicine." They both laughed. "In that case, you will have to give me another sign instead of a fee," Dr. Ren said. They laughed again. The doctor got up and they came away.

---

* This expression also means "medicine given gratis."

CHAPTER 55
The Imperial Tutor

When Dr. Ren had finished his examination of Li Ping'er, they went back again to the great hall and sat down. "I want you to tell me the truth," Ximen Qing said. "What do you think of the case?"

"The lady did not take sufficient care after the birth of her child," Dr. Ren said. "Now her blood is impoverished, and her face is pale. She has no appetite, and she does not care to move about. Her pulse beats strongly enough, but it is not steady. That is a symptom that her liver is inflamed and that her blood circulates irregularly. Without the most careful attention, I fear she will not get well."

"What medicine are you thinking of giving her?" Ximen Qing asked.

"The first thing to do is to break down the fever and stop the flow of blood. I shall use yellow cedar and *Jinmu* as the base and a few other things. I think she will be all right."

Ximen Qing told Shutong to seal a tael of silver and give it to the doctor for the medicine. The doctor left, and shortly afterwards the medicine arrived. It was made ready in the rooms of Li Ping'er. Ximen returned to Ying Bojue.

"Li and Huang came to me this morning," Bojue said. "They say they must have the money and asked me to plead with you to help them."

"I suppose I must do what you wish," Ximen said. "Tell them to come tomorrow." He went with Ying Bojue to another room and they had something to eat.

"Is Li Guijie still here?" Bojue asked. "It seems to me that the man who went to the Eastern Capital should be back by now."

"Yes," Ximen said, "I want him myself. I am anxious to send him to Yangzhou. I don't see how he can be much longer."

After the meal, Ying Bojue went away.

The next day when Ximen Qing returned from the office, Ying Bojue was already waiting for him with Li and Huang. When he came in, they rose. Ximen went to change his clothes. He asked Wu Yueniang for the two hundred and fifty taels that Xu had paid. He added another two hundred and fifty taels and told Chen Jingji to give the money to Li and

Huang. "I am really very short of money," Ximen Qing told them, "and I am only giving you this because Brother Ying has pressed me to do so. I must have it back as soon as possible."

"You have been so kind to us," Li said, "that, of course, we shall not be slow to pay. As soon as we recover the money, we will bring it to you before we touch a penny ourselves." They checked the silver, thanked Ximen Qing repeatedly, and withdrew.

Ying Bojue was going too, but Ximen pressed him to stay. While they were talking, Ping'an came and said: "Laibao has come back from the Eastern Capital."

"There," Bojue said, "didn't I tell you yesterday that he was due back?"

Laibao came in and kowtowed to Ximen Qing. "Did you see Uncle Zhai? What happened about this business of Guijie's?" Ximen asked him.

"I saw Uncle Zhai himself," Laibao said. "As soon as he had read your letter, he sent a man to the Minister. I went with the man, and the Minister told me that he would have had all the prisoners released, seeing that we came from his Eminence's palace, but, unfortunately, the matter had been taken up by Grand Marshal Huang, and all he could do was to prevent any further pursuit of those who had escaped. He said he must keep in jail those who had already been taken. But eunuchs, he said, never carry things to a conclusion and, before long, the Grand Marshal will have forgotten all about the matter. Then it will be easy to settle the matter of the prisoners."

"In that case, Qi Xiang'er will not be arrested," Bojue said. "The little strumpet is in luck's way."

"Uncle Zhu and the others will probably receive some slight punishment," Laibao said, "but I don't think they will be sentenced." He took Zhai's letter from his pocket and gave it to his master.

"Old Sun and Pockmarked Zhu can never have dreamed that I would come to their rescue," Ximen Qing said.

"But you have such a kind heart, Brother," said Bojue.

"Uncle Zhai seemed very pleased to see me," Laibao continued. "He asked whether you were going to the Capital to congratulate the Imperial Tutor on his birthday. I did not dare to say you were not going, so I said very probably you were. Uncle Zhai said it would be very nice of you to go and see him."

"I never had any idea of going," Ximen Qing said, "but, after what you have said, I shall have to go." Then he said: "You must be tired. Go to the inner court for some refreshment and then rest. I shall want you to go to Yangzhou in a day or two."

Laibao went out. Ximen Qing went to tell Li Guijie. He said to Bojue:

"You stay here. I shall be back in a moment." But Bojue was anxious to go after Li and Huang. He said: "I must go now, but I will come back." He went away.

When Ximen Qing came to Wu Yueniang's room, Guijie had already heard the news. She hastened to kowtow to Ximen Qing and Yueniang. "Father and Mother," she said, "it is only by your kindness that I have been rescued from desperate straits. I don't know what I can do for you in return."

"Since you came to us," Yueniang said, "we could do no less than get things put right for you. If we had not done our best, there would have been no point in your coming."

"Father and Mother," Guijie said, "you have saved my life, but that little whore Qi Xiang'er had no claim on you, and you have saved her too. She made a lot of money; she involved me in her own trouble, and we have treated her well. I can't help feeling she is in our debt."

"Yes, indeed," Ximen Qing said, laughing, "the little whore has come out of it very well."

They talked for a while, then Guijie prepared to go away. "My mother has not heard the news," she said. "I must go and tell her or she will go on worrying. I will come again with her to thank you."

"Very well," Ximen said. "I will not keep you. Go home and tell your mother."

"You must have something to eat before you go," Yueniang said. Guijie declined. Again she thanked Ximen Qing, Yueniang, and the others.

"You are safe now," Ximen Qing told her, "but see that in future you have nothing to do with that young man Wang."

"Father," Guijie said, "what are you talking about! How could I even let him touch me! Why! if I meet him in the street, I shall be done for. It was not I who asked him to come the other day."

"That is all right," Yueniang said. "Only don't see him any more. There is no need to be so positive about it." They sent for the sedan chair and saw the girl off.

Ximen Qing told Yueniang he was thinking of going to the Eastern Capital.

"If you make up your mind to go," said Yueniang, "we must begin to get things ready at once, or you will be rushed."

"I have already got ready the things for the Imperial Tutor's birthday, the dragon gong, the embroidered stuffs, and the golden flowers," Ximen said. "Only my personal baggage is not ready yet."

"Oh, your things will be no trouble," Yueniang told him. Ximen Qing went to see Li Ping'er.

The next day Ximen was sitting in the arbor. He told Chen Jingji to write a letter to Censor Cai. This was the letter for Laibao to take. He gave Laibao some money and told him to start for Yangzhou the following morning.

Several days passed. The Imperial Tutor's birthday was drawing near. Ximen Qing picked out an auspicious day and told Qintong, Daian, Shutong and Huatong that they were to accompany him. They were to get their things ready. Wu Yueniang, Meng Yulou, Pan Jinlian, and the others packed Ximen's clothes and the things he needed for the journey. With the presents there were more than twenty loads. On the eve of his departure, the ladies gave a feast in honor of their husband, and afterwards he went to Yueniang's room to sleep with her.

The next day he sent off in advance the loads and his baggage and procured a passport so that his things might be cleared through all the stages on the way. When he had attended to these details, he went to see Li Ping'er and his little son Guan'ge.

"Take care of yourself," he said to Li Ping'er. "Whenever you need any medicine, just send somebody to Doctor Ren. I shall be back before long."

Li Ping'er said good-bye to him with tears in her eyes. "Be careful on the way," she said to him. Then she went with him to the great hall where Yueniang, Yulou, Jinlian, and the others were waiting. All together they escorted him to the gate. Ximen got into a light sedan chair and, with the four boys on horseback, set out for the Eastern Capital. Every day they rose early to continue their journey, and every night they rested at an inn or post stage. The scenery was delightful. The travelers they met were mostly civil and military officers going with their presents to the Capital to congratulate the Imperial Tutor on his birthday.

In ten days they reached the Capital. They entered by the Gate of Ten Thousand Blessings, and, as it was late, they went straight to the Arch of Dragon Virtue to see Zhai.

When the Comptroller heard that Ximen Qing had come, he hurried out to welcome him. They greeted one another and tea was served. Ximen Qing told Daian to have the baggage brought in, but Zhai bade his own servants attend to it. A banquet was served in honor of Ximen's arrival. A table of carved horn was set and there were some very rare dishes. It would have been perfection if only there had been dragons' livers and phoenix marrow. Even the Imperial Tutor himself could not have done better. The servants brought wine. Zhai offered a cup to Heaven, then to Ximen Qing. Ximen offered a cup in return. Fruits and dishes followed one another like water flowing in a stream.

After drinking two cups of wine, Ximen Qing said: "I have come specially to celebrate his Eminence's birthday and have brought with me a few trifling gifts for him. But I am afraid he may refuse them, and, to be candid, I should like you to go to him and speak to him about me. Besides, I hope that his Eminence may take me under his guardianship. If he will do this, I shall be happy all the rest of my life. But it may be difficult to persuade him."

"There will be no difficulty," said Zhai. "Though his Eminence is the most powerful of his Majesty's subjects, he is somewhat susceptible to praise and flattery. Let him but see the value of the presents you have brought him, and not only will he accept you as his ward, he will see that you get promotion."

Ximen Qing was delighted to hear this. They went on drinking and, after some time, Ximen said he had drunk enough. Zhai pressed him to drink one more cup, but Ximen said he had serious business to attend to on the morrow and he dared not drink too much. But, being pressed, he did drink one cup more.

Zhai saw that the boys were served with refreshments and invited Ximen Qing to go and rest in a study in the inner court. A bed with silken curtains and bedclothes, exquisitely perfumed, had been made ready and there were many servants to wait upon him. Ximen Qing lay down alone upon the bed. This was something to which he was not accustomed, and he found it hard to pass the night. Before dawn he was anxious to get up, but all the doors were shut and he had to wait till sunrise. Then a man came with a key and opened the doors; boys came with water and towels, and Ximen Qing dressed. Zhai came in and sat with him. A servant brought a red box in which were thirty different kinds of delicacies and a silver wine pot. The wine was poured and they ate their breakfast.

"After breakfast," the Comptroller said, "I will go before you to the palace and speak to his Eminence about you. I will let you know when to send the presents."

Ximen thanked him. They took a few cups of wine with their breakfast and the table was cleared. "Sit here," Zhai said to Ximen Qing. "I must go, but I shall be back very soon." It was indeed only a short time before he was back again. "When I got to the palace," he said, "his Eminence was washing. There was a host of civil and military officers waiting to congratulate him on his birthday, but not one of them had seen him yet. I spoke of you to him, and you must go at once. There is a crowd at the palace. I will go first and you can join me there." He went away again.

Ximen Qing was delighted. He ordered his own servants and asked some of Zhai's servants to carry the presents to the palace. Dressed in ceremonial robes and hat, he got into his sedan chair. A host of officials, great and small, all come to congratulate the Prime Minister, were pressing shoulder to shoulder and back to back. In the distance Ximen Qing saw one officer, also sitting in a sedan chair, near the Arch of Dragon Virtue. When he looked more closely he recognized his old friend Miao of Yangzhou. At the same time Miao recognized him. They got down from their sedan chairs, bowed, and saluted one another. Miao was a rich man and now held a very comfortable position. He had attached himself to the Imperial Tutor's faction, and had come, like the rest, to congratulate his Eminence on his birthday. So they chanced to meet. They were both eager to get on to the palace and did little more than greet one another, exchange addresses, and then separate. Ximen Qing came to the palace, bowed, and entered through the Great Archway. There Zhai met him.

Ximen Qing noticed that the middle gate was shut and that the officers were all coming in by the gates at the side. He asked Zhai the meaning of this and was told that the Emperor had once passed through that door and, ever after, it must be closed to ordinary men. Ximen Qing followed the Comptroller through one door after another. Each was guarded by a military officer. There was excellent order everywhere. The military officers bowed to Zhai and asked who Ximen Qing was. Zhai told them that Ximen was his relative from Shandong, come to congratulate his Eminence. They went through more doors and down more passages. Everywhere were carven pillars and painted beams. Music could be heard faintly. It seemed to come from heaven. "The palace is far distant from any other place," Ximen said. "Where is the music coming from?"

"His Eminence," Zhai said, "has commanded the attendance of twenty-four girl dancers. They know all such dances as the Dance of the Evil One, the Rainbow Skirt Dance and the Dance of Guanyin. They play every day when my master breakfasts, dines, and sups. At present he is taking his breakfast."

Ximen Qing smelled some incense that he had never smelled before, and the music seemed nearer. "Step softly," said Zhai, "we are quite close to his Eminence's study."

They went through another passage and came to a great hall that seemed to Ximen Qing like the palace of the angels. Outside were storks and peacocks and many strange birds. There were the Hortensia flowers that confer Eternal Life, Flowers of the Sacred Cloud, and the *Fusang* Plant; flowers that never faded, blossoming so luxuriantly that the eye could scarce bear to dwell on them. Ximen Qing did not dare to press forward. He asked Zhai to go before him.

They went into the hall. In the midst of it stood a great throne with a tiger skin thrown over it, and, on the throne, sat a man robed in a gown with dragons embroidered upon it. This was his Eminence the Imperial Tutor. Behind a screen were twenty or thirty exquisite maidens in a row, all dressed after the fashion of the court. Some held kerchiefs, and some held fans with which to refresh his Eminence. The Comptroller stood beside him, and Ximen Qing kowtowed four times. His Eminence rose and, standing upon a rug, returned the salutation. It was the first time they met.

The Comptroller approached the Imperial Tutor and whispered. Ximen Qing knew that he was being spoken about, and again kowtowed four times. Now the Imperial Tutor did not rise. It was a sign that he was prepared to accept Ximen as his ward. Then Ximen spoke and called him "Father."

"Your son," he said, "has nothing to offer. I have brought no more than a few trifles in honor of your most illustrious birthday. It is as though one brought a feather for ten thousand *li*. But may your Eminence live as long as the Mountains of the South!"

"You are very kind," the Imperial Tutor said. "Please sit down."

An attendant gave Ximen Qing a chair. He bowed twice and sat down. Tea was brought. Zhai went out and ordered the presents to be brought in. There were more than twenty loads. They were brought and laid before the steps. A small box was opened and the inventory taken from it. It said: One crimson dragon robe; one green dragon robe; twenty rolls of Han-figured satin; twenty rolls of Sichuan silk; twenty rolls of foreign cloth; other rolls, forty, both plain and figured; a girdle of a lion's head in jade; another girdle mounted in gold of tagaraka wood; of jade goblets and horn goblets, each ten pairs; four pairs of golden wine cups with flowers for decoration; ten fine pearls and two hundred taels of gold. These were the present.

The Imperial Tutor looked at the inventory and then at the twenty loads of offerings. He was pleased and thanked Ximen Qing. Then he told Zhai to have them sent to the treasury and called for wine to entertain Ximen Qing. But Ximen remarked that his Eminence was very busy. He rose and prepared to take his leave. "Very well," said the Imperial Tutor, "but come this afternoon." Ximen Qing bowed and went out, the Imperial Tutor taking a few steps with him. Zhai went farther, but he too was busy and had to return, and Ximen Qing went back alone to the house. There he took off his hat and girdle and had dinner. After dinner, he went to the study and slept for a while. Then a man came and asked him to go and see the Imperial Tutor. Ximen gave the man some gold and put on his robes. He told Daian to make up a number of parcels of silver and put them into a box. The four boys followed him as he made his way again in a sedan chair to the Imperial Tutor's palace.

His Eminence sent invitations to all who came to congratulate him upon his birthday, but these invitations were spread out over a period of three days. The first day was reserved for members of the Royal Household and the eunuchs, the second for ministers and officials of high rank, and the third for the commoner class of officers. But Ximen Qing was a stranger and had offered so magnificent a present that his Eminence was pleased with him and gave him a special invitation. He even came to receive his guest. Ximen very politely begged the Imperial Tutor to go before him. He bent his back and walked delicately.

"It has been very kind of you to come such a long way especially on my account, and to give me such a splendid present," his Eminence said. "I trust you will take a meal with me that I may at least show my inclination for you."

"My life in this world," Ximen said, "is entirely dependent upon your Eminence's kindness. The trifles I brought are not worth mentioning."

They chatted and joked together as though they really were father and son. The twenty-four beautiful maidens played for them, and attendants brought wine. His Eminence desired to offer Ximen a cup of wine. Ximen expressed his unworthiness, but, being pressed, rose and drank a single cup. They sat down. Then Ximen Qing bade Shutong bring a peach-shaped cup of gold. He filled it to the brim and, taking it, knelt down before his Eminence and said: "Live for a thousand years." The Imperial Tutor smiled.

"Stand up, my son," he said. He drank the wine.

Ximen Qing rose and took his place again. The food served was so rare and varied that it can hardly be described. Ximen Qing stayed until sunset. Then he distributed the packets of silver among the attendants and took his leave of the Imperial Tutor. "Father," he said, "you have much to do and I must not detain you. I shall not trouble you again." Then he left the palace and returned to Zhai's house.

The next day he decided to visit Master Miao and told Daian to find out where he was staying. Daian discovered that he was at a house outside the Imperial City belonging to a eunuch named Li. Ximen Qing went there with Daian. The boy presented Ximen's card and Master Miao came out. "I was hoping that some good friend would come and have a chat with me," he said. "You have come at the right moment." He insisted that Ximen should stay for dinner. There was a magnificent spread of food of every kind. Two very handsome singing boys came and sang several songs.

"These two foolish boys," Ximen Qing said, pointing to Daian and Qintong, "can only eat and drink. They cannot compare with your two boys."

Miao smiled. "I'm afraid they will not be of much use to you, but, if you really like them, I shall be only too glad to give them to you."

Ximen Qing said: " I dare not accept anything that you must appreciate so much yourself." They did not stop drinking till very late. Then Ximen said good-bye to Miao and returned to Zhai's house.

For eight or nine days, nearly all the important officials at the palace sent invitations to Ximen Qing. Then he felt anxious to get home and ordered Daian to pack up his baggage. The Comptroller pressed him to stay one day more. This he did. The two men drank together and treated one another as though they were blood relations. Then Ximen Qing set off on his way back to Shandong.

While Ximen Qing was away, Yueniang and the others stayed in their own rooms doing needlework, and none of them went out to play. So they waited for his return, all except Jinlian, who dressed herself exquisitely and mingled with the maids, sometimes playing at guessing fingers and sometimes at dominoes. She laughed and talked merrily, not caring what anybody thought about her. She was anxious to meet Chen Jingji, and every day went to the garden and many times to the cavern, hoping to find him there. Jingji was always thinking about her, and he went there frequently. Whenever they met they would play and kiss. But they were afraid of someone seeing them and dared not fully satisfy their longing for each other.

One day Yueniang, Yulou, and Li Ping'er were sitting together when, suddenly, Daian came in and kowtowed. "Father is nearly here," he told them.

"Where is he now?" Yueniang asked.

"I came first with the passports," Daian said. "He must still be twenty *li* away."

"Have you had anything to eat?" Yueniang asked.

"I have had breakfast but not lunch."

Yueniang ordered food to be prepared, then she, with the other ladies, went to the great hall to await her husband. They waited a long time.

At last Ximen Qing arrived. The ladies went out to welcome him. He made a reverence to Yueniang, then greeted all the others. Shutong, Qintong and Huatong kowtowed and went to the kitchen for something to eat. Ximen Qing told the ladies about the hardships of his journey, how he had stayed with Zhai, how the Imperial Tutor had invited him, and how he had gone to many parties with the eunuchs and other officials. Then he asked Li Ping'er about his baby. "And how do you feel," he said, "after taking Doctor Ren's medicine? Was it any good? Though my body went to the Eastern Capital, my heart was always here with you."

"The baby is well, and I am better than I was," Li Ping'er assured him.

Yueniang saw that all the luggage was brought in and the presents that Ximen Qing had been given. She gave orders for a meal to be made ready for her husband.

That night the ladies gave a feast to celebrate his return. He went to Yueniang's room to sleep, and it seemed to them like a refreshing rain after a long period of drought, or the meeting of old friends in a strange land. They took extreme delight in one another.

The next day, Chen Jingji and his wife came to pay their respects to Ximen Qing and discussed business matters. Ying Bojue and Chang Zhijie heard that Ximen had returned, and they came to call. Ximen greeted them. "So long a journey must have been very trying," they said. Ximen told them about the beauty and greatness of the Eastern Capital and how the Imperial Tutor had accepted him as a ward. They congratulated him. Ximen asked them to stay and have some wine.

When Chang Zhijie was about to leave, he said to his host: "There is something I should like to ask you, but I don't know whether I should or not." He bent his head and seemed embarrassed.

"Please tell me what it is," Ximen said.

"Well," Chang Zhijie said, "my house is not so convenient as it might be. I should like to find another, but I have no money. Perhaps you will lend me some and let me pay you back with interest."

"Why talk about interest?" Ximen Qing said. "We are too good friends for that. But, at the moment, I simply haven't any ready money. You must wait till Han comes back, and I will certainly do what you wish." Ying Bojue and Chang Zhijie thanked him and went away.

Master Miao had promised to give two singing boys to Ximen Qing. But Ximen Qing had been so anxious to get home that he did not stay to say good-bye to Miao. Miao thought he was still at the Capital and sent his servants to Zhai's place to make inquiries. So he learned that Ximen Qing had gone. "A gentleman's word," he thought, "is like a whip on a mettlesome horse, I must do what I promised." He sent for the two singing boys and said to them: "I promised to give you to his Lordship Ximen Qing, and now I am going to send you to his place. You must pack your things."

The two boys knelt down. "We have been with you many years," they said. "You have done much for us and taught us to sing. Now you don't want us any longer: you are going to send us away." They wept.

Miao himself was not at all happy about it. "Don't think I wish to get rid of you," he said, "but a man must keep his word. We must observe the teaching of Confucius. He says: A man who does not keep his word is a man no longer. There is no help for it. We cannot disobey these precepts, and I must not take your point of view into account. I am going to write a letter and send you to him. I will ask him to treat you kindly."

The two boys could only submit. They stood up. Miao told his family tutor to write a letter for them to take to Ximen Qing. He also wrote a card to go with a present of silk, books and handkerchiefs. Then he ordered his servant Miao Shi to take the letter and the two boys to Ximen Qing. The boys said good-bye to their old master, shed many tears, then mounted their horses and set off for Shandong. When they reached Qinghe district, they dismounted and inquired where Ximen lived. Then they went to the house.

After Ximen's return from the Eastern Capital, he was very busy. Many people sent him presents and many sent him invitations. Every day three or four friends came to see him, and he could not even attend to his duties at the office. But this day things were easier and he had gone to the office. He went to the Great Hall and, with Magistrate Xia, examined some of the prisoners. After this, he got into his sedan chair and, with several policemen to clear his way, went home. When he reached home, Miao Shi and the two boys had been waiting for some time. They followed him into the hall. Miao Shi knelt down.

"I come from Master Miao of Yangzhou," he said. "This is his letter." He took out the letter and the list of presents.

"Please stand up," Ximen Qing said to him. He opened the letter and read it carefully, pleased that Master Miao had sent him the two boys. "It was quite by chance I met your master," he said. "We were very friendly and when we were drinking together he was good enough to promise me you two boys. Now he has sent you to me even all this long way. Your master is certainly a man whose words are worth a thousand gold pieces. It is most unusual."

The two boys came forward and kowtowed. "Our master bade us come and serve you," they said. "He asks that you will be kind to us."

Ximen Qing told them to rise. "I will see that you are given a worthy task," he said. He called for food and wine to be given them and Miao Shi, prepared some valuable presents for Master Miao, and had a letter written to accompany them. He told the two boys that they should serve him in his study.

*   *   *

Han Daoguo's wife, Wang Liu'er, knew that Ximen was very busy and was anxious to find someone to take a message to him. Her young brother, Wang Jing, was a fine-looking lad about sixteen years old and, that same day, she decided to send him to Ximen Qing. Ximen accepted him and sent him to work in his study.

While Ximen Qing was making arrangements about these boys, Ying Bojue came to see him. Ximen told him how Master Miao had sent the two boys. He told Daian to bring refreshments and invite Bojue to dine. Then he asked the boys to sing some songs of the South. They came in and stood side by side with castanets in their hands. They sang "Last Night the Plums in the Garden Blossomed." Their voices were sweet, and the melody they sang was exquisite. Bojue was delighted. He jumped out of his chair. "Brother," he said, "what extraordinary luck to get two boys like this. It was indeed kind of Master Miao."

"I shall have to give him something in return," Ximen Qing said. He gave the two boys new names. One he called Chunhong and the other Chunyan. He told them to sing two or three short songs. The two men drank their wine after a while, and Ying Bojue went away.

CHAPTER 56

Chang Zhijie Buys a New House

Ximen Qing kept the two boys. He gave a letter of thanks to Miao Shi to take to his master with some presents, and some silver to Miao Shi himself. Then Miao Shi went home. Not long afterwards Chunyan died, and Chunhong was left alone.

Though Chang Zhijie had asked for Ximen Qing's help, the days passed and he was still without money. His landlord pressed him continually. Unfortunately for him, Ximen Qing, after coming back from the Eastern Capital, was kept busy going to one party after another. Chang Zhijie could not get hold of him. The proverb says: If friends meet, they cannot fail to help each other; but, when they do not meet, nothing is done. Chang Zhijie asked Ying Bojue to go to Ximen for him. Ximen was not at home. Chang Zhijie went mournfully home and his wife told him what she thought about him. "You call yourself a man," she said, "yet you can't get a house fit to live in, and here we are in utter misery. You have always bragged about your friendship with Master Ximen, but it doesn't look as though he would do much for you."

Chang Zhijie had a mouth but, after this, he dared not open it. He seemed dazed and did not utter a single word. The next day he got up very early in the morning and went to see Ying Bojue. He took him to a wine house and invited him to drink. "I do not wish to cause you any expense," Ying Bojue said, but Chang Zhijie pushed him into a chair. He ordered wine, a plate of smoked meat and another of fish. When they had drunk a few cups, Chang Zhijie said:

"I have bothered you several times to speak to his Lordship about my affairs, but, so far, we have not been able to see him and this business of my house is getting desperate. Last night my wife kept at me all night about it. I could not bear it. That is why I am up so early this morning. Now, Brother, won't you go to his Lordship again? I don't suppose he has gone out yet."

"Since you ask me," Bojue said, "I will certainly go, and I have no doubt we shall manage it today."

They drank more wine, then Ying Bojue said he must not drink too much so early in the day. Chang Zhijie pressed him to drink still one more cup, then he paid for the wine and they came out together and went to Ximen's house.

It was the beginning of autumn, and a pleasant wind was blowing from the west. Ximen Qing had been going to one party after another and was beginning to feel the strain. This day he had been invited by Eunuch Zhou, but he excused himself and did not go. Instead, he went to the garden with Wu Yueniang, Meng Yulou, Pan Jinlian, and Li Ping'er. They enjoyed the flowers and were all very happy together.

Chang Zhijie and Ying Bojue were delighted to find Ximen at home. They went to the hall and sat there for a long time, but there was no sign of Ximen Qing. Shutong and Huatong came in with a large chest filled with silken clothes. As they passed, they shouted: "We've been carrying these things half a day, and we're nowhere near finished yet." Bojue asked them where Ximen Qing was.

"He is amusing himself in the garden," Shutong said.

"Then may I trouble you to tell him we are here?"

The two boys went on with their chest. After a while Shutong came out again and said: "Father says, will you wait a moment and he will be with you." They waited and, at last, Ximen came to them. They bowed to him and sat down.

"Brother," Bojue said, "you have been drinking much wine these last few days, and you must be very busy. What are you doing at home today?"

"Since I saw you last," Ximen Qing said, "I have had invitations every day. I have been drinking too much, and I'm tired of it. Today I ought to have gone to another party, but I made some excuse for not going."

"I have just seen a chest full of clothes," Bojue said. "Where have they come from?"

"It is nearly autumn," Ximen Qing said, "and we must have autumn clothes, you know. Those you saw are my first wife's, but that was only half of them. We haven't finished them all yet."

Chang Zhijie put out his tongue. "With six wives you must have to have six chests. What a nuisance! We poor people find it bad enough even to get a roll of cloth. You must be a rich man, Brother." Ying Bojue and Ximen Qing laughed.

"How is it that the things from Yangzhou have not arrived yet?" Bojue said. "We know nothing of the way business has been going or whether Li and Huang have let you have their money yet."

"Perhaps the boat is delayed," Ximen said, "I have not heard a word, and I am rather worried. Li and Huang have told me that they will not get their money till next month."

Bojue drew nearer to Ximen Qing. "You may remember," he said, "that the other day Brother Chang asked your help. The last few days you have been very busy, and we have not had an opportunity of mentioning the matter to you. Brother Chang's landlord is being very harsh, his wife grumbles every day, and he is at his wits' end. The weather is getting colder and colder and his fur coat is still in the pawnshop. Brother, you must show your kindness to him. You can't have forgotten the proverb: If we would help a man, let it be when he most needs help. If you help him so that his wife ceases to nag at him and he can find a house to live in, all the more credit to you. Brother Chang has asked me to come and beg you to help him at once."

"I certainly did promise to help him," Ximen Qing said, "but I spent a great deal of money on my visit to the Eastern Capital and I shall have to wait until Han comes back. Why is Brother Chang in such a hurry?"

"It isn't Brother Chang: it's his wife. She is the one who grumbles. You must do something for him without delay."

Ximen Qing thought for a while. Then he said: "Well, perhaps I may just be able to manage it. How many rooms will they need?"

"They are only husband and wife," Bojue said. "They will need an outer room, a reception room, a bedroom and a kitchen. They can't do with less than four rooms. They must have three or four pieces of silver. Brother, do this for them. Help them to get a house at once."

"I can only let him have a few taels today," Ximen Qing said. "With them he can buy clothes and furniture. When he has got his house, he shall have some more."

Ying Bojue and Chang Zhijie stood up together and thanked him. Ximen Qing said to Shutong: "Go and ask the Great Lady to give you the silver that I have in a leather case." The boy went away and soon returned with the silver. "This is the money—about ten taels, I think— that I had at the Eastern Capital to give to the servants at his Eminence's Palace," Ximen Qing said. "Take it and buy a few things with it." He opened one of the packets and showed it to Chang Zhijie. "The silver is in packets of three or five *qian*," he said.

Chang Zhijie took them and put them in his pocket. He thanked Ximen Qing.

"Don't think I have deliberately kept you waiting," Ximen said. "But you hadn't fixed upon your house and I didn't have the money. When I do get some, you shall have more."

Chang Zhijie thanked him. They all sat down again.

"I have heard of men of past generations who were generous and openhanded," Bojue said. "The consequence was that their sons and grandsons were an honor to their family, and improved and extended their patrimony. On the other hand, I have heard of others, mean men who hoarded away their gold and treasure, whose sons and grandsons were anything but desirable. Sometimes they failed to preserve even the tombs of their ancestors. The justice of Heaven is unfailing."

"Yes," Ximen Qing said, "money should be made to circulate. It ought not to be buried away in one place. It is given us to use. If one man keeps a huge store of it for himself, someone else must go short. It is a crime to hoard away money and treasure."

Shutong brought food for them and the three men ate it. Chang Zhijie stood up, the money in his pocket, and went away in great delight. When he got home, his wife came out shouting and scolding as usual. "Now you barren fig tree! you impecunious rascal!" she cried. "Would you go away and leave your wife to starve? You seem quite pleased with yourself, but you ought to be ashamed. Here we are with no house to live in and the landlord always badgering us. I suppose you think I like to hear the sort of thing he says."

Chang Zhijie did not open his mouth. He waited until his wife had finished, then quietly took the silver from his pocket and put it on the table. He opened the packet. "Hullo, my square-holed brother, my dear square-holed brother! How bright and good you look! You make my body tingle all over. What a pity I can't swallow you down with a drop of water. If only you'd come to me earlier, that whore would not have been so rude to me."

His wife saw him set down twelve or thirteen taels of silver. She dashed to the table and tried to grab them.

"Ah," said Chang, "you have been nagging at me all this time, yet, the moment you set eyes on the silver, you seem to have become quite friendly. Tomorrow I am going to buy some clothes and get a place to live by myself. I'm tired of putting up with your tricks."

Mistress Chang smiled sweetly at him. "Brother," she said, "where did you get this silver?"

But Chang had nothing to say to her.

"Are you angry with me, Brother? I only want us to get a home. Now the money is here we must talk the matter over. We will buy a house and settle down. Why are you so angry? I have been a good wife to you. If you are angry with me, you are unjust."

Chang did not speak.

The woman continued, but he paid not the slightest attention. She began to feel abashed and started to cry. Chang sighed.

"You woman," he said, "you do no work in the fields. You do not weave. All you do is nag at me."

Mistress Chang shed more tears. Then they both shut their mouths tight and sat there silently, for there was no one to make peace between them. But Chang began to reflect. "The woman," he said to himself, "is in a very difficult position. Perhaps I ought not to be angry with her even if she does grumble about everything. It seems hardly kind not to speak to her. If Ximen Qing got to know about it, he would undoubtedly say that I am to blame." He smiled and said to his wife: "I am joking with you. I am not angry really. But you so often talk to me in this horrible strain, and I have never complained. I have just gone out of your way. Now I'll tell you all about this money. This morning you were so cantankerous that I could stand it no longer. I went to Brother Ying, gave him a drink and then we went to see his Lordship. By a stroke of luck, his Lordship happened to be at home. He had not gone to a party. Brother Ying was most kind. He did his utmost with his Lordship, and I got this money. He has promised that, when we find a house, he will give me some more. These twelve taels are for expenses and buying the things we need immediately."

"Now that you have this money," his wife said, "we must take care not to waste it. First of all, we must buy some winter clothes so that we won't freeze."

"Yes," Chang Zhijie said, "I was just going to suggest that. Here are twelve taels. We can buy a few clothes and some furniture. When we get the new house and are ready to move in, we shall look more respectable. I don't know how to express my appreciation of his Lordship's kindness. We shall certainly have to send him an invitation when we get into our new house."

"We will see about that later," said his wife.

The woman asked him if he had had anything to eat. "Yes," Chang Zhijie said, "I had something with his Lordship. But, doubtless, you have not. I will take some money and go and buy you some rice."

"Be careful you don't lose it, and please come straight back."

Chang Zhijie took a basket and went down the street. He bought mutton at the butcher's and rice at the rice shop. He took them home. His wife came to the door to meet him.

"Why did you buy this piece of mutton?" she said.

"You said you had a hard life, and, really, I ought to have killed an ox or two for you. This is but a trifling piece of meat."

Mistress Chang shook her finger at him. "You hardhearted thief. You still hate me. But I don't believe there is anything you can do about it."

"Probably," said Chang, "I shan't forgive you though you call me Brother and Darling and ask for forgiveness a thousand times. I will show my authority."

The woman laughed and went to the well to draw some water. Then she cooked the food, set a piece of mutton on the table and asked him to have some. "I have just had something," he said. "Eat it all yourself." The woman ate the food alone. She cleared the table and told him to go and buy some clothes. Chang Zhijie took some silver and went down the street. He went to several shops before he found what he wanted. He bought a black silk gown for his wife, a green silk skirt, a blue jacket and a white silk skirt, five pieces in all. For himself he bought a goose-yellow coat and a clove-colored gown. All this, with a few other things, cost him five taels and six *qian*.

"The things are not a bargain, but they are worth the money," his wife said. She put the clothes into a chest and decided to go and buy furniture the next day. She was thoroughly delighted, and all her grumblings vanished in the Eastern Ocean.

When Chang Zhijie had gone, Ximen Qing and Ying Bojue still sat in the great hall. "Though I am only a military officer," Ximen said, "I have a fairly important position. I have made a number of friends in the Capital, and I am in close relation with the Imperial Tutor. Letters pour in upon me like a stream. I am too busy to attend to my own correspondence, and I must find a scholar who can save me the trouble. Unfortunately, I don't know any genuinely learned man. If you do, please say so."

"You have set me a very difficult problem," Bojue said. "We want a learned man, but he must be honest. He must be a man easy to get on with, yet one who does not talk too much. We must have someone who can keep his own counsel. And we don't want a man who is a profound scholar in deceit and cunning and a fool at everything else. I have a friend who is a graduate. He has, it is true, several times failed to pass the final examination, but he is a learned man and will stand comparison with Ban and Sima. *He is a follower of Confucius. He and I have been good friends for ages. So far as I remember, ten years ago he went in for the examination and the examiners spoke very highly of his work. Unfortunately, another man was slightly better than he was, and he failed. He has made several other attempts since then and he still reads though his hair is gray now. He owns about a hundred acres of land and three or four houses."

"If he is in comfortable circumstances, why should he take a job?" Ximen said.

"His land and his houses have been bought by wealthy families, and now his two hands are his only capital."

---

* Ban Gu and Sima Qian.

"Why did you tell me he had land if he has sold it?"

"Well, if that doesn't appeal to you, perhaps this will. He has a pretty young wife about twenty years old, an excellent woman. She has two three-year-old babies."

"If he has a beautiful wife, he certainly won't come," Ximen Qing said.

"Fortunately, about a couple of years ago, his wife ran off to the Eastern Capital with another man. The two babies died of smallpox, so he is all alone in the world. I'm sure he will come."

"You are talking rubbish," Ximen said, laughing. "What is his name?"

"He is called Shui. His learning is incomparable. If you engage him, I guarantee your letters will be a source of pride to you. He is a very learned man indeed."

"I don't believe a word you say," Ximen said. "It is all a pack of lies. If you can remember anything he has written, tell me, and, if I think it is any good, I'll engage him and provide him with quarters. Since he is a single man, there will be no difficulty about that."

"I remember getting a letter from him asking me to help him to find a job," Bojue said. "I will tell you what I can remember of it."

A letter this for Brother Ying.
I think of you, but cannot find
Words to express my feelings.
All here are well.
If you should hear of a job for a tutor
Pray get it for me.
I may flatter myself, but it seems to me
My brush is as great as a beam.
I do not write often, but when I do
Look out for clouds and mist.

Ximen Qing roared with laughter. "If he wanted you to get him a job, why didn't he write a letter instead of sending you doggerel like that? Horrible doggerel too! I'm sure the fellow is both an ignoramus and a rogue."

"Oh, dear me, no," said Ying Bojue. "You must not judge him by that. He and I have been friends for three generations. We used to go to school together when we were boys. I remember our teacher saying that Ying and Shui were one as clever as the other. 'They will turn out well,' he used to say. We did our exercises and our compositions together and never felt the least bit jealous. You see, we are really good friends. We are never formal with one another. That's why he wrote me that little ditty. It's quite entertaining, isn't it?"

"Perhaps you can tell me what the fifth line means?" Ximen said.

"Ah, Brother," said Bojue, "don't you see? That is a very clever piece of character analysis. When you write *she* [residence] on the left-hand side and *guan* [official] on the right, and you have the other *guan* [a mansion]. He is saying to me, perfectly obviously: 'If you hear of a *guan,* a position, recommend me for it.' Not a single unnecessary word. How could he write more plainly what he wants to say?"

Ximen Qing could think of no further objection to make. He said to Ying Bojue: "What kind of man is he?"

"His behavior is even more admirable than his scholarship," Bojue said. "Two years ago he was tutor in the household of a certain Vice President Li. There were a host of beautiful maids there and several good-looking boys. Master Shui was there for four or five years and an impure thought about them never entered his head. In course of time the maids and boys were so impressed by his wisdom that they all deliberately set to work to seduce him. Master Shui is a soft-hearted man and he yielded. His employer drove him out and the neighbors said he was a scamp. As a matter of fact, even if a girl sits on his knee, he remains perfectly calm. If you engage him, let your maids and your boys go to him and you'll find out soon enough how he behaves."

Ximen Qing laughed. "You funny dog, you can never stop joking. The other day, my colleague Xia's tutor, Master Ni, told me of a friend of his called Wen. When he has been to see me, we will decide."

CHAPTER 57

Ximen Qing Becomes a Benefactor

The temple stands bare on the mountainside
There are shrines among the towering crags
But the Buddhas of days gone by can be discerned no more.
Their stone bodies are covered with moss
The ancient sanctuary stands alone
The image of the world-honored one is shrouded in dust,
As though he heard the mourning of the dragons and the elephants

And the hearts of the faithful are filled with sadness.
If a general goes to war in vain
Let him give freely the four gifts and tarry not.
I know that the fan palm tree
Still grows beside the lotus blossom tower.
Thus will he bring joy to the gods
And the demon host will bear no grudge against him.

In Dongpingfu of the province of Shandong there was a temple called the Temple of Eternal Felicity. It was built in the second year of the Putong reign of the Emperor Wu of the Liang dynasty. Its founder was a certain patriarch named Wanhui [Returns-from-afar]. If you ask why the patriarch was so called, I must tell you that, when he was about seven or eight years old, his brother was sent to serve as a soldier in the marches. He did not write to his family, and none knew whether he was alive or dead. So his old mother was unhappy about him and often shed tears. One day the younger boy said to his mother: "Mother, the world is at peace and our life is comfortable. What makes you weep so much? Tell me and I will share your grief."

"You are only a boy," his mother said, "and you do not know. When your father died, your elder brother went to the marches. He was an officer in the army. For four or five years no word has come from him, and I do not know whether he is alive or dead. How can I be happy?" She cried again.

"If I had known this before, I would soon have put things right. Mother, tell me where my brother is, and I will go and find him and get a letter from him."

The old woman laughed before her tears had dried. "You foolish child!" she said, "if it were only a hundred *li* or so away, we could go. But he is in Manchuria and that is more than ten thousand *li* away. It would take a strong man five months to get there. You are only a boy, and you would never get there at all."

"If he is in Manchuria," said the boy, "Manchuria is not in the skies. I will go, and you shall have me back in no time." He fastened his shoes, straightened his coat, bowed to his mother, and went off like a streak of smoke. The old woman called him back but he did not answer, and when she ran after him she could not catch him. She was more melancholy than ever. Many of her neighbors came to console her. "The boy cannot possibly go very far," they said. "He is sure to come back." The old woman dried her eyes and sat down sadly.

The sun was sinking in the west when the old lady went out to see if she could see anything of him. In the distance was a faint shadow that might have been a boy. She besought Heaven and Earth and the Three Luminosities and said: "May my little son return as a reward for my fastings and my sacrifices." And indeed, her son suddenly stood before her.

"What, Mother," he said, "have you not gone to bed yet? Here I am, back from Manchuria, and here is the letter from my brother."

The old woman laughed. "You did right not to go, but don't tell me any more lies. You couldn't possibly go more than a thousand *li* in one day."

"So you don't believe me, Mother?" the boy said. He took a packet from his sleeve. In it was a letter. It had indeed been written by his brother. And he brought a shirt to be washed that was one the old woman remembered making. Everybody heard of this, and so the boy came to be called Wanhui. Afterwards, he became a monk and was known as Abbot Wanhui. He was a man of outstanding virtue and performed a number of striking miracles. Once he swallowed two pints of needles before the stone tiger of the Emperor Zhao, and once he brought three pagodas from his head before the heir apparent of the Emperor Wu of Liang. So the Temple of Eternal Felicity was built expressly for him and immense amounts of money were spent on its construction.

Years and months flew like a weaver's shuttles. The patriarch Wanhui went back to Paradise, and, one after the other, his pious monks passed away. There were left but a handful of idle scroungers who kept women, drank wine, and did everything that is unbecoming. It was not long before they reached such a pitch that they pawned their religious habits and sold their bells. The tiles and bricks of which the temple was built were sold for wine, and the rain and wind soon affected the sacred images. A place of veneration became the prey of mists and weeds. For forty years nobody troubled to rebuild it. Then there came a monk from India who was impressed with the greatness of China. He crossed the River of Shifting Sands and the Sea of the Zodiac, and, after traveling eight or nine years, came at last to China. Then he came to Shandong and so to the ruined temple. There, for nine years he stayed with his face to the wall and did not speak a single word.

One day, an idea suddenly came into his head and he said to himself: "This temple is utterly in ruins, and these hairless asses care only for eating and drinking. It has become a waste place. This is a sad business. If I do not make up my mind to do something about it, no one else will. I must go out. I hear that his Lordship Ximen, a military officer and a very rich man, one day when he was entertaining his Excellency Cai here, saw the ruin and spoke of restoring this temple. If I can only persuade him to take the initiative, everything will be plain sailing. I must go at once." He beat the gong, assembled all the monks in the Great Hall, and told them what his purpose was. He bade one of them bring him ink and a brush. Then he wrote an appeal for funds. This veritable Buddha of a monk then left his fellows, put on sandals and a straw hat, and went to see Ximen Qing.

Now to return to Ximen Qing. When Ying Bojue had left him, he went to Wu Yueniang's room and told his wife about Bojue's recommendation of Master Shui. Then he said: "When I came back from the Eastern Capital, my friends and relations all gave parties in my honor and we must do something in return. I am not particularly busy today and I think we might do it at once." He told Daian to see to the preparations, and sent the other boys around with invitations. Then he took Yueniang's hand and went to see Guan'ge in the rooms of Li Ping'er.

The Sixth Lady welcomed them smilingly, and told the nurse to bring out the baby. He had grown very handsome. The child smiled at them and went readily to Yueniang. She took him in her arms. "My son," she said, "you are a clever boy and you will do well. When you are grown up, you will be a good son to your mother."

"When he is grown up and gets a position, the robes of ceremony will be yours," Li Ping'er said.

"My son," Ximen Qing said, "don't follow in your father's footsteps. When you are a man, be a civil officer, not a military officer like me. Mine is a good post, but it has not the dignity of a civil officer's; and, though I am rich, I do not enjoy the respect that is paid to the others."

Pan Jinlian was standing outside and heard all this. She was very angry. "You shameless, boasting, dirty strumpet!" she muttered. "Do you think you are the only woman who can bear a child? He hasn't passed three yellow plum seasons or four summers yet. He isn't through smallpox, and his schooldays are not over. He lives still with the God of Hades. What right have you to talk about his getting a government appointment and your being honored as a lady? And that rascal has no shame. Why should the child get a civil position different from his own?"

While she was muttering angrily to herself, Daian came. "Fifth Mother," he said, "where is Father?"

"You little thief!" Jinlian cried, "how do I know where your father is? Do you expect to find him in my room? Why not with the honored lady to whom he pays so many delicate attentions? Why do you come and ask me?"

Daian saw that there was no purpose in his questioning her any further, and went to Li Ping'er's room. There he coughed warningly and said: "Uncle Ying is in the great hall."

"Why! He has only just gone," Ximen Qing said. "What has brought him back so soon?"

"He will tell you when he sees you," the boy said.

Ximen Qing left Yueniang and Li Ping'er and went to the outer court. He was just about to speak to Ying Bojue when the old monk arrived. Outside the gate, he called loudly upon Buddha and asked: "Is this the noble Ximen's house? Tell him, Master Comptroller, that I am here. Tell him that I will bless his son, send him prosperity and long life. I am a monk from the Eastern Capital come to ask for alms."

Ximen Qing was a man who never troubled about money. He was delighted to have a son and was only too glad to do anything he could for the child. The servants knew this well and they came and told him without hesitation. "Bring him in," Ximen said. The old monk came in and made reverence to Ximen Qing.

"I come from India," he said. "I was at the Eastern Capital for a while, but for nine years I have remained in solemn meditation at the Temple of Eternal Felicity. I have come to know the Sacred Principle. Now the temple is in ruins, and the rooms are falling down and it seemed right to me that, as a humble disciple of Buddha, I should do something for the temple. So I determined. The other day, you, my lord, took leave of some other noble gentlemen at the temple. You were sorry to find it in such disrepair, and it was your kind intention to assist us. At that moment the host of Buddhas were your witnesses. I remember that we read in the sacred scriptures: If the pious men and women of this generation spend their wealth for the glory of the image of Buddha, reward shall come to them; their sons and grandsons shall be fair and strong; they shall pass all their examinations and their wives shall be honored. I have come especially to you. Help me to accomplish this good deed, whether you give me five hundred or a thousand." He took out a silken cloth and, from it, the subscription list, and handed it with both hands to Ximen Qing.

Ximen was moved by the monk's words and gladly took the appeal. He told a boy to bring tea for the monk and meanwhile looked at what was written.

A humble supplication [he read]. When, after the White Horse had borne the Sacred Books here, the Religion of the Buddha was made known, the glorious doctrines that had come from India were established in their various schools. Then all the monks of this great country were converted to the teaching of the Buddha. The Three Thousand Worlds were beautified. Now we have seen that this temple is in ruins and no longer worthy of its great name.

If we do not give alms, how shall we pride ourselves that we are disciples of the Buddha and men of virtue? This Temple of Eternal Felicity is a religious foundation of great antiquity, a holy place of sacrifice. It was built in the days of the Emperor Wu of Liang, and its founder was the Great Teacher Wanhui. In those days it had splendid proportions and was modeled upon the garden of the Buddha himself. The floor was paved with gold and the adornments were of exquisite delicacy so that it resembled the monastery of Qi Yuan. The staircases were of white jade. Lofty towers soared to the heavens. So the religious atmosphere was made manifest in the skies. The foundations were solid and the main sanctuary could contain a thousand monks. The wings were magnificent with beautiful buildings. The cloisters were spotless and the whole building was like the dwelling of the Immortals.

In those days bells and drums announced the sacred principle of the Buddha and all men said: "Here is the abode of the Buddha in this world." The monks were learned, and it was a paradise upon earth. But now, many years have passed and things have altered. Evil monks gave way to drink and broke their vows; so fond of sleep were they and idle that they never swept their monastery. Gradually it declined; the number of the monks decreased. It became a desert place, and few came to worship there.

Snakes and rats made their holes in the walls; wind and rain wore them away. Pillars and walls, one after another, fell. The monks did nothing to repair them, and the place crumbled into ruin. Day succeeded day, year followed year, and none thought to restore the buildings. Instead, the painted balustrades and panels were burned by the monks themselves to heat wine and tea; great pillars and beams were taken to exchange for salt and rice. The weather tarnished the gold upon the Lohan's body; the rain streamed upon the Buddhas, and their bodies crumbled into dust. Alas, thus was so gorgeous and beautiful a place, a treasure-house of gold and color, transformed into a desert of weeds and brambles. Things prosper for a while and then decay, yet prosperity will return when ill fortune has done its worst.

This monk can no longer bear to see the ruin of the House of Buddha. He has sworn a great oath that he will go to all good people for their charity and stimulate their generous feelings. Whether they give a column, a beam, or simply wood; whatever it is, their names shall be remembered forever. Whether they contribute silver or cloth, whatever we receive, their names shall be entered upon the roll of benefactors.

Trusting in the might and the wisdom of the Buddha, we call down blessings upon all good people that they may prosper forever. We have confidence in the All-knowingness that father, son and grandson shall obtain high office and that their household shall be continued forever. They shall beget wise sons who shall bring repute upon their families; their gold shall be piled as high as mountains and, whatever they ask for, it shall be granted them.

You to whom this shall come, may the spirit of parsimony depart from you.

When Ximen Qing had finished reading, he laid the writing on the table very carefully.

"Though I cannot call myself a rich man," he said to the monk, "I have a few thousands. I am a military officer, and for long no son was born to me. Last year, my sixth wife bore a child and I was content. The other day I happened to come to your monastery to take leave of some friends, and I thought then of giving money for the restoration. It is good of you to come and see me. I shall not refuse."

He took a brush and wondered how much he should put down. Ying Bojue said: "Brother, since you seem so well disposed, why not pay the whole cost? I'm sure it would not be too much for you."

Ximen Qing laughed, the brush in his hand. "No," he said, "I cannot do that."

Bojue said: "Well, at least a thousand."

Again Ximen Qing laughed. "No, that's too much."

Then the monk spoke. "Noble sir," he said, "we monks of Buddha never press people to give. We take whatever they choose to give us. Write what you can afford. I only ask that you will commend the cause to your relatives and friends."

"You speak with wisdom, Master," Ximen said, "I will not give less than five hundred." This sum he wrote down. The monk thanked him. "All the eunuchs and officers of the prefecture and the district are friends of mine. Go and see them. I am sure they will put down three hundred, two hundred, one hundred, or at least fifty, and you will certainly be able to restore your monastery." He gave the monk some vegetarian food and saw him to the door.

When he returned to the hall, he said to Ying Bojue: "I was just wishing to see you when you came. When I came back from the Eastern Capital, my friends and relatives gave parties in my honor. Today I am making a return and I should like you to stay. The monk interrupted us."

"A good monk that," Bojue said. "Certainly a very holy man. I was quite touched while he was talking to you, and even I made my little contribution."

"What did you contribute?" Ximen Qing asked. "I didn't see you write it down."

Bojue laughed. "Ah, Brother," he said, "I fear that you do not understand. The Sacred Scriptures tell us that good will is the finest form of charity; then the teaching of religion; and, last of all, the giving of alms. Did I not urge you to give him money? That was charity of the first order."

Ximen Qing laughed. "You certainly did, but I don't believe there was any particular good will about it."

They both laughed. "I will stay until your guests come," Bojue said. "If you have anything to attend to, please don't mind me, but go and discuss it with your lady." Ximen left Bojue and went to the inner court. Jinlian was grumbling there, but he paid no attention. She yawned and went to her room to sleep.

Li Ping'er, Ruyi'er, and the maids were trying to amuse Guan'ge, who was crying. Yueniang and Sun Xue'e were superintending the cooks in the kitchen. Ximen Qing went to them and told them about the monk and the contribution he had made. He also told them the joke Ying Bojue had made. They laughed.

Yueniang was a good woman. She said something to Ximen Qing that touched him deeply.

"Brother," she said, "you have been blessed by Heaven. A son has been born to you. Now you have had this generous idea of giving your money and the whole household will be the better for it. But the more good ideas the better, while evil ideas should be uprooted utterly. Brother, in days past you have not been all that you ought to have been. You have gone after whores and behaved improperly. This must stop. Then you will grow in virtue, and it will be better for your son."

Ximen Qing laughed. "That's a nice way to talk. And you're quite wrong. The world is based upon the interaction of the male and female principles, and it is natural for men and women to be drawn together. Any irregular little affair that may happen in this present life was predetermined in a former one. It is all written down in the register of marriages. One cannot say that anything we do is out of depravity and evil passion. Besides, they tell me that gold is not despised, even in Paradise, and, in the ten regions of Hell, money is at a premium. So, if we are generous in almsgiving now, it won't do us any harm if we debauch the angels and run off with the daughters of the Mother of the Gods."

Yueniang laughed. "Dogs eat filth and think it's nice. They can't change their habits, because they are made that way."

They were still laughing when the two nuns, Wang and Xue, came in with a bowl. They greeted Yueniang and Ximen Qing. Yueniang asked them to sit down.

Nun Xue was not one who had been brought up in a convent from her youth. She had been a married woman, and her husband had sold buns outside a temple. But the business did not prosper, and she started a business of greater profit with the monks of the temple. Five or six of them enjoyed her favors. They used to send her bread and other things that the faithful had given them for sacrifice. They gave her money for ornaments and cloth that pious donors had presented to the temple, and she used the cloth to make shoes for her feet. All this was without her husband's knowledge. When he died, as she had developed a keen enthusiasm for monasticism, she became a nun. She sent about conducting services in pious households and assisting wicked women in their unlawful love affairs. Seeing that Ximen Qing was a wealthy man with several wives, she favored his household with very frequent visits, hoping always to get more money.

The Buddhist nuns, of course, have not a hair
Upon their heads.
Night after night, they sport with the monks.

Three bald heads
The teacher and his two disciples.
What are the little cymbals doing on the bed?

Nun Xue sat down and opened a small box. "We have really nothing to offer you," she said, "but I have brought a few fruits that have been offered to Buddha. They are perfectly fresh."

"It is good of you to come at all," Yueniang said. "There is no reason why you should trouble to bring presents."

Jinlian woke up and heard somebody talking. She thought it must be Ximen Qing again with Li Ping'er, and she got up to peep at them. But Li Ping'er was playing with the baby. When she knew that the two nuns were there, she determined to ask their advice about the child and went to Yueniang's room. When she had come and greeted the nuns, Ximen told them about the monk who had come to ask for alms. Jinlian was annoyed and went off muttering to herself.

When Xue had listened to Ximen Qing, she rose and made a reverence to him. "With generosity such as yours," she said, "you must assuredly live a thousand years. You will have five sons and two daughters and they will live together with you. I have a suggestion to make. It will cost you very little, and it will make you even more prosperous. If you accept this suggestion, even old Gautama who lived an ascetic life upon the Mountains of Snow, or the great Kāśyapa who could sweep the ground with his beard, or the Second Great Teacher who cut himself to shreds to feed a tiger, or old Ji Gu who poured the yellow gold upon the ground, will not be able to rival you in merit."

Ximen Qing laughed. "Sit down, most worthy Sister," he said. "Tell me what I must do and I will do it."

"Our Lord Buddha," the nun began, "has given us the Dharani Sutra to teach men the way to Paradise. Because those who see with the eyes of the flesh do not truly see and cannot truly believe, the Lord Buddha gave this teaching urging men to serve him faithfully that so they may attain to Paradise and escape from the turning of the wheel. The Buddha said: He who reads this book or prints it for others to read shall receive blessings unbounded. And in that book are charms for the protection of children. If people would engender boys and girls, first they should secure this text and recite it. Then their children will be easy to rear. No calamities will fall on them and blessings will be showered upon them. I know that the type of this book still exists but no one has reprinted it. Now, my lord, if you will spend a little money and print a few thousand copies, they can be sewn and distributed and you will have done a truly meritorious work."

"I see no objection," Ximen said, "but first I must know how much the paper, the printing, and the binding will cost. Tell me that, and I will have the work done."

"My lord," Nun Xue said, "there is no need for you to be troubled with such details. Nine taels of silver will do to begin with. The printer can print a few thousand copies and, when the binding is finished, you can pay whatever else is needed."

Meanwhile Chen Jingji was looking for Ximen Qing. He came to the arbor, and there had the good fortune to find Jinlian. When she saw him, it was as though a cat suddenly espied a fish. Her melancholy disappeared at once, and the soft winds of Spring brought color to her face. They saw that no one was about, held each other's hands and kissed, but they feared lest Ximen Qing might suddenly appear and were like a couple of rats, glancing about on one side and another as though they watched for the cat. They realized that there was no possibility for them to go further. Chen Jingji ran away without telling Ximen Qing what he had come to say.

After hearing what Nun Xue had to say, Ximen was once more persuaded. He told Daian to take thirty taels of silver from a box and gave them to the nuns. "I will have five thousand copies printed," he said. "When the work is done, I will check the accounts."

Then Shutong came and said that all the guests had arrived. There were Uncle Wu, Uncle Hua, Xie Xida, Chang Zhijie and the others. Ximen hastily dressed and came out to see them. He ordered tables to be set and they took their places in due order. Then fish, meats and fruits were brought. Those who were present were all good friends, so formal politeness was dispensed with. They guessed fingers and played all sorts of games. Some of them sang songs. They all heartily enjoyed themselves.

CHAPTER 58
Zheng Aiyue

Ximen Qing drank wine with his friends and relatives and got very drunk. When the party was over, he went to Sun Xue'e's room. She was in the kitchen watching everything being cleared away, but, when she heard that Ximen had gone to her room, she hurried away. Miss Yu was in her room. Xue'e asked her to go to Wu Yueniang's room, where she could share a bed with Yuxiao and the other maid. There were only three rooms in Xue'e's apartment. One had a couch and another a *kang* or stove bed. It was more than a year since Ximen Qing had visited her. She quickly took his clothes and put them on a chair. Then she made the bed, washed herself with perfumed water, and went to make him some tea. When he had drunk it, they took off their clothes and went to bed.

The next day was the twenty-eighth, Ximen's birthday. When he had burned some paper offerings, a boy called Hu Xiu came with a message from Han Daoguo. The servants told Ximen Qing, and Ximen gave orders that he should be brought to the hall. He asked the boy where the boat was. Hu Xiu gave him a letter with some accounts. "Uncle Han has bought silk in Hangzhou worth ten thousand taels," he said. "He has brought it as far as Linqing and there he is waiting for money to pay the duty. Without it, he can't bring the goods to the city."

When Ximen Qing had read the letter and looked at the accounts, he was delighted. He ordered Qitong to give Hu Xiu something to eat and told the boy that, when he had done, he must go and take the news to Master Qiao. He himself went to see Yueniang. "Han," he said, "has arrived at Linqing and he has sent this boy Hu Xiu with the statements. We must get busy clearing the house opposite. We can store the goods there, and I must look about for a man to take charge of the shop."

"Yes," Yueniang said, "there is no time to lose. It is late enough already."

"I will talk to Brother Ying about it when he comes," Ximen said.

When Bojue came, Ximen took him to the hall and explained the situation.

"I came to congratulate you on your birthday," Bojue said. "But now that your goods have come, I have still further reason to congratulate you. Their arrival on such a day is a good omen. You say you need a man. I happen to have an old friend who is the very fellow for you. He knows the silk trade inside out, but he has had bad luck and is out of employment at the moment. He is about forty years old. He is a good judge of silver; he can write and keep accounts, and all things considered, he is an excellent business man. His name is Gan and his second name Chushen. He lives in a house of his own in Stone Bridge Alley."

"Splendid!" Ximen Qing said. "Tell him to come and see me tomorrow."

Li Ming, Wu Hui and Zheng Feng came and kowtowed. In a short time the other musicians followed them. They were entertained in one of the side rooms. Then one of the servants came and said he had been to summon the singing girls. "But I cannot get Zheng Aiyue to come," he said. "Her old woman says she was all dressed and ready to start, when somebody came from the princely family of Wang and took her away. So I only got Qi Xiang'er, Dong Jiao'er and Hong Si'er."

"What rubbish!" Ximen Qing declared. "Not come indeed! and why not?" He turned to Zheng Feng. "What does your sister mean by refusing to come? Is it true that anybody from Wang's place took her away?"

Zheng Feng knelt down. "I do not live at home," he said, "I know nothing about it."

"She thinks if she says she is going to sing at Wang's place, that will settle the matter and I shall not be able to touch her." Then he said to Daian: "Take my card and two soldiers and go to Wang's. Ask for the young lord Wang. Tell him that I am entertaining a few guests here today and that Zheng Aiyue promised to come. We should be very much obliged if he would see that she does come. If there is any demur, arrest the old woman and throw her into jail. Let her see how she likes that." He told Zheng Feng to go too. The boy dared not refuse, and went out with Daian.

"Brother," Zheng Feng said to Daian, "you go in, and I'll wait outside. I have no doubt that my lord Wang did send for her, but perhaps she has not gone yet. If she has not, tell her she really must come with us."

"If she has gone to Wang's place, I shall take my master's card there," Daian said, "but if she is still at home, you had better go and tell your mother to dress her quickly and we will all go back together. I will say what I can for you to Father, and it will be all right. You don't understand him. When he was at Master Xia's place, he arranged with her to come, and he is naturally annoyed when she does not turn up." Zheng Feng went home and Daian, with the two soldiers, followed him.

Meanwhile, Ximen Qing said to Ying Bojue: "The beastly little strumpet! She is ready enough to go and sing for others, but, when I tell her to come here, she won't come!"

"She is a little baggage," Bojue said. "But she is not very experienced, and does not realize what a great man you are.

"I met her at a party," Ximen said. "I thought she talked prettily so I told her to come and sing here, the young scamp."

"Brother," Bojue said, "the four wenches you have here today are as fine as any of their kind."

"But you haven't seen Zheng Aiyue, Uncle," Li Ming said.

"Oh, yes I have," Bojue said. "Your father and I went and drank wine at her place one day. She was very young then. But it is some years since I last saw her, and I don't know what she is like now."

"The girl is well made," Li Ming said, "but she puts on rather too much paint. She knows a few songs, but she is not half as good as Li Gui-jie. And what kind of a place does she imagine this house to be that she dares to refuse to come here? She ought to be grateful for the chance. She certainly does not know her luck."

While they were talking, Hu Xiu came back. "I have been to see Master Qiao," he said. "Now I await your orders."

Ximen Qing asked Chen Jingji to get fifty taels from Wu Yueniang and told Huatong to write a letter and seal it. Then he ordered a soldier to start early next morning and go with Hu Xiu to the customs office. "Go and see Master Qian," he said, "and ask him to be lenient when he looks over the goods."

Chen Jingji brought the money. It was handed to Hu Xiu, who took it with the letter and the papers connected with the payment of duty and arranged to leave the next morning.

Shortly after Hu Xiu's departure, they could hear the shouts of men clearing the way. Ping'an came and announced the two eunuchs, Liu and Xue. Ximen put on his robes and received the two eunuchs in the great hall. When they had exchanged greetings, he invited them to go to the arbor to take off their ceremonial robes. They sat down, the two eunuchs in two large chairs in the place of honor, Ying Bojue in a more lowly seat.

"Who is this gentleman?" said Xue.

"You met him last year," Ximen Qing said. "It is my old friend Ying the Second."

"Ah," said Xue, "the gentleman who made such excellent jokes!"

Bojue bowed. "Your Excellency has an excellent memory. It was I."

Tea was brought. Ping'an came and said: "Major Zhou has sent a man with a card to say that he is engaged elsewhere and will not be able to come early. He asks that you will please not wait for him."

Ximen Qing looked at the card. "Very good!" he said.

"Sir," Eunuch Xue said, "who is this who is coming late?"

"Zhou Nanxuan. He is engaged elsewhere and has sent a man to ask us not to wait for him."

"We will leave a place for him," said the eunuch.

Then Wang Jing brought two cards and said: "The two scholars have arrived." Ximen looked at the cards. On one was written Ni Peng, and, on the other, Wen Bigu. Wen was the man whom Master Ni wished to recommend to him. He hastened out to welcome them and found the two scholars in academic dress. He paid particular attention to Wen Bigu, who was a man of about forty years of age, of dignified and discreet appearance. There was hair upon his cheeks, and his manner was urbane and gentle.

> Though he possessed incomparable talents
> Often he went to the place where the Rites are despised.
> His name and his achievements held no glory
> And his ambition was, perforce, content with lowly things.
> His fortunes had declined, and with them self-respect.
> Philosophy and letters he left to Confucius.
> The career of a public officer,
> Or the desire to make a name for himself and his ancestors
> Such notions as these he cast into the East River.
> Now he foregathered with the scum of the earth
> Only money was his goal.
> Hail-fellow-well-met,
> Without a care for shame or prudence.
> He was tall of stature, and broad girdled
> He could see no one before him.
> He talked with an air and sang a pretty song
> But his brain was empty.
> Every three years, for the examination he would enter
> But even a low degree was too much for him.
> So now he has abandoned hope of climbing high
> And sits with others to drink a cup of wine
> To lessen melancholy,
> Like a retired minister
> Exiled to the mountains.

Ximen Qing took them to the hall and each of them offered him a book and a handkerchief as a birthday present. They sat down in the places appropriate to host and guests.

"I have often heard of your great learning," Ximen Qing said. "Will you tell me your honorable name?"

"My second name is Rixin," said Master Wen, "and Kuixuan is my honorific name."

"Master Kuixuan, in what department of learning do you excel?"

"I am only a mean scholar," Master Wen said, "so I have begun upon the Book of Changes. Your great renown has long been known to me, but I have never ventured to call upon you. Yesterday, my old school friend, Ni Guiyan, spoke to me of your extraordinary virtues, and I felt I must come and see you."

"It is very kind of you to pay me the first visit. I shall hope to return your call one of these days. I am a military officer and know little of litera-ture, and I have no one able to attend properly to my correspondence. The other day when I was visiting my colleague Xia, I made the acquaintance of Master Ni, and he spoke most highly of your attainments. I intended to call upon you, but you have come to me first and been good enough to bring me these gifts. I don't know how to express my appreciation."

"You flatter me," said Wen. "I am really devoid of learning and virtue."

When they had drunk tea, Ximen asked them to go to the arbor where the two eunuchs were sitting. Xue suggested that they should take off their academic robes, and they took off their gowns and joined the party, only taking their seats after they had been pressed to do so for some time.

As they were chatting, Uncle Wu and Captain Fan arrived, and Daian and Zheng Feng came to say that the four singing girls were now all pres-ent. "Is it true," Ximen Qing asked, "that she had been sent for by the princely family of Wang?"

"Yes," Daian said, "but she had not started. I was about to arrest the old woman; that frightened them, and Zheng Aiyue decided to come with me."

Ximen Qing went out and stood on the steps to look at the four girls. They came forward together and kowtowed. Zheng Aiyue wore a long violet gown with a white-ribboned skirt beneath it. Her waist was like the willow, supple and full of the promise of delight. Her face was like a lotus blossom.

"Why did you not come when I sent for you?" Ximen Qing said to her. "Did you imagine you could escape me?"

Zheng Aiyue kowtowed without a word, then stood up and went smilingly to the inner court with the other girls. They kowtowed to Wu Yueniang and the others, and, finding Li Guijie and Wu Yin'er with the ladies, they greeted them too. "You came early," they said.

"We have been here two days," Guijie said. "What makes you so late?"

"It is all Zheng Aiyue's fault," said Dong Jiao'er. "We were ready, but she wouldn't come and we had to wait." Zheng Aiyue hid her face with her fan, laughed, but still said nothing.

"Who is this girl?" Yueniang said.

"Don't you know her, Mother?" said Dong Jiao'er. "She is Zheng Aixiang's younger sister, and her name is Zheng Aiyue. It is only six months since she was made a woman."

"She has a very fine figure," Yueniang said.

Pan Jinlian pulled up Zheng Aiyue's skirt and looked at her tiny feet. "Your shoes are too pointed; they are not like ours," she said. "In ours the proportions are as they should be, but your heels are too large."

"How impertinent she is," Yueniang said to Aunt Wu. "Why should she interfere in matters that do not concern her?"

Jinlian took a gold pin shaped like a fish from Zheng Aiyue's head and said: "Where did you get this?"

"It was made by our own silversmith," Zheng Aiyue told her. Tea and cakes were brought, and Yueniang told Guijie and Wu Yin'er to join the others. The six singing girls sat down together.

After tea, Guijie and Wu Yin'er invited the other girls to go to the garden with them, but Dong Jiao'er said; "We must go to the outer court first." Li Guijie and Wu Yin'er went with Pan Jinlian and Meng Yulou. They kept away from the great arbor because there were many guests there, and, after looking at the flowers for a while, they went to Li Ping'er's room to see Guan'ge. The baby was ill again. He kept waking up out of a bad dream and he would not take his milk. Li Ping'er had to spend all her time in her own room looking after him. When they came, she asked them to sit down.

"Is the baby asleep?" Guijie said.

"He has been crying all day long, but he has gone to sleep now," Li Ping'er said.

"The Great Lady tells me she is going to send for old woman Liu," Yulou said. "Why don't you send a boy and ask her to come at once?"

"It is Father's birthday today," Li Ping'er said, I think I will wait until tomorrow."

Then the four singing girls came with Ximen Dajie and Xiaoyu. "So you are here," said Ximen Dajie. "We have been looking all around the garden for you."

"There were so many people about we did not stay long," Yulou said.

"What were you doing all that time in the inner court?" Guijie said to Hong Si'er.

"We were having tea in the Fourth Lady's room."

Pan Jinlian looked at Meng Yulou and Li Ping'er. Then she laughed. "Who told you she was the Fourth Lady?"

"She asked us to go and take tea in her room," Dong Jiao'er said, "and, since we had not been presented to her before, we asked her what was her position in the household and she said: 'I am the Fourth Lady.' "

"The hussy!" Jinlian cried. "It would have been more becoming if somebody else had said so for her. In this house she is of no account at all. Nobody calls her the Fourth Lady. But she has had her husband in her room for one night. Now she has managed to scrape a little color together and is all agog to start a dye works. If it hadn't been that Aunt Wu was in the Great Lady's room, Guijie in the Second Lady's room, Aunt Yang in the Third Lady's room, the Wu Yin'er in the Sixth Lady's room, and my mother in mine, he would never have dreamed of going to her."

"You ought to have seen her this morning," Yulou said. "When she had seen Father to her door, she flaunted herself about the courtyard, with a 'Here, Zhang!' and a 'Now, you Li!' making a tremendous fuss of herself."

"Well," Jinlian said, "the proverb says: Never indulge a slave, and never spoil a child." She said to Xiaoyu: "I hear your father told the Great Lady he was going to buy that woman a maid. Last night, when he was in her room, he found it a complete mess. He asked her, and the little strumpet seized the opportunity and told him she was so busy all day she had not time to clean her room. She said she only went there to sleep and that was all. So he said: 'Don't worry about that any more. I will ask the Great Lady to get you a maid.' Is this true?"

"I know nothing about it," Xiaoyu said. "Perhaps Yuxiao heard it."

"Your father would never have thought of going to her," Jinlian said to Guijie, "if all our rooms had not been occupied. I am not one to talk about people behind their backs, but she is a very undiscerning sort of woman. And she has a very nasty tongue. I never speak to her if I can avoid it."

Yingchun brought tea. While they were drinking it, sounds of music reached them from the outer court. The guests had all arrived and the banquet was ready. Daian came and called the four singing girls. Master Qiao did not come that day.

First there were some varied amusements, then music and songs and dances. After a few comic sketches, food was brought in. Cold appetizers were served, followed by a soup. Then Dr. Ren arrived, dressed in robes of ceremony. Ximen Qing took him to the great hall. Dr. Ren brought out a handkerchief with the symbol for longevity embroidered on it and offered it, with two pieces of white gold, to Ximen as a birthday present.

"Yesterday," he said, "Han Mingchuan told me of your birthday. I am sorry I am so late."

"I am most grateful for your coming," Ximen Qing said. "With these delightful presents too. And I must congratulate you on the wonderful medicine you were good enough to send us."

Dr. Ren wished to offer a cup of wine to Ximen Qing as a mark of respect, but Ximen politely refused to allow it. Then Dr. Ren took off his ceremonial robes and they joined the others. He sat at the fourth seat on the left, next to Uncle Wu. When soup and rice had been served, Ximen Qing gave Dr. Ren's servant a box of food. Dr. Ren thanked him and told the servant to take it away.

Then the four singing girls sang a suite of birthday songs, accompanying themselves with stringed instruments. More food was brought and wine was passed around. The actors brought their repertory list and the eunuchs selected the play *Han Xiangzi Saves Chen Banjie*. When the first act was done, they heard the noise of men clearing the way. Ping'an came in to announce the arrival of Major Zhou. Ximen Qing hastened to welcome him and, without waiting for the usual greetings, asked him to take off his ceremonial clothes. "But let me first offer you a cup of wine," Major Zhou said.

"No," said Eunuch Xue, "do not offer him wine, noble Zhou. Greet each other with a simple reverence." This they did and Major Zhou bowed to the other guests. He sat down in the third place on the left. Food was brought for him, then soup, two types of snacks, two plates of meat, and two jars of wine. This was for Major Zhou's servants. Major Zhou thanked his host and bade his servant take the food away. They passed wine to each other. With singing, dancing and music, they had a very happy time.

They drank until sunset. Dr. Ren was the first to leave. Ximen Qing took him to the gate. "How is your lady?" the doctor said. "Is she better?"

"She was better immediately after she took your medicine," Ximen Qing said, "but for some reason or other she has been none too well these last few days. You must come and see her again." Dr. Ren mounted his horse and rode away.

The two scholars Ni and Wen rose. Ximen urged them to stay longer but they would not. Ximen went to see them off. "I will come and see you," he said to Wen. "I will have a study prepared for you to live in and you must bring your family. Every month I shall offer a small sum for your beans and water."

"You are most kind," said Master Wen.

Master Ni exclaimed: "A noble gentleman indeed, who recognizes literature so handsomely!"

When they had gone, Ximen Qing returned and drank with his guests. The party did not come to an end until the first night watch. The four singing girls went to Yueniang's room and sang a few songs for the ladies. In the front court, Ximen asked Ying Bojue and Uncle Wu to stay. He gave food to the actors and dismissed them. The servants cleared the tables and Ximen called for dessert. Then he bade Li Ming, Wu Hui and Zheng Feng come and sing, and gave them wine.

"Brother," Bojue said, "this has been a splendid entertainment and your guests have been well pleased."

Li Ming said that the two eunuchs, Liu and Xue, had been very generous in their presents and they had left a packet of silver for Guijie and Wu Yin'er. "His Excellency Xue is younger than the other," the boy said, "and that makes him more lively."

Huatong brought dessert. Bojue noticed some pastries among the different dishes. He picked out one and put it in his mouth. It melted away at once. It seemed like exquisite dew falling upon his heart. "This is excellent," he said.

"Oh, when it comes to eating, you know well enough how to pick out something good," Ximen said to him. "Your sixth mother made those."

Bojue laughed. "To show her daughterly devotion to me," he said. Then he said: "Uncle, won't you try one?" picked one out and put it into Uncle Wu's mouth. He gave one to Li Ming and Zheng Feng.

While they were drinking, Bojue said to Daian: "Go to the inner court and tell the four little strumpets to come here. I can do very well without them, but I want them to sing for your uncle. He cannot stay much longer and, after all, they have only sung one or two songs all day. It won't do to let them off too lightly."

Daian did not move. He said: "I did speak to them, but they are singing for the ladies now. Doubtless they will be here in a few moments."

"When did you speak to them, you young rascal?" Ying Bojue said. He told Wang Jing to go, but Wang Jing paid no attention. "You won't go, won't you?" said Bojue. "Then I will go myself." But, as he spoke, the scent of perfume came to them and they could hear laughing voices. The four singing girls came in, dabbing their faces with handkerchiefs.

"What!" cried Bojue, "are you going without singing for us? That's too much of a good thing! Your sedan chairs alone cost four *qian* of silver, and for that money we could buy quite a lot of rice, enough to keep your whole households for a month."

"Brother," Dong Jiao'er said, "if you think we can earn a living so easily as all that, why don't you come and join us?"

"It is very late," Hong Si'er said, "almost the second night watch. We really must go."

And Qi Xiang'er said: "We have to get up very early in the morning to go to a funeral."

"Whose funeral?" said Bojue.

"At a house where the doors open underneath the eaves," Qi Xiang'er replied.

"Doubtless young Master Wang's," said Bojue. "You got into trouble over that young man before, but luckily for you this gentleman sent to the Eastern Capital and had the matter hushed up for Li Guijie's sake. You were forgiven too. Now you put on the airs of a bird that has escaped from a cage."

Qi Xiang'er laughed. "Don't talk nonsense, old oily mouth!"

"Are you making fun of me because I am old?" Bojue said. "I fancy I still have some good points. Anyhow, I can manage you four little strumpets without any difficulty."

Qi Xiang'er laughed again. "Brother," she said, "I can't see you very well but it is obvious that you are boasting."

"When I spend my money," Bojue returned, "I insist upon having something worth paying for. You young strumpets of the Zheng family appear to have eaten something that makes you talk too much. You seem lost."

"After listening to you," said Dong Jiao'er, "she dare not open her mouth."

"I don't care whether she is afraid of me or not. Bring your instruments and each of you sing a song. Then I will let you go."

"Very well," Ximen Qing said, "two of you shall serve us with wine and the other two shall sing."

Then Qi Xiang'er said: "I and my sister will sing." Zheng Aiyue took her lute and Qi Xiang'er her zither. They sat down and sang very sweetly "Darkness Has Gone, the Dawn Is Here." Dong Jiao'er offered wine to Uncle Wu, and Hong Si'er to Ying Bojue.

After they had drunk several cups of wine and the girls had finished singing, Ximen Qing still pressed Uncle Wu to stay and sent for Chunhong to sing some songs of the South. Only then did he tell Qitong to saddle a horse and take a lantern to see Uncle Wu to his home. But Wu said: "Brother, don't order a horse for me. I will go with Brother Ying." Ximen bade Qitong accompany them with a lantern. He himself went as far as the gate with them. As they were standing at the gate, Ximen said to Ying Bojue:

"Don't forget about Gan. I am going to make a contract with him.

Then I will join with my kinsman Qiao, and we will get the house ready for the storage of the goods."

"I will not forget," Bojue said. He went away with Uncle Wu. Qitong, carrying a lantern, went with them.

"My brother-in-law spoke about getting the house ready. What house does he mean?" Uncle Wu said.

"Han Daoguo has arrived with the goods he has bought," Ying Bojue said, "and his Lordship is going to start a silk shop in the house facing his own."

"When is he going to open it?" Uncle Wu said. "We are his kinsmen and friends, and we ought to do something to mark the occasion."

They left the main street and came to the lane in which Ying Bojue lived. Uncle Wu said to Qitong: "Take Uncle Ying to his door."

Bojue declined. "No," he said, "go with your uncle. I don't need a light. My house is close by." They separated and Qitong went with Uncle Wu.

Ximen Qing paid and dismissed Li Ming and the others and went to sleep in Yueniang's room.

The next day Ying Bojue brought Gan Chushen to see Ximen Qing. Gan was wearing black clothes. They discussed terms, then Ximen sent for Cui Ben and told him to go and see Master Qiao and find out what Qiao thought about the arrangement of the house, and when they should open their shop. "I will do everything your master wishes," Qiao said to Cui Ben. "He need not worry about me." So Ximen Qing made a contract with Gan, with Ying Bojue as the witness. It was decided that, out of the profits, three parts of every ten should be for Ximen Qing, three for Qiao, and the remaining four should be divided equally between Han Daoguo, Gan Chushen and Cui Ben. They set to work upon the warehouse, had signs painted, and only waited for the merchandise to come so that they might start business. At home, Ximen Qing cleared one of the courts for Master Wen to occupy as his secretary. He arranged to pay his new secretary three taels of silver as salary each month, and to make him appropriate gifts at the different seasons. Huatong was instructed to wait upon the scholar. When all these arrangements were completed, Ximen gave a series of parties.

After his birthday celebrations, he sent for Dr. Ren to see Li Ping'er. Then he went to the house opposite to see how the men were getting on with their work. Aunt Yang went home, but Guijie and Wu Yin'er still remained. Yueniang took three *qian* of silver and bought some crabs. She boiled them and, when dinnertime came, invited Aunt Wu, Guijie, Wu Yin'er and the ladies to come and enjoy them.

Yueniang had sent for old woman Liu to come and see Guan'ge. After taking tea, the old woman went with Li Ping'er to her apartments. The baby, she said, had been frightened and could not digest his food. She gave Li Ping'er some medicine for him. Yueniang gave her a small fee and dismissed her.

Meanwhile, Yulou, Jinlian, Guijie, Wu Yin'er and Ximen Dajie were in one of the flower arbors. They had a small table and played dominoes. Xue'e was there too. She lost her game and was made to drink seven or eight cups of wine. Then she went away and the others asked Li Ping'er to take her place. Jinlian asked Guijie and Wu Yin'er to sing for them. They made merry all day, and, at sunset, Yueniang had the food boxes of the two singing girls filled and sent them home.

Jinlian had had too much to drink. She saw her husband going again to Li Ping'er and remembered that, the same morning, he had sent for Dr. Ren to see her. She was consumed by jealousy but she dared not go to him because she knew the baby was not well. As she was going in the dark to her own room, she trod upon some filth. When she reached her room, she asked Chunmei for a light. Her scarlet silk shoes were ruined. Her eyebrows went up and her eyes opened wide. She told Chunmei to get a stick, take a lamp, close the corner door, and give the dog a beating. The dog set up a terrible howling. Li Ping'er sent Yingchun to say that the baby had just taken old woman Liu's medicine and gone to sleep. She asked that Jinlian would stop beating the dog. But Jinlian sat and made no answer. The dog beating continued. At last she allowed the dog to run away and began to grumble at Qiuju. The more she looked at her shoes, the more her anger increased. She called Qiuju and said: "It was your business to drive the dog out. What do you mean by letting him stay there? Is that dog your lover that you can't bear to part with him? My new shoes, that I've only worn for three or four days, are completely ruined. You know you ought to have had a light showing for me when I came in. Why did you pretend not to know I was coming?"

"Before you came," Chunmei said, "I told her to feed the dog and put him out. She wouldn't listen but looked at me like a fool."

"Oh, yes, the bold slave!" Jinlian cried. "I know you must be beaten before you will do anything. Come here and look at my shoes."

Qiuju went forward and stooped to look at them. Jinlian struck her in the face with one. The girl's face was cut: she drew back and tried to stop the blood with her hand.

"You slave! You slave! Would you try to escape me?" Jinlian cried. Then to Chunmei: "Pull her here: drag her here, and go get the whip. Take off her clothes and let me give her thirty stripes. If she tries to get away, I'll give her more."

Chunmei pulled off Qiuju's clothes. Jinlian bade her hold the girl's hands, and the blows fell upon her body like raindrops. Qiuju shrieked and cried like a pig being killed.

Guan'ge had only just closed his eyes, and now he was waked up by the noise. Once more Yingchun came to Jinlian. "Mother asks you please to forgive Qiuju. She is afraid the noise will frighten the baby."

Old woman Pan was lying on the bed in the inner room. When she heard the noise, she got up. She asked her daughter to stop, but Jinlian would not listen to her. When Li Ping'er sent her maid again, old woman Pan took the whip from her daughter's hands. "Daughter," she said, "don't beat the girl any more. Your sister is afraid that the noise will upset the baby. I don't mind your beating this donkey, but we must not harm the treasure of the household."

Jinlian was already wild enough, but when she heard her mother's words she was infuriated. Her mind was so enraged that her face became purple. She pushed her mother away and the old woman all but fell down. "You old fool," she screamed. "Keep yourself in your place and don't interfere with me. What treasure indeed? What donkey? You are in league with everybody else to injure me."

"Why! nothing of the sort," the old woman said. "I only come to get a little cold food. Why do you treat me so badly?"

"Take your old cunt off tomorrow," Jinlian said. "I can tell you that nobody is going to get the better of me in this place."

The old woman went to her room and wept. Jinlian went on beating Qiuju. She beat her twenty or thirty stripes with the whip, then gave her another ten with a cane. Qiuju's skin and flesh were torn before she let the girl go. Then she drove her nails into her cheeks and scratched her face all over.

Li Ping'er covered the baby's ears with her two hands. Tears coursed down her cheeks. She was furious, but she did not dare to say anything more.

That day Ximen Qing had been taking wine in the house opposite with Ying Bojue, Cui Ben and his new manager, Gan. Afterwards he went to sleep with Yulou.

The next day Major Zhou invited him to go to a birthday party and he went. Li Ping'er saw that her child was no better, although he had taken old woman Liu's medicine, and, as a result of the noise in the night, his eyes were upturned. The two nuns, Xue and Wang, came. Li Ping'er went to Yueniang's room and said: "Here are a pair of silver lions that I have taken from the baby's bed. I am going to give them to Sister Xue so as to have some Buddhist scriptures printed and given away in the temple on the fifteenth day of the eighth month."

Nun Xue took the silver lions and was going away with them when Yulou stopped her. "Wait a moment," she said. "Sister, you must get Ben the Fourth to weigh them. When we know the weight, Ben the Fourth can go with her and we shall know how much we shall have to pay for these copies of the scriptures. Ben the Fourth had better see to it, for our teacher, Xue, is not expert in such matters."

"You are right," Yueniang said. She sent Laian to fetch Ben the Fourth. When Ben the Fourth came, he made a reverence to the ladies and weighed the silver. It came to forty-one taels and five *qian*. Yueniang told him to go with Nun Xue to the printer to arrange for the printing of the texts.

Jinlian said to Yulou: "We will take the two teachers to the gate and then go to see Ximen Dajie. She is making shoes in her room." Holding each other's hands, they went to the outer court. Ben the Fourth and the two nuns went out, and Jinlian and Yulou went to the rooms at the side of the great hall. They found Ximen's daughter making shoes under the eaves. Jinlian picked up the shoes and looked at them. They were of green Nanjing silk.

"You shouldn't have made the designs in red," Yulou said. "Blue would have been better, for you will have to have red heels."

"I have a pair with red heels," Ximen Dajie said. "That is why I am making this pair in red with blue heels."

They sat down. Yulou asked if Chen Jingji was in. "He is asleep indoors," said Ximen Dajie. "He has been drinking somewhere, I don't know where."

"If I hadn't spoken as I did," Yulou said to Jinlian, "that foolish Sixth Sister of ours would have given all that silver to the nuns. If they had once gone off with it, we should never have seen them again. That is why I suggested sending Ben the Fourth with them. They could have taken refuge with some people of importance and we should never have been able to get them out again."

"The nuns would be fools if they didn't make money out of rich ladies," Jinlian said. "To get a sum like that from her is like pulling a hair out of a cow. She wishes to save the baby's life because she knows she will never get another if this one dies, even though she gives mountains and rivers for charity. This printing of a few texts is a trifle. In our house it seems that some people are allowed to set the house on fire, but we mayn't even light our lamps. You are no stranger and this is our sister, so there is no harm in my saying that that lady indulges herself too much. She sends for the doctor even in the early morning. Of course, it is no business of ours. What annoys me is the way she says in front of others: 'Your father comes to see the baby and wants to sleep with me, but I always send him to the other ladies.' I am good-natured enough in all conscience, yet she is always complaining about me. The Great Lady always seems to take her side. Yesterday, Father did not go to her room. What does she do but send a maid to the corner door to ask him to go and look at the baby. Then she took some medicine and told her husband to sleep with Wu Yin'er. You see how clever she is. He was delighted, of course, and the Great Lady didn't seem to mind. Yesterday, when I was going to my room, I got my shoes all dirty and told my maid to drive the dog out. That displeased her, and she sent Yingchun to say the noise was frightening the baby. That old fool of a mother of mine told me to stop and said she was afraid of frightening the precious treasure. I was angry. I said something nasty to my mother, and now she has gone off in a huff. The best thing she could do, perhaps. We can manage well enough without that poor old woman."

Yulou laughed. "How badly you have been brought up," she said. "You should not talk like that about your own mother."

"Well, she annoyed me. She always was deceitful and ready to take anybody's part but mine. Anyone who will give her half a bowl of rice can always count on her support. If anyone gives her a little something she likes, she will remember it with gratitude forever. As for the other, after that baby's birth she got our husband to stay there as if he had taken root. If he were to make her his first wife, she would throw us in the mud and trample on us. But Heaven has eyes, and that accounts for the baby's illness."

Then Ben the Fourth came back. He was on his way to Yueniang's room, but, seeing the three ladies, he stopped outside the second door and did not venture to go farther. Laian came and said: "Ladies, Ben the Fourth is here."

"Well, you rascal, let him come in," Jinlian said. "We saw him only a moment or two ago."

Laian told Ben the Fourth. He put something over his head and hurried through to the inner court to see Yueniang and Li Ping'er. He explained that the two nuns had given the printer forty-one taels and five *qian*. Five hundred copies were to be printed with silk covers, each of which would cost five *fen*, and a thousand copies in thinner silk that would cost three *fen* apiece. That would be fifty-five taels all together. We still have to pay the printer thirteen taels and five *qian*," he said. "He has promised to send all the copies here on the fourteenth."

Li Ping'er went to her room and brought a silver perfume box. She gave it to Ben the Fourth, who weighed it and found it to be fifteen taels. "Take it," Li Ping'er said, "pay the printer and keep the rest for your expenses when you go to the temple to give out the texts. It will save you the trouble of coming to ask me again." Ben the Fourth took the box. As he was going away, Li Ping'er said: "Fourth Brother, I thank you."

Ben the Fourth bowed. "You are very kind," he said. Then he went to the front court. There Jinlian and Yulou stopped him.

"Have you given the silver to the printer?" Yulou asked.

"Yes," he said. "I have arranged for the printing of fifteen hundred copies. I paid forty-one taels and five *qian,* and now the Sixth Lady has given me this silver box." Jinlian and Yulou looked at the box but said nothing. Ben the Fourth went out.

"Our Sixth Sister is wasting her money," Yulou said. "If the baby is destined to live, nothing can kill him. If he is destined to die, his life won't be saved by any distributing of texts. If she trusts the nuns, they will make a fool of her."

They got up. "Let us go and look out of the gate," Jinlian said. They asked Ximen Dajie to go with them but she declined. Pan Jinlian took Meng Yulou by the hand, and they went to the gate together. When they got there, she asked Ping'an if the house opposite had been made ready.

"Yesterday," Ping'an said, "Father made the workmen clear it out and fix up the rooms in the back court as a warehouse. The Master of the Yin Yang came and blessed the starting of operations. The ground floor is being divided into three rooms, and shelves are being set up for the silk. The rooms at the front are to be made into a shop, and the painters have been told to decorate them. Next month the shop will be opened."

Yulou asked if Master Wen's family had move in.

"Yes," Ping'an said, "they came yesterday. This morning Father gave instructions that they were to be supplied with a bed, two tables, and two chairs."

"Did you see his wife?" Jinlian said.

"She came in a sedan chair," Ping'an said, "and it was too dark for me to see her."

As they were talking, they heard 'Ting, Ting, Ting', and an old man came along shaking a brass rattle. "Here is the polisher of mirrors," Jinlian said to Ping'an. "My mirror needs polishing. It is very tarnished. I told you to look out for a polisher, and you forgot all about it. Now, the very minute we come here, one comes along."

Ping'an stopped the old man, who put down his things. "If you have any mirrors to clean," Jinlian said to Yulou, "tell the boys to bring them out." Then she said to Laian: "Go to my room and ask Chunmei for my mirrors, the large one and the two small ones and the square one I use for dressing. See that he gets a good polish on them."

Yulou said to him: "Go to my room and ask Lanxiang for my mirrors." Laian went and came back with mirrors large and small, eight altogether in his hands, and the square one pressed against his chest.

"You foolish boy," Jinlian said, "you can't carry all those mirrors. Why didn't you make two journeys? You will make dents in them, holding them all together like that."

"I have never seen that big mirror of yours," Yulou said to Jinlian. "Where did you get it?"

"It came from the pawnshop," Jinlian said. "I like its brightness. That's why I keep it in my room." She said to the boy: "Only three of those mirrors are mine."

Yulou said: "and only two are mine."

"Whose are the rest?" Jinlian said.

"The other two are Sister Chunmei's," the boy said. "She gave them to me so that they might be cleaned with yours."

"The cunning little wretch!" Jinlian said. "She never uses her own mirrors but always mine. That's why mine are so dull."

The boy gave the mirrors to the old man who sat down on a bench, brought out his quicksilver and, in a very short time, polished them all till they shone again. Jinlian took one up and looked at herself. The mirror was like pure clear water.

> The lotus and the water chestnut
> Cast their reflection on the water.
> The breeze brings ripples to the surface
> And the green shadows move darkly.
> In a pool of autumn waters the lotus appears
> Like Chang E in the moon.

She gave the mirrors to Laian to take back. Yulou told Ping'an to go to the shop and ask Fu for some coins for the old man. He took the money but did not move away. "Ask the old man why he doesn't go away," Yulou said to Ping'an. "Perhaps he thinks we have not paid him enough." The old man wept.

"My mistress wants to know why you are so distressed," Ping'an said to him.

"Brother," said the old man, "I am sixty-one years old, and I have a son who is twenty-one. He is unmarried but he will do nothing for a living. He gads about everywhere, and I have to come out to the street day after day to earn a little money to support him. He is such an undutiful son that he even takes my money and goes gambling with it. The other day he was mixed up in some trouble and they took him to the courts. There they dealt with him as a pickpocket and beat him twenty strokes. When he came home, he took his mother's clothes and pawned them all. That upset his mother so much she had to take to her bed and she has stayed there this last fortnight. I upbraided him and he went away. He did not come back and I have looked everywhere for him in vain. Sometimes I think I will not bother to look for him any more, but I am old and he is my only son. There is only he to take care of me in my old age. Yet when he is at home he makes me angry. Life isn't worth living. I suffer so much and have no place to complain. I would cry my heart out if I could."

"Go and ask him how old his wife is," Yulou said to Ping'an.

"She is fifty-five," the old man said. "She has no children of her own, and she has been ill ever since this trouble. She is getting better now, but I have nothing to give her to feed her. She keeps asking for dried meat. I have been begging everywhere these last few days, but nobody will give me any."

"Never mind," Yulou said, "I have some in my room." She told Laian to go and ask her maid for two pieces.

Jinlian said: "Would your wife like some millet gruel?"

"Would she not?" cried the old man. "Where is there any? If she could only have some, she would be delighted."

Jinlian told Laian to ask Chunmei for two measures of new millet from that which old woman Pan had brought her, and two dried melons. When he returned, he brought the preserved meat, two measures of millet and two pickled cucumbers. "Old man," he said, "you are in luck's way. If she doesn't feel well enough to eat this, she must be just getting over childbirth, and this millet will help settle her stomach."

The old man reached out both his hands and took what was brought for him. He put it with his tools, bowed to the ladies, slung everything over his shoulder and went off sounding his rattle.

"Mothers," said Ping'an, "you shouldn't have given him so much. He has defrauded you. His wife is a go-between. I saw her on the street only a day or two ago. She hasn't been at home at all."

"Why didn't you tell me so before, you rascal?" Jinlian said.

"I told him he was lucky to have met you two ladies," Ping'an said.

CHAPTER 59

The Death of Guan'ge

The maple leaves are turning red
The other leaves are already yellow.
Her hair is white as the morning frost
For he of whom she thinks
Is at the gate of the underworld
And she will see him no more.

Though she cries out her heart
There is none to carry her message to the other world.
It is far distant, and the way is covered
With the mist of sorrow.
The pearl is buried
And all earthly things are forgotten.
If her tears were drops of rain
They would fill the Eastern Ocean
With sorrow eternal.

The old mirror cleaner had just gone when suddenly a man came from the East galloping towards them on muleback. He was wearing eye-shades and a broad-brimmed hat. He pulled up at the gate and the two ladies hastily withdrew. When he took off the eyeshades, they knew it was Han Daoguo. Ping'an asked him if the merchandise had come.

"All the wagons are inside the city," Han said; "I want to know where we are to unload them."

"Our master is at Major Zhou's place," Ping'an said, "but he told me that everything has to be put into the house opposite. Please come in."

A moment later, Chen Jingji came to take Han Daoguo to see Wu Yueniang. When he came out, he brushed the dust and dirt from his clothes and told Wang Jing to take his baggage home. Yueniang ordered a meal to be served for him. Soon all the wagons arrived. Chen Jingji took the key and unlocked the doors. The porters carried in box after box of merchandise, ten great wagonloads in all, and did not finish till evening. Cui Ben was there to help, and everybody took a hand in the work. The doors were locked again and sealed. Then the porters were paid and dismissed.

Daian went to Major Zhou's house to tell Ximen Qing that the goods had come, and Ximen, after drinking a few more cups of wine, came home. Han Daoguo was waiting for him in the great hall. They sat down and Han told his master the whole story from beginning to end.

"Did you give my letter to his Lordship Qian?" Ximen asked. "Did he make things easier?"

"Oh, yes!" Han Daoguo said. "Because of that letter, though we had ten wagonloads we paid very much less than the amount due. At the customs I reckoned two boxes as one, and we made out that only two-thirds of them contained silk and that the rest held only tea and incense. So, though we had ten big wagonloads we only paid thirty taels and five *qian* duty. His Lordship accepted my list without going through the boxes, and passed everything through."

Ximen Qing was delighted to hear this. "We must send his Lordship a handsome present," he said. He told Chen Jingji to entertain Han Daoguo and Cui Ben. Afterwards, Han Daoguo went home.

When Wang Liu'er heard that her husband had returned, she bade her maid prepare an especially good meal and waited until the evening. When he came in, he made a reverence before the domestic shrine, took off his clothes, washed, and they began to talk. Han Daoguo told his wife that his mission had been very successful. Wang Liu'er remarked that there seemed to be a good deal of money in his pockets. He told her he had bought two hundred taels' worth of goods on his own account, wine and rice and so forth. These he had left outside the city and, when he came to sell them, he would certainly do well out of them. Wang Liu'er was very pleased. "Wang Jing," she said, "tells me that there is now a new manager called Gan, and it has been arranged that we and Brother Cui are to share equally with him in the profits. This will be all to our advantage. The shop is to be opened next month."

"If there is someone here to look after the shop," Han Daoguo said, "we shall need a man to go to the South to make the necessary purchases. I suppose our master will send me."

"You silly fellow," Wang Liu'er said, "a man who is really capable always gets more work than other people. If our master trusts you, it is because you are such a clever businessman. The proverb says: No man can make money without working for it. If you are sent away for a year or two, I will speak to his Lordship and have you brought back; Gan or Lai-bao can be sent in your place. Then you will be able to work at home."

"Oh, I don't mind," Han Daoguo said. "After all, I have a good deal of experience in this outside trade."

"You must not let it upset you," his wife said. "You will have more to do than if you were at home."

Wine was brought. Husband and wife pledged each other. Then they went to bed and enjoyed a pleasant night.

The next day was the first of the eighth month. Ximen's merchandise had come and he was free. He decided to go and visit Zheng Aiyue. He quietly gave Daian three taels of silver and a light dress and told him to take them to the girl. When the old procuress heard that Ximen Qing was coming, she was delighted. He might have been a gift from Heaven. She took the presents and said to Daian: "Tell his Lordship that both my girls are waiting anxiously for him. He must come early." Daian returned and told Ximen Qing in his study.

That afternoon, Ximen told Daian to have his sedan chair brought around. He dressed in a large hat, a black summer gown, and a pair of black shoes with white soles. Before leaving he went to the house opposite and saw how the workers were getting on. Then he got into the chair and pulled down the bamboo blind. Qintong and Daian went with him. Wang Jing was left at home and Chunhong was sent in advance with Ximen Qing's things.

Zheng Aixiang, dressed in her best clothes, stood smiling at the door to receive Ximen Qing. She led him to the reception room and made reverence to him. Ximen told Qintong to take the chair home and return that evening with a horse. Only Daian and Chunhong remained.

The old procuress came to welcome Ximen. "My daughter troubled you the other day," she said, "and now you have been kind enough to visit us. But why did you send those presents? I must thank you very much indeed for the dress you sent my daughter."

"Why didn't she come when I sent for her?" Ximen said. "Why did you say she had to go to Wang's?"

"I haven't forgiven Dong Jiao'er and Li Guijie yet," the old woman said. "They never told us it was your birthday. So, that day, they both brought you presents and my poor girl had nothing to offer. Besides, if we had known, we should have got out of that engagement at Wang's place. You would certainly have had the first claim. Then you sent your servant for her. I got into a flurry, and, without letting Wang's people know anything about it, I sent her off to you by the back door."

"I spoke to her about it when I was taking wine with Magistrate Xia," Ximen said. "If it had not been for that, I should not have minded. What made me so angry was that she never sent me word, but simply stayed away. I want to know why that was."

"Since that little baggage has become a woman," the old woman said, "she has not been at all eager to go out to sing. She knew that there would be a number of guests at your house, and she was shy. She has been brought up very tenderly. She has only just got up now, as you see, and I had to urge her several times. I said to her: 'You must get up at once because his Lordship Ximen is coming,' but she has only just done so."

The maid brought tea, and Zheng Aixiang offered a cup to Ximen Qing. Then the old procuress invited him to go to the inner court. Zheng Aixiang took him to her sister's room. He saw a scroll hanging on the wall with the words "Aiyue Hall." He sat down; the lattice was raised, and Zheng Aiyue came in. She wore no net upon her hair. It was simply dressed in the fashion of Hangzhou. It shone with a glossy blackness, coil upon coil like a black mist. Her double-breasted gown was of white silk, and her skirt was purple with green embroidery. Beneath it he could see two small red shoes. When she moved, the tinkling of the pearls and jewels made her seem still more beautiful.

Zheng Aiyue came towards him and greeted him rather carelessly. Then she sat down, hiding her pale face behind a gilded fan. Ximen Qing looked at her and thought her more desirable than ever. His eyes sparkled, his mind was troubled, and he found it hard to contain himself. The maid brought tea. Zheng Aiyue drew her sleeve back a little and, with her dainty fingers, offered him a cup. She and her sister Zheng Aixiang each took a cup and drank together with Ximen Qing. Then the cups were removed. She asked him to take off his long gown and go to her room. Ximen summoned Daian to take his cloak and the boy put it over a chair.

In Zheng Aiyue's room the hangings, curtains and bedclothes were all of silk. It was a most attractive room and exquisitely perfumed. "Indeed," Ximen said, "this is a dwelling place for the Immortals to which no mortal man should come."

They talked and laughed together for a while. Then the maid came to set the table. The food was well chosen and well prepared. First, they offered him lotus-blossom cakes. Then Zheng Aiyue picked out a mince-meat roll and offered it to him on a golden plate. When the food was done with and everything cleared away, she laid a scarlet cloth on the table and brought out thirty-two ivory pieces and they played dominoes. After the game, wine was brought and many fine fruits. The wine was poured into a golden cup, and the two sisters offered it to him. Then they took their instruments, Zheng Aixiang a zither, and Zheng Aiyue a lute, and together sang the song "Love Is in Our Hearts." So from exquisite lips came exquisite melody. Their voices would have melted a piece of marble. When the song was over, they cast dice. Then Zheng Aixiang made a show of going to change her clothes and left Zheng Aiyue alone with Ximen Qing.

Ximen took from his sleeve a white silk kerchief in which was wrapped a tiny gold box. Zheng Aiyue thought there were fragrant tea leaves in it and was going to open it, but Ximen said: "That is not for tea leaves. It holds my medicine." He took a packet from his sleeve and unfolded it, taking from it a lozenge of fragrant tea that he handed to her. She wished for more and put her hand into his sleeve. She found a purple kerchief with a pair of gold toothpicks in it. She admired it exceedingly.

"Guijie and Wu Yin'er have kerchiefs like it," she said. "You must have given them to them."

"Yes," Ximen said, "they were brought from Yangzhou. I don't suppose there is anyone else who could have given them such kerchiefs. Have it if you like it. I will send one for your sister in the morning." He took the wine cup and drank wine with his medicine. He put his arms around Zheng Aiyue and they drank mouth to mouth. He stroked her breasts. They were small and very soft. He pulled aside her shift. Beneath it her skin was as clear as the whitest jade. His passion was aroused, and his penis rose in anticipation. He pulled down his trousers and asked her to stroke it, but it was so big that she was afraid. She put her arms around his neck and said, "My sweet, this is the first time we have met. Be merciful and give me only a half. If you put in all there is, you will kill me. You've made it that size with your medicine. Nothing else would make it so red, so hot, so fearful."

Ximen laughed and said, "Get down, girl, so that you can find out what it knows."

"Another time I will do that for you," Zheng Aiyue said, "for we shall meet as often as there are leaves upon the trees, but not today, the first time we have come together."

Ximen Qing was anxious to begin. Zheng Aiyue asked if he would not have more wine. "It is not wine I want," he said, "but to lie with you."

Zheng Aiyue summoned the maid to clear away the wine table and take off Ximen's boots. Meanwhile, she went to the inner court to take off her clothes and wash herself. When the maid had taken off his boots, Ximen gave her a piece of silver, then he got into bed and she lighted some incense. Zheng Aiyue came back and asked if he would like some tea. "It is not tea I want," he said. Then she fastened the door and pulled down the curtains, put the pillow on the bed and joined him there. They were like a pair of lovebirds or the phœnix and his mate.

Ximen Qing saw that the girl's skin was smooth and fine, and her cunt dainty and without a hair upon it. It was like a piece of pastry made of the finest flour, tender and delicate and perfectly adorable. He clasped her waist with both his arms. It was as soft as jade and fragrance issued from it. Not for a thousand gold pieces could such perfection have been bought. He wrapped her white legs around his body, put on the clasp, and surged to the inmost recess of her flower of pleasure. But his penis was so stiff that it could not enter. He struggled long, with little success. She grimaced, and, gripping the pillow, begged him to stop. This only made his movements fiercer.

They sported together until the third night watch. Then Ximen Qing went home.

The next day Wu Yueniang was sitting in her room with Meng Yulou, Pan Jinlian and Li Jiao'er. Daian came and asked for the silk that was to be sent as a present to Magistrate Xia upon his birthday.

"Yesterday your father called for his sedan chair," Yueniang said. "Where did he go? It was very late when he came back and I suspect he went to Han Daoguo's house. You young rascal, you are always trying to throw dust in my eyes when you go off with him on sly expeditions of that sort."

"No," Daian said, "it was not to Han Daoguo's house my father went, for Han has only just come home."

"Where did he go, then?"

Daian smiled. He made no answer and took away the silk.

"Great Sister," Jinlian said, "you will never get the truth out of that young scamp. But I believe the young Southerner went with him too. Send for the young Southerner. We may get the truth from him."

Chunhong was sent for, and Jinlian said to him: "Where did you go with your father yesterday? Tell us the truth or the Great Lady will have you beaten."

Chunhong knelt down. "Don't beat me, lady," he said, "I will tell you. Daian, Qintong and I went with Father through a great gateway. We went up several streets and down others, and at last we came to a house where the doors were partly open, protected by sharp-edged bars. Inside the door there stood a very beautiful young lady."

Jinlian laughed. "You rascal. Don't you know what a house like that is? Calling a singing girl a lady too!" Then she asked: "What did the girl look like? Have you ever seen her before?"

"I didn't recognize her," Chunhong said. "She wore a net upon her head just as you ladies do. When we went in, a white-haired old lady came and made reverence to Father. Then we went to the inner court. There was another young lady there, but she didn't wear a net. Her face was the shape of a melon seed and her lips were painted very red. She drank wine with Father."

"Where did you go then?" Jinlian asked.

"Daian, Qintong and I went to the old lady's room. She gave us wine and cakes."

This amused Yueniang and Yulou roared with laughter. They asked him if he knew the second of the two girls.

"She looked like one who was here the other day."

"Ha! Guijie!" Yulou said.

"So he went there, did he?" said Yueniang.

"But there is no half-finished gate at our house," Li Jiao'er said.

"Perhaps they have built one lately," Jinlian suggested.

When Ximen Qing returned, he went straight out again to congratulate Magistrate Xia upon his birthday.

Pan Jinlian had a long-haired white cat. It was white all over except for a black streak that went down from its head along its back. It was called Coal in the Snow and sometimes Snow Lion. It could pick up fans and handkerchiefs in its mouth. When Ximen Qing was away, Jinlian often took it to bed with her. It never made a mess of her clothes. When it was wanted, it would come at once, and when it was not wanted, it would go away at once. Sometimes the woman called it Snowy Bandit. It ate not ox liver or dried fish, but raw meat, and this made it fat and strong. So long was its hair that you could hide an egg in it. Jinlian was fond of this cat, and often used to wrap a piece of meat in a red handkerchief and made the cat pounce forward to snatch it.

Guan'ge had been ill, but, after taking old woman Liu's medicine, he improved considerably. Li Ping'er dressed him in a red silk shirt and put him on the bed to play. Yingchun and the nurse were there, and the nurse was having something to eat. Snow Lion was sitting on the bed. The baby was wearing a red shirt and moving about, and the cat imagined that the red shirt was the handkerchief in which Jinlian often wrapped up a piece of meat for him to play with. Suddenly, the cat pounced forward and scratched the child. The baby gave one shriek and began to choke. Then he had convulsions. The nurse was alarmed, put down the bowl she was holding, and took up the baby. She succeeded in stopping the convulsions, but the cat still came after the baby and tried to scratch him. Yingchun drove him away.

Ruyi'er thought that the baby would now be better, but he had one fit after another. She asked Yingchun to go at once to the inner court for Li Ping'er. When the maid told her mistress what had happened, Li Ping'er was terribly upset. Yueniang ran with her to her room. Guan'ge's eyes were turned so that the pupils could not be seen. There was foam on his lips and the only sound he made was like the chirping of a young chicken. His hands and feet were trembling.

Li Ping'er felt as if her heart had been cut by a knife. She rocked the child in her arms and kissed him. "Oh, my baby," she cried, "you were so well when I went to the inner court. What has made you have a fit like this?" Yingchun and Ruyi'er told her about the cat. Li Ping'er wept more bitterly than before. "Baby," she said, "nobody has loved you, and now you have fallen into this trap."

When Yueniang heard this, she said nothing, but sent for Jinlian and asked her whether it was her cat that had frightened the baby.

"Who said it was my cat?" Jinlian said.

Yueniang pointed to the nurse and Yingchun. "They said so," she said.

"Then they have too much to say," Jinlian cried. "My cat is asleep in my room. How can it have frightened the baby? What right have they to say such a thing? Just as, when they take a melon, they always pick out the soft spot, so, whenever anything goes wrong, the blame is put down to me."

"How did the cat get in here?" Yueniang said.

"It often comes," Yingchun told her.

"Then why hasn't it scratched the baby before?" Jinlian cried. "As for you, young woman, don't goggle at me like that. Don't raise your eyebrows and don't have so much to say. Oh, I never have any luck." She went angrily to her own room.

Jinlian had secretly trained her cat with intent to kill the baby. If the child died, she hoped to win back Ximen Qing. It was the same as the very old story in which Tu'an Gu trained a dog to kill Zhao Dun, the minister.

When Yueniang and the others saw the child in such a state, they poured ginger broth down his throat and sent Laian for old woman Liu. The old woman came and felt the baby's pulse. She tapped her foot upon the floor and said: "This is serious. I fear the child will die." She hastily made a decoction of peppermint and Jinlian, then she produced a ball of gold foil, pounded her decoction in a cup, and filled the gold foil with it. Yueniang took a golden pin to open the baby's mouth. It was tightly closed but they got the medicine down his throat. "If that cures him, well and good," said the old woman. "If it doesn't, I fear we shall have to burn moxa on him."

"We can't decide that," Yueniang said. "We shall have to wait until his father comes home or he will be angry."

"Mother," Li Ping'er cried, "we must save the child's life. If we wait, it may be too late. If Father scolds us, I will take all the blame."

"Well," Yueniang said, "it is your boy. I will leave it to you, for I dare not take the responsibility."

Old woman Liu burned moxa on the baby in five places, between his brows, on his neck, on both wrists and on his breast. Then he seemed to go to sleep. In the evening, when Ximen Qing arrived, he had not yet awakened. When the old woman knew that Ximen Qing had come, she took five *qian* of silver from Yueniang and slipped away by a back door. Ximen came to Yueniang's room and she told him all about the child. He hurried to Li Ping'er's room. Her eyes were very red. "What has made the boy ill?" Ximen asked her. She only wept and made no answer. Then he asked the maid and the nurse, but they dared not tell him. He noticed that the child's hands were scratched and that he was burned in several places. He rushed back to question Yueniang. She could keep silence no longer and told him about the cat. "Old woman Liu declared that the boy had been terrified," she said, "and that the only thing to do was to use the needle and burn moxa on him. She was afraid it would be too late if we waited for you. Since then the child has slept. He has not waked at all."

Ximen Qing flew into a furious rage. He dashed to Jinlian's room and, without a word, took the cat by the legs and dashed out its brains on the stone flags underneath the eaves. There was a crash. The cat's brain was scattered like ten thousand peach blossoms, and its teeth like broken jade.

When Jinlian saw her cat destroyed, she sat on her bed and did not move. "You thief," she muttered as Ximen Qing went away, "taking people's property and killing it. That's the sort of hero you are. All this fuss about a cat. Of course, the cat won't demand its life at your hands when it meets you in Hades! You treacherous villain! you changeable creature! You will come to a bad end."

Ximen Qing went back to the Sixth Lady's room. "You were looking after the baby," he said to Ruyi'er and Yingchun. "How did it happen that you allowed the cat to frighten and scratch him? Then you listened to old woman Liu and allowed her to burn the child. If he gets better, well and good. But if he doesn't, that old whore shall go to the courts and I'll have the screws on her."

"What would you have done," Li Ping'er said, "if you had thought the baby was at the point of death? Doctors only do the best they can to help people."

Li Ping'er had hoped that after the operation the child would be better, but the only result was to drive the trouble farther in. The convulsions developed into a slow fit. The child's water and motions issued freely and were strangely colored. His eyes opened and closed convulsively; he dozed, and took no food all day. In a terrible state of anxiety, Li Ping'er consulted fortune-tellers, but the omens were all unfavorable. Yueniang, without Ximen Qing's knowledge, again sent for old woman Liu to come and work a charm. Then they sent for a doctor who specialized in children's ailments. He proposed to blow some powder into the baby's nostrils. "If the child sneezes," he said, "well and good, but if he doesn't, I fear there is no hope." They blew the powder into the child's nostrils but nothing happened. Not once did he sneeze. Li Ping'er gazed and gazed at the child all day and all night. She never dried her tears and she never wished to eat or drink.

The fifteenth day of the eighth month was Yueniang's birthday, but she would not keep it. Her relatives sent presents but no invitations were sent to them. Only Aunt Wu, Aunt Yang and the two nuns came. The two nuns had not shared the money equally and they were not on the best of terms.

On the fourteenth, Ben the Fourth and Nun Xue went to the printer's and brought back with them fifteen hundred copies of the texts. Li Ping'er gave him a string of coppers to buy paper offerings, incense, and candles, and, on the fifteenth, he went with Chen Jingji to the temple, burned the paper offerings and the incense, and distributed the scriptures. Then he returned and told Li Ping'er what he had done. Every day the Qiao family sent old woman Kong to see Guan'ge. They recommended a certain Dr. Bao of the Imperial College of Medicine, who was a specialist in children's diseases. When he came, he called the illness by a long name and said that it was hopeless. They gave him five *qian* of silver and dismissed him. Then they tried to pour some medicine down the baby's throat, but he rejected it. He closed his eyes, clenched his teeth and made a gurgling noise. All night long Li Ping'er never took off her clothes. She carried the baby in her arms, crying all the time. Ximen Qing, except for his duty at the office, never went out, and, whenever he came back from the office, he went at once to see his son.

One night at the end of the eighth month Li Ping'er was lying on the bed with Guan'ge in her arms. A single lamp was burning on the table and the maids and the nurse were sound asleep. She looked at the window. The moonbeams shone through it and she could hear the mournful sound of the night watchman. To her sad heart it sounded like ten thousand knockings. Her grief was beyond expression.

> The Milky Way is still, is still.
> The stars are far, are far away.
> The gleaming moon casts her cool beams through the window
> And the cold night breeze drives through the door.
> On the watchtower the drum beats quickly

One watch and then another.
In someone's house, beating laundry,
A thousand strokes, and then again a thousand strokes.
The wind chimes ring under painted eaves:
It breaks the grieving woman's heart.
The lamp, burning on its silver stand,
Serves but to point out her unending sorrow.
One thought alone is in that heart
The longing for her child's recovery.

Li Ping'er lay on her bed half sleeping, half waking. She dreamed that her old husband Hua Zixu came to her door, wearing white, and looking as he had looked in life. "Strumpet," he said harshly, "what right had you to steal my wealth and give it to Ximen Qing? At this moment I go to accuse you." Li Ping'er seized him by the sleeve. "Good Brother," she pleaded, "be merciful." But Hua Zixu escaped from her. She woke to find her hand grasping Guan'ge's sleeve and knew it was a dream. "Strange! Strange!" she gasped. She heard the drum sounding the third night watch. Her hair was standing on end and her body was bathed in a cold sweat.

The next day when Ximen Qing came, she told him of her dream. "Where he is now we do not know," Ximen Qing said. "It was only your fancy. Try and be calm and do not worry so much. I will get Wu Yin'er to come and stay with you, and old woman Feng to come and wait on you." Daian was sent to bring Wu Yin'er.

That afternoon Guan'ge, lying upon his nurse's breast, seemed hardly able to breathe. Ruyi'er was frightened. She called Li Ping'er. "Mother," she cried, "look at the baby. His eyes are upturned and he seems able only to breathe out, not in." Li Ping'er took the child from her, weeping. She told the maid to go at once for Ximen Qing and tell him that the baby was dying.

Chang Zhijie was there, telling Ximen Qing how he had found a house with four rooms and needed thirty-five taels more. When Ximen heard how ill his son was, he said to Chang Zhijie: "You must go now. I cannot take you to the gate. I will send you the money and come to see you in your new house." He hurried to see Li Ping'er. Yueniang and the other ladies were already there, watching the child struggling in the last agony. Ximen Qing could not bear to look. He went into another room, sat down on a chair, and sighed deeply. Before he had time to drink half a cup of tea, Guan'ge died. It was around four in the afternoon of the twenty-third day of the eighth month. The boy had lived a mere fourteen months.

They all set up a great crying. Li Ping'er beat her ears, tore her cheeks, dashed her head upon the ground, and wept until she fell into a swoon. For a long time she stayed unconscious, then she came to herself and rocked the dead child in her arms, sobbing.

"Oh my poor unfortunate child," she cried, "my heart is broken. Why could I not die with you? I will not live long in this world. Why have you left me so cruelly?"

Ruyi'er and Yingchun cried bitterly. Ximen Qing told some of the boys to prepare a room at the side of the great hall, and was going to put the child upon his bed on two benches there, but Li Ping'er clung to him with both hands and would not let him go. "My unfortunate child, my precious baby," she cried, "you have taken my heart with you. Now all my labor is wasted. I can never see you more, my heart!"

Yueniang and the others cried with her and tried to console her. Ximen Qing, when he saw her torn face and her hair in disorder, said: "Do not take it so hard. He was not fated to be our child. We reared him for a spell but now his little life is done. Cry and be done with it. We cannot bring him back to life by weeping. Remember that you are dear to me. Now we must take him away and I must send for the Master of the Yin Yang." He asked what the time was and Yueniang told him.

"As I thought," Meng Yulou said, "he waited for this hour and then went. At this hour he was born and at this hour he has died. It was the twenty-third day too, only the month is different. He has lived one year and two months exactly."

When Li Ping'er saw the boys waiting to take the body of her child away, she began to cry again. "Oh, why must you be in such a hurry? Great Mother, put your hand upon him. He is still warm. Oh, my son! How can I give you up? You cannot leave me so cruelly." Again she threw herself upon the ground and sobbed bitterly.

The boys took Guan'ge and laid him in the room they had prepared. Yueniang said to Ximen Qing: "We must let our relatives the Qiaos know, and send for the priests."

"We will send for the priests tomorrow," Ximen said. He sent Daian to bear the news to Master Qiao. Xu, the Master of the Yin Yang, was summoned to write the certificate. Ben the Fourth was given ten taels of silver and told to buy a set of fir-wood boards and get the carpenters to make a little coffin for the child.

As soon as the Qiaos got the message, Mistress Qiao came. She cried. Yueniang and the others cried with her and told her all that had happened. Then Xu, the Master of the Yin Yang, came. "My young brother," he said, "departed this life exactly at the hour of the monkey." Yueniang told him to look at the black book. Master Xu took up his black book and read:

The young master was born at the hour of the monkey on the twenty-third day of the sixth month of the *bingshen* year in the Zhenghe reign period, and died at the hour of the monkey on the twenty-third day of the eighth month of the *dingyu* year of the same reign. This combination of a *renzi* day and a *dingyu* month indicates that another life and death are before him. We must have no mourners except the relatives, and, when he is put into the coffin, no one who was born under the sign of the Snake, the Dragon, the Rat or the Hare, must be present. It says in my black book that one who dies on a *renzi* day will go upwards to the Temple of the Precious Vase, or down to Qi (Shandong). In his previous existence he was a scion of the house of Cai in Yanzhou. He extorted money from people by violence and spent his substance in wild living. He paid no worship to Heaven and Earth and was lacking in due reverence for his kinsmen. He caught a chill, took to his bed, fouled his bedclothes, and died. He was born again, suffered from convulsions, and, ten days ago, some animal terrified him. On that day his evil star was in the ascendant; his spirit was taken from him. On that day, too, he was born again in a family named Wang. He will grow to be a military officer and live to be sixty-eight years old.

This was what Master Xu found in his book. He asked whether Ximen Qing intended to bury or burn the body the following day.

"I do not wish him to be taken from here tomorrow," Ximen Qing said. "I will have the appropriate ceremonies on the third day, and he shall be buried in my family sepulchre on the fifth day after his death."

"The twenty-seventh will be a *bingchen* day and not inauspicious so far as the members of your household are concerned," the Master of the Yin Yang said. "The burial should take place at noon." He wrote a certificate and the child was placed in the coffin. It was the third night watch. Li Ping'er went to her room and, weeping, gathered together some of the child's tiny religious garments and put them, with hat, shoes, and socks, into the coffin with him. It was nailed up. Everybody began to cry again. The Master of the Yin Yang went away.

The next day Ximen Qing was too busy to go to the office. Xia heard of his bereavement and came to offer his condolences. Ximen sent a man to give the news to Abbot Wu and ask him to send eight priests to sing a dirge on the third day after the decease. The Abbot and Master Qiao both offered the customary offering of three animals. The four uncles, Wu, Shen, Han, and Hua, did likewise and came to burn paper offerings. Ying

Bojue, Xie Xida, Master Wen, Chang Zhijie, Han Daoguo, Gan, Ben the Fourth, Li and Huang, all made contributions and came in the evening to watch before the body with Ximen Qing. When the monks had performed their part and had gone away, the customary offerings were made before the baby's coffin. Ximen Qing had tables set in the great hall for the entertainment of those who had come to condole with him.

Li Guijie, Wu Yin'er, and Zheng Aiyue sent offerings.

Li Ping'er, thinking always of her child, was very sad. She would take nothing to eat and cried so much that she lost her voice. Indeed Ximen Qing was afraid she might try to kill herself, and told the nurse, the maids, and Wu Yin'er to stay with her all day. He himself spent three nights with her and did all he could to console her. Nun Xue read the Lengyan Sutra to her and an exorcism for freeing the troubled spirit, and tried to persuade her to stop crying. "This was not really your child," she said. "He was one to whom you were beholden in a former existence. We read in the Dharani Sutra of a woman who bore three children, all of whom died before they were two years old. She cried as she took the last dead baby to the river's bank, and could not bear to cast it in. Then the Blessed One took the form of a monk and said to her: 'You should not so bewail. This is not your child, but one who was your enemy in your last life. Three times he has come to you to try to bring about your death. If you do not believe me, here is proof.' The Blessed One pointed at the baby and it appeared in devil's form. Standing on the water, the devil cried to the woman: 'Because you have read the Dharani Sutra with devotion, angels have watched over you day and night and I have had no chance to kill you. Now the Blessed One has changed my heart, and I will be your enemy no longer.' So saying, he sank beneath the waters and disappeared. I assure you, this baby must have been your enemy. He came to you to be an expense and a hurt to your body. The other day you gave fifteen hundred copies of the Dharani Sutra to be distributed, so establishing yourself in virtue, and, thereafter he could no longer endure to be with you and so died. Now you will have a child who will be your true child."

Li Ping'er listened but she did not forget Guan'ge. Whenever the baby's name was mentioned she wept.

Five days passed. On the morning of the twenty-seventh, eight small boys wearing black gowns and white hats carried banners, white parasols, white flowers and willows, and walked before the coffin of scarlet and gold. A great red scroll was borne beneath a canopy and on it was inscribed: "The Coffin of a son of the house of Ximen." Abbot Wu had sent twelve Daoist novices in black robes. They chanted exorcisms about the coffin. Musicians played mournful tunes. Then came all the relatives and Ximen

Qing dressed in plain clothes. They went on foot to the end of the street, near the city gate, and there got into carriages and mounted horses.

Ximen Qing feared that Li Ping'er would cry if she went to the grave with them, so he would not let her go, but all the other ladies went in sedan chairs. Sun Xue'e and Wu Yin'er stayed at home to keep company with Li Ping'er. She, forbidden to go to the grave, went after the coffin to the gate. There she cried: "Oh my baby, you have broken my heart," and fell swooning. As she fell, her head struck the gate; her cheeks were bruised, and the golden pins fell out of her hair. Xue'e and Wu Yin'er went forward and lifted her up. They took her to her own room. There she saw the lonely bed with the little drum shaped like the God of Longevity lying upon it. This reminded her again of her lost child. She beat her hands upon the table and sobbed bitterly.

Wu Yin'er grasped her hands. "Mother," she said, "please don't cry any more. The baby has gone and cannot come back to you however much you cry. You must console yourself. Don't be so sad."

Xue'e said: "You are still young and you will certainly have another child. I must not say all I think, because, in this place, there are holes in the wall and eyes to look through them, but it was she who schemed for this and she will pay for it. It was she who killed the baby and the baby will demand his life from her. You and I have had much to suffer. She wants her husband all to herself and, whenever he goes to anyone else, she is very angry. You know that our husband has not been to me for a long time. Well, the other day he did come, and you saw what a fuss she made about it and what she said about me to his daughter. I say nothing, but I keep my eyes open and watch. We shall see to what sort of an end that strumpet comes."

"Yes," said Li Ping'er, "she has made me suffer. But I do not know when I shall die. It may be today or it may be tomorrow, and I cannot make trouble with her. I can only leave her to go her own way."

The nurse Ruyi'er came in. She knelt down and said: "There is something I must say to you. I have not dared to do so before. The baby is dead and that is bad luck for me. I am afraid his Lordship and the Great Lady will send me away. My husband is dead and I have nowhere to go."

Li Ping'er was distressed again. "The baby is dead," she said, "but I am still alive. And even if I should die tomorrow, you have served me well. I am sure they will not send you away. One of these day, the Great Lady may have a boy or a girl. They will let you be his nurse, and it will be all the same for you. There is no cause for you to worry."

This satisfied Ruyi'er.

Li Ping'er began to cry again. Wu Yin'er and Xue'e did their best to console her and tried to get her to eat something. They asked Yingchun to go to the inner court and bring some food. But when it was set upon the table Li Ping'er could not bring herself to eat any. She tried a few mouthfuls and then gave up the attempt.

When the funeral procession came to the grave, Ximen Qing asked Master Xu to determine the site. Guan'ge was buried beside the tomb of Ximen's first wife, the lady Chen.

Master Qiao and the other relatives made offerings at the tomb and were entertained in the new arbor. When they returned, Li Ping'er came to kowtow to Yueniang, Mistress Qiao and Uncle Wu. Again she wept. "Lady," she said to Mistress Qiao, "who could have such evil fortune as myself whose baby has died so young? Your daughter is widowed before her marriage, and all that we have done for them is thrown away. I trust you will not scorn me now."

"Lady," Mistress Qiao said, "you must not talk like that. We can never be sure how long anyone will live. There is an old saying that those who have arranged an alliance between their families can never cease to be friends. You are not old. You will very likely bear another child. We must be patient and not give way to melancholy." Mistress Qiao went home.

In the hall, Ximen Qing asked Xu, the Master of the Yin Yang, to purify the house. They hung yellow paper charms over all the doors to drive away evil spirits. The charms said: 'The spirit of our departed one is thirty feet high. It goes towards the northeast. If it meets the god of the day, it will return and not go forth again. Or it will destroy it, and all will be well. The relatives will have nothing: to fear.

Ximen Qing gave a roll of cloth and two taels of silver to Master Xu and took him to the gate. That evening he went to Li Ping'er's room and tried to comfort her. He was afraid she would be sad if she saw the baby's toys, so he told Yingchun to put them all away.

CHAPTER 60

The Opening of the New Shop

After Guan'ge's death, Pan Jinlian was as pleased as could be. She would say, pretending to scold her maids: "Ha, you strumpet! You thought you were like the sun at its zenith, but now you are brought low. Now you are like a turtle dove brought down by the bow, stretching out its tongue in vain. You are like a chair without a back and nothing to lean upon. You are another old woman Wang, who sold her corn and can never have it again to grind, or an old procuress whose singing girls are dead who has no one else to depend upon. Yes, we are now on the same footing again."

Li Ping'er in her room could hear all this. She said nothing, but her tears flowed faster. With the anger in her heart and her great grief, her spirit drooped more and more and she had no peace even in her dreams. Her appetite decreased day by day. On the second day after Guan'ge's funeral, Wu Yin'er went away.

Old woman Feng brought a maid, thirteen years old, and sold her to Sun Xue'e for five taels of silver. She was given the name Cui'er.

Li Ping'er never ceased to think of her baby, and there was a furious hatred within her for Jinlian. So her old illness returned; she had a continual issue of blood. Ximen Qing sent for Dr. Ren, but his medicine did her no good. It was like watering a rock; the more medicine she took, the worse she became. In less than a fortnight, she grew very ill and thin. All her beauty and charm left her and she looked like a handful of bones. Her sorrow was too great for her to bear.

One day, at the beginning of the ninth month, it was cold and the west wind blew chill. She was in her room alone. The bed was cold: the lonely moon cast its beams upon the window. She was thinking of her baby and sighed deeply several times. Suddenly she seemed to hear someone tapping on the window. She called her maid, but the maids were sleeping soundly and there was no reply. She rose from her bed, put on her shoes and an embroidered gown, went to the door, opened it and looked out. Hua Zixu was there with Guan'ge in his arms. He told her that he had a new house and asked her to go with him. But she would not leave Ximen Qing. She refused him and tried to take the child from him. He pushed her and made her fall upon the ground. Then she woke up and found it was a dream. Her body was bathed in sweat and she sobbed till dawn.

About this time, the merchandise that Laibao had bought in Nanjing arrived. Laibao sent Wang Xian before him to get the money to pay the duty. Ximen Qing wrote a letter and sent it to Rong Hai with a hundred taels of silver. He sent presents of wine, silk, and other things to the customs officer asking that, when the merchandise was checked, a lenient reckoning might be made. The shop was ready, and it was arranged that it should be opened on the fourth day of the ninth month. On that day the merchandise was brought, twenty large loads of it. Kinsmen and friends sent presents and scrolls to be hung up in the new shop, and there were twenty guests or more. Magistrate Xia sent a man with gifts and red favors; Master Qiao sent twelve musicians. Ximen Qing himself engaged Li Ming, Wu Hui and Zheng Chun. The two clerks, Gan and Han, were in the shop, one to check and test the silver, the other to determine the price of the goods. Cui Ben received the goods and set them in their proper place. Ximen Qing, in his ceremonial dress, burned paper offerings; then the relatives and friends offered the presents they had brought. Fifteen tables were laid in the hall. There was an abundance of food and, when all had taken their places, the musicians began to play. Everybody seemed to be present and the seats were all occupied. The three singers sang the song of the World's Beginning; the wine was passed around several times, and several courses of food were served. The musicians played and those in the company urged each other to drink. Ying Bojue and Xie Xida took the largest cups. They did not stop drinking till sunset. Then the guests departed, but Ximen Qing urged Uncle Wu, Uncle Shen, Uncle Han, Master Wen, Ying Bojue and Xie Xida to stay. The tables were relaid and they sat down again. This was the first day the shop had been open, and, when the clerks reckoned up, they found they had done business to the value of more than five hundred taels of silver. Ximen Qing was delighted. When the shop had been closed, he invited Gan, Han and Fu with Cui Ben, Ben the Fourth and Chen Jingji to join their party. When the musicians had finished playing, they were dismissed. Only the three singers remained to sing for them.

Ying Bojue was drunk. He went to the front to wash his hands. Then he said to Li Ming: "Who is that good-looking young singer with his hair in a knot?"

"Uncle," Li Ming said, "don't you know him? That is Zheng Feng's younger brother, Zheng Chun. A few days ago, his Lordship had a party with Zheng Aiyue at Zheng's house."

"Ah," Bojue said, "now I understand why she was at the funeral the other day." He went back to join Ximen Qing and the others.

"I see I have to congratulate you on a new brother-in-law," he said to Ximen Qing.

Ximen Qing laughed. "Don't talk nonsense," he said. He told Wang Jing to give Bojue a large cup of wine.

"What do you think about it, venerable Uncle?" Bojue said to Uncle Wu. "Don't you think he is punishing me without due cause?"

"I am punishing you, you dog, because of the lies you tell," Ximen Qing said.

Ying Bojue bent his head, considered for a while and said: "Very well, I will drink it. I don't suppose it will kill me. But I never drink without music. Kindly tell Zheng Chun to sing me a song."

The three boys came in together. Bojue said to Li Ming: "You and Wu Hui can go away. I only want Zheng Chun. I want him to play the zither and sing a song for me."

Xie Xida said to Zheng Chun: "Come and sing for your Uncle Ying."

"Beggar Ying," said Ximen, "please understand that you will have to drink a cup of wine for every song he sings." He told Daian to set two great silver cups before Bojue. Zheng Chun took up his zither and sang.

> A girl of sixteen years or so
> Watching a pair of butterflies at play,
> On the white wall rested her dainty shoulders
> And dried her tears with tender fingers.
> To her slave she said
> Drive them away and make them play elsewhere.

When Zheng Chun had finished his song, he invited Ying Bojue to drink. Bojue did so. Daian quickly refilled his cup. Zheng Chun began again.

> He passed beyond the sculptured screen and came to her
> Leaning against the arbor of wild roses.
> Shyly she pretended to put straight her phœnix pins.
> She would not speak of what had passed the night before,
> But smiled and gathered flowers to cast at him.

Bojue drank another cup of wine. Then he turned to Xie Xida. "This is too much for me," he said. "Two great cups of wine are more than I can manage."

"What, you foolish beggar!" Xie Xida said. "When you can't drink, you would make me drink for you? I am not your slave."

"Foolish beggar yourself," Bojue said. "When one of these days I get an official position, you certainly will be my slave."

"Oh, you dog," Ximen Qing said, "the only appointment you'll ever get will be that of musician in a brothel."

"Well, my boy," Bojue said, "if I am you shall have the hall."

Ximen Qing laughed. He said to Daian: "Go and fetch the knuckle cracker and crack this rascally beggar's knuckles."

Xie Xida went quietly over and tapped Bojue on the head. "Beggar," he said, "Master Wen is here, yet you talk all this nonsense."

"Master Wen is a man of learning," Bojue said. "He won't mind our being frivolous."

"You two gentlemen are my patron's very good friends," Master Wen said. "It is right and fitting that you should behave like this when drinking wine. Otherwise, enjoyment never could reach the pitch we desire. Happiness is in our hearts but it demands expression and, when it is expressed, it is natural that we should let go a little."

Uncle Shen said to Ximen Qing: "Now let us try something else. Allow us to have a game of some sort—dice, or guessing fingers, or dominoes, and then a poem or a song or a tongue twister. He who fails must drink. That is fair, and there will be no disputes."

"An excellent idea!" Ximen Qing said. He poured a cup of wine, set it before Uncle Wu and asked him to begin.

Uncle Wu took up the dice box and said: "Gentlemen, I will begin, and after me, everyone in turn. I must have the name of a flower to correspond to the markings of the dice. The first word of the second sentence must be the same as the last word of the first. It must be a quotation from a song or a poem. He who fails must drink a large cup of wine. Here goes: I cast the first and get one point red. The red plum blossoms stand beside the white plum blossoms."

Uncle Wu cast the dice and got a two. He drank a cup of wine and passed the box to Uncle Shen.

"For the second cast: upon one stem I see two lotus blossoms. 'The lotus blossoms are the delight of the gaily colored mandarin ducks.' "

He threw a two, drank two cups of wine and passed the dice to Uncle Han.

"For the third cast," said Uncle Han, "I have three spring plums. 'The plums fall, but I do not put straight my hat.' "

He cast the dice but did not say what turned up. Then he drank his wine and gave the box to Master Wen.

"The fourth cast makes the *Zhuang Yuan* red," said Master Wen. " 'Red and purple are not the wear for common men.' "

Master Wen drank a cup of wine. It was Ying Bojue's turn. "I can't read a word," Bojue said. "You will get no quotation from me. I shall have to give you a tongue twister."

> Flip-flop, flip-flop, a fast-footed old fellow
> Bearing beans by the bushel in his right hand
> And a beggar's broad begging bag firm in his left
> Scuffled steadily straight to his front.
> A mangy mongrel, all yellow and white
> Bit the beggar's broad begging bag.
> Flip-flop, flip-flop, the fast-footed old fellow
> Dropped the basket with the bushel of beans
> Strove stoutly to stampede the mangy mongrel all yellow and white
> But who can say whether he beat the dog, or the dog beat him?

Ximen Qing laughed. "You boil-breaking, mad creature!" he said. "Have you ever seen a man drive off a dog with his fist?"

"Well, he shouldn't have gone out without a stick. Nowadays, all beggars take sticks with them. That's the only way they can deal with the dogs."

"Sir," said Xie Xida, "Beggar Ying is speaking for himself. He is the beggar here."

"We shall have to punish him," Ximen Qing said. "He hasn't played the game properly. Now, friend Xie, it is your turn."

"I will give you a better tongue twister than his," Xie Xida said.

> On the wall there is a bit of broken brick.
> Beside the wall there is a horse.
> If the bit of broken brick falls upon the horse,
> Will the bit of broken brick break the horse's back,
> Or will the horse break the bit of broken brick?

"You said mine was no good," Bojue said. "Do you flatter yourself that your 'bit of broken brick' was any better? If you ask me, your wife is that horse and I the bit of broken brick. I and your wife would make a fine pair. It would be a case of a skinny donkey going around a broken millstone."

"Your wife, the old whore," said Xie Xida, "has only black beans to feed the pigs with. If she offered them to a dog, the dog would refuse them."

They joked with one another and each filled up his own cup. It was Han Daoguo's turn. "Master, you are here," Han Daoguo said. "How dare I go before you?"

"Don't stand on ceremony," Ximen Qing told him. "We must follow the order of the game." Han Daoguo said:

"The fifth cast gives the winter plums. 'Among the plums, I meet an angel.'"

Then it was Ximen's turn. "I will throw a six," he said. "The sixth cast fills the sky with stars. 'The stars are cold: the dark green waters mirror them.'"

Ximen did throw a six. Ying Bojue said: "I am sure promotion will come to you this winter. Fortune will turn your way." He filled a cup for Ximen.

Li Ming and the other singers came and sang for them. The party did not break up until the night watch had sounded. Ximen Qing dismissed the boys, watched the servants clear everything away, and told the four clerks to take charge in turn and see carefully to the doors and windows. Then he went home.

The next day, Ying Bojue came with Li and Huang to make a settlement of their debt. They said to Ximen Qing: "So far we have only got back fourteen hundred and fifty taels. That is not enough to cover the expenses; we can only offer his Lordship three hundred and fifty. When we receive the next payment from the authorities, we will pay the remainder." Bojue spoke on their behalf, and Ximen Qing told Chen Jingji to weigh the money and accept it.

Huang and Li then went away, leaving the money on the table. Ximen Qing said to Ying Bojue: "Brother Chang told me that he had got a house. He wants thirty-five taels. He came the other day, but I could not attend to him because the baby was ill. I don't know whether he mentioned the matter to you or not."

"I told him he had no business to worry you when your little son was ill," Bojue said. "I said you couldn't be expected to discuss matters of that sort when you were so terribly anxious. 'Keep the landlord quiet,' I said to him, 'and I will see our brother and get it fixed up for you.'"

"We will have something to eat and then you can take him fifty taels," Ximen said. "This is an auspicious day and he can settle the matter now. Tell him to spend anything that is left over on setting up a small shop so that he can make a little money for himself. That ought to be enough for his wife and himself."

Bojue thanked him. Food was brought, and they ate it together. Afterwards, Ximen told Bojue that he would not detain him, and asked him to go and arrange about Chang's house.

"I should like one of your servants to go with me," Ying Bojue said.

"Nonsense," said Ximen Qing. "Put the money in your sleeve and take it to him. That's all that's necessary."

"I don't mean that," Bojue said, "but I have other matters to attend to. It is my cousin Du's birthday. I sent him a present this morning and he sent a boy to ask me to go and see him this afternoon. I shan't be able to come back and report to you. If you will let one of your boys come with me, he can come and tell you when we have arranged about the house."

"Wang Jing shall go with you," Ximen said.

Wang Jing went with Bojue to see Chang Zhijie. Chang was at home and invited Bojue to go in. Bojue showed him the money. "His Lordship," he said, "told me to come and arrange with you about the house. I am very busy and have to go and see my cousin Du. Let us get the matter settled quickly. Then I must go."

Chang Zhijie hastily told his wife to make some tea. "His Lordship is really very kind," he said. "I can't think of anyone else who would have done it." They drank their tea and went to New Market Street. There they signed the contract and paid the landlord. Bojue told Wang Jing to go home and report to his master; then he gave the remaining silver to Chang Zhijie and went to see his cousin. Ximen Qing looked at the contract and told Wang Jing to take it back to Chang Zhijie.

CHAPTER 61

Li Ping'er Falls Ill

The cricket chirps mournfully in the dew
It frightens her as she lies on the autumn pillow.
Her tears moisten the embroidered coverlets.
Lonely she lies, her exquisite limbs are cold.
The night seems as unending as her sorrow.
The rain pours down. The lamp is very dim.
She cannot sleep.
Now the crow cries and the golden pit is cold.

One night, when Han Daoguo was at home from the shop, his wife Wang Liu'er said to him: "Through our master's kindness we have made a good deal of money. I think we ought to prepare some sort of a feast and invite him to come. Besides, he has just lost his son and we should do something to console him. It need not be a very expensive entertainment, but it should be well done. When the people at the shop see it, they will realize that you are on very good terms with his Lordship. Such friendships as that between our master and yourself are not by any means usual. It will help when you go to the South."

"That is just what I have been thinking," Han Daoguo said. "Tomorrow is the fifth, but that is not a favorable day. Why don't we give our party on the sixth? I will engage two singing girls and take my card around myself and ask him to come. At night, I will go and sleep at the shop."

"Why should you engage singing girls?" Wang Liu'er said. "After dinner, he may wish to stay a while, and it will be awkward if there are singing girls about. Our neighbor, Mistress Luo, knows a girl called Shen. She is young and has an excellent voice. She has the advantage of being blind. We might get her to come. We can send her away when we have done with her."

Han Daoguo agreed. The night passed. The next day he went to the shop and asked Master Wen to write an invitation card for him. Then he went himself to Ximen Qing. "Tomorrow," he said, "I am arranging to have a very small party, and I beg you to come." He handed his card to Ximen Qing. Ximen looked at it.

"You should not take so much trouble," he said. "I shall be free tomorrow, and I will come as soon as I get back from the office." Han Daoguo went away. The next morning, he sent Hu Xiu to buy food and engaged a cook. He sent a sedan chair for Miss Shen. His wife and the maids prepared some excellent tea and waited for Ximen Qing.

In the afternoon, Qintong brought a jar of grape wine and, later, Ximen Qing came in a sedan chair, followed by Daian and Wang Jing. He was wearing a *zhongjing* hat, a black silk gown, and black shoes with white soles. Han Daoguo welcomed him and thanked him for the wine. Ximen sat down on a chair that was set by itself in the place of honor. Wang Liu'er, in a dainty dress, came and kowtowed four times to him. Then she went out to see about the tea. Wang Jing brought it, and Han Daoguo offered a cup to Ximen; then he sat down and took a cup himself. When they had drunk their tea, Wang Jing took the cups away.

"Both when I have been here and when I have been away," Han Daoguo said, "you have been very kind to me and my wife. I find it hard to express my gratitude. The other day, when your son died, I was not at home, and, unfortunately, my wife had a very bad cold and could not call to offer our sympathy. We have ventured to invite you today, partly in the hope of making you merry and partly as a sign of our sincere sympathy."

"You are both very kind," Ximen Qing said.

Wang Liu'er came and sat with them. "Have you told his Lordship?" she asked her husband.

"Not yet," he said.

"What is that?" Ximen Qing said.

"He was going to ask two singing girls to come, but 1 thought they might be in the way and I wouldn't let him send for them. We know a young lady who often visits my neighbor Luo, a certain Miss Shen. She knows all the latest songs. The other day, when I was at your house, I saw Miss Yu. She sings well, but not so well as Miss Shen. I have asked Miss Shen to come and sing for you. If you like her singing, you may think fit to get her to sing for your ladies."

Han Daoguo told Daian to take his master's cloak, and the table was laid. Hu Xiu brought in the food. Wang Liu'er opened the jar and heated the wine. She carried the pot and her husband offered a cup of wine to Ximen Qing. Then Miss Shen came. Her hair was dressed high upon her head, and the ornaments and flowers she wore were very simple. Her gown was green, her skirt red. Her feet were very small. Her cheeks were the color of peach flowers, and her eyebrows long. She kowtowed to Ximen Qing. He bade her rise and asked how old she was.

"I am twenty-one," she said.

"How many songs do you know?" Ximen asked.

"More than a hundred; some long, some short."

Ximen asked Han Daoguo to give her a seat, and, after making a reverence, she sat down. Then she took a zither and sang "The Arbor of Fragrance in Autumn." When they had finished their soup and other dishes had been brought, she sang "The Five Thousand Rebels." They drank again, and Ximen Qing asked her to put down the zither and sing a short song to the accompaniment of the lute. Miss Shen was anxious to display her skill. Gently waving her silken sleeves, she took up the lute delicately, tuned it softly, and sang. The song she sang was "Sheep upon the Mountains." Han Daoguo asked his wife to fill up a cup of wine and offer it to Ximen Qing.

Wang Liu'er said to Miss Shen: "You know another fine song. I should like you to sing it for his Lordship."

At the first meeting with her lover
No more than twice ten springs had welcomed her.
Black is her hair like a black cloud
Her cheeks as rosy as a peach blossom
As tender as the soft shoots of the bamboo.
If she had been born of a good family
She would have been a great lady.
Alas, she has thrown away her virtue in a house of ill fame.
If she could give up that evil life and marry,
It would be better than having always to dismiss one man
To give welcome to another.

At the first meeting with her lover
She is as perfect as the moon, as graceful as a flower
A jewel amid the dust and wind
With a slim waist that a hand can encircle
And a clever mind that needs no telling.
He is full of regret that they did not meet before
Now, as they lie on the bed drinking, they repine
They pour their wine, sing softly to each other, and embrace.
One looks long and is charmed
The other gazes and is filled with delight.
They know that their joy may last for but a moment
And strive to throw foreboding to the winds.

The songs reminded Ximen Qing of his first meeting with Zheng Aiyue. He was pleased. Wang Liu'er filled his cup again and said, smiling: "My Lord, do not hurry over your wine: Miss Shen has several songs to sing yet. She has only made a beginning. You may decide to send for her to sing for your ladies. In my opinion, she is certainly cleverer than Miss Yu."

"Miss Shen," Ximen Qing said, "if I send someone for you at the Double Ninth festival, will you come?"

"Whenever you think fit to command me, I will come," Miss Shen said.

Ximen Qing was pleased with the intelligent way she spoke. They drank again. Wang Liu'er thought that the girl's presence might prove hampering to her dealings with Ximen Qing, so, after a few more songs, she told her husband to send Daian with Miss Shen back to Mistress Luo's house. Ximen Qing gave her three *qian* of silver to buy strings for her instruments. When Miss Shen had thanked him, he told her that he would send someone for her on the eighth day. "My lord," Wang Liu'er said, "you need only tell Wang Jing. I will do the rest." Miss Shen went away. Han Daoguo went to the shop and left his wife alone with Ximen Qing. Wang Liu'er threw dice and drank with him. Their hearts began to grow warm. Ximen Qing pretended that he was going to change his clothes and went to her room. She followed him; they fastened the door and set to their pleasure. Wang Jing took a lamp and went to another room where he joined Daian and Qintong and drank wine with them.

The boy Hu Xiu stole a few cups of wine in the kitchen. Then he dismissed the cook and went to the room where Wang Liu'er had her domestic shrine. There he set down a mattress and went to sleep. But the room was next to Wang Liu'er's, and soon the boy woke up. He could hear sounds coming from the next room. Through a crack in the partition he could see a light. He thought that Ximen Qing had gone and that Han Daoguo was sleeping there. He took a pin and made a hole in the paper. Through the hole he peeped. The candles were shining brightly. He was surprised to see Ximen Qing sporting vigorously with his master's wife, whose legs were plainly to be seen over the frame of the bed. Ximen Qing was wearing a short silken vest and nothing at all upon the lower part of his body. At the edge of the bed, he was coming and going, plunging and prancing, making a considerable noise. The woman was saying all kinds of endearments to him. Hu Xiu heard: "My darling, if you would like to burn your naughty sweetheart, do so. Burn me whenever and wherever you like. I shall not forbid you. My body is all yours, and whatever you like to do with it, you may do."

"But your husband may not like it," Ximen Qing said.

"Even if that turtle had eight heads and eight galls, he would not dare not to like it; it is only by your bounty that he exists."

"If you will love me only," Ximen said, "I will send him and Laibao to stay in the South. I can keep them busy there buying merchandise for me."

"Then send him," the woman said. "Why should you keep him here? Send him away by all means, and when he comes back I will find another woman for him. I belong heart and soul to you, so I want him no longer. Do with me whatever you think fit, I shall be quite content. And if I lie to you, may this unworthy body rot utterly away."

"You need take no oaths," Ximen said.

Hu Xiu heard all that they said and saw all that they did.

Han Daoguo, before he left the house, had seen no sign of the boy and supposed that he had gone to the shop. But when he got to the shop and made inquiries of Wang Xian and Rong Hai, they told him that the boy was not there. Han Daoguo went home again and looked for Hu Xiu at the front and the back, but could see him nowhere. In the front court, Wang Jing, Daian and Qintong were drinking.

When Hu Xiu heard Han Daoguo coming, he hurriedly lay down again on his mattress and pretended to be asleep. His master came into the room with a light. There the boy was, snoring. Han Daoguo kicked him. "Get up at once, you rascal," he said. "I thought you were at the shop. You have no business here. You can find a place to sleep there. Get up and come with me." Hu Xiu got up, rubbed his eyes, and went to the shop with Han Daoguo.

Ximen Qing and Wang Liu'er enjoyed the pleasures of love for a long time. He burned the woman in three places, at the pit of the stomach, on the mount of Venus, and on the tail bone. Then she got up, dressed herself, and called her maid to bring water that she might wash her hands. Fresh wine was heated; food was brought, and they talked together. After drinking a few cups of wine, Ximen Qing mounted his horse and went away with the three boys, Daian, Wang Jing and Qintong. It was the second night watch when they reached home.

He went to see Li Ping'er. She was lying on her bed. She noticed that Ximen Qing had been drinking and asked where he had been.

"Han Daoguo invited me to go to his place. He wished to express his sympathy in the loss of our child. There was a young woman named Shen there. She sings very well, certainly more sweetly than Miss Yu, and I am going to send for her at the festival. She shall sing for you. I know how melancholy you have been, but now you must not think about the baby any longer."

He was going to tell Yingchun to take his clothes and make ready to go to bed with Li Ping'er. "No," she said, "I am still unwell, and the maid is making some medicine for me at this moment. Won't you go and sleep with someone else? You must have seen how ill I have been looking lately. There is hardly any breath left in my body. You will take no more pleasure with me."

"My dearest one," Ximen said, "I love you too dearly ever to forsake you. I want to stay with you."

Li Ping'er looked at him and smiled. "Who can believe that deceitful tongue of yours?" she said. 'If I were to die tomorrow, would you not forget me? Wait till I am better and, if you still wish to sleep with me, you shall."

"Very well," Ximen said, "if you won't have me, I'll go to Pan Jinlian."

"Yes, do," Li Ping'er said. "That is exactly where you should go. She is waiting for you in a fever of anxiety. If you do not go, she will think I have prevented you.

"In that case, I will go now."

Li Ping'er smiled bitterly. "I was teasing you," she said. "But please go."

When he had gone, she got up and sat on the bed. Yingchun brought her medicine. She could not restrain her tears, and her fragrant cheeks were wet with them. She sighed as she took the medicine.

Jinlian had gone to bed when Ximen Qing came to her room. "You have gone to bed very early," he said.

"What kind of wind has blown you here?" she said. "Where have you been drinking today?"

"Han Daoguo asked me to go to his place," Ximen said. "He wished to distract me after my bereavement, and to make some return for the kindness I've shown him."

"Looking after his wife when he was away on business, I suppose!" Jinlian said.

"Oh, no," Ximen said, "between master and man, anything of that sort would be improper."

"Improper, do you say? Did you put a strap about your loins to make sure that you would not overstep the mark? It is no use trying to hood-wink me. I have known all about it for some time. On your birthday, that strumpet was here flaunting a pin with the character *shou* that you had secretly sneaked from Li Ping'er and given to her. The Great Lady and Meng Yulou both noticed it. I told her what I thought, and she flushed crimson. But I don't suppose she mentioned that to you. So that is where you have been today. Oh, you shameless fellow! A flat-footed, lanky, ugly-looking strumpet like that with the hair all over her forehead and lips as red as blood! What a woman! A great purple-faced wanton hussy. I can't imagine what you find in her. And you keep her brother here so that he can run messages between the pair of you."

Ximen Qing kept on denying. "You funny little slave," he said, laughing, "why do you talk such nonsense? There is nothing at all between us. Besides, her husband was there today, and I did not even see her."

"You are lying again," Jinlian said. "Everybody knows her husband is a barefaced pander. He is the sort of man who guards his sheep and goes picking tinder at the same time. He lets you have his wife and takes your money. You silly fellow, you can only hear guns forty *li* away."

Ximen Qing undressed and sat down on the bed. Jinlian stretched out her arm and pulled down his trousers. She touched his staff. It was soft. The clasp was still about it.

"Oh, you dried duck, boiled in a cauldron!" she cried. "Your body may be exhausted, but your mouth is never so. Look at this gentleman! Not a word to say for himself! Now, you villain. How dare you play tricks with that strumpet all this time? See the state you've brought him to! And your mouth is as assured as ever. Will you take an oath? I will tell Chunmei to bring a cup of cold water. If you dare drink it, I will believe you. Salt is salt, and vinegar is vinegar all the world over. But I need not tell you that. You are like a bald-headed man putting on a wig. If I let you do as you would like to do, there won't be a woman in the world safe from you. You shameless scoundrel! It is a good thing you are a man. If you were a woman, you would be carrying on with every man in the street."

Ximen Qing laughed. He could not think of anything to say. He got ready for bed and told Chunmei to heat some wine. Then he took a pill from the little gold box, swallowed it and lay down on the bed.

"My dear," he said, "taste it. If you bring it to life again, good for you."

Jinlian swore she would do nothing of the sort. "You filthy creature! And it has just been busy in that dirty strumpet's mill. If I did a thing as foul as that, it would kill me.

"You funny little whore," Ximen said, "don't talk nonsense. I tell you I have had nothing to do with her."

"If you have not, why won't you take an oath?"

The argument continued for some time. Finally, she invited Ximen Qing to wash. He would not. She took a handkerchief from under the pillow and wiped his penis, then took it in her mouth so that it soon regained its fire. Ximen mounted her fiercely and began; pressing her legs with his arms, he moved his penis noisily. The candle gleamed; he rejoiced at the sight. She lay on the bed and moved up to meet him, arousing his passion still more. He put some of his red powder onto his prick, which he pushed in again. Gripping her legs, he thrust three hundred times. Jinlian's eyes closed and she began to tremble. "Darling," she whispered, "you must do no more. You should not have put the powder on him."

"Now, little strumpet," Ximen Qing cried, "are you afraid of me or not? Will you ever treat me disrespectfully again?"

"Darling, forgive me," Jinlian said. "I will never dare to talk like that again. Don't thrust so roughly, you will make my hair untidy."

They played happily far into the night, till at last they were tired and went to sleep.

On the day of the Double Ninth festival, the ninth day of the ninth month, Ximen Qing said to Wu Yueniang: "A day or two ago, when I was drinking wine with Han Daoguo, I saw a certain Miss Shen. She is good-looking and she sings well. I will send a boy for her and she shall stay a few days to sing for you." He told the cooks to prepare a feast, and tables were set in the garden in the Hall of the Lovely Prospect. There Ximen and his household kept the festival. Wang Jing brought Miss Shen. She kowtowed to all the ladies. Yueniang thought her very pretty and asked how many songs she knew. Miss Shen said she knew a great many. Yueniang offered her some refreshments and asked her to sing for a while in the inner court before she went to the garden.

Ximen Qing did not go to the office that day. He superintended the planting of the Qiujus and invited the ladies to go to the garden. Chunmei, Yuxiao, Yingchun and Lanxiang were there to serve the wine. Miss Shen sang, and accompanied herself on the lute.

Li Ping'er, who was still anything but well, did not come until she had been sent for several times. She was indeed not fit to come; her body was so weak that the wind might have blown her over. Everybody asked her to drink, but she could take only a little. Ximen Qing and Yueniang, seeing her so melancholy, did their best to encourage her. "Sister," they said, "you must cheer up. We have brought Miss Shen to sing for you."

"Tell her any song you like," Meng Yulou said. But Li Ping'er did not answer them.

While they were drinking, Wang Jing came and said that Ying Bojue and Chang Zhijie had come. "Tell them to wait for me in the small arbor," Ximen said, "I will be there in a minute."

"Uncle Chang has brought two boxes," Wang Jing said.

"He has brought me some presents because I have helped him to get a house," Ximen said to Yueniang.

"We must see about something for them to eat," Yueniang said. "We can't allow them to go away with empty stomachs. You go to them, and I will arrange for them to have some food."

Before Ximen left the ladies, he said to Miss Shen: "Sing the best of all your songs for the Sixth Lady." Then he went to see Bojue.

"Sister," Jinlian said to Li Ping'er, "tell Miss Shen what song you would like. Father sent for her specially on your account, and you must choose something."

Li Ping'er asked for the song "Red Dust in the Purple Street."

"Yes, I know it," Miss Shen said. She took up her lute and sang it with particular care. When the song was done, Yueniang said: "Sister, drink a cup of this wine. It is beautifully sweet." Li Ping'er could hardly refuse. She took a cup and drank a mouthful, no more. Soon she felt too ill to stay and went back to her room.

Ximen Qing went to the Hall of the Kingfisher. Ying Bojue and Chang Zhijie were standing beside a pine thicket admiring the chrysanthemums. Twenty pots of the most renowned blooms stood there, all more than seven feet high. Among them were such famous flowers as Scarlet Cloak, Doctor's Red, Purple Cloak, Golden Girdle, White *Fenshi* and Yellow *Fenshi,* and many others. Bojue and Chang Zhijie came forward and made a reverence to Ximen Qing, then Chang called the man who had come with him to bring the boxes.

"What is this?" Ximen Qing said.

Bojue answered. "Brother Chang," he said, "is eager to express his sense of your kindness in helping him to get a house. He had nothing to give you, but his wife has prepared this box of crabs and a couple of roast ducks and he asked me to come with him so that we can enjoy them together."

"Brother Chang," Ximen Qing said, "there was no need for you to trouble. Your wife is only just better. She should not have bothered to cook these things."

"I told him so," Ying Bojue said, "but he thought it would be better than anything else he could get."

Ximen Qing told a boy to open the box. There were forty large crabs, ready dressed with peppers, ginger, garlic and herbs, and prepared with oil, sauce and vinegar. They smelled very tasty and promised excellent eating. The two roast ducks were done in the most attractive style. Ximen Qing told Chunhong and Wang Jing to take them to the kitchen. He gave a small present to the porter and thanked Chang Zhijie. Qintong raised the lattice and they went into the Hall of the Kingfisher. Bojue could not find words to express his admiration of the chrysanthemums. He asked where they had come from. "Eunuch Liu, the warden of the brick kilns, sent me these twenty pots," Ximen told him. "Not only the plants but the pots as well."

"Indeed!" said Bojue. "They are the genuine official pottery too. The clay is of the highest quality: it is put through the finest of sieves and pressed by the workmen's feet. That is how such flower pots as these are made. They are made like Suzhou bricks, and they are by no means easy to get hold of these days."

Ximen Qing called for tea. "Brother Chang," he said, "when did you move into your new house?"

Bojue answered: "He moved in three days after the money was paid. Yesterday was a lucky day. He bought a number of things, and opened a small shop. Mistress Chang's younger brother keeps the books."

"We must buy presents and celebrate the occasion," Ximen said. "We don't want a crowd of people, Xie Xida perhaps, and you and I will arrange for food to be taken to Brother Chang's house, so that he may not be put to any expense. We will engage two singing girls and have a merry housewarming."

"I should have invited you myself," Chang said, "but I did not dare. The house is so small I thought you would not like it."

"Not at all!" Ximen said, "we don't wish you to spend your money. I will send word to Xie Xida myself." He said to Qintong: "Go and ask your Uncle Xie to come and see me."

"Which singing girls are you going to send for?" Ying Bojue asked.

Ximen Qing laughed. "Oh, Zheng Aiyue and Hong Si'er, I think."

"Brother," Bojue said, "you didn't wish to tell me which two girls you would have, but I guessed. Now what do you think of Zheng Aiyue? Is she more tasty than Li Guijie?"

"There is none better," Ximen said.

"Why wouldn't she talk to us on your birthday?" Bojue asked. "It seems to me she is a very cunning girl."

"Next time I go to see her," Ximen said, "I will take you with me. She and her sister play backgammon very well, and we will have a game with them."

"By all means," Bojue said. "I will certainly go and have a game with the young lady. I don't intend to let her off altogether."

"You naughty dog," said Ximen, "don't play your tricks on her."

Xie Xida came, made a reverence, and sat down. "Brother Chang has just bought a new house," Ximen said to him. "He has moved into it without a word to us. I suggest that we all contribute a small sum and I will have a feast prepared here and send it around to his house. We will engage two singing girls and have a gay time there. But he must not be put to any expense."

"Brother," Xie Xida said, "you have only to say the word and the money shall be sent to you at once. Will anyone else be at the party?"

"Nobody else," Ximen Qing said. "Each of us will give two pieces of silver."

"His place is not very big," Bojue said. "It will not hold many people."

Then Qintong came and said that Uncle Wu had come. Ximen told the boy to bring him in. Uncle Wu made reverence to the three guests, then to Ximen Qing, and sat down. A boy brought fresh tea, and they drank it together. Then Uncle Wu rose and said to Ximen Qing: "Brother, will you come with me to the inner court for a moment? I should like to speak to you." Ximen Qing got up, and they went to the inner court together. They went to Yueniang's room, but she was in the arbor with the other ladies drinking wine and listening to Miss Shen singing. When she was told that her brother had come, she went back to her room and told Xiaoyu to bring tea.

Uncle Wu took ten taels of silver from his sleeve and gave them to Yueniang. "I have only had three pieces of silver from the office," he said, "so I can only pay my brother these ten taels. I shall have to pay the remainder by degrees."

"There is no hurry about it, Brother-in-law," Ximen Qing said.

"I am afraid I am very late already," Uncle Wu said.

Ximen Qing asked him if the work upon the granary was finished. "There is still another month's work to be done," Uncle Wu told him.

"Well," said Ximen, "when it is complete, you will reap your reward."

"Brother-in-law," Uncle Wu said, "this year, I understand, a number of military officials are to be appointed. I hope you will do anything you can for me by way of recommendation."

"Certainly," Ximen Qing said, "anything I can do for you, I will."

"You will go to the outer court, Brother?" Yueniang said.

"Perhaps I had better not go," Uncle Wu said. "The other three gentlemen may have business to transact."

"No," Ximen said, "a short time ago, Brother Chang borrowed a few taels from me and took a new house. He has just moved into it, and today he brought me a present of food, and I asked them to stay and enjoy it. You will be very welcome." He took Uncle Wu to the outer court. Yueniang went and bade the cooks get food ready for them. Qintong and Wang Jing prepared the table. Ximen Qing gave orders that the cellar should be opened and a jar of chrysanthemum wine brought. It had been given to him by Magistrate Xia. The wine was brought and opened. It was pale green in color and very sweet. Before it was poured into the wine pot, a jar of cold water was mixed with it to make it milder. It had a very delicate flavor, finer than that of grape wine.

Ximen Qing told Wang Jing to give a small cup to Uncle Wu, then to Ying Bojue and the others. They sipped it and spoke of it appreciatively.

Then food was brought, and after they had had some, the crabs and roast ducks were served. Ying Bojue urged Uncle Wu to eat freely. Xie Xida was astounded: he could not imagine how they could be made so tasty and tender.

"They are a present from Brother Chang," Ximen Qing said.

"I have lived to be fifty-two years old," Uncle Wu said, "and never in all my life have I known crabs cooked in this way to be so good."

"Brother," Ying Bojue said, "have you given the ladies a taste?"

"I have," said Ximen.

"Mistress Chang's cooking is really marvelous," said Bojue.

Chang Zhijie smiled. "Oh," said he, "my poor wife does not really cook very well. I brought these things thinking perhaps they might afford a little pleasure."

They enjoyed their crabs with the wine while, at Ximen Qing's bidding, Chunhong and Shutong sang Southern melodies. Bojue thought he heard music. "Is Li Guijie here?" he said. "Who else can be playing like that?"

"Listen again," Ximen Qing said.

"If it is not Guijie, it must be Wu Yin'er."

"You are guessing, Beggar Ying," Ximen said. "This girl is blind."

"It must be Miss Yu, then?" Bojue said.

"No, it is a Miss Shen. She is young and pretty and an excellent singer."

"Then why not tell her to sing a song for us?"

"I brought her here to sing for the ladies," Ximen said. "Your ears are very sharp if you can hear all this way off."

"Yes, my eyes are so clear that they can see a thousand *li* and my ears can hear a bee buzzing forty *li* away."

"Beggar," Xie Xida said, "you ears are as sharp as a rabbit's. Of course you can hear."

Then Bojue said: "Brother, you really must send for her. I should like to see her. Tell her to sing just one song for Uncle Wu. You can't refuse, for his sake."

At last, Ximen Qing told Wang Jing to go and ask Miss Shen to come and sing for Uncle Wu. She came, kowtowed, and sat down. Bojue asked her age and she told him she was twenty-one. Then he asked how many songs she knew and she said she knew a number for lute accompaniment, and more than a hundred short songs. "That is not bad," Bojue said.

"Miss Shen," Ximen Qing said, "we do not wish to put you to any trouble, but will you be good enough to take your lute and sing for us 'The Four Dreams and the Eight Spaces'?" He told Wang Jing to fill up his guests' glasses. Miss Shen played and sang sweetly.

When Li Ping'er reached her apartment, she went to wash her hands. Suddenly, the blood gushed from her, and her eyes were dazzled. She got up as quickly as she could, and pulled up her skirts, then fainted and struck the ground with her head. Yingchun was there and did what she could, but Li Ping'er hurt herself. Yingchun and Ruyi'er got her to bed. She lay there unconscious. Yingchun was frightened and told her fellow maid to go for Yueniang. All the ladies hurried to see what was amiss. Yingchun and the nurse were on the bed, holding up Li Ping'er.

"She was quite well a moment ago," Wu Yueniang said. "What has happened to make her like this?" Yingchun showed her the chamber pot.

Yueniang was startled. "Perhaps," she said, "the blood has flowed more freely because of the wine she drank."

"But she only drank a little," Meng Yulou and Pan Jinlian said together. They made ginger broth and poured it down her throat, but it was a long time before she came around and was able to speak to them.

"Sister," Yueniang said, "what is the matter?"

"Nothing very much," Li Ping'er said. "I got up and pulled up my skirt. Then my eyes seemed to go black. Everything whirled round and round, and I couldn't keep myself from falling."

Yueniang was going to tell Daian to go for his master and also for Dr. Ren, but Li Ping'er said: "No, don't say anything about it. I should not like to disturb their party."

Yueniang told Yingchun to straighten the coverlets and help Li Ping'er to go to bed. She and the other ladies gave up their amusements and went to their own rooms.

Uncle Wu and the others stayed until the evening, then Ximen Qing went to Yueniang's room. She told him how Li Ping'er had fainted. Ximen went at once to see her. She was lying, pale as wax, upon the bed. She held him by the sleeve and cried. He asked her what the trouble was. "As soon as I came in," she said, "the blood poured from me like water. Then I fainted."

Ximen saw that her head was slightly bruised. "What were the maids doing to let you fall and hurt your face?" he said.

"It was a very good thing for me the maid and the nurse could come to my help," Li Ping'er said. "If they hadn't, I should have been very much worse hurt."

"I will send for Doctor Ren the first thing in the morning," Ximen said. He spent the night in her room, sleeping on another bed.

The following morning, after he had been to the office, Ximen sent Qintong for the doctor. It was a little after noon when Dr. Ren arrived. Ximen Qing received him in the great hall and they had tea. Then he sent a boy to tell the ladies. They had the room cleaned and incense burned, and Dr. Ren was asked to go and see Li Ping'er. When he had examined her, he came back to the great hall.

"The lady is much worse than she was before," he told Ximen Qing. "The trouble has gone to her liver and the lungs are much inflamed. The wood element gets stronger and stronger and the earth element weaker. Her blood is overheated and circulates too violently. It comes down like a mountain torrent and nothing can hold it back. If the blood that comes from her were dark in color, she might still be saved, but it seems lighter; it is, in fact, fresh blood. I will send her some medicine and, if it does her any good, there may be some hope. If it does not, I fear there is nothing I can do for her."

"Master," Ximen said, "I beg you to make some medicine for her with all the skill at your disposal. You shall be handsomely rewarded."

"Do not speak of reward," Dr. Ren said. "You and I are good friends. I will certainly do my best for her." They took more tea, and the doctor left. Ximen Qing told Qintong to take a roll of Hangzhou silk and two taels of white gold to the doctor and bring the medicine back with him. The medicine he brought was called a tonic for the spleen. Li Ping'er took it very hot, but the blood poured from her more than ever. Then Ximen Qing, very much distressed, sent for Dr. Hu, who lived in the same street. Dr. Hu said that anger had disorganized the pulse, and that the blood had become feverish. He too sent some medicine. Li Ping'er took it, but it was like a pebble thrown into the depths of the ocean.

Now that doctors were visiting the house all the time, Yueniang decided not to keep Miss Shen for more than one night. She gave her five *qian* of silver, some clothes and some ornaments. Miss Shen went away in a sedan chair, and a box of food was sent with her.

When Hua Ziyu was at the party given to celebrate the opening of the shop, he heard that Li Ping'er was ill. He told his wife, and his wife brought a box of presents and came to see the invalid. When she saw how thin and pale Li Ping'er had become, both women cried. Yueniang ordered tea and took Mistress Hua to the inner court.

Han Daoguo suggested to Ximen Qing that Dr. Zhao, a graduate of the Imperial College of Medicine and a specialist in the diseases of women, might be called in. "He is an expert on the pulse," he said. "My wife once had trouble of much the same sort and Doctor Zhao cured her. I commend him to you for your lady."

As soon as he heard this, Ximen Qing told Qintong and Wang Jing to go at once on horseback outside the Western Gate and ask Dr. Zhao to come. Then he sent for Ying Bojue and discussed the matter with him. "My sixth wife," he said, "is very ill. What can I do about it?"

"I heard she was better," Bojue said in surprise. "Is she worse again?"

"She has been very sad ever since the baby died," Ximen said, "and now her old trouble has returned. Yesterday, on the festival day, I got Miss Shen here especially for her. But she didn't take any interest. She went back to her own room and there fainted, fell on the floor, and bruised her face. I sent for Doctor Ren. He said she was worse than she had ever been. She took his medicine, but the blood only poured from her the more."

"I hear you sent for Doctor Hu, too," Bojue said. "What did he say?"

"He said that anger had disorganized her pulse. She took his medicine, but it did her no good. Today, my clerk Han recommended Doctor Zhao. His name is Chao Longgang and he is a specialist in women's diseases. I have sent two boys to fetch him. I am very very anxious about her. It is all on account of the baby. She thinks about him day and night. Women never know where to stop. I have tried to console her but she won't listen to me and I don't know what to do."

Ping'an came and announced Master Qiao. Ximen Qing took him to the hall and there they sat for a while with Ying Bojue.

"I hear that your Sixth Lady is not well," Master Qiao said. "I have come to inquire about her."

"It is the child's death," Ximen said. "It has made her so melancholy that an old trouble has returned. It was very kind of you to come."

"Have you sent for any particular doctor?" Master Qiao asked.

"First she took Doctor Ren's medicine," Ximen said. "Then, yesterday, I sent for Doctor Hu. There was no improvement, and now I have sent for Doctor Zhao."

Then Qiao said: "Near the office there lives an old gentleman named He who has a great knowledge of medicine. His son, He Qixuan, has become a very famous doctor. Why don't you ask him to come?"

"I will send for him when Doctor Zhao has gone."

"I would suggest having them together," Qiao said. "Then they can hold a consultation about the cause of the illness. They can prescribe afterwards, and their prescription ought to be effective."

"You are right," said Ximen. He told Daian to take his card and go with Qiao Tong to ask old master He to come. When Master He came, he bowed to Ximen Qing and Qiao, and they made him take the seat of honor. "It is several years since I last saw you," Ximen said politely, "and now your hair is quite white."

"How is your son doing?" Qiao asked the old man.

"He goes to the office every day," He said, "and that does not leave him much time for anything else. I myself have to go and see those patients who are not of official rank."

"You are very old," Ying Bojue said, "yet you seem very strong."

"Yes," said the old man, "I am eighty-one years old." They had tea and a boy was sent to give warning to the ladies. Then the old gentleman went to see Li Ping'er. He came back to the hall.

"I will tell you what is the matter with the lady," he said to Ximen Qing and Master Qiao. "The seed got into her blood. Then she had a fit of anger. This intermixture of anger and blood has caused the trouble. Whether I am correct or not, I do not know."

"Yes, you are right," Ximen Qing said, "but what I want to know is, can you cure her?"

Just then, Qintong and Wang Jing came back with Dr. Zhao. Old Master He asked who he was. "This is a doctor who was recommended to me by one of my clerks," Ximen Qing said. "Don't mention the fact that you have examined her. When he has seen her, you can consult with him."

Dr. Zhao came in and made a reverence to them all. The two old men, He and Qiao, sat in the places of honor, and made room on their left for Dr. Zhao. Ying Bojue sat on the right, and Ximen Qing in the host's place. Dr. Zhao asked the names.

"This is He, and I am Qiao," said Qiao.

"My name is Ying," said Ying Bojue. "I presume you are Doctor Zhao."

"I am," said Zhao, "and my second name is Longgang. My grand father was an official in the Imperial College of Medicine; my father was a doctor of high standing, so that I have the experience of three generations behind me. Every day I work very hard upon the theories of Wang Shuhe, Dong Yuan, and Wu Tingzi. I read the poem upon the Nature of Medicine, the Su Wen of Huangdi, the Nan Jing, and, of living masters, the Secret Art of Dan Xi, the cure of heart troubles also by Dan Xi, Jie Gu's Secret of Pulse Examination, the Thirteen Prescriptions, and so forth. I have read nearly everything that is written about medicine, so that, when I have to prescribe, I have a very harmonious system at my disposal. My fingers are able to discern the most profound workings of the pulse. I can diagnose the conflict between Yin and Yang according to the seasons. I determine the sinking or the floating of the pulse according to internal and external relations. And, in cases of fever or chill, I leave no detail unconsidered. There is nothing about the pulse I do not know, but, really, I cannot attempt to explain how much I do know."

Old Master He listened attentively. "May I ask what is the first thing to be done in the consideration of a patient's case?" he said.

"According to the ancient masters," Dr. Zhao said, "when one deals with any patient, one should look at him, listen to him, question him, and examine him. Then a miraculous cure is certain. I always begin by asking my patient questions, then I feel his pulse and consider his general appearance. Unless we see a patient as Zi Ping, the reader of fortunes, sees him, it is impossible to be quite definite about the ailment."

"Please, doctor, come and see my wife," Ximen Qing said. He told Qintong to warn the ladies in the inner court, and took Dr. Zhao to see Li Ping'er. She had just gone to sleep and had to be waked up again. Then she sat up in bed propped up with pillows and bedclothes. Dr. Zhao examined first her left hand, then her right.

"Lady," he said, "please raise your head." Li Ping'er did what she was told. Then the doctor said to Ximen Qing: "Kindly ask the lady who I am."

"Who is this gentleman?" Ximen said to his wife.

Li Ping'er looked at Zhao. "A doctor, I suppose," she said.

"There!" said Dr. Zhao, "you have no need to worry, Sir. She can still distinguish between one person and another."

"Be very careful," Ximen said, "and your fee shall be correspondingly large."

Dr. Zhao studied Li Ping'er for a long time. "Judging by her general appearance and her pulse, I think she must be suffering from a fever or some wasting disease. She must have been ill either before she had a baby, or afterwards."

"You are quite wrong," Ximen Qing said. "Kindly examine her again."

Dr. Zhao gazed at Li Ping'er and murmured: "Why is her face so pale? Her stomach must be out of order— or is it her blood?"

"Let me tell you, Doctor," Ximen Qing said. "My wife suffers from an issue of blood. It is that which makes her so thin and weak. If you have any medicine that will do her any good, I will pay you well for it."

"I said it was the blood," Dr. Zhao said. "Have no fear. I have some excellent medicine."

Ximen Qing took him back to the hall. Old Master He and Master Qiao asked what the doctor thought.

"In my opinion she is discharging too much blood," Dr. Zhao said.

"And what medicine are you going to give her?" said the old gentleman.

"I have a perfectly wonderful medicine that will certainly cure the lady. It is made of these drugs—liquorice, spurge, *gangsha,* hellebore, croton, coriander flowers, a mixture of ginger juice with raw pinella, aconite and almond *tianma.* Make all these into a pill with honey and take it with spirit in the morning."

"But, it seems to me, those drugs are much too strong," the old gentleman said. "I can't believe that would do at all."

"Why not?" said Dr. Zhao. "Doctors have always agreed that strong medicine, bitter to the taste, is excellent for invalids."

Ximen Qing realized that the doctor was talking nothing but rubbish. He gave him two *qian* of silver and dismissed him. He did not go with him to the gate, but he made no complaint because Han Daoguo had recommended him.

"The man is a fool," he said to Master Qiao.

"I did not venture to say so before," old Doctor He said, "but the fellow is very well known outside the gate. People call him Zhao the Trickster. He is always defrauding people and strolling about the streets. What should he know of medicine? As for your lady's illness, I will make up some medicine for her when I get home. If, when she has taken it, the flow of blood stops and she feels more comfortable, I will continue the treatment, but, if this medicine does not help, there is nothing else I can do." Ximen Qing gave the old gentleman a tael of silver and he went away.

Daian was sent for the medicine. Li Ping'er took it that evening, but there was no improvement in her condition.

"Do not give her any more medicine," Yueniang said. "She has had nothing to eat or drink, and medicine on an empty stomach is useless. Don't you remember that Wu the Immortal said she would have a blood disorder when she was twenty-seven years old? She is twenty-seven now. You would do well to send for Wu again. He can tell us whether she will live or not. If some evil star is overshadowing her life, we will ask the Immortal to offer sacrifice for her."

Ximen Qing at once sent a boy with his card to make inquiry at Major Zhou's house. Major Zhou's people said that Wu was a man who never stayed long in the same place. "When he is here," they said, "he always lives at the Temple of the Guardian Spirits of the Soil, south of the city, but, in the fourth month of this year, he went to the Wudang Mountains. If it is a fortune you wish to have told, there is a certain Master Huang who lives at the Daoist temple. He is well skilled in the art. He will not accept more than three *qian* of silver, but he will not leave his temple."

This was reported to Ximen Qing. He immediately told Chen Jingji to take three *qian* of silver and go to the Daoist Temple to consult Master Huang.

Outside the temple hung a sign on which was written: "Here, by the divinely blessed method of the Book of Changes, the decrees of Fate are interpreted. The fee is three *qian*." Jingji went in and bowed to Master Huang. He gave him the three *qian*.

"The fortune I would ask you to tell," he said, "is that of a woman twenty-seven years old, born at noon on the fifteenth day of the first month."

Master Huang made a calculation upon the abacus and said: "In this fate we have the year *Xinwei,* the month *Gengyin,* the day *Xinmao,* and the hour *Jiawu.* The life would appear to be one in well-to-do circumstances. The fate seems to run in the years with a four. The fourth year is *Jiwei,* the fourteenth *Wuwu,* the twenty-fourth *Dingsi,* and the thirty-fourth *Bingchen.* This year is *Dingdu,* and the evil stars are all in the ascendant. The *Jidu* star commands her life, and the five evil spirits are always busy making trouble for her. The *Jidu* star is the star of darkness, its form is that of a bundle of tangled silk that has neither beginning nor end. There is a great deal of unhappiness and some illness. The first month, the second, third, seventh and ninth are all months in which illness appears. This year, too, is unpropitious as regards children. There are other sources of anxiety, quarrels, losses of property, and, because she is a woman, the situation is more disastrous."

Master Huang wrote down what he had said, and Chen Jingji went back with it. Ximen Qing was with Ying Bojue and Master Wen. When Jingji gave him the paper, he took it to the inner court and read it to Yueniang. It was obvious that what destiny had in store for Li Ping'er was more to be feared than hoped for, and they were full of sorrow.

CHAPTER 62

The Death of the Sixth Lady

When Ximen Qing realized that no medicine seemed to cure Li Ping'er, and when all the fortune-tellers assured him that her case was hopeless, he did not know what to do. At first, Li Ping'er still tried to get up, dress, comb her hair, and leave her bed when she had to attend to the intimate details of her toilet, but, by degrees, she came to eat less and less and grew thinner and thinner. In a very short time, she who had been such a flower-like creature was faded and withered. She could no longer get out of bed. Papers were put on her mattress, and she told her maids to burn incense all the time so that there might not be an unpleasant odor. Ximen Qing saw that her arms were as thin as threads. He was nearly always in her room, weeping, and only went to his office every other day.

"Dear man," Li Ping'er said to him, "you must not neglect your duties. I am afraid you will get behind with your official business. Don't worry about me. I have this trouble, but if the blood will only stop, and I can manage to eat and drink a little, I shall be better. You are a man. It is not fitting that you should stay at home with me all the time."

"Sister," Ximen said, and he wept as he spoke, "how can I leave you when I see you like this?"

"Oh, you foolish man, if the Fates have decreed that I must die, who can prevent it? I only wish to say one thing to you. I don't know why, but, when I am alone, something terrible seems to overshadow me. Shadowy forms are always before my eyes and, at night, I am haunted by evil dreams. Men with swords and staves quarrel and struggle with me. They snatch my baby from my breast and make to throw me on the ground. Then my former husband comes and says that he has a new house and wants me to go with him. But I did not mean to tell you this."

"When a man dies," Ximen Qing said, "he is as a light blown out. No one can say whither he has gone. It is because you have been ill so long. You are weak. I don't believe any evil spirit really comes to trouble you. But I will get Abbot Wu to give me some charms and I will put them up at your door. Then we shall see if there are devils in this house."

He went to the outer court and told Daian to go to the Temple of the Jade King to get the charms.

On his way, Daian met Ying Bojue and Xie Xida. He hastily dismounted. "Where are you going?" Ying Bojue said to him. "Is your master at home?"

"Yes," said Daian, "and I am going to the Temple of the Jade King for some charms."

The two friends went on to see Ximen Qing.

"When Brother Xie heard how ill your lady is, he was terribly shocked," Bojue said. "We have come to ask how she is."

"These last few days," Ximen told them, "she has grown so thin that she looks like another woman. Really, I don't know what to do."

"Why did you send Daian to the temple?" Bojue said.

Ximen told them about the evil dreams Li Ping'er had. "I fear there may be devils about the house," he said, "so I have asked for some charms to drive them away."

"Oh," Xie Xida said, "I am sure it is only because she is so weak. There are no devils here."

Then Bojue said: "Brother, if you wish to get rid of devils, it is a very simple matter. Priest Pan, of the Temple of the Five Sacred Mountains outside the city gate, has power over the Five Thunders and he can exorcise devils of every sort. He is known as Pan the Expeller of Demons. With his charms and wonder-working philters he often gets people out of difficulties of this sort. Send for him, Brother, and then we shall know whether there are devils at work here or not. And indeed, if you ask him, he may be able to cure your lady."

"As soon as the boy comes back from Abbot Wu, I will send him with you to Pan," Ximen said.

"We won't wait for him," Bojue said. "I will go at once. I most sincerely hope that your lady may be cured, and, if there is anything I can do to help, I will do it, even if I have to go on my head instead of my feet." He went off with Xie Xida.

When Daian came back with the charms, they were put upon the door of Li Ping'er's rooms. But that night she was terrified once more. She said to Ximen Qing: "He has been with two other men to carry me off. They ran away as you came in."

"Don't believe it," Ximen Qing said. "Brother Ying says it is all due to your weakness. He tells me that he knows a priest called Pan who will give us some very efficacious charms and medicine, and who has the power to drive out devils. I have told Brother Ying to get him to come tomorrow morning, and I'm sure he will get rid of all the disturbing influences."

"Oh, Brother," said Li Ping'er, "send for him this very moment. The dead man has gone away in a fury, and I am afraid he will come back and take me with him. Send for him now."

"If you are afraid, I will send for Wu Yin'er to keep you company," Ximen said.

Li Ping'er shook her head. "I don't wish to trouble her," she said, "I shouldn't like her to lose business."

"What about old woman Feng, then?"

Li Ping'er nodded, and Ximen Qing sent Laian for the old woman. But the door was locked, and the old woman was not to be found. Laian told the Beanpole that, when she came back, she must be told to go at once to Ximen Qing's house because the Sixth Lady needed her. Ximen Qing told Daian that, early next morning, he must go with Ying Bojue to the Temple of the Five Sacred Mountains to bring the priest Pan.

The next day, Nun Wang came. She brought a box of specially treated rice, twenty large milk biscuits and a small box of preserved eggplants. When she arrived, Li Ping'er bade Yingchun help her to sit up in bed. Nun Wang made a reverence, and Li Ping'er asked her to sit down.

"Teacher," she said, "I have not seen you since you had those texts printed for me. Though I have been so very ill, you have never come to see me."

"I did not know about your illness, Lady," the nun said. "It was only yesterday that the Great Lady sent a servant to the convent and I heard for the first time that you were ill. And, speaking of the printing of those texts, you don't know what trouble I had with that wicked old nun Xue. You remember it was arranged that we should both make terms with the printer. I got nothing out of it, but she secretly persuaded the printer to give her five taels. She did not even let me see a penny. Lady, when that bad old woman dies, she will go to the very depths of Hell. She put me in such a state that I even forgot the Great Lady's birthday, and I did not come."

"Let her go her evil way," Li Ping'er said, "but do not quarrel with her."

"I had no intention of quarreling with her," the nun said.

"The Great Lady is annoyed with you," Li Ping'er said. "She says you have never read the scriptures for her."

"Oh, Buddha!" Nun Wang cried, "I don't profess to be a saint, but I should not dare to forget a thing like that. I have been reading them all the time. I only stopped yesterday when the month was up. I have just seen her and told her about my troubles. I told her that I had only just heard about your illness, and I have nothing to offer but this rice, the preserved fruits, and the biscuits you will perhaps make into sop. The Great Lady told Xiaoyu to bring me here to see you."

Xiaoyu opened the boxes. Li Ping'er looked at them and thanked the nun. Then the nun said: "Sister Yingchun, please go and warm two of these biscuits. I want to see your lady take something to eat."

Yingchun took away the things and Li Ping'er ordered tea to be brought for the nun.

"I have had tea in the Great Lady's room," the nun said. "I only want to see you eat some porridge."

Yingchun set the table and brought in four kinds of tea cakes for Nun Wang. For Li Ping'er she brought some porridge with a plate of preserved fruits and two steamed milk biscuits. There were two bowls of porridge and a pair of small ivory chopsticks. Yingchun and Ruyi'er held the bowls and assisted Li Ping'er. But she only took two or three mouthfuls of porridge and nibbled at the cakes. Then she shook her head and would eat no more. She told them to take the things away.

"We must eat and drink," Nun Wang said. "Do have a little more. This porridge is so good."

"I would if I could," Li Ping'er said.

Nun Wang helped to pull the bedclothes over her and, as she did so, noticed how wasted Li Ping'er had become. She was shocked. "Lady," she said, "you were fatter than this when I saw you last. What has made you so thin?"

"She was better for a while," Ruyi'er said. "Then something angered her, and her illness came back again. Father sent for the doctor and he gave her some medicine that made her very much better. But, in the eighth month, the baby took fright and was very ill. My lady watched him day and night and never slept at all. She hoped he would recover, but, alas, he died. Then she cried and sobbed all day. Then, too, she was made angry, and, all things considered, got into a state that no one could stand, even if she were strong as iron or stone. Anybody but my lady would have complained and so got rid of her trouble, but she never tells anybody, only reluctantly when she is made to do so."

"Who upset her?" the nun asked. "Your master loves her, and the Great Lady respects her. There are only the few other ladies, and I can't think any one of them would offend her."

"Ah, you don't know," Ruyi'er said. She told the younger maid to go and see if the door was fast and continued: "It was the Fifth Lady. It was her cat that scratched the baby and made him have a fit. Master came and asked my lady, but she would not tell him and, in the end, the Great Lady told him. He killed the cat. The Fifth Lady never relented. She went on making trouble with us. In the middle of the eighth month the baby died. The Fifth Lady was delighted and has insulted us every day since. We can hear clearly everything she says, and my lady cannot help being upset. She weeps nearly all the time. Anger and sorrow together have gradually brought her to this pass. Only Heaven knows what a good heart she has. She never shows an angry face to the other ladies. If she has nice clothes, she will not wear them unless the other ladies have dresses like them. There is not a single person in the house to whom my lady has not been kind at some time or another. The trouble is that, though they are ready enough to take things from her, they never have a kind word to say about her."

"What do you mean?" Nun Wang said.

"There is old lady Pan, the Fifth Lady's mother. Whenever Father stays the night in the Fifth Lady's room, the old lady comes and sleeps here. And when she goes away, my lady never lets her go without stuff for making clothes or shoes. She gives her money too. Yet the Fifth Lady never has a good word to say about it."

"Oh, woman!" cried Li Ping'er, "why do you have so much to say? Let them do what they like. Heaven is mighty, yet Heaven never boasts; and Earth is solid, yet Earth never speaks."

"Buddha!" said Nun Wang, "who would have known that you had such a sweet disposition? But Heaven has eyes. Heaven will see your good works and reward you."

"Teacher," Li Ping'er said, "what reward shall I receive? Not even my child is left to me. I suffer so much pain, and have an ailment so unpleasant that even as a spirit I shall be unclean. I am going to give you some money so that, when I am dead, you can employ a few nuns to read as many texts as you can find so that this nasty disease may not cling to me forever."

"You are looking too far ahead," Nun Wang said. "Your heart is so good that Heaven cannot fail to protect you."

While they were talking, Qintong came. "Father says this room must be cleaned," he told Yingchun. "Uncle Hua has come to see your lady. He is in the outer court now."

Nun Wang stood up. "I must go to the inner court," she said.

"Teacher," said Li Ping'er, "don't go away. I wish you to stay for a few days. There is something I should like to say to you." The nun promised to stay.

Ximen Qing brought in Uncle Hua. Li Ping'er lay still upon her bed and did not speak.

"I never knew you were ill until yesterday," Uncle Hua said. "I have come especially to see you."

"It is very good of you," Li Ping'er said. She turned her face to the wall.

Hua stayed a short time, then went back to the outer court with Ximen Qing. "Our late noble relative," he said to his host, "when he was Governor of Guangnan, had some *gynura* medicine. It is a certain cure for all those troubles from which women suffer. If she takes five *fen* of it, mixed with a little wine, it will stop that flow of blood. I know she has this medicine. Why has she not tried it?"

"She has tried it," Ximen Qing said. "Yesterday the Prefect Hu came to see me. I told him about her illness, and he, too, told me of some medicine. That was white cockscomb flowers. It is mixed with a little charcoal and taken with wine. She took it, and, for a day, the flow of blood ceased, but the next day it was worse than ever."

"It is a very difficult case," Hua Ziyu said. "I think, brother-in-law, that you would do well to look out for a coffin for her. I will send my wife to see her tomorrow." He went away.

While the nurse and Yingchun were changing the bed for Li Ping'er, old woman Feng came. She made a reverence, and Ruyi'er said to her: "You are a fine one, Mother Feng! You have never been near your mistress, and yesterday Master had to send for you. Laian said your door was locked. Where were you?"

"I can't tell you what a hard life I have," old woman Feng said. "Every day I go to the temple for my religious devotions. I set off in the morning and, for some reason or other, I never get back till night. When I get home, there is always some priest to come and see me. Father Zhang, or Father Li, or Father Wang."

"An old woman like you, and so many priests to visit you!" said Ruyi'er. "This is the first time we have heard of Father Wang."

Li Ping'er smiled. "The old woman always talks nonsense," she said.

Then Ruyi'er said: "Old woman, you refuse to come when you are sent for. For the last few days my lady has had nothing to eat, and she has been terribly depressed. You have only just come, yet you have made her laugh already. If you will only stay a few days, I'm sure she will soon be better."

"Yes," old woman Feng said, "I am a good doctor when it is a question of driving care away." She laughed. Then she looked at Li Ping'er. "Lady," she said, "I had hoped to find you better. Are you able to get out of bed when you wish to relieve nature?"

"If only she could, it would be splendid," Yingchun said. "Until a few days ago, she could just manage to get up, we helping her, of course, but lately she has not been able, and we have had to put papers in the bed."

As they were talking, Ximen Qing came in. "Old woman Feng," he said, "you ought to be here nearly all the time. Why have you been so long away?"

"My Lord," the old woman said, "you know this is the season for preserving vegetables. I have been preserving some, so that if anyone is brought to me, I shall be able to give her something to eat. I have no other way of buying them."

"Why didn't you tell me?" Ximen Qing said. "Yesterday I was having the vegetables on my farm dug up, and you might have had a bushel or two."

"I am greatly obliged to your Lordship," the old woman said. Then she went to another room. Ximen Qing sat down beside the bed and Yingchun burned incense.

"How do you feel today?" Ximen asked Li Ping'er. Then he said to Yingchun: "Has your mother had any gruel?" Yingchun told him that the nun had brought some milk biscuits but that her mistress had only tasted them and taken a tiny bit of porridge.

"Brother Ying and the boy went for Priest Pan," Ximen Qing said, "but he was not at his temple. Tomorrow I will send Laibao."

"Oh, do send for him at once," Li Ping'er said. "I see that dead man whenever I close my eyes."

"It is all because your mind is so enfeebled," Ximen said. "Try to pull yourself together and don't let such ideas get hold of you. When the priest comes he will exorcise any evil spirits there may be about. He will give you medicine too, and you will soon be well again."

"Brother," Li Ping'er said, "there is no hope for me. I had always hoped to live long years with you, and now I am dying when I am only twenty-seven. What an evil fate is mine that I must leave you! I shall go and never see you again until you come to the gate of the spirits." She held his hand in hers and cried, sobbing softly, for she was too weak to make a noise. Ximen cried with her.

"Sister," he said, "if there is anything that you would say to me, say it."

In the midst of their grief, Qintong came and said: "An officer has come from your court. He says that tomorrow is the fifteenth, and there is a great deal of important business to be done. They wish to know whether you will be there or not."

"I cannot go tomorrow," Ximen Qing said. "Give the man a card, and tell Magistrate Xia that he must do all that is necessary."

"Brother," said Li Ping'er, "you must go to your office and not neglect your duties. Though I am dying, I shall not be gone so soon."

"But I am going to stay and watch over you," Ximen said. "I want you to keep firm hold on yourself and not let your thoughts bother you so much. Uncle Hua told me that I should get the boards for your coffin and so keep the evil ones away. When I have done so, you will certainly begin to improve."

Li Ping'er nodded. "Very well," she said, "but don't let yourself be cheated. You must not spend more than ten taels on the wood. And, if you really look upon me as your wife, don't have my body burned, but lay me beside your dead wife. So, perhaps, I may benefit from some of the offerings made at her tomb. And do not spend too much money on those boards for my coffin. You have a great household, and you must think of the future."

These words pierced Ximen's heart as though they had been a sword. "Sister," he said, "why do you talk like this? Even if I were a poor man, I would not treat you so disgracefully."

Then Wu Yueniang came with a small box of apples. "My sister-in-law has sent these especially for you," she said to Li Ping'er. She told Yingchun to wash and peel them.

"It is very kind of Mistress Wu," Li Ping'er said. When Yingchun had peeled some of them, she cut them into slices, put them on a plate and tried to help Li Ping'er to eat one. But she could only suck it and spit it out. Yueniang was afraid they might be disturbing her, so she made her turn her face to the wall, and she and Ximen Qing went out to talk about her.

"I am afraid she is in a very bad way," Yueniang said. "You ought to go and buy some boards for her coffin before it is too late."

"So Brother Hua has just said, and I have spoken to her about it. She said I must not spend much money because I have so many people to provide for and I must think of the future. It went to my heart. But I think I will wait until Priest Pan has been, and then I'll see about the coffin."

"You don't realize the situation," Yueniang said. "Look how she has changed. She has lost appetite till she cannot even drink a drop of water. You still hope for her recovery. We must face the facts. If she does get better, we can give the coffin to somebody for charity. It will not cost us much."

"I will do what you say," Ximen Qing said. He went to the great hall and sent for Ben the Fourth. "You know who has good coffin boards for sale," he said. "Go with Chen Jingji, my son-in-law, and see if you can find a good set. Take the money with you."

"I believe that Captain Chen, in the Main Street, has some good boards," Ben the Fourth said.

Ximen Qing sent for Chen Jingji and said to him: "Go to the Great Lady and ask her for five pieces of silver. Then go to look at the boards with Ben the Fourth." Chen Jingji hurried away, got the money, and went out with Ben the Fourth. In the afternoon they came back.

"We went to Chen's place and looked at all the boards he has," Jingji said, "but we did not think them either particularly good or very cheap.

On our way back we met Master Qiao. He told us that a scholar named Shang had a very fine set of boards. His father bought them at Chengdu in Sichuan, where he used to be a judge. He brought them for his own lady. There were two sets originally and they have used one. They are of the kind known as Peach Flower Cavern. The set is complete in five pieces—sides, cover, top and bottom. They are asking three hundred and seventy taels. We went with Master Qiao to see the set, and it certainly is a very fine one. Master Qiao bargained with Scholar Shang for a long time, and at last the scholar agreed to reduce his price by fifty taels. He would not have sold the boards at all, he said, if he had not wanted the money to pay for his expenses when he goes to the Capital next year to sit for the public examination."

"Take three hundred and twenty taels at once and secure the boards," Ximen Qing said. "There is no time to lose."

"He has taken two hundred and fifty taels as a deposit," Jingji said, "so that leaves us with seventy more to pay." They went again to the inner court and Yueniang gave them another seventy taels. Then they went to Master Shang's. That evening a number of porters brought the boards, carefully wrapped in red drugget. They set them down in the courtyard. Ximen Qing examined them and found them excellent. He sent for carpenters to saw them, and the wood gave out a delightful fragrance. The main piece was about five inches thick, two feet five inches broad and seven feet five inches long. Ximen Qing was quite satisfied. He sent for Ying Bojue to come and look at them and asked him if he had ever seen such a fine set of coffin boards in his life before. Bojue expressed his admiration.

"A perfect example of the fitness of things!" he exclaimed. "Everything in the world has its proper owner somewhere. You have bought these boards for my sister-in-law, and it is clear evidence that she did well when she married you."

Ximen said to the workmen: "Make these boards up carefully and you shall have five taels of silver." The workmen set to work with a will and soon had put the coffin together.

Ying Bojue said to Laibao: "Tomorrow morning go and see Priest Pan. If he will come, bring him with you. We must avoid all further delay." Then he stood with Ximen Qing and watched the carpenters working in the courtyard. It was the first night watch before he went away.

"Come early tomorrow," Ximen said to him. "The priest may be here early." Bojue promised and went away.

In the evening, old woman Feng and Nun Wang went to Li Ping'er's room. They had seen Ximen Qing in the front court. They proposed to stay the night with Li Ping'er, but she would not allow them. "This is a foul place," she said, "and it would be disagreeable for you. Go and sleep somewhere else." Ximen, seeing that the nun and the old woman were there, went to sleep with Pan Jinlian.

Li Ping'er told Yingchun to fasten the corner door and bolt it. Then she said: "Take a light and open my chest." Yingchun took out some dresses and ornaments. Li Ping'er asked the nun to go nearer and gave her five taels of silver and a roll of silk.

"When I am dead," she said, "read the texts for me, you and a few other nuns."

"Lady," Nun Wang said, "you are looking too far ahead. Heaven will take pity on you, and you will certainly get better."

"Keep the money," Li Ping'er said, "and say nothing about it to the Great Lady. Tell her I gave you the silk for the sacred offerings you made for me." Then she called old woman Feng. "Old Feng," she said, "you are my old nurse. You waited on me when I was a child. Now I am dying. I have nothing to give you but these old dresses and this pin. I give them to you as a keepsake. And here is some silver that you may buy yourself a coffin. You need have no anxiety. I will ask his Lordship to let you stay on in that house as caretaker. I'm sure he won't send you away."

Old woman Feng took the silver and the clothes and knelt down. Weeping, she said: "This is the end of me. As long as you have lived, I have always had someone to depend upon. If you die, I shan't know where to go."

Then Li Ping'er called the nurse and gave her a purple silk gown, a blue silk skirt, an old silk cloak, two gold-headed pins, and a silver ornament.

"You took care of my baby," she said, "and even when my baby died, I still hoped you might take care of another child of mine. I did not want you to leave me while I lived. But there is no hope for me now, and I am going to ask your master and mistress to keep you after my death, so that, if the Great Lady has a child, you may nurse it. I give you these clothes as a little token of remembrance. Do not think that I am mean."

Ruyi'er knelt down and kowtowed. She cried. "I hoped that I might serve you always," she said. "You have always been so kind to me. And it is really my fault that the little master died and you are so ill. Please speak to the Great Lady for me. My husband is dead, and, if I am sent away from here, there is nowhere for me to go." Then Ruyi'er took the clothes and the ornaments and stood, drying her tears.

Now Li Ping'er summoned Yingchun and Xiuchun. They came and knelt down beside the bed. "You two have served me since your childhood. You have served me well, but there is little I can do for you now.

You have already clothes enough, and there is no need for me to give you more. Here, for each of you, are two pairs of gold pins and two gold flowers. As for you, Yingchun, your master has made a woman of you, so, of course, you will not leave here, and I will ask the Great Lady to look after you. And you, Xiuchun, I will ask the Great Lady to find a good home for you, for I would not have you stay on here to be ill used by anyone else. I don't wish my maids to suffer when I am gone, and I don't think you will find anyone else as indulgent as I have been."

Xiuchun knelt and cried. "Mother," she sobbed, "I would like to stay here forever."

"Oh, you silly maid! Whom will you serve when I have gone?"

"I will look after your tablet."

"My tablet will not be here for long. It will be burned and you will have to go away."

"Then I and Yingchun will both serve the Great Lady."

"That is one way," said Li Ping'er.

Xiuchun did not quite understand the situation. Yingchun took the ornaments and cried. She could not speak.

So Li Ping'er gave them all her last instructions. In the early morning, Ximen Qing came. She asked him about the coffin. "We bought the boards yesterday," he told her, "and the men are working on it now. Remember, it is to drive your illness away. When you get better, we shall give it away in charity."

"How much did it cost? I do not wish you to waste your money."

"Oh, not much," Ximen Qing said. "A hundred taels, or something like that."

"It is a great deal of money for so useless an end," Li Ping'er said. "Well, have it made up ready for my death."

Ximen Qing went out to see the carpenters at work. Yueniang and Li Jiao'er came to see her. It was clear that she was very ill indeed. "How do you feel today, Sister?" Yueniang asked.

Li Ping'er took her hand. "Mother," she said, "there is no hope for me."

The Great Lady wept. "Sister," she said, "is there anything you would like to say to me? Here is the Second Lady, too. Tell us both."

"I have nothing to say," Li Ping'er answered. "We have been sisters together for a few years and you have always been very kind to me. I had hoped we should grow old together, but the Fates were against me. My baby died, and now I am dying. When I am dead, my two maids will be left. The older of them has already been made a woman, and you will doubtless keep her in your apartments. As for the younger, keep her if you want her, but, otherwise, please find a young man for her and let her be free. I don't wish people to speak of her as a maid without a mistress. I say this because she has served me so long, and I shall be the easier after my death for telling you. Ruyi'er does not wish to leave, so, Mother, for the sake of the care she took of my baby and for my own sake, keep her to look after the child you will bear."

"Sister," said Yueniang, "think no more about any of these matters. I take them all upon myself. If you leave us, I will have Yingchun to live with me and Xiuchun shall wait upon the Second Lady. The maid the Second Lady has now is not as honest as she might be and she is lazy. One of these days I shall have to dismiss her. The nurse, Ruyi'er, as you have said, has nowhere else to go, and I will keep her whether I have a child or not. I will try and find a husband for her."

"Don't worry about any of these things," Li Jiao'er added. "The Great Lady and I will hold ourselves responsible. If Xiuchun comes to me, I will let her wait upon me, and treat her kindly."

Li Ping'er called the nurse and the two maids and bade them kowtow to the two ladies. Yueniang began to cry again.

Meng Yulou, Pan Jinlian, and Sun Xue'e then came to visit Li Ping'er and she said a few kind words to each of them. Then all but Yueniang went away. "Mother," Li Ping'er said to her softly, "if you bear a child, Mother, look carefully after him. Bring him up that he may continue the family after you. Do not be careless as I was, so that you suffer from the evil plottings of others."

"I understand, Sister," Yueniang said. These words made a great impression upon her, and, when Ximen Qing was dead, the remembrance of them was the reason why Jinlian was no longer allowed to live in the family.

While they were still talking, Qintong came and said they must burn incense. Priest Pan had come. Yueniang told the maids to clean the room, make tea, get pure water, and burn some precious incense. She and the other women went to the inner room to listen to what the priest should say. Ximen Qing brought him in.

The priest came in by the corner door, past the screen. Before he entered the room where Li Ping'er was, he went backward two steps before the stairs. Then he murmured something; the servants raised the lattice, and he went in. He sat down beside the sick woman's bed. It seemed as if all his strength was concentrated in his two eyes; it was a sign that he was summoning all the power of spiritual vision at his command. He held a sword in his hand, and his fingers were bent in a definite and peculiar position. He murmured again, and it seemed as though his eyes saw through everything. Then he went to the other room and set out the table for incense. Ximen Qing burned some incense and the priest set fire to a charm. Then he cried:

"Come quickly, all ye spirits that serve!"

He cast around him a mouthful of water. Immediately there seemed to be a whirlwind of furious intensity outside the room, and in the whirlwind some of the marshals of the host of angels.

"In this house of Ximen," said the priest, "a woman, Li, is ill. She has appealed to me. I bid you, bring the guardian of the soil and the six tutelaries of this household. Bring them that I may examine them and learn the reason for this illness. Go then, forthwith, and delay not."

The priest closed his eyes. His color changed, and he sat stiffly upright. He put his hands on the table and hammered with a piece of wood as a judge does when he tries a case. This he did for a long time. Then he came out. Ximen Qing invited him to go to the outer court and tell what he had seen in his vision.

"This woman," the priest said, "is suffering the punishment that has been due to her for several generations. She has been accused in Hades, and there is no devil's work here. I can do nothing."

"Master Priest," Ximen Qing said, "is there no sacrifice that you can offer?"

"Hatred and debt," said the priest, "always find their quarry. Even the officers of Hades themselves could do nothing." But when he saw how very much in earnest Ximen Qing was, he said: "How old is the lady?" Ximen told him she was twenty-seven. "Well," said the priest, "I will offer sacrifice to the star of her life, and we shall see the manner of its burning." Ximen Qing asked when he would do so and what he would need.

"Tonight, at the third night watch," the priest said. "I shall need some white powder to mark the boundary. I shall make an altar and cover it with yellow silk. Then I shall arrange the stars according to their order and make an offering of five kinds of grain and soup and dates. I shall need neither meat nor wine. I shall need a lamp to represent the light of her life, and twenty-seven lanterns. I shall require an umbrella to cover the lanterns. That is all. You must fast, put on black clothes and come here to make your obeisance. I will offer the sacrifice. See that dogs and chickens are kept away, for I do not wish to be disturbed."

Ximen went at once to get everything ready. He went to his study, bathed, and changed into clean clothes. He asked Ying Bojue to stay with him. They had a vegetarian meal with the priest and, about the third night watch, the altar and the lanterns were made ready. The priest took his seat upon a dais with the altar of the lanterns below him. They were set out according to the position of the stars. Over everything were three large umbrellas and, around the dais, the master stars, twelve in number. Below them were the lanterns representing the life of Li Ping'er. These were twenty-seven in number.

The priest recited a preamble. Then Ximen Qing, dressed in black clothes, came and knelt down. The servants all withdrew. None was allowed to remain. The lanterns were lighted. The priest sat on the seat, his head bent down, his sword in his hand. He murmured something, then gazed at the sky and set his feet in a certain position. Three times he burned incense that he might be granted knowledge of the three worlds. And every command he gave sounded like thunder. It was a bright clear night; the stars were shining in the heavens. Suddenly the whole world darkened and a mighty hurricane blew.

> This is not the roaring of tigers
> Or the muttering of dragons
> But a wind that rushes through the doors
> And around the screens
> A wind that blasts the flowers, rips off the leaves
> And drives the clouds to leave the mountains
> And send rain to the ocean.
> The wild geese have lost their mates and cry bitterly
> The wild ducks and the herons are frightened
> And seek trees for refuge.
> The angel of the moon shuts her palace door in haste
> And the immortal Liezi cries for help
> Away in the sky.

Three times the wind blew. It was followed by an ice-cold blast that put out all the twenty-seven lamps. The priest saw a man in white garments and two black-robed attendants with him. They came, bringing a paper that they set down upon the table. The priest looked at it. It was the final judgment of Hades. There were three seals upon the paper. He came to Ximen Qing and said: "Your lady has sinned against Heaven. Our prayers are useless. The light of her life has gone out. There is no hope, and death is not far distant from her."

When he heard this, Ximen Qing bowed his head and was silent. He wept. At last he said: "Teacher, you must help her."

"It is the will of Heaven," said the priest. "There is nothing I can do." He asked to be allowed to go. Ximen Qing urged him to stay the night. "Being a priest, to walk through the dew and pass the night upon the mountains is nothing to me," the priest said. Ximen Qing could not persuade him to stay. He told his servants to give the priest a roll of cloth and three taels of silver. "It is God's will that I should make use of the knowledge I possess," the priest said. "I have taken an oath that I will never take anything from the world. I cannot accept your gift." But, being pressed, he told a novice to accept the roll of cloth and make a gown for him. Before he left he said to Ximen Qing: "Sir, you must not go to her room tonight. If you go, you too will have trouble. Be cautious! Be cautious!" He went out of the gate and walked swiftly away.

Ximen Qing went back to the courtyard. He saw that all the lanterns had been extinguished. This made him very sad, and he wept before Ying Bojue. "Brother, this is her destiny," Bojue said. "We cannot take her back against the will of Heaven. You must not be so sad. The fourth night watch has sounded." Then he said: "Brother, you are weary, go and rest. I will go away now and come again tomorrow morning."

"You must have a light," Ximen Qing said. He ordered Laian to take a lantern and light Ying Bojue home. Then he went back to his study. There he sat by himself with the light of a solitary candle. His heart was torn by distress, and he could only sigh. He thought how the priest had said to him that he must not go to his loved one's room. "But how can I desert her now?" he said to himself. "I will go and see her even if I die for it. She may wish to say something to me." So he went to the sickroom.

Li Ping'er was sleeping with her face to the wall, but she wakened when she heard Ximen Qing. She turned to him and said: "Brother, why have you come?" Then she asked him about the lanterns.

"Be easy in your mind," Ximen said. "There was nothing wrong with the lanterns."

"Brother," Li Ping'er said, "do not try to deceive me. I saw him who is dead come with two others and stir up trouble for me again. He told me that you had sent for a priest to get me back from death. But, he said, the accusation against me in Hades had been accepted and I could not escape him. He went off in a raging fury and said: 'Tomorrow I shall come and take you.'"

Ximen Qing sobbed aloud when he heard this. "Oh, Sister," he said, "do not worry about him. I had hoped that we should live long years together. I never thought you would go away and leave me. I would rather die myself. It would be better than this agony."

Li Ping'er put her hands upon Ximen's neck. "Brother," she said, "I had longed to live with you always, but now I am going away. Before I close my eyes I would say one thing to you. You have a great household, and you alone can control it. You must always be careful and not do things without thinking. And be kind to the Great Lady. I know that one day soon she will bear a child to you, and he will carry on your family after you are gone. You are an officer now, but you must not go drinking so much as you have been doing. You must come home early. Your household affairs are of more importance than feasting. If I could have lived, I would have given you counsel. When I am dead, I fear there will be none to advise you."

These words cut Ximen's heart like a sword. "Sister," he said, "I know it. But do not worry about me. Heaven has put an end to our happiness together. It will not permit us to be husband and wife any longer. This will kill me, even though it is the will of Heaven."

Li Ping'er spoke to him about Yingchun and Xiuchun. "I have spoken to the Great Lady," she said, "Yingchun is going to serve her, and Xiuchun the Second Lady. The Second Lady has promised me."

"Say no more of this, Sister," Ximen Qing said. "Nobody shall send your maids away when you are dead. I will not even allow the nurse to go. I mean them all to guard your tablet."

"What tablet?" said Li Ping'er. "There will be nothing but a wooden board, and it will be burned thirty-five days after my death."

"Oh, no!" Ximen said. "I shall keep it as long as I live and make offerings before it."

Then Li Ping'er said: "It is late now. Go and sleep."

"I don't wish to sleep," Ximen answered her. "I am going to stay and look after you."

"I am not likely to die yet," Li Ping'er said, "and there is such a nasty mess here, it will make you sick. Besides, you will be in the way when the maids have to attend to me."

So Ximen Qing told the maids to look well after their mistress and went to Yueniang's room. He told Yueniang about the sacrifice, and said: "I have been to her room. She is still able to speak quite well. Perhaps Heaven will, even yet, allow her to get better."

"Her eyes are sunken, her lips are parched, and her ears burn," Yueniang said. "I fear there is no hope. She has the kind of illness in which she is able to talk up to the last moment."

"She has been in this house only a few years," Ximen Qing said, "and she has never harmed anyone, whether of high or low degree. And so sweet is her nature that she has never spoken an unkind word about anyone. I cannot bear to lose her." He cried, and Yueniang cried with him.

*   *   *

Li Ping'er asked Yingchun and the nurse to place her so that she faced the wall. Then she said: "What is the time?" The nurse told her:

"The cock has not yet crowed: it is the fourth night watch."

Yingchun put some new paper beneath her, and they helped her over till she faced the wall. Then they pulled the bedclothes over her. Everybody had been up all night. Old woman Feng and Nun Wang at last went to sleep. Yingchun and Xiuchun put something on the floor and slept there. In less than an hour, Yingchun dreamed that Li Ping'er got out of bed and touched her. "Look after my room," she said, "I am going now." Yingchun woke up with a start. The lamp was still burning on the table. She looked at the bed. Li Ping'er was there, facing the wall, but, when Yingchun put her hand over her mistress's mouth, she could feel no breath. She could not say when her lady had died.

So this beautiful and charming lady became a dream of the Spring.

Yingchun quickly woke the others. They saw that Li Ping'er was dead. She was lying in a pool of blood. They were greatly excited and ran to the inner court to tell Ximen Qing. He and Yueniang hurried to the room as fast as they could. They lifted the bedclothes. The Sixth Lady's face had not changed and there was still a little warmth in her body. There was a red stomacher about her. Ximen Qing did not trouble about the blood. He gathered her in his arms and kissed her.

"Oh, my ill-fated sister, my dear sweet sister! How could you leave me like this? I will die too. I know I have not long to live." He cried and threw himself into the air in his grief. Wu Yueniang cried; Li Jiao'er, Meng Yulou, Pan Jinlian, and Sun Xue'e, and the household, maids and nurse and all cried, so that the sound of their crying shook the earth.

"We did not know when she was going to die," Yueniang said, "so we never dressed her properly."

"Her body is warm," Yulou said, "I think she must have just gone. We must wait no longer but dress her now, while her body is limp."

Ximen Qing still held Li Ping'er in his arms. "Heaven wills my death," he was crying. "You have been in this house three years and not a single day's real pleasure have you had. It is all my fault."

This made Yueniang a little impatient with him. "Cry if you will, but put her down," she said. "You must not cry face to face with her like that. If the foul air from her mouth comes to you, it will make you ill. And what do you mean by saying that she never had a single happy day? If she did not, who did? We ourselves cannot decide how long we shall live. We shall all have to go the same way." She bade Yulou and Li Jiao'er take the key and get some clothes so that they might dress her. She told Jinlian to help dress her hair.

"Get the clothes she used to like best," Ximen Qing said.

Yueniang said to Li Jiao'er and Yulou: "Get that new scarlet silk gown, and the satin skirt of willow yellow, the clove-colored silk dress and the light blue skirt she used to wear when she went to visit Mistress Qiao, and the dresses that were made for her lately."

Yingchun took a light and Yulou the key, and they went to the room and opened a chest. After searching a long time, they found the three dresses, a purple silk vest, a white silk underskirt and a scarlet undergarment, with white silk socks and a pair of drawers. Li Jiao'er carried them to Yueniang who, with Jinlian, was dressing the dead woman's hair. They used four gold pins to keep in place a green kerchief.

"What kind of shoes must she have?" Li Jiao'er asked.

"She used to like that scarlet pair with high heels," Jinlian said. "She did not wear them more than twice. Let us have those."

"No," said Yueniang, "I will not have red shoes put on her. It would look as though we wished her to jump into the fire of Hell. Bring the violet shoes with high heels that she wore when she went to her sister-in-law's place." Li Jiao'er told Yingchun to bring those shoes. They all worked together dressing Li Ping'er.

Meanwhile, Ximen Qing sent the boys to the great hall. They took down the pictures and covered the screens. They got a large piece of board and carried it to the hall, then put a silken coverlet on the board and a paper cover over that. Then they prepared a table for incense and a lamp to be kept lighted continually. Ximen Qing appointed two boys to be with the body all the time, one to beat the gong, the other to keep paper offerings burning. Then he sent Daian for Xu, the Master of the Yin Yang.

Yueniang took all the clothes that were to go with the dead woman into the coffin, and locked up the rooms that had belonged to her. Only the bedroom was left unlocked. The maids and the nurse were placed in charge of it.

When old woman Feng saw that her mistress was dead, tears rolled down her nose like a river. Nun Wang muttered texts for the soul of Li Ping'er. There was the *Duoxinjing*, the *Yaoshijing*, the *Jieyuanjing*, the *Lengyanjing* and incantations to invoke the compassion of the Blessed One, that he might receive the dead lady's soul and set her on the right way in the realm of the dead.

In the great hall, Ximen Qing was beating his breast. He cried so much that he had no voice left, saying: "My kind, sweet sister!" It was nearly dawn.

Then the Master of the Yin Yang came. "I am sorry to hear of your lady's death," he said. "At what hour did she die?"

"We cannot say exactly," Ximen Qing told him. "I only know that she went to sleep about the beginning of the fourth night watch. Everybody was tired. There was no one awake when she died."

"It does not matter," the Master of the Yin Yang said. He asked a servant to give him a light. Then he lifted the paper coverlet. The fingers of Li Ping'er indicated the hour of the Ox. *"She died," he said, "two degrees after the fifth night watch. We may say that she died at the hour of the Ox." Ximen called for ink and brushes and asked Master Xu to write the certificate. Xu asked for the dead lady's name and her eight characters. Then he wrote:

> The deceased lady Li, the wife of Ximen, was born at noon on the fifteenth day of the first month in the year *Xinwei* of the reign *Yuanyu,* and died at midnight on the seventeenth day of the ninth month in the year *Dingyu* of the reign *Zhenghe.* This was a *Bingzi* day, and the order of the month *Wuzu,* Her spirit is ten feet high. It will be useless to wail for her until the mourning dress has been worn. And, when she is put into her coffin, none should be present whose animal is the Dragon, the Tiger, the Cock, or the Snake, unless he is a kinsman.

Yueniang told Daian to ask Master Xu to look into his black book and tell them the destiny of Li Ping'er. The Master of the Yin Yang opened his secret book and said: "This was the hour of the Ox on a *Bingzi* day. If the departed goes to Heaven, she will go to the Palace of the Precious Vase, but if to the world again, then to the land of Qi. In a former existence she was born as a man named Wang in Binzhou. As this man she killed a ewe with child, and, for that reason, her animal was the sheep. Though she married a rich man, she suffered much from illness and the backbitings of others. Her child lived for a very short time, and she has died from a combination of disease and anger. Nine days ago her soul went to a family named Yuan in Kaifengfu to be reborn as a girl. There she will suffer poverty, but, when she is twenty years old, she will marry a rich man, much older than herself. She will have an easy life and die when she is forty-two, again as the result of anger." He ended his reading of the black book. The ladies all sighed.

Yueniang inquired what would be a suitable day for the funeral. Xu asked how long they wished to keep the body at the house.

"I cannot let her go yet," Ximen Qing said, crying. "She must not be buried for thirty-five days, at least."

---

*   Between 1 and 3 a.m.

"If you keep her thirty-five days," Xu said, "there will be no day suitable. But after twenty-eight days there is one. I suggest that you have her grave dug about noon on the eighth day of the tenth month and bury her on the twelfth, about the hour of two. Both those days are suitable from every point of view."

"Very well," Ximen said, "we will have the funeral on the twelfth day of the tenth month."

The Master of the Yin Yang wrote out his certificate and placed it on the dead woman's body. Then he said to Ximen Qing: "About the hour of the Dragon[†] on the nineteenth, we will put her in her coffin. Please have everything ready." Then he went away. It was now broad daylight.

Ximen Qing told Qitong to get a horse and ride to tell Uncle Hua. Then he sent servants in all directions to give the news to his relatives, and a man to the office to ask for leave of absence. He sent Daian to Lion Street for twenty rolls of thin white cloth and thirty rolls of coarser material. He told Tailor Zhao to bring a number of assistant tailors and set to work in the rooms beside the hall to make hangings and curtains and tablecloths for the funeral, skirts and gowns for all the ladies, and a long gown of white cloth for every servant. He gave Ben the Fourth a hundred taels of silver and sent him to buy thirty rolls of linen and two hundred rolls of yellow funeral silk. He sent for the arbor builders to make a great arbor in the courtyard.

Ximen never ceased thinking of Li Ping'er, her appearance and her actions. Suddenly he thought of having a portrait of her painted. He summoned Laibao and said to him: "Where can we find a good artist to paint her portrait?"

Laibao said: "Once a man named Han painted some screens for us. He used to be employed in the Imperial Household. He was dismissed but he paints excellent portraits."

"If you know where he lives," Ximen said, "bring him here at once." Laibao went away.

Ximen Qing had not slept all night. What with his grief and what with the strain he had had, he became very irritable about the fifth night watch. He cursed the maids and kicked the boys. Still he remained in the great hall watching his wife's body. From time to time he sobbed aloud. Daian was there too, and he cried bitterly. Yueniang, Li Jiao'er, Yulou, and Jinlian busied themselves distributing mourning to the maids and serving women behind the curtain. They could hear Ximen Qing still crying though he had no voice left. They asked him if he would take some tea, but he would not answer.

---

† 8 a.m.

"She is dead," Yueniang said to him, "and you will not bring her back to life by crying. You have not slept properly for several nights; you have not combed your hair or washed your face. This morning you have worked very hard and have had nothing at all to eat. It would be more than anybody could stand even if he were made of iron. Go and do your hair, and have something to eat. We will attend to things. You are not very strong, and if you have to take to your bed, I don't know what we shall do."

"He has not dressed his hair or washed his face," Yulou said.

"A moment ago," Yueniang told her, "I sent a boy to ask him to do so, but he kicked the boy out, and I dare not ask him again."

Then Jinlian spoke. "You may not know it, but a short time ago, I spoke to him quite kindly. I said, 'If you cry like this, you will lose your flesh and your bones too. You must eat something. You can see about things afterwards.' He opened his red eyes wide and called me a swine of a woman. I won't bother about him any more. The unreasonable fellow! There's nothing swinish about me. And he always talks about others upsetting him!"

"She died so suddenly that he is naturally rather upset," Yueniang said, "but he should keep the sorrow in his heart and not make such a fuss about it. You saw, dead though she was, he didn't care. He kissed her and cried so loud. Really, it is not good breeding. She had been here for three years, he said, and had never had a single day's happiness. I have no recollection of her ever having had to draw water or do any other hard work day by day."

"He loved her more than any of us," Yulou said, "but he was right. Such a woman as our Sixth Sister was!"

As they were talking, Chen Jingji came with nine rolls of white silk. "This silk," he said, "Father tells me, is for kerchiefs and skirts."

"Ask your father to come and have some food," Yueniang said to him as she took the silk. "He has had nothing to eat."

"I dare not," Jingji said. "When a boy went to ask him, he nearly killed him. I dare not go near him."

"If you won't go, I shall have to send somebody else."

After a while she called Daian and said to him: "Your father has not had anything to eat, and he has been crying so long. Take him some food. Master Wen is there now; try and get your father to have something to eat with him."

"We have been for Uncle Ying and Uncle Xie," the boy said. "As soon as they come, we will take some food in. They need only say a word or two, and I promise you, Father will eat something."

"You cunning young rogue," Yueniang said. "You are the worm in your father's stomach. It looks as though we poor old women are not as good as you are. How do you know he will eat when they come?"

"You don't realize, Mother, what good friends they are with Father. Whenever he gives a party, no matter who else is there, they are sure to be invited. If Father has three *qian* worth of food to eat, so have they; if he has only two *qian* worth, they have it just the same. However bad a temper he may be in, they have only to speak a few words, and he is laughing and smiling again."

Qitong brought Ying Bojue and Xie Xida. They went in, knelt down before the body, and wept for a long time. They bewailed their kind sister-in-law. Jinlian said: "The rascally oily-mouthed rogues! So we are not kind!" Then they stood up. Ximen Qing made a reverence to them and they cried again.

"How unhappy you must be, Brother," they said. They were asked to go to a room in the wing. There they greeted Master Wen and sat down.

"When did my sister-in-law die?" Bojue asked.

"It was sometime about the hour of the Ox," Ximen told them.

"It was after the fourth night watch when I got home," Bojue said. "My wife asked after her, and I said: 'By Heaven's will, the poor lady is at the point of death.' As soon as I went to sleep, I dreamed a dream. I dreamed you sent a boy to fetch me. He said you were giving a feast in your house to celebrate your promotion. I came at once. You were wearing scarlet robes. You took two jade pins from your sleeve and showed them to me. 'One is broken,' you said. I looked at them for a long time and then I said: 'It is a pity the broken one is made of jade, while the other is only crystal.' But you said: 'No, they are both made of jade.' I woke up feeling that the dream boded no good. My wife saw me sucking my lips and asked me whom I thought I was talking to. I said: 'You don't understand. Wait, and, when the dawn comes, I'll tell you.' Then the day broke, and I saw your boy coming dressed in white. It was a shock, but here you are wearing mourning dress."

"I too had a dream," Ximen Qing said, "it was rather like yours. I dreamed that my kinsman Zhai of the Eastern Capital sent me six pins. One of them was broken, and I said: 'What a pity!' Then I woke up. I was just telling my wife about the dream when she in the front court died. What an unkind Heaven to bring such a calamity upon me. I would rather have died myself. I only lost sight of her for a moment, and at that moment she died. Even in years to come, how shall I think of her without my heart breaking? I have never wronged anyone, why should Heaven snatch my loved ones from me? First my child is taken, now she lies here, dead.

What have I to live for in this world? Even if my money reached to the North Star, what use is it to me?"

"Brother," Bojue said, "it is no use talking like this. You and she were such a perfect couple that, of course, you cannot help feeling miserable now that she has died so suddenly. But you have a fine home; you have an official appointment, and you have a houseful of people dependent upon you. If anything should happen to you, what would become of them? Remember the old saying: If one lives, three live; but if one dies, three die. Brother, you are an intelligent man and I do not need to tell you this. If you loved your wife dearly and you wish to do justice to that love, send for the Buddhist and the Daoist priests to read their dirges, and give her a splendid funeral. Then you will be easy in your mind because you will know that you have done well by my sister-in-law. I don't believe that there is anything else you can usefully do. You must see this, Brother."

Then Ximen Qing realized the situation and stopped crying. The servants brought tea and they drank it. Ximen told Daian to go to the inner court. "Bring some food," he said, "and I will eat it with your uncles and Master Wen."

"Haven't you had anything to eat yet?" Bojue asked.

"I have been busy all the time since you went away, and I haven't had a bite of anything."

"It was foolish of you," Bojue said. The proverb says: 'It is better to lose money than to be starved.' The dead are dead; the living must go on living. You must think of yourself."

CHAPTER 63

The Sixth Lady's Funeral

His loved one is gone
Darkly, darkly.
He thinks of her so far away
Bitterly, bitterly.
The realms of light and darkness are ten thousand miles apart
Each has its own sun, its own moon.

He seems to see her in the play
But the day is late.
So long have they been parted, he cannot tell
Whether his dream is true
When he dreams of her.

Ximen Qing dried his tears and sent a boy to the inner court to ask for food. The two brothers Wu came. They made obeisance before the body, then greeted Ximen Qing, and expressed their sympathy. Ximen took them to the room in the wing, and they sat down with the others.

Daian, when he came to the inner court, said to Wu Yueniang: "Mother, you ladies would not believe me. Now that Uncle Ying has come, a few words from him have made Father ask for something to eat."

"Oh, yes, you cunning little rogue," Pan Jinlian said, "you are always acting as a go-between for him, so of course you know him well."

"I have served my master ever since I was a child," Daian said. "I can't help knowing what is in his mind."

"Who is with him now?" Yueniang asked.

"The two uncles have just come," the boy said. "Master Wen is there, Uncle Ying, Uncle Xie, Clerk Han and brother-in-law. There are eight of them altogether."

"Ask your brother-in-law to come here to have something to eat," Yueniang said. "Why should he have to join that crowd?"

"He has already sat down," Daian said.

Yueniang told him to take some other boys and go to the kitchen for food. "Take some porridge for him," she said, "I don't suppose he had any rice this morning."

"But who is there to go with me?" Daian said. "I am the only one at home. Some of the boys have gone shopping, and others have gone with messages about our lady's death. Wang Jing has gone to Zhang's place to borrow a funeral gong."

"What about Shutong? Are you afraid of upsetting his dignity?"

"Shutong and Huatong are both in the death chamber. One is beating the gong, the other attending to the burning of incense and paper offerings. Father sent Chunhong with Ben the Fourth to change some silk. He didn't like the silk they brought. He is going to pay six *qian* a roll."

"I should have thought five *qian* a roll was quite enough," Yueniang said. "Why should he change it? Go and get Huatong and take the food to them at once. Don't waste time like this."

Daian and Huatong carried large plates and large bowls to the outer court and set them out on a square table. While the men were eating, Ping'an came with a large card. "His Lordship Xia has sent his secretary and a guard of honor to do your bidding," he said. Ximen Qing went to inspect them and gave orders that the man should be given three *qian* of silver and a card of thanks with the name in mourning. He asked the man to express his thanks to Xia.

They had finished their meal and everything was cleared away when the artist Han, whom Ximen Qing had sent for, came. Ximen greeted him and said: "May I trouble you to paint a portrait for me?" Han said he would do his best.

"You must not be too long setting to work," Uncle Wu said. "Her appearance may change."

"That does not matter in the least," Han said, "I can paint it without seeing her if necessary."

When they had finished their tea, Ping'an said that Uncle Hua had come. Ximen Qing and Hua Ziyu went together before the body and cried there. Then they greeted each other and sat down with the rest. Uncle Hua asked when Li Ping'er had died.

"It was about the hour of the Ox when she breathed her last," Ximen said. "She spoke quite sensibly up to the last. She went quietly to sleep, and when the maid got up to look at her, she was dead."

Uncle Hua saw the artist and a boy carrying a palette. He was taking brushes and colors from his sleeve. "I see you are having her portrait painted," Hua Ziyu said.

"I loved her so much that I must have one," Ximen Qing said. "It will remind me of her whenever I look at it."

He warned all the womenfolk to withdraw. Then the curtain was raised, and Ximen Qing took the artist, Uncle Hua and the others to the death chamber. The artist put aside the coverings and looked at Li Ping'er. A green handkerchief was bound about her head. Though she had been ill so long, her face still seemed as beautiful as when she was alive. Her pale yellow cheeks and her scarlet lips were as delightful as ever. Ximen Qing could not help weeping again. Laibao and Qintong stood beside the artist with his brushes and colors. Han looked once only, but that was enough for him. Those who were standing around asked him to begin his painting. "Sir," Ying Bojue said, "you will bear in mind that this is the face of an invalid. When she was in health, the lady's face was rounder. She was very beautiful."

"I need not trouble you for instructions," the artist said, "I think I know. May I ask if this is not the lady who went to the temple on the first day of the fifth month? I saw her then."

"Yes," Ximen said, "at that time she was still quite well. If you can remember her, paint two portraits, one full-length and one half-length. Then we can make our offerings before her picture. I will give you a roll of silk and ten taels of silver."

"I will do my best," the artist said. He sketched out a half-length figure, and it looked very handsome, the flesh like jade and almost fragrant. He showed them the sketch and they thought it very good indeed.

When Ximen Qing had examined it he told Daian to take it and show it to the ladies. "Let them see whether they think it good or not," he said. "If there is any little point they don't like about it, they have only to say so and it shall be put right."

Daian took the sketch to the inner court. "Father told me to bring this to you," he said. "He says if there is anything about it that seems to you not exactly like the Sixth Lady, you must say so, and he will get the artist to correct it."

"This seems to me very unnecessary," Yueniang said. "We do not know where the dead woman has gone. What need was there to have a portrait painted?"

"And where are the children to kowtow before it?" Jinlian said. "I suppose, when all six of us are dead, he will have six portraits made."

Meng Yulou and Li Jiao'er examined the picture. "Mother," they said, "it looks bright and lifelike, but the lips seem rather flat."

"Yes," said Yueniang, looking at it, "and the left side of her brow is not quite high enough. Her eyebrows were more curved. But how could the man draw such a picture when he had only glanced at her dead body?"

"He saw the Sixth Lady at the temple once and he has drawn her chiefly from memory," Daian told them.

Then Wang Jing came and asked the ladies if they had done with the portrait: his master wished to have it back. "Master Qiao has come," the boy said, "and he is anxious to see it."

Daian took the picture back to the outer court and told the artist that the ladies thought the lips too flat and the eyebrows not sufficiently arched. They thought, too, that the left side of the forehead was not high enough. Han said: "I can easily put that right." He took his brush and corrected the sketch. Then he showed it to Master Qiao.

"A fine portrait!" Qiao said. "It only lacks breath."

Ximen Qing was perfectly satisfied. He offered the artist three cups of wine, and entertained him. Then he gave him a roll of silk and ten taels of silver, telling him to finish the half-length portrait first, because he wished to put that up at once, and to complete the larger one in time for the funeral. Both were to be painted in green with ceremonial headdress and robes. They were to be on silk, and the rollers were to have ivory ends. The artist took the silver and told his boy to bring his things. Then he went away.

Master Qiao and the others went to look at the coffin. It was now finished. "I suppose that the informal ceremony of encoffining will take place today?" he said.

"Yes," said Ximen, "the undertakers are coming and we shall have the informal ceremony today. The formal ceremony will take place three days hence."

Qiao finished his tea and went away. Then the undertakers came. They rolled up the papers and set out the clothes. Ximen Qing himself performed the rite of "lighting the eyes" for Li Ping'er, and appointed Chen Jingji to take the part of her son and dry them for her. He took a bright pearl and put it into her mouth. So the informal ceremony was performed. The body was set up again, and the whole household bewailed the dead woman. Laixing had ordered various things to be made at the paper shop, four sets of gilt paper offerings, a washing basin, towels, combs, and figurines. These were set on either side of the body. Before it were incense burners, vases, candlesticks and incense boxes that the metal smiths had made. They were placed upon a table and looked very fine and bright. Ten taels of silver were given to the silversmith to make three sets of silver goblets.

Ximen Qing asked Ying Bojue to look after the account books and records for the funeral. He gave out five hundred taels of silver and a hundred strings of coppers. Clerk Gan was detailed to keep the accounts; Ben the Fourth and Laixing to buy what was necessary and keep in touch with the kitchen. Ying Bojue, Xie Xida, Master Wen and Clerk Gan were to act in turn as ushers. Cui Ben's duty was to attend to the accounts for the purchase of mourning. Laibao was to have charge of the temporary stores, Wang Jing to attend to the cellar, and Chunhong and Huatong were to be in attendance at the coffin. Ping'an and the soldiers of the guard were to sound the funeral gong, and bring incense and paper offerings for the guests who came. A writer and four soldiers were detailed to keep the visitors' book at the gateway, to see that the dates were correctly given when the religious ceremonies took place, and to hold the canopies and banners.

These orders were written on a sheet of paper and posted upon a screen, and all the different members of the household went about the duties that were appointed them.

Eunuch Xue sent men with sixty long poles, thirty bamboos, three hundred pieces of matting, and a hundred hempen ropes. Ximen Qing gave the man who brought them five *qian* of silver and a card of thanks for his master. He gave orders that a great shelter should be set up, which was to have a lofty center ridge and an entrance on either side. In the middle was to be a screen: in front of it a kitchen, and behind, a smaller shelter about the size of three rooms. Outside the great gateway was to be another temporary building, seven rooms wide.

Twelve priests from the Temple of Thanksgiving were summoned to sing the dirge. Two servants each day were to be employed doing nothing else but serve tea and water.

Uncle Hua and the younger Wu went away. Ximen Qing asked Master Wen to compose an obituary notice to be printed. Ximen Qing told him to write: "My humble wife has died." Master Wen wrote it without comment, then showed it to Ying Bojue.

"This will not do at all," Ying Bojue said. "It is contrary to polite usage. His wife is still alive and, if this is sent out in the way he wishes, people will talk. Uncle Wu, especially, will be offended. Don't do anything about it for the moment. I will speak to him later." They sat down again with Ximen Qing and, after a while, Ying Bojue went away.

That evening, Ximen Qing did not go to the inner court. He had a bed set up beside the body of Li Ping'er, put a screen around the bed, and so passed the night alone. The two boys Chunhong and Shutong attended him. The next morning he got up and went to Yueniang's room to wash. He dressed in a white hat and gown, with white shoes, white socks, and a white girdle.

Magistrate Xia came to offer his condolences. When Ximen Qing had greeted him, Master Wen came and they had tea together. When the magistrate went out and passed through the gate, he bade the writer do his work well and keep an eye on the soldiers of the guard. If any of them should absent himself, word must be brought him and he would have the man punished. When he had given these instructions, he mounted his horse and rode home.

Ximen Qing asked Master Wen to send out invitations for the funeral and sent servants around to ask the relatives to come on the third day after the death.

In the afternoon, the temple servants came and set out the place for the ceremony. They hung up pictures of Buddha and made other preparations.

When the news was brought to Wu Yin'er, she got into a sedan chair and came to bewail and burn paper offerings. She kowtowed to Yueniang and said, weeping: "How sorry I am that nobody told me sooner. I never knew my Sixth Mother was dead. It has upset me terribly."

"You were her ward," Yulou said, "and you ought to have come as soon as you knew that she was ill."

"Good Lady," Wu Yin'er said, "I swear I had no idea. If I had known, I should certainly have come."

"Well," said Yueniang, "whether you came or whether you did not, she did not forget you. She left a keepsake for you and I have put it aside." She told Xiaoyu to get the things that Li Ping'er had left for Wu Yin'er. Xiaoyu went to the inner room. When the parcel was opened, it was found to contain silken dresses, two gold pins, and a golden flower. Wu Yin'er looked at them and cried so bitterly that her tears fell like drops of rain.

"If I had only known that she was ill," she cried, "I would have come to wait on her." She thanked Yueniang. Yueniang gave her tea and asked her to stay until the third day after the death.

On the third day the priests beat their gongs and chanted a dirge. Paper money was hung up and everyone in the household put on mourning clothes. Chen Jingji, dressed in the deepest mourning, made obeisance before the pictures of Buddha. Neighbors, friends, kinsmen and the gentlemen from the office came to offer their sympathy and to make paper offerings. Not a few indeed made special offerings. Xu, the Master of the Yin Yang, was there early. When the great offering was over, the body was lifted into the coffin. Ximen Qing asked Yueniang for four more complete dresses to put into the coffin. In each corner of it was placed a piece of silver.

"Brother-in-law," Hua Ziyu said, "I should leave the silver out. Neither gold nor silver will stay there long."

But Ximen Qing would not listen. He insisted on placing the silver in the coffin. Then the board of the seven stars was placed in position and the lid of the coffin put in its place. The undertakers nailed it down with longevity nails on every side, and all the people cried aloud. Ximen Qing cried so much that he seemed demented. "Oh, my sweet sister," he sobbed repeatedly, "I shall never see you again." It was long before they finished their lamentations. They entertained Master Xu with vegetarian dishes, and he went away.

All the people belonging to the household and all who served in the shop wore mourning, and the incense wafted from the gate seemed like a white cloud. Master Wen acted as Master of the Ceremonies, and Du, a writer of the Great Secretariate, came to write the Sixth Lady's name upon the banner. Du's name was Zichun. In the reign of Zhenzong he had been an official at the Ninghe palace, but now he was living in retirement. Ximen Qing had sent a present of gold and silk and asked him to come. Special delicacies were prepared for his refreshment. When he arrived, Ximen offered him three cups of wine, and Ying Bojue and Master Wen sat down to keep him company. A piece of red silk was set before him, and upon this he was to write the obituary title for the dead lady.

Ximen Qing wished him to write: "The coffin of the Lady of Ximen, Captain of the Royal Guard."

"But we can't say that," Bojue objected. "The 'lady' is still alive."

"This lady bore a son," Master Du said. "It is perfectly in order. There can be no possible objection to the title."

They discussed the matter for some time and finally decided to write "wife" instead of "lady."

"'Lady' is the word used to designate one of official rank," Master Wen said, "and 'wife' one who lives in your apartments. Both are commonly used in a very wide sense."

Master Du wrote the inscription in white, except for the word "Royal," which he wrote in gold. Then the silken banner was hung before the coffin, and Du was asked to write the tablet. Afterwards, Ximen Qing thanked him very heartily, entertained him with food and wine, and he went away.

The same day, Master Qiao and the three uncles, Wu, Hua and Shen, came to make their offering of the three carcasses. Mistress Qiao, Aunt Hua, and the two ladies Wu came in sedan chairs to express their condolences. They wailed before the coffin, and Wu Yueniang and the others cried with them. Then they were asked to go to the inner court and there given tea and something to eat. They were all dressed in mourning, Uncle Hua and his wife in very deep mourning. Li Guijie had been sent word, and she came in a sedan chair to make paper offerings. When she found Wu Yin'er there, she said: "When did you come? Why didn't you tell me? You are a fine one, always looking out for yourself."

"I did not know my mother was dead," Wu Yin'er said. "If I had known, I should have been here before this." Yueniang took them to the inner court and entertained them there.

The seventh day came. Sixteen priests came from the Temple of Thanksgiving. Priest Lang was in charge of them and presided over the ceremony. They recited the Lotus Sutra and performed the ritual for the dead. The relatives, friends, and those who served in the shops attended again. Abbot Wu of the Temple of the Jade King came to make an offering, and also to secure an invitation for the second week's mind. Ximen Qing asked him to stay and gave him vegetarian food.

A boy came and said: "The artist has brought the portrait." Everybody examined it. The painting showed Li Ping'er in a golden ceremonial headdress, wearing pearl ornaments and a scarlet embroidered gown. Her face was as fair as though she lived. Ximen Qing was delighted. He set the picture up beside the coffin, and everybody said that the only thing it lacked was breath. Ximen entertained the artist and asked him to take even more pains with the large portrait.

"Be assured that I will take the utmost care over it," said the artist. Ximen gave him a handsome present, and he went away.

About noon, Master Qiao came to make his offering. He brought a pig, a sheep, and other things for sacrifice, gold and silver mountains, and paper offerings of all sorts, paper money and incense. There were fifty loads in all, and they created a great impression as they were brought with carriages and music. Ximen Qing and Chen Jingji, standing before the body, made reverence in return. Then Master Qiao invited Scholar Shang, President Zhu, Uncle Wu, Scholar Liu, Captain Hua, and his relative Duan, one after the other to offer incense. When the three offerings had been made, they all knelt down on the floor to hear the Master of the Yin Yang read the panegyric:

> On the twenty-second day of the ninth month of the seventh year of the reign Zhenghe, Qiao Hong and the other relatives, with all due reverence, offer the stiff-bristled and the soft-haired animals and other sacrifice of food before the coffin of the deceased lady, the wife of Ximen, and there bewail her loss.
>
> The deceased lady was generous and kind. She managed her household prudently. She governed those in subjection to her with sympathy and goodwill. She was, in truth, the very acme of perfection in womanhood and her good fame was on the lips of all who lived about her. Most glorious of women, most fragrant of blossoms!

When she married, she lived in absolute harmony with her lord. To him she bore a son with the brightness of a river pearl. We trusted that they might live together in married blessedness until a ripe old age, but, suddenly, she fell ill and vanished like a dream.

How shall we restrain our grief when we realize the departure of a lady so estimable? My little daughter is still in her mother's arms, yet she is the bond between this departed lady and ourselves. It was the will of heaven that the marriage should never be consummated. We must live in different worlds, and we shall never meet again.

With this cup I would express all my love and sincerity. May she who is gone know this, come, and enjoy it!

After this offering, the gentlemen were taken to the temporary building and entertained. Then the ladies came. Mistress Qiao, Mistress Cui, President Zhu's wife, Scholar Shang's wife and Miss Duan came to make their offering to the dead. Drums and gongs were beaten, and a number of dancers dressed as spirits performed before the coffin. Yueniang accompanied the ladies and afterwards took them to the inner court and gave them tea. Then they were entertained.

While Ximen Qing was drinking with the others, he suddenly heard the funeral gong being sounded, and a servant hurried in to say that the prefect Hu had come and his sedan chair was waiting at the gate. Ximen Qing, wearing his mourning robes, went to the coffin to await his guest, and asked Master Wen to dress and go to receive the prefect. Servants came in with incense and paper offerings, and, behind them, the prefect in plain dress and gold-buckled girdle. A number of officials followed him, some to hold his robes, others to adjust his girdle, and so on. When the prefect came to the coffin, Chunhong knelt and offered him incense. The prefect took it and burned it before the body, twice making a reverence.

"I pray your Excellency to rise," Ximen Qing said. "I am very grateful to you." He made reverence in return.

"I only heard yesterday that your lady had died," the prefect said. "I am sorry I come so late."

"My wife's illness was incurable," Ximen said. "It is very good of you to come."

Master Wen was with them. They went to the hall and offered the prefect a cup of tea. Then he went away, Master Wen accompanying him to the gate.

That day the people who came to make offerings to the dead did not leave until the evening. The next day Zheng Aiyue came and burned paper offerings before the coffin. Yueniang saw that the girl made an offering of eight plates of cakes and three of other refreshments, and she called for a white silk skirt for the girl. Li Guijie and Wu Yin'er each made an offering of three *qian*. Yueniang told Ximen Qing, and he said: "Give each of them a silk skirt, no matter what they offer." Yueniang took them to the inner court, and there they had tea. In the evening, a number of friends and kinsmen came to spend the night. A troop of actors had been engaged and were waiting to perform their plays. Li Ming, Wu Hui, Zheng Feng and Zheng Chun were with them. Ximen Qing had fifteen tables arranged for his guests in the temporary building. Master Qiao was there, the two uncles Wu, Uncle Hua, Uncle Shen, Uncle Han, the two scholars Ni and Wen, Dr. Ren, Li and Huang, Ying Bojue, Xie Xida, Zhu Shinian, Sun Guozui, Bai Laiguang, Chang Zhijie, the clerks Fu, Han, and Gan, Ben the Fourth, the two nephews of Wu Shun, and six or seven others. The tables were all large, and more than ten great candles were lighted. The ladies were near the coffin, hidden from the view of the guests by screens and hangings, but so that they could watch the play.

All the guests made reverence to the dead, and Ximen Qing and Chen Jingji made reverence in return. Then everybody sat down and the actors and musicians began to play. The first play was the *Romance of Wei Gao and Yuxiao*, and their betrothal in two generations. First upon the stage came the hero Wei Gao and sang, then the heroine, Yuxiao, and she sang, too. The cooks brought soup and rice and meat and goose. Ying Bojue said to Ximen Qing: "I hear that the three young ladies from the bawdy-house are here. Why not ask them to come and offer a cup of wine to Master Qiao and the two Masters Wu? It is too great an indulgence to let them simply stay and listen to the play."

Ximen Qing would have told Daian to bring the girls, but Qiao said: "We can't do that. They have come to make offering to the dead, and we can't ask them to serve wine."

"Sir," Bojue said, "you are mistaken. Little whores of their sort must not be allowed to be idle." He turned to Daian. "Go at once and drag them out. Tell them: Uncle Ying says that, although you have come to pay your due respects to the Sixth Lady, you must come and do something for us as well."

Daian went, but he soon came back. "They say they will not come if Uncle Ying is here."

"In that case I must go myself," Bojue said. He stood up, walked two steps and sat down again.

Ximen Qing laughed. "Why have you come back?" he said.

"I had it in mind to go myself and fetch those little whores," Bojue said. "But wait till I think what I'm going to say, and then I'll go and let them have a piece of my mind." After a while, he told Daian to go again and ask them.

The three girls came slowly. They were all wearing white silk gowns and blue skirts. They greeted the company, then stood smiling.

"Since we are here, why didn't you come at once?" Bojue asked them. They did not answer. They served all the gentlemen with wine and then sat down together at one table. The music began again. Wei Gao and Bao Zhiben had come together to Yuxiao's house, and her mother had come out to welcome them.

Bao Zhiben said: "Go and fetch the girl out," and the old woman replied:

"Master Bao, you are lacking in courtesy. My daughter is not at every man's disposal. You should say, not: 'Fetch her out,' but, 'Please ask her if she will be so good as to come out.'"

This made Li Guijie laugh. "Master Bao," she said, "was like Beggar Ying. He did not know how to behave."

"You little whore," Bojue said, "if I don't know how to behave, why is your mother so much attached to me?"

"She is attached to you the other way around," said Guijie.

"Attend to the play," Ximen Qing said to them. "If you talk any more, you will have to be fined." Bojue kept silence.

The play went on. In the great hall, on one side of the large screen, sat the two aunts Wu, Aunt Yang, old woman Pan, another Aunt Wu, Aunt Meng, Miss Zheng and Miss Duan, with the ladies of Ximen's household. On the other side were Chunmei, Yuxiao, Lanxiang, Yingchun and Xiaoyu. They stood in a group and watched the play. A maid passed with a plate of fruits and a pot of tea. Chunmei stopped her and said: "For whom are you taking the tea?"

"The ladies on the other side want some," the maid replied.

Chunmei took a cup for herself. Xiaoyu had observed that the girl in the play was called Yuxiao. She took hold of her fellow maid and said to her: "You little whore! See, two men have come to visit you, and your wicked old woman wishes you to welcome them. Why don't you go?" She pushed Yuxiao, and she stumbled over Chunmei. Chunmei was holding the cup of tea in her hands and she spilled it over her clothes.

"What are you doing, spilling the tea all over me!" Chunmei cried. "It is only a matter of luck that you didn't make me break the teacup."

Ximen Qing heard the noise and sent Daian to see who was making it. The boy saw Chunmei sitting on a chair. "Go and tell our master," she said, "that that whore Yuxiao got quite out of control when she saw the man on the stage."

Ximen Qing heard what was said, but he was too much occupied to think about it. Yueniang came and scolded Yuxiao. "What have you been doing here all this time?" she said. "You ought to have gone to see who is in my room. Do you know who is there?"

"Yes," Yuxiao said, "your daughter has gone to the inner court, and the two nuns are in our room."

"There is always trouble if I let you stay and watch the plays," Yueniang said.

Then Chunmei, seeing Yueniang, rose and said: "Mother, you might think they were crazy. They seem to have forgotten both their senses and their manners. They laugh and talk and never trouble in the least whether the guests see them or not."

Yueniang scolded them again and went back to her place.

Master Qiao and Scholar Ni were the first to go away. Uncle Shen, Uncle Han and Dr. Ren were about to follow their example, but Ying Bojue stopped them. "Host," he said to Ximen Qing, "you must speak to them. I am only a friend, but I am not going yet. They are your relatives and they ought to stay. Uncle Shen lives within the walls. Even if Uncles Han and Hua and Doctor Ren live outside the city, it is so late now that they can't get out, so what's the use of their hurrying? Come back all of you and sit down. Besides, the play is not finished."

Ximen Qing told the boys to get four jars of Magu wine. When it was brought, he said: "We won't keep this any longer." He took a large cup, set it before Uncle Wu and said: "He who tries to break up this party shall be punished by Uncle Wu." So they all sat down again, and Ximen Qing bade Shutong tell the actors to perform the most lively part of their play. The music began, and one of the actors came to ask whether they should play the scene in which the portrait is painted. "I don't care what it is," Ximen Qing said, "but let it be something lively."

The girl, Yuxiao, again appeared upon the stage. While she was singing "Never more shall I see you in this world, so I make this portrait of you," Ximen suddenly thought of all the suffering through which Li Ping'er had gone, and he was moved to tears. He took a handkerchief from his sleeve and dried his eyes. Pan Jinlian saw him with her cold eyes. "Look at that rascal," she said to Yueniang, and pointed to him, "he even sheds tears when he hears something on the stage."

"In spite of all your cleverness," Meng Yulou said, "you don't appear to understand. Plays are intended to express sorrow, joy, separations and meetings. He saw something that touched his heart. He is not the first to weep when he sees a play. It is like thinking about a dead horse when we see a saddle."

"Oh, I don't believe a word of it," Jinlian said. "People who cry when they hear a tale or see a play are all pretending. If the actors can make people shed real tears, they must be very fine actors."

"Be quiet, ladies," Yueniang said. "Listen to the play."

"I can't think what makes this sister of ours so self-opinionated," Yulou said to Aunt Wu.

The play went on until the fifth night watch, and then the party began to break up. Ximen Qing took a large cup and, standing by the door, stopped his guests and pressed them to drink again. But, when he found he could keep them no longer, he allowed them to go. The servants cleared away, and Ximen told the actors to leave their boxes because he wished them to perform another day when the two eunuchs, Liu and Xue, were coming. The actors agreed, and, after being entertained with food and wine, went away. Li Ming and his three companions went home. It was nearly dawn and Ximen Qing went to the inner court to rest.

CHAPTER 64

Shutong Runs Away

The jade is perished and the pearls are lost
Sadly he thinks of it.
In public he sheds tears, and in secret mourns.
Often he painted butterflies playing on the wall
And remembered the joy of the love birds
In the green curtains.
Now, only in dreams may he enjoy her.
She may not hope to emulate Fei Yin
Red lips and pearly teeth have joined the yellow dust.
Mournfully he longs to meet her
In the world to come.

It was almost dawn when all the guests went home and Ximen Qing went to rest. Daian took a large pot of wine and several dishes and went to the shop to enjoy them with Clerk Fu and Chen Jingji. Clerk Fu was getting old. He did not feel like sitting up any longer. He made his bed and lay down, saying to Daian: "You and Ping'an had better have these things. I don't believe Brother-in-law Chen is coming." Daian went to fetch Ping'an. They encouraged one another to drink and finished everything off. Then they cleared away the dishes and plates, and Ping'an went to his own place. Daian shut up the shop and went and lay on Clerk Fu's bed, feet against feet.

"Well," Clerk Fu said, "the Sixth Lady is no more, but she has had a good send-off. Her coffin and the funeral are as fine as anyone could desire."

"Yes," said Daian, "if she had lived longer, she might have been accounted a very fortunate woman. Father has been to all this expense, but, after all, it was not his own money. She was very well off when she married him. I happen to be one of the few who know this. She had not only money but gold, pearls, jade, embroideries and valuable ornaments of all sorts. They were the attraction. It wasn't the lady, but her money that our master wanted. But there wasn't a more agreeable lady in the whole household. She was unassuming and pleasant always. She had a

smile and a kind word for everybody she met, even the slaves. When she
sent us out to buy anything, she would pick up a piece of silver and hand
it to us. And if we said, as we sometimes did: 'Mother, won't you please
weigh the silver?' she would smile and say: 'Take it away. Why should I
weigh it? You wouldn't be working here if you didn't hope to make a little
for yourselves now and again. So long as you bring me something good
I won't worry.' Everybody in the place borrowed money from her, and
nobody ever paid her back. She never troubled whether they did or not.
The Great Lady and the Third Lady are generous too, but the Fifth Lady
and the Second are as mean as mean can be. If it ever falls to them to run
the household, we shall have a very bad time. The sort of thing they do is
to give us short money when they send us out to buy things, nine *fen* or
something like that when the thing they want costs a *qian*. I suppose we
are expected to make up the difference ourselves."

"The Great Lady is not so bad as that," Clerk Fu said.

"She is not so bad as that, certainly," Daian said, "but she loses her
temper very easily. When she is in a good mood, one can talk to her and
find her very agreeable, but when she is displeased, she scolds everybody
without exception. The dead lady was far better than she is, for she never
did harm to anyone and often spoke kindly for us to our master. If we
got into scrapes, no matter how awkward, we used to go to her, and she
would speak to our master. He never refused anything she asked. But the
Fifth Lady always has words upon her lips like 'Wait and see if I don't tell
your father' or 'You shall have a beating.' Her maid Chunmei is another
evil star. My word! They are a fine pair!"

"She has been here several years," Clerk Fu said.

"Yes, and you know what she was like when she came. She does not
even treat her own mother decently. The poor old lady often goes away in
tears. Now that the Sixth Lady is dead, I can see the Fifth Lady ruling the
roost completely. Anyone who goes to clean up the garden will get a good
cursing from her if he doesn't do it as she would have it."

Clerk Fu was soon fast asleep and snoring. Daian had had some wine.
He, too, was not long before he closed his eyes and was dead to the world.
The sun was high in the heavens before they woke.

Ximen Qing often slept beside the coffin. Every morning, Yuxiao
came and took away the bedclothes, and Ximen Qing went to the inner
court to dress. Then Shutong, his hair undressed, would come to play and
joke with the maid, and Yuxiao would dally there a long time. But today,
Ximen Qing did not sleep there but in Yueniang's room. Yuxiao got up
before the others and slipped out quietly. She went with Shutong to the
study in the garden and there they had a merry time together.

Pan Jinlian also got up early that day. She went to the hall and saw that the light before the coffin had gone out. The tables and chairs were in disorder. Nobody was to be seen but Huatong, who was busy sweeping.

"What are you doing here alone?" Jinlian said to him. "Where are the others?"

"They are not up yet," Huatong told her.

"Put down your broom," Jinlian said, "and go and ask Brother-in-law for a roll of white silk. I want it for my mother. I want a girdle for her too. She is probably going away today."

"I think Brother-in-law is still in bed, but I will go and see," Huatong said.

When he came back, he said: "Brother-in-law says it isn't his business. Shutong and Cui Ben are responsible for the mourning. You must ask Shutong."

"How do I know where he is?" Jinlian said. "Go and look for him."

Huatong looked into the room beside the hall and said: "He was in here a few moments ago. Perhaps he has gone to the garden to dress his hair."

"Go on with your work, and I'll go and look for him myself," Jinlian said. She went to the garden. When she came to the study, she heard the sound of somebody laughing. She pushed the door open, Shutong and Yuxiao were enjoying a full measure of delight.

"Ah, you slaves!" Jinlian said, "excellent work you're doing there!"

Shutong and Yuxiao were scared. They plumped down on their knees and begged to be forgiven.

"You slave," Jinlian said to Shutong, "go and get me a roll of white silk and another of cloth. I am going to give them to my mother when she goes away."

Shutong hastened to bring them for her, and she went to her own room. Yuxiao went with her, knelt down, and said: "Fifth Mother, please say nothing to my Father about this."

"Tell me," Jinlian said, "how often have you played this game with him? If you tell me the truth, I will say nothing."

Yuxiao told her the whole story.

"I will forgive you," Jinlian said, "on condition that you promise me three things."

"If you will only forgive me, I will do anything you wish," Yuxiao said.

"First, whatever happens in your mistress's room, whether important or unimportant, you must tell me all about it. If I hear it from anybody else, and you have not told me, I will never forgive you. Secondly, you must get anything I want. Thirdly, I wish to know how it is that your mistress, who was never with child before, is now going to have a baby."

"The truth is," Yuxiao told her, "that my mother took some medicine made out of an afterbirth that Nun Xue brought for her."

Jinlian did not forget this, but she did not say anything to Ximen Qing.

When Shutong saw that Jinlian took Yuxiao away with her, smiling in a manner that boded ill, he decided that the matter was going to have unpleasant consequences. He went to the study, opened the cabinet, and took a number of handkerchiefs, kerchiefs and pins, together with some of the presents that had come from relatives. He had about ten taels of silver of his own and he went to the shop and got another twenty by deceiving Clerk Fu, telling him that he had to buy some silk. He went outside the city, hired a mule for a long journey, and went to the river. There he took boat and went to Suzhou, his native place.

This day Li Guijie, Wu Yin'er, and Zheng Aiyue went away. The two eunuchs, Xue and Liu, sent food and paper offerings as offerings for the dead, and a tael of silver. They also sent two storytellers to discourse upon a religious theme, and announced that they would come in person to visit Ximen Qing. Ximen wished to send some silk to the eunuchs and looked about for Shutong who kept the keys. He could not find the boy. Clerk Fu told him: "This morning he asked me for twenty taels and said you had given him orders to buy some silk. He may have gone outside the city for it."

"I never gave him any such orders," Ximen Qing said. "How dared he ask you for the money?" He sent people to look for the boy in all the silk shops, but in vain.

"I always believed there was something crooked about that slave," Wu Yueniang said to Ximen. "He has got into a scrape of some sort, stolen the money and made off. Go and look around your study. Then we shall know if he has taken anything else."

Ximen Qing went to the study. The key was hanging on the wall. Handkerchiefs, presents, and pins had disappeared from the great cabinet. He was very angry and gave orders to the police to arrest the boy wherever they found him. But they never found him.

About noon, Eunuch Xue came in his sedan chair. Ximen Qing had invited Uncle Wu, Ying Bojueand Master Wen to meet him. The eunuch came to the coffin and made reverence. "I deeply sympathize with you," he said to Ximen Qing. "What was the cause of your lady's death?"

"She suffered, unfortunately, from an issue of blood," Ximen Qing said. "It is good of you to come."

"I had nothing worthy to offer," Xue said, "and such things as I have sent are merely to indicate something of what is in my mind." He looked at the portrait that hung before the coffin. "How beautiful she was. And how sad that, when she was still so young and seemed to have such a happy life before her, she should have died."

"Such are the changes and chances of life," said Master Wen, who was standing beside them. "Such is the inevitability of fate. Some are poor, others rich. Some live long; others only for a short while. Yet all are governed by their destiny. Even the sages must submit to fate."

Eunuch Xue turned and looked at the speaker. He noticed that Master Wen was wearing academic robes and said: "Brother, may I ask to which academy you belong?"

Master Wen bowed low. "I am a man of very small learning," he said, "and my name is inscribed only in the records of the academy of our prefecture."

Xue asked if he might look at the coffin. Ximen bade a servant draw back the curtains and the eunuch examined the coffin closely. "What a magnificent coffin!" he said. "How much did it cost?"

"I bought it from a relative," Ximen Qing said.

"Venerable Sir," Ying Bojue said, "guess how much it cost, and tell us where it came from and what the wood is called."

Xue again examined it very carefully. "I should say it came from Jianchang or, if not, from Zhenyuan," he said.

"If it had come from Zhenyuan," Bojue said, "it would not be so fine."

"I believe the best elm comes from Yangxuan," the eunuch said.

"The Yangxuan elm is short and thin. It is not to be compared with this. This is made of much finer wood called Peach Flower Cavern. The tree grows in Wuling in Huguang. Long, long ago an old fisherman came to that cavern and saw some maidens of the Qin dynasty who had gone there to escape the soldiery. It is a place to which travelers seldom go. The boards of which this coffin is made were seven feet long, four inches thick, and two feet five inches broad. His Lordship paid three hundred and seventy taels for them, although he is a kinsman of the owner. Ah, Venerable Sir, you should have seen it before it was made up. Such fragrance! Such exquisite markings on both sides of the wood!"

"Fate was generous in allowing this lady to enjoy so wonderful a coffin," the eunuch said. "We court chamberlains can hardly hope for such a funeral when our time comes."

"It is very kind of you to say so," Uncle Wu said, "but, Sir, you are in the closest relations with the Imperial Court, and we, who are merely officers of the external administration, can in no way approach you. You, Sir, were but lately basking in the favor of the Son of Heaven. To us, you represent His Majesty's precious words. His Excellency Tong has been given the title of Duke, and those who follow after him will wear ceremonial dress. There is, I am sure, a glorious future before you."

"May I ask your name?" the eunuch said, "you speak with great discretion."

"This is Wu, my wife's brother," Ximen said. "He is a captain in our district."

"Is he the dead lady's brother?" Xue asked.

Ximen Qing explained that Uncle Wu was his first wife's eldest brother.

"You must please excuse me, worthy Sir," Eunuch Xue said to Uncle Wu, bowing. Ximen Qing then took them all to the temporary hall. He offered a chair to the eunuch and the servants brought tea.

"I wonder why Liu has not come yet," Xue said. "I must send one of my servants for him." One of the eunuch's servants knelt down.

"I did go to bring His Worship," he said, "and his sedan chair was waiting for him. I am sure he will be here soon." Xue asked if the two storytellers had come. Ximen Qing told him that they had. They were summoned, and came to kowtow. Xue asked them if they had had anything to eat, and, when they told him that they had, bade them do what they had been sent to do with all due care, promising them a good reward.

"Venerable Sir," Ximen Qing said, "I have engaged some actors. Perhaps you would like to hear them."

"Where are they from?" the eunuch asked.

"They are a company from Haiyan," Ximen told him.

"These barbarous dialects sound so impossible," Xue said, "I can't understand a word they say. Poor devils of students, who put their noses to the grindstone for three years, and then wander all over the place for another nine, carrying a zither, a sword, and a box of books, then come to the capital for the examination, and, when they have got a job, have to leave their wife and children behind—they are the people to enjoy actors of this sort. I'm just a single old chamberlain. Why should I bother about them?"

Master Wen smiled. "Venerable Sir," he said, "I am afraid I cannot agree with you. When in Qi, do as the Qi people do. Even though you occupy such an exalted position, there is a possibility that these actors may amuse you."

Xue laughed and clapped his hands. "Ah," he said, "I had forgotten Master Wen. Of course he takes the part of the officers who serve away from the court."

"Scholars and officers stand or fall together," Master Wen said. "If you cut down a branch, you injure a hundred forests. When anything happens to the hare, the fox grieves. If you disapprove of one, you disapprove of all."

"Not at all," Xue said. "In the same place you find both fools and wise men."

At that moment a servant came and told them that Liu had come. Uncle Wu went out to welcome him. After making a reverence before the coffin, he greeted the others.

"What has made you so late?" Xue asked.

"Xu came to call on me. I could not get away without sitting down with him for a while."

They sat down, and the servants brought tea. Liu asked his attendants if the food to be offered to the dead was ready. The servant told him that everything was arranged. "Let us go and burn some paper offerings," Liu said.

"Venerable Sir," Ximen said, "do not disturb yourself to such an extent. You have already made reverence to her."

"I came for that purpose," Liu said. "I must offer something to her with my own hands."

A servant brought incense. The two eunuchs together offered it and three cups of wine to Li Ping'er. They made reverence again to the dead lady. Then Ximen prayed them to stand up. They made only two reverences, and Ximen Qing made reverence to them in return. Then they went back to the arbor. A table was set.

When the two eunuchs had taken their places, Master Wen, Uncle Wu and Ying Bojue sat down, Ximen Qing sat in the seat of the host. The music began and the actors brought out their list of plays. The two eunuchs went through the list and bade them play the *Story of the White Rabbit*. But before the play had proceeded very far, the two eunuchs were tired of it. They sent for the two storytellers, who played and told the story of how the snow stopped Han Wengong in Languan.

Eunuch Xue began to talk to his colleague. "Brother Liu," he said, "I don't suppose you have heard, but the other day, the tenth day of the eighth month, there was a terrible rainstorm, and the roof figures at the palace were struck by lightning. A number of people at the court died of fright. Even His Majesty was alarmed. He admonished all the officials to take the greatest care in the performance of their duties, ordered the *Ling-shujing* to be read every day in Shangqing Palace, and forbade the killing of animals for sacrificial purposes for ten days. For the same space of time, the courts were not permitted to give sentence and no reports might be made to the Emperor.

"Then an ambassador came from the people of Jin and demanded the surrender of three of our towns. The old villain Cai Jing suggested that this should be agreed to. As for the troops that had been under Tong's command, the Censor Tan Ji, Huang An and others were to take them over. Tong was to withdraw from the three districts in question, but he refused to come back and the case has been referred to a council of ministers.

"The other day was the Winter Festival, and his Majesty went to the Temple of His Ancestors to offer sacrifice. There is a certain doctor in the Department of Imperial Ceremonies called Fang Zhen, and, in the morning, when he went to inspect the temple, he discovered blood issuing from the courses between the bricks. At the northeastern corner, the floor had given way. He told the Emperor about this, and one of the censors told His Majesty that this was a sign that Tong had assumed a power beyond his due, there being no justification for the appointment of a eunuch as a duke. After this, the Emperor at once sent an envoy with his Golden Decree summoning Tong to return."

"Well," Liu said, "you and I do our duty here. What happens at the Court is no concern of ours. Let us enjoy whatever the day brings forth. Even if the sky seems about to fall, still, as the proverb says, there are four giants to hold it up. It looks to me as if this Empire of Song would be ruined by busybody ministers. Let us drink."

He told the storytellers to sing the story of Li Bo and his fondness for wine. This they did. About sunset, the two eunuchs called for their sedan chairs. Ximen Qing could not persuade them to stay longer and went with them to the gate. When he returned, he gave orders for the candles to be lighted and sat down again with Uncle Wu, Ying Bojue and Master Wen. He sent boys to bring Clerk Fu, Clerk Gan, Han Daoguo, Ben the Fourth, Cui Ben and Chen Jingji. Then he bade the actors perform the play of the Jade Ring that they had played the day before.

"The eunuchs do not understand these Southern plays," he said to Ying Bojue. "If I had realized that, I would not have asked them to stay."

"Brother," Ying Bojue said, "they did not appreciate the compliment you were paying them. Eunuchs are very ignorant. They like such things as the story of Languan, simple tales, folk songs and all that sort of thing, but the higher forms of art, compositions of a really great order, are completely beyond them."

The music began, and the actors played that part of the Jade Ring that had not been finished the day before. Ximen Qing called for good wine to be brought.

Ying Bojue, sitting at Ximen's table, asked if the three singing girls were still there. "Why don't you send for them and make them serve the wine?" he said. But Ximen said: "You must be dreaming. They have been gone a long time."

"Then they only stayed a day or two," Bojue said.

"Wu Yin'er was here longest," Ximen Qing told him.

It was the third night watch before the party broke up. The play was finished. Ximen asked Uncle Wu to come early the following day to welcome the guests for him. Then he gave the actors four taels of silver and dismissed them.

The next day, Major Zhou, General Jing, Captain Zhang of the militia, and Magistrate Xia came with other officers to make their offering to the dead lady. They made a reverence before the coffin, and someone was appointed to read their panegyric. Ximen Qing offered them refreshment. Li Ming and the other three young actors were in attendance. It was about noon when the offerings were brought. Uncle Wu, Ying Bojue and Master Wen stood at the gate to welcome the officers. They came in and changed their clothes in the great hall. Then the offerings of food were set out, and they came together to make reverence before the coffin. Ximen Qing and Chen Jingji were there to return their salutation. The Master of Ceremonies conducted the appropriate ceremonies and, when the triple offering had been made, knelt down to read the panegyric. When it was done, Ximen Qing thanked his visitors, and the officers were taken to the temporary hall. They took off their robes and had tea. Tables were set, and they sat down to enjoy themselves. The young actors played and sang to them. About sunset they went away. Ximen Qing would have liked Uncle Wu and the others to stay, but Uncle Wu said: "It seems to me that we are all rather tired, especially you, and we must have a rest." He went away with the rest.

CHAPTER 65
The Burial of Li Ping'er

The twenty-eighth day of the tenth month was the fourteenth day after the death of Li Ping'er. This was the second week's mind, and Abbot Wu with sixteen monks from the Daoist Temple of the Jade King came to make sacrifice. They brought banners and set up an altar in the house. A letter came from Secretary An. Ximen Qing entertained the messenger and dismissed him.

Abbot Wu brought a table of food and a roll of silk as his personal offering. The monks sang dirges, and the abbot solemnly made reverence before the coffin. Ximen Qing and Chen Jingji returned the reverence.

"Teacher," Ximen said, "you should not have done so much. We really do not know how we can accept this offering."

"I am ashamed of my unworthiness to offer sacrifice for your lady," Abbot Wu said. "These little things are no more than a trifling indication of my regard for her." Ximen Qing accepted the offerings and the men who had brought the boxes were sent away. The monks busied themselves most diligently with their ceremonies. They sought the dead lady in the nine dungeons of Hell; they summoned her spirit; they prayed for her relief.

The next day, the first to arrive was Uncle Han, who lived outside the city gates. With him came Meng Yulou's brother, Meng Rui, who had returned from his business abroad. Hearing that there was a bereavement in Ximen Qing's household, he came with Uncle Han, brought an offering of his own, and asked to be permitted to wear mourning. After paying his respects to Ximen Qing, he went to see his sister. Later, Ximen Qing entertained him.

About noon, a number of civil officers came. There were Li Gongji, the District Magistrate; Qian Sicheng, the Assistant Magistrate; Ren Linggui, the Deputy Assistant Magistrate; and the Jail Warden, Xia Gongji. The District Magistrate of Yanggu, Di Sixiu, came with them. The five gentlemen were all wearing mourning and brought with them presents and paper offerings. Ximen Qing, with Uncle Wu and Scholar Wen, entertained them, and three young actors sang for them.

While they were drinking, Ximen Qing was told that his Excellency, Huang, the Controller of the Brickfields, had come to offer his condolences. He hastily put on his mourning robes again and went to the coffin. Master Wen went out to the gate to welcome his Excellency. Servants came bringing incense, paper offerings, and silk, and they walked in procession to the coffin. Huang burned incense and made a reverence to the dead. Ximen Qing and Chen Jingji returned the reverence.

"I did not know that your lady was dead," Huang said, "or I should have been here sooner. I am sorry to be so late."

"It is a long time since I have been to see your Excellency," Ximen Qing said, "and now you come to me with such gifts. I don't know how to thank you." He took Huang to the hall. There Ximen Qing and Master Wen sat down with him, and the servants brought tea.

"Song Songyuan sends his love to you," Huang said. "He has heard of your lady's death and would have liked to come and see you, but he is very busy at the moment and has had to go to Jizhou. You may not have heard that His Majesty is going to set up an artificial mountain on the north of the imperial city. He has appointed Grand Marshal Zhu Mian to proceed south of the Yangzi River to collect the Taihu stones. The boats have been coming down one after another, and the first of them has now reached the Huai and will come down the river into Shandong. The stones are beautifully marked and in pieces about twenty feet long and several feet wide. Each piece is covered in yellow wrappings, and the boats, which are very many, all carry yellow flags. The river is shallow just now and people have been brought together from all around to tow the boats. It has been a most unpleasant time for officials and people alike, and the people, especially, are finding life very hard. Our friend Song has to see to everything himself and direct all the underlings in his district. There are so many orders and instructions that they would make a mountain. Song is busy all day and all night, and never has a moment to himself.

"Now, Grand Marshal Huang is coming from the Capital, and friend Song, with all his staff, is going to receive him. He has asked me to say that, as he has no other friend here to whom he is able to appeal, he hopes you will entertain the Grand Marshal."

He bade his servants summon the messengers whom Song had sent. Two officials in black robes came and knelt down. They brought presents of gold silk, incense, candles and paper. "These are the things Song has sent on his own account. The other parcels contain the presents from his staff. From the Provincial Treasurer and the Provincial Judge, twelve; and from the officers of the Prefecture, eight. In all there are twenty-two presents, a hundred and six taels."

He offered the gifts to Ximen Qing and again asked if he would entertain the Grand Marshal.

Ximen Qing hesitated. "I am in mourning, and I do not know what I ought to do. When is His Grace coming?"

"There is plenty of time," Huang said, "he won't be here for another six weeks. He has not left the Capital yet."

"My wife is to be buried on the twelfth day of the tenth month," Ximen Qing said. "Since you and his Lordship are good enough to give me such a proof of your confidence, I will do what you wish. But I cannot accept these presents. Say what you would have me do and I will make the necessary preparations."

"Nothing of the sort," Huang said. "Song asked me to approach you on the matter, and these presents have been sent by all the officers of the province. They are not from Song alone. You can't possibly refuse them. If you insist, I shall take them back and we will not ask you to do anything for us."

"In that case," Ximen Qing said, "I have no option in the matter." He told Daian and Wang Jing to remove the presents. Then he asked what preparations it would be necessary to make.

"For his Grace," said Huang, "a long state table. For Song, the Provincial Treasurer and the Provincial Judge, a table on the floor level, and, for the lower officers, tables of the common sort. We ourselves will provide for the servants and musicians. You need not trouble about them."

Tea was brought a second time and Huang stood up to take leave. Ximen Qing asked him to stay, but the Controller said: "I am on my way to see Shang Liutang. He used to hold the post I have now, and afterwards he was made a judge at Chengdu. His son, Liangquan, passed the examination when I did."

"I did not know you were a friend of Liangquan," Ximen Qing said. "He is a good friend of mine too."

Huang made ready to go. "Please give my respects to his Excellency Song," Ximen said, "and tell him I await his pleasure."

"When the time comes, he will send word," Huang said. "Do not be too extravagant in your preparations."

Ximen Qing escorted Huang to the gate. He mounted his horse and rode away.

When the magistrate and the officers heard that Huang had come with officials from the provincial government, they were tremendously alarmed, and ran away to hide in the small arbor near the artificial mound. They told their servants to take their horses and sedan chairs away. When Ximen Qing rejoined them, he told them that Song had asked him to entertain Grand Marshal Huang the following month. With one voice they made complaint: "Our district is poor enough already. If the Grand Marshal comes, we shall have to provide all kinds of things, banquets, materials and servants, and we shall have to extract the money from the people. What more dreadful calamity could have overtaken us? We only hope you will speak to his Excellency on our behalf, for we are all friends of yours." They went away.

The days passed until it was the twenty-first day after the death of Li Ping'er. The abbot Daojian of the Temple of Eternal Felicity outside the gates came with sixteen monks to perform the appropriate rites. They wore embroidered vestments and large hats, and, with their drums and great gongs, performed a very imposing ceremony.

On the twenty-eighth day the priests of Baoqing Temple came to sing the Buddhist liturgy for the dead. Ximen Qing was not at home. He had gone to the grave with Xu, the Master of the Yin Yang, to watch the pit being dug. He came back in the afternoon, and, in the evening, all the monks departed. The next day, he sent wine, food, and other things to the grave, and instructed his servants to put up a temporary building, the size of three rooms, near the site of the grave. The neighbors were entertained and, afterwards, everybody was given a present.

On the eleventh day, very early, a troop of singing boys came with their gongs and instruments to perform some farewell plays before the coffin. They played *The Five Demons Playing Pranks on Ban Guan; Zhang Tianshi Being Led Astray by Devils; Zhong Kui and the Little Ghosts; Laozi Passing over Han Guan; The Six Thieves Deceiving Amida; Plums in the Snow; Zhuangzi Dreaming of the Butterflies; The Heavenly Prince Sending Down Earth, Water, Fire, and Wind;* and many another. The ladies watched the plays from the other side of the screen. When they were over, all the relatives came and burned paper offerings before the coffin. They made loud lamentation.

The next day was the funeral. At a very early hour the obituary banner was brought out, together with a host of other banners and objects made of paper. Musicians and Buddhist and Daoist clergy came. Ximen Qing had arranged with Major Zhou for fifty soldiers, all fully equipped with arms and horses. Ten of them were on duty at the house; the other forty marched on either side of the coffin. Another twenty men from his own department marched in front and attended to the paper objects. Still another twenty had gone before to the funeral ground to guard the gate and receive the offerings that might be sent there.

Officers, scholars, relatives, friends and neighbors assembled for the funeral. There was a great din of horses and carriages arriving, and the street was full of people. Many more than a hundred sedan chairs brought ladies. Even the smaller sedan chairs of the singing girls might have been counted in scores.

Xu, the Master of the Yin Yang, selected the moment for the procession to start.

Ximen Qing gave directions for Sun Xue'e to stay at home with the two nuns.

Ping'an and two soldiers stood at the gate.

Chen Jingji, on his knees before the coffin, broke a cup into many pieces. Then sixty-four undertakers lifted the coffin upon their shoulders, their directors standing upon a raised platform and signaling instructions by striking a wooden gong. The priests of the Temple of Eternal Felicity chanted a dirge and the procession started down the main street and turned to the south. The masses of people on either side of the street seemed like a sea of men, a human mountain. The weather was fine, and it was a magnificently imposing funeral.

> Banners bearing characters of gold; banners with characters of silver
> Following close behind the coffin.
> Parasols of white silk and parasols of green silk
> Carried by those who walk before it.
> Banners for worthiness fluttering in the breeze.
> Cries and groans of lamentation all the way.
> Soldiers marching to clear the road
> Brandish staves of olive wood.
> Acrobats coming to meet the god, trying to display their skill
> Tumble and twist to left and right
> With bodies lithe as falcons
> Clambering like monkeys over their horses
> Standing on their heads
> Turning somersaults
> Passing coins through their bellies
> And standing on one leg like golden cockerels.
> The people applaud
> Each trying to praise more loudly than his neighbor.
> Shoulder to shoulder and back to back
> Wise and foolish undistinguishable
> Nobles and commonalty, all are there to see.
> Zhang the Fifth, the big blockhead
> Puffing and blowing.
> Li the Fourth, the dwarf

On his toes all the time.
White-haired old gentlemen
Propping their beards on their sticks.
Dark-haired beauties
With babes in their arms
All come to look at the funeral procession.

There were more than ten sedan chairs for Wu Yueniang, Li Jiao'er and the other ladies. They followed the coffin one behind the other. Ximen Qing, wearing a hempen hat and mourning dress, walked with the others immediately after it. Chen Jingji placed his hand upon the coffin, and so they came to the beginning of East Street. There Ximen Qing, in accordance with the Rites, called upon Abbot Wu of the Temple of the Jade King to set up the portrait. The Abbot wore a gown embroidered with a scarlet stork, a hat of the Nine Thunders, and a pair of orange-colored shoes. In his hand was an ivory tablet. He rode in a sedan chair carried by four men. He advanced towards the coffin, bearing the large portrait of Li Ping'er. Chen Jingji knelt down, and the procession halted. Then, while all listened attentively, the Abbot began to read.

"This is the dead lady of Ximen, officer of the Royal Guard. She was born at noon on the fifteenth day of the first month of the year *Xinwei,* and departed this life very early in the morning of the seventeenth day of the ninth month of the seventh year of the reign Zhenghe. She lived for twenty-seven years. The glorious dead was an excellent lady of high degree, most beautiful of wives. Nature endowed her with a loveliness like that of flowers and the moon. Her disposition was as fragrant as the orchid. In temper and behavior, she was gentle and sweet; in character, agreeable and harmonious. And as she was wise and gentle when in her own family, so, after her marriage, she lived most perfectly with her husband. A child she bore, like the jade of Lantian, but he drooped as the blossom of an orchid. We hoped that a hundred years of happy life might be before her, but, alas, she lived but twenty-seven. As the bright moon always fades, so the treasures of this world easily elude us. She, this excellent lady, died suddenly, for whether we die young or live to old age is for the Fates to decide.

"Now we bear her coffin through the streets, and mourning banners wave in the breeze. Her worthy husband laments before her bier, and her household, here in the street, are broken-hearted. So deep is their affection that they can never forget her. But lest, being dead, the remembrance of her appearance should be dimmed, we, who unworthily assume this hat and these ornaments of the Daoist faith, unworthily because we failed to restore her to health, can only, with all due reverence, follow the traditions of our ancestors and set forth her portrait for exhibition.

"We cannot bring back the butterfly of Zhuangzi's dream, but we hope that in Paradise she may partake of sweet dew and precious refreshment. When she comes face to face with the True God, she will be adorned with a hundred jewels and her pure spirit will not long remain in Hades. Then will her mind forget all things, for all things, in very truth, are but illusion.

"So, as her body is buried, may her spirit become a pure breeze. This true spirit will go away and return no more, and she will enter into eternal life. Hearken now, while we bid her a last farewell. We know not whither her spirit goeth, but her portrait will remain for people of future generations to gaze upon."

The sedan chair, with the Abbot sitting upright within it, slowly withdrew. The music played and there was a great lamentation. The funeral procession moved forward. When it came to the East Gate, the relatives and Ximen Qing mounted horses, but Chen Jingji continued on foot behind the coffin all the way to the grave. Captain Zhang and two hundred soldiers, and the two eunuchs, Liu and Xue, were at the burying place, stationed on the hillock. There they received the coffin with music. Paper offerings were burned, and the smoke reached the skies. When the body was brought to the hill, the undertakers set it down while Xu, the Master of the Yin Yang, went with them to examine the grave with a compass. When everything was ready, sacrifice was made to the god of the place; the coffin was lowered into the grave, and earth cast upon it.

Then Ximen Qing changed his clothes, and, taking two rolls of silk to Major Zhou, asked him to put the final dot upon the tablet. After this, the officials of Ximen's office, and his relatives and friends, offered wine to him. The music thundered and fireworks blazed everywhere. It was a magnificent scene.

After taking some refreshment, they prepared for the return journey. Yueniang sat in the Spirit's sedan chair, with the tablet and the banner. Chen Jingji went back with the Spirit's bed, the fourteen Daoist novices accompanying him, playing music all the way. Both uncles Wu, Master Qiao, uncles Hua, Shen and Meng, Ying Bojue and Xie Xida, Master Wen and the clerks, came back with Ximen Qing. The ladies' chairs followed. When they reached the gate, a fire was lighted. Then they went in, and set up the tablet in the room of Li Ping'er. Master Xu performed various ceremonies, purified the whole house, and set yellow charms upon all the doors to keep away evil spirits. He was given a roll of silk and five taels of silver, and went away. The other guests went too. Ximen Qing took twenty strings of small money, five for the policemen, five for the soldiers of his own department, and ten for those of Major Zhou. He sent a servant with his card to thank Major Zhou, Captain Zhang and Magistrate Xia. He urged Master Qiao and the others to remain, but they declined and went away.

Laibao came. "The men who set up the temporary buildings await your orders," he said. "They propose to remove everything tomorrow."

"I do not wish them taken down yet," Ximen said. "Tell the men to come after I have entertained Censor Song."

In the inner court, Mistress Hua and Mistress Qiao waited to see the tablet set up, then they made a last lamentation and went away.

That evening, Ximen Qing, still thinking of Li Ping'er, went to her room. The tablet was placed in the position of honor, facing her portrait. The smaller portrait was next to the tablet. There was a small silver bed and silver coverlets in a shrine, complete in every way with ornaments, and, beneath it, a pair of tiny shoes. On a table were incense, flowers, candles, plates, bowls and all kinds of things offered to the dead. Ximen Qing cried again. He bade Yingchun make a bed for him opposite the tablet. In the middle of the night he watched the lonely lamp and the moon shining through the window. He tossed about on his bed and sighed. All the time, he thought of the beauty he had lost.

> Mournfully he sighed before her shuttered window
> Lonely and broken-hearted, like the phœnix
> That has lost his mate.
> The orchids are withered, and the rain of autumn falls
> The maple leaves drop into the river
> In the frosty night.
> Their longing to be together was in vain
> In this life he will never more behold her.
> If the dead know what passes in the world
> Then there must be two heartbroken lovers
> One still on earth, the other in the underworld.

When day came, Ximen Qing watched the maids offer food and tea to their dead mistress, and he took his own meals there. When he took up his chopsticks, he looked towards the tablet and invited his dead lady to eat with him. Seeing this, the maids and the nurse shed tears. When he was alone, Ruyi'er used to come and give him tea and things to eat. She would find means to touch him, and an excuse for saying something or other, and soon they were on very good terms with one another.

One day, Ximen Qing invited a number of ladies and gentlemen to a service at the grave, and, when he came back, he was drunk. Yingchun helped him to bed. In the middle of the night he wished for some tea, but Yingchun was not there and Ruyi'er brought it for him. She noticed that his bedclothes had almost fallen on the floor, so, when she had given him the teacup, she gathered them up for him. This touched him; he put his arms around her neck and kissed her. Then he slipped his tongue between her lips. She let it pass, but did not speak. Ximen told her to undress, and they got into bed together and played with great delight.

"Now my mistress is dead," Ruyi'er said, "I will stay here and serve you, if you love me."

"If you serve me well," said Ximen Qing, "you need not worry."

After this, the woman did all she could to give him satisfaction, and was ready to do everything he wished. This pleased him.

The next day she got up and brought his shoes and socks, made the bed, and would not allow Yingchun to do anything for him. Ximen took four pins that had belonged to Li Ping'er and gave them to her. She kowtowed and thanked him. Yingchun knew this and joined forces with her. Ruyi'er, realizing that her position was now secure, and that she no longer needed help from anyone else, became quite different in manner. Every day she dressed beautifully and mingled with the other maids. She talked and joked so much that Pan Jinlian remarked it.

One morning, Ximen Qing was sitting with Ying Bojue, when one of the servants told him that a man had come from Song the Censor. He had brought a set of gold and silver wine cups, a pair of gold wine pots, two pairs of gold goblets, ten pairs of small silver cups, two pairs of silver jars, four pairs of large silver cups, two rolls of scarlet silk, two rolls of gold silk, ten jars of wine, and two sheep. He said that the Grand Marshal's boat had now arrived at Dongchang, and brought a message asking Ximen Qing to prepare for his entertainment on the eighteenth. Ximen accepted all these things, and gave the man a tael of silver and his card. He ordered Ben the Fourth and Laixing to buy whatever might be necessary.

"Ever since my sixth wife's illness," Ximen said to Ying Bojue, "I have never had a moment to myself. Now the funeral is over, there comes this business, and I shall be more occupied than ever."

"You must not complain, Brother," Bojue said, "it is not of your seeking. They came to you. You will certainly have to spend a little money, but the presence of the high officers of the province will make your house glorious."

"That is not what is troubling me," Ximen said, "but I expected they would come sometime after the twentieth. If they come on the eighteenth, things will have to be done in a hurry. It will be the thirty-fifth day after her death, too. I have made arrangements for a service with Abbot Wu, and I cannot alter the date. Even if I could alter it, I couldn't manage with these two things coming on the same day."

"I don't see any difficulty about it," Bojue said. "My sister-in-law died on the seventeenth day of the ninth month, and the fifth week's mind will be on the twenty-first. You have this reception on the eighteenth and the service on the twentieth. That does not seem too late to me."

"Very well," Ximen said, "I will send a boy to explain matters to the Abbot."

"There is another matter," Bojue said. "His Holiness, Huang, who has been deputed by his Majesty to go to Taian to offer incense, and also to accomplish the solemn sacrifice to Heaven that lasts for seven days and seven nights, is staying at present at our temple here. Before he goes away, you might get Abbot Wu to invite His Holiness to come and hold a service here. We should be only too glad to have a cleric of such great renown."

"Yes," said Ximen, "everybody says that Huang is a real saint. I would ask him to come, but Abbot Wu, you know, sent me a number of presents the other day; he displayed the portrait of my dead wife, and his priests came to the funeral. There was nothing I could do in return for all these attentions except to ask him to come and perform the sacrifice. If I now invite Huang, I don't know how I can make things right with Wu."

"Ask Wu to arrange the whole affair," Ying Bojue said, "and suggest that he invites Huang for the final ceremony only. If you spend a few more taels, there need be no difficulty. And, after all, you are spending money for your wife and not for anybody else."

So Ximen Qing told Chen Jingji to write a letter to the Abbot, requesting him to invite Huang, and saying that the day for the service would be the twentieth. Twenty-four monks would be wanted and the service should last for a day and a night. Five taels more were sent with the letter, which Daian was ordered to deliver on horseback immediately. Ying Bojue went away and Ximen Qing joined Wu Yueniang in the inner court.

Yueniang told him that Ben the Fourth's wife had brought her daughter Changjie to present her on the occasion of her engagement. They had brought two boxes of presents with them. Ximen Qing asked to whom the girl was engaged.

Mistress Ben the Fourth and her daughter, who was wearing a red silken gown, a yellow skirt, and many ornaments upon her hair, came and kowtowed to Ximen Qing. Yueniang stood beside them. "I hear," she said, "that Magistrate Xia has made choice of this young lady. The arrangement was yesterday, and the wedding is to be upon the twenty-fourth. He gave only thirty taels of silver for her. She is good to look upon, and no one would think she was only fifteen. She seems more like sixteen or seventeen. She has grown so much in the short time since I saw her last."

"He told me the other day," Ximen Qing said, "that he was thinking of securing two young ladies and having them taught music, but I never thought of asking who they were."

Wu Yueniang entertained Mistress Ben the Fourth and her daughter, and Li Jiao'er, Meng Yulou, Pan Jinlian, Sun Xue'e and Ximen Dajie came and joined them. When Mistress Ben went away, Yueniang gave her a complete outfit of heavy silk and a tael of silver. Li Jiao'er and the other ladies all gave her something: flowers, ornaments, kerchiefs, powder, or something of the sort.

In the evening, Daian returned and said that Abbot Wu had accepted the silver. "His Holiness Huang," he said, "is still here and will remain until after the twentieth. They will come on the morning of the nineteenth and prepare the altar and the dais."

The next day, Ximen Qing gave instructions to the cooks, insisting that everything should be of the very best. At the great gate he set up a seven-storied pagoda, and, before the great hall, one of five stories.

On the seventeenth, there came two officers from Song to see what preparations had been made. At the upper part of the hall they saw a peacock screen. The floor was covered with colored rugs. The chair cushions and tablecloths were all embroidered. The food that had been prepared for the Grand Marshal was the finest imaginable and the delicacies were delightful to eat as well as to look at. Two smaller tables were set for the two provincial officers, and there were a few other tables for provincial officers of rank. Outside the hall, in the temporary building that had been put up, were a number of tables for five courses of food and five of dessert for the officials of the eight districts. When the officers had finished their inspection, Ximen Qing gave them tea, and they went back to report to their superiors.

The next day the provincial dignitaries came with a host of officers to await the arrival of the Grand Marshal's boat. They had with them a yellow banner with the words imperial commissioner, and before them was carried the imperial decree. The officers, guards and soldiers of every kind were in full dress, marching behind their banners. The procession stretched for miles.

Then came Grand Marshal Huang. He wore a robe with the scarlet dragon embroidered upon it and rode in a sedan chair carried by eight men. Another eight men marched beside it. This chair had a silver top and the canopy above it was tea-colored. A host of officers and attendants followed, all mounted upon splendid horses. The procession was as fine as a bouquet of ten thousand flowers. They marched along to the strains of martial music. The road was strewn with yellow sand. As the procession advanced, there was such a silence that even the dogs did not bark or the cocks crow. Not a soul dared step forward.

They passed through Dongpingfu and arrived at Qinghe. The officials of the district knelt on either side of the road, till the Grand Marshal's guard called out: "Stand up, stand up!" Messenger after messenger was dispatched to Ximen's house.

At last they arrived, and the noise of the music was great enough to reach the skies. Beside the gate, in double ranks on either side, stood officers robed in black. Ximen Qing himself, also in black robes and hat, bowed low to the dust. The soldiers marched past, and the Grand Marshal's chair appeared. The Grand Marshal came in, followed by a crowd of people of high and low degree. He entered the great hall and the music played again, stringed and wind instruments together.

First, the Governor of Shandong, Hou Meng, and the Censor, Song Qiaonian, came to greet the Grand Marshal, and he returned their salutations. Then the Provincial Treasurer of Shandong, Gong Qi; State Counselor He Qigao; Provincial Treasurer Chen Sizhen; State Counselor Li Kanting; Counselor Feng Tinggu; Counselor Wang Boyan and a number of other provincial officers came to salute his Excellency, and he received them with pleasant affability. They were followed by the Prefects of the eight Prefectures. These made reverence from the courtyard, and the Grand Marshal bowed low to them in return. The captains and military officers came then, but the Grand Marshal sat still and took no notice of them. All the officers went back to remain in waiting outside.

Ximen Qing and Xia came to offer tea to the Grand Marshal. The two officers of highest rank present, Hou and Song, themselves handed the cup to His Grace. The music played. Then they offered a golden flower, and wine in a goblet of jade. The Grand Marshal moved towards his table, and, when he had seated himself, the Governor, the Censor and the other officers sat down in due order. Ximen Qing sat down too. The manager of the company of actors brought his repertory and the dance began. Both dancing and music were extremely well performed. They played the first act of *Pei Jingong returns the Girdle*. When this was over, cooks brought meat, venison and pork, with all manner of sauces and dressings, soup, a hundred kinds of the richest and rarest of viands, with rice and *shaomai*. Then four actors, with zithers, flute, lute and cittern, sang songs unaccompanied by dancing. While two courses of soup were being served, the music played three times. Song appointed two officers to entertain the Grand Marshal's attendants in the temporary rooms, while Ximen Qing had arranged for the entertainment of the military officers in the outer court.

The Grand Marshal bade his attendant to distribute ten taels of silver among the servants. Then he called for his sedan chair and prepared to leave. He could not be persuaded to remain longer, and the officers escorted him to the gate. Then the music played again; banners and insignia were ranged in order on either side of the street. Officials went forward to clear the way, and the soldiers set out with a fine martial step. A number of officers prepared to mount their horses to accompany His Grace, but this he would not allow. He stepped into his sedan chair and was carried away, and all the soldiers were ordered to escort him to his boat. The two senior officers, Hou and Song, had arranged for supplies of food, and these, with their cards, they entrusted to Hu Shiwen, the Prefect of Dongpingfu, and the Captain of the Bodyguard, Zhou Xiu, to take to the boat.

The Governor and the Censor returned to the hall and thanked Ximen Qing. "This has really put you to grave inconvenience," they said, "and we do not know how to thank you. You must tell us whether the money we sent was adequate, so that we may make up any deficiency."

Ximen Qing bowed. "I am grateful to you," he said, "for entrusting to me so pleasant a duty, and making so magnificent a present. I only fear that, in my poor house, the entertainment has been unworthy of the occasion. Will you forgive me if there has been anything amiss?"

Song thanked him again, then called for his sedan chair and went away with the Governor. All the other officers hastened after them. Ximen Qing went back to the hall and gave food to the musicians and actors and they, too, went away. Four young actors alone were bidden to stay. Then all that belonged to the officers was taken away by their servants.

Seeing that it was still early, Ximen Qing had the tables cleared, and the food collected upon four of them. Then he sent boys to invite Uncle Wu, Ying Bojue, Xie Xida, Scholar Wen, the clerks, and his son-in-law, Chen Jingji. Many of them had risen before dawn that day and had been busy all the time, and he wished to offer them a feast in return. Before long, they all arrived and sat down to drink.

"Brother," said Ying Bojue, "how long did the Grand Marshal stay? Was he pleased with his entertainment?"

"I am sure His Grace must have been pleased when he saw such a splendid feast," Han Daoguo said. "The Governor and the Censor were perfectly satisfied. They thanked his Lordship repeatedly."

"I can think of no other house that could offer so magnificent a reception," Bojue said. "In the first place, no other house here is so spacious, and, secondly, no other house could welcome so many official people. You must have entertained at least a thousand today. Well, it may have been rather expensive, but your fame will spread throughout the province."

"My old teacher Chen was here too," Scholar Wen said.

"Who was your teacher?" Ximen Qing asked him.

"Chen Zhenghui," Scholar Wen said. "He is the son of the censor, Chen Liaoweng, a native of Zhengcheng in Henan. When he was only eighteen years old, he passed the senior examination. Now he is President of the Board of Education and a very learned man."

"He is about twenty-four years old now," Ximen Qing said.

Food was brought in. While they were eating it, Ximen Qing sent for the four young actors and asked their names. They were Zhou Cai, Liang Duo, Ma Zhen and Han Bi. Ximen Qing said to the last of them: "Are you any relation of Han Jinchuan?"

Han Bi knelt down and said: "Han Jinchuan and Han Yuchuan are my younger sisters."

The mention of the girls' names reminded Ximen of Li Ping'er. It made him sad to think that on such a glorious occasion as this she was no longer with him. "Take your instruments," he said to the boys, and sing 'The Flowers of Luo-ang and the Moon of Liangyuan.'" Han Bi and Zhou Cai tuned their instruments and sang.

> Flowers of Luoyang
> Moon of Liangyuan.
> Perfect blossoms we may buy and keep a little while
> Bright moon, which, for a moment, we may borrow.
> The flowers on the trellis seem so beautiful
> We stretch out our wine cups to the full moon.
> The moon is full, and then it wanes
> The flowers blossom and then fade.
> Parting is the bitterest thing in life.
> The flowers fade, but Spring has still her beauty.
> The moon wanes slowly, but the Autumn Festival will come again.
> Only we mortals die and never return.

When the song was over, Bojue saw tears in Ximen Qing's eyes. "Brother," he said "you told them to sing that song. Are you still thinking about your dead lady?"

Ximen noticed the plates of dessert at the other side of the table. "Brother Ying," he said, "you think my mind is always upon her. Look at those dishes. When she was alive, she used to arrange them with her own hands. Now she is dead, the maids do it. You can see for yourself whether the dishes are properly set out or even fit to eat."

"Judging by this meal," Scholar Wen said, "I do not see that you have any reason to complain of your ladies."

"Brother," said Ying Bojue, "you cannot get over your grief at her loss, but to talk in this way is hardly fair to the other ladies."

As they talked and drank together, Pan Jinlian was listening to them behind a curtain, secretly. When she had heard what Ximen Qing said, she went straight to the inner court and told Wu Yueniang all about it.

"Let him say what he likes," said Yueniang, "it's no use your imagining you can do anything to stop him. While she was still living, she promised Xiuchun to the second lady. Now he says she has only been dead a little while and we must not give her maids to anybody yet. I said nothing, but you have seen for yourself what airs the nurse and those two maids have been giving themselves lately. If I begin to say a word to them, he says I am too rough with them."

"Ruyi'er has certainly been different the last few days," Jinlian said. "I am very much afraid she will turn out to be a troublesome baggage. He spends all his time with her. I hear, too, that he gave her two sets of pins and she put them in her hair so that everybody could see them."

"They are a rubbishy lot," Yueniang said, "and none of them seems to have any morals."

CHAPTER 66

The Solemn Sacrifice

His breast is filled with a thousand griefs.
The sun seems to hang over the treetops
Green leaves give shade and Spring has come
The grass grows thick and the oriole sings.
He cannot hear her dainty footsteps
The music of her voice comes to him only in dream
The mountain masses beyond the gate
Cannot bar the way to sorrow.

Ximen Qing was drinking wine with Uncle Wu, Ying Bojue and the others. He said to Han Daoguo: "When will the boats be ready to start? We must see about getting the goods packed up."

"Yesterday," Han Daoguo said, "I had word to say that the boats will sail on the twenty-fourth."

"After the twentieth we will have everything made ready," Ximen Qing said.

"Who is going this time?" Bojue asked.

"Three in all," Ximen told him. "I propose that Cui shall come back first next year with a cargo of merchandise from Hangzhou. Han Daoguo and Laibao are going on to Songjiang and elsewhere to buy cloth. We have silk enough already in store."

"Really, you are a wonderful manager," Bojue said. "The proverb says: A good businessman must think of everything."

It was now the first night watch. Uncle Wu rose. "Brother-in-law," he said, "you have been working very hard lately and we have all had quite enough to drink. I think we ought to leave you to rest."

Ximen Qing would not hear of their going. He ordered the young actors to pour out wine and sing more songs. But after three more cups of wine or so, they went away.

Ximen Qing offered six *qian* of silver to the four young actors, but they declined the money. "We came on the instructions of his Excellency," they said. "We have done no more than our duty. How can we accept a present from you?"

"It is true you have been on duty," Ximen said, "but I see no reason why you should not take the silver." The four actors took it, kowtowed and went away. Ximen Qing went to bed in the inner court.

The next day when he returned from the office, he found that Abbot Wu had sent one of his novices and two men to make preparations for the ceremony. Ximen Qing had monastic fare served to the novice, who afterwards went away. Ximen asked Scholar Wen to send invitations to kinsmen, friends and neighbors, both men and women. The cooks were instructed to make the necessary preparations and especially to prepare vegetarian food to be offered to the dead lady.

Before dawn next day the priests arrived. They went upon the dais, lighted candles and burned incense. Then they began to play their instruments and recite the appropriate prayers. Outside the gate hung a long banner with an inscription, and, on either side of the gateway, a scroll of yellow paper. Upon one was written: "By the gracious mercy of the Ruler of the East may the soul of this lady, in the light of dawn, ascend to the mansions of the blessed," and on the other: "By the efficacy of the *Nandan* may she be granted forgiveness of her offenses, that her spirit, strengthened and purified, may mount to the Heavens."

Over the dais on which the altar stood hung a scroll that announced that thirty-five texts, charms and spells were to be read to relieve from travail the soul of the dead lady, and that sacrifice would be made to bring her safely through the perils of Hades.

His Holiness Huang, wearing a scarlet robe with a gold girdle, and with many attendants following, arrived in a sedan chair shortly after sunrise. Abbot Wu and the other clergy went to receive him. They led him to the altar. Ximen Qing, in black robes, came to welcome him and offered him tea. The priests were given monastic fare beside the altar. The table on which the food was set was made of red lacquer and the table covers were all embroidered. Two boys waited beside the table. While the attendants were preparing the texts, Ximen Qing made his offering of a roll of gold silk.

Before he went up to the altar, his Holiness put on a Hat of the Nine Thunders and a scarlet vestment with golden clouds and the hundred cranes embroidered upon it. He recited the prologue; the priests washed their hands and offered incense. Then his Holiness incensed the altar. He burned spells to summon the angelic host, and with invocations and charms made announcement to the three Heavens and the ten Earths. They presented the three offerings. The music began, and incense was burned processionally. Ximen Qing and Chen Jingji both had censers, and soldiers marched before them. Before them and behind were borne four parasols of gold embroidery, and banners adorned with pearls. When the procession returned, they took their places, and the music struck up again. Then they went to the tablet of Li Ping'er and summoned her spirit to appear that they might assist her on her way to Paradise. A small table was set apart especially so that the dead lady's spirit might come there, listen to the reading of the scriptures, and hear the teaching of the true faith.

At noon, his Holiness, still wearing his hat and vestments, offered sacrifice to the stars and burned charms to dispatch angelic messengers to the underworld.

This holy man, Huang, was not more than thirty years old. His appearance was most remarkable. Vested in his robes and engaged in the execution of these ceremonies he looked almost divine.

After this, Abbot Wu read before the altar from the Heavenly Treasures from the Jade Book with the Tiger Seal. Then incense was burned again, and everyone went to the temporary hall for refreshment. The most imposing table was that of his Holiness; the Abbot's was slightly smaller. The others had ordinary tables. Ximen Qing offered his Holiness and the Abbot each a roll of satin, four pairs of flowers and four rolls of silk. The other priests each received a roll of cloth. Food for his Holiness and the Abbot was sent to the temple, and the priests bade their servers put their food into a large box. After the meal, they all went to take the air in the garden. The tables were cleared and fresh ones set for the entertainment of the kinsmen and friends who had come to the ceremony.

Meanwhile, a messenger arrived from the Eastern Capital with a letter from Zhai. Ximen Qing received him in the hall. He was an official of the Imperial Tutor's household, wearing a black gown, tight-fitting trousers, with a swastika hat and yellow boots. He was fully armed. He made a reverence to Ximen Qing, and Ximen returned his greeting. Then he produced a letter and ten taels of silver. Ximen Qing asked his name.

"My name is Wang Yu, and his Lordship Zhai has bidden me bring this letter to you. Until he heard the sad news of your lady's death from his Excellency An, he knew nothing about it."

"When did his Excellency's letter reach the Capital?" Ximen Qing asked.

"In the tenth month," the messenger said. "His Excellency completed his work as Warden of the Royal Forests within the year, and he has now been made Senior Secretary of the Board of Waterways. He will return to the Capital when he has finished his present work."

Ximen Qing told Laibao to entertain the messenger and said that he would give him a letter to take back the following day. The messenger asked where Han Daoguo lived, saying that he had a letter to deliver to him, and that he would like to see him at once because he had to return to the Capital with the least possible delay. Ximen sent for Han Daoguo and the two men had a meal together, after which the messenger went with Han Daoguo to his house.

Ximen was greatly pleased to receive this letter and showed it to Scholar Wen. "When you write the answer for me," he said, "the style must be as good as this. I am sending him ten kerchiefs, ten kerchiefs of silk, ten pairs of gold toothpicks and ten gold wine cups. The messenger will come tomorrow for my letter."

Scholar Wen read the letter:

Zhai Qian, your kinsman in the Capital, presents his most humble salutations. At the onset of winter he sends this letter to his Lordship Ximen Siquan, officer of the Imperial Guard.

Since we last parted at the Capital, there has been no opportunity for us to meet, and this is a matter of great regret to me. I have told my master how much I long to see you.

The first sad news of your lady's death came to me from An Fengshan. It distresses me beyond measure that I cannot come in person to offer my sympathy. It is most unfortunate, most unfortunate! I can only hope that you will not allow yourself to give way utterly to your grief. As a slight token of my feeling for you, I send a small present, which I trust you will accept.

I am informed that your activities in the public service are so meritorious that the people of Qinghe cannot too loudly sing your praises. There can be no doubt that after the general inspection this year, you will receive promotion. The other day report was made of those officers whose work merited the highest approbation, and I asked my master to place your name in the list. When the work is completed, his Majesty will distribute awards and you will be given the post of Senior Magistrate. His Lordship Xia's period of office will shortly expire, and he will receive a higher appointment. I tell you this before the matter is made public.

I trust this letter will give you pleasure, but pray keep its contents to yourself and do not say anything to his Lordship. Keep the matter a complete secret.

The noble Yang died in prison on the twenty-ninth day of last month.

Scholar Wen finished reading this letter and was putting it into his sleeve when Ying Bojue took it from him and read it again. When he gave it back to the scholar, he said: "Sir, you must take great pains over the answer. There are many men of learning at the capital, and we mustn't have them laughing at us."

"I," said Scholar Wen, "am like a dog's tail. It can be used instead of ermine when there is no ermine to be had. There is little depth to my learning, and who am I to wield a battle ax among the military gentlemen? I can only do what my duty requires of me."

"Scholar Wen will do admirably anything he is asked to do," Ximen Qing said. "What do you understand about matters of this sort, you dog?"

When they had finished their meal, he told Laixing to give food to the kinsmen, friends and neighbors who had come. He bade Daian take return gifts to the singing girls who had sent presents. To each of them he gave a roll of cloth and a tael of silver. In the afternoon, he sent for Li Ming, Wu Hui and Zheng Feng.

The priests returned to the altar. They beat their drums, made obeisance to the gods, and chanted their texts. Then they set up lanterns, burned paper offerings, and so went on until it was dark. By the time they were done, it was already the first night watch. Uncle Hua decided to remain, Ximen Qing having detained him, but Master Qiao and Uncles Shen and Meng went away. The two uncles Wu, Ying Bojue, Xie Xida, Scholar Wen and Chang Zhijie stayed with the clerks to watch the ceremonies during the night.

In the great court, a high dais had been erected with a decorated arch. A tank of water and a pool of fire had been prepared with offerings of food for the spirits. The tablet of Li Ping'er was placed upon a table, and offerings of every sort were set out before it. Beside the tablet were three banners, one for her spirit, one red one, and one yellow one. There was an inscription that read: "Away, ye evil spirits! This is holy ground. The purification of the Southern Palace has here been made."

The priests played their instruments, sitting in two ranks. Beside them stood four young novices, one bearing a wand, another a basin, another a double-edged sword. His Holiness put on a golden miter for the banishment of demons, and an embroidered vestment. Then going up to the highest point, he chanted the following verses:

> May the mercy of the ineffable one descend
> And the gates to the passes of the underworld
> Shall open one by one.
> Novices, walking two by two, lead the way

And the soul of the departed, purified and cleansed,
Shall reach the abode of the blessed.

Then he burned incense again and sang: "The Mighty One hath revealed the way of truth and shown mercy to them that dwell in darkness. He hath said that all who mortify the flesh shall come to immortality. He bestoweth blessings upon the people, both of this world and of the world to come. His mercy is outpoured over all in danger, famine or distress. We burn incense, and implore the Most High, the Most Gracious, the Ineffable One, and all the Immortals in all the Worlds, to come to our aid this day. All we who live in this world of dust are fettered by the things of this world. Death is a mystery to us; we long for life. Few there are who plant good seed, and many are they who go on the wrong path. We are foolish and do not understand; we yield ourselves to greed and passion. We believe that we shall live forever and forget the death that cometh so easily. One day we die and all is over. Yet our sin remaineth, and we suffer punishment in Hell.

"Therefore, as Thou hast taught us, we make sacrifice for this dead woman. She departed and went to the world of darkness, and, if we offer not sacrifice for the remission of her sins, she must suffer the most dreadful torments. We implore Thee, O Most High, grant Thy mercy and save us who cry to Thee. Let Thy most gracious light shine upon us that we may be enlightened. Bid Thine angels be merciful unto us, and send forth Thy decree to the Powers of Hell that they cease their examination of her who is dead. Bid them open the prison gates and set the prisoner free. Pardon her sins and let hatred be stilled.

"Let all obey Thy commands and come forth from the gates of Hell.

"Let her pass over this fire that her weakness may become strength, and that she be not as a. faded flower.

"Grant unto her another life, and bring her safely to the shores of Truth.

"To this end we burn these sacred spells, beseeching Thee to hear our prayer."

The priests dipped the spirit's banner into the pool of water and burned charms. They took the red banner, put it into the pit of fire and burned charms again. Then they took the yellow banner. His Holiness said: "From Heaven cometh the water and from Earth the fire. From their meeting cometh life itself." So the ceremony came to an end. The tablet was carried over the decorated bridge to pay respect to the God and to take refuge with the Three Divinities of the Daoist Faith. Then five sets of offerings were made.

"Now," said his Holiness, "she has found the three refuges. We will pronounce the nine commandments." The nine commandments were read. The priests played their instruments and recited many charms. Then they implored a blessing upon the soul of the dead woman and all other souls.

His Holiness came down from the dais. The others, still playing their music, followed him and went out of the gate to burn paper money, treasure chests and other things. This was the end. The priests returned and took off their vestments. People from the temple rolled up the pictures.

In the great hall, Ximen Qing had ordered many tables to be prepared. The lights shone very brightly. The three young actors sang, and all the relatives and friends sat there. Ximen Qing offered his Holiness a cup of wine, with two rolls of silk and ten taels of silver. Upon his knees, he said: "Now that my dead wife has had the benefit of your blessing, she will be able to enter paradise. I am most grateful to you, and this offering is a token of my gratitude."

"I am ashamed," said his Holiness, "that my priest's robe should cover one so unworthy to profess Holy Religion. Not any virtue of mine but your own sincerity will send your wife to paradise. I feel that I ought not to accept your gift."

"It is but a trifle," Ximen Qing said, "and really utterly unworthy of you. I can only pray that you will smile and accept it."

His Holiness then bade his novices remove the gifts.

Ximen Qing offered a cup of wine to Abbot Wu, with a roll of silk and five taels of silver. Ten taels more were for the expenses of the ceremony.

"I will accept the fee and no more," said the Abbot. "You have always been extremely generous to me, and I could do no less than perform this ceremony for your lady. Indeed I ought not even to take the fee, so how dare I accept the rest?"

"Teacher," Ximen said, "though his Holiness performed the actual ceremony, you had all the trouble of the preparations. I must insist."

The Abbot was obliged to accept. He thanked Ximen Qing. Then Ximen offered wine to all the other priests, spreading the blessing, as it is said. Uncle Wu and Ying Bojue helped him, Uncle Wu passing the cups, and Bojue pouring out the wine. Xie Xida took around the food. They knelt down.

"Today," Bojue said, "we have done excellent work. We are delighted to have his Holiness with us, and we are greatly obliged to Abbot Wu for the trouble he has taken. I have no doubt that all that has been done will greatly benefit my dead sister-in-law. Though this is largely due to the supreme powers of his Holiness, yet, Brother, your earnest sincerity must have had its part." He offered a cup of wine to Ximen Qing.

"Gentlemen," Ximen said, "I have troubled you greatly these last few days and I do not know how to thank you." With these words he drained the cup.

Ying Bojue filled another cup. "Drink this, Brother, and make it a pair. I would not have you drink a single one." Xie Xida helped Ximen to some food. In return, Ximen Qing offered wine to them, and they sat down. The actors sang and the cooks brought more and more food. They guessed fingers, played games and, with music and singing, drank until the second night watch. Then Ximen Qing was drunk, and everybody went away. He gave three *qian* of silver to the actors, and went to the inner court.

CHAPTER 67

Ximen Qing Dreams of Li Ping'er

The wind blows from the north
And the ground is covered with flakes of jade.
The white earth and the river are made one.
A cold mist rises above the waves: it is like a screen.
The mountains are covered with gray cloud
And the cloud links them with the water.
The withered grass seems to be dead.

His thoughts were far as the red cloud
The gentle spirit was sad, and the memory bitter
Night after night, only a kind dream
Could give him sleep.

Do not stand alone on the high building
When the moon is waning.
The wine descending to a sorrowing breast
Turns to tears of love.

Ximen Qing was very tired when he went to the inner court to sleep. He did not rise next day until the sun was high in the heavens. Laixing came and said to him: "The builders are here. They wish to know if they shall pull down the temporary buildings."

"Yes, tell them to demolish everything," Ximen answered angrily. "Why do you come and bother me?"

The builders unfastened the mats and ropes and took down the pinewood posts. They carried them to the house on the other side of the road and there stored them.

Yuxiao came and said to Ximen: "The weather is very threatening." He told her to bring his clothes so that he might get up.

"You are very tired, and the weather looks bad," Wu Yueniang said. "Stay in bed. What is there for you to do if you get up so early? Don't go to the office today."

"I am not going to the office," Ximen said, "but Zhai's messenger is coming for my answer."

"Then you had better get up," Yueniang said, "and I will tell them to make some gruel for you."

Ximen Qing got up but did not wash. He put on a velvet gown and a felt hat and went to his study in the garden. Now that Shutong had gone, Ximen Qing had told Wang Jing to wait upon him in this study and Chunhong to look after the study in the outer court. In winter Ximen usually came to this garden study. There was a fire beneath the floor and a large bronze brazier. The winter blinds were drawn. In the middle room were some *jiazhi* peaches, chrysanthemums of many different kinds, a few slender bamboos of great delicacy, and orchids. Writing materials and vases with the plum-blossom pattern books, and musical instruments were set out with great care.

When Ximen Qing came in, Wang Jing hastened to burn incense in a small gold burner. Ximen bade him tell Laian to go for Ying Bojue. Then Ping'an came and told Wang Jing that Little Zhou, the barber, had come. Ximen Qing gave orders that he should be sent in. The barber came and kowtowed.

"You have come at the right moment," Ximen said to him. "Now comb my hair and massage my body." He asked the barber why it was so long since he had last been there.

"I heard that the Sixth Lady had died and that you were very busy."

Ximen Qing sat down on a comfortable chair, and Little Zhou dressed his hair. Laian came with Ying Bojue. Bojue was wearing a felt hat, a green velvet gown, and a pair of old black boots with palm-leaf galoshes over them. He made a reverence to Ximen Qing. Ximen, who was still having his hair dressed, told him not to stand on ceremony but to sit down. Ying Bojue pulled out a chair and sat down beside the brazier.

"Why are you dressed like this?" Ximen said.

"Don't you know?" said Bojue. "It is snowing and very cold. I did not get home before cockcrow, and this morning I did not feel at all anxious to get up. If you hadn't sent your boy, I should have been asleep still. You must be strong, or you wouldn't be able to get up so early. If I were in your place, I should never get up at all."

"No," said Ximen, "I don't suppose you would. You know all I have had to do of late. First the funeral, then Grand Marshal Huang to entertain, and now this last ceremony. I have had no rest at all. This morning, my wife said to me: 'You must be tired; stay in bed for a while,' but I remembered that Zhai's messenger was coming for an answer to the letter he brought, and I wanted to see the temporary buildings pulled down.

On the twenty-fourth, Clerk Han and the others are to start for the South. Then, during the funeral ceremonies, my kinsmen and friends have been very kind. I ought to go and visit them but, in the circumstances, perhaps I may be excused. But at least I must go and see the officers of rank who came to the funeral."

"I am afraid you can't escape that," Bojue said, "but, as for the others, if I were you, I should get somebody to go and call on them on your behalf. You can thank them when you see them. They all know how busy you are, and they will understand."

As they were talking, Huatong brought two cups of milk with sugar and cream. Bojue took one. The milk was so white that it looked like goose fat with the cream floating on the top. "This is a great treat," he said. "Nice and hot too!" He drank the milk, and found it so sweet that he had no difficulty in finishing it. Little Zhou finished Ximen Qing's hair and began to clean his ears. Ximen set down his cup of milk.

"Drink your milk, Brother," Bojue said. "Don't let it get cold. A man like you ought to drink milk. It is so nourishing."

"I don't want it," Ximen Qing said. "You drink it. My gruel will be coming shortly."

Ying Bojue liked it very much. He picked up the cup and drank it straight off.

The barber finished cleaning Ximen's ears and took a roller to massage his body.

"Do you enjoy being rolled like this?" Bojue said.

"I have a good deal of pain in the back," Ximen said. "I need the massage."

"Well, you are very stout, and you have such rich food every day you must have a good deal of heat inside you."

"Doctor Ren has said to me more than once: 'Sir, though you seem so stout, you are really not very strong,' " Ximen Qing said. "He gave me a box of tonic, reinvigorating pills. He told me that these pills had originally been made for his Majesty by his Holiness Lin, and recommended me to take one every morning with human milk. But the last few days I have had so much to do I forgot all about the pills. You are always saying that I have too many ladies and that I see too much of them, but since the Sixth Lady died, I have had so much on my mind I have never thought about such things."

Then Han Daoguo came in. "I have just heard that our boat has been chartered," he said. "We shall be able to start on the twenty-fourth as we proposed."

Ximen Qing told Clerk Gan to go into the accounts, get the silver ready, and see that everything was packed up the following day. He said to Han Daoguo: "How much money have we made in our two shops?"

"About six thousand taels all together," Han Daoguo said.

Ximen told him to give two thousand taels to Cui Ben so that he could go and buy goods at Huzhou, and to take the remaining four thousand to buy cloth at Songjiang with Laibao. "You will come back by one of the first boats next year," he said. He told each of them to take five taels and go home to get ready.

"There is one matter I must mention," Han Daoguo said. "I am detailed to a tour of duty in Duke Yun's palace. They say I must go in person and will not accept substitute money. What shall I do?"

"You are in the same position as Laibao," Ximen said. "He gets out of it by simply paying three *qian* of silver every month."

"Brother Laibao was appointed by his Eminence the Imperial Tutor," Han Daoguo said. "The papers came, and the authorities at the palace dare not say a word. But I have to serve because my ancestors have always served. I can't do what he does."

"Go and write out a statement of your case and I will ask Doctor Ren to go to the palace and arrange matters with Master Wang. I am sure they will take your name off the register and allow you to give money in place of service. After that, you will only need to send a man there once a month."

Han Daoguo bowed and thanked him.

"Brother," Ying Bojue said, "if you can arrange this matter for him, he will be much easier in mind when he starts for the South."

By this time the massage was finished, and Ximen Qing went to the inner court to dress. He told a servant to give Little Zhou something to eat. Sometime later he returned, wearing a white velvet hat and a velvet cloak, and gave the barber three *qian* of silver. He told Wang Jing to go for Scholar Wen. The scholar came, wearing a tall hat and a broad girdle. They greeted one another, and a servant laid the table and brought in gruel. Ying Bojue and Scholar Wen sat in the places of honor, Ximen Qing in the host's seat, and Han Daoguo in the lower place. Ximen called for another bowl of gruel and a pair of chopsticks for Chen Jingji. Jingji, wearing a white hat and white gown, bowed to Bojue and the others and sat down beside Han Daoguo. They soon finished the gruel, and the things were cleared away. Han Daoguo left them.

Ximen Qing asked Scholar Wen whether he had written the letter. "I have a rough draft here," Scholar Wen said, "and when you have approved it, I will write it again." He took the draft from his sleeve and gave it to Ximen Qing. It read:

To the great and virtuous statesman, my worthy kinsman Yun Feng.

The time has flown since we parted at the Capital, and already half a year has passed. Sorrow has come upon me and I have lost my wife. You, from so great a distance, have been gracious enough to send an offering. And you have sent a letter that I value highly, an earnest of your kind feeling and generous actions. I am greatly indebted to you and shall never forget your kindness. My only fear is that my delinquencies in the office may bring disgrace upon you, since my position there is due to you. I trust that you will speak kindly for me to his Eminence. All that I have is of your giving.

I take this opportunity of asking after your well-being. I have thought of you continually.

With this letter I send ten silken Yangzhou handkerchiefs, ten of colored silk, twenty gold toothpicks and ten gold cups. These are but a slight token of my regard, and I trust you will accept them with indulgence.

Your kinsman Ximen Qing of Qinghe.

When Ximen Qing had read the letter, he told Jingji to pack up the presents. He asked Scholar Wen to copy the letter upon fine paper and seal it with his seal. Then he gave five taels of silver to the messenger Wang Yu.

The snow was heavier than before. Ximen invited Scholar Wen to stay with him in the study and admire the beauty of the landscape. The servants cleared the tables and brought wine. Then Ximen Qing saw someone peeping through the blind and asked who was there. Wang Jing told him it was Zheng Chun. Ximen called the boy in, and he came, carrying two boxes. He lifted them high before him, then knelt down before Ximen Qing. A small golden square box was opened and Ximen asked what was in it. "My sister Zheng Aiyue," said the boy, "knows how busy and tired you have been, and she sends you these two boxes of cakes." One of the two boxes contained pastries filled with fruits, and the other, pastries shaped like a spiral shell. "My sister prepared them with her own hands," Zheng Chun said. "She knows you like them and made them especially for you."

"It is only a day or two since you brought me some tea," Ximen said, "and now your sister has sent me these delightful pastries. I am very grateful to her."

"Splendid!" Ying Bojue said. "Hand them to me. I'll see what they're like. My daughter, who used to make these pastries so well, is dead, but now, I see, I have another daughter who knows how to make them." He picked up one and put it in his mouth. Then he took another and gave it to Scholar Wen, saying: "Here, old gentleman, try this. You will find it will make your teeth grow again and give new life to your flesh and bones. I give you my word: to have rare things like this is better than ten years added to one's life."

Scholar Wen put the pastry into his mouth. It seemed to melt at once. "Cakes like this," he said, "come from the West. They are not the kind of thing one sees every day. They ease the lungs and bring a feeling of genuine delight. A rarity indeed!"

"What is in the little box?" Ximen Qing asked Zheng Chun.

The boy knelt down again and handed the box to Ximen. "My sister has sent this for you alone," he said, softly.

Ximen Qing put the box on his knee, but, before he could open it, Ying Bojue snatched it away from him and opened it. There was a red silk handkerchief inside, embroidered with a pattern of entwined hearts, and in the handkerchief were melon seeds that Zheng Aiyue had cracked with her own teeth. Bojue tossed the handkerchief to Ximen Qing, grabbed two handfuls of melon seeds and crammed them into his mouth. Ximen Qing tried to stop him, but by this time there were only a few seeds left.

"You dog," cried Ximen, "are you starving? She sent them for me. Give them to me at once."

"It was my daughter who sent them," Bojue said, "so it is right and proper that I should have them. You, my son, have too many good things already."

"If Scholar Wen were not here," Ximen said, "I would tell you what I think about you. You dog, you really go beyond all bounds." He put the handkerchief in his sleeve and told Wang Jing to take the boxes to the inner court. Food and wine were brought. When they had drunk a cup of wine, Daian came and said that Li and Huang had come to pay their debt.

"How much have they brought?" Ximen Qing asked.

"They have brought a thousand taels," Daian said, "and they say they will pay more later."

"The ungodly scoundrels," Bojue cried, "they have deceived me. They never said a word to me about it. No wonder they did not put in an appearance during the ceremony. They must have been to Dongpingfu for the money. Take it, Brother, and have done with them. They have had credit enough. I shouldn't be surprised if, later, they weren't able to pay. I knew that Eunuch Xue was going to Dongpingfu to get some money for himself yesterday. I hoped that all the money would not go to that old ox, because I knew there wasn't any hope that you would get your money back if he got hold of it."

"I am not worrying about him," Ximen Qing said. "If they don't pay, I shall clap them into jail." He told Chen Jingji to get the scales and weigh the silver. "Then I will go and see them," he said.

Jingji came back. "I have weighed the silver," he said, "and there are exactly a thousand taels. I gave it to the Great Lady. Huang the Fourth says he would like to speak to you."

"Go and tell him I am entertaining some guests," Ximen Qing said. "He must come back after the twenty-fourth. I know he wants to get out of his contract."

"No," said Jingji. "He says it is another matter about which he would like to speak to you. It is a favor he wishes to ask."

"Then I will go and see him," Ximen said.

When he came to the hall, Huang the Fourth kowtowed and said: "I have now paid a thousand taels to your son-in-law, and I will pay shortly the remainder. There is another matter about which I should like to ask your help." He knelt down and burst into tears.

Ximen Qing raised him and asked what was the matter.

"My wife's father, Sun Qing, and his partner, Feng the Second, are in the cotton business at Dongchang. Feng the Second has a son, Feng Huai, a very unfilial fellow, who spends all his time at bawdy houses. One day he stole two bales of cotton. My father-in-law remonstrated with his partner, and Feng the Second gave his son a beating. Then the young man made trouble with my wife's brother, Sun Wen, and there was a fight. He knocked out one of my brother-in-law's teeth, but not before he had taken a hard knock on the head. Bystanders stopped the fight, and Feng's son went home, but something went wrong, and he died about a fort-night later. The dead young man's father-in-law is a notorious scamp of Hexi. His name is Bai the Fifth, but he is nicknamed Profiteer Bai and is a harborer of rogues and villains. He put up Feng the Second to bring an accusation, and Feng went to the court to accuse the Suns. The magistrate appointed Captain Li to investigate the case, but his Lordship was then awaiting the arrival of the Imperial barge and the matter was delegated to Tong, one of the magistrates of the Prefecture. Bai bribed the magistrate and persuaded some of the neighbors to give false evidence. They swore that, when the two young men were fighting, my father-in-law encour-aged them. Tong has sent to arrest my father-in-law. I have come to you to beg you to have pity and write a letter to Captain Li on his behalf. What I suggest is that, when my father-in-law has been in prison for a few days, Captain Li should be approached again. In the first place, my father-in-law had nothing whatever to do with the fighting, and secondly, the young man died so long after the actual fight that it was beyond the recognized limit. Besides, his own father had punished him first, so that it cannot be definitely said that Sun Wen was the cause of his death."

Ximen Qing looked at the paper Huang the Fourth had brought. It said: 'Sun Qing and Sun Wen, now held in prison at Dongchang, implore your favor and your gracious help.'

"Captain Li was here only the other day," Ximen said. "It was the first time we had met, so we can hardly be called intimate friends. How can I approach him in this matter?"

Huang the Fourth knelt down again. He cried and said: "You must have compassion on them, or both father and son will perish. If Sun Wen cannot be saved, at least let us save my father-in-law. It will be a noble act on your part. My father-in-law is sixty years old. If he is kept in prison during the wintry weather, it will certainly kill him."

Ximen Qing thought for a long time. Then he said: "I will write to his Lordship Qian of the Customs. He will speak to Captain Li. They passed their examination in the same year."

Once more Huang the Fourth knelt down. He took from his sleeve a card that said: "A hundred sacks of finest rice." He handed this to Ximen Qing and then brought out two parcels of silver. Ximen said he wanted none of his money.

"If it is no use to you," Huang the Fourth said, "you might perhaps pass it on to his Lordship Qian."

"Don't trouble about that," Ximen said. "If the matter is settled, I will send him some presents."

Ying Bojue came through the corner door.

"Brother," he said, "do nothing for this fellow Huang the Fourth. He is the sort of man who never burns incense to Buddha yet comes to fall before the knees of Buddha when he is in difficulties. Remember that, when you had the service for your dead lady, he never even sent you tea. Nor did he come himself. Why should you trouble about him?"

Huang the Fourth bowed to Ying Bojue. "Good uncle!" he said, "this is a serious matter and you are sentencing men to death. For the last month this business has kept me on the run, and I couldn't find a moment to come here. Yesterday I went to the office for the money, and today I have come to pay my debt and to ask his Lordship's aid to save my father-in-law. His Lordship refuses to take my offering, and I fear he is not willing to help me."

Bojue saw a hundred taels of snow-white silver. "Brother," he said, "are you going to do anything for him?"

"I don't know Captain Li well enough," Ximen said, "but I will buy a present of some sort and ask Qian to do what he can. I don't think I can take this money from Huang the Fourth."

"Then you make a mistake," Bojue said. "He comes and asks you for help, and it is not right that you should be put to expense in the matter. If you refuse to accept it, it will look as though you thought the gift too small. Take my advice and accept the money. If you don't need it yourself, pass it on to his Lordship Qian. Now, in Brother Huang's presence, I say that the fate of his father- and brother-in-law is entirely a question of luck. There is no knowing whether, even if the letter is delivered, they will get off scot-free. His Lordship here is no money-grubber. I think you ought to offer us a feast at the bawdy house."

"Uncle," Huang the Fourth said, "if you do this for me, you may be sure I shall offer you wine. Indeed, I shall make my brother-in-law come and kowtow to you. I may tell you that I have busied myself day and night over this affair and, hitherto, I have failed to get anyone to help me. If you refuse, I shall not know where to turn."

"You silly thing!" Bojue said, "of course it is a serious matter for you. You sleep with his daughter."

"Yes, indeed," Huang the Fourth said, "and she cries all the time."

Ximen Qing yielded to Bojue's persuasion and took the card, but he still refused the silver. Huang the Fourth implored him to take it, and went out, leaving it behind. Ying Bojue called him back and asked when he wanted the letter.

"It is very urgent," Huang the Fourth said, "and I should like it at once. Tomorrow morning I will send my son with your servant to deliver it. I should like to speak to the servant you decide to send."

"I will write the letter now," Ximen said. He sent for Daian and said to him: "Tomorrow morning you will have to take a letter." Then Huang the Fourth spoke to the boy, and they went out. When he came to the gate, he asked Daian to get for him the purse in which he had brought the silver. The boy went to the inner court to ask Wu Yueniang for it. She was making clothes with her two maids. Daian waited, but Yueniang said to him:

"We are too busy. We can't give it you now. Tell him he shall have it tomorrow."

"But he wants it very urgently," Daian said. "He has to go to Dongchang tomorrow, and he won't be able to come back. Please take the silver out of it and let me have the purse."

"Go and give him the thing and get rid of him," Yueniang said to Yuxiao.

Yuxiao went to the inner room and emptied the silver on to the bed. She brought the purse to Daian. "Take it away, you rascal," she said to him. "Nobody is going to eat it. What a nuisance you are!"

"If it hadn't been wanted, I shouldn't have troubled you," the boy said. He went out with the purse. When he reached the second door, a piece of silver, about three taels in weight, dropped out. One of the wrappers had been torn, and, when Yuxiao had emptied the silver in such a hurry, she did not notice that this piece had been left in the bottom of the bag. "What a stroke of luck," Daian said to himself. "Money for nothing!" He put it in his sleeve. He gave the purse to Huang the Fourth and promised to bring the letter the next morning.

Ximen Qing went back to the study and asked Scholar Wen to write the letter. Then he gave it to Daian.

They looked out over the snow. It seemed like willow fluff blowing in the wind, or withered pear blossoms dancing. Ximen Qing had a jar of doubly strong Magu wine opened, and told Chunhong to warm some. Meanwhile Zheng Chun played for them. Ximen Qing bade him play "The Wind Blows Softly through the Willows."

Qintong came and said that Han Daoguo had given him a paper to show his master. Ximen read it and said to the boy: "Take this to Doctor Ren's house and ask him to go to the palace and have Han's name taken off the list."

"It is too late now to go outside the city," Qintong said. "Shall I go tomorrow morning?"

Ximen Qing agreed. Then Laian brought a square box with several dishes and two large plates of pastries made of goose fat and rose flowers. Chen Jingji shared their meal. Ximen Qing told Wang Jing to give three dishes and some pastries to Zheng Chun and two large cups of wine. Zheng Chun knelt down and said: "I never drink wine."

"You foolish boy," Ying Bojue said, "it is very, very cold, and, besides, it is your father who offers it to you. You know your brother always has some."

"My brother may drink wine, but it is not for me," said the boy.

"Drink one cup," Bojue said, "and I will ask Wang Jing to drink the other for you."

But Wang Jing said he never touched wine.

"Foolish boy," Bojue said, "I am asking you to drink one for Zheng Chun. You ought to know by now that young people should not refuse anything their eiders give them. You must drink it." He stood up. Wang Jing held his nose and swallowed the wine.

"Dog!" Ximen Qing said. "What right have you to force him to drink?"

The boy drank only half a cup. Ying Bojue told Chunhong to drink the rest and asked him to sing some Southern songs.

"Wait a moment," Ximen Qing said, "I am going to have a game with Scholar Wen, and he can sing while we drink. That will be fun." He told Wang Jing to get the dice box and asked Scholar Wen to throw the dice first.

"I dare not," said Wen. "I ought to ask Master Ying to begin. What is your honorable name, worthy Sir?"

"My poor name is Nanpo,"* Bojue said.

"I will explain it to you, Master," Ximen Qing said jokingly. "So many gentlemen come to his place that there is no chance for him to get at the thing he keeps under the bed. In the evening, when he can get at it, he dare not pour it out in the street for fear his neighbors will curse him, so he tells his maid to take it to the south and empty it against the granary wall. That's why his second name is Nanpo."

Scholar Wen laughed. "But that is a different *po*. The character for 'pouring' has the water radical on one side and the word *fa* on the other. This *po* has the earth radical and the word *pi.*"

"*Pi* is the very word, Master," Ximen said. "There are always *pizi* (Southerners) with his wife."

"I did not mean that," Scholar Wen said, laughing.

"Master," Bojue said, "you don't know him. He is always making nasty jokes about people."

"A little joking serves to liven things up," the scholar said.

"Let us begin our game," Bojue said. "Don't bother about him. His mouth is always dribbling. Please begin. Don't stand on ceremony."

"When I throw the dice," Scholar Wen said, "we will have a quotation from some poem, or song, or some classical work, which must have the word 'snow' in it. If we can think of one, we drink a small cup; if not, a large one." He threw a one. "I know," he said, "it is long since snow fell on the wild bird's island." He passed the dice box to Ying Bojue, who threw a five.

Bojue thought for a long time but could not think what to say. "This is really terrible," he muttered. Finally he cried: 'I've got it! The plum flowers in the snow open their snow-white blossoms. What do you think of that?"

"That won't do," Scholar Wen said. "You said 'snow' twice."

"That's all right," Bojue said, "big snow and little snow!"

"What nonsense you always talk, you dog," Ximen said. He told Wang

---

*   This means, literally, "pouring at the south."

Jing to give Bojue a large cup of wine, and bade Chunhong sing a Southern song.

> The night was chill and the traveler hungry
> He went to the village to seek an inn.
> Snow hovers gently over the temples
> And drops thickly on the places for dancing.
> Now he must stay awhile.
> On the bank of the river he goes cheerfully
> To see the plum blossoms.
> In the courtyard, people with silver candles
> Go to appreciate the snow
> White snow, falling endlessly
> Dancing in the air like willow fluff.

Bojue was enjoying his wine when Laian brought fresh pastries and dessert. There were conch-shaped light pastries and things that looked like small black balls, wrapped in orange leaves. Bojue picked one up and put it to his nose. It smelled very sweet. He put it into his mouth. It tasted like honey, and he thought it most delicious. He could not imagine what it was. Ximen Qing told him to guess.

"Sugar-coated soap," Bojue said.

Ximen Qing laughed. "Sugar-coated soap would hardly be so pleasant," he said.

"I would say 'Plum pastry balls,' but there is a kernel."

"Come here, you dog, and I'll tell you," Ximen said, "for I don't suppose you will ever guess. They were brought for me from Hangzhou by one of my people, and are called coated plums. There are various kinds of medicine inside. The medicine is mixed with honey, and the plums are steeped in the mixture. Finally, they are covered with peppermint and orange leaves. That is why they taste so pleasant. Taken every morning, they are excellent for the chest. They get rid of foul breath, are useful against phlegm, tone down the effects of wine, and are splendid for the digestion. They are much better than plum pastry balls."

"How should I ever have thought of that if you hadn't told me?" Bojue said. "Master Wen, I think I'll have another." He said to Wang Jing: "Bring me some paper, I'm going to take a couple home to my wife." He picked up one of the shell-shaped pastries. "Is it true," he asked Zheng Chun, "that your sister made these herself?"

Zheng Chun knelt down and said: "Do you think I would lie to you? Zheng Aiyue spent hours over these few pastries."

"She did good work," Bojue said. "Look! They are marked exactly like real shells. The colors, red and white, stand out ever so clearly."

"My son," Ximen Qing said, "when you talk like this you make me think of her who is gone. She was the only one in my house who could make them, and, now she is no more, there is no one here to take her place."

"I told you sometime ago that that does not trouble me," Bojue said. "One of my daughters is dead, but there is still another to make such pastries for me. I must say you are a wonderful man to discover such wonderful people."

Ximen Qing laughed until his eyes were no more than a narrow slit. He slapped Ying Bojue and told him not to talk such nonsense. Scholar Wen said: "Gentlemen, no one can help seeing what good friends you are."

"Don't say that," Bojue said, "he is your nephew, you know."

"For twenty years, Master," Ximen Qing said, "I have been his step-father."

Seeing them making fun with one another, Chen Jingji stood up and went away. Scholar Wen put his hand before his mouth and laughed. Ying Bojue drank his wine. It was Ximen Qing's turn to throw the dice. He threw a seven. For a long time he racked his brains for a verse. Then he said: "I will give you a quotation from the 'Perfumed Girdle': 'The Lord of the East will go away, for the pear flowers look like snow.'"

"No," Ying Bojue said, "that won't do. The word 'snow' must be the ninth. You must drink a large cup." He filled a cup of wine to the brim, gave it to Ximen Qing, and told Chunhong to sing. "My child," he said to him, "if one may judge by the number of date stones in your belly, you must know more than a song or two." Chunhong sang another song.

It was getting dark and lights were brought. When Ximen Qing had finished his wine, Bojue said: "Your son-in-law has gone, so Scholar Wen will have to finish the game." Scholar Wen again threw a one. As he was thinking what to say, his eyes caught sight of a pair of scrolls hanging on the wall. On them was written, "The wind rustles the tender willows. It is night upon the bridge. The snowflakes gently touch the frozen plums.' There is Spring in the tiny courtyard." He took the line beginning "Snow-flakes" for his quotation.

"We can't have that," Ying Bojue said. "That doesn't come from your memory. You must drink a large cup." Chunhong offered wine to Scholar Wen. He drank it, and it made him drowsy. He nodded his head. Then he got up and excused himself. Bojue would have kept him, but Ximen Qing said:

"No, a scholar is a man of education and cannot drink much wine."

He told Huatong to take Master Wen home. This was what Scholar Wen desired. He got up and took leave of them.

Bojue said to Ximen Qing: "Scholar Wen is really a poor creature. He has had very little to drink, yet he is drunk already." He and Ximen Qing went on with their drinking.

At last Bojue himself stood up. "The ground is slippery, and I must go now," he said. "Don't forget, Brother, to see that Daian takes the letter tomorrow."

"Didn't you see me give it to him?" Ximen said. "He will go in the morning."

Ying Bojue pulled aside the lattice. The sky was full of clouds, and the ground was like ice. He asked for a lantern and for Zheng Chun to go with him. Ximen Qing gave the boy five *qian* of silver, and filled a jar with the coated plums and put them in a box for Zheng Aiyue. As they were going away, Ximen said to Bojue: "Be good with your younger brother."

"That is enough!" Bojue replied. "We are father and son and shall behave as such. But I may go and have a chat with that little whore Zheng Aiyue."

Qintong took them to the gate. Ximen Qing saw that the tables were cleared, then, supported by Laian, who carried a lantern, he went to the corner door. He passed by Jinlian's door, which was closed, and quietly went on to the rooms of Li Ping'er. He knocked gently and Yingchun opened the door. Laian went back. Ximen entered the room and looked at the portrait of his dead wife. He asked whether they had offered food before it. "We have just made an offering," Ruyi'er told him.

Ximen sat down on a chair and Yingchun brought him tea. He told her to help him undress. Ruyi'er, finding that he was going to spend the night, quickly made the bed and warmed it with a hot-water bottle. Then she helped him to bed, and Xiuchun went out to shut the corner door. The two maids went to sleep in the other room.

When he asked for more tea, the maids were too sleepy to wish to get it. They told Ruyi'er to hurry. She took off her clothes and got into bed with him. The wine he had drunk had aroused Ximen's passions. He took some of the secret medicine and put the clasp on his penis. She lay on her back, he parted her legs and pushed hard until her tongue froze and her cunt ran with abundant stream. She called him all the tender names she could think of. It was the middle of the night and so silent that the noise they made might have been heard far away. Ximen Qing found the woman's body as yielding as down. He put his arms around her and kissed her, then told her to squat upon the bed and suck. She did so, to his great satisfaction.

"My child," Ximen said to her, "your skin is as white as the Sixth Lady's was. Being with you is like being with her. Treat me well and faithfully, and I will be kind to you."

"You must not say that," Ruyi'er said. "Comparing me with her is like comparing Earth with Heaven. But my husband is dead, and, if you do not hate a creature so ugly as I am, look at me sometimes and I shall be more than content."

Ximen Qing asked how old she was.

"My animal is the Hare, and I am thirty-one."

"You are a year younger than I am," he said. He was delighted to find that not only did she talk sensibly, but she was no mean performer on the bed. Next morning she waited upon him hand and foot, put on his shoes and socks, and helped him to dress his hair. The two maids, Yingchun and Xiuchun, could not get near him. Ruyi'er asked him to give her some white silk to make a mourning gown for her dead mistress. Ximen Qing sent a boy to the shop to get three rolls of white silk so that both she and the maids might have white gowns. He gave them money and clothes and ornaments, and Wu Yueniang knew nothing about it.

But Pan Jinlian knew, and she went to see Yueniang. "You really must speak to him," she said. "The shameless fellow went and slept with that woman yesterday. The wretch might be starved. He is ready to carry on with anybody he can get. We can't let him go on like this. What shall we do if she has a baby? She would play the same game as Laiwang's wife did. We ought not to allow her such liberties."

"You always try to get me to do things of this sort," Yueniang said. "He is carrying on with this woman. You all want to keep in his good graces and let me bear the brunt. Why should I be such a fool? You tell me to talk to him about it. Well, I'm not going to do anything of the sort."

Jinlian went back to her room without another word.

The snow had stopped, and Ximen Qing told Daian to set out with the letter for Qian. When he returned from the office, Ping'an told him that Zhai's messenger had come for his answer. Ximen Qing gave it to him and asked why he had not come the day before. The messenger told him that he had been delayed because he had had to go to Governor Hou. He took Ximen's letter and went away.

When he had had his dinner, Ximen went to the shop and watched his men weighing out silver and packing up. On the twenty-fourth, they burned paper offerings and started for the South. Han Daoguo and Cui Ben took with them the two boys Rong Hai and Hu Xiu. Ximen gave them a letter and some presents for Miao Xiaohu.

By the twenty-sixth, Ximen had finished paying his visits of thanks to relatives and friends. One morning he was sitting in Yueniang's room, having his breakfast. His wife said to him: "The first day of next month is Zhangjie's birthday. We ought to send some sort of present to the Qiaos. The proverb says: 'Once a relative, always a relative,' and we ought not to cease these courtesies now that our baby is dead."

"I see no reason why we should," Ximen said. He told Laixing to buy enough presents to fill four boxes, silken clothes, two kerchiefs and a box of ornaments. Then he wrote a card and told Wang Jing to take the things to Master Qiao's house. After this he went to his study in the garden.

Daian came back. "His Lordship Qian," he said, "received your letter. He wrote a letter to Captain Li and gave it to the officer with whom Huang the Fourth's son-in-law went to Dongchangfu. Captain Li asked the magistrate Tong to send the prisoners and all the documents to him, so that he could go into the case himself. Old Sun was discharged and all that happened was that they had to give ten taels of silver to pay for the other man's funeral expenses. Sun Wen was sentenced for some trivial offense, given seventy stripes, and made to pay a small fine. The officer came back to tell his Lordship Qian, and now we have Captain Li's letter."

Ximen Qing was very pleased with Daian for handling the matter so adroitly. He opened the letter and read it. It was from Li to Qian and explained the situation.

I have received your letter [it read] and the matter is now quite clear. Feng the Second beat his son and, when his son fought with Sun Wen, both parties received injuries. The man's death took place after the statutory limit. It would be unjust to condemn the other man to death, and I have adjudged that he shall pay Feng ten taels of silver towards the funeral expenses. So there is an end to the case.

The letter was signed Li Jiyuan.

Ximen Qing asked where Sun Wen was now.

"He went home as soon as he came out of prison," Daian said. "Tomorrow he is coming with Huang the Fourth to kowtow to you. Huang gave me a tael of silver."

Ximen Qing told the boy to spend the money on shoes and socks and anything else he needed; Daian made a reverence to his master and went away. Ximen Qing lay down on the bed and went to sleep. Wang Jing burned some incense in a small burner and went out quietly.

Suddenly, Ximen Qing heard someone pushing aside the lattice. Li Ping'er came in. She was wearing a violet coat and a white silk skirt.

Her hair was disordered and her face very pale. She came forward and, standing beside the bed, said to him: Brother, you are sleeping here. I have come to see you. You know I was accused by that fellow, and I have been in prison. I still suffer from an issue of blood and I have suffered greatly, for I have been unable to escape from the unpleasantness. The other day you were kind enough to pray for mercy for me, and my sentence was reduced by three parts. Still that fellow insists that I must be punished severely. He demanded your arrest. I have come to warn you lest, sooner or later, you should fall into his hands. Now I am going to find a place for myself. Take care of yourself. Do not go to too many parties, and, when you go, come back early. Remember what I say." She threw her arms around him and sobbed.

"Sister," Ximen Qing cried, "tell me where you are going." But she pulled her hands away from him. He woke up and found it was a dream. And, when he woke, his eyes were filled with tears. From the shadow of the blind upon the floor, he knew that it was about noon. He was very sad.

> The snow has settled
> Its brightness shines upon the window.
> The fire is nearly out and the bed is cold.
> They meet again in a dream of love
> And the breeze sends the fragrance of plum blossom
> Through the curtains.

That morning they had sent presents to the Qiaos. Now Mistress Qiao sent Qiao Tong with an invitation to Yueniang and the other ladies. Yueniang was told that Ximen Qing was asleep in his study, so she did not wish to disturb him. She entertained Qiao Tong in the inner court. But Jinlian said: "Give me the card. I will go and see what he says." She came to the study and found Ximen lying on the bed. She sat down on the bed. "My son," she said, "you are talking to yourself. What is the matter with you? No wonder nobody ever sees you nowadays. You are too comfortable here."

As she talked, she looked more closely at him and saw that he had been crying. "What makes your eyes sore?" she said.

"Perhaps because I fell off the pillow," Ximen said.

"No, you have been crying."

"You silly slave," Ximen said. "Why should I cry?"

"You have been thinking of someone who is still dear to you."

"Don't talk nonsense about people dear to me or not dear to me," Ximen Qing said.

"You were thinking about Li Ping'er," Jinlian said. "And the nurse, Ruyi'er, is in your mind too. As for us, we find no place there. We don't count at all."

"Don't be so silly, you little strumpet," Ximen said. "I want to ask you something. That day when the Sixth Lady was put into her coffin, what clothes did you wear?"

"Why do you wish to know?"

"No particular reason," said Ximen, "I just wish to know."

"There must be some reason," Jinlian said. "Well, I wore silk, a white silk coat and a yellow silk skirt. And underneath, I wore a purple jacket, a white skirt and red vests." Ximen Qing nodded. "I have been an animal's doctor for twenty years," Jinlian continued, "but what is the matter with your donkey's stomach, I can't for the life of me make out. If you are not thinking about Li Ping'er, of whom are you thinking?"

"I have seen her in a dream," Ximen Qing said.

"Yes," Jinlian said, "that's just what you would do. When my nose tickles, it is a sign that I am going to sneeze. Now, even though she is dead, you still think of her warmly. It is a clear sign that you care nothing for the rest of us. When we die, nobody will bother about us."

Ximen Qing put his arms around her and kissed her. "Little oily mouth," he said, "you always think of something nasty to say."

"My son," Jinlian said, "I can see through you as clearly as I can see a cat with a black tail."

Their tongues met, and soon the sweetness softened their hearts. There was fragrance upon her lips, and the room in which they were was exquisitely perfumed. Ximen Qing was stirred. He kissed her. Then, lying on the bed, he displayed his penis and asked her to play with it. She bent her head and fondled it with her lips. She was wearing a gold tiger-headed pin. There were many pearls and plum flowers in her hair, and jewels and ornaments of all kinds on her head.

Suddenly, as they were sporting very pleasantly together, they heard Laian's voice saying that Ying Bojue had come. Ximen Qing told him to bring Bojue in, but Jinlian, greatly excited, cursed Laian. "Don't let him come until I am up," she cried.

"He is already in the courtyard," Laian said.

"Then tell him to keep out of the way."

Laian went to Ying Bojue. "Please wait outside a moment," he said. "There is someone in the study." Bojue went towards the pine hedges and looked at the bamboos, some of which were still covered with snow. Wang Jing pulled aside the lattice, and there was a rustle of skirts as Jinlian ran away like a wisp of mist.

Bojue came in and made a reverence to Ximen Qing. Then he sat down.

"It is several days since you were here," Ximen said. "Why is that?"

"Brother," Bojue said, "I am absolutely tired of life."

"Why?" Ximen asked.

"Lately," said Bojue, "I have been hard pressed for money, and, yesterday, without the slightest excuse, Chunhua went and had a baby. It would not have been so bad if it had been in the daytime, but it was in the middle of the night. She was in a bad way and I had to jump out of bed, get ready papers and bedclothes, and go out for the midwife. Ying Bao had gone with my brother to get some fodder, and there was I, as busy as could be, and not a soul to help me. I got a lantern and went down the street for old woman Feng. When she got there, the baby was born."

"A boy or a girl?" Ximen asked.

"A boy," Ying Bojue said.

"Well, you silly fellow, are you sorry to have a son? So that slave Chunhua has presented you with a son."

"*Aunt* Chun to you," said Bojue, laughing.

"Why did you marry her, you dog, if it is too much trouble for you to go for the midwife?"

"You don't seem to understand," Bojue said. "I am not like you, and, in this cold weather, I know it only too well. You are a rich man and a person of importance. When one of your ladies has a baby, it is as though fresh flowers were added to a piece of embroidered satin. Of course you are pleased. But poor people like us can't even bear the sight of our own shadows. What point is there in adding to our number? Each member of the household has to be fed and clothed. No! I feel as hard as hard can be. There's Ying Bao goes out to work every day. My brother never gives a thought to me. My eldest daughter has gone and got married, and now, Heaven be my witness! the second one is all ready to be. She will be thirteen years old at the end of this year. The other day some old woman came to ask about her. I said: 'There is no hurry. She is young enough yet. Don't worry me any more.' Then, if you please, this disgusting creature must choose to be born in the middle of the night. Heaven and earth seem dark to me. Where am I to turn for money? My wife saw me worrying, gave the old woman a silver pin, and sent her off. Tomorrow will be the baby's third day. A host of people know this and they are sure to come. And what about the ceremony when the child is a month old? When that day comes, the best thing I can do is to disappear and spend a few days at a temple."

Ximen Qing laughed. "If you do go," he said, "one of the priests will come and take your place in the bed. You seem to have some sense, you dog." He laughed again, but Bojue looked sulky and would not speak.

"Cheer up, my son," Ximen Qing said. "How much money do you need? You have only to say and you shall have it."

"Not very much," Bojue said.

"You must have enough to cover the expenses, or you will have to pawn your clothes again."

"Since you are so kind, Brother," Bojue said, "I think twenty taels will be sufficient. I did, in fact, write out a note, but I was ashamed to mention the matter, for I have troubled you so many times. I did not fill in the amount. Give me what you think fit, Brother."

"What are you talking about?" Ximen said. "We are friends, and I don't require any note from you."

As they were talking, Laian came in with tea. Ximen Qing told him to put down the cups and go for Wang Jing. When Wang Jing came, Ximen said to him: "Go to the inner court, and tell your mistress that, in the cabinet behind the bed, there are two packets of silver that came to me from his Excellency Song. Ask her to give you one of them."

The boy went away. He was soon back with the silver.

"Here are fifty taels," Ximen said, handing the packet to Ying Bojue. "Take them. I haven't opened the packet. You'd better open it yourself and see what is in it."

"But this is too much," Bojue said.

"You say your second daughter is growing up," said Ximen; "buy her some new clothes, and, later on, she will be glad of them."

"That is a good idea, Brother," Bojue said. He opened the packet. It was some of the silver that the officers had sent, divided into pieces of three taels each, of very fine quality. He was delighted and bowed to Ximen Qing. "Brother," he said, "how generous you are. No one else would help me as you do. But you will take this note, won't you?"

"You foolish lad," Ximen said, "why should I trouble about that? This is your parents' house or you would not come here to ask help so often. The baby does not belong only to you, he belongs to me too. It is my duty to help you rear him. When the ceremony of the first month is over, I will send for your wife. She will do for the interest on the money I have just given you."

"These last few days," Bojue said, "your aunt has been as thin as your mother."

They laughed and joked together. Then Bojue asked what had happened to Huang's relations.

"Qian wrote to Li," Ximen told him, "and Li sent for the accused and examined them himself. Both Sun Wen and his father were set free, with only ten taels to pay towards the funeral expenses."

"What luck for them!" Bojue exclaimed. "They would never find anybody else like you. No, not even if they took a lantern to look. And you wouldn't take anything from them, either dry or wet. But though you would not accept a present from them, you must take the money you had to spend on Qian. And don't forget to tell Huang he must give us a feast. If you won't tell him, I will. We have saved his brother-in-law's life, and that is no small matter."

Wu Yueniang was sitting in her room when Meng Yulou came. "My brother, Meng Rui, will soon be leaving for Sichuan and Guangtong," Yulou said. "He is going to buy stock. He has come to say good-bye and would like to see his Lordship. My brother is in my room. I don't know where his Lordship is. Will you send a boy for him?"

"He is with Ying the Second, in the garden," Yueniang said. "But, talking about asking him to come, Jinlian went to speak to him about the invitation Mistress Qiao sent us. Qiao Tong was here, waiting for the answer. I gave him tea, and we waited and waited, but she never came back. Qiao Tong lost patience and went off. A long time afterwards, I saw her and asked her if she had spoken to him about it. It was hard to get an answer out of her, but at last she said she had forgotten all about it. The card was still in her sleeve. She is like a donkey that has lost its tail. I don't know what she was doing with him, but she was there a very long time. She would tell me nothing, and I gave her a scolding. Then she went away."

After a while, Laian came in. Yueniang said to him: "Go and tell your father Uncle Meng is here."

When he heard this, Ximen Qing got up. He asked Bojue not to go away, saying he would be back in a moment. Then he went to the inner court. Yueniang told him about the invitation.

"Yes," Ximen Qing said, "but you must go alone. We are still in mourning, and it would not look well for a crowd to go."

Yueniang told him that Meng Rui was waiting to see him in Yulou's room. "He has come to say goodbye before he sets out to Sichuan and Guangtong," she said. She asked why he had sent for the silver.

"Last night Brother Ying's wife had a baby," Ximen said. "He needs some money. And he says that his second daughter is coming to a marriageable age. He is anxious about it."

"Brother Ying is getting on in years," Yueniang said. "Now that he has this child, his wife will be pleased. We must send her some rice to make gruel."

"Yes, indeed," Ximen said, "and we will ask Beggar Ying to send us an invitation to the ceremony of the first month. Then we shall see what Chunhua looks like."

"I don't suppose she's any different from any other woman," Yueniang said, laughing. "She has eyes and a nose, just like everybody else."

They sent Laian to ask Meng Rui to come. Meng Yulou came with her brother. When they had greeted one another and talked for a while, Ximen Qing took Uncle Meng to the study where Ying Bojue was. He told the boys to bring something to eat. The table was set and they sat down to drink. Ximen Qing told them to set an extra cover and sent Laian for Master Wen. But the boy came back and said the scholar had gone to call on Scholar Ni. Then Ximen said: "Go and fetch your brother-in-law." After a little while, Chen Jingji came. He greeted Meng Rui and sat down on the other side of the table.

"When are you starting?" Ximen Qing asked Meng Rui, "and how long do you expect to be away?"

"I am leaving on the second of next month," Meng Rui said, "but how long I shall be away I cannot tell. I am going to Jingzhou to buy paper, then to Sichuan and Guangtong for incense and wax. That will take me a year or two. When I have finished buying, I shall come back. I propose to go through Henan and Shaanxi by land but, when I come back, I shall come by water. That means taking the river to Jingzhou. I suppose, all together, it will be a journey of seven or eight thousand *li*."

Bojue asked how old he was. "I am twenty-six," the young man told him.

"You are a young man," Bojue said, "but you seem to know all there is to know about traveling and business. I myself have wasted my life at home."

More food was brought. Plates and dishes filled up the whole table. It was evening when Meng Rui went away. Ximen Qing took him to the gate and returned to Bojue. He happened to see two paper chests and told Jingji to fill them up. He asked Yueniang to get some of the clothes that had belonged to Li Ping'er and put them into the chests with some paper money. He said to Ying Bojue: "It is forty-two days now since she died. We haven't sent for any priests, but we are going to burn these chests."

"How quickly time passes," Bojue said. "It is more than a month since my sister-in-law died."

"Yes," Ximen Qing said, "the fifth of next month will be her last week's mind, and I must ask some priests to come and hold a service for her."

"This time, you ought to have the Buddhist priests," Bojue said.

"My wife tells me," Ximen said, "that when the sixth lady was alive, when her child was born and she suffered from continually flowing blood, she promised that our two nuns and some others should come and read prayers for her."

Bojue saw that it was getting late. "I must go," he said, "and you will have to be burning these papers for my sister-in-law." He bowed low and added: "Brother, you have been very kind to me and I will never forget it."

"Forget it or not," Ximen said, "don't try and make out that you are dreaming. When the time comes for the ceremony of the first month, all my ladies are going to take presents and congratulate you."

"There is no need for them to bring presents," Bojue said. "It will be good enough of them to come to my poor house."

"I tell you what," Ximen said; "you must dress up old Chunhua and fetch her along here for me to see."

"Your aunt tells me that, now she has a son, she won't require your services any more," Bojue said.

"Wait!" Ximen said. "I shall know how to deal with her when I see her."

Bojue laughed and went away. Ximen Qing told the boys to clear away. Then he went to the room of Li Ping'er. Chen Jingji and Laian had packed the paper chests. That day, offerings of paper things had been sent from all the neighboring temples. Ximen Qing watched Yingchun prepare the table and offer cakes, food, and soup to the dead lady. Incense was burned and candles lighted. Then he told Xiuchun to bid the ladies come and he, with them, burned paper offerings before the tablet. Chen Jingji took out the paper chests and burned them out of doors.

CHAPTER 68

The Party at Zheng Aiyue's House

So deep is her passion, even when she is old
She cannot restrain it.
The moon, the dew, the mist, the cloud,
In all of them is something to incite her love.
When a real man stands before her
How shall she control her yearning?

They whisper softly, one to the other,
Then love weaves its chains about them.
Even if their bowels were made of iron
They must melt.
It is time to say farewell
The water runs onward, but the flowers are faded.

When Ximen Qing had burned the paper offerings for Li Ping'er, he went to spend the night with Pan Jinlian. The next day, Ying Bojue sent him a present of lucky noodles. Then Huang the Fourth came with his brother-in-law, Sun Wenxiang. They kowtowed to Ximen Qing and offered a pig, a jar of wine, two roast geese, and two boxes of fruits. Ximen showed great reluctance to accept them, but Huang the Fourth fell on his knees and begged him to do so. "My Lord," he said, "you have saved our lives, and we and all our households feel that we must do something to show our gratitude. We can't think what to do. These are only trifles that you may care to give your servants." After much argument, Ximen Qing agreed to accept the pig and the wine, though only on the understanding that he would send them on to Qian.

"Well," Huang the Fourth said, "it would seem that since I cannot make you accept them, we shall have to take the rest away." Then he said: "When you are at liberty, we should very much like to give a little entertainment to Brother Ying and yourself."

"Oh, you mustn't pay attention to anything he suggests," Ximen Qing said. "He plays the fool too much. You have been good enough to offer me these presents, and there is no reason why you should go to all the trouble of entertaining me." Huang the Fourth and his brother-in-law thanked him repeatedly and went away.

On the first day of the eleventh month, when Ximen Qing had returned from the office, he set out again to take wine with Magistrate Li. Wu Yueniang, dressed in white, went alone to the Qiaos' to celebrate the birthday of Zhangjie. The same afternoon, Nun Xue came with two boxes of presents. She had heard that Yueniang wished to have a service on the fifth, and she slipped out quietly, without any of the other nuns knowing what she was about. As Yueniang was not at home, Li Jiao'er and Meng Yulou took tea with her. "The Great Lady," they said, "has gone to a birthday party at the Qiaos', but you must not go away, for she has something to say to you." The nun stayed.

Jinlian had not forgotten what Yuxiao had told her. She had said that Yueniang had conceived after taking some medicine the nuns had brought her. Ximen Qing had taken a fancy to the nurse, Ruyi'er, and Jinlian feared that the nurse might have a child, and win Ximen's favor for herself. So, secretly, she invited Nun Xue to go to her room, and gave her a tael of silver to get some medicine for her.

In the evening Yueniang returned and invited Xue to stay. The next day she asked Ximen Qing to give the nun five taels of silver. Xue, ignoring her sister in religion, Wang, arranged with eight other nuns to come to Ximen's house on the morning of the fifth. An altar was set up in the garden house. There they recited Dhāranīs from the Avatamsaka and Diamond Sutras and fulfilled the ceremonies of the Blood Vessel Sutra In the evening there was the ceremony of feeding the Hungry Ghosts. Aunt Wu, Aunt Hua, Uncle Wu, Ying Bojue and Scholar Wen were invited to eat monastic fare. The nuns chanted their liturgy, but used no musical instruments except the wooden fish and the sounding stone.

With Ying Bojue there came a servant from Huang the Fourth bringing a card of invitation. They were asked to go on the seventh to Zheng Aiyue's house. Ximen looked at the card and smiled. "I cannot go on the seventh," he said, "because I have an engagement at a birthday party on that day. But I shall be free tomorrow, if that will do. Will anybody else be there?"

"Only Li the Third and myself," Bojue said, "and four singing girls who will play selections from the *Story of the Western Pavilion*."

Ximen Qing gave orders that Huang the Fourth's messenger should be entertained, and then dismissed him. It was settled that the party should be held the following day.

"Huang the Fourth sent out some presents today, I believe," Bojue said.

"Yes," Ximen Qing said. "I didn't want to take anything, but he pressed me so hard that, in the end, I accepted a pig and some wine. I sent them with two rolls of white silk, two rolls of cloth made at the Eastern Capital, and fifty taels of silver to his Excellency Qian."

"Brother," Bojue said, "you wouldn't take their money in the first instance, and now you have given these four rolls of material to Qian. It will cost you at least thirty taels, all out of your own pocket. You treat them far too generously. Besides, you saved the lives of both father and son."

At sunset Ying Bojue went away. Ximen Qing asked him to come again the next day.

The nuns did not finish their service until the first night watch. Then they burned paper treasure chests and went away. Early next morning, Nun Wang, who had found out about the service that had been held the day before, came to complain. Xue, she said, had taken everything for herself, and she wanted her fee. Yueniang was surprised. "Why didn't you come yesterday?" she said. "I understood from Nun Xue that you had gone to a birthday party at Wang's place."

"That old whore Xue played a dirty trick on me," Nun Wang said. "She told me that the service was put off until today. Surely she hasn't taken all the money and not left me a penny?"

"I'm afraid you are too late," Yueniang said. "She had the money before the service, so that is all over and done with. But perhaps I can find a roll of cloth for you." She told Xiaoyu to give the nun a meal and to get the cloth for her.

Wang cursed and cursed. "The wicked old whore!" she cried. "She got the poor dead lady to have some scriptures printed and made a lot of money. She promised to share it with me, but every last bit of it went into her own pocket."

"That may be," said Yueniang, "but she told me that you had five taels for chanting texts to free the poor lady from her blood trouble. Why didn't you do it?"

"On the thirty-fifth day after the lady died," the nun said, "I and a number of other nuns kept chanting those texts for hour after hour in our temple."

"Why didn't you tell me so before?" Yueniang said. "I might have given you something for your pains."

Nun Wang said no more. She sat down, but could not keep still and, before very long, she went away to find Nun Xue and tell her exactly what she thought about her.

Ximen Qing came home from the office. He had hardly finished his meal when Ying Bojue arrived. Bojue was wearing a new silk hat, a gown the color of incense, and black boots with white soles. "It is past noon already," he said to Ximen Qing, "and time we were off. Huang has sent several times to summon us."

"We will take Master Wen with us," Ximen said. He told Wang Jing to go and summon the scholar, but, when the boy came back, he said Master Wen was not at home. He had gone to visit a friend.

"Don't let us wait for him," Bojue said. "These scholars are always running about visiting their friends. There is no telling when he will be back. We mustn't waste time."

Ximen Qing told Qintong to bring the yellow horse for Ying Bojue. "No," said Bojue. "None of your horses for me! When I go riding, I wobble about like the clapper of a bell. I'll go first, and you can come in a sedan chair at your leisure."

"Well, well," Ximen said, "do as you please."

Bojue went away and Ximen Qing called for his sedan chair. He ordered Qintong, Daian and four soldiers to attend him. Just as he was about to set out, Ping'an hurried in with a card. "The honorable gentleman from the Office of Works is on his way to see you," he said. "This is his card. His sedan chair will be here in a moment."

Ximen Qing ordered food to be prepared, and sent Laixing out to buy some special delicacies. An arrived, and Ximen Qing, wearing his ceremonial robes, went to meet him. An was wearing an embroidered ceremonial gown with a round collar, and a girdle with carved gold buckle. They sat down and the servants brought tea. The two men talked politely to one another.

"Sir," Ximen Qing said, "it was a great disappointment to me that I could not come in person to congratulate you upon your appointment. The other day you were good enough to write to me and send me presents on the occasion of my bereavement. I am very sorry indeed that I have not had any opportunity to show my appreciation of your kindness."

"I cannot say how much I regret that I could not come to the funeral," An said. "When I was at the Capital, I told the sad news to Zhai Yunfeng. Possibly he sent something to mark the occasion?"

"He did indeed," Ximen Qing said. "Even all that long way."

"I imagine that promotion is in store for you this year," An said.

"I am so unlettered and incompetent that I dare not hope for anything," Ximen said. "You, Sir, have been promoted, and at last you have an opportunity to display your talents. The splendid work you have done upon the river is well known."

"You flatter me," said An. "I am but a poor scholar, and, had it not been for his Eminence's kindness, I should never have been given that appointment. You can imagine what terribly hard work it has been in these days when people are so desperately poor. Then, a little while ago, his Majesty required marble. A great many of the bridges over the river had to be pulled down so that the boats could pass under them, and everywhere the Imperial vessels passed, officials and people had a very bad time. Again, the country is overrun by thieves and bandits, and things are at such a pass that even the most efficient administrator would find it impossible to do anything very much."

"Sir," said Ximen Qing, "a man of your undoubted gifts will certainly make short work of difficulties and obtain still further promotion. Does his Majesty's decree specify any particular time limit?"

"The work must be completed within three years," An said, "and the Emperor is going to appoint an envoy to make sacrifice to the God of the River."

While they were talking, Ximen Qing had ordered a table to be prepared, but An said: "It is very kind of you, but I am on my way to see Huang Taiyu."

Ximen Qing said: "You must stay long enough to take some light refreshment." A great number of delightful dainties were brought in, and wine was poured into golden cups. Meanwhile, An's attendants were entertained elsewhere. An drank three cups of wine and got up to go, promising to come again. Ximen Qing escorted him to the gate; he got into his sedan chair and was carried away.

Ximen Qing went back to the hall, took off his robes of ceremony, and put on a plain hat and a purple gown. He asked if Scholar Wen had returned. Daian said: "No, but Zheng Chun and Huang's boy, Laiding, have come for you. They have been waiting a long time." Ximen Qing went out, got into his sedan chair, and set off with his attendants for Zheng Aiyue's house.

When he arrived, the people of the house withdrew respectfully, one servant stood on either side of the door. Zheng Chun and Laiding went in to announce his coming. Ying Bojue was playing double-sixes with Li the Third, but, when they heard that Ximen Qing had come, they put aside their game. Zheng Aiyue and her sister Zheng Aixiang wore sealskin caps upon their hair, which was dressed in the style of Hangzhou. They looked as dainty as flowers. They both came out to welcome Ximen Qing and he got out of his sedan chair and went with them to the guest room. He had given orders that there should be no music upon his arrival, so the musicians did not play.

Li the Third and Huang the Fourth were the first to make reverence to him. Then came the old procuress, and lastly the two sisters. Two large chairs had been set in the place of honor and Ximen Qing and Ying Bojue sat down in them. Li, Huang, and the two girls sat opposite. When Daian asked if the sedan chair should be dismissed, Ximen said that the soldiers and the chair men might go away. He sent Qintong to see whether Master Wen had come home yet, saying that he was to be given the yellow horse to bring him more quickly.

Bojue asked what had kept Ximen so long. Ximen Qing told him about An's unexpected visit. Zheng Chun brought tea. Aixiang took a cup and offered it to Ying Bojue and Zheng Aiyue offered one to Ximen Qing. Bojue held out his hand for this one too. Then he said: "Oh, I beg your pardon. I thought it was meant for me."

"I would not pay you so much honor," said Aiyue.

"You never bother about anybody but this naughty husband of yours," Bojue said. "You ought to treat his friends as well as you treat him."

"I don't consider you are one of his friends," Aiyue said, laughing.

After tea, the four players kowtowed to Ximen Qing, and he asked their names. "When it is time for them to play," he said, "please tell them to use their drums only, no other instruments."

"Just as you wish," Huang the Fourth replied.

Thinking that Ximen might feel cold, the old procuress told Zheng Chun to pull down the blinds and put more coal upon the fire. Some of the band of ne'er-do-wells heard that Ximen Qing was at a party at Zheng Aiyue's house. They came to the door and poked their noses around the corner, but did not dare to go any farther. One of them, who knew Daian, asked the boy to speak to his master on their behalf. Daian went softly and told Ximen Qing, but the only response was a growl, and the men went off as fast as their legs would carry them.

Two tables were laid in the place of honor, one for Ximen Qing by himself, the other for Ying Bojue and Master Wen. The scholar had not yet come, but a place was left for him. Two other tables were set opposite, one for Li and Huang, the other for Zheng Aiyue and Aixiang. An excellent meal was served, and the tables were decorated with flowers in golden vases. Zheng Chun and Zheng Feng sang.

The party had just settled down when Scholar Wen arrived. He was wearing a tall hat, and a green gown. When he came in, he bowed to the company. "What makes you so late, Scholar?" Bojue said. "We have been waiting for you a long time."

"I am very sorry," Scholar Wen said, "I did not know you wanted me. I have been to see a poor old schoolfellow of mine. We talked about books and that made me late."

Huang the Fourth hastened to set a cup and chopsticks at Wen's place and the scholar sat down with Ying Bojue. Fresh dishes were brought for him. The two boys sang again. Afterwards the four singers began to play one of the acts of the *Story of the Western Pavilion*.

Then Daian came and said that Wu Yin'er had sent Wu Hui and another boy with some tea.

Zheng Aiyue's house and that of Wu Yin'er were in the same lane, only a short distance from one another. Wu Yin'er heard that Ximen Qing was taking wine at Zheng Aiyue's, and decided to send him some tea. Ximen called for the boys. They came and kowtowed. They told him their errand, then opened their tea baskets and each of them offered a cup of fragrant tea with melon seeds.

"What is Wu Yin'er doing today?" Ximen asked them.

"She is at home," the boy said.

Ximen Qing drank the tea and gave each of the boys three *qian* of silver. Then he told Daian and Wu Hui to go and fetch Wu Yin'er.

Zheng Aiyue was quick-witted enough to send Zheng Chun with them. "You go too," she told him, "and if she shows any signs of not wanting to come, tell her I won't love her any more."

"It makes me laugh," Ying Bojue said, "to think of you as partners in your particular trade."

"My good friend," Master Wen said, "you don't seem to understand. It is well known that people of the same profession and the same disposition are fondest of one another. He who finds he has more to hope from Heaven looks always Heavenward, and he whose help comes from the Earth, looks towards the Earth. It is perfectly natural that this young lady should invite another young lady to come and join her."

"Beggar Ying," said Zheng Aiyue, "you and Zheng Chun are just as much partners. You both are always to be found wherever there is anything to be had for the asking."

"My poor foolish child," Bojue said, "I was a rascal long before you were born. I was making love to your mother while you were still in her belly."

They laughed and joked till the players returned to play another act. Ximen Qing called the girl who played the part of Ying Ying and asked who she was. "Don't you recognize her, Father?" Aixiang said. "She is a niece of Han Jinchuan, and her name is Xiaochou. She is thirteen years old."

"She will turn out very well," Ximen said. "Even now, she has a most fascinating manner and she sings delightfully." He bade her serve wine to them. Huang the Fourth pressed everybody to eat and made himself most agreeable.

After a while, Wu Yin'er came. Upon her head was a white headdress with a band of pearls around it. She wore a white double-breasted silk coat with an embroidered hem. Beneath it, a light green silk skirt with a golden fringe. Her shoes were made of dark green silk. She smiled as she came and kowtowed to Ximen Qing. She made a reverence to the others. "You make me wild the very moment you come in," Ying Bojue said. "Am I the son of a concubine that you kowtow to his Lordship and only make a reverence to the rest of us? Really, you little strumpets give yourselves too many airs. If ever I am called upon to go to the court, I shan't forget this."

"Beggar Ying," Zheng Aiyue shouted at him, "you are nothing but an unmannerly scamp. In your slovenly rags, how can you expect to be taken for anyone of consequence?"

Once again the tables were set. Wu Yin'er sat down beside Ximen Qing. He noticed that she was wearing a white headdress and asked her for whom she was wearing mourning.

"Why, you must know," Wu Yin'er said, "it is for the Sixth Lady, of course."

This pleased Ximen Qing, and they talked together very fondly. Food was brought and Aiyue came to offer wine to Ximen. Wu Yin'er rose. "I must go and see my Aunt Zheng," she said. She went to the old procuress's room and made reverence to her. The old woman invited her to sit down and told a maid to bring a brazier, for she was afraid the girl might feel cold. After a while, Wu Yin'er went back to the others. Fresh courses were brought, but she took no more than a mouthful or two of soup and a piece of cake. Then she put down her chopsticks. "I understand you had a special service for my lady's last week's mind," she said to Ximen Qing.

"Yes," he said, "I must thank you for sending the tea."

"It was very poor tea I sent," Wu Yin'er said, "yet you thank me even for that. Rather should I thank you for the splendid presents you sent in return. They set my mother all in a flutter. I suggested to Zheng Aiyue and Li Guijie that they should send tea to you for my lady's last week's mind, but we did not know you were having any service."

"There were only a few nuns to chant a dirge," Ximen Qing said. "We did not invite any of our relatives and friends. I was overtired."

They drank their wine and talked. Wu Yin'er asked after Ximen's ladies. He told her they were all well.

"Father," Wu Yin'er said. "My lady died so suddenly, you must feel lonely when you go to her room. Do you still think about her?"

"Indeed I do," Ximen said. "The other day I was in my study, and, though it was broad daylight, I dreamed of her and found myself sobbing."

"I can quite understand," Wu Yin'er said. "You see, she died so suddenly."

"Now then!" Ying Bojue cried. "You two are talking about your loves while the rest of us are as dry as dry can be. If somebody doesn't come and offer me a cup of wine and sing a song, I shall go."

Li the Third and Huang the Fourth were greatly put out and hurriedly asked Aiyue and Aixiang to serve the wine. They sent for the musicians, and the two sisters, with Wu Yin'er, sat together near the fire and sang "Dallying with the Plum Blossoms." The sound of their voices was enough to break the rocks and make the clouds course more quickly. When they had finished their song, Ximen Qing said to Bojue: "You made them sing, now you must offer them wine."

"Oh, that's all right," Ying Bojue said. "They shall have all they want from me before they die. How would they like it? Shall I lie on my back with my limbs outstretched, or on my side, or shall I stand on one leg like a golden cockerel? I can do any of those things. Or perhaps they would like me to imitate a wild horse stampeding around the courtyard, a monkey offering nuts, a yellow dog piddling, or an angel pointing the way? Tell me, Brother, which way shall I deal with them?"

"I can't find words bad enough to curse you with, you dirty scoundrel!" Aixiang cried. "You are always talking nonsense."

Bojue put three cups on a plate. "Daughters," he said, "drink this from my hand. If you don't take it, I'll throw it all over you."

"I am not drinking any wine today," Aixiang said.

"Get down on your knees before my sister Aixiang and let me box your ears," Aiyue said. "Then I'll drink."

"And what do you say, Sister Wu Yin'er?" Bojue said.

"I am not very well today. I will only drink half a cup."

"If you don't go on your knees," Aiyue said, "you can implore me for a hundred days, but you won't get me to drink any."

"Uncle," Huang the Fourth said, "if you refuse to kneel down, it will show you don't know how to take a joke. Kneel down. I will ask them not to box your ears."

"I won't box his ears more than twice," Aiyue said, "that is, provided he kneels down."

"Master," Bojue said to Scholar Wen, "you see how these little strumpets carry things to extremes." There was no escape. He knelt down. Zheng Aiyue pulled up her sleeves and held out her slender hands.

"Now, you rascally beggar, will you ever be rude to me again? You must promise out loud, if you wish me to drink the wine." Bojue could not help himself. He promised that he would never be rude to her again. Zheng Aiyue slapped him twice, then drank the wine.

Bojue got up. "Well, most excellent little strumpet," he said, "are you going to drink all the wine and leave none for me?"

"Kneel down again," Aiyue said, "and I will give you another cup." She filled one and poured it down Bojue's mouth.

"Oh, you little whore," he cried, "you've spilled it all over my clothes. Let me tell you this is the very first time I've worn this suit. If you make a mess of it, I shall have to ask your sweetheart to buy me another one."

They laughed and went back to their places.

It was getting late, and lights were brought. Ximen Qing called for the dice box. He asked Scholar Wen to throw first, but Wen declined, saying it was not fitting that he should throw before his master. So Ximen Qing and Wu Yin'er played. They used twelve dice and played Catch the Red. Meanwhile, the four players sang and played. The wine was passed around again. Wu Yin'er went to Scholar Wen and played dice with him and Ying Bojue, while Aixiang went to Ximen Qing and guessed fingers with him. Then Aiyue went back to Ximen and played dice again. Wu Yin'er devoted herself to Li the Third and Huang the Fourth and offered wine to them.

Zheng Aiyue went to her room and dressed again. She put on a double-breasted coat of figured satin, a skirt of the color of the finest down, with blue spots and golden fringe. Her trousers were embroidered; her shoes scarlet, designed like a phoenix's bill. Upon her head she wore a small white sealskin cap. In the candlelight she looked more beautiful than ever. The sight of her aroused Ximen Qing's desire. He had drunk deeply, but he remembered what Li Ping'er had said to him in his dream: "When you are away from home, never drink too much." He got up and went to the inner court to wash his hands. The old procuress sent a maid with a lantern to light him, and Aiyue followed him. When he had done what he went to do, she held his hand, and they went together to her room. Moonlight was pouring through the windows, and the candles were burning brightly. The air was as warm as Spring, and sweetly perfumed. Ximen Qing took off his outer clothes and sat with her upon the bed, his legs intertwined with hers.

"Will you stay the night?" Aiyue asked.

"No, I must go home," Ximen said. "Wu Yin'er is here, and that makes me a little uncomfortable. Then I have to remember my official position. The Inspector is coming this year, and I must not run the risk of any scandal. I can only come to you in the daytime." He thanked her for the cakes she had sent. "But when I saw them," he said, "I could not help feeling sad. The Sixth Lady, when she was alive, was the only person who ever made them for me. Now she is dead, there is no one in my house who can do it."

"They are not hard to make, if you are careful about the right proportions," Aiyue said. "The melon seeds I sent you, I cracked with my own teeth. But I hear Beggar Ying ate them all."

"He did. The rascal took two handfuls and left me hardly any."

"Lucky for him," Aiyue said. "I might have sent them especially for him! Thank you very much for the coated plums. My mother took some and found them very good indeed. When she has a coughing fit, she coughs all through the night and upsets everybody in the house. But one of those coated plums in the mouth keeps her throat moist. My sister and I did not take many of them. We gave the jar to my mother because we thought it was good for her to take them morning and night."

"Tomorrow, I will send another jar for yourselves," Ximen promised.

"Have you been to see Li Guijie lately?" the girl asked.

"I have not seen her since the funeral."

"Did she send any tea for the fifth week's mind?"

"Yes, Li Ming brought it for her."

"I will tell you something," Aiyue said, "if you promise to keep it secret."

Ximen Qing asked what it was, but Aiyue thought for a while and then said she would not tell him. "If I do," she said, "it will look as though I talk about the other girls behind their backs."

Ximen put his arms around her. "Little oily mouth, tell me what you were going to say. I won't say a word to anybody."

They were talking when Ying Bojue burst into the room. "Ah, you good people! So you leave us behind and come here to talk secrets to one another?"

"Why do you always poke your nose into other people's business?" Aiyue said. "How dare you rush in here and frighten me like that?"

"You dog!" Ximen said. "Go back to the front court at once. What do you mean by leaving Master Wen and Wu Yin'er to come and see what we're about?"

Bojue sat down on the bed. "Let me kiss your arm," he said to Aiyue, "then I'll go away and leave you to amuse yourselves." He drew the girl's arm from her sleeve and praised it. "My child," he said, "one has only to see these hands of yours to realize that Heaven intended you for the life you lead."

"Oh, you rascal," Aiyue cried, "no words are bad enough for you."

Bojue took her hand and bit it. She cried out and cursed him. "Oh, vile Beggar Ying, you never stop playing these horrible tricks of yours." Then she said to Taohua, her maid: "Go after him and, when he is once outside the door, bolt it."

Then Aiyue told Ximen Qing all about Li Guijie and young master Wang. "Sun Guazui," she said, "Pockmarked Zhu, Little Zhang and some others went with young Master Wang to Guijie's place. He had given up Qi Xiang'er and taken on with Yuzhi, at the Qin's place. At both places, he has spent a great deal of money and, recently, he had to pawn his fur coat for thirty taels. He stole a pair of his mother's gold bracelets and gave them to Guijie for a month's enjoyment of her favors."

"The wicked little whore!" Ximen Qing said. "I told her to have nothing to do with that young scamp. She promised me faithfully she would give him up, and swore she would never see him again. She has deceived me."

"Father, don't be annoyed," Aiyue said. "I will tell you a way to get even with young master Wang. You will have no more reason to be angry."

Ximen Qing took her on his knees. "What is your idea?" he said. "Tell me."

"I will tell you if you promise not to say a word to anybody else, not even Beggar Ying. I don't want it to get about."

"I am not a fool," Ximen said. "Why should I mention it to anyone?"

"Master Wang's mother, Lady Lin, is not yet forty years old," Aiyue said. "She is a very fascinating woman. She pencils her eyebrows, paints her face, and gets herself up as cleverly as a fox. Her son spends all his time at the bawdy house and she receives gentlemen at home. She pretends to go to the nunnery, but, as a matter of fact, it is old woman Wen she really goes to see. That old woman arranges everything for her. I understand she is very expert in the arts of love. Now this is what I have to say. If you would like to make her acquaintance, it ought not to be very difficult. Then there is the young man's wife. She is about nineteen years old, and a niece of Grand Marshal Huang of the Eastern Capital. She is as pretty as a picture. She can play backgammon and chess, but she might as well be a widow, for her husband, young Wang, never spends any time with her. She is a very disappointed woman and more than twice has tried to hang herself. Somebody cut her down. If you can only get hold of the mother, you will not have much difficulty in making sure of the daughter."

Ximen Qing was delighted with the idea. He put his arms around Aiyue's neck. "How do you come to know all this, my child?" he said.

Aiyue often went to Wang's house herself, but she did not think fit to say so to Ximen Qing. "One of my friends told me," she said, "and once old woman Wen introduced me to her."

"Who was the man who visited her?" Ximen asked. "Was it Zhang the Second, the nephew of that wealthy Master Zhang of the High Street?"

"No," Aiyue said, "not that ugly fellow. His face is covered with pock-marks, and his eyes are all screwed up. He is not good-looking enough for an adventure of this sort. Nobody but the Jiang girls would take him on."

"Well, I can't guess who the man is," Ximen Qing said.

"I will tell you," Aiyue said. "He is a Southerner, the man who made a woman of me. He comes here on business twice a year, but he only stays here one or two nights. He is too fond of poaching."

Ximen was thrilled. "My child," he said, "you seem to be very fond of me, and I am going to give you thirty taels of silver every month. You can give the money to your mother and then it will not be necessary for you to have any other visitors. I will come and see you whenever I am free."

"Why so much as thirty or twenty taels, Father? A few taels for my mother will be enough. I shall be glad not to have to receive everybody who comes, and to belong to you alone."

"Most certainly I shall give you thirty taels," Ximen said. "Say no more about it."

They began to sport upon the bed. It was piled deep with coverlets. "Won't you take off your clothes, Father?" Aiyue asked.

"I am afraid I must keep my clothes on," Ximen Qing said. "They will be out of patience waiting for us." He pulled up the pillow for her. She took down her trousers and stretched herself upon her back. Ximen Qing lifted her dainty feet over his shoulders, then unloosed his blue silk trousers and put the clasp on his penis. The heart of the flower lay sweetly folded before him; the tender willow-like waist quivered.

This is a flower so delicate
It cannot endure violence.
The wind of Spring blows over it unceasingly
And when it reaches the flower's heart
Still seems unsatisfied.
There are no limits to their love.
Softly she calls him her precious boy.
There are no words can tell
The happiness of this night of Spring.

For a long time their love followed its course to their great delight. Ximen Qing breathed heavily, and she made strange little noises without ceasing, her hair spread out over the pillow. "My love," she murmured, "do not be so furious." Then their satisfaction reached its height, and sperm flowed from him in a stream. The rain ceased, and the clouds dispersed. They rose, dressed themselves, and washed their hands. Then, hand in hand, they went back to the hall.

Wu Yin'er, Aixiang, Scholar Wen and Ying Bojue were throwing dice and guessing fingers, all the time encouraging one another to drink, and being very merry together. When Ximen Qing came in, they rose and begged him to sit down. "A nice thing!" Bojue said. "You leave us here all this time and then come to have some wine. To steady your head, I suppose."

"We have been talking," Ximen Qing said.

"Talking indeed!" Bojue said. "I know the sort of secrets you have to tell one another." He took a large cup of wine already warmed, and they invited Ximen to drink. The four players sang.

Then Daian came and said: "The sedan chair is here." Ximen Qing pursed his lips as a sign that he was ready and Daian went out to bid the soldiers light their lanterns. As Ximen had made clear his intention not to stay any longer, everyone stood up and drank with him. He ordered the four players to sing "When First We Met, Shyness Restrained Us." Then Xiaochou took her lute and sang.

When the song was done, Wu Yin'er offered Ximen Qing a cup of wine while Aixiang and Aiyue offered wine to Ying Bojue and Scholar Wen. Li and Huang drank too. The four players sang again. When the cup had been emptied, they urged each other to drink again and the wine passed around twice more. The singers sang two more songs, and the wine and the music were finished at the same time.

Then Ximen Qing made ready to go. He told Daian to give packets of silver, some large, some small, to all who had waited on him. There were three *qian* of silver for each of the four players, five for the cook, and three for Wu Hui, Zheng Chun, and Zheng Feng. There were two *qian* for all the other servants, except Zheng Aiyue's maid, Taohua, who was given three. They kowtowed to express their thanks. Huang the Fourth did not wish them to accept these presents yet. "Uncle Ying," he said to Bojue, "won't you say something to his Lordship? It is still early, and he must sit down, just to show that he enjoys our entertainment." He turned to Aiyue. "Sister, you must help me to persuade him to stay."

"I have tried already," Aiyue said, "but he will not."

"I shall be very busy tomorrow, and I must go," Ximen Qing said. He bowed to Huang the Fourth. "I have had a very pleasant time," he said.

"Indeed I fear you have been starved," Huang the Fourth said, "and that is why you won't stay. It seems obvious that we have entertained you very poorly."

The three girls kowtowed. "When you get home," they said, "please give our humble duty to the Great Lady and the others. When we are free, we will come to see them."

"Yes, do," Ximen said. "Come any time and spend the day."

Lanterns were brought, and Ximen Qing went down the steps. Old woman Zheng came to make a reverence to him. "My lord," she said, "why must you go in such a hurry? I fear our cooking cannot have pleased you. There is another course to come yet."

"I have had everything I wanted," Ximen said. "Unfortunately, I have to get up very early in the morning to go and attend to some important business at the office. Brother Ying has nothing to do: ask him to stay."

Ying Bojue was going away with Ximen Qing, but Huang the Fourth stopped him. "If you go too, Uncle," he said, "it will be the last straw."

"Don't keep me," Bojue said. "Try Scholar Wen. If you can persuade him to stay, I shall believe you are a hero."

Scholar Wen tried to slip away, but Huang the Fourth's boy and Laian caught him by the waist and held him. Ximen Qing reached the gate. He asked Qintong whether he had brought anything for Scholar Wen to ride. "There's a donkey here," Qintong said. "Huatong is in charge of it."

Ximen called out to Scholar Wen: "There is an animal here for you to ride. You and Brother Ying stay. I must go now." They all went with him to the gate. Zheng Aiyue was holding his hand. She gave it a squeeze.

"Remember what I have told you," she said, "but keep it to yourself." She bade Zheng Chun go with Ximen to his house. Ximen got into his sedan chair and went away.

Outside the gate, Wu Yin'er said good-bye to everybody, and was going home with Wu Hui when Zheng Aiyue said: "If you see Guijie, don't say a word about this." Then they went back to their tables; the fire was replenished, and more wine poured out. With music, songs and wine, they passed the time very pleasantly, and the party did not break up until the third night watch. The entertainment cost Huang the Fourth about ten taels of silver.

Ximen Qing, with two soldiers carrying lanterns, reached home in his sedan chair, dismissed Zheng Chun, and went to bed.

The next day, Magistrate Xia sent a servant to ask Ximen Qing to go early to the office. There was a thief to be tried. He went, heard the case and did not return until midday. When he had finished dinner, Shen Ding came with a young man named Liu Bao, whom Uncle Shen introduced as a cook for the silk shop. Ximen Qing agreed to engage him and went to the study to get a return card to give to Shen Ding. There he found Daian and asked him what time Scholar Wen had come back the night before.

"I was in the shop," Daian said, "and had been in bed a long time before I heard Qintong knocking at the door of the house opposite. I think it must have been the third night watch. This morning, I asked him if he had been drunk. 'No,' he said, 'but Uncle Ying was, and he was sick all over the floor. Then Zheng Aiyue thought it was getting very late, and she sent Zheng Chun home with him.'" This made Ximen Qing laugh. He called the boy closer to him.

"You remember old woman Wen, who arranged my daughter's marriage. If you know where she lives, go and tell her I want her to come and see me at the house across the road."

"I don't know where she lives," Daian said, "but I will ask Brother-in-law."

"Yes, make sure, and then go right away," Ximen said.

Daian went to the shop and asked Chen Jingji where the old woman lived.

"What do you want with her?" Jingji said. "Go along East Street towards the south. Turn to the left when you have passed the bridge. You will find yourself on the Wangs' estate. In the middle of it is a guardhouse, and, close by, a small stone bridge. Cross the bridge and you will come to a lane that passes a nunnery. Go up there and the third house you come to will be a bean curd shop. A little farther along is a house with red doors. That is the place. Shout: 'Old Mother Wen,' and she will come out to you."

"It sounds like a witch directing a tinker," Daian said. "What a rigmarole! Tell me again. I shall never remember all that."

Jingji told him again.

"A fine walk!" Daian said. "I must have a horse." He went and got the big white horse, mounted it, whipped it up, and went off at a gallop. He followed all his instructions until he came to the guardhouse near the ruined stone bridge, and saw the red walls of the nunnery. He went up the lane until he reached a house with a sign to show that bean curd was sold there. Outside was an old woman drying horse dung.

"Does an old woman named Wen live about here?" Daian asked her.

"Yes," the old woman said. "The next house on the other side."

Daian went on and came to a house with red doors. He jumped down from his horse and knocked at the door with his whip. "Is Sister Wen at home?"

Wen Tang, the old woman's son, opened the door and asked Daian what he wanted.

"I have come from his Lordship Ximen to ask Madam Wen to go and see him at once," Daian said.

As soon as Wen Tang heard this, he asked Daian to go in. The boy tied up his horse and went into the house. Lucky papers were hanging up, and a number of people were engaged in reckoning up the amount of offerings. He waited some time, then a cup of tea was brought to him. "My mother is not at home," Wen Tang said, "but as soon as she comes back I will tell her, and she will come to see his Lordship tomorrow morning."

"If she is not at home," Daian said, "what is her donkey doing here?" He stood up and went to the inner court. Old Woman Wen was drinking tea with several other old women. She had no time to hide.

"Surely this is Sister Wen," Daian said. "Why was I told you were not at home?"

The old woman laughed and made a reverence. "Brother," she said, "would you mind going back and telling his Lordship that I have a party? I don't know what he wants, but I will come to see him tomorrow morning."

"I don't know what he wants you for," Daian said. "I only know he does want you. What an out-of-the-way hole of a place you live in. Getting here has made me quite exhausted."

"For the last few years," old woman Wen said, "when your master has bought any maids or arranged any marriages, he has always gone to Feng or Xue or Wang. He has ignored me completely. Why does he suddenly want me now? It is as though one saw beans burst before the pan is put on the fire. Perhaps, now that his Sixth Lady is dead, he wishes me to find him another lady to take her place?"

"I know nothing about that," Daian said. "You will find out when you see him."

"Well, Brother, sit down for a while and, when my guests go away, I'll go with you."

"My master wishes you to go at once," Daian said. "He told me so repeatedly. He is waiting to talk to you before he goes out."

"Stay until I've given you something to eat, then we'll start together."

"I don't want anything to eat."

Old woman Wen asked if Ximen's daughter had any children. Daian told her she had not. Then the old woman gave him some cakes and went to change her clothes. "You go first on your horse," she said, "and I'll follow on foot."

"Your donkey is here," Daian said. "Why don't you ride it?"

"My donkey?" said the old woman. "That donkey belongs to my neighbors of the bean curd shop. They leave it here to graze, and you think it is mine."

"But you used to have a donkey," the boy said.

"Yes, but sometime ago one of my young women hanged herself. I had to sell my old house to pay off her people, so you can hardly expect me to have kept the donkey."

"The house didn't matter very much," Daian said, "but I'm surprised you parted with the donkey. I should have thought you would have kept him with you day and night. If I'm not mistaken, that donkey was splendidly finished."

Old woman Wen laughed merrily. "Oh, you young monkey!" she cried, "I'm afraid you'll come to a bad end. I was taking you seriously. Well, it's some years since I saw you last and a fine clever-spoken lad you've become. You'll have to come to me when you think of finding a wife."

"My horse goes at a good pace, and you walk slowly. If you don't come soon, my master will be in a fine temper. Come on, up you get behind me."

"You young rascal," the old woman said, "I'm not your shadow. What do you think people in the street will say if they see me riding behind you?"

"Then hire this donkey. We will pay them when you get there."

"That sounds better," said the old woman. She told her son Wen Tang to saddle the donkey and put a pair of blinkers on him. Then she climbed on to his back and went with Daian to Ximen Qing.

CHAPTER 69

Lady Lin

When Daian and old woman Wen reached the house, Ping'an told them that Ximen Qing was at the shop across the road. Daian went to see him. He was in the study with Scholar Wen but, as soon as Daian came in, he went into another small room.

"Old woman Wen awaits your pleasure," Daian said to him. Ximen Qing bade the boy bring her in. The old woman raised the lattice quietly and came in. She kowtowed to him.

"Sister Wen," Ximen said, "it is a very long time since I saw you last."

"Yes," the old woman said. "I have been very busy."

"Where are you living now?" Ximen asked her.

"Unfortunately," the old woman said, "I had a lawsuit and was compelled to sell my old house. I am living now on the Wangs' estate, at the south end of the street."

"Stand up," Ximen said, "I have something to say to you." The old woman got up, and Ximen sent the boys out. Ping'an and Huatong went to the corner door, but Daian hid himself behind a curtain to listen.

"You frequently call to see ladies of quality," Ximen said. "Tell me, who are they?"

"The Princely family in the High Street, Major Zhou's, Master Qiao's, Master Chang's and Magistrate Xia's. I see them constantly."

"Do you happen to know the lady at General Wang's place?"

"She is one of my most regular patrons. The lady herself and her daughter-in-law are always buying flowers from me."

"If you know them well, I should like you to do something for me," Ximen said. He took up a piece of silver weighing five taels and gave it to her. "If you devise a scheme for getting the lady to your place, so that I can meet her only once, there will be more for you."

Old woman Wen laughed. "Who told you about her?" she said. "How did you come to hear of them?"

"There is a common saying," Ximen answered, "that as trees have their shadows, so people have their names. Why shouldn't I know of them?"

"The Lady is thirty-five years old," old woman Wen said, "and she is all you could desire. She is charming and intelligent, and she looks not a day over thirty. If she does carry on like this occasionally, she does so only in the strictest secrecy. Generally, when she goes out, she is accompanied by a train of servants. She goes wherever she has to go and comes straight back. Her son is now grown up, so, of course, she does not wish people to talk about her. Probably the stories you have heard are untrue. She has, indeed, a great big house and, when her son is not at home, it is possible a gentleman may sometimes come to visit her, but nobody ever hears about it. It would be quite impossible for her to come to my place. There are no conveniences there. Even if you offered me more money, I dare not take it. I would rather go and tell her what you have said to me."

"If you will not take my money, it means you will do nothing for me, and I shall be very much offended. Take it, and if this little business comes off, you shall have some silken clothes."

"You are so wealthy that that side of the affair does not trouble me," the old woman said. "I shall consider myself lucky if you so much as look my way." She knelt down and took the money. "I will go and speak to the lady. When I come back, I will tell you what she says."

"You must take every pains," Ximen said. "I shall expect you here. I won't send a boy for you."

"Very well," the old woman said. "Tomorrow perhaps, or maybe the day after. As soon as I am in a position to say anything, I will come and see you."

She went out. Daian came up and spoke to her. "Sister Wen," he said, "one tael is all I ask from you. It was I who told you to come, and you mustn't keep everything for yourself."

"You little monkey," old woman Wen said. "When we hear someone sifting grain on the other side of a wall, we have no means of telling whether the results are good or bad. It is just the same with this business." She went out, mounted the donkey, and her son led it away.

Ximen Qing and Scholar Wen chatted together for a while, then Magistrate Xia came. Ximen put on his hat and robes and went with Xia to see the Sub-Prefect Luo, whose name was Luo Wanxiang. It was late when he returned.

Old woman Wen was very pleased with the five taels she had received from Ximen Qing. In the afternoon when the tea party at her house was over, she went to call upon Lady Lin. She made a reverence to the lady, who asked why it was so long since she had called. Old woman Wen said she had been having a tea party and that she had been busy making preparations to go on a pilgrimage in the twelfth month.

"Why not send your son instead?" Lady Lin said.

"If I find I can't go, I shall have to send Wen Tang," the old woman said.

"When the time comes, I will give you some money for him."

The old woman thanked her. Lady Lin invited her to sit near the fire. The maid brought tea.

"Is the young master in?" old woman Wen asked, while she was drinking her tea.

"No," Lady Lin said, "he has not been home for two nights. He is always going with some villain or other to spend his nights in the haunts of vice. He seems to care nothing for his wife, who is an exquisite creature, and I don't know what can be done about it."

"Where is the young mistress?" the old woman said.

"She is in her room," Lady Lin said.

When the old woman was sure they were alone, she said: "I don't think you need worry any longer, Lady. I think I know a way to dispose of these bad companions, and get the young master back to his home, so that he never sets foot in a brothel again. But I dare not suggest it to you without your leave."

"I always listen to any suggestions you make," Lady Lin said. "If you have anything to say, speak out."

"His Lordship Ximen, who lives near the Town Hall," the old woman began, "is now an assistant magistrate and a military officer. He lends money to all the officials, and has four or five shops where he sells silks and medicines, cloth and thread. He has boats upon the river going up and down for his purchases. He buys salt from Yangzhou and incense and candles from Dongpingfu. Dozens of clerks are employed in his service. He is a ward of the Imperial Tutor Cai in the Eastern Capital, and a subordinate of Grand Marshal Zhu. He and Zhai, the Comptroller of the Imperial Tutor's household, are upon a footing of kinship. He is on friendly terms with the highest officers of the Province, not to mention their underlings. He has acre upon acre of property and so much rice that it rots in his barns. His wife, by his second marriage, is a daughter of Captain Wu. He has five or six ladies and scores of singing boys and dancing girls. There is continual feasting in his house. He is about thirty-one or thirty-two, in the very prime of life. He is tall and handsome, and he takes medicine to strengthen his weapon. In matters of love, none is more skilled than he. He plays backgammon and chess, and is an expert ball-player. He is well up in the philosophers and every kind of amusement. He profits by everything he sees. Indeed, so clever a man can only be compared to a fine piece of jade or a lump of pure gold.

"Now, Lady, he has heard that your family has held high rank for generations, and he knows that the young master has been in the military academy. He would very much like to make your acquaintance. Of course, he cannot do that without a preliminary meeting. The other day he was given to understand that your birthday is not far distant. He would like to be allowed to come in a friendly way to celebrate the occasion. He spoke to me about the matter. I said to him: 'I can quite see that you don't feel you can call without an introduction of some sort. Let me go and speak to the lady and ask her leave.' Lady, I don't regard this simply as a question of becoming friendly with him. You will be able to ask him to help you to get rid of the young master's bad companions. I do not think a man of his sort will be in any way damaging to the good fame of your house."

Lady Lin was already persuaded, but she said to the old woman: "We have never met. How can we suddenly pick up an acquaintance?"

"That need not trouble you," the old woman said. "I will go to him and say that you would be glad of his help about an accusation you propose to send to the courts against these rascals, and that you would be very much obliged if he would come and talk the matter over with you."

Lady Lin was satisfied, and it was arranged that she should expect him two days later, in the evening.

At dinnertime next day, the old woman came to see Ximen Qing. He was in his study when Daian came to tell him that she had come. He went to the inner room and pulled down the lattice. The old woman came and kowtowed to him. Daian, who knew well enough what was afoot, went out. Old woman Wen told Ximen she had succeeded in persuading Lady Lin. She had spoken highly of him, she said, explained his position, praised his generosity and amiability, spoken of his gay and lively nature. "She believed what I told her," the old woman said, "and she is willing to meet you tomorrow night. Her son will not be at home. She will offer you a meal and make a show of discussing legal matters with you."

Ximen Qing was delighted. He told Daian to get two rolls of fine silk for the old woman.

"When you go tomorrow," the old woman said, "don't be too early. Go at night, when it is quiet in the streets, and enter the house by the back door. Close to the back door is a house belonging to a woman called Duan. I shall be waiting there for you. Knock at the door, and I will come out and take you to Lady Lin's house. We shall have to be careful that none of the neighbors see us."

"I understand," Ximen Qing said. "Go to Madam Duan's and wait there for me. Don't go away. I shall certainly not be late."

Old woman Wen went back to tell Lady Lin the result of her conversation with Ximen.

That night, Ximen Qing went to Li Jiao'er's room. He was impatient for the next day and was sparing in his attentions. When the day came, he put on a white hat and went with Ying Bojue to Xie Xida's place to celebrate his birthday. Two singing girls were there. He drank only a few cups of wine and, as soon as it was dark, escaped from the party and mounted his horse. Daian and Qintong followed him. It was the nineteenth day of the month, and the moon was full. He set eyeshades on his eyes and turned into the road that led from the main street to Lady Lin's backdoor. It was late, and the street was quiet. Before he came to the door, he pulled up his horse and bade Daian knock at Madam Duan's door. This house belonged to Lady Lin. Old woman Wen had introduced Madam Duan to Lady Lin as a kind of guard for the back door and, whenever any business of this sort was to be done, the back door was always the place chosen as the rendezvous.

Old woman Wen heard the knocking and came to the door at once. She waited until Ximen Qing had dismounted and taken off his eyeshades. She told Qintong to wait with the horse beneath the eaves of a house close by. Daian went to wait in Madam Duan's house. Then the old woman took Ximen through the back door and fastened it securely behind them. They went through a passage that led to a courtyard. On one side were the five rooms that formed Lady Lin's apartments. The small door that led to them was closed. Old women Wen knocked softly. The sound was delightful to Ximen's ears. A maid came and opened the door. The old woman took Ximen Qing to the hall. When the screen was pulled aside, he saw that the place was brightly lit up by lamps and candles. In the place of honor was a portrait of Wang Jingchong, Commander-in-Chief of Taiyuan, and Duke of Fenyang. He wore a red dragon embroidered gown, with a jade girdle, and sat upon a great chair covered with a tiger skin, reading a book upon the art of war. Had his beard been longer, he would have looked like the God of War himself. Above the portrait was an inscription: "The Hall of Virtue and Righteousness." There were two scrolls written in the Li style, of which one read: "The Tradition of Integrity in this House stands ever firm as the pine tree and the bamboo." The other bore the legend: "His services to his country were many as the stars and glorious as the mountains."

Ximen Qing was looking at them when he heard a tinkling of the bells upon the door. Old woman Wen brought him a cup of tea. "Please ask the lady to come and see me," he said.

"Pray, Sir," the old woman said, "drink your tea. I have told her ladyship that you are here."

Lady Lin had hidden herself behind the door and was secretly taking stock of him. She found him tall and good-looking. He was wearing a white silk hat with sable ear covers, a purple woolen gown, and a pair of black shoes with white soles. She liked the looks of him. She quietly summoned old woman Wen and asked for whom he was wearing the white hat.

"His Sixth Lady died in the ninth month," the old woman said, "but though she is no more, he has still as many ladies as there are fingers on his hand. He is like a quail just let out from his cage, smart at the attack."

Lady Lin was more pleased than ever. Old woman Wen urged her to come and see Ximen, but she said it would embarrass her and she would rather he came to her room. The old woman went back to Ximen Qing and said: "The Lady would like you to go to her." She pulled aside the screen and he went in.

There were red hangings about Lady Lin's room and the floor was covered with carpets and rugs. There was a delightful odor of orchids and perfume, and the atmosphere was as balmy as that of Spring. The bed had embroidered curtains. The screens shone like the moon. Lady Lin wore a headdress of gold thread and jade, a full gown of white silk, and a coat of figured satin, with a gold design upon an incense-colored background. Her skirt was of the scarlet satin worn by ladies of the court, and her white silk shoes were high heeled. She was, indeed, an exquisite woman of the embroidered chamber, a goddess who, as it were, made sacrifice of her body for the love of men.

Ximen Qing bowed. "Lady," he said, "will you not sit in the place that is your due, that I may make reverence to you?"

"My lord," she said, "I pray you, do not."

Ximen Qing kowtowed to her twice, and she returned his greeting. Then he sat down on a chair and she sat on the edge of a small couch shaped like a comb. She was on the other side from him, but not immediately facing him.

Old woman Wen saw that the door to the courtyard was safely fastened. The servants withdrew. The door that led to young master Wang's apartments was secured. A maid brought tea.

"The lady," old woman Wen said, "has heard of your name and your position as an officer of the law. She would be very glad to know if you are disposed to help her."

"Pray tell me what I can do," Ximen said.

Lady Lin spoke for herself. "In truth," she said, "though I have inherited a title, I have not been well off since my husband's death. My son was brought up without the discipline that would have been good for him, and even now he has not passed his examination. He has studied at the military academy, but I fear his education has been neglected. Then, too, he has fallen into the clutches of some very objectionable fellows. They have carried him off to places of ill-fame, and, over and over again, he has brought my family to the verge of ruin. There are times when I think of going to the courts to make accusation against him, but I feel I cannot bring shame upon my dead husband. I have asked you to come, and, since I am telling you the truth, it is the same as though I actually went to the court. I shall esteem it a great favor if you will rid my son of these evil companions and so enable him to make a fresh start. If he will only change his present mood and attend to his studies, he will become a worthy successor to a worthy family. If you can bring this about, I shall be eternally grateful and try to make you a suitable return."

"Most estimable lady," Ximen Qing said, "please do not speak of reward. For generations your family has been one of exalted rank. Your son is at the military academy now, and, of course, he ought to think of his future and the title that will come down to him. Unfortunately, he has got mixed up with a pack of rascals and is giving himself up to wine and undesirable young women. It is only because he is young. Now that you have issued your commands, I will go to the office and have the rascals punished. You shall have no further trouble."

Lady Lin stood up and made a reverence. "I hope to be allowed to make you a present," she said.

"Please don't mention it," Ximen said. "We are such good friends."

As they talked, they exchanged glances that were more than affectionate. Old woman Wen set the table and put wine upon it. Ximen Qing made a show of reluctance to accept such an honor. "This is my first visit," he said. "I have come empty-handed. How can I accept such kindness at your hands?"

"Indeed," Lady Lin said, "it is I who should apologize for being taken unawares and having nothing more than this poor wine to offer you. I can only hope that it will serve to keep out the cold."

The maid poured out the wine. Lady Lin rose to offer him a cup. He stood up too and said: "I should be the first to offer wine."

"Today, perhaps," old woman Wen said, "you may be dispensed from offering wine to her Ladyship. The fifteenth day of the eleventh month is her birthday and, I suppose, you will come to congratulate her."

"Why didn't you tell me so before?" Ximen said. "Why, this is the ninth. There are only six days left. Of course I shall come to pay my respects."

Lady Lin smiled. "You are too kind," she said.

Sixteen bowls of delightful food were brought. Candles in silver candlesticks burned brightly on the table; a golden brazier on the floor gave forth splendid heat. They offered wine to one another, played games, and guessed fingers. Their smiles and merriment were an omen of clouds and rain, and, as we know, wine never fails to arouse the passions. The water clock dripped and dripped; the moon cast its beams upon the window. Their minds were obsessed by the same idea. Old woman Wen had withdrawn, and, though they called her several times, she made no answer. Seeing that they were alone, Ximen Qing gradually moved his chair nearer and nearer to her; his words became more and more affectionate. He pressed her hands, touched her arm, drew closer. Then he put his arms about her neck. She smiled but did not repulse him. She opened her red lips and he slipped his tongue into her mouth. They kissed, and smiled still more lovingly.

Lady Lin got up and fastened the door. She took off her long gown and some of her ornaments. Gently, she pulled aside the bed curtains and spread the embroidered coverlets. The pillows were set at one end of the bed. There was a delightful odor of perfume. Their perfect bodies met in an embrace; he felt the sweetness of her breasts.

Ximen Qing had been warned of the woman's skill in matters of love, and had brought his instruments with him. With the secret drug to encourage him, his passion blazed like fire. Their outstretched limbs quivered with a madness like that of butterflies and bees.

Ximen spent himself to the utmost to satisfy the woman, and they went on till it was very late. Lady Lin's hair was disordered; her pins had fallen out of place. She seemed like a weary flower, a tired willow. They lay down quietly together.

When they were up again and had put on their clothes, Lady Lin snuffed the candles and unlocked the door. She dressed herself before a mirror and told a maid to bring water for them to wash their hands. Again they pressed each other to drink. Ximen Qing drank three cups and got up to leave. Lady Lin could not persuade him to stay. She asked him to visit her again. Ximen Qing bowed and promised to come. She went with him as far as the door into the courtyard. Old woman Wen opened the back door and told Daian and Qintong to bring their master's horse.

The watchman was already beating his rounds from street to street. It was very still and the sky was white with frost. Ximen Qing went home.

The next day, when he had gone through his ordinary business at the office, he summoned two police runners and ordered them to find out who had been going about with Wang the Third, and the places to which they resorted. "Report to me," he said, "when you have made inquiries." He explained this to his colleague Xia by saying that "Young Wang the Third appears to be neglecting his studies. Yesterday his mother sent a man to me to say that it is not really his fault, but that he has got into the clutches of a pack of rascals. Unless we make an example of them, I'm afraid they will be the ruin of this scion of a famous house."

"You are right. We will deal with them as they deserve," said Xia.

The runners, armed with Ximen Qing's order, went around to find out the names and, in the afternoon, they came to his house and made their report. Ximen Qing examined their list. Upon it were the names of Sun Guazui, Zhu Shinian, Little Zhang, Nie Yue, Xiang the Third, Yu Kuan and Mohammedan Bai. The girls were Li Guijie and Qin Yuzhi.

Ximen Qing took up a brush and crossed out the names of the two girls and of Sun Guazui and Zhu Shinian. Then he gave orders that all the others should be arrested and brought before him the following day.

In the evening, the runners discovered Wang the Third and the others drinking and playing ball at Li Guijie's house. They surrounded the house, and, in the middle of the night, raided it. They arrested Little Zhang, Nie Yue, Yu Kuan, Mohammedan Bai and Xiang the Third. Sun Guazui and Zhu Shinian crawled away to the back of the house, and Wang the Third crept beneath Guijie's bed. Guijie and the others were terrified and did not know what to do. They came out to ask what the raid meant, but Wang the Third, in his hiding place, dared not move an inch. The old procuress imagined that the runners must have come again at the orders of some authority in the Capital. Before dawn, she made Li Ming dress and take Wang the Third home.

The police took Little Zhang and the others and threw them into jail for the night. The next day, when Ximen Qing arrived at the office, he went with Magistrate Xia to the hall of audience. The underlings were all in attendance. The prisoners were dragged forward. Each of them was placed in the screws and then beaten twenty times. Their skin was torn, their flesh bruised, and blood streamed from them. There was such a sound of beating that it reached the skies, and the noise of their groanings shook the earth.

"You outrageous scoundrels!" Ximen Qing cried. "You are always leading astray young men of good family and taking them to the bawdy house. I ought to give you most severe punishment, but, for this once, I am being kind to you and letting you off with a few stripes. If ever you come into my hands again, I will have you put in the cangue and make a show of you outside the Town Hall." He bade the officials kick them out, and they ran for their lives.

Having settled this matter, Ximen Qing and Xia retired to a room to drink tea.

"Yesterday," Xia said, "I had a letter from my kinsman, Grand Secretary Cui, in which he says that a report upon our work has reached the capital, but, as yet, its consequences are unknown. I think we might send a man to Huaiqingfu to see whether any news is to be had from Lin Cangfeng, our colleague there."

Ximen Qing agreed. They summoned a man and said to him: "Here are five *qian* of silver. Take them and go to Huaiqingfu and call upon Captain Lin. Take our cards and find out what you can about the report and when we are going to know what has happened in regard to it." The man took the silver and the cards, went to his room to get his things ready, called for a horse, and started on his journey. Ximen Qing and Magistrate Xia went home.

When Little Zhang and his friends escaped from the court, they could not imagine why they had, so unexpectedly, got into trouble. One blamed another, but they found it impossible to decide who had given them away.

"I think somebody in the Eastern Capital is responsible," Little Zhang said.

"No," said Mohammedan Bai, "if it had been that, we should not have got off so easily."

There is an old saying: Goldsmiths are the greatest thieves, and singing girls can never be outdone in cunning. So it was with these rascals. They were as artful as could be. Nie Yue hit upon the solution.

"I know what it is," he said. "Ximen Qing is anxious to put young Master Wang in his place. You see, he was playing with Ximen's own girl. When there is a fight between a dragon and a tiger, the little wolves come off badly."

"It sounds likely," Little Zhang said, "and we come off the worst. Sun Guazui and Zhu Shinian were there with us, but we were the only ones who got into trouble."

"Don't be silly!" Yu Kuan said, "you know they are friends of Ximen. If he had arrested them, they would have been on their knees and he would have been sitting there, and it would not have been very pleasant for him."

"Why weren't the girls taken?" Little Zhang said.

"He is very fond of both of them," Nie Yue said. "Guijie is his own girl, and he would never think of arresting her. It's no use complaining. Put the blame on our bad luck. It's that which has brought us to this pass. By the way, I noticed that Magistrate Xia never spoke a word. That is how I know this is one of Ximen's tricks, and his alone. Let us go to Guijie's house and see what Wang the Third has to say. We can't have our backs broken for nothing. If we don't get some money out of him, the girls will think we're fools."

They went to Guijie's house. The door was closed as though it were of iron. They knocked for a long time, and, at last, a maid came and asked who was there. She did not open the door.

"We have come to see Master Wang," Little Zhang said.

"He is not here," the maid said. "He went home last night. There is nobody here. I can't let you in."

They went to Wang's house and marched into the parlor. Wang the Third heard that they had come and hid himself in his own room, terrified. After a long delay, he sent a boy to say he was not at home.

"Ah," they cried in chorus, "if he is not at home, where is he? Send for him."

Yu Kuan said: "Look here! It's no use his pretending to be half asleep. We have been hauled before the courts, beaten and kicked. Now they want him there." He pulled up his gown and showed the boy his legs. "Go and tell your master that we have been beaten on his account," he roared.

One after the other, they lay down on the benches and groaned and yelled. Wang the Third was less inclined than ever to come out. He said to his mother: "Mother, you must save me."

"What can I do?" his mother said, "I am only a woman."

The men began to lose patience and demanded that Lady Lin should speak to them. She did not go to them, but spoke from behind a screen.

"Wait a while," she said. "Really, he is not at home. I know, for a fact, that he is at my estate outside the city. I will send for him."

"Do, Lady," Little Zhang said, "and please be quick about it. This business must be settled, and the only thing to do with a wart is to cut it. Your son is the cause of this trouble, and we have had to bear the brunt of it. We have been dismissed now, but the court has still to deal with him. Until he comes, there will be no end to the trouble."

Lady Lin bade her servants take them some tea. Wang the Third was as frightened as a ghost. He implored his mother to find someone to get him out of the difficulty. At last, Lady Lin said: "I believe old woman Wen knows his Lordship Ximen. Some years ago, she acted as intermediary in his daughter's marriage. She must know him well."

"If she does, send for her," Wang the Third said.

"But a few days ago," his mother said, "you insulted her and she has not been here since. You offended her. I don't see how I can ask her now, and I don't suppose she would come if I did."

"Good Mother," Wang the Third said, "this matter is extremely serious. Send for her, and I will beg her pardon."

Lady Lin sent Yong Ding, the boy, to fetch the old woman. Yong Ding went quietly out by the back gate and brought her.

"Old mother Wen," Wang the Third said, "you know his Lordship Ximen and you must save my life."

The old woman pretended she could do nothing. "I arranged his daughter's wedding some years ago, but I have hardly been to his house since. It is a very big establishment. I can hardly expect to go there very often."

Wang the Third knelt down. "Old mother Wen," he said, "if you will only help me, I will see you do not lose by it. I will remember your kindness as long as I live. These fellows are trying to get me to go to the court, and I don't want to go."

Old woman Wen looked at Lady Lin. "Yes," the young man's mother said, "help him if you can."

"I am not going alone," the old woman said. "Put on your hat and clothes, Sir. I will take you to see his Lordship, and you can settle the business for yourself. I will say what I can on your behalf and, doubtless, everything will soon be all right."

"These fellows are very anxious to find me," Wang the Third said. "I am afraid they will see us as we go out."

"Don't worry about that," old woman Wen said. "I will go and pacify them. I'll arrange for them to have something to eat and drink and, while they are eating, I'll get you out by the back door. They won't see us."

She went to the outer hall and made a reverence to Little Zhang and the others. "I have come on behalf of her Ladyship," she said to them, "to assure you that the young gentleman is not at home. She has sent for him, and he will be here shortly. Sit down a while. We know you have suffered, but, when the young master comes back, he will certainly make it up to you. We don't blame you for coming since you have been mixed up in this affair. Besides, you came by order of the court and not of your own accord. I'm sure that, when the young master comes back, it will all end happily."

When they heard this, they cried, with one accord: "Old woman, you are talking sense. If you had come before and spoken to us in this strain, we should not have been so impatient and ill-mannered. But, you see, we could get nothing out of them but: 'He is not at home.' Nothing else. And it looked as if we were held responsible for all the trouble. He was the cause of our being beaten, and now the police are after him. What's the use his trying to get out of it with a 'not at home'? Does he get someone else to take his place when he is eating meat or drinking wine? Old woman, you seem to see things in the proper light. Here is a hint for you. If he likes to spend a little money and get the matter settled, well and good. It might even be managed without his seeing us, if he doesn't wish to do so. This is a military court, and things are more easily settled in it."

"Brothers," the old woman said, "there is much wisdom in what you say. I will ask the lady to have food and wine served for your entertainment. You must be hungry."

"Old mother," they said, "you seem to be sympathetic. To tell the truth, not a drop of water has passed our lips since we left the court."

Old woman Wen went back to the inner court, and foraged about till she got two *qian* worth of wine, one *qian* worth of cakes, and several large plates of pork, mutton, and beef. These were taken to the men, and she encouraged them to set to. Meanwhile, Wang the Third dressed himself in academic robes and wrote a petition. Old woman Wen smuggled him through the inner court. He put on a pair of eyeshades and they walked to Ximen's house.

When they reached the gateway, Ping'an, who knew old woman Wen, said: "My master is in the great hall. What do you want with him?"

The old woman handed him a visiting card and said: "Brother, kindly take this to your master." She asked Wang the Third to give two *qian* of silver to the boy. Ping'an took the card to Ximen Qing. Ximen looked at it. It bore the inscription: 'The young student, Wang Cai.'

He sent for old woman Wen, and she told him what had happened. He went into the hall and sent the boy to ask Wang the Third to go in. He did not change his clothes before going to receive the visitor. When he saw Wang the Third dressed in full ceremonial attire, he said to the old woman: "Sister Wen, why didn't you tell me? I am not suitably dressed." He said to the servants: "Bring my clothes at once." Wang the Third hastily stopped them.

"Uncle," he said, "pray don't trouble. I have come to see you, but I beg you not to put yourself to any inconvenience."

When they were in the great hall, Wang the Third insisted upon making a most profound reverence to Ximen Qing. Ximen smiled. "This is my house," he said, "I can't possibly allow it." He made the first reverence himself.

"How sorry I am that I have never called on you before," Wang the Third began.

"I hardly feel that we are strangers," Ximen said.

Again, Wang the Third pressed Ximen Qing to accept the honor. "I am your nephew," he said, "and you must accept it. It will show that you forgive me for having troubled you."

They compromised. Ximen Qing asked the young man to sit down. Wang the Third sat politely upon the edge of his chair. Tea was brought.

"I am very anxious for your assistance," Wang the Third said, taking a paper from his sleeve. He handed it to Ximen Qing and knelt down.

Ximen pulled him up again. "Tell me what I can do for you," he said.

"I am utterly ashamed of myself," Wang the Third said. "Only for the sake of my ancestors and their good fame do I venture to ask your forgiveness. Save me from the courts, and I will remember your kindness forever. I am afraid, afraid."

Ximen Qing unrolled the paper and looked at it. The five names were written on it.

"What?" he said. "These rogues again? I have given them one beating today. Why have they come to you?"

"They said that, when you had done with them, you ordered them to come for me. They are at my house now, roaring and shrieking insults. They demand money. There was nothing I could do but come and implore your help." He brought out a list of presents and gave it to Ximen Qing.

"Why do you offer me this?" Ximen said. "When I threw out those rogues, I had no idea they would come and make trouble with you." He returned the list of presents to the young man. "Go home," he said, "I will send and have the scoundrels arrested at once. I hope I may see you again soon."

"Since you have been so kind," the young man said, "I will certainly come to offer my thanks." He went out uttering innumerable protestations of gratitude.

Ximen Qing went with him as far as the second door. "I will not go farther with you," he said, "since I am not wearing my ceremonial dress." Wang the Third put on his eyeshades and went away with a boy. Old woman Wen waited to see Ximen Qing. "Not a word to those fellows," he said to her, "I am sending men to arrest them at once." Old woman Wen rejoined Wang the Third.

Ximen Qing sent four soldiers and a sergeant to the young man's house. The rascals were drinking and making a terrible din. The soldiers went in and arrested them. So frightened were they when the chains were put on them that they became as pale as death.

"Wang the Third has deceived us finely," they said. "He got us to stay here and then played this trick upon us."

"No nonsense now!" said the soldiers, "you had better beg for mercy from his Lordship Ximen."

"You are right," Little Zhang said.

They came to Ximen's house. The soldiers and Ping'an held out their hands for money, saying if they did not get it, they would not take them in. The men could not help themselves. Some took off their cloaks, others gave their pins, and, at last, word was taken to Ximen Qing. There was a long delay, then Ximen Qing came to the hall and they were taken in. They fell upon their knees.

"Now, you rogues," Ximen said, "I sent you about your business, and you went and pretended you had come from me, in an attempt to get money from these people. How much did you get? If you don't tell me, it will mean the screws again."

At this, the soldiers got busy with the thumbscrews, new and strong ones. Little Zhang and his companions kowtowed and begged for mercy. "We didn't get a penny," they said. "It is true we told them the court had ordered us to go there, but they only gave us something to eat. We never asked for anything else."

"You had no business there at all," Ximen Qing said. "You scoundrelly fellows are always leading honest young men astray. I loathe the very sight of you. If you do not confess, you shall be thrown into jail and, tomorrow, I will try you and have cangues put about your necks."

They all cried: "Heaven have mercy on us! Be merciful, and we will never go and cause them trouble again. Even if we don't get the cangue, to have to go to jail at a cold season like this will certainly be the death of us."

"Once again I forgive you," Ximen Qing said, "but you must repent and give up your evil ways. Henceforth, devote yourselves to steady honest work and don't go leading young men into evil courses. If you come before me again, I will have you beaten to death." He told the soldiers to kick them out. They ran for their lives. Ximen Qing went to the inner court.

"Who was your young visitor?" Wu Yueniang asked him.

"It was Wang the Third, the heir to General Wang. You remember the trouble there was sometime ago at Li Guijie's house? It was the same young man. He has been keeping that little strumpet and giving her thirty taels a month. No wonder she has been behaving so strangely. She had this young fellow completely at her feet. I found out about it and sent to arrest the rogues and have them brought before me. I had them beaten. Then they went to the Wangs' place and created a disturbance in the hope of getting money out of the young man. They told him I wanted him. He has never been before the court, and he was frightened and came with old woman Wen to ask me to help him. He brought fifty taels. I had the fellows re-arrested and put a stop to their games. They will make no more trouble. But what an unfortunate thing for that family to have such a bad young man. His grandfather was a man of great eminence, a general, in fact. This young man is at the military academy, but he never gives a thought to his career, neglects his flower-like young wife, and goes with these rascals to the bawdy house every night. All these bad habits before he is twenty."

"You seem to me like a young blackbird making disparaging remarks about a black pig," Yueniang said. "You only see things from your own point of view. You fancy yourself an angel, but, to me, you and he appear to have drunk from the same well. Are you a better man than he is that you should find fault with his goings on?"

Ximen Qing made no reply to this. Food was brought. Then Laian came and said Ying Bojue had come. "Take him to the study. I will be there in a few minutes," Ximen said to the boy. Wang Jing opened the study and showed in Bojue. Sometime later, Ximen Qing joined him. The two men sat down to talk.

"Why did you leave Brother Xie's place so early the other day?" Bojue asked.

"I have been very busy, and it is almost time for the inspection. I have sent people to the Capital to see what they can find out. You mustn't compare me with yourself, you, who never have anything to do."

"Has there been anything of interest at the office lately?" Ying Bojue said.

"There is always something," Ximen Qing said.

"I hear you had Little Zhang and some others arrested at Guijie's place the other evening. Old Sun and Zhu escaped, but the others got a beating at the office. When they had left there, they went and made trouble at Wang's place. Why wouldn't you tell me?"

"You dog!" Ximen said, "where did you hear all this? You have got hold of the wrong story, It was not my court, but Major Zhou's."

"Nothing of the sort," Bojue said, "Major Zhou had nothing to do with it."

"Perhaps somebody came from the Eastern Capital."

"Li Ming told me all about it this morning," Bojue said. "He said his people were in a terrible state, and Guijie, who was almost frightened to death, is still in bed. They thought the runners had come from the Eastern Capital but, this morning, they found it was your office."

"I haven't been to the office for several days," Ximen Qing said. "I know nothing about it. As for Guijie, she swore an oath that she would never have anything more to do with Wang the Third. I don't believe she is so frightened that she is still in bed."

Ying Bojue caught the flicker of a smile about Ximen's lips. "Brother," he said, "you almost took me in. Do tell me. How did old Sun and Zhu manage to escape? I can't believe the runners are so careless when they arrest people. You had a finger in the pie somewhere.

You evidently determined to punish the sheep so as to teach the young horses a lesson. I suppose you meant to frighten Guijie, and let her realize what a powerful man you are. You wouldn't go so far as to arrest her—that would have been too hard, so you treat one set of people in one way and another set in another way. If old Sun and Zhu meet you, they wont know what to say for themselves. It was a very clever move on your part, making a show of repairing the bridge in one place and secretly posting your soldiers in another. Without flattering you, Brother, I must say it was a very clever scheme. A brilliant man never gives himself away. If you had done this openly, there would be nothing very remarkable about it. How deep you are, and how you understand human nature!"

Ximen Qing laughed softly. "There is nothing in that," he said.

"Surely someone gave you a hint?" Bojue said. "You would never have known so much about it otherwise. Why, neither ghosts nor gods could ever have found it out."

"You dog," Ximen said, "if people don't wish things of this sort to come out, they had better refrain from doing them."

"Aren't you going to have Wang the Third before the court?"

"Why should I?" Ximen said. "When the case was first brought to my notice, I crossed out the names of Wang the Third, Zhu, old Sun, Li Guijie and Qin Yuzhi. I only had those few scamps arrested."

"Why did they make trouble with Wang the Third?"

"They hoped to get money out of him. But Wang the Third came to see me. He kowtowed and begged my pardon, so I had the rogues arrested once more and told them I would have cangues put about their necks. They begged for mercy and swore they would never go near him again. As for Wang the Third, he addressed me as 'Uncle' before he said a word. He brought me a present list representing about fifty taels, but I told him to take it away. He has promised to ask me to go to his place so that he may thank me."

Bojue was surprised. "Did he really and truly apologize to you?" he said.

"Do you think I'm lying to you?" Ximen Qing said. He told Wang Jing to go and get Wang the Third's card. Wang Jing came back with the card. Bojue examined it. "The young student, Wang Cai," it said.

"Really, it was a brilliant scheme," he said.

"If you see any of them," Ximen Qing said, "don't tell them I know all that is to be known."

"I understand," Bojue said. "You don't wish them to realize it was all your idea. Of course, I won't say a word."

They had tea. Then Bojue said: "I must go. Old Sun and Zhu might come to see you. If they do, don't tell them I have been here."

"I shall not see them, if they do come," Ximen said. He sent a boy to tell the doorkeeper that, if the two men came, they were to be told he was not at home.

After this, Ximen Qing did not go near Li Guijie. When he had a party at his house, he did not engage Li Ming. Relations between them were completely broken off.

CHAPTER 70

Ximen Qing Visits the Capital

The Emperor said
That he would choose strong men and scholars,
That the wise should be as his arms and legs.
Now the art of letters is purified,
Rites and Music have regained their influence.
Men of nobility go to the palace
And the gate of guests is entered by men of worth.
The royal bounty is bestowed upon the people
Beyond all expectation.
The benevolence of the Ruler is above all things.

Ximen Qing had sent a man to Huaiqing to get news from Captain Lin. The captain gave him a copy of the Imperial Gazette and five *qian* of silver, and the man traveled back post-haste to Qinghe. Xia and Ximen Qing were waiting for him at the office. They opened the envelope. First they read the document that dealt with the inspection of the officials in their district. It related his Majesty's approval of the project to investigate the conduct of the officers, and spoke of Xia and Ximen Qing in these terms:

Xia Yanling, Captain and Magistrate in the Province of Shandong. An officer of excellent reputation and considerable experience. In a former appointment he kept his district in admirable order, and, in the position he now holds, has done even better. He deserves promotion as a thoroughly capable official and one worthy of high rank in the service.

Ximen Qing, Vice Captain and Deputy Magistrate, is also an efficient officer. He is renowned for the subtlety of his judgments, and, being a wealthy man, he does not accept bribes. He is attentive to his duties and carries them out satisfactorily. He has never received a penny that is not justly his due. He maintains the dignity of the law and the people respect him. His promotion to the full rank of Captain is suggested, and he should be confirmed in his appointment as Magistrate.

Ximen Qing was delighted with his promotion. But Magistrate Xia, when he learned that he had been appointed to the Imperial Escort, changed color and could not speak for several minutes.

The other document was from the Office of Works. It related his Majesty's satisfaction with the work that had been done in the transport of materials for the North Mount, ordered that half the taxes should be remitted in districts that had suffered from the work of transport, and that the dikes and weirs that had been destroyed should be replaced by officers of the Office of Works and the Provincial Authorities. Among the rewards granted in this document was a step in rank to Ximen Qing.

When Xia and Ximen had finished reading it, they went home. That afternoon, Wang the Third sent old woman Wen and a boy to invite Ximen Qing to go and see him on the eleventh of the month. He wished, he said, to express his gratitude for the favor Ximen Qing had done him. Ximen accepted the invitation with considerable pleasure, thinking that, in good time, Wang the Third's wife would fall into his hands.

On the evening of the tenth, orders came from Headquarters in the Eastern Capital summoning all the military officers of the Province to the Capital. They were to arrive before the day of the Winter Festival, and to attend at Court to express their gratitude to the Emperor. The order declared that anyone who arrived late would be punished.

The next day Ximen Qing went to discuss the matter with Magistrate Xia, then both men went home and set about the preparation of their luggage. They made ready presents and prepared to start in good time.

Ximen Qing sent Daian for old woman Wen and asked her to tell Wang the Third that he would be unable to keep his engagement because he had to go to the Eastern Capital to see the Emperor. The old woman hurried to Wang the Third and told him. Wang the Third said he would renew his invitation when Ximen came back.

Ximen Qing summoned Ben the Fourth and told him he was going to take him to the Eastern Capital. He gave him five taels of silver for household expenses. Daian and Wang Jing were also detailed to go, but Chunhong was left behind. Ximen asked Major Zhou for an escort of four horse soldiers. Sedan chairs and horses were made ready.

Magistrate Xia took with him only Xia Shou, but, in all, there were more than twenty attendants.

They started from Qinghe on the twelfth. It was winter and the days were short, but they traveled night and day. At Huaiqing they hoped to join Captain Lin, but he had started before them. They went on. When it was particularly cold, they stayed in their sedan chairs, but, on the warmer days, they rode on horseback.

At last they reached the Eastern Capital and entered the city by the gate of Ten Thousand Blessings. Ximen Qing proposed to stay at a temple, but Xia insisted that they should go together to his kinsman, Secretary Cui. Ximen, who did not know Cui, sent his card before him. When they reached the house, the Secretary was at home. He came out to welcome them and led them to the hall. They exchanged greetings. Cui said how delighted he was to see Magistrate Xia; they sat down, and tea was brought.

"May I know your honorable name?" Cui said, bowing to Ximen Qing.

"My humble name is Siquan," Ximen said. He asked Cui's name.

"I am a very insignificant fellow," Cui said, "and I am living in retirement. My humble name is Shouyu, and I am also called Xunzhai. My kinsman, Xia, has often told me of your preeminent virtue. I trust your favor may always uphold and support him."

"He has taught me all I know," Ximen Qing said. "Now that he has been promoted, I shall be dependent upon him in many ways. I owe him much."

"Why do you flatter me?" Xia said. "It would seem as though we were strangers."

"Siquan is right," Cui said, "you are his senior in rank."

They laughed. Their luggage was carried into the house. It was growing late. Secretary Cui ordered a meal to be prepared for them and they spent the night in his house.

The next morning they set off very early with their presents and visiting cards to the palace of the Imperial Tutor. His Eminence was still at the Court, but officers and people flocked like bees outside his palace. Xia and Ximen Qing had great difficulty in forcing their way through the crowd. They made a present to the gatekeeper, and their cards were taken in.

Zhai came out to greet them and took them to his own house. Magistrate Xia saluted him and Ximen Qing greeted him. They sat down. Xia presented his list of gifts. He offered two rolls of golden satin, two rolls of figured satin to the Imperial Tutor and ten taels of silver to Zhai. Ximen Qing had brought a roll of scarlet silk with embroidered dragons, a roll of black silk, also embroidered, and two rolls of official silk for the Imperial Tutor. To Zhai he offered a roll of dark green velvet and thirty taels of silver.

Zhai told the servants to take the presents for the Imperial Tutor to his palace, and to inscribe their names in the visitors' book. He accepted the velvet that Ximen Qing had brought for him, but would not take the silver from either of them.

"It would not be right," he said. "If I took money from you, it would look as though we were not good friends."

He told a servant to prepare a meal for them. "Today," he said, "his Majesty has set the finishing touch to the building he began at the behest of Heaven, and the title is being set up. His Eminence is presiding over the sacrifice. He will not be able to get away before the afternoon. When he comes back, he is going with Li Bangyan to a party at the palace of the Zhengs, who are connected with the Imperial Household. I doubt whether you will care to wait so long, and your other business may be delayed. Do not wait. When his Eminence is at liberty, I will speak to him for you. That will be just as good as if you saw him yourselves."

"It is extremely kind of you, kinsman," Ximen Qing said.

Zhai asked Ximen where he was staying. Ximen told him he was with Xia at Secretary Cui's house.

The meal was now ready. There were a great many dishes, prepared in the manner of the court and served in huge plates and dishes. The food was delicious. When Ximen and his colleague had drunk three cups of wine, they rose and prepared to leave, but Zhai begged them to stay and pressed them to drink again.

"Kinsman," Ximen Qing said, "when shall I be able to see his Majesty?"

"You will not be so fortunate as his Lordship Xia," the Comptroller said. "He is now one of the officers of the Capital. You and the newly appointed Vice Captain, He Yongshou, Chamberlain He's nephew, who are law officers —he is to be your assistant—will have to wait until his Lordship Xia has seen his Majesty. He will wait for you and, after your audience, you will get your commissions together. Whatever you wish to do after that, you will have to consult his Lordship."

Xia listened but said nothing.

"Kinsman," Ximen Qing said, "will it be possible for me to see his Majesty when he has returned from the worship of Heaven on the day of the Winter Festival?"

"Can you wait all that time?" Zhai said. "When he comes back, all the officials of the Empire will offer their congratulations and there will probably be a royal banquet. I don't see how you can wait till then. You had better go to the Registry today, and tomorrow go to Court and see his Majesty. Then you will be able to go home as soon as you have secured your papers."

"Thank you," Ximen said, "I will do as you command. I don't know how I can ever repay your kindness."

As they were going away, the Comptroller took Ximen Qing aside. "When I sent you that letter," he said reproachfully, "didn't I tell you to be most careful and not let your colleague know what should have been a secret between ourselves? What made you tell Xia? He wrote to his Holiness Lin, and Lin persuaded Marshal Zhu to come to his Eminence and say that Xia did not wish to come to the Capital to take a post in the Imperial Escort. He wished to remain another three years at Qinghe. Chamberlain He brought the matter before his Majesty's favorite concubine, and she herself approached both Marshal Zhu and his Eminence and urged the appointment of He Yongshou as the deputy. This produced a most awkward situation. His Eminence was placed in a very difficult position. If I had not spoken to his Eminence on your behalf, and persuaded him to refuse Lin's petition, you would have found yourself without any appointment at all, my dear kinsman."

Ximen Qing was greatly disturbed. "I am most grateful to you," he said, "but, really, I never mentioned the matter to anyone. I can't imagine how it came out."

"If a man doesn't keep things like that secret, so much the worse for him," Zhai said. "You must be more careful in the future."

Ximen Qing thanked him again and went away with Xia. They returned to Cui's house. Ximen sent Ben the Fourth to the Registry to put down their names, and the next day, he and Xia, dressed in black robes and hats of ceremony, went to the Imperial Palace to express their gratitude for his Majesty's favor.

As they were coming out by the West Gate, a man in plain clothes came up and said: "Which of you gentlemen is Master Ximen, the law officer from Shandong?"

Ben the Fourth asked the man who he was.

"I am from Chamberlain He, the Bailiff of the Imperial Palace. He would like to speak to Master Ximen."

The words were hardly out of his mouth before a eunuch, wearing a scarlet robe embroidered with dragons, a ceremonial hat, and black boots, came out upon the Imperial roadway and said: "Greetings, my lord Ximen."

Ximen Qing left Magistrate Xia. The eunuch took him by the hand and led him to a place apart. The eunuch bowed and Ximen knelt down to make a reverence in return.

"You do not know me, my Lord," the eunuch said, "I am He, the Bailiff of the Imperial Palace, and the Chamberlain of his Majesty's fourth lady. Recently, when I had completed my service, his Majesty was graciously pleased to appoint my nephew, He Yongshou, Vice Captain and Deputy Magistrate in your district of Qinghe. He will be your colleague."

"I must apologize for not recognizing your Excellency," Ximen Qing said. He bowed again. "This is a prohibited place and I cannot salute you here in a manner befitting your dignity. I trust you will allow me to visit you in your own palace."

They sat down and a servant brought tea. A food box was opened and many delicacies were set upon a table. Cups and chopsticks were brought.

"We will not use the small cups," the eunuch said, "I know you have just come from the Court, and you must be feeling cold. Besides, I have made such meager preparation for you, that it would not be right. Such food as this will only give you an appetite."

"I must not put you to any trouble," Ximen said.

Eunuch He filled a large cup and offered it to Ximen Qing.

"Since you are so gracious," Ximen said, "I must accept it, but I have to call upon a number of other officers, and I fear my face will be unbecomingly red."

"Oh, a cup or two to keep out the cold will not do you any harm. My nephew is very young," the eunuch continued, "He knows nothing of the law. I shall consider it a favor to myself if you will teach him whatever is necessary for him to know."

"Your Excellency," Ximen said, "pray do not be formal with me. Your nephew may be young, but I have no doubt that, having been brought up in so exalted a household, he is extremely intelligent."

"That is very kind of you. But the proverb says: Though we keep learning to the end of our days, we still know very little. The things one should know are as many as the hairs on an ox. Even Confucius was only able to acquire a legful. I am afraid he is sure to make mistakes, and I hope you will correct him."

"At your Excellency's service," Ximen Qing said. "Will you be good enough to tell me where your palace is situated, that I may come and call upon you?"

"My humble dwelling is in the Wenhuafang, east of the Bridge of the Heavenly River. There are two lions outside the door. We use them as mounting blocks. Tell me where you are staying, and I will send someone to call on you."

"Secretary Cui has been good enough to give me a room," Ximen Qing told him.

He drank a large cup of wine and rose. Eunuch He took him to the gate. "Do not forget what I have said," the eunuch said. "Perhaps you will wait for my nephew and get your commissions together."

"Certainly," Ximen said.

He left the palace and went to the Ministry of War, where he found Xia. They went together to pay their respects to the officials of the Ministry. When they came to the office of their own regiment, they went to call upon Grand Marshal Zhu. They handed in their records of service and then visited the Military Secretary and other officials.

It was now late in the afternoon. Xia changed his clothes, put on the robes of his new office, and sent in his card to the Grand Marshal. Zhu would not allow him to kowtow. Xia reported the date upon which he would enter upon his duties and came away. Ximen Qing was waiting for him. Ximen hesitated to ride side by side with Xia any longer. He asked him to mount his horse first, but Xia insisted that they should go together as before. Ximen kept addressing him as 'Sir' and 'My Lord' till Xia said: "Siquan, you and I have always been colleagues. Why do you speak to me in this formal way?"

"You are of higher rank now, and it is right that I should. Now that your Lordship has attained this high position, you will not be returning to Shandong, I suppose. When will you bring your family here?"

"I would have brought them with me, but there is nobody to look after my house," Xia said. "I think I shall stay with relatives here and send for my family next year. Perhaps you will be good enough to keep an eye on them. If you can find anyone who will buy my house, I hope you will sell it for me. I shall be glad to make it worth your while."

"How much is your house worth?" Ximen asked.

"I paid one thousand three hundred taels for it," Xia said. "Then I built another wing, and that cost me two hundred taels more. I am prepared to sell it for what it cost."

They went back to Secretary Cui's house. Wang Jing reported that Master He had been to call upon Ximen. "I told him," the boy said, "that you were not yet back from the Ministry. He asked me to present his compliments to his Lordship Xia, and left two cards. A man came and brought two rolls of silk from him."

Ximen Qing told Wang Jing to get two rolls of Nanjing five-colored silk, and wrote a card to go with them. He had something to eat as quickly as possible and hastened to the eunuch's house. When he entered the great hall, Captain He came out to greet him. The young man was dressed in black ceremonial hat and boots. He seemed not more than twenty years old and looked so handsome that one might have thought his face was powdered and his lips rouged. He saluted Ximen Qing modestly yet with the utmost grace.

Ximen told Daian to bring in the presents. "I hear that you have been good enough to call upon me and to bring me most precious gifts," he said. "I am sorry I was not there to receive you. This morning, his Excellency your uncle was kind enough to entertain me at the palace. I am grateful to him."

Captain He made a reverence. "I have been made an officer of the lowest grade," he said, "and count myself supremely fortunate to have been appointed to your office. I hope to benefit by your instruction."

They continued to exchange compliments.

"My lord," Captain He said, "have you called upon the Grand Marshal?"

"Yes," Ximen Qing said. "I went to the Ministry immediately after leaving his Excellency, your uncle. I went to our headquarters, handed in my record of service and called on the officers there. When I came away, it was my intention to call upon you. I never dreamed you would call on me first."

"Did you go to the Palace with his Lordship Xia?"

"Yes," Ximen Qing said. "We went together to the court, but as he has been appointed to the Imperial Escort, when we called at the Ministry, we handed in our papers and sent in our cards separately."

"Do we send presents to the Minister, or wait till we receive our commissions?" Captain He said.

"My kinsman tells me," Ximen Qing said, "that we should send our presents first. Then the Marshal will present us at court, and afterwards we shall get out commissions."

"In that case," He said, "we had better send our presents tomorrow morning."

They discussed the question of a suitable present. Captain He decided to offer two rolls of silk and a jade buckle. Ximen Qing would offer a roll of scarlet satin, a roll of black silk and a gold ring inlaid with jade. Each would offer four jars of Jinhua wine in addition. They arranged to meet outside the Marshal's house. They had tea, and Ximen Qing took leave of his new colleague and went home. He said nothing to Xia of the arrangements he had made.

The next morning, Ximen Qing went to Captain He's place. He had prepared an excellent meal, and Ximen Qing and his servants were admirably provided for. Ben the Fourth and He's servants were given charge of the presents, and Ximen Qing and He Yongshou went together to the Marshal's house.

Marshal Zhu was not at home. Officials of every grade were waiting with their presents in a crowd outside the gate. Captain He and Ximen Qing dismounted and went into a nearby house, whose master they knew. They sent a man to watch for the Minister's return. They waited until the afternoon. Then the man came running to say that the Marshal was coming back from the sacrifice by the South Gate. Already, he said, orders were being given to clear the way for him.

Soon afterwards, the man came again. "The Marshal has reached the Bridge of the Heavenly River," he said. There came an escort of officials and soldiers, with banners and weapons. They marched in pairs, shouting. Then, still a long way off, Ximen and his companion could see Marshal

Zhu. He was sitting in a sedan chair carried by eight footmen; another eight footmen followed. He was wearing a ceremonial hat and a scarlet gown; a piece of white jade formed the clasp of his girdle. He wore a golden fish, the insignia of his office, and looked extremely dignified.

The escort reached the gate and halted. Then they turned inwards to form a guard. There was perfect silence among the onlookers. No one dared even to cough. The officers came forward to greet the Grand Marshal and knelt on the ground before him. As the sedan chair approached, the command was given to stand up, and the officers immediately obeyed. The sound of their acclamations reached the skies.

Suddenly there came from the east the strains of music. The principal officers in the Minister's department had arranged for this in honor of the exalted rank that had been conferred upon him by the Emperor's recent decree, and also to celebrate his son's entry into official life.

When the Minister got down from his sedan chair, the music stopped. The officers were preparing to present themselves to him when, suddenly, a messenger in black clothes, carrying two red cards, rushed forward and handed the cards to another official. "Their Excellencies, Chang of the Board of Rites and Vice Chancellor Cai, are here." The man went into the house to give warning to his master. Then, in two sedan chairs, came Zhang Bangchang and Cai Yu. They were both wearing scarlet ceremonial robes with peacocks embroidered upon them. One had a buckle of rhinoceros horn upon his girdle, the other, one of gold.

Following them came Wang Zudao, President of the Board of Civil Service, with Han Lü the Minister of the Left, and Yin Jing, the Minister of the Right. Marshal Zhu offered them tea, and they came away at once.

Then came the Duke of Xiguo, a kinsman of the Imperial House, the President of the Privy Council, Zheng Juzhong, and the Master of the Household, the Imperial Son-in-law, Wang Jinqing. They all wore girdles with jade buckles. Zheng rode in a sedan chair, but the others were on horseback.

When they had gone, the six officers of the Marshal's own department paid their respects to him. First came the Commander-in-chief of the troops at the Capital, Sun Rong; then, in order, Liang Yinglong, Commissioner of Police; and the others, all wearing red cloaks and fur hats. Sun Rong had a jade buckle to his girdle by virtue of his rank, but the rest wore gold buckles. They all brought presents.

There was music within the palace as the generals, wearing golden flowers, offered wine to the Grand Marshal. There was music in the courtyard while the banquet proceeded within. When they had offered wine, the generals sat down. Five singers came in, and to the accompaniment of

lute and zither, sang a song in celebration of the occasion, beating time
with ivory castanets.

When the wine had been passed three times, the song ended. The six
generals rose and the Grand Marshal went with them as far as the gate.
Then he returned to the hall, and the music died away. A servant told
him that many officers wished to see him. He ordered a great table to be
brought and set in the middle of the hall.

"Let the noblemen of the Court and those of high family be first
admitted," he commanded.

They came in, and retired again immediately. Then all the officers of
his own department were introduced. They came with their cards, and
these were handed to him. Then came the law officers of the thirteen
provinces in relays. Ximen Qing and Captain He were in the fifth party.
Their presents were brought in, and an attendant took the list and placed
it on the table. They came in and stood at the foot of the steps waiting
for their names to be announced. While they waited, Ximen looked up
and admired the magnificent proportions of the great hall and the great
red sign with four characters upon it that had been written by the Emper-
or's own hand. Their names were called and the two men went forward,
bowed, knelt down and waited.

"Why have you two gentlemen troubled the venerable chamberlain to
send me a present?" the Grand Marshal said. He told his servants to take
their gifts. "Do your duty, and I will treat you justly," he told them. "Stay
until you have been to the Court and, afterwards, come to my Ministry
for your papers."

The two men acknowledged the command the Marshal gave them.
Then the attendants warned them to withdraw, and they went out by a
door on the left. As they passed through the gateway, Ben the Fourth and
the other servants were carrying out the empty boxes. They were about to
go away, when a man, carrying a red card, galloped towards them. "Their
Excellencies Wang and Gao are coming," he cried as he passed.

Ximen Qing and Captain He went into a house to watch the two
noblemen pass. Soldiers cleared the way. Then came Wang Hua, Duke
of Longxi, Commander of the Royal Guard, and Marshal Gao Qiu. They
rode in sedan chairs, and wore red jade buckles on their girdles. The officers rushed out of the palace in a crowd, and Ximen Qing and Captain
He lost sight of the two dignitaries. They went to a quiet place, took their
horses from the servants, and rode home.

CHAPTER 71

The Son of Heaven

The flowers droop and the sweet grass is faded
He is a stranger in a strange place.
In the little courtyard
He thinks of her whom he has lost.
It is evening, and his tears
Drop red as blood.
Mountain and river are parted
His eyes are dim, his spirit ill at ease.
It seems that her sweet spirit has vanished utterly.

When, at the fifth night watch, he woke from his dream
His heart was broken.
The wind brought the sound of horns
And swept away the moon and the plum blossom.

Ximen Qing and Captain He came to the principal street. He asked Ximen to take wine with him at his house, but Ximen Qing very politely declined. Then He bade his servant take Ximen's bridle. "You must come," he said, "I am anxious to talk to you." So they went to He's place, and Ben the Fourth took the empty present boxes back to Secretary Cui's house.

Captain He had made special preparations for his guest. In the great hall, animal charcoal was burning in the braziers, and the smoke of incense went curling upwards from golden burners. There was a table in the middle of the hall, and beside it two other tables, one nearer the door and the other at one side. Bowls piled with rare fruits stood on the tables and flowers in golden vases.

"Are you entertaining any other guests?" Ximen Qing asked Captain He.

"No," He said. "My old uncle will dine with us when he comes back."

"Since we are to be colleagues," Ximen Qing said, "you should not have gone to all this trouble on my account."

"I beg your pardon," He said, "but, as a matter of fact, my venerable uncle has done this."

When they had drunk tea, Ximen asked if he might pay his respects to the eunuch. He said he would not be long and, in a short time, Eunuch He came from the back of the house. He was wearing a green dragon gown, ceremonial hat and boots, and a jewel at his girdle. Ximen Qing bowed to him and asked leave to kowtow, but the eunuch would not allow him to do so.

"Your Excellency is distinguished both by age and virtue," Ximen Qing said. "You are a nobleman of the Court and, as your nephew and I are colleagues, you must permit me to do so."

They wrangled for some time, and, at last, the old eunuch accepted a compromise. He asked Ximen Qing to take the place of honor, seated himself in the host's chair, and put his nephew on one side. Ximen Qing protested. "We are fellow officers," he said. "I cannot allow him to take a lower position than myself. It would be seemly so far as your Excellency and he are concerned, for you are uncle and nephew, but it is not right for me."

The eunuch smiled. "Sir," he said, "you seem to understand the Rites very well. I am an old fellow. I will take the lower place and let the officer take mine."

"That would be even more insupportable," Ximen said. They finally sat down as they had before.

"It is cold," the eunuch said to the servants, "put more coal on the fire."

The servants brought fine water-polished charcoal and put it in the brazier. They pulled down the oiled-paper blind outside the hall. It was so arranged that, when the sun shone, it shone through the paper and gave light to the hall.

"Sir," the eunuch said, "will you take off your ceremonial clothes?"

"I have nothing underneath," Ximen said, "I must send my servant for something."

"Don't trouble to do that," the eunuch said. He bade one of his servants bring his green gown.

Ximen Qing smiled. "How dare I put on the robes of your Excellency's rank?"

"Don't let that worry you," the eunuch said. "Put it on by all means. His Majesty gave me this new robe yesterday. I shall have no further use for the old one, and I should be glad if you would accept it and use it as a cloak."

When the servant brought it, Ximen Qing took off his ceremonial clothes and gave them to Daian. He put on the green robe, bowed to express his thanks to the eunuch and asked him, in turn, to take off his robes of ceremony. Tea was brought again.

"Let the boys come in," the eunuch commanded.

He had twelve boys being trained as singers. They were brought in by their instructors. They kowtowed. The eunuch bade them begin, and they went to their places. The eunuch himself prepared to offer wine to Ximen Qing, but Ximen hastily begged him not to do so.

"Your Excellency, pray do not offer me wine yourself," he said. "The Captain will do it for you. I shall be more than happy if you set the cup on the table before me."

"I must do so," the eunuch said. "My nephew has now secured his first appointment. He is quite ignorant. I am placing my confidence in your kind assistance. With it, I am sure, all will be well."

"Your Excellency," Ximen said, "the old proverb says: When men become fellow officers, there will be friendship between them and their descendants for three generations. I am in your hands. How can I fail to do my utmost for your nephew?"

"You are both in the service of his Majesty," the eunuch said. "For that reason, you must help one another."

Ximen Qing did not wait for the eunuch to pour the wine for him. He took the cup from his hands and set it down on the table. In his turn, he offered a cup to the eunuch and to Captain He. They bowed to each other and sat down.

After a prelude, three boys and their instructors played the banjo and the lute and sang the songs "Visiting Zhao Pu" and "The Silken Hangings in the Palace of Crystal." When they had finished their songs they withdrew.

The wine was passed several times and the second course brought. It was growing dark, and the lamps were lighted. Ximen Qing told Daian to give some money to the cooks and the musicians. He rose and said: "I have troubled you sufficiently. I must go now."

The old eunuch would not hear of this. "I happen to be free today," he said, "and I wish you to stay. I have not made any special preparations for you. This is very ordinary food, and I fear you must be starved."

"Starved!" Ximen cried, "starved, with all this delightful food. I only wish to go back and rest because, tomorrow morning, I have to go with your nephew to pay a round of visits, have our names registered, and get the necessary documents."

"If you are going to be occupied with my nephew," the eunuch said, "why not send for your luggage and spend a few days here? There is a small apartment in my garden that you would find very quiet. You could discuss everything you have to discuss with my nephew, and you would find it most convenient."

"I should very much like to come," Ximen Qing said, "but I must not offend his Lordship Xia. If I come here, he may regard it as a sign that I am no longer anxious to be on good terms with him."

"Oh, you mustn't bother about that," the eunuch said. "Men who have been together in the same office are separated one morning, and, the same evening, do not even bow to one another. Officers come and go. You have served with him; he is now promoted and you succeed him. That's all there is to it. If he thinks otherwise, he is not a reasonable man. No, we must have the pleasure of your company for the night. I shall not allow you to go."

He said to his attendants: "Give something to eat to his Lordship's servants, and send somebody for his luggage. Get the apartment ready in the courtyard of the western garden, make up beds there, and get a fire going."

One word from his Excellency was sufficient. A hundred eyes were on the watch. Servants hurried to do his bidding.

"Your Excellency," Ximen Qing said, "this is very kind of you, but I am sure Xia will be displeased."

"He has nothing more to do with your office," the eunuch said. "It doesn't matter what he thinks. He is now officer of the Imperial Escort, and has no more to do with affairs of the law. I don't believe he will mind in the least."

The eunuch said no more, but sent Daian and the other servant to have their evening meal. A number of other servants took poles and ropes and went to Cui's place for Ximen Qing's things.

"There is one point I wish especially to mention to you," the eunuch said. "When my nephew assumes office, he will need a house. I hope you will help him to find one. I am anxious that his family should join him at Qinghe as soon as possible. I think he had better go with you, and I will arrange for his family to follow when you have secured a house for them. It is not a very large household, only about thirty people, including all the servants."

"How much is your Excellency prepared to spend?" Ximen said.

"I suppose something more than a thousand."

"Now that Xia is going to remain in the Capital," Ximen said, "he will be getting rid of his house. You might buy that. It would be to the advantage of both parties. It is a good-sized house, seven rooms wide and five deep. When you go in by the second door, there is a large hall with side rooms. The living rooms branch out in different directions behind that, and there are quite a number of other rooms. The house is in a good broad street. It ought to suit Captain He very well."

"How much does Xia want for it?" the eunuch said.

"He told me he paid thirteen hundred for it," Ximen said, "and later, he built an extra wing and made a garden. If your Excellency cares for the idea, I should offer any sum you consider suitable."

"I will leave the matter to you," the eunuch said. "You shall arrange it for me. I am at home now, so why not send someone to tell Xia we think of buying his house and ask him for the title deeds? We shall be lucky if we get it. My nephew will have somewhere to live as soon as he gets to Qinghe."

Daian and a host of servants came with Ximen's luggage. Ximen Qing asked him if Ben the Fourth and Wang Jing had come.

"Wang Jing is here," Daian said, "but Ben the Fourth is still at Secretary Cui's house, making arrangements about the sedan chair."

Ximen Qing said softly to Daian: "Go and see his Lordship Xia, and ask him for the title deeds of his house. His Excellency here would like to see them. Bring Ben the Fourth back with you."

Daian went. Ben the Fourth, wearing black clothes and a small hat, soon came back with him. He brought the document.

"His Lordship Xia," Ben the Fourth said, "told us to say that, since his Excellency would like to have the house, there will be no difficulty about the price. Here are the title deeds. He says that, though he built the wings and spent a great deal of money on the place, he will leave the price to you."

Ximen Qing handed the papers to the eunuch. The sum mentioned was twelve hundred taels.

"Xia has lived in the house a good many years," the eunuch said, "and I expect it needs doing up. But since you, Sir, are seeing the business through for me, I will give him the price he paid for it."

Ben the Fourth knelt down. "Your Excellency does well," he said. "The proverb says: The establishment of an estate is an expensive business, and though in a thousand years, a house may change hands a hundred times, each new master will have it redone his own way from top to bottom."

"Who are you?" said the eunuch. "You talk like a man of sense. You are right when you say that a man who is setting up an establishment mustn't mind how much he spends. What is your name?"

"He is called Ben the Fourth," Ximen Qing said.

"Well, I don't see that we need look any further," the eunuch said. "You shall act as our representative, and get the thing fixed up for us. This is an auspicious day, and I will pay Xia his money."

"It is late now," Ximen said, "why not pay him tomorrow?"

"No," the eunuch said, "I have to be at the Palace before dawn tomorrow. It is the day when all the officers come to pay their duty to his Majesty. We will settle with him today."

"At what time will the Emperor come out tomorrow?" Ximen Qing asked.

"His Majesty will go to make sacrifice about midnight," the eunuch said. "An hour or two before dawn he will return and breakfast at the Palace. Then he will hold his court. All the officers of the Empire come at the Winter Festival to offer their congratulations. All the Ministers and some of the higher officials will remain for a banquet. You gentlemen simply attend the court."

The eunuch told Captain He to put twenty-four large bars of silver into a box, and ordered two servants to go with Ben the Fourth and Daian and take the money to Xia at Secretary Cui's house.

Xia was pleased. He signed the document and gave it to Ben the Fourth to take back to the eunuch. The eunuch, too, was satisfied. He gave ten taels of silver to Ben the Fourth and three taels each to Daian and Wang Jing.

"They are only boys," Ximen Qing said, "your Excellency should not have troubled to give them anything."

"It is only something to buy food with," the eunuch said.

The three kowtowed and thanked him.

Then the eunuch bowed to Ximen Qing. "I am placing all my confidence in your kindness," he said.

"I am entirely at your Excellency's service," Ximen Qing said.

"Now, Sir," the eunuch said, "please ask Xia to have his place made free as soon as possible so that I can make arrangements for my nephew's family to take possession."

"I will certainly tell him," Ximen Qing said. "Perhaps, when Captain He arrives at Qinghe, he will stay a few days at the office while Xia's family make their preparations to leave for the Capital. Then we will have the place put in order, and you will send your nephew's family."

"No," the eunuch said, "I think we will leave the question of repairs until next year. I will send his family before then. He will not be comfortable if he has to live so long alone at the office."

It was now the first night watch. Ximen Qing said: "Will not your Excellency retire and take some rest? I have had wine enough."

The eunuch went to bed, but Captain He bade the musicians play, and went on drinking with Ximen Qing. When it was time to go to bed, Ximen Qing went to the garden. There was a small three-roomed apartment used as a study. The garden was very delightful with its buildings, arbors, lake, hillocks, flowers, and woods. Candles burned brightly in the study, and fragrant incense burned. It was quiet and delightful. Captain He chatted for a while with Ximen Qing, and they took tea together. Then he said good night and went to his own rooms to sleep.

Ximen Qing took off his hat, girdle and clothes and went to bed. Wang Jing and Daian waited on him, then went to their own place.

Ximen Qing, lying on the bed, watched the moonbeams playing on the windows. He tossed about but could not sleep. He heard the drip, drip, drip of the water clock. He saw the tall shadows of the plants upon the casement. The cold wind rattled the windowpanes. He had now been away from home for some time and was thinking of calling Wang Jing to sleep with him. Suddenly, he heard a woman speaking very softly outside the window. He wrapped his cloak around him, put on his slippers, and quietly opened the door. He looked out. Li Ping'er stood there, her hair like mist. She was dressed in simple, beautiful clothes, and a white coat covered her snow-white body. She wore soft slippers, yellow in color, upon her dainty feet. She stood there in the moonlight.

Ximen Qing went forward, took her into the study and kissed her. "My darling!" he cried, "what has brought you here?"

"I have sought you," she said, "because I wanted to tell you that I have a new home now. I was anxious to let you know, because, sooner or later, I must go to it."

"Where is this house?" Ximen asked her.

"Not far from here. It is in the middle of the Zaofu Lane, east of the main street."

Ximen Qing put his arms about her, and they went to bed that they might enjoy each other the more fully. When they had taken their pleasure, she made her clothes tidy and dressed her hair, but she was loath to go away.

"Brother," she said to Ximen Qing, "don't forget what I said to you. Do not drink wine late at night. Go home early. That fellow is only waiting his chance to destroy you. Remember."

Holding each other by the hand, they went to the main street. The moon shone so brightly that it might have been day. They came to a lane leading eastwards from the street. In the middle of it was a house with white double doors. Li Ping'er pointed to it. "That is the house," she said. She loosed her hand from his, and ran in. Ximen dashed forward to stop her.

Then he awoke. It was a dream. The moon was still shining upon the window; the flowers cast a deeper shadow than before. He passed his hand

over the bedclothes. There was a pool upon them that seemed to show
that all had not been in his imagination. He could still smell the delicate
scent of her body upon the bed, and the lips which she had kissed were
still sweet. He was very sad, but restrained his sobs.

There was no sleep for Ximen Qing. He longed for the day to break.
At last, when dawn was near, he began to doze.

The next morning, Captain He sent his own servants to help Ximen
to dress, and himself came early to call upon him. They drank tea and
breakfasted together.

"Why does his Excellency not come?" Ximen asked.

"He went to the court before it was light," Captain He said.

They were served with gruel; then with buns stuffed with forcemeat,
and soup of chickens' brains. They called for their horses, put on their
ceremonial dress and went to the Ministry with their servants following.
When they came out, Captain He went home, but Ximen went to the
Xiang Guo Temple to visit the Abbot, Zhi Yun. The Abbot entertained
him with monastic fare, but Ximen Qing would only eat one cake and
gave the rest to his servants. Then he went away, passing through the
main street on his way to Secretary Cui's house to see Xia. They went
through the Zaofu Lane. Halfway down it, he saw a house with white
double doors exactly like the one he had seen in his dream. An old woman
was selling bean curd nearby, and Ximen told Daian to ask her who lived
in that house. "It is General Yuan's house," the old woman said.

Ximen Qing sighed with curiosity and amazement. He came to Secretary Cui's house. Xia was setting out to pay a call. He immediately
ordered his servant to take the horses away, and took Ximen Qing to the
great hall. Ximen told Daian to bring the presents that he wished to offer
to Xia upon his appointment. There was one roll of black silk and another
of figured silk.

"I have not congratulated you," Xia said to him, "yet you do so much
for me. Yesterday you took a great deal of trouble over my house."

"Chamberlain He asked me about a house," Ximen said, "and I told
him about yours. He asked for the title deeds, and agreed to the price without the slightest ado. That is just like a eunuch. They think they can build
a bridge in a couple of seconds. But, after all, it was to your advantage."

They laughed. "I have not yet called on Captain He," Xia said. "Is he
going back with you?"

"Yes," Ximen said. "And his family will follow later. His Excellency
told me to ask you to be so good as to vacate the place as soon as you can
so that he can send the Captain's family. Until you have done so he will
have to stay at the office."

"That will not be very long," Xia said. "I am looking for a house here and, as soon as I find one, I will send for my family. I don't see why the house should not be ready for him next month."

Ximen Qing rose. He left a card for Cui. Xia took him to the gate and waited till he had mounted his horse. Ximen Qing went back to Captain He's house. He was waiting to entertain him. Ximen told him that Xia had promised that his house should be free the following month. The Captain was delighted. "It is all due to your good offices," he said.

After dinner, while they were playing chess in the great hall, a servant came and said that a number of presents had come from the Imperial Tutor's comptroller Zhai. They had been taken to Cui's house, and the Secretary had sent them on. Ximen Qing looked at the list. A roll of gold silk, a roll of patterned hempen material, a pig, a sheep, a jar of palace wine, and two boxes of cakes. All these were set down upon the card, and at the end of the list was written: "Your kinsman Zhai Qian makes most humble salutation."

"Your master has troubled himself once again on my account," Ximen Qing said to the servants who brought the things. He accepted the gifts, wrote a return card, and gave two taels to the servant and five *qian* to each of the porters. To the servant he said: "You will understand that, as I am a stranger here and not versed in the usual customs, I am ashamed to offer such a reward." The man kowtowed and accepted the money.

Wang Jing, who was standing beside his master, whispered: "I was told to go to the palace to see Han Aijie. I have brought something for her."

"What have you brought?" Ximen asked him.

"Two pairs of home-made shoes," Wang Jing said.

"That is not enough," Ximen said. He told Daian to look in his chest and take out two jars of rose-flower biscuits. He gave them to Wang Jing, with a card of thanks for the presents, and the boy put on black robes and went to the Imperial Tutor's palace with the servant.

Ximen wrote a card and sent it, with the sheep and a jar of wine, to Secretary Cui. He told a servant to offer the pig, a jar of wine, and the boxes of cakes to the eunuch. "We are such good friends," Captain He said to him, "that really there is no need for you to do anything of the sort."

Wang Jing came to the palace, and was received by Han Aijie in the great hall. She was dressed so exquisitely that she looked like a tree of jade, not at all like the girl who had lived with her mother at Qinghe. She had grown taller. She asked the boy many questions about her family, and gave him some food. She thought Wang Jing's clothes were very thin. She brought a blue silk gown, lined with fur, and gave it to him with five taels of silver. When the boy got back, he showed the cloak to Ximen Qing.

Captain He and Ximen were playing chess, when, suddenly, there was shouting outside. The doorkeeper came in and said: "His Lordship Xia has come to call." He handed one card to Ximen Qing and another to Captain He. They hurried to the great hall to meet Xia. He thanked him for the expedition with which he had settled the question of the house. Xia presented gifts to each of them, and they thanked him cordially. Then he gave ten taels of silver to Ben the Fourth, Daian, and Wang Jing. They had tea, and Xia asked if he might see the old eunuch, but He said:

"His Excellency is at the Palace now." Then Xia presented a red card.

"Please give my humble respects to his Excellency," he said. "I am sorry I am too late to see him." He took leave of them.

Captain He immediately sent him a present in return. It was getting late. Captain He entertained Ximen Qing in one of the small rooms in the garden. During the meal, the boys sang for them, and it was the second night watch before they went to bed.

Ximen Qing had not forgotten what had happened the night before. He told Wang Jing to bring his bedclothes to the study and sleep there. In the middle of the night the boy went to him. They kissed each other and he found the boy's lips very fragrant.

The next morning, Ximen was up before dawn and joined Captain He. They went together to the Palace to wait for the opening of the East Gate. After a while the gates of the Throne Hall were swung open, and they heard the sound of gongs and cymbals. Then the Gate of Heaven was opened, and they caught a glimpse of the most glorious and august diadem. The Son of Heaven was returning from the altar of the south, and all his officers, civil and military, waited to receive him. Gongs were beaten and bells rung, as the Emperor came back to his palace to receive the homage of his officers. Clouds of incense streamed towards the skies. The great ceremonial fans waved to and fro.

His Majesty ascended the throne, and the cracking of whips gave the signal for silence. The officers, holding their tablets of office before their breasts, made five salutations and kowtowed three times before the throne, doing homage to the Sacred Majesty.

Then, from the palace, came an officer and spoke the words of the Emperor that all might hear them.

"We have reigned for twenty years," he said, "and at last We have completed the building of the *Genjue*. Heaven has been Our helper. Now as We enter upon another new year, We pray that the good fortune Heaven has bestowed Upon Us, may be shared by you."

There came out from among a group of high officials, one whose ceremonial boots trod proudly, whose sleeves waved in the breeze. This was

Cai Jing, the Chancellor, Minister of the Left, President of the Board of Civil Service, Imperial Tutor and Duke of Lu. Carrying his ivory tablet low before him, he knelt down upon the golden steps.

"May Your Majesty live forever! In awe and humility, we kowtow before the Son of Heaven. As Your Majesty has said, you have governed this Empire for twenty years. During those years the Empire has enjoyed peace and prosperity, and the harvests have been plentiful. Heaven has observed Your Majesty's conduct, appreciated Your Majesty's labors, and given many signs of favor. There has been no war or disturbance upon the frontier, and people from all lands have come to pay tribute before Your Heavenly Throne. Your Majesty's palace is as a mountain of silver towering in the sky, and Your Majesty's capital of jade is unique in all the world.

"The Most Precious and Sacred Will is expressed in Your Majesty's exalted palace; purple candles have been burned in the palace of Heaven. How fortunate are we, that we should live in a world so blessed.

"The relations between Your Majesty and the people are perfect. We pray that You may be spared to live as the mountains, that the light of the sun and the moon may always shine upon us. Your Majesty's graciousness is beyond our power to express: we can only enjoy the blessings that come to us through it. We offer Your Majesty our most humble congratulations and praise."

There was a long delay. Then the Emperor's word was announced to them again.

"You, Our worthy officers, have offered Us your praises. Once again, We appreciate your loyalty and fidelity. We are content. It is Our purpose upon the first day of the New Year to change the title of Our reign to the first year of Chonghe. This We shall duly make known to Heaven. There shall be a general amnesty throughout the Empire, and reward for all those who serve Us."

After listening to this, the Chancellor withdrew.

"It is his Majesty's command," the herald said, "that if anyone has any business to bring forward, he shall do so now. Otherwise his Majesty will retire."

A man stepped out of the crowd, wearing a scarlet gown, with a jade clasp to his girdle, and a golden fish as his badge of office. He lowered his ivory tablet and bowed towards the Emperor, then knelt upon the golden steps.

"Zhu Mian, Grand Marshal, Commander-in-Chief of the Royal Guard, presents twenty-six magistrates to Your Majesty. Inspection has been made of their work, and the question of their promotion or dismissal determined. They have come to the Capital to obtain their new commissions, and since I dare not myself make the decision, I bring them before Your Majesty and await Your Majesty's command.

The twenty-six magistrates knelt down behind the Grand Marshal.

After a while, the Imperial Decree issued. "Let them be given their commissions in accordance with precedent."

Marshal Zhu retired.

The Emperor waved his arms, and the officers withdrew. His Majesty went into the palace.

The officers poured out of the two gates, headed by twelve elephants that marched unattended. The grooms and servants of the Ministers hurried to the service of their masters. There was a crowd of carriages outside the palace gates, and the shouting of the people made a noise like a storm at sea, while the neighing of their horses seemed like an earthquake. The magistrates came out and mounted their horses, and all rode together to their headquarters to wait for orders. A messenger came out to them. "The Grand Marshal," he told them, "will not be here. He is going to celebrate the Winter Festival at the Imperial Tutor's palace." The magistrates dispersed.

Ximen Qing returned to Captain He's place and spent another day there. The next day, they went together to their headquarters and secured their documents. Ximen went to say good-bye to Zhai, then went back to pack up his luggage, so that he would be ready to return to Qinghe with Captain He.

That evening, the old eunuch entertained them to dinner. He bade his nephew consult Ximen Qing in all things, and not make any decisions for himself.

On the twentieth day of the eleventh month, they set out for Qinghe, with more than twenty servants following them. They traveled upon the high road to Shandong. It was the season of greatest cold and every drop of water was frozen. They saw nothing but barren hills and deserted paths. Upon the withered trees only the blackbirds sat in the feeble sunshine. Snow and frozen clouds hung above the river. Over one hill they went, and found another one before them. They passed one village, and came to another. When they had crossed the Yellow River and had come to a town on the other side, they were suddenly overtaken by a violent windstorm.

> Not this the roaring of the tiger
> Or the muttering of the dragon.
> The cold air stung their faces; the sharp wind
> Pierced their very hearts.

There was at first no sign of its coming
But soon the mist and cloud were swept away.
It rocked the trees and made mad the sea
It hustled the pebbles and urged the stones
And the skies were dark.
The high trees moaned without ceasing
And the lonely goose lay broken in the ditch.
The sand drove across the ground
The dust screened the sky.
The small stones were flung about as in a whirlwind
And the dust was as the dust set up
By millions of soldiers on the march.
This tempest was so violent
It smashed the trees on the frontier of hell
And carried away the dust from the palace
Of the god of the underworld.
Chang E, the angel of the moon,
Shut the doors of her palace in haste.
Liezi, walking in the skies,
Called out for help.
The Jade Monarch could hardly stay
On the summit of the Koulkun Mountains.
Heaven and Earth alike
Were in a mad confusion.

Ximen Qing and Captain He were in sedan chairs, wrapped in rugs and blankets. The wind was so fearful that they could not advance even a single step. It was late, and they feared that highwaymen might come out from the woods and attack them. Ximen Qing sent some of his men forward to try to find a shelter for the night, saying that they would go on again when the wind abated. It was some time before a place was found. Then they discovered an old monastery with a few bare willow trees outside it. The walls were half in ruins.

The walls and the memorials were covered with rank grass
The corridors and the ancient sanctuaries were on the point of fall-
    ing.
The monks at midnight had no light.
When the moon had set, it made the heart grieve
To see the monks at meditation.

The two officers hastened there. It was called the Temple of the Yellow Dragon. There were only a few monks, engaged in meditation without fire and without light. The rooms were nearly all in ruins, and many of them were patched with boards.

The abbot came to welcome them and made a fire to make them some tea. Hay was brought for their horses. When the tea was ready, Ximen Qing took from his bag preserved chicken, meat, cakes and fruit, and Captain He and he made their supper on this food, together with some porridge that the abbot prepared for them. They stayed the night in this place.

The next day, the wind had stopped and the skies were clear. They gave the monks a tael of silver, and set out again.

CHAPTER 72

Pan Jinlian Quarrels with Ruyi'er

They flourish their arms and shrug their shoulders
Sometimes warm and sometimes cold.
Even a eunuch may raise a family
And a stone virgin bring forth a child.
Loss of power is the one thing to escape.
To some, their own children are not so much to be loved
As other people's children.
Father and Mother are not of great account
At any moment their own children
May pass them by.

While Ximen Qing was away, Wu Yueniang was a little anxious. There were so many ladies in the household, and she was afraid there might be trouble. She exhorted them all to keep the peace, and made sure that the main gate was closed and the back door locked, every night. The ladies stayed at home, doing needlework. Whenever Chen Jingji had to go to the inner court for clothes or anything, Yueniang took care that either Chunhong or Laian went with him. She was particularly careful about the closing of doors and windows and made quite sure that everything was safe.

Pan Jinlian could see nothing of Jingji.

One day, the nurse, Ruyi'er, gave her an opportunity to make trouble. Yueniang took some of Ximen Qing's clothes, shirts, and underclothes to Ruyi'er, and told her and Madam Han to wash and iron them. Chunmei was washing at the same time, and she sent Qiuju to borrow the dolly pin. Ruyi'er and Yingchun were using it, and they would not give it up. "You borrowed it only the other day," Ruyi'er said, "and here you are, after it again. We have all these shirts and clothes of our master's to do while Madam Han is here."

Qiuju, in a very ill humor, went back and said to Chunmei: "You are always sending me there to borrow things, and now they won't lend me the dolly pin. Yingchun was willing enough. It was Ruyi'er who wouldn't do it."

"What's that?" Chunmei cried. "Why shouldn't we borrow a lamp in the daytime? She won't lend us a dolly pin, won't she? Here I am with Mother's foot binders to wash. What am I going to beat them with? Go to the inner court and borrow one from somebody else."

Jinlian was washing her feet in her room. She overheard this. She hated Ruyi'er and was glad of the opportunity to make trouble. "How dare that strumpet refuse to lend us the dolly pin?" she cried. "Go yourself. And, if she makes any bones about it, curse her well. That ought to settle her."

Chunmei dashed away like a whirlwind. "Who is the stranger in this house?" she said, "are you or are we? You refuse to lend me this dolly pin. That means, I suppose, that there is a new mistress here now."

"If I hadn't been using it," Ruyi'er said, "I shouldn't have kept it."

She got angry in her turn. "The Great Lady," she said, "thought that, with Sister Han here, it was a splendid opportunity to get these shirts and trousers washed. I told Qiuju she could have the dolly pin as soon as I had finished with it. Then she went and told you I wouldn't lend it to her. It was a lie. Yingchun heard what I said."

Jinlian came along. "Now, woman," she said, "don't try any tricks on me. Since your mistress died, you have been taking her place in this apartment. You are washing his Lordship's clothes. I suppose you are trying to make out that, if you didn't, nobody else would. We might all be dead, and you the only one to attend to his clothes. I know. You think you will be able to score over the rest of us. But you needn't think you're going to frighten me by games of this sort."

"Fifth Lady," Ruyi'er said, "it is really nothing of the sort. If the Great Lady had not given me orders, you don't think I should have taken it upon myself?"

"You wicked bone," Jinlian cried, "you have far too much to say. I ask you: who was it served his Lordship with tea in the middle of the night? Who made his bed for him? Who asked him for a new dress? You think I don't know the games you play with him on the sly. But I do know, and I'm not afraid to say so."

"My mistress died, even though she had borne a son," Ruyi'er said. "What chance have I against you?"

This made Jinlian wild. Her face, which was already red, became redder. She ran forward, caught Ruyi'er by the hair, and thumped her in the belly. Fortunately, Madam Han was there to separate them. Jinlian went on cursing. "You shameless strumpet! You husband-stealer! We have been neglected long enough, and now you try to get our husband away from us. What are you doing here at all? Even if you are Laiwang's wife come to life again, I'm not afraid of you."

Ruyi'er cried. She put her hair straight. "I have not been long in this household," she said. "I don't know anything about Laiwang's wife. I only know I came here as a nurse."

"If you are a nurse, you should behave as a nurse," Jinlian said. "Why do you set the whole place on its head like a disturbing spirit? I know what I'm about, and I'll see you don't get away with it."

Meng Yulou came from the inner court. "Sister," she said, "I asked you to play chess with me. Why didn't you come? What is the matter?" She pulled Jinlian away to her own room.

When they had sat down, she asked Jinlian what was wrong. The woman was now calmer. Chunmei brought them tea.

"See!" Jinlian said. "That strumpet has made my hands quite cold. I can't lift my cup. I was in my room, making a pattern for my shoes, when your maid came for me. I told her I was going to lie down and rest a while before I came. I lay on the bed, but did not go to sleep. Chunmei was washing my skirt, and I told her she might as well wash my foot binders too. A few moments later, I heard a great to-do, and found that Qiuju had gone to borrow a dolly pin, and the woman wouldn't lend it to her. She said we had had it the other day, and she wasn't going to lend it to us again because she was washing his Lordship's clothes. That annoyed me, and I told Chunmei to go and curse her. You see, she has been misbehaving herself for some time, and I was determined to teach her a lesson. What sort of a woman does she think she is? His Lordship never married her. She is worse than Laiwang's wife, and I wasn't going to forgive her. She wouldn't give way, and I gave her a real good cursing. If Madam Han hadn't been there to stop me, I would have pulled the strumpet's guts out. The Great Lady is very much to blame. You remember how she spoiled Laiwang's wife by being too indulgent. When I had a row with her, all the blame fell upon me. The Great Lady even went so far as to say I was responsible for Laiwang being kicked out. Now she is dealing with this woman as she dealt with Laiwang's wife. If the woman is a nurse, let her mind her own business. We are not going to let her carry on before our very eyes. We are not going to have dust thrown in our eyes. The shameless hussy! Her mistress is dead, but she still stays on in that apartment. Every time he comes home, he goes and bows to the portrait and mumbles something or other. Nobody knows what he says. During the night he asks for tea and this strumpet ups and gets it for him. Then she pulls the bedclothes over him, and they start their tricks. It is the maids' business to serve tea. Why should she take it upon herself? Why did she ask him for a new dress? The shameless fellow went to the shop immediately and got a roll of silk for her. You remember the last week's mind for Li Ping'er. He went there to burn some paper things for her. The maid and this strumpet were lying on the same bed, playing knuckle-bones. Did he say a word to stop them? Not he! He said: 'You can have the food and wine that have been offered to the dead lady.' That's how he treats them. One day I overheard the strumpet saying: 'I wonder what is keeping his Lordship so long. We must be ready for him.' I went in, and she was alarmed and didn't say any more. What a woman! The rascally strumpet! But he is so anxious for fresh meat he will take anything that comes along. He never troubles whether it is good or bad. The lustful fellow! The strumpet says her husband is dead; but who was that fellow with a baby in his arms looking around the gate the other day? She is deceiving us. She is like Li Ping'er come to life again, quite a changed woman. And the Great Lady spends all her time in her own room and acts as though she were deaf and dumb. Whenever we go and say anything to her, she says: 'You are mistaken.' "

Yulou could not help laughing. "How do you manage to get all this information?" she said.

"It's common gossip," Jinlian said. "Everybody knows it. If you bury a body in the snow, it always turns up again when the snow melts."

"She said her husband was dead," Yulou said. "Who is this husband, then?"

"The clouds never disperse unless there is wind," Jinlian said, "and business is never done without telling a lot of lies. She would never have got the job if she hadn't deceived us. You remember what she looked like when she first came. Half starved, yellow-faced, as thin as a lath, and her limbs shaking. Now she has enjoyed good food for a couple of years, she starts stealing our husband. If we don't put a stop to it, she will have a baby one of these days, and, if that happens, where shall we be? And whose baby would it be?"

"There is something in what you say," Yulou said, laughing. They stayed talking for a while and then went to the inner court to play chess.

One afternoon, Ximen Qing reached Qinghe. He told Ben the Fourth and Wang Jing to take the luggage home, and went with Captain He to the office. He helped to make the necessary arrangements there, then mounted his horse and rode home.

Wu Yueniang received him in the hall and gave him water to wash his face. He ordered a maid to set up a table in the courtyard that he might offer incense to Heaven and Earth in thanksgiving for his safe return. Yueniang asked him why he did this.

"Oh, it was terrible," Ximen Qing said, "I very nearly lost my life. On the twenty-third, when we had crossed the Yellow River and come to the place called the Town of the Eight Corners, there was a frightful storm. Dust and sand filled our eyes and we could make no progress at all. It was late and for a hundred miles we had not seen a soul. We were alarmed because we had so much luggage and we were afraid highwaymen might suddenly attack us. Then we came to an old monastery. The monks were so poor that they were going without light. The only thing they could give us was porridge. We spent the night there and started off again the next morning. The wind had stopped. It was a much worse journey than the last one. The last was during the hot season, but it was more agreeable than this, because, not only was the weather terribly cold this time, but we always felt so insecure. It was a good thing for us we were on the plain when the storm arose. If it had come on while we were crossing the Yellow River, I don't know what might have happened. I vowed to offer a pig and a sheep to Heaven and Earth on the first day of the twelfth month."

"Why did you go to the office before you came home?" Yueniang asked.

"Magistrate Xia has been promoted to be an officer of the Imperial Escort," Ximen said. "That is an appointment in the Capital and he is not coming back here. The new captain is He Yingshou, a nephew of Eunuch He. He is a boy of about twenty. He is quite ignorant and the old eunuch begged me to look after him. I couldn't leave him to find his own way to the office. He knows nothing about the place. He has bought Xia's house for twelve hundred taels. I arranged it all for him. He is going to send for his family as soon as Xia's people have left.

"I can't imagine who told Xia about these promotions. He sent a large sum of money to his Holiness Lin, and his Holiness told Marshal Zhu that he would like to retain his present position for another three years instead of going to the Capital. The Marshal spoke to his Eminence about the matter and it made matters most awkward. If it hadn't been for our kinsman Zhai speaking on my behalf, I might have lost my position. Our kinsman was very much annoyed. He said I had been very careless. I can't think who told Magistrate Xia."

"If you will forgive my saying so," his wife said, "you are indeed careless. Whenever you hear anything, you tell it first to one person and then to another. You like to show people how rich and powerful you are. You carelessly let things slip, and those who hear do not lose the opportunity. Then there is trouble. People worm secrets out of you and go off and use the information to their own advantage. You never hear about it till they have done all they wish to do."

"When I left Magistrate Xia," Ximen said, "he begged me repeatedly to do anything I could for his family. We must send them a present and call."

"It will be Mistress Xia's birthday on the second of next month," Yue-niang said. "We will go then. As for you, you must be careful. Remember the saying: Never let people know more than a quarter of what you know yourself. Even your own wife may take advantage of you, not to mention other people."

As they were talking, Daian came and said: "Ben the Fourth would like to know if you are going to his Lordship Xia's place."

"Tell him to go when he has had something to eat," Ximen said.

Li Jiao'er, Meng Yulou, Pan Jinlian and Ximen Dajie came to welcome him home. They sat down together and talked.

Ximen Qing remembered that the last time he had returned from the Eastern Capital, Li Ping'er was still alive. He went to her room, bowed before her tablet and wept. Ruyi'er, Yingchun, and Xiuchun came to kowtow to him. Then Yueniang sent Xiaoyu to ask him to go to dinner in the inner court. He gave orders that those who had accompanied him on his journey should be given five taels of silver.

He sent a card to Major Zhou, and told Laixing to get half a pig, half a sheep, forty measures of fine flour, a sack of white rice, a jar of wine, two hams, two geese, ten chickens, and take them, with a supply of condiments, to Captain He. He also sent a cook.

He was in the hall when Qintong came and said that Scholar Wen and Ying Bojue had come to see him. Ximen Qing ordered the boy to bring them in. They bowed several times and said: "What a rough journey you must have had." Ximen thanked them for looking after his house in his absence.

"This morning, when I awoke," Bojue said, "I heard the crying of the magpies on the roof, and my wife said to me: 'I expect that means his Lordship Ximen is back. Why don't you go and see?' I said: 'Brother started on the twelfth and he hasn't been away a fortnight yet. How can he be back already?' 'Well,' my wife said, 'whether he is back or not, you must go.' She told me to dress and come, and here you are. I congratulate you."

He saw the wine and rice and other things collected outside the hall. "To whom are you sending these things?" he said.

"I came back with Captain He, the new magistrate," Ximen said. "His family has not come yet and he is staying at the office for the time being. I am sending him some provisions. I have invited him to dinner tomorrow, and I am going to ask you and Uncle Wu to come too."

"I must remind you," Bojue said, "that Uncle Wu and you are officers. Master Wen wears a scholar's hat. I am only a private person, and it seems hardly fitting that I should join you. I don't know what he may think. He may laugh at me."

"If that's all that is worrying you," Ximen said, laughing, "I will lend you my silk hat, and, when Captain He asks who you are, I'll tell him you're my eldest son. Will that suit you?"

They laughed. "I am serious," Bojue said. "My size in hats is eight and three-tenths. Yours won't fit me."

"I take a hat eight and three-tenths too," Scholar Wen said. "Perhaps you would like my scholar's hat!"

"No," Ximen Qing said. "Don't let him have it. When he goes to pawn himself, he might wear it."

"Well said, Sir," Scholar Wen said, "the joke is on both of us."

Tea was brought. "I suppose his Lordship Xia will stay at the Capital," Scholar Wen said, "or is he coming back

"He is now an officer of the Imperial Escort," Ximen said. "He wears embroidered robes and carries a wand. It is an exalted position and he will not come back."

He looked at the card that was to go with the provisions for Captain He, and bade Daian take them. Then he went with Ying Bojue and Scholar Wen to the side room and sat down on the stove bed. He sent Qintong to tell Wu Hui, Zheng Chun, Zheng Feng and Zuo Shun that they would be wanted the following day. The table was set and they began to drink. Ximen told a servant to get another pair of chopsticks and invite his son-in-law.

Chen Jingji came and sat down with them. They sat near the fire and, while the wine went around, Ximen Qing told them of the dangers he had passed through.

"Brother," Bojue said, "you have a heart stout enough to carry you through a hundred dangers. Even if there had been ruffians about, they could not have harmed you."

"'If a good man were to govern the country for a hundred years,'" Scholar Wen said, "'he would be able to make evil men into peaceful citizens, and could do away with the punishment of death.'* You are doing the Emperor's service, and Heaven will not let you come to harm."

Ximen Qing asked how things had been in the household.

"There was nothing of any consequence," Jingji said. "His Excellency An of the Office of Works sent twice to ask if you had returned. Only yesterday a man came from him, and I told him you were not back."

Then Ping'an came and said that the junior officers and their men were outside. Ximen Qing went to the hall and gave orders that the two officers should be admitted. They came and knelt down. "When will you assume your office?" they asked, "and what money will you require?"

---

* A quotation from the *Analects of Confucius*, Book XIII, Chap. 11.

"Let everything be as before," Ximen told them.

"Last year, you were alone," they said, "but now you are promoted to a higher office, and Captain He comes to the office also. It is not the same. There are two officers instead of one."

"Take ten taels more, then," Ximen Qing said.

As the two men were going away, Ximen stopped them. "You had better ask Captain He when he wishes to assume office."

"Captain He says on the twenty-sixth," they said.

"Very well. See that everything is ready on that day." When the two junior officers had gone, Master Qiao came. Ximen Qing asked him to stay, but he went away as soon as he had taken tea. Ximen Qing went back to Ying Bojue and Scholar Wen, and they drank together until evening. That night, Ximen slept with Yueniang

Old woman Wen heard that Ximen had returned. She told Wang the Third, and he sent a card of invitation to Ximen Qing. In return, Ximen sent Daian with a pair of pig's trotters, two live fish, two roast ducks and a jar of wine as a belated birthday present to Lady Lin. Lady Lin gave Daian three *qian* of silver.

The next day Ximen Qing entertained Captain He to dinner. It was laid in the great hall. Very careful preparations had been made. Uncle Wu, Ying Bojue, and Scholar Wen came early and took tea with Ximen Qing. He sent a man to remind Captain He. Then the singing boys came and kowtowed to Ximen.

"Why haven't you engaged Li Ming today?" Bojue asked.

"If he doesn't come of his own accord, I shall not send for him," Ximen said.

Ping'an brought a card and announced Major Zhou. Uncle Wu, Scholar Wen, and Ying Bojue withdrew to a side room while Ximen Qing put on his ceremonial clothes and went to receive Major Zhou in the great hall. The Major congratulated Ximen on his promotion, and Ximen thanked him for the men who had acted as his escort on the journey to the Capital. They sat down and Zhou asked what he had seen at the Capital and in the Court. When Ximen had told him, he said: "I suppose Xia will be taking his family to the Capital?"

"Yes," Ximen said, "but not before next month. For the time being, Captain He is living at the office, but he has bought Xia's house. I made the arrangement myself."

"Excellent!" Major Zhou said. Seeing the tables all set out, he asked what guests Ximen was expecting.

"It is only a very plain meal in honor of Captain He," Ximen said. "It is the least I can do seeing that we are both in the same office."

When Major Zhou had drunk his tea, he stood up. "One of these days," he said, "I shall bring the officers of my command to offer you two gentlemen our congratulations."

"You are too kind," Ximen said. Thank you for troubling to come and see me."

They bowed to each other. Major Zhou went away and Ximen Qing rejoined his three friends.

It was late in the afternoon when Captain He came. Ximen Qing introduced Uncle Wu and the others and they exchanged greetings. After tea, they took off their ceremonial clothes. Captain He soon realized that Ximen Qing was a very rich man, so splendid was the repast served to him. There were four singing boys playing different instruments. They drank together till the first night watch, then Captain He went back to the office. Uncle Wu, Ying Bojue, and Scholar Wen went away at the same time. Ximen Qing dismissed the singing boys, told the servants to clear everything away, and went to Pan Jinlian's room.

Jinlian had taken particular pains to make herself look pretty and she had washed her body with perfumed water. She was expecting him and, when he came, she smiled sweetly. She took his clothes and told Chunmei to make tea. They went to bed, and, under the coverlets, embraced and pressed their tender bodies closely together. She used every one of her hundred charms to give him pleasure. They enjoyed each other for a while, then Ximen Qing found that he could not sleep. He told her how he had longed for her while he had been away. Then, as he was still unsatisfied, he asked her to play the flute for him. She was ready to do anything he asked, so that she might the more firmly establish her hold over him. They had been separated for a long time. She had been starved for love so long that passion set her afire. She would have made herself a part of him. She grasped his penis and wanted to suck it almost all night. He wished to make water, but she would not let him go. "Darling," she said, "never mind how much there is; my mouth can take it all. It is chilly tonight and you might take cold if you got out of bed. It would be more trouble."

Ximen Qing was delighted. "Dearest," he said, "I don't believe anyone else would love me as you do." He made water into her mouth and she drank it gradually. "Do you like it?' said Ximen.

"It is a little bitter," she replied. "Give me some fragrant tea leaves to take the taste away."

"The tea leaves are in my white silk coat," Ximen said. "Get them for yourself." Jinlian pulled the coat to her, took the tea leaves, and put them into her mouth.

Readers, concubines are always ready to lead their husbands on and to bewitch them. To this end, they will go to any length of shamelessness and endure any shameful thing. Such practices would be abhorrent to a real wife who had married her husband in the proper way.

Ximen Qing and Jinlian enjoyed ecstasies of pleasure that night.

The next day, Ximen Qing went to the office with Captain He. It was their first appearance in their new posts. There was a banquet, and musicians played for them. In the afternoon Ximen went home and the soldiers of his office sent a present of food. Wang the Third sent a man to ask him to dinner. Ximen was about to leave for Wang's house, when a servant came and announced the arrival of An, of the Office of Works. Ximen Qing hurriedly put on his robes and went to welcome him.

An, who now held the rank of a Vice President, wore a girdle with a golden clasp, and a silver pheasant as the badge of his office. He was followed by a host of officers. They entered the hall, smiling, and congratulating one another.

"I have asked several times when you were expected to return," An said, when they had sat down, "but I was told you were not yet back."

"I could not leave the Capital until I had been presented at Court," Ximen said.

"I wanted to ask a favor of you," An said. "Cai Xiaotang, his Eminence's ninth son, is governor of Jiujiang. He is on his way to the Capital and I have had a letter from him to say he will be here very shortly. Song Songquan, Qian Yunye, Huang Taiyu and I would like to entertain him. But, for that, we should need your house, and I don't know whether you would be willing to lend it to us or not."

"Certainly you may have it," Ximen said. "When is he coming?"

"On the twenty-seventh," An said. "I will send the necessary money tomorrow. It is extremely kind of you."

They drank tea, and Vice President An went away.

Ximen Qing went to Lady Lin's house and sent in his card. Wang the Third came out to receive him and took him to the great hall. Above the place of honor hung a golden scroll with the words: "The Hall of Loyalty Continuing." There were other scrolls on either side. One said, "The Wind and Frost wear down the mighty Trees," and the other, "Mountains and Rivers, Girdles and Whetstones are always new."

Wang the Third made a reverence to Ximen Qing and asked him to take the place of honor. Tea was brought, and he himself handed it. After tea they talked for a while until dinner was served. Two boys sang to them.

"Will you not ask her Ladyship to come?" Ximen Qing said.

Wang the Third sent a servant to invite his mother to join them.

Very soon the servant returned. "Her Ladyship asks that you will go to the inner court to see her," he said.

Wang the Third asked Ximen Qing to go, and Ximen asked Wang the Third to lead the way. So they went to the hall.

Lady Lin was wearing pearls and ornaments on her head, a scarlet, straight-sleeved gown, and a girdle decorated with gold and green jade. She wore a silken skirt embroidered with the design of the hundred flowers. Her face was powdered till it was as white as silver. Ximen Qing prepared to make a reverence to her and asked her to take the place of honor. "You are my guest," she said. "The place of honor is due to you." Finally, they made equal reverences, and sat down.

"My young son," Lady Lin said, "is very inexperienced. He was unfortunate enough to incur your displeasure, but you were generous and punished the fellows who led him astray. I don't know how to thank you. I have prepared this very simple entertainment for you, but I feel that really I should kowtow. Why have you sent me presents? I shall feel embarrassed if I accept them, and lacking in courtesy if I decline them."

"I had to go to the Eastern Capital on duty," Ximen Qing said, "I could not come to congratulate you on your birthday. These trifling presents you speak of are really intended for your servants."

Old woman Wen was standing beside Lady Lin. Ximen said to her: "Madam Wen, please give me a cup that I may offer her Ladyship some wine." He called Daian, who brought a dress of very fashionable style, embroidered with gold. This was put on a tray, and offered to Lady Lin. The dress was so bright that it was dazzling to the eyes. Lady Lin was delighted. Old woman Wen brought gold and silver cups. Wang the Third was going to send for the boys to sing, but Lady Lin said it would be better if they played outside. When Ximen had offered wine to her, she offered it to him in return. Then Wang the Third offered wine to him. Ximen would have made a reverence to the young man in return, but Lady Lin said:

"My lord, you must stand and allow him to pay you the respect that is your due."

"I dare not," Ximen Qing said, "the Rites do not allow it."

"My lord," Lady Lin said, "surely you are wrong. Your rank is now such that you might be his father. My son, in his earlier youth, was very poorly educated. He never associated with gentlemen. If you are well disposed to him, you may, perhaps, be willing to teach him something of the ways of the world. I would even venture to suggest that you might take him under your guardianship and treat him as your son. If he gets into trouble, correct him. I will not stand in your way."

"Lady," Ximen Qing said, "you speak wisely, but your son is really both intelligent and amiable. He is still young and only on the threshold of life. As he acquires more experience, he will amend his ways. You must not worry about him."

Ximen Qing was persuaded to take the place of honor. Wang the Third offered him three cups of wine and made reverence to him four times. Then Ximen Qing made a reverence to Lady Lin, and she, smilingly, returned it. After this, whenever Wang the Third was in the presence of Ximen Qing, he called him Father.

After this simple ceremony, Lady Lin bade her son take Ximen Qing to the outer court to take off his ceremonial clothes. Daian brought a hat and he changed. The two men sat down, and the singing boys played and sang for them. When the cooks brought in food, Daian gave them a small present of money. When five courses had been served, and the singers had sung two songs, lights were brought. Ximen Qing stood up to take leave, but Wang the Third begged him not to go so pressingly that he remained. The young man took him to a small courtyard attached to the study. There were only three rooms, but there were delightful flowers and trees about, and the furniture was very handsome. A golden sign bore the words: "Sanquan's Ship of Poesy." There were five old pictures on the walls.

Ximen Qing asked who Sanquan was. Wang the Third was reluctant to tell him, but at last he said: "It is your son's name." Ximen Qing said nothing.

Tall jars were brought. They played darts and drank, and the singing boys sang for them again. Lady Lin, in the inner court, looked after the cooks and servants, sending them with dishes and fruits.

It was the second night watch before Ximen Qing went away. He was almost tipsy. He distributed money to the cooks and singers, and went home.

When he reached home, he went at once to Jinlian's room. She had not gone to bed, but had taken off her headdress and painted her face very delicately. She had made tea and burned incense in a golden burner. Now she was waiting for him, and when he came, she was delighted. She took his clothes and told Chunmei to make him a special cup of Sparrow-Tongue Tea. Chunmei helped him to take off his clothes and girdle. He went to bed. Jinlian took off her ornaments, put on a pair of bed shoes, and went to bed too. They lay down together and entwined their legs. Ximen Qing made a pillow of one arm and pressed her close to him with the other. Her body seemed to him as smooth as a piece of soft jade. His breast touched hers; their cheeks were close together. They kissed; their hearts seemed to melt away within them, and they were thrilled to the very center of their beings.

"My child," Ximen said, "did you ever think of me when I was away?"

"I never forgot you for a single second. The nights seemed so long. When I lay down, I could not sleep. I heated my bed and made it as warm as I could, but I still felt cold, so cold, indeed, that I could not stretch my legs out. I had to suffer and keep them drawn up. I kept thinking you would come, but you never came. Oh, many tears fell upon this pillow. Then dear little Chunmei saw how melancholy I was and sighing, and she cheered me as best she could. She used to play chess with me in the evenings. We stayed up till the first night watch, then went to bed and slept together. That was how I felt, Brother. I wonder how it was with you.

"Little oily mouth," Ximen said, "I have several wives, but, as everyone knows, I love you best."

"No, you are deceiving me," Jinlian said. "You are like a boy who takes rice from the bowl but keeps his eyes on the jar all the time. You think I don't know it. Do you remember how you and Laiwang's wife were as close together as honey and oil mingled? You never thought about me then. Li Ping'er had a baby, and you treated me like a black-eyed hen. Now they are gone, and I am still strong and well. You are like a willow catkin blown about by the wind. You have been secretly carrying on with Ruyi'er. You don't seem to care what sort of creature she is. After all, she is only a nurse, and, besides, she has a husband. If you take her on, one of these days her husband will bring all his sheep outside your door. You are an officer now. What are you going to do when the scandalmongers begin to talk about it? When you were away, that woman quarreled with me, screamed at me, and wouldn't give way an inch. That was when I sent Chunmei to borrow a dolly pin from her."

"Dear, dear!" Ximen Qing said. "It doesn't matter who she is, she must not forget that she is a servant here. I am surprised she had the audacity to quarrel with you. If you raise your hand, it should be a sign to her to pass, and if you lower it, she should know that she is barred from going any farther."

"Oh, you can always talk!" Jinlian said. "Now that Li Ping'er is dead, Ruyi'er has taken her mistress's place. I suppose you said to her: 'Serve me well, and you shall have everything that belonged to your mistress.' Did you say that?"

"Don't be so silly. I said nothing of the sort. If you will forgive her, I will make her come and kowtow to you tomorrow."

"I don't want her apologies. I forbid you to go to her."

"When I go there to sleep," Ximen Qing said, "I have no other purpose than to remember your dead sister. I go to look at her tablet, and I have nothing whatever to do with the woman."

"You are such a liar, I don't believe you," Jinlian said. "It is more than a hundred days since Li Ping'er died. Why should you go to gaze upon her tablet? You don't go to watch before the tablet, you go to make the place like a miller's grinding place. Before midnight we hear the sound of the bell and, after midnight, the sound of the winnowing."

Ximen Qing pulled her to him and kissed her. "You funny little strumpet," he said "where did you get such sharp ears?"

He told her to turn over, and inserted his penis from behind. He held her legs and moved in and out noisily. "Do you fear me or not?" he cried. "Will you try to control my actions any more?"

"If I didn't," Jinlian said, "you would fly off in the air. I know you can't give the woman up, but, if you wish to have her, you must ask my permission, and, if she asks you for anything, you must tell me before you give it to her. I won't have you giving her things without my knowledge. If you do, and I find out, you shall see whether I make trouble or not. I and that strumpet will die together. It is the story of Li Ping'er over again. You could think of no one but her, and I was as little to you as the lowest of your women. You rotten peach! You are like bean sprouts that haven't been tied with proper string. But your old mother is too clever for you."

Ximen Qing laughed. It was the third night watch before they were content to put their arms around one another and go to sleep. They slept till nearly dawn.

Before it was light, Jinlian, still hungry for more, fondled his weapon with her slender fingers till it was ready once more for action.

"Darling," she said, "I want to lie on you." She climbed on to him, and played the game of making a candle upside down. She put her arms around his neck and wriggled about. She asked him to grip her firmly by the waist. Then she lifted herself up and dropped herself again; soon his penis entered her up to its very root, and the only part that stayed outside was that bound by the clasp.

"Darling," she said, "I will make a red silk belt for you, and you can keep in it the medicine the monk gave you. And I will make two supports that you can tie at the root of it and fasten around your waist. When they are tightly tied, it will be soft and go in all the way. Don't you think that better than this clasp, which is so hard and such a nuisance?"

"Yes, my child, make it by all means. The medicine is in my little box. Put it in for yourself."

"Come back tonight," Jinlian said, "and we will see what it is like."

Daian came with a card and asked Chunmei if his master was out of bed. "His Excellency An," he said, "has sent money, two jars of wine, and four pots of flowers."

"Father is not up yet," Chunmei told him. "Ask the man to wait."

"He has a long way to go," Daian said. "He is on his way to the new wharf."

Ximen Qing overheard this. He asked what was the matter, and the card was brought to him. Upon it was written: 'I send you eight taels for the refreshment of Xiaotang. The food for the others may be what is customary. I trust you will instruct your servants to make careful preparations, and thank you for your kindness. I send you also four pots with seasonable flowers in the hope that you will like them. The two jars of wine may, perhaps, serve for the entertainment of the guests. Please accept them indulgently.

Ximen Qing got up. He did not dress his hair but, putting on a felt hat and a gown, went to the hall. He sent for his Excellency's messenger. The man presented the silver and the pots of flowers. One contained red plum, another white plum, the third jasmine and the fourth, magnolia. And there were two jars of Southern wine. Ximen was very pleased. He gave the man a card in return and five *qian* of silver for himself.

"When will the gentlemen arrive?" he asked. "Will it be necessary to engage actors?"

"Their Excellencies will be early," the man said. "They would like to have the Haiyan company." He went away.

Ximen Qing told the servants to take the flowers to his study and sent Daian to engage the actors. As it was Meng Yulou's birthday, he arranged for them to come in the evening also. Laian was sent to buy provisions.

We now return to Ying Bojue. On the twenty-eighth day of the month, his baby would be one month old, and there was to be a celebration. He took five cards and sent Ying Bao with a box to the house opposite Ximen Qing's. He was going to ask Scholar Wen to write invitations to Ximen's five ladies.

He had left his own house and turned into the street when he heard a voice behind him calling: "Uncle! Uncle!" It was Li Ming. Bojue stopped, and Li Ming asked where he was going.

"I am going to see Scholar Wen on business," Bojue said.

"I was just coming to see you," Li Ming said. "There is something I want to tell you."

Ying Bojue saw a porter carrying a box behind Li Ming, and he took Li Ming to his house. The boy kowtowed to him and presented the box. There were two roast ducks and two bottles of spirits in it.

"I have nothing but these trifles to offer you," Li Ming said, "but I should like to ask your help." He knelt down and could not be persuaded to rise. Bojue finally pulled him up.

"You silly boy. If you have anything to say, say it. There was no need for you to bring these presents."

"I have served his Lordship Ximen ever since I was a little boy," Li Ming said. "Now he is giving his patronage to others and leaving me out in the cold. I have nothing to do with Li Guijie's affairs. We are not in the same boat. His Lordship is angry with her, and he seems to be angry with me too. I have had no opportunity to explain matters. So I have come to you. I beg you to go and speak for me. Tell him that I had nothing to do with Guijie's naughty behavior. Since I have incurred his displeasure, all the boys in my business make fun of me."

"You haven't been to his place for a long time," Bojue said.

"No," the boy said.

"That explains why, the other day, when Captain He was at his place, I only saw Wu Hui, Zheng Chun, Zheng Feng and Zuo Shun. You were not there, and I asked why. His Lordship told me that you never came near the place and he wasn't going to send for you. Now, you silly boy, pull yourself together and don't be such a blockhead."

"When he didn't send for me," Li Ming said, "I felt too shy to go of my own accord. The other four were there two or three days ago and, today, I find Laian is engaging two of them for the Third Lady's birthday. There is a party tomorrow, and the four boys will be there again without me. I am very miserable about it. Uncle, I want you to explain matters for me. I will come and kowtow to you again."

"I spend all my time helping others," Bojue said, "and I will do the best I can for you. I have done many, many things for people, and this trifling business of yours is nothing at all. Take these presents away. I know how you get your money, and I won't take them. Come with me, and let me make everything all right."

"I will not go unless you accept my present," Li Ming said. "You do not need the things, of course, but I am anxious to show my humble respect for you."

He implored Ying Bojue to take them, and, at last, Bojue did so. He gave thirty coppers to the porter who had carried the box. Then they set out together. They went first to the house opposite Ximen Qing's. They went into the courtyard. Bojue knocked at the door and asked if Scholar

Wen was at home. The scholar was in the study, writing a card. "Please come in," he cried. Huatong opened the door, and Bojue went into the study. Scholar Wen greeted him. They sat down, and the scholar said: "You are early today. What have you been doing?"

"I have come to ask you to write a few invitations with your masterly brush. It will be the end of my little son's first month of life on the twenty-eighth, and I am inviting his Lordship's ladies."

"Give me the cards," Scholar Wen said, "I will write them for you with pleasure."

Bojue told Ying Bao to take out the cards and give them to Scholar Wen. The scholar took them to the inner room and had written two when Qitong came hurrying in and said: "Master, please write another two cards for my lady. She wishes to invite Mistress Qiao and Mistress Wu. Did you give Qintong the cards for Mistress Han and Mistress Meng?"

"Yes," Scholar Wen said, "they were sent off sometime ago."

"Master," Qitong said, "when you have finished those two cards, please write another four. They are for Mistress Huang the Fourth, Mistress Fu, Mistress Han, and Mistress Gan. Laian will come for them."

Qitong went away and Laian came for the four cards. Bojue said to him: "Is your master at home or at the office?"

"He has not been to the office today," Laian said. "He is in the hall receiving presents."

"It was very late when his Lordship came back from Wang's place last night," Scholar Wen said.

"Which Wang's?" Bojue asked.

"The general's," Scholar Wen told him.

This was the first Ying Bojue had heard of this business.

When Scholar Wen had finished the cards for Laian, he began again on those for Ying Bojue. When they were done, Bojue went across the road to Ximen's house with Li Ming.

Ximen Qing's hair was still undressed. He was in the hall, accepting presents and sending cards in return. Tables were being set out for the reception. He asked Bojue to sit down. Bojue thanked him for the gifts he had sent some days before and asked why the tables were being arranged. Ximen told him that his Excellency An was making use of the house for a reception to the Imperial Tutor's son.

"Are you having actors or singing boys?" Bojue asked.

"We are having the Haiyan company of actors," Ximen Qing said, "but I have engaged four singing boys as well."

"Who are they, Brother?" Bojue asked.

"Wu Hui, Zheng Feng, Zheng Chun and Zuo Shun," Ximen said.

"Why not Li Ming?"

"He has climbed too high to care about my patronage any more," Ximen said.

"Why should you say that, Brother?" Bojue said. "He can hardly come if you don't send for him. I didn't know you were angry with him. And the business for which you are angry with him is really not his concern at all. He can't help what happens at the bawdy house. We must not be unfair to him. This morning he called at my house and said, with tears in his eyes, that, apart from the relations that have existed between you and his sister, he has served you himself for several years. Now, he says, you send for the others and will have nothing to do with him. He swore on his oath that he had nothing to do with that business at the house. If you are angry with him, it will be very awkward indeed for him. He is only a boy. He can't earn a great amount of money and, if you stop sending for him, his position will be impossible."

"Li Ming, come here!" he called. "Tell your father all about it. Why are you hiding there? Come here, I tell you. Even an ugly bride must meet her father-in-law sometime."

Li Ming was standing outside the hall. He bowed and then stood upright, like the image of a little devil. He had been listening to what they were saying and, when Bojue called him, he came in quickly and knelt down. He kowtowed repeatedly.

"Father," he said, "you must think about this again. If I had anything to do with that business, may my bones be broken to pieces by horses or carts, and may I die at the hand of the executioner. Your kindness to me in the past has always been so splendid. My people and I can never repay you. If you are angry with me, the others in my profession will laugh at me and look down on me. I can never find another master like you."

He cried aloud, knelt on the floor, and would not get up.

"We must settle this," Bojue said. "A gentleman never holds a lesser man's faults against him. Besides, it wasn't his fault and, even if it had been, you would have to forgive him now that he comes to apologize." He said to Li Ming: "I am wearing black clothes so I have to stand near a black pillar. Now you have spoken to your father, I am sure he won't be angry with you any more. But, in future, you must take care."

"Yes, Uncle," Li Ming said, "I will amend my ways."

"Since your uncle asks me to forgive you, I will do so," Ximen said slowly. "Stand up."

"Kowtow," Bojue said.

Li Ming kowtowed and rose to his feet.

Ying Bojue asked Ying Bao for the cards of invitation and gave them to Ximen Qing. "It will be my baby's month-day on the twenty-eighth," he said. "I am inviting my sisters-in-law to my humble dwelling."

Ximen Qing looked at the cards, and told Laian to take them with the box to Wu Yueniang. "I don't think they will be able to come that day," he said. "Tomorrow is the Third Lady's birthday, and there is this reception as well. On the twenty-eighth, my wife is going to call on Mistress Xia. I don't see how she can manage to come to your place."

"Brother," Bojue said, "would you seek my death? If my sister-in-law won't go, whom else can I count upon? Since the fruits are in the garden, I will go myself and ask them."

But Laian came in with the box empty. "The Great Lady says I am to tell Uncle Ying she accepts his kind invitation."

Bojue gave the empty box to Ying Bao. "Brother," he said, laughing, "you are always making game of me. If my sister-in-law had really refused to come, I would have bashed my head against the wall, and she would have been compelled to give way."

"Stay till I have done my hair," Ximen Qing said to Bojue, "and we will have something to eat." He went to the inner court.

"Now what?" Bojue said to Li Ming. "If it hadn't been for me, he would not have forgiven you. Don't mind what he says. Wealthy people are always bad-tempered, but you mustn't forget the proverb: An angry fist will never smite a smiling face. In these days, people like to be flattered. Even if you have money and set yourself up in business, you have always to be agreeable to your customers. If you pull a long face, nobody will bother about you. What you have to do is to fit yourself to circumstances and make yourself as adaptable as running water. Then you will make money. If you always try to ride the high horse, others will get good food but you will starve. You have served his Lordship for a long time, but you don't understand him yet. Tell Li Guijie to come tomorrow. If she is hot upon your heels, she will kill two birds with one stone. It is the Third Lady's birthday. She can come to congratulate her and apologize to him at the same time. Then everything will be well."

"Uncle," Li Ming said, "you are right. I will go home at once and tell my aunt."

Laian came in to set the table. "Uncle Ying," he said, "if you will wait a few moments, Father will be here."

Soon Ximen came in, properly dressed. They sat down.

"I haven't seen old Sun and Pockmarked Zhu for a long time," Ximen said.

"I told them to come," Bojue said, "but they declared you were offended with them. I told them that, thanks to your generosity, when the mosquitoes and grasshoppers were brought before the court, they were allowed to escape. They swore to me they would never have anything to do with young master Wang again. I hear you were at Wang's place yesterday. I hadn't known of it before."

"Yes," Ximen said. "There was a little party, and I was invited. I was asked if I would take the young man under my protection and treat him as a son. I didn't get back until the second night watch. Why shouldn't they go there any more? They can go if they like. It won't worry me. Why should I bother about the young man? I'm not really his father."

"If you mean what you say, Brother," Bojue said, "I am sure they will come to apologize and explain the whole business."

"There is nothing for them to apologize about," Ximen said. "Tell them to come, that's all."

Daian brought the food. There were all sorts of delicious things. Ximen Qing had porridge, and Bojue, rice.

"Why haven't the two singing boys come yet?" Ximen asked.

"They are here," Laian said.

"Go and have something to eat with them," Ximen said to Li Ming. One was Han Zuo, the other Shao Qian. They came and kowtowed before Ximen Qing, then went to have their dinner. Before long, Ying Bojue stood up. "I must be going now," he said, "I expect my people are waiting anxiously for me. In humble families like ours, it is very hard to get anything done. We have to buy everything. Buy, buy, buy from the bottom of the cooking stove to the sitting-room door."

"Go and do what you have to do," Ximen said, "and come back this evening to kowtow to the Third Lady and show what a good son you are."

"I will certainly come," Bojue said, "and my wife will send some presents." He went away.

CHAPTER 73

Qiuju in Trouble

I was called a great lover
I remembered my love.
He who called me a great lover and accepted my love
That man despised me.
Because I am a great lover
My love grows ever deeper and stronger
If I die of love I shall not complain
My love shall be ever steadfast.

When Ying Bojue had gone, Ximen Qing went to the Cave of Spring to watch the masons putting in a warm bed. It was heated by a furnace outside the wall, so that the flowers should not be spoiled by the smoke.

Ping'an brought him a card and told him that Major Zhou had sent a present. There was a box with five separate contributions from Major Zhou himself, General Jing, Captain Zhang, and the two eunuchs, Liu and Xue. Each of them sent five *xing* and two handkerchiefs. Ximen told a servant to accept the things, and gave a card to the man who had brought them.

Aunt Yang, Aunt Wu and old woman Pan came early. Nun Xue, Nun Wang, the two novices, Miao Qu and Miao Feng, and Miss Yu came with gifts for Meng Yulou. Wu Yueniang gave them tea in her own room. The ladies were all there to welcome the guests, but after tea they went to their own rooms.

Pan Jinlian was eager to make the red silk belt she had promised Ximen Qing. She went to her room and brought out her sewing box. From it she took a piece of red sarcenet. Then, from a porcelain box, she took some of the aphrodisiac drug and sewed it, with fine delicate stitches, into the material. Everything was now ready for the work of darkness. Suddenly, Nun Xue came to the door. She had brought Jinlian the potion she was to take to make her conceive. They sat down to talk. Nun Xue saw that nobody was about.

"Wait until a *Renzi* day," she whispered. "Then take it before you have anything to eat. That night, sleep with your husband and you will conceive without fail. The Great Lady has a big belly. It was I who gave her the medicine. And I will tell you something else. Make yourself a little bag, and I will give you a spell written in red ink to put in it. Carry it on your body, and you will bear a son. You have my word for that. It has never been known to fail."

Jinlian was delighted. She put the medicine and the charm into a box. Then she consulted a calendar. The next *Renzi* day was the twenty-ninth. She gave the nun three *qian* of silver. "This is very little," she said. "It will buy you some vegetarian food. But when I have a baby, I will give you some silk to make clothes with."

"Don't trouble about that," the nun said, "I am not so greedy as Nun Wang. You remember when I held that service for the dead lady. She said I had done her out of it, and quarreled with me. Now, she never meets me without saying something horrid. But she can go to Hell. I am not going to argue with her. My only aim in life is to do all the good I can and save people from misfortune."

"Do the best you can," Jinlian said. "We can't expect everybody to be as kind as we are. Don't mention this business to her."

"Oh, I shall say nothing about it," Xue said. "It shall be a secret between ourselves. Last year, when I did this for the Great Lady, Wang said I had been too well paid, and nagged at me until I gave her half of what I got. A fine god-fearing creature she is! She never fasts, and she is far too fond of money. She takes alms from everybody and never does anything in return. When she dies and is born again, she will be something worse than a horned animal. I'm sure of it." ·

Jinlian told Chunmei to give the nun some tea. When she had drunk it, she went to Li Ping'er's room to pay her respects to the tablet. Then she went back to the inner court.

In the afternoon, Yueniang had tables laid in her room and invited all the ladies and the nuns. She also had a table set in the middle room and a fire lit, so that they could drink wine there in honor of Yulou's birthday.

The wine was poured into jade cups. Yulou, herself like a jade statue, raised a cup aloft. She offered it to Ximen Qing. Then she made a reverence to each of the other ladies in turn. Jingji and his wife were there. They greeted her. They all sat down, and special birthday dishes were brought in. While they were drinking, Laian came in with a box and said Ying Bao had brought presents. Ximen Qing asked Yueniang to accept them. He told Laian to get an invitation card written for Mistress Ying, and to invite Ying Bojue and Uncle Wu to come also.

"I know Mistress Ying will not come," he said, "so we had better ask Uncle Ying. We will send presents in return another day." Laian gave Ying Bao a card, and the boy went home.

Ximen Qing remembered Yulou's last birthday, when Li Ping'er was still alive. Now, all the other ladies were there, but she was gone. The thought grieved him and he shed tears.

Li Ming and the other two boys came in. "Can you sing the song of the lovebirds?" Yueniang asked them. Han Zuo said he knew it, took up his instrument and was going to sing, but Ximen Qing stopped him.

"No," he said. "Sing 'I Remember the Flute Playing.'" The boys changed the tune and sang: "I remember the flute playing. Where is that exquisite creature now?" They went on till they came to the line: "For me she took off her silken skirt. There was blood on the red azalea flower."

Jinlian knew that Ximen Qing was thinking about Li Ping'er. and when this line was sung she deliberately teased him.

"My son," she said, "you are like Zhu Bajie sitting in a butcher's shop without a fire. No one could look as sour as you do. She wasn't a virgin: she was a married woman. Why do you think of the blood on the red azalea in connection with her? That is going too far. You are a shameless piece of goods."

"Listen to the song, you slave. I wasn't thinking anything of the sort."

The two boys sang: "The lovesick maiden in the palace made up her mind to run away. But how shall I do so? I must gather the flowers upon the walls."

Ximen Qing listened with bowed head. When the song was over, Jinlian was so jealous she could not leave him alone. They began to bicker. Yueniang would not have this. "Sister," she said, "be silent. What are you squabbling about? Aunt Yang and my sister-in-law are in the other room with nobody to keep them company. Perhaps two of you will go and join them. I will come myself in a few moments."

Jinlian and Li Jiao'er went to the inner room.

Laian came back. "I took the card to Mistress Ying," he said. "Uncle Ying and Uncle Wu are coming."

"Go and fetch Master Wen," Ximen Qing said to him. He said to Yueniang: "Tell the cooks to bring food to the outer court. I will take my friends there."

Then, with Li Ming, he went to the room in the eastern wing. Bojue was waiting for him. Ximen thanked him for his presents and told him he must let Mistress Ying come the following day.

"I'm afraid she won't be able to come," Bojue said. "There is nobody she can leave behind to look after the house."

Master Wen came in. Bojue bowed to him and said: "I am afraid I was a great trouble to you this morning."

"Not at all," Master Wen said. "It was a pleasure."

Uncle Wu came and sat down. Qintong brought lights, and they all sat around the fire. Laian brought wine and cups and set them on the table.

Ying Bojue noticed that Ximen Qing was wearing a dark green silken gown with a dragon in five colors embroidered upon it, over his white jacket. The dragon's claws were outstretched, and it showed its teeth. The head and horns were noble and impressive. The whiskers were bristling and the hair stood on end. The gold and green seemed alive and the dragon was coiled around Ximen Qing's body. Bojue was almost startled.

"Where did you get that gown?" he said.

Ximen Qing stood up. "Look at it," he said. "Can you guess where it came from?"

"I have no idea," Bojue said.

"Eunuch He of the Eastern Capital gave it to me," Ximen said. "I was drinking with him one very cold day, and he gave it to me then. It is, as you see, a flying dragon. The Emperor had given him another, and he had no further use for this. But it was a great honor to me."

"It must be worth some money," Bojue said. "Brother, it is a good omen. One of these days, you will become governor of a province and wear a dragon robe and a jade girdle. You will go a long way yet."

Qintong warmed wine and set the cups before them. Li Ming sang.

"I must go and offer a cup of wine to your Third Lady," Ying Bojue said. "Then I'll come back and join you."

"My son," Ximen said to him, "if you have such a sense of filial devotion, go, and don't talk so much about it."

"I wouldn't mind going and kowtowing to her," Bojue said, "if the others wouldn't be jealous. But, as a matter of fact, it wouldn't do for me to kowtow to her, because I am the one in authority here. You must go and do it for me."

Ximen Qing tapped him on the head. "You dog," he said, "what do you care about authority?"

"I care a great deal," Bojue said. "Haven't you just hit me on the head?"

They laughed and joked together. Qintong brought them some birthday noodles. Ximen Qing pressed them to set to, and went to eat his own with the ladies in the inner court. Li Ming had something to eat too, then came back to sing for them again. Ying Bojue asked Uncle Wu to tell him what to sing.

"I will be kind to him," Uncle Wu said. "He may sing anything he knows."

"Uncle Wu is very fond of 'The Earthen Jar,'" Ximen Qing said. He told Qintong to fill up the cups. Li Ming tuned his instrument and sang: "She looked out over the countryside, and spoke no word. All day she stood there, and her lovely face grew sad." Then Li Ming withdrew.

Laian came and said: "In the kitchen they want to know how many cooks you will need tomorrow."

"Six cooks and two scullions," Ximen said. "We must have five especially good courses."

Laian went away.

"Who will be your guests tomorrow?" Uncle Wu said.

Ximen Qing told him that Vice President An had invited the Imperial Tutor's ninth son.

"I am glad his Excellency will be taking wine here," Uncle Wu said.

"Why?"

"Because of that old business of the granary," Wu said. "My work is controlled by his Excellency's department. I should be glad if you would ask him to look indulgently on me, and tell him that I hope he will speak well of my work when the inspection is over. I shall be very much obliged to you."

"Let me have your record of service," Ximen Qing said. "I will speak to him for you."

Uncle Wu rose and bowed to Ximen.

"You ought to be satisfied," Bojue said to him. "His Lordship wouldn't do it for anybody but you. But, after all, if he doesn't look after your interests, whom will he bother about? A little effort on his part and, I'm sure, everything will turn out well."

They went on drinking until the second night watch. When Li Ming was about to go away, Ximen told him to come the following day. Li Ming went out. The boys cleared everything away. When the ladies in Yueniang's room heard that the guests in the outer court had gone, they went to their own apartments.

Pan Jinlian expected Ximen Qing to go to her room and hurried there but, as she reached the second door, she saw Ximen Qing going towards Wu Yueniang's room. She hid herself behind the shadow wall and watched him pass. Then she went quietly after him. Yuxiao was standing at the door.

"Why haven't you gone to your room, Fifth Mother?" she said. "Where is Grandmother?"

"Oh, that old thing has a pain," Jinlian said, "she has gone to bed."

She heard Yueniang say: "What made you send for those two new boys? They are no use at all. They sing the same old tune over and over again."

"When you told them to sing 'The Lotus Pool,' they were not so bad," Meng Yulou said. What are the little turtles called? They did nothing but play about all the time they were here."

"One is Han Zuo, and the other Shao Qian," Ximen Qing said.

"They might call themselves by any name," Yueniang said. "We know nothing whatever about them."

Jinlian tiptoed into the room, and stood behind the bed. Suddenly she said: "Sister, you told them to sing a song. He stopped them and told them to sing 'I Remember the Flute Playing.' That confused the little turtles. They didn't know whom to obey."

Yulou turned around quickly. "Where have you come from?" she said. "You gave me a fright, speaking suddenly like that. You might have been a ghost. How long have you been there?"

"The Fifth Lady has been standing behind you a long time," Xiaoyu said.

Jinlian nodded her head. "My son," she said, "don't think yourself so clever. You always flatter yourself that nobody sees through your little tricks. What right had you to compare her to a virgin in the palace? She and I were both in the same boat; we had both been married before. How could she take off her skirt for you, so that you saw the blood upon the red azalea? I should like to know how you would prove that. I can put up with a good deal, but this is too much. You told your friends that, since she died, you have never been able to enjoy your favorite dishes. Now that Butcher Wang is dead, you have to eat your pork with the hair on. Have you had nothing but dung to eat? You regard us as beneath contempt. We don't mind that. But the Great Lady manages the household for you, and you pay no heed to her. She who is dead is the only one worth thinking about. Why didn't you save her when she was dying? How did you live before you met her? Now everything is wrong. Whenever her name is mentioned, you are upset. But you have taken someone to fill her place and, what's more, you seem very glad of the chance. It looks as though the only water fit to be drunk in this house comes from her room."

"Sister," Yueniang said, "the good are short-lived; the wicked live a thousand years. If you have not a lathe to turn a ball, you must shape it with a chisel. Since we are dull and don't suit him, he must do as he pleases."

"I don't want to be nasty," Jinlian said, "but the things he says are so hurtful. I can't let them go by."

"When did I say anything of the sort, you little strumpet?" Ximen Qing said, laughing.

"The day you entertained his Grace Huang," Jinlian answered, "you were talking to Ying the Second and Scholar Wen. If she were here, you wouldn't care if the rest of us died tomorrow. You had better marry some-body to take her place, you rascally scamp."

Ximen Qing jumped up and kicked her. She ran away as quickly as she could. Ximen followed her, but when he reached the door she had disappeared. Chunmei was there. He put his hand on the maid's shoulder and went back to the inner court.

Yueniang saw that he was drunk and was anxious to get rid of him because she wished to listen to the nuns. She told Xiaoyu to take a light and take him away. Jinlian and Yuxiao were standing in a dark passage, and Ximen Qing passed them without seeing them.

"Father seems to be going to your room," Yuxiao said.

"Yes, he is drunk. He can go to bed. I am in no hurry."

"Mother, wait here a moment for me," Yuxiao said, "I am going to get some fruit for you to give the old lady." She brought the fruit. Jinlian put it in her sleeve, and went to her room. On the way, she met Xiaoyu, coming back.

"Father is looking for you," the maid said.

Jinlian came to her door but did not go in. She peeped through the window. Ximen Qing was on the bed amusing himself with Chunmei. She did not wish to disturb them, so she went around to the other room and gave the fruit to Qiuju. She asked whether old woman Pan was in bed, and the maid told her she had been asleep for a long time. Jinlian bade her put the fruit away and went back to the inner court. The ladies were all assembled, Nun Xue was sitting on the bed, and incense was burning on a small table. They were listening with great attention to the nun's words.

Jinlian came in suddenly, smiling. "You have had trouble already," Yueniang said to her. "He has gone to your room. Why have you come back here instead of seeing that he gets to sleep? I am very much afraid he will beat you."

"Do you think he'd dare?" Jinlian said, smiling.

"You talked to him too roughly," Yueniang said. "He was drunk and, if he had got into a rage, he would certainly have beaten you. We were all very anxious. You really are naughty."

"I am not afraid of him, even when he is in a temper," Jinlian said. "And what a performance! You told the boys to sing one song. He stopped them and told them to sing another to suit himself. It is the Third Lady's birth-day and not the time for songs of that sort. The dead are dead. He is always trying to show how much he thought about her, and I don't like it."

"What is the matter, ladies?" Aunt Wu said. "I don't understand. His Lordship came in and suddenly went out again."

"Sister," Yueniang said, "you don't understand. He remembered that, on the Third Lady's last birthday, Li Ping'er was still alive. He cried because she was not here today. He told the boys to sing 'I Remember the Flute Playing.' The Fifth Lady didn't like it and began an argument with him. He flew into a temper and kicked her. Then she ran away."

"Lady," Aunt Yang said, "you should let your husband do what he pleases. What is the use of arguing with him? I can understand how sad he must have felt at the Sixth Lady's death, after you had all been so long together."

"We should never have thought of complaining about the song," Yulou said, "but Jinlian knows all the allusions. She realized that, when he picked out that particular one, he wished to praise her who is dead, and even went so far as to compare her with an historical personage. The song describes their loves, and tells how they lived for one another. It was too much for the Fifth Lady, and she quarreled with him. That caused all the trouble."

"How clever you are, Sister," Aunt Yang said to Jinlian.

"There are no songs she doesn't know," Yueniang said. "Give her the first line and she can always tell you the last. Whenever my husband calls for a song, there is always trouble. She knows what is in his mind. She often makes him angry."

"Of all my children," Yulou said, jokingly, "this is the only one who has any brains."

"I make trouble for everybody," Jinlian said, laughing, "and now you laugh at me."

"Sister," Aunt Yang said, "you must let your husband have his own way. The proverb says: One night of married bliss, and love stays for a hundred nights. Even if husband and wife live together only a short time, they must love one another. When the Sixth Lady died so suddenly, it must have seemed to him as though he had lost one of his fingers. It is only natural that he should grieve when he thinks about her."

"Let him think about her, by all means," Jinlian said, "but with moderation. We are all his ladies. He ought not to exalt one and treat the rest of us like dirt. He was angry because we didn't wear mourning for her long enough. We did so for fifty days. Why shouldn't that have been enough?"

"You must not be too hard on him," Aunt Yang said.

"How quickly time flies," Aunt Wu said. "It must be nearly a hundred days since she died."

"When is the hundredth day?" Aunt Yang said.

"The twenty-sixth day of the twelfth month," Yueniang said.

"We ought to have a service for her," Nun Wang said.

"We can't have a service every time," Yueniang said. "Perhaps we will have one on New Year's Day."

Xiaoyu brought tea and gave each of them a cup. When they had drunk it, Yueniang washed her hands and burned incense. Nun Xue preached to them again. After some opening verses, she told them how the holy man, Wu Jie, broke his vows and fell in love with Hong Lian, and how, in a later life, he became Dong Po. She went on for a long time.

Lanxiang brought two boxes of vegetarian food and cakes. She took the incense burner from the table and put down the food and a pot of tea. The nuns had this, then the maid brought food and a jar of wine for the other ladies as they sat around the fire.

Yueniang cast dice with her sister-in-law, and Jinlian guessed fingers with Li Jiao'er. Yuxiao stood behind Jinlian's chair to serve the wine and, at the same time, suggested how she should play. Li Jiao'er was beaten.

"I will guess fingers with her now," Yulou said. "She seems to win all the time. But I won't have her putting her fingers in her sleeves, or Yuxiao standing behind her, either."

Jinlian was beaten and was made to drink several cups of wine. She went to her room. She had to knock at the corner gate for a long time before Qiuju, rubbing her eyes, came to open it.

"You have been to bed, you slave," Jinlian said.

"No," said Qiuju.

"You are lying, you have only just this moment got up. What an idle good-for-nothing you are! You didn't even come to meet me. Has your father gone to bed?"

"He has been in bed a long time," Qiuju said.

Jinlian went to the inner room, pulled up her skirts, and warmed herself at the fire. Then she demanded tea. Qiuju hastily poured out a cup for her.

"Your hands are dirty, and I don't want stewed tea. Go and tell Chunmei to get the small kettle and boil some fresh water. Put some more tea leaves in the pot and make it strong."

"Chunmei has gone to bed. Shall I wake her?"

"No, don't disturb her. Let her sleep."

Qiuju went in. Chunmei was sleeping at Ximen Qing's feet. Qiuju woke her up. "Mother has come," she said. "She wants some tea. Get up at once."

Chunmei spat at her and cursed her.

"You slave! What do you mean by coming here and startling me like that? 'Mother has come,' indeed! Well, what about it?"

She got up, however, and slowly dressed herself. Then she went to Jinlian and stood, rubbing her eyes. Jinlian scolded Qiuju.

"You saw she was asleep, you slave. Why did you wake her?" Then she said to Chunmei: "The kerchief on your head is rumpled. Pull it down a little. And what have you done with the other earring?"

Chunmei looked at herself and saw that one of her earrings had gone. She took a light and went into the other room to look for it. After searching a long time, she found it on the footstool.

"Where did you find it?" Jinlian asked.

"It was Qiuju's fault," Chunmei said. "She woke me up suddenly and my earring caught in the curtain hook. I found it on the footstool."

"I told her not to wake you," Jinlian said, "but she didn't pay any attention."

"She said you wanted some tea."

"I wouldn't let her make it. She has such dirty hands."

Chunmei filled the small kettle and put it on the fire. She put coal on the brazier, and the water was soon boiling. She washed a cup, made some very strong tea, and gave it to her mistress.

"Has your father been in bed long?" Jinlian asked.

"Yes, I helped him to bed a long time ago. He asked where you were, and I told him you were still in the inner court."

Jinlian drank her tea. "Yuxiao gave me some fruits and things for my mother. I gave them to this slave. Did she hand them over to you?"

"No, I haven't seen them. I have no idea what she's done with them."

"Where are the fruits?" Jinlian said to Qiuju.

"I put them in the cabinet," the maid said. She went and brought them. Jinlian counted them and found that an orange was missing. She asked what had become of it.

"I took them and put them in the cabinet just as you gave them to me," Qiuju said. "Surely you don't think I was so near starvation I had to go and eat it."

"You thief!" Jinlian cried. "You are far too cheeky. If you haven't stolen it, where is it? When I gave them to you, I counted them. Why is there one short? Did you think I brought them for you?"

She turned to Chunmei. "Give her ten slaps on each side of her face."

"I should soil my hands if I touched those dirty cheeks," Chunmei said.

"Send her to me, then," Jinlian said.

Chunmei pushed the girl to her mistress and Jinlian pinched her cheeks.

"Did you eat that orange, you thief? Tell me the truth, and I will let you off. Otherwise, I will get the whip and beat you without mercy. Don't think I'm drunk. You deliberately stole that orange, and now you are trying to deceive me."

"Am I drunk?" she asked Chunmei.

"Certainly not," Chunmei said. "You are perfectly sober. It might be well to look in her sleeves. We might find some orange peel there."

Jinlian took Qiuju's sleeves and began to feel in them. Qiuju, in a great flurry, struggled to prevent her. Chunmei caught her hand. They found some orange peel.

Jinlian pinched the girl's face as hard as she could, and boxed her ears. "You thievish slave!" she cried. "You are as ignorant as can be, yet you are cunning enough when it comes to cheating and stealing. I catch you red-handed, and you still try to make excuses. I am going to have my tea, so I shall not punish you now. I'll deal with you tomorrow."

"Mother," Chunmei said, "don't let her escape you. The best thing we can do is to take off all her clothes and get one of the men to give her a good thrashing. If we do that, she may learn to have some respect for us. If we use a stick as though we were prodding a monkey, she won't take it seriously."

Qiuju's face was swollen. She went to the kitchen, sulking. Jinlian divided an orange into two parts and gave one to Chunmei. She gave her half the apples and pomegranates, saying: "These are for you. My mother can have the rest." Chunmei put them into her sleeve without looking at them, as though they were of no consequence at all. Jinlian was going to give her some of the other things, but Chunmei asked her not to.

"I don't care much for sweet things," she said. "Please give them to Grandmother."

Then Jinlian went to the chamber and made water. She asked Chunmei to get a tub of water so that she could wash. Then she asked what the time was.

"I have been asleep some time," the maid said, "it must be about the third night watch."

Jinlian took down her hair, and went to the inner room. The lamp was nearly out. She pulled up the wick. Then she went to the bed. Ximen Qing was snoring. She undressed and lay down beside him. After a while, she began to toy with his weapon. But Ximen had been playing with Chunmei; she could not excite it, for it was too soft. She was fiery with wine, and squatting on her heels on the bed she put the prick in her mouth. She titillated the hole, moved the head backwards and forwards, and sucked it inside and outside without ceasing. Ximen Qing woke up.

"Now, you funny little strumpet, where have you been all this time?"

"We were drinking in the inner court," Jinlian said. "The Third Lady gave us a feast and Miss Yu sang. We guessed fingers, threw dice, and played for a long time. I beat Li Jiao'er, but Yulou beat me. I had to drink a few cups of wine. Lucky for you that you got away and came here to sleep in peace, but don't think I will let you escape."

"Have you made the belt of ribbon?" Ximen said.

"Yes, it is here." She took it from underneath the bedclothes, showed it to him, then tied it about his prick and around his waist. She tied it very tightly.

"Have you taken anything?" she asked him.

He told her that he had, and she continued her attentions until the sinews of the prick stiffened and it surged erect, a fingerbreadth longer than usual. She lay on his body, but the penis was so big that she had to stretch her cunt with both hands before it would fit. But when it entered she embraced his neck and asked him to hold her around the waist; and gradually the prick, pressing on one side, pressed from the other, buried itself completely. "Darling," she said, "put a silk cloak below yourself." Ximen folded a red gown twice and put it beneath his thighs. She started again, and absorbed the whole prick. "Delight of my heart," she said, "feel. It's gone right in. It has filled me completely. Are you satisfied?"

Ximen felt with his hand and found that the penis had entered so far that nothing, not even a hair's breadth, remained outside. Only the testicles were left, and he was suffused with deepest pleasure.

"I'm cold," she said. "Let us move the candle. It was nicer in summer." And again, "Don't you think this ribbon is better than the clasp? It doesn't hurt me, and makes your prick longer. If you don't believe me, put your hand on my belly. I can feel it touching my bowels. Embrace me and let me sleep on top of you."

"Sleep, girl," said Ximen. "I'll hold you."

She put her tongue in his mouth, closed her eyes, put her arms around him, and slept. But soon desire woke her. She pressed his shoulders, sat up, and bounced up and down so fast that his penis went right in and out. "I am dying, my dearest," she cried. Man and woman enjoyed three hundred thrusts, and Ximen was the first to withdraw from the struggle. "Embrace me," she said, and gave him a breast to suck. Then she relaxed, and the juices of love flowed from her. A stag seemed to leap within her. Her arms and legs were limp; her hair covered her body. The penis, although it had withdrawn, was still erect, and she wiped it with a handkerchief. "What shall we do, darling?" she said. "It is not enough for you even yet."

"Let us go to sleep now," Ximen said. "We will settle that question afterwards."

"I feel as though I were paralyzed," Jinlian said.

So the mystery of clouds and rain was performed once more. They lay down to sleep and did not wake again till dawn.

CHAPTER 74

Li Guijie Is Forgiven

Wealth and dignity are as the dew of morning
Friends and companions as the gathering of sand.
It is better to sit before a bamboo window
And meditate upon some sacred book.

Contemplation benefits the soul as truly
As any listening to sermons.
When the soul is purified, you may make a cup of tea.
The crowing of the cock is all you fear
For in the morning the entanglement of earthly things
Is as a bundle of hemp.

At dawn, Pan Jinlian and Ximen Qing awoke. Jinlian saw that his weapon was still upright like a ramrod. "Darling," she said, "you must forgive me, but I can stand no more. I shall suck your prick."

"Suck it," said Ximen. "If you can soften it, all will be well." She squatted on her buttocks, put her hand between his legs, and took his prick in her mouth. She played with it for a whole hour, but it did not flag. Ximen held her white neck and dragged his prick this way and that inside her mouth with all his might. Soon her lips were wet with white spittle, and the prick was as red as they.

"Ying the Second has invited us to go and see his wife," Jinlian said. "Are we going?"

"Why not?" Ximen Qing said.

"I have a favor to ask of you," Jinlian said. "I wonder whether you will grant it me."

"What is it, you little strumpet?"

"Will you give me the Sixth Lady's fur coat? If we go, they will all be wearing fur coats, and I have none."

"We have the coat that General Wang's people pawned. Won't that do?"

"I don't want that. Li Jiao'er can have it. Let Sun Xue'e have the one Li Jiao'er had and give me the one that belonged to the Sixth Lady. I will make a pair of scarlet sleeves, with golden storks to go with it, and wear a white silk skirt. If you give it to me, it will be a proof that it has been worthwhile being your wife all this long time."

"You little strumpet, you never lose a chance of doing well for yourself. That fur coat is worth at least sixty taels of silver. If you put it on, will you look well in it?"

"You rascal," Jinlian said, "you would give things to any other woman. I am your wife and, if I wear it, so much the more credit to you. If you talk like this, I shall be angry with you."

"One moment you ask for something, and the next you are riding the high horse."

"I am not a maid. There is no reason why you shouldn't do something when I ask you."

She softened the penis with her cheeks and put it in her mouth. She teased the hole and titillated the sensitive spot with her tongue. She held it firmly between her lips and moved it gently. Ximen was delighted; his pleasure mounted, and he prepared to give way.

"Hold tight and let the sperm come out," he cried, and at once the sperm flowed into her mouth. After a while she swallowed it.

It was the day of the reception. Ximen Qing dressed and went out. Jinlian stayed in bed.

"Bring me the coat now," she said. "If you put it off, you will be too busy."

Ximen went to the room of Li Ping'er. The nurse and the maids were up, making tea to set before their mistress's tablet. Ruyi'er was dressed and her face and eyebrows painted. She smiled and offered him a cup of tea, and talked to him as he drank it. Ximen Qing told Yingchun to get the key. Ruyi'er asked him why he wanted it.

"I am going to give the Fifth Lady the fur coat," he said.

"The sable coat?" Ruyi'er asked.

"Yes," Ximen Qing said, "I am giving it her because she wants it."

Yingchun went to do his bidding. He took Ruyi'er on his knee and touched her breast. "My child," he said, "though you have had a baby, your breasts are still small." They kissed each other.

"I have noticed that you often go to her and seldom to the other ladies," Ruyi'er said. "She would be very pleasant if she were not so suspicious and touchy. The other day, when you were away, she quarreled with me about the dolly pin. Fortunately, Sister Han and the Third Lady were there to separate us. I did not mention the matter to you when you came back. I can't imagine who told her that you care for me, or when she found out. Has she spoken to you about it?"

"Yes, she has," Ximen Qing said. "I think the best thing you can do is to go to her and say you're sorry. She can never resist flattery, and she is very easily pleased. Her mouth may be sharp, but her heart is in the right place."

"That is so," Ruyi'er said. "We had that quarrel, but the next day, when you came home, she was quite pleasant. She said you were very fond of her, but that the other ladies were not able to rival me. I was to tell her everything, she said, and she would be my friend."

"In that case, there is nothing to bother about," Ximen Qing said. "I will come to you tonight."

"Are you sure?" Ruyi'er said. "Don't tease me."

"Why should I tease you?" Ximen said.

Yingchun brought the key. Ximen Qing told her to open the cabinet door and take out the fur coat. The maid shook it, then wrapped it up again.

"I badly need a good skirt and coat," Ruyi'er said softly. "Will you get one for me while there is a chance? And I should like a short coat, if there is one, belonging to my mistress."

Ximen Qing brought out a light blue silk coat, a yellow skirt of soft silk, a pair of embroidered drawers and some blue trousers. He gave them to Ruyi'er. She kowtowed and thanked him. He locked up the cabinet.

Ruyi'er took the fur coat to Jinlian. She was getting up, dressing her feet as she sat on the bed. When Chunmei told her Ruyi'er had come with a fur coat, she understood. Ruyi'er went in.

"Did your father send you?" Jinlian said.

"Yes, he told me to bring you this fur coat."

"Did he give you anything?"

"He gave me a dress for the new year, and told me to come and kowtow to you."

"There is no need for that," Jinlian said. "Your master has taken a fancy to you. Well, there is an old saying that, though there are many boats on the river, they do not block it; and though there are many carriages upon a road, there is still room for traffic. If it amuses you to go in for this kind of thing, do so, but you must do nothing that will injure me. I shall not bother about you any more, and I shall do nothing to interfere with you."

"My mistress is dead," Ruyi'er said, "and though the Great Lady still keeps me here, you are the one on whom I really depend. If you help me, I shall never dare to be ungracious in return. Falling leaves always come back to the root again."

"Perhaps you had better tell the Great Lady about the clothes he gave you," Jinlian said.

"I asked her to give me some clothes, and she said Father would give me some when he was free."

"That is all right, then," Jinlian said. Ruyi'er went back to her room. Ximen Qing had gone to the great hall.

"When you went for the key," Ruyi'er said to Yingchun, "did the Great Lady say anything?"

"She asked what he wanted it for. I didn't tell her about the coat. I said I didn't know. She said no more."

Ximen Qing, in the great hall, watched the preparations for the banquet. The actors of the Haiyan company, Zhang Mei, Zhou Shun, Gou Zixiao, came with their properties, and Li Ming and the other boys also came and kowtowed to Ximen Qing. He ordered food to be given to all of them, then told Li Ming and three others to perform in the outer hall, and Zuo Shun to entertain the ladies at the back.

Han Daoguo's wife, Wang Liu'er, could not come that day. She bought two boxes of presents and sent Miss Shen, in a sedan chair, with her boy Jin Cai, to congratulate Meng Yulou on her birthday. Wang Jing took them in and dismissed the chair men. Aunt Han and Aunt Meng came, then Mistress Fu, Mistress Gan, Cui Ben's wife, Miss Duan, and Mistress Ben the Fourth.

Ximen Qing, who was in the great hall, saw Daian taking in a short lady who wore a silver-gray coat and a red skirt. Her face was not powdered and her eyes were very narrow. She looked rather like Zheng Aixiang. As she was in the passage, Ximen Qing asked who the lady was. Daian told him it was Ben the Fourth's wife. Ximen said no more. They went on to the inner court to see Wu Yueniang, in whose room all the ladies were having tea. Ximen Qing himself came for porridge. He gave Yueniang the key.

"Why did you wish to open the cabinet?" his wife asked.

"Pan Jinlian told me she was going to Brother Ying's place. She wanted the Sixth Lady's fur coat."

Yueniang looked at him sharply. "You don't keep your word," she said. "When she died, you were very angry if anyone suggested getting rid of her maids, but now it seems all right for you to give her clothes away. Why doesn't the Fifth Lady wear her own fur coat? It is a good thing the owner of the coat is dead. If she were alive, I don't know what Jinlian would do."

Ximen Qing could not think of any answer to make to this.

Then a servant came to say that Liu, the Provincial Director of Studies, had come to pay back some money, and Ximen went to the great hall to receive him. Daian brought a card and said that people had come from General Wang's place with presents. Ximen asked what the presents were. The boy said: a roll of silk, a jar of wine, and food. Ximen told Wang Jing to give the messenger a card in return and five *qian* of silver for himself. Then Li Guijie came, with the house porter, bringing four boxes of presents. Daian took the wrapper. "Please step into the passage, Aunt Guijie," he said hastily. "There is a gentleman in the hall." Guijie went into the passage and Daian carried the boxes to Yueniang's room.

"Has your father seen them?" Yueniang asked.

"No," Daian said, "he has a gentleman with him."

Yueniang told him to put the boxes in an adjoining room.

When his visitor had gone, Ximen Qing came to have something to eat.

"Guijie has come and brought some presents," Yueniang told him.

"This is the first I have heard of it," Ximen Qing said.

Yueniang told Xiaoyu to open the boxes. There were buns with mincemeat, a special birthday gift; crystallized roses; two roast ducks, and a pair of pig's trotters. Guijie came in from the other room, pearls and jewels all over her head. She was wearing a scarlet double-breasted coat and a blue silk skirt. She kowtowed four times to Ximen Qing.

"That will do," Ximen said. "Why did you go to all this expense?"

"Guijie has just told me she is afraid you are still angry with her," Yueniang said. "It was really not her fault at all, but her mother's. Guijie had a headache and, that day, Wang the Third and his friends were on their way to Sesame's place, and called in to have some tea as they were passing. Then the trouble began, but she never saw him."

"She didn't see him this time, and she didn't see him that time!" Ximen Qing said. "I don't know how she has the face to say so. I'm not interested any more. In a place like yours, everything is all right so long as the money comes in. I'm not angry with you in the least."

Guijie knelt on the ground and refused to get up. "Father," she said, "you are right. But may I rot to pieces if I ever let that fellow touch me! May every pore of my skin come out in boils! It is all that old whore's doing. She has no sense at all. She would let anybody in, no matter whether he is handsome or hideous. That is what has made you so angry."

"Now she is here," Yueniang said, "let us consider the matter ended. Don't be angry with her any more."

"Stand up, and I'll forgive you," Ximen Qing said.

But Guijie, with her most winning manner, said: "You must smile at me, Father. Then I'll get up. If you won't, I shall stay here for a year."

Jinlian joined them.

"Guijie," she said, "stand up. If you kneel there, and use pretty words to him, he will make all the more fuss. Now you are kneeling before him, but, I tell you, in future when he comes to you, make him kneel down before you and keep him there."

Ximen Qing and Yueniang laughed. Guijie rose to her feet.

Daian came. He was greatly excited. "Their Excellencies have arrived," he said. Ximen Qing put on his robes and went to meet them.

"From today," Guijie said to Yueniang, "I will give up my father if I may be your daughter."

"I don't believe in your oaths," Yueniang said. "You forget them as soon as you have taken them. He went to see you twice, and you were not there."

"Heavens!" Guijie cried, "when did he come to my place and find me not there? If he did, may I die this very moment. Somebody has been telling lies. He must have gone to some other place. I know he went to Zheng Aiyue's house and played with the girls there. They are jealous, Probably they are responsible for the whole affair. I don't see how Father could be angry with me otherwise."

"Why don't you girls attend to your business, instead of talking scandal about one another?" Jinlian said.

"Mother, you don't know. There is always jealousy among people of our profession. Each one is anxious to get the better of the others. Whenever one seems to be securing a little favor, the others conspire to cast her down."

Yueniang gave her tea.

Ximen Qing took Censor Song and Vice President An to the great hall. After the usual greetings, each of them presented him with a roll of silk and a case of books. They saw that the tables were very well set out, and thanked him repeatedly. Then they sat down to tea.

"I have still another favor to ask you," Song said. "Hou Shiquan has just been appointed Master of the Court of Sacrificial Worship. I and those under me would like to entertain him, if possible, here at your house, on the thirtieth. He is to leave for the Eastern Capital on the second of next month. Will you do this for us?"

"Your Excellency has only to command, and I obey," Ximen Qing said.

"The money is here," Song said. He summoned an attendant, who brought twelve taels of silver, which the officers had contributed. "We should like one large table and six small tables. Perhaps a few actors."

Ximen Qing promised to make the necessary arrangements. He took his guests to the arbor. Before long, Assistant Secretary Qian arrived. The three gentlemen played chess together.

Song was impressed by the magnificence and convenience of Ximen Qing's house. The books, pictures and furniture were all the best of their kind. In front of the screen stood a gilded tripod with the figures of the Eight Immortals. It was of very fine workmanship and several feet high. Incense was burning in it, and the smoke came out through the mouths of deer and storks. He went and examined it more closely.

"This tripod is beautifully made," he said to Ximen Qing. He turned to the others. "I wrote some time ago to Brother Liu to ask him to get me a pair of tripods like this. I am going to present them to Cai, but they haven't come yet. Siquan, where did you get yours?"

"It came from a man in Huai," Ximen Qing said.

They went on with their game. Ximen Qing ordered some dainty cakes and other refreshments to be brought, and bade the actors sing songs of the South.

"Our guest has not come yet," Song said. "It won't look right if we meet him with red faces."

"I don't believe a cup will do us any harm," An said. "It is terribly cold."

Song was about to send someone to hasten his guest, but one of his attendants said: "We have been already. Their Excellencies are playing chess, but they will be here soon." An told the actors to sing the Spring Song. Before it was over, Cai and Huang were announced. Song ordered everything to be cleared away. They put their robes straight and went out to welcome their guest.

Cai was wearing a plain gown and a gold-buckled girdle. He presented a card to Ximen Qing. An said: "This is his Lordship Ximen. He holds the office of Captain and is one of his Eminence's wards." Cai bowed to Ximen.

"I have long wished to meet you," he said.

Ximen Qing replied: "I shall do myself the honor of paying you a visit." After these greetings, they took off their ceremonial clothes, tea was brought, and they sat down to talk. Sometime afterwards, the tables were laid, and Cai took the place of honor. Cooks brought soup and cutlets and rice. The actors came with their list of plays, and Cai bade them play the story of the two faithful lovers. They played two acts, and the wine went around several times. Then the singers came and sang "With a Whip of Jade and a Prancing Steed, He Leaves the Imperial City." Cai laughed.

"Songyuan," he said, "this promises well for you. The black horse is a censor's horse, and the third noble seems like Liu of the long beard."

An said: "But we can't say that this is the day on which the Magistrate of Jiangzhou made his black gown wet with tears."

Everybody laughed. Ximen Qing told Chunhong to sing "We Have Made Report to the Golden Gate of Peace upon the Frontier."

Song was delighted. He said to Ximen Qing: "What a charming boy!"

"Ximen said: "He is one of my household, and comes from Yangzhou." Song took the boy's hand, and asked him to pour wine for him. Then he gave him three *qian* of silver, and the boy kowtowed to thank him.

The sun was going down. Cai saw that it was getting late, and told his servant to bring his clothes. He made ready to go. The others tried to persuade him to stay, but in vain. They went with him to the gate. Two officials were bidden to take presents to the wharf. As Song was going, he said to Ximen Qing: "I will not thank you today, since I am putting you to still further trouble." Then they all went away.

Ximen Qing went back and dismissed the actors. "I shall want you again the day after tomorrow," he said to them. "Be sure to bring some especially good singers. His Excellency is going to invite Governor Hou."

He called for wine and sent Daian for Scholar Wen. He sent Laian for Ying Bojue. The two men came almost at the same moment, made a reverence to their host, and sat down. The three boys sang and wine was served.

"The ladies are all coming to see you tomorrow," Ximen Qing said to Ying Bojue. "Have you engaged any singers or entertainers for them?"

"That's a nice thing to ask!" Bojue said. "How can you expect me to do all that, when I'm so poor? I've engaged a couple of singers, and I hope my sisters-in-law will come early."

In the inner court, the two Mistresses Meng were the first to go away. Aunt Yang was about to follow them, but Wu Yueniang asked her to stay longer. "Nun Xue has sent her novices to fetch the sacred texts," she said, "and you might as well stay and hear them read this evening."

"I should very much like to stay," Aunt Yang said, "but I have been asked to go to my nephew's betrothal party tomorrow. I cannot very well fail to go."

When she had gone, the ladies drank together. When the lamps were brought, the wives of the three clerks went away. Miss Duan stayed, and old woman Pan went to Jinlian's room. Aunt Wu, L Guijie, Miss Shen, Miss Yu, the nuns, Meng Yulou, Li Jiao'er, and Pan Jinlian, were left in Wu Yueniang's room.

When the boys began to bring in the things, they knew that the party in the outer court had broken up. Jinlian hurriedly went out and stood silently at the corner door. Ximen Qing, supported by Laian with a lantern, came rolling by. He had meant to go and see Ruyi'er, but, seeing

Jinlian, he took her hand and went to her room. Laian went on to Yue-niang's room to give her the cups and chopsticks.

Yueniang thought Ximen Qing was coming to her room, and she had sent Miss Shen, Miss Yu, and Guijie to stay with Li Jiao'er. "Is your father coming?" she said to Laian.

"He has gone to the Fifth Lady's room," Laian told her. Yueniang was annoyed.

"The fellow doesn't know what he's doing," she said to Yulou. "I was sure he would come here and go with you. I can't imagine why he has gone to her again. But, now I come to think of it, she has been looking lovesick these last few days. She doesn't seem able to leave him for a moment."

"Oh, never mind, Sister," Yulou said, "if we talk like this, it will look as though we wished to beat her at her own game. Didn't you notice how the nun poked fun at us, saying that, no matter where he went, he could not go beyond these six rooms? Let him do what he likes. We cannot control him."

"They must have arranged it beforehand," Yueniang said. "When she heard that the party in the outer court was over, she dashed out as though her life depended on it." She said to Xiaoyu: "There is no one in the kitchen. Shut the second door and tell the nuns to come. We will listen to their preaching." She asked Li Jiao'er, Miss Shen, Miss Duan, and Miss Yu to come back again.

"I have sent one of the young nuns to fetch the *True History of the Lady Huang*," she said. "Unfortunately, Aunt Yang has left us."

She told Yuxiao to make some good tea.

"You and I will take our turn with the tea," Yulou said to Li Jiao'er. "We must not trouble the Great Lady all the time." So they gave orders for tea. The table was set. The three nuns came and sat on the bed with their legs crossed, and the other ladies sat down and disposed themselves to listen. Yueniang washed her hands and burned incense. Then Nun Xue opened the text of the *True Story of the Lady Huang* and read:

We know that the Law never perisheth. It proceedeth into the void. The DAO is without life, and, when it giveth life, it advan-tageth us in no way. From the Holy Body are manifested the Eight Incarnations, and from the Eight Incarnations is manifested the Holy Body. Such is the brightness of the Lamp of Wisdom that it openeth a window to the world: so clear is the Mirror of Buddha that it shineth to the bottom of the dark way.

A hundred years is as the twinkling of an eye.

The four bodies of illusion are but shadows.

Yet, every day, people busy themselves in the dust; they make haste all day to compass their own ends. They know not what they do.

Only Nature is glorious and perfect.

As for them, they pursue the six roots of vanity and concupiscence. Though their achievements and their renown are known to all the world, yet they are but a dream. Though their dignity and their wealth make men amazed, they cannot escape a sudden end. As wind and fire they die away, and there is no exception either for old or young. The water wears away many a mountain.

After this, the nun read some short homilies and sang hymns. Then she began to tell the story of the Lady Huang, whence she sprang, how she read the sacred books and gave alms. How she died and was born again as a man, and how five men and women went up to Heaven at the same moment. She did not end her story before the second night watch.

Li Jiao'er's maid brought tea for the ladies, and Yulou's maid brought fruit and food, a large jar of wine, and a big pot of tea. Yueniang told Yuxiao to give the nuns cakes and dainties to eat with the tea.

"Now that the teachers have done," Guijie said, "it is my turn to offer you a song."

"You are very kind," Yueniang said.

"I will sing first," Miss Yu said.

"Very well," said Yueniang.

Then Miss Shen said: "When she has finished, I will sing."

Guijie would not have this. "What song would you like, Mother?" she asked. Yueniang asked her to sing "The Stillness of the Late Night Watch." Guijie offered wine to all the ladies, then took her lute and sang to them. When she had finished, Miss Yu was about to take the lute, but Miss Shen took it from her.

"I will sing 'The Hanging of the Portraits in the Twelfth Month.' She began: "The fifteenth day of the first month is the merry Feast of Lanterns. We take handfuls of incense and do homage to Heaven and Earth."

Aunt Wu was sleepy. Before Miss Shen had finished, she drank her tea and went to Yueniang's bedroom to sleep. Afterwards, Guijie went to sleep with Li Jiao'er, Miss Duan with Yulou. The nuns went to Xue'e and Miss Yu and Miss Shen to Yuxiao. Yueniang herself slept with her sister-in-law.

There is an ancient tradition that when a woman is with child she should never sit down on one side, or lie on one side. She should never listen to exciting music or look upon any immodest color. She should occupy all her time with poetry and books, with gold and jade. If she does this, she will give birth to a boy or a girl who will be intelligent and good. This we call the education of the child in the womb. Now that Yueniang was with child, she should not have allowed the nuns to tell these stories of life, death and reincarnation. In consequence of this, one of the Holy Ones came to her and, afterwards, her son mysteriously disappeared, so that the family of Ximen came to an end. It was very sad.

CHAPTER 75

Pan Jinlian Quarrels
with Wu Yueniang

Butterflies hover in couples among the flowers beside the stream
South of the hills and west of the river.
The wind and the moon are distraught with love.
In the ancient palace
The beautiful woman is filled with discontent
Clouds and rain are in wild confusion.
She opens her fragrant mouth, and the words flow from her lips
She presses her delicate cheeks in wild abandon.
Say not that the life of love is without substance
When one oriole has finished its song,
Another takes up the melody.

Pan Jinlian met Ximen at the corner door and went with him to her
room. He sat down on the bed. "Why don't you undress?" she said to
him.

He smiled and kissed her. "I came to tell you I am going somewhere
else tonight. Please give me my love instruments."

"You rascal," Jinlian said, "do you think you can get around me with
soft words like these? If I had not been standing at the door, you would
have been with her already. You would never have come near me. I know.
This morning you arranged everything with that evil slut. That was why
she brought me the fur coat and kowtowed to me. What do you take me
for? You won't get over me in that sort of way. When Li Ping'er was alive, I
counted for nothing. But that bird is no longer in the nest. I'm not going
to make the same mistake a second time."

"Rubbish!" Ximen Qing said, laughing. "If she hadn't come and kowtowed to you, you would have had just as much to say."

Jinlian was silent for a long time. "I will let you go, but you shall not
have the instruments," she said at last. "You want to use them for your dirty
work with that bad bone. When you come back to me, they will be filthy."

"But I am so accustomed to them I don't know what to do without
them."

He badgered her for a long time, and she gave him the silver clasp. "Take it, if you must have it," she said. Ximen Qing put it into his sleeve and went out staggering.

Jinlian called him back. "Tell me. Are you going to spend all night with her? If you do, you'll have all the maids laughing at you. You'd better stay a little while and then send her packing."

"I shall not stay very long," Ximen Qing said. He went out again.

Again Jinlian called him back. "Come here," she said, "I am talking to you. Why are you in such a hurry?"

"What do you want now?" Ximen Qing said.

"I am allowing you to go and sleep with her, but I forbid you to talk a lot of nonsense. If you do, she will give herself airs in front of me again. If I find out you have done anything of the sort, I will bite off your weapon the next time you come to me."

"Oh, you funny little whore," Ximen Qing said, "you talk enough to kill anybody." He went out.

"Let him go," Chunmei said. "Why do you try to keep him in order? You know the old saying: if a mother-in-law has too much to say, the daughter-in-law will become deaf. If you go on like that, people will only hate you more. Let us have a game of chess."

She told Qiuju to shut the corner door. Then they sat at the table and played chess.

Ximen Qing went to Li Ping'er's room and pulled aside the shutter. Ruyi'er, Yingchun, and Xiuchun were having supper on the bed. When Ximen came in, they all got up.

"Don't mind me," Ximen Qing said. He went to the inner room and sat down in a chair before the tablet of his dead wife. After a while, Ruyi'er came out to him.

"It is cold here, Father," she said, smiling, "come into the other room."

Ximen Qing put his arms around her and kissed her. They went into the other room together. Tea was boiling on the fire and Yingchun offered him some. Ruyi'er stood before the bed, near the fire.

"You have had no wine," she said. "We have had a pot of Jinhua wine and some food for my dead lady and we kept some for you."

"You take the food and give me some of the fruit," Ximen Qing said. "I don't want any Jinhua wine." Then he said to Xiuchun: "Take a lantern and go to my study. There is a jar of grape wine there. Ask Wang Jing for it and warm some for me."

Yingchun set the table. "Sister," Ruyi'er said to her, "open the boxes and let me find something for Father to eat with his wine." She picked out some special dainties and fruits and put them on the table. Then Xiuchun

came with the wine, opened the jar and warmed some. Ruyi'er poured
out a cup and offered it to Ximen Qing. He tasted it and found it very
good. Ruyi'er stood beside the table to wait on him. She gave him some
chestnuts.

Yingchun knew why he had come and went to spend the night with
Xiuchun. When she had gone away and there was no one else in the room,
he made the woman sit on his knee and they drank wine from mouth to
mouth. He unfastened her dress and uncovered her tender white bosom.
He touched her nipples. "My child," he said, "I know nothing so sweet as
your lovely white skin. It is as beautiful as your lady's, and when I hold
you in my arms I feel as if I held her."

Ruyi'er smiled. "No, Father, hers was whiter than mine. The Fifth
Lady is beautiful, but her skin is not so pure. It is not so white as the
Third Lady's. But the Third Lady, unfortunately, has a few pock marks
on her face. Sun Xue'e is white and pretty." Then she said: "Yingchun
is going to give me one of her ornaments. I wish you would give me the
golden tiger that belonged to my dead lady. It is something to be worn in
the new year, and I would like her to have it."

"If you have nothing to wear, I will give the silversmith some gold and
get him to make something for you. The Great Lady has all your lady's
ornaments. I can hardly ask her for them."

"I should like a gold tiger," Ruyi'er said. She stood up and kowtowed
to him.

When they had been drinking for some time, she said: "Father, will
you ask my sisters to come and have some wine with us? They will be
unhappy if you don't."

Ximen Qing called Yingchun, but there was no answer. Ruyi'er went
to the kitchen and told the two girls that their master wanted them. Yingchun came. Ximen Qing asked Ruyi'er to give her some wine and a plate
of food. Yingchun took them, standing. "Please make Xiuchun come,"
Ruyi'er said, "I should like to offer her something." The maid went away
but returned and said Xiuchun would not come. Then she took her bedclothes and went to the kitchen to sleep with Xiuchun.

Ximen Qing drank more wine. Then Ruyi'er cleared everything away
and gave him some tea. She found fresh silken bedclothes, and an embroidered pillow. She warmed them and asked him whether he would rather
sleep on the large bed or the small one. "I prefer the small one," he said.
Ruyi'er put the bedclothes on the small bed and helped him to undress.
She went to the other room to wash, came back, and fastened the door.
When she had put the lamp beside the bed, she undressed and got into
bed with him.

The woman touched the warrior. The clasp was already in position. It was very hard and frisky and she felt pleased and terrified at the same time. They kissed each other and set to. Ximen, seeing her lying on the bed without any clothes on, was afraid she might catch cold. He picked up her vest and covered her breast with it. Then he took her by the legs and thrust forward violently. Ruyi'er gasped for breath and her face became very red.

"Mother gave me that vest," she said.

"My dear," said Ximen, "never mind about that. Tomorrow, I will give you half a roll of red silk to make underwear, and you shall wear that when you wait on me."

"Thank you," Ruyi'er said.

"I have forgotten how old you are," Ximen Qing said. "What is your surname, and your place in the family? I only remember that your husband's name was Xiong."

"Yes," Ruyi'er said, "his name was Xiong Wang'er. My own name is Zhang, and I am the fourth child. I am thirty-two years old."

"A year older than I am," he said.

They went on with their lovemaking, and he called her Zhang the Fourth. "My daughter," he said, "serve me well, and, when the Great Lady's baby is born, you shall have charge of it. And, if you yourself bear a son to me, I will make you one of my ladies and you shall take the dead lady's place."

"My husband is dead, and I have no relatives of my own," Ruyi'er said. "I have no other wish than to serve you, and I never want to leave you. If you take pity on me, I shall always be grateful."

Ximen Qing was very pleased with the way she spoke. He grasped her white legs firmly and plunged forward violently again. She murmured softly and her starry eyes grew dim. Soon he asked her to lie down with legs spread-eagled like a mare's, and, covered with a red blanket, he rode her. He thrust with his prick, pressing on as he fondled her white buttocks in the candlelight. "Call me your darling without stopping," he said. "Let me bury myself in you." She rose to receive him, and called him her darling in a trembling voice. They played for a whole hour before Ximen wished to yield. At last he withdrew his prick, and she wiped it with a handkerchief. They slept in each other's arms. Before dawn she woke up excited and put his prick in her mouth. "Your Fifth Mother," said Ximen, "sucks all night. She does not let me get up if I want to piss because she is afraid that I'll catch cold, and she drinks my water."

"What does that matter?" she cried. "I'm also thirsty"; and Ximen made water in her mouth. They made love in every possible way.

The next day, she rose first, opened the door and lit a fire. Then she helped Ximen Qing to dress. He went to the front court and told Daian to send Ben the Fourth with two soldiers to take the golden tripod with his card to Censor Song's place. "When they have delivered it," he said, "they must wait for a return card." He told Chen Jingji to pack up a roll of gold silk and a roll of colored satin. He bade Qintong get a horse ready and take them to his Excellency Cai. Then he took breakfast in Yueniang's room.

"I don't see how we can all go to see Mistress Ying," Yueniang said, "Somebody must stay at home to keep Aunt Wu company."

"But I have got five presents ready," Ximen Qing said. "Of course, you must all go. My daughter is here. She can stay with Aunt Wu. I have promised Brother Ying." Yueniang said no more.

Guijie came and kowtowed to them. "I am going home today, Mother," she said.

"There is no hurry," Yueniang said. "Stay another day."

"My mother is not well," Guijie said, "and there is no one to look after her. I will come and see you again in the fifth month."

She kowtowed to Ximen Qing. Yueniang gave her some cakes and a tael of silver. When she had had some tea, she went away.

Ximen Qing had put on his ceremonial clothes and was on his way to the outer court when Ping'an came and said that General Jing had come. Ximen Qing went to greet him, and they made reverences to one another in the great hall.

"I haven't been to see you, and I have not yet congratulated you upon your promotion," General Jing said.

"And I have not called to thank you for sending me such a splendid present," Ximen Qing replied.

When they had exchanged greetings and taken tea, General Jing said: "I see your horse is waiting for you. Where are you going?"

"Yesterday," Ximen said, "Censor Song and their Excellencies An, Qian, and Huang, used my house for a reception to Cai the new Governor. Cai is the Imperial Tutor's ninth son. He gave me a card, and I am going to call upon him. I must go now because he may be leaving at any moment."

"I have come to ask a favor of you," General Jing said. "You know that Song's term of office will expire early in the new year. I expect there will be an inspection of all the officers, and I have come to you in the hope that you will mention my name to him. I discovered that he was here yesterday, and that is why I have called. If any promotion comes to me, I shall owe it to you."

"We are good friends," Ximen Qing said, "I shall be glad to do anything I can. Give me your record of service. He will be coming here for another party the day after tomorrow and I will speak to him then."

Jing rose and bowed. "I am very much obliged to you. Here is my record of service." He took it from an attendant and handed it to Ximen Qing. It said:

Jing Zhong, Garrison Commander of Qinghe, and officer in command of troops in various districts of Shandong. Thirty-two years of age. Born at Tanzhou. In consequence of the exploits of his ancestors, he was given the rank of captain. He passed through the military academy and has been promoted by degrees to his present post in command of troops in Jizhou, etc.

When Ximen Qing had read this, Jing brought out a list of presents and asked him to accept them. Ximen saw: "Two hundred measures of fine rice."

"What is this?" he said, "I cannot possibly accept it. If I did, there would be no point whatever in our friendship."

"Siquan," Jing said, "if you do not want it, you can give it to his Excellency. You must not refuse. If you do, I will never trouble you again."

After much demur, Ximen accepted. "When I have spoken to him, I will let you know," he said.

They drank tea again, and Jing went away. Ximen Qing mounted his horse and, with Qintong in attendance, went to see Governor Cai.

When Ximen had gone, Yuxiao, who had helped him to dress, went to see Jinlian.

"Mother," she said, "why didn't you stay longer in the inner court last night? Mother said several nasty things about you. She said that, as soon as you heard Father coming from the other court, you dashed after him. She said you got hold of him so tightly that you wouldn't let him go, even to the Third Lady, whose birthday it was. And the Third Lady said she wasn't going to enter into a competition with you; he might go to any room he liked."

"What can I do to clear myself?" Jinlian said. "They are not blind. Why couldn't they see that he never came here at all?"

"He comes to you so often," Yuxiao said. "And now the Sixth Lady is dead, they don't see where else he can go."

"Chickens cannot piddle, but they have to get rid of their water somehow," Jinlian said. "One woman has died, but there is another to take her place."

"Mother was angry with you because you asked for the fur coat without speaking to her about it first. She scolded Father when he gave back the key. She said it was lucky for you the Sixth Lady was dead or you wouldn't have had a chance to get the things. If she had been alive, you would only have been able to look at them."

"How absurd!" Jinlian said. "He is at liberty to do what he thinks fit. She is not my mother-in-law. It is not for her to control me. So she said I wouldn't let him go, did she? Well, I didn't put a cord about him. What nonsense!"

"I have come to tell you this so that you will know how matters stand. You mustn't mention it to anybody else. Guijie has gone, and the Great Lady is getting ready to go out. You will have to get ready too."

Yuxiao went away again. Jinlian decked herself with flowers and ornaments and powdered her face before the mirror. She told Chunmei to go and ask Yulou what color she was going to wear.

"Since we are still in mourning, Father wishes us all to wear plain clothes," Yulou said.

The ladies decided to wear white hairnets with pearl bandeaux, and plain-colored clothes. Yueniang alone wore a white headdress with a gold top, an embroidered coat, and a green skirt. One large sedan chair and four small ones were waiting for them. They took leave of Aunt Wu, the nuns, and old woman Pan, and set out to Ying Bojue's house to celebrate his baby's first month.

Ruyi'er and Yingchun had the food that Ximen Qing had left and a jar of Jinhua wine. They set out these things, took another pot of grape wine from the jar, and, at midday, invited old woman Pan, Chunmei, and Miss Yu to come and enjoy them. Miss Yu played and sang for them.

"I understand that Miss Shen sings that song about hanging up the portraits very well," Chunmei said, as they were enjoying their meal. "Why shouldn't we send for her and get her to sing to us?"

Yingchun was going to send Xiuchun but, at that moment, Chunhong came in to warm his hands at the fire.

"Now, you thievish little Southerner," Chunmei said to him, "didn't you go with the ladies?"

"No," Chunhong said, "Father told Wang Jing to go and said I was to stay here."

"You must be frozen, you little Southerner, or you wouldn't have come to warm your hands." She asked Yingchun to give him some wine. "When he has had it," she said, "we will get him to go for Miss Shen, and she shall come to sing for Grandmother."

When Chunhong had drunk his wine, he went to the inner court.

Miss Shen was drinking tea with Aunt Wu, Ximen Dajie, Yuxiao, and the nuns.

"Sister Shen," Chunhong said, "my aunt wants you to go and sing for her."

"Your aunt is here," Miss Shen said. "What are you talking about?"

"I mean Aunt Chunmei," the boy said.

"Why does she want me?" Miss Shen said. "Miss Yu is there."

"Go, Miss Shen," Aunt Wu said, "and come back to us later." But Miss Shen would not go.

Chunhong went back and told Chunmei that he could not persuade her to come.

"Tell her I want her. Then she will come," Chunmei said.

"I did tell her, but she wouldn't pay any attention. When I said my aunt wanted her, she cried: 'What aunt are you talking about?' I said: 'Aunt Chunmei.' Then she said: 'Why should I bother about her? Miss Yu is there, and that's enough. Who is she to have the audacity to send for me? I am busy. I'm singing for Aunt Wu.' Aunt Wu told her to come, but she wouldn't."

Chunmei flew into a temper. Her ears grew red, and her face became purple. Nobody could stop her. She rushed to Yueniang's room, shook her finger at Miss Shen, and upbraided her.

"How dare you say to the boy: 'What aunt are you talking about?' and: 'How has she the audacity to send for me?' Who are you? Are you a general's wife that I have no right to send for you? You are just a thievish strumpet who runs around from one family to another. Before you have been here any time at all, you begin trying to give yourself airs. What songs do you think you know? You know about a couple of lines, one here and one there. The sort of stuff you sing is the veriest doggerel, never written down on paper. You know a few heathenish songs and a few crazy tunes, and you make all this fuss. I have heard some of the finest singers there are. You simply don't count. That whore, Wang Liu'er, may think a lot about you, but, I assure you, I don't. I don't care how much you try to follow in her footsteps, I'm not afraid of you. Get out of here at once."

Aunt Wu checked her. "You must not be so uncivil," she said.

Miss Shen, surprised at being scolded in this way, could only blink. She was angry but she dared not speak. At last she said: "Sister seems to be very annoyed, but I didn't say anything wrong to the boy. Why does she come and insult me like this? If this is no place for me, there are plenty of other places I can go to."

This made Chunmei more angry still. "You wandering vagabond of a strumpet! If you are such a high-principled woman, why do you go begging clothes and food outside your own family? Get out of here and never come back again."

"I don't depend upon this place for my living," Miss Shen said.

"If you did, I should tell the boys to pull your hair out."

"You maid," Aunt Wu said, "what makes you so uncivil today? Go to the other court."

Chunmei did not move. Miss Shen cried and got down from the bed. She said good-bye to Aunt Wu, packed her clothes, and went away without waiting for a sedan chair. Aunt Wu told Ping'an to send Huatong with her to Han Daoguo's house.

Chunmei, still fuming, went back to the outer court. Aunt Wu looked at Ximen Dajie and Yuxiao. "Chunmei must have been drinking," she said. "She would not have been so unmannerly if she hadn't. It made me very uncomfortable. She ought to have let Miss Shen go in her own good time. Why should she tell her to get out at once? She wouldn't even let a boy take her away. It is too bad."

"I imagine they have been drinking," Yuxiao said.

When Chunmei got back to her party, she said: "I wish I had boxed her ears. Then she would have known what sort of woman I am. I wasn't going to let her get away with behavior like that."

"You must remember that, when you cut one branch of a tree, you hurt the other branches," Yingchun said. "Don't forget Miss Yu is here."

Miss Yu is a very different sort," Chunmei said. "She has been coming here for years and everybody likes her. She never refuses to sing if she is asked. She is not in the least like that strumpet. What songs does she know? Always the same few lines from the same few ditties, extremely vulgar, and not at all the sort of thing to be Song in a decent house like this. I don't want to hear her sing. I believe she is trying to put herself in Miss Yu's place."

"That is true enough," Miss Yu said. "Last night, when the Great Lady asked me to sing, she took the lute away from me. But don't be angry with her. She has no idea how she ought to behave here, and she doesn't know the respect that is due to you."

"That's what I told her," Chunmei said. "I said: 'Go and tell Han Daoguo's wife. I don't care.'"

"Sister," old woman Pan said, "why let yourself be so upset?"

"Let me give you a cup of wine to make you calmer," said Ruyi'er.

"This daughter of mine always flies into a temper when she is provoked," Yingchun said. "Now, Miss Yu, pick out one of your best songs and sing it for her."

Miss Yu took up her lute. "I will sing 'Ying Ying Made Trouble in the Bedchamber' for Grandmother and Sister Chunmei."

"Sing it well and you shall have some wine," Ruyi'er told her.

Yingchun took a cup of wine and said to Chunmei: "Now, Sister, no more tempers. Drink this cup of wine from your mother's hand."

This made Chunmei laugh. "You little strumpet!" she said, "how dare you call yourself my mother? Miss Yu, don't sing that song. Sing 'The River Is in Flood, and the Water Has Reached My Door.'"

Miss Yu took her lute and sang the first line: 'The flowers are dainty and the moon delightful.' They enjoyed their wine.

When Ximen Qing returned from the wharf where he had visited Cai, Ping'an said: "A messenger has been from Captain He to ask you to go early to the office tomorrow. Some robbers have been arrested, and they are to be tried. Prefect Hu has sent a hundred copies of the new calendar; and General Jing, a pig, a jar of wine, and four packets of silver. I gave them to brother-in-law, and he took them to the inner court. We did not send a card in return because the servant said he would call again this evening. I gave a return card and a *qian* of silver to his Lordship Hu's servant. Your kinsman, Master Qiao, has sent a card asking you to take wine with him tomorrow."

Then Daian came, bringing a return card from Song. "I took the things to his office," the boy said. "His Excellency said he would settle up with you tomorrow, and he gave me and the men five *qian* of silver and a hundred copies of the new calendar."

Ximen Qing went into the great hall. Chunhong hurried to warn Chunmei and the others.

"Are you still drinking?" he said. "Father has come back."

"What if he has, you little Southerner?" Chunmei said. "He won't interfere with us. The ladies are not at home, and he won't come here."

They went on drinking and joking, and nobody left the party. Ximen Qing went to Yueniang's room. Aunt Wu and the nuns went to the adjoining room. Yuxiao took his clothes and got something ready for him to eat.

Ximen Qing summoned Laixing and said to him: "You must see about preparing another feast. On the thirtieth, Censor Song is going to have a party here, and, on the first, the two eunuchs, Liu and Xue, Major Zhou and the others, are coming."

When Laixing had gone, Yuxiao asked Ximen what kind of wine he would like.

"Open the jar that General Jing has just sent," he told her. "I would like to taste it and see if it is any good."

Then Laian came and said he was going to take a man to meet Yueniang and the other ladies. Yuxiao asked him to unseal the jar. Then she poured out some wine and handed it to her master. It was a beautiful shade of green, and rather pungent. Ximen Qing asked for more. Food was brought, and he had his meal. Laian took some soldiers with lanterns to escort the ladies home.

They came in, wearing their fur coats. Sun Xue'e was the only one to kowtow to Ximen and Wu Yueniang. Then she went to the other room to see Aunt Wu and the nuns. Yueniang sat down and said: "Mistress Ying seemed very glad to see us. Her neighbor, Madam Ma, and Brother Ying's sister-in-law, Miss Du, and several other ladies were there, perhaps ten in all. There were two singing girls. The baby is big and chubby, but Chunhua seems thinner and darker than she used to be. Her long face is not very beautiful. It looks just like a donkey's. She is not at all well, and the household is in a mess, for there are not enough people to look after it. When we came away, Brother Ying kowtowed and thanked us most effusively. He asked us to thank you for the presents you had sent."

"Did Chunhua dress and come out to see you?" Ximen Qing asked.

"Of course, she did. She has eyes and a nose like everybody else. She is not a spirit. Why shouldn't she come out to see us?"

"Oh, the poor maid!" Ximen said. "If I put a few black beans on her, I'm sure some pig would run off with her."

"You shouldn't talk like that," Yueniang said. "You always try to make it appear that nobody is worth looking at except your own wives."

Wang Jing, who was standing beside them, said: "When Uncle Ying saw the ladies coming, he didn't come out to welcome them. He ran to a little room and peeped through the window. I caught him there, and I said: 'Old gentleman, you are lacking in propriety. 'What are you looking for?' He kicked me out."

"The rascal!" Ximen Qing said, laughing. "When he comes tomorrow, I will cover his face with dust."

"Yes," Wang Jing said, and laughed too.

Yueniang shouted at him. "Don't tell such lies, you young rascal. He didn't look at us at all. You are telling stories. We never saw him all day long, except when we were leaving and he came to kowtow to us."

Wang Jing went away. Yueniang got up and went to see her sister-in-law and the nuns in the next room. Ximen Dajie, Yuxiao, and the maids and serving women came to kowtow to her.

"Where is Miss Shen?" Yueniang said.

Nobody answered. At last Yuxiao said: "Miss Shen has gone."

"Why didn't she wait for me?" Yueniang asked.

Aunt Wu saw that the business could not be kept hidden. She told Yueniang of the quarrel between Chunmei and Miss Shen. Yueniang was angry. "If she didn't wish to sing, why should she?" she said. "The maid has no business to be so conceited and undisciplined as to curse her. The master of this house does not behave properly himself, and the maids do what they like. The whole household is topsy-turvy." She turned to Jinlian: "You ought to keep her in order instead of letting her behave so outrageously."

"I have never seen such a blind mule as Miss Shen," Jinlian said, laughing. "If the wind didn't blow, the trees wouldn't shake. She goes from one person's door to another, and singing is her business. When she is asked to sing, she should do so with a good grace. If she made a fuss and gave herself airs, Chunmei was right to tell her what she thought about her."

"All very well," Yueniang said, "but if she goes on like this, people, whether good or bad, simply won't stand it. They'll go away. You will do nothing to keep her in order."

"I don't see why I should punish my maid because she put this blind strumpet in her place."

Yueniang grew angry. Her face flushed.

"Very well, spoil your maid, and she will drive all our relatives and neighbors away."

She went to Ximen Qing, and he asked her what was the matter.

"I expect you know," Yueniang said. "You have such polite young ladies for your maids. Now, one of them has been cursing Miss Shen and making her go away."

"But why wouldn't she sing for her?" Ximen said, smiling. "Don't worry. Tomorrow, I'll send her two taels of silver, and that will put matters right."

"Miss Shen's box is still here. She didn't take it away," Yueniang said. She saw that Ximen Qing was laughing. "There you are, laughing, instead of sending for the maid and giving her a scolding. I don't see anything to laugh at."

Li Jiao'er and Yulou were there but, seeing how angry Yueniang was, they went to their own rooms. Ximen Qing went on drinking wine. Yueniang went to the inner room to take off her ornaments and ceremonial dress.

"Where have those four packets of silver on the chest come from?" she said to Yuxiao.

Ximen Qing answered her. "General Jing sent them. He wants me to speak to Song for him."

"Brother-in-law brought them. I forgot to tell you," Yuxiao said.

"Silver belonging to other people should always be put in the chest at once," Yueniang said.

Yuxiao put it in the chest.

Jinlian was still sitting there, waiting for Ximen Qing to go to the outer court. It was a *Renzi* day. She was going to take the medicine Nun Xue had given her and hoped that, after she had slept with him, she would conceive.

Ximen Qing showed no sign of moving. At last, she pulled aside the lattice. "If you are not coming, I shall go," she said. "I haven't patience to wait any longer."

"You go first," Ximen Qing said. "I will come when I've finished my wine."

Jinlian went away. Then Yueniang said: "I don't wish you to go to her. I have something to say to you. The pair of you wear the same pair of trousers, and you are making my life unbearable. She even has the audacity to come to my room and call you away. The shameless hussy! She might be your only wife and the rest of us nobodies. You are a foolish scamp. No wonder people talk about you behind your back. We are all your wives and you ought to treat us decently. You needn't make everybody aware of the fact that she has got you body and soul. Since you came back from the Eastern Capital, you haven't spent a single night in the inner court. Naturally people are annoyed. You should put fire into the cold stove before you begin on the hot one. You have no right to allow one woman to monopolize you. So far as I am concerned, it doesn't matter. I don't care for games of this sort, but the others will not stand it. They don't say anything, but they think a great deal. Yulou didn't eat a thing all the time we were at Brother Ying's place. She has probably caught a chill on the stomach. Mistress Ying gave her two cups of wine, but she couldn't keep it down. Will you go and see her?"

"Is that true?" Ximen Qing said. "Have these things taken away. I won't drink any more." He went at once to Yulou's room. She was undressed and lying on the bed, sick. She was retching painfully. "My child, how do you feel?" Ximen said. "I will send for a doctor for you." Yulou was vomiting. She did not answer. He helped her to lie down, but she pressed her hands to her breast.

"My dear, how are you? Tell me."

"I have a good deal of pain. Why do you ask? Go and attend to your own affairs."

"I didn't know," Ximen said. "The Great Lady has only just told me."

"Of course you didn't know," Yulou said. "I am not your wife. You only love the one who has established herself in your heart."

Ximen Qing took her in his arms and kissed her. "Don't tease me," he said. "Lanxiang, make some strong tea for your mother at once."

"I have some already made," Lanxiang said. She brought a cup. Ximen took it and held it to Yulou's lips.

"Give it to me," she said, "I will drink it by myself. Don't try to be pleasant. Go and sell your hot buns where they are wanted. I am not jealous. The sun must have risen in the west today, since you come to see me. I can't imagine why the Great Lady said anything to you about it."

"You don't understand," Ximen Qing said. "The last few days, I have really been too busy to come."

"Yes," Yulou said, "you have too much to think about; you can't think about anyone but your sweetheart. We are stale. We're only fit to be thrown into the dustbin. Perhaps in ten years' time you will remember us."

Ximen Qing still went on kissing her. "Go away," she said, "I can't bear the smell of the wine you've been drinking. I have had nothing to eat all day and I haven't strength enough to play with you."

"If you have had nothing to eat, let me tell the maid to bring something. I haven't had my supper yet. I will have it with you."

"No," Yulou said. "I feel too ill. If you want anything to eat, go and have it elsewhere."

"If you won't eat," Ximen said, "neither will I. Let us go to bed. Tomorrow I will send for Doctor Ren."

"Doctor Ren or Doctor Li, it's all the same to me. I shall send for old woman Liu. She'll give me medicine that will cure me."

"Lie down," Ximen said, "and let me stroke your stomach. That will make you better. You know I am an expert at massage." Then he suddenly remembered. "The other day," he said, "Liu, the Director of Studies, gave me ten cow-bezoar pills from Guangdong. If you take one with some wine, you will be all right in no time." He said to Lanxiang: "Go to the Great Lady and ask her for the medicine in the porcelain jar. And bring some wine with you."

"I'm sure you will be well as soon as you have taken it," he said to Yulou.

"I can't think of anything horrid enough to say to you," Yulou said. "What do you know about medicine? And, if you want wine, there is some here."

Lanxiang came back with two pills. Ximen Qing made her heat the wine. He took off the outer wax. There was a golden pill inside it. He gave it to Yulou.

"Now heat another cup of wine for me," he said to Lanxiang. "I am going to take some medicine myself."

Yulou looked at him. "You dirty creature! If you are going to take medicine, go somewhere else to do it. What do you think you're going to do here? You've decided I'm not going to die just yet, so you think you'll begin your tricks. In spite of all the pain I've had, you are ready to begin. No, I'll have none of it."

Ximen Qing laughed. "Very well, my dear. I won't take any medicine. We'll go to bed."

When she had taken the pill, they went to bed. Ximen Qing fondled her soft breasts. With one hand he pressed her sweet nipples, and, with the other, drew her white neck closer.

"How do you feel now that you've taken the pill?" he said.

"Not so bad as I did, but still bad enough."

"Don't worry," Ximen said, "you'll soon be better. Today, while you were out, I gave Laixing fifty taels of silver. We are going to give a banquet for Song the day after tomorrow. On the first of next month we must burn paper offerings, and, on the third, we must devote a couple of days to entertaining people. We can't accept presents and give nothing in return."

"What do I care whether you have people coming or not?" Yulou said. "On the twentieth, I am going to get the boys to settle up the accounts, and I shall give up this housekeeping business. You will probably hand it over to Jinlian. It is time she did some work. Only yesterday she was saying there was nothing very hard about it, and there is no reason why I should always be bothered with it."

"You shouldn't pay any attention to that little whore," Ximen said. "She is always bragging, but, if she is given anything of importance to do, she can't do it. If you really mean to hand it over to her, wait until these parties are over."

"Oh, you are very clever, Brother," Yulou said. "You pretend you don't love her more than the rest of us, but now you are giving yourself away. You say I am to hand the accounts over to her when the parties are over. Why should I have all the hard work? In the morning, when I am dressing my hair, the boys come in and out, measuring silver and getting change. It takes my breath away and uses me up. And nobody even says: 'Well done!'"

"My child," Ximen said, "don't you know the saying: 'When anyone has managed the house for three years, even the dog hates him'?"

He slowly lifted up one of her legs and put it over his arm. He embraced her, still holding it. He saw that she was wearing a pair of red silk slippers. "My child," he said, "what could be more delightful to me than this white leg? If I had all the women in the world to choose from, I could never find one so tender and so lovable as you."

"Oh, chatterbox!" Yulou said. "Do you imagine anybody believes that wooly mouth of yours? Other women have legs just as white. You really mean that my skin is rough, and you are calling black white."

"My dear, if I am lying to you, may I die this minute!"

"Don't take any oaths," Yulou said.

Ximen Qing put on the clasp and slipped his staff into her.

"I know the fellow you are," Yulou cried. "You always come to this." Then she saw the clasp. "When did you put that thing on? Take it off at once." But Ximen ignored her words, grasped her legs, and strove with all his might. Soon her juices of love flowed with a sound like that of a dog eating a fowl. She wiped her cunt with a handkerchief. She trembled and could not speak.

"Don't go any further, darling," she said. "My back has recently been hurting and some white fluid has been escaping."

"We will get some medicine from Doctor Ren tomorrow. That will cure it."

Yueniang was talking to Aunt Wu and the nuns. By degrees they came to the subject of Chunmei and Miss Shen, and the whole story came out.

"Chunmei was really very rude," Aunt Wu said. "She insulted Miss Shen in words that cut like knives. I was obliged to interfere. It was not surprising that Miss Shen was angry. I would never have believed that Chunmei could curse people like that. I'm sure she must have been drinking."

"Yes," Xiaoyu said, "she and four others were drinking."

"It is all that unreasonable fellow's fault," Yueniang said. "He has encouraged her to give herself such airs. She doesn't care who it is. She won't suffer anybody to speak to her. I shouldn't be surprised if, in the future, all sorts of people don't get driven away, and nobody will have anything to do with us. Miss Shen is a girl who goes from one house to another. It won't be very pleasant for us if this story gets about. People will say Ximen Qing's wife must be a dreadful creature. In this household, it is impossible to say who is master and who the slave. People will not say she is an undutiful slave, but that we are a bad bunch. And what will that mean?"

"Never mind," Aunt Wu said, "since your husband says nothing about it, why should we bother?"

The ladies went to their own rooms to sleep.

When Jinlian realized that Yueniang had prevented Ximen Qing from going to her, so that she missed the *Renzi* day, she was very angry. Very early the next morning, she told Laian to fetch a sedan chair for old woman Pan.

When Yueniang got up, the nuns were ready to go away. She gave each of them some cakes and five *qian* of silver, and promised that Nun Xue should hold a service in her own temple in the first month. She gave her another tael of silver to buy incense, candles and paper things, and said she would send oil, wheat flour, rice, and vegetarian food as an offering.

The nuns had tea with Aunt Wu in the upper room, and Yueniang sent for Li Jiao'er, Yulou, and Ximen's daughter, Ximen Dajie.

"How do you feel after taking the pill?" she asked Yulou. "Is your stomach still painful?"

"I brought up a little water this morning," Yulou said, "but I feel better now."

Yueniang told Yuxiao to go for Jinlian and old woman Pan. Yuxiao said: "Xiaoyu is seeing about the buns. I will go myself." She went to Jinlian's room.

"Where is Grandmother?" she said. "They want you to go and have tea with them."

"I sent her away this morning," Jinlian said.

"Why did you send her away without telling anybody?" Yuxiao said.

"Why should she stay any longer? She seems to have made herself a nuisance."

"But I have a piece of dried meat and four preserved melons for her. I never dreamed she would go. You keep them for her." The maid gave the food to Jinlian, who put it in a drawer.

"Last night, when you had gone away," Yuxiao said, "the Great Lady told Father you were the one who governed this household, and that you and he wore the same pair of trousers. She said you were a shameless thing, monopolizing him as you did, so that he was afraid to go to the inner court. She persuaded him to go and sleep in the Third Lady's room. Then she told Aunt Wu and the nuns that you spoiled Chunmei so much that she even dared to insult Miss Shen. Father is going to send a tael of silver to Miss Shen to make things all right."

Yuxiao went back to Yueniang and said that the Fifth Lady was coming, but that her mother had gone home.

Yueniang looked at Aunt Wu. "You see! I said something to her yesterday, and now she flies into a temper and sends her mother away without a word to me. She must be up to something, but what form the storm will take I can't think."

Yueniang did not know it, but Jinlian was already in the room on the other side of the lattice. She came in suddenly.

"Great Sister," she said, "I have sent my mother home. Did you say that I monopolize our husband? I wish to know."

"Yes, I did say so," Yueniang said. "What about it? Ever since he came back from the Eastern Capital, he has spent all his time in your room.

He never comes near the inner court. Do you flatter yourself that you are his only wife, and the rest of us nothing? Whether the others realize what you are about, I don't know, but I do. A few days ago, when Guijie went away, my sister-in-law asked me why she was in such a hurry and why our husband was angry with her. I told her I didn't know. You pushed yourself forward and said you were the only one who knew all about it. Of course you know. You never lose hold of him for a moment."

"If he didn't wish to come to my room," Jinlian said, "do you imagine I should keep him there with a pig's-hair cord? Do you suggest that I am a whore?"

"Aren't you?" Yueniang said. "Yesterday, when he was here, you pulled the lattice aside and dashed in to take him away. What do you mean by it? Our husband is a man. He does a man's work. What crime has he committed that you should tie him with a cord of pig's hair? You foolish creature! I said nothing about it until you made me do so. On the sly, you asked him for a fur coat. You didn't say a word to me about it, even when you put it on. If everybody behaved like that, my function here might as well be to look after the ducks. It is time you realized that, even in a poor house, there must be someone in authority. You allowed your maid to sleep with him. It was like cat and rat sleeping together. You indulge her in every possible way, and now she has the audacity to insult people. Yet you still stick up for her and won't be contradicted."

"What about my maid?" Jinlian cried. "You think she is bad, and you would like to get rid of me. As for that fur coat, I did ask him for it, but it wasn't only to get that for me that he opened the door. He got clothes for other people too. Why don't you mention that fact? I spoil my maid. I am a whore. And I make my husband happy. Why don't you say that woman is a whore too?"

Yueniang became more and more angry. Her cheeks became crimson. "No," she said, "not you, but I am the whore! But when I married him, I was a virgin, not a married woman who got him into her clutches. I am no whorish husband-stealer. It is clear enough which of us is a whore and which is virtuous."

"Sister, don't lose control of yourself," Aunt Wu said.

But Yueniang went on. "You have killed one husband already, and now you are trying to kill another."

"Mother," Yulou said, "why are you so angry today, beating us all with the same stick? You, Fifth Lady, must give way to the Great Lady. You must not quarrel with her."

"The proverb says: When there is fighting, no hand is gentle: when there is quarreling, no words are soft," Aunt Wu said. "When you quarrel like this, it makes your relatives ashamed. If you won't pay any attention to me, I shall take it that you are angry with me and call for my sedan chair and go home."

Li Jiao'er hastily begged her not to do so.

Jinlian sat down on the floor and rolled about. She banged her face on the ground and knocked the hairnet from her head. She cried aloud.

"Let me die!" she shouted. "Why should I go on living a miserable life like this? You were married in due and proper manner: I only followed him to the house. Very well! There need be no more difficulty, I will ask him to set me free. I will go, but I fear that, if you imagine you will capture a husband thereby, you are mistaken."

"Now, you disturber of the peace," Yueniang said, "before one can get a word out, you pour forth a stream of words. You roll about on the floor. You put all the blame on us. Will you ask my husband to divorce me? Don't think anybody is afraid of you, even if you are so clever."

"No, indeed!" Jinlian cried, "you are the only good and virtuous woman here. Who would dare to quarrel with you?"

"Am I not good and virtuous? Do you suggest that I have had a lover in this house?" Yueniang was growing still more angry.

"If you haven't, has anybody else? Let me see you point to any lover I have had."

When the quarrel had reached this pitch, Yulou went forward and tried to pull Jinlian away. "Don't behave like this," she said. "These holy nuns will be ashamed of you. Stand up, and I will go with you to your room."

Jinlian would not get up. Yulou and Yuxiao pulled her up. They took her to her own room.

"Sister," Aunt Wu said to Yueniang, "you ought not to get into a state like this when you are in such delicate health. There is really nothing very much the matter. When you sisters are happy, I am content; but, if you spend all the time quarreling and will not listen to what I say, I shall not be able to come any more."

The nuns gave their novices something to eat. Then they took their boxes and came to say good-bye to Yueniang. "Teachers," Yueniang said, "you must not scorn me."

"There is some smoke to every fire," Nun Xue said. "A tiny flame in our mind can give rise to much smoke. My advice is: give way to each other. As Buddha says: Our minds should be as calm as a ship at anchor. We must cleanse our hearts and make them pure. If we leave the lock open and loose the chain, ten thousand diamond clubs can not control us. The first step towards Buddhahood is self-control. Thank you for all your kindness to us. We hope you will be very well."

They made reverence to Yueniang, and she returned it. "I feel that, this time, I have entertained you very poorly," she said, "but I will send you something later." She asked Li Jiao'er and Ximen Dajie to see the nuns to the gate. "Mind the dog," she said.

When the nuns had gone, she sat down again with Aunt Wu. "This business has made my arms numb and my fingers as cold as ice," she said. "I only had a mouthful of tea this morning, and there is nothing but that in my stomach."

"Over and over again, I have advised you not to quarrel," Aunt Wu said. "You never listen to me. Now you are getting near your time. Why do you make this trouble?"

"You saw the whole affair," Yueniang said. "Am I the one who causes the trouble? You might as well talk about a thief arresting a policeman. I can give way to everybody but nobody will give way to me. There is only one husband here, and she wants him all for herself. She schemes and plots with that maid of hers. They do things that no other person would ever dream of doing. Though they are women, they have no idea of decency. She never looks at herself, but opens her mouth and pours forth insults. When Li Ping'er was alive, she was constantly having rows with her. She was always coming and telling me one thing and another that Li Ping'er had done wrong. She is the kind of woman who is always causing trouble. She has an animal's heart and a human face. She never admits saying anything. She takes such dreadful oaths they would frighten anybody. But I will keep my eyes open and watch her. I will see what sort of an end she comes to. When we had tea, I sent for her mother. How could I have dreamed she would send her away? She was all ready to make trouble with me. She sneaked up here determined to do so. Well! I am not afraid of her. Let her tell my husband, and he can divorce me."

"We were all in the room," Yuxiao said. "I was standing near the fire, but I did not hear the Fifth Lady come in. I never heard a sound."

"She walks like a spirit," Xue'e said. "She always wears felt shoes, so she doesn't make any sound. Don't you remember the trouble she used to make for me when she first came here? She said all sorts of things about me behind my back, and my husband beat me twice in consequence. At that time, Sister, you said it was my fault."

"She is accustomed to burying people alive," Yueniang said. "Today she thought she would try her hand on me. You saw her beating her head on the ground and rolling about. When he comes back and finds out about it, I shall come off worst."

"You mustn't say that, Mother," Li Jiao'er said, "the world cannot be turned upside down."

"You don't know," Yueniang said. "She is one of those nine-tailed foxes. Better people than I have died at her hands. How shall I escape? What flesh and bones have I that they can withstand her? You have been here several years, and you came from the bawdy house, but you are worth a dozen of her. See how desperate she was yesterday. She dashed into my room and called him. She said: 'I'm not going to wait for you if you don't come.' It looked as though he belonged to her, and she had the right to have him. I shouldn't care if he hadn't gone to her room every night since he came back from the Eastern Capital. Even when it was somebody's birthday, she wouldn't let him go. She wants all ten fingers to put into her own mouth."

"Why do you worry about it so much?" Aunt Wu said. "You are nearly always ill. Let him do what he likes. If you are trying to fight other people's battles, you will be the one to suffer."

Yuxiao brought some food, but Yueniang would not touch it. "My head aches, and my heart feels very queer," she said. She told Yuxiao to put a pillow on the bed so that she might lie down, and asked Li Jiao'er to keep Aunt Wu company. Miss Yu was going, so Yueniang gave orders that a box of cakes and five *qian* of silver should be given to her. Then the girl went away.

It was about noon when Ximen Qing came home after trying the case at his office. General Jing's man came to ask for his return card. Ximen Qing said to him: "Thank your master for these valuable presents, but they are really too much. I should like you to take them back now, and I will accept them when I have been able to do what he wishes."

"My master gave me no orders," the man said, "and I dare not take them back. It will be just as well if they are kept here."

"In that case," Ximen Qing said, "thank your master for me. Here is a card to take back to him." He gave the man a tael of silver.

Then he went to Yueniang's room. She was lying on the bed. He spoke to her several times, but she would not answer. He asked the maids what was wrong, but none dared to tell him. Then he went to Jinlian's room. She, too, was lying on the bed, and her hair was in disorder. He asked her what the trouble was, and again he got no answer. Then he went to pack up some silver, and, when General Jing's man had gone, he went to Yulou's room. Yulou knew that the secret could not be kept so she told him about the quarrel between Yueniang and Jinlian.

In a great state of excitement, Ximen Qing went to Yueniang's room again. He held her up in his arms. "Why did you have this quarrel?" he said. "You know you are not in a fit state of health. Why do you take that little strumpet seriously? Why did you have a row with her?"

"I did not quarrel with her," Yueniang said. "It was she who started the trouble, I didn't go to her: she came to me. If you wish to prove it, ask the others. This morning, out of kindness, I got tea ready and asked her mother to come and join us, but, in a temper, she had sent her mother away. Then she came herself, tossing her head and shouting. She rolled about on the floor and beat her head on the ground. She got her hairnet in a mess. It was a marvel she didn't strike me, and, if it hadn't been for the others keeping us apart, we might have rolled about together. She is so used to bullying people that she thinks she can bully me. She said several times that you married her irregularly and that she would ask you to divorce her and she would go away. For one word I said, she said ten. Her mouth was like the Huai River in flood. How could a weak person like me withstand her? She knows how to put the blame on others. She made me so angry I didn't know where I was. As for this baby, he will never be born, not even if he is a prince. She made me so ill my belly feels ready to burst, and my guts hurt as though they were dropping out of me. My head aches and my arms are numb. I have just come back from the closet, but the child didn't come away. It would have been better if it had come, then I shouldn't have been troubled any longer with it. Tonight I will get a cord and hang myself. Then you will be free to go to her. If I don't hang myself, I shall surely be murdered as Li Ping'er was. I know you will think things very unfortunate if you can't get rid of more than one wife in three years."

Ximen Qing was terribly excited. He put his arms around Yueniang. "Good Sister," he said, "don't worry about that little whore. She doesn't know the difference between high and low, what is sweet and what is sour. Don't be angry. You are worth more to me than all the others put together. I will go and beat her."

"Dare you?" Yueniang said. "She will tie you with a pig's-hair cord."

"Let her say so to me," Ximen said. "If I get angry with her, I will kick her till she doesn't know where she is. How do you feel now? Have you had anything to eat?"

"I haven't tasted a thing," Yueniang said. "This morning, I got the tea ready and waited for her mother. Then she came and screamed at me. Now I feel very ill. My belly hurts and my head aches. My arms are all numb. If you don't believe me, come here and feel my hands. They are still cold."

Ximen Qing stamped his feet on the ground. "What shall I do?" he cried. "I know. I'll send the boys for Doctor Ren."

"What is the use of sending for Doctor Ren? He can do nothing. If it is to live, it will live, and, if not, it will die. If it dies, so much the better for everybody. A wife is like the paint on the walls. When it is faded, another coat is put on. If I die, you will make her your first wife. She is clever enough to manage this household."

"I'm surprised you have patience even to quarrel with her," Ximen Qing said. "You ought to treat her as dung and leave her alone. If we don't send for Doctor Ren, the anger will get into your system and we shan't be able to get it out again. Then it will be too late to do anything."

"Send for old woman Liu, and I will take her medicine," Yueniang said. "I will ask her to use a needle on my head and get rid of the headache."

"That's absurd," Ximen Qing said. "What does that old whore know about women's ailments? I shall send a boy with a horse for Doctor Ren at once."

"You can do so if you like, but I won't see him."

Ximen Qing paid no attention. He went to the outer court and said to Qintong: "Get a horse at once and go for Doctor Ren. Be quick. Bring him back with you." Qintong got a horse and was away like a cloud of smoke. Ximen Qing went back to Yueniang's room and told the maids to make some gruel. But when the gruel was brought, Yueniang would not eat it.

Qintong came back and said Doctor Ren was at the palace and his people said he would come the next morning.

Yueniang saw that messengers had come several times from Master Qiao to invite Ximen Qing. "The doctor will be here tomorrow," she said. "You had better go or our kinsman Qiao will be angry."

"If I go, who will see to you?"

Yueniang laughed. "You silly fellow," she said. "None of this. Off you go. There is nothing seriously wrong with me. Leave me alone. Perhaps I shall feel better. If I do, I'll get up and have something to eat with my sister-in-law. Don't be so excited."

Ximen Qing said to Yuxiao: "Go for Aunt Wu at once, and ask her to stay with your mother. Where is Miss Yu? Tell her to come and sing for your mother."

"Miss Yu has been gone a long time," Yuxiao said.

"Who told her to go?" Ximen said, "I wanted her here for another two days." He kicked Yuxiao.

"She saw this was no place to be at, so she went away," Yueniang said. "Yuxiao is not to blame."

"You wouldn't kick the one who insulted Miss Shen," Yuxiao murmured.

Ximen Qing pretended not to hear this. He dressed and went to Master Qiao's house. Before the first night watch, he returned and went to Yueniang's room. Yueniang was sitting with Aunt Wu, Yulou and Li Jiao'er. Aunt Wu hurriedly went away as soon as he came in.

"How do you feel now?" Ximen Qing said.

"I have had two mouthfuls of gruel with my sister-in-law," Yueniang said, "and my stomach feels rather easier. But I still have the headache and backache."

"That is all right," Ximen said, "Doctor Ren will be here tomorrow and he will give you some medicine to expel the anger and strengthen your womb. You will soon be well again."

"I told you I didn't want the doctor, but you would send for him. This is nothing serious, and I don't want any man to come and fiddle with me. You will see whether I am able to go out or not tomorrow. What did kinsman Qiao want with you?"

"Oh, it was only an entertainment to celebrate my coming back from the Eastern Capital. He was very kind, and had made a lot of preparations. There were two singing girls, and his Honor Zhu was there. But I was so anxious about you, I couldn't eat a thing. I had a few cups of wine and came back as soon as I could."

"You smooth-tongued rascal," Yueniang said. "These flowery phrases and flattering expressions are too much for me. What is making you so extraordinarily pleasant? Even if I were one of Buddha's incarnations, you would give me no place in your heart. If I died, you wouldn't think me worth a jar of earthenware. What did Qiao say to you?"

"He is thinking of applying for honorary rank, and he has prepared thirty taels of silver. He wants me to speak to Prefect Hu about it. I told him there would be no trouble about that because, yesterday, Hu sent me a hundred copies of the new calendar, and I hadn't sent him anything in return yet. When I did, I said, I would send a card and ask him for a nomination. Qiao wouldn't agree. He said he must offer his thirty taels. If I help him, he said, it would be very much to his advantage."

"Did you take his money?" Yueniang said. "You ought to do something for him if he asks you."

"He is going to send the money tomorrow. He was going to send presents too, but I stopped him. I think if I send Hu a pig and a jar of wine, that ought to be enough."

That night, Ximen Qing stayed with Yueniang.

The next day was Censor Song's party. Tables were arranged in the great hall, and everything was made ready. Thirty musicians from the Prefecture came early in the morning, with four conductors and four soldiers. Shortly afterwards, Dr. Ren came on horseback. Ximen Qing took him to the hall, and they greeted one another.

"Your servant called for me yesterday," Dr. Ren said, "but I was on duty. When I came home last night, I found your card, and I have come this morning without waiting for my carriage. May I ask who is ill?"

"My first wife has suddenly become disturbed in health, and I should be glad if you would examine her," Ximen said.

They drank tea. Then Dr. Ren said: "Yesterday, Mingchuan told me you had been promoted. I must congratulate you now and send my presents later."

"It is really not an occasion for celebration," Ximen said, "I am so ill-fitted for the office I hold."

He said to Qintong: "Go to the inner court and tell the Great Lady that Doctor Ren has come. Ask them to get the room ready." Qintong went. Aunt Wu, Li Jiao'er and Meng Yulou were with Wu Yueniang. He gave them Ximen's message. Yueniang did not move.

"I told him not to send for the doctor," she said. "I don't want any man here, staring at me and putting his fingers on my hand. I want some medicine from old woman Liu, nothing more. Why should he make a fuss like this to satisfy that man's curiosity?"

"But he is here now, Mother," Yulou said, "we can't tell him to go away without your seeing him."

Aunt Wu also insisted. "He is a physician to the royal family," she said. "You must let him feel your pulse. We don't know what is wrong, or where the trouble lies. This is the only way we can find out. It will be good for you to take his medicine and put your blood and air in order. You mustn't let the thing go too far. Old woman Liu knows nothing about medicine."

Yueniang went to dress her hair and put on her headdress. Yuxiao held the mirror for her, and Yulou climbed on the bed and brushed her back hair. Li Jiao'er arranged her ornaments, and Xue'e put her clothes straight. In a very short time she looked like a carving in jade.

CHAPTER 76
Master Wen Falls into Disgrace

The golden cups are always in their hands
They pledge each other without ceasing.
No thought of earthly things disturbs their quiet hearts.
Year after year, men are the same
In every place, the same flowers bloom.
Let us sing and recite poems
To increase the joy that comes from this inspired wine
And when we have drunk our fill,
Call for the flute and strings.
When we are in our cups, things are today
As they were yesterday.
Only the scholar Wen is here no more.

When Ximen Qing found that Wu Yueniang was not yet ready, he came himself to hurry her. When she was dressed, he asked Dr. Ren to come. Yueniang came from her bedroom and made a reverence towards the visitor. Dr. Ren turned and bowed. Yueniang sat down on a chair facing the doctor, and Qintong put an embroidered cushion on the table. She held out her arm, and Dr. Ren felt her pulse. After this, she made a reverence and went back to her room. One of the boys brought the doctor tea.

"Your lady," said Dr. Ren, "appears to be suffering from disorder both of air and blood. Her pulse is feeble and sluggish. As regards the air, it is partly because she is with child, but also because she has not been taking sufficient nourishment. Then, too, she has been angry and so stirred up the fire in her liver. This makes her head and eyes ache. She takes things too seriously, and the result of this is a certain melancholy in the abdominal region. The blood and air in her body are not evenly matched."

Yueniang sent Qintong to tell the doctor that her head ached, her arms were numb, and her belly very painful. She had backache and no appetite.

"This is evident," the doctor said. "I have already said as much."

"As you say, she is with child," Ximen Qing said. "Indeed, she is near her time. She has had occasion to be angry, and her anger has been unable to find a satisfactory outlet. She feels depressed in consequence. I hope, Doctor, you will give her the best medicine you can think of. I shall be more than grateful."

"I will do what I can," the doctor said. "I will send her something to make her stomach easier, to set the air in the right channels and, generally, to strengthen her internally. But when the lady has taken the medicine, she must avoid all further occasion of anger, and she must be careful what she eats,"

"You will remember the baby, Doctor?" Ximen said.

"My medicine will nourish and soothe it."

"My third wife, too, has pains in the stomach," Ximen Qing said. "If you have anything likely to do her good, will you be so kind as to prescribe for her?"

"Certainly. I will send her some pills," Dr.. Ren said.

He went to the outer court. On the way, he saw the company of musicians and asked Ximen Qing whom he was entertaining.

"His Excellency Song and his officers are entertaining Governor Hou here today," Ximen told him.

The doctor was astonished. His respect for Ximen Qing increased accordingly. Indeed, when he was taken to the gate, he bowed so often that he paid twice the usual degree of honor to his patron.

Ximen Qing went back, packed up a tael of silver and two handkerchiefs, and told Qintong to take them on horseback to the doctor's house and bring back the medicine.

Li Jiao'er, Meng Yulou and the other ladies were busy in Yueniang's room, getting the fruit ready and cleaning the silver.

"You didn't want to come out to see the doctor," Yulou said to Yueniang, "but, you see, he knew exactly what was wrong the moment he looked at you."

"I am not a good respectable wife," Yueniang said, "and, if I am going to die, why don't you let me die in peace? That woman said I was not her mother-in-law. The only difference between us, I suppose, is that I am eight months older than she is. If she hadn't made sure of our husband, do you think she would have dared to shout and rave at me as she did? If you hadn't taken her away, I should not have escaped in ten years. If I am to die, let me die. As the proverb says: when one cock dies, there is always another to take his place, and the new cock's crowing is sweeter than the last. When I am dead and she has taken my place, all will be peace and quietness. When the turnips are pulled up, there will be more room in the field."

"Oh, Great Sister, you mustn't talk like that," Yulou said. "I will answer for her. I admit she often behaves badly, and she is always trying to score over people, but she isn't so bad as she sounds. You mustn't fall out with her completely."

"Isn't she as clever as you are? I tell you she is cunning personified. If she were not, she wouldn't always be sneaking up to listen to other people's conversation. And why should she say such horrid things?"

"Mother, you are the mistress here. You are the source from which we draw our water, and you must not be ungenerous. A gentleman can afford to be indulgent to ten commoner folk. If you raise your hand, she may pass, but if you are as obstinate as she is, she can never get by."

"No, our husband is behind her," Yueniang said, "I, the first wife, must stand aside."

"That is not true," Yulou persisted. "Now that you are not very well, he does not even venture to go near her."

"Why?" Yueniang said. "She talked about binding him with a pig's-hair cord. He is a wild horse. When he loves a woman he must have her, and no power on earth can stop him. If we try to do anything about it, we are called whores for our pains."

"Mother," Yulou said, "you have got this off your chest, and now the anger must be out of your system. I will go and fetch her. She shall kow-tow and say she's sorry. Aunt Wu is here, and I want you both to smile at each other in her presence. If you refuse to make up this quarrel, you will put our husband in a very awkward position. He won't know what to do. When he wants to go to her, he will be afraid of your displeasure, and, if he doesn't go, she won't have anything to do with him. Here we are, all busy getting things ready for the party, and she is in her room, doing nothing. We can't have her staying there any longer. Am I not right, Aunt Wu?"

"Sister," Aunt Wu said to Yueniang, "the Third Lady is right. It isn't simply a misunderstanding between you two ladies. It puts your husband in a hole, and makes it very embarrassing for him whichever of you he goes to see."

Yueniang did not speak until Yulou was on the point of going for Pan Jinlian. Then she said: "Don't go. It is of no consequence whether she comes or not."

"She will not dare refuse to come," Yulou said. "If she does, I'll drag her here with a pig's-hair cord."

She went straight to Jinlian's room. Jinlian had not dressed her hair. There was no powder on her face, and she was sitting on the bed, alone.

"Fifth Sister," Yulou said, "why are you making such a fool of yourself? Get your hair done. There is to be a party in the outer court, and we are all very busy, yet you stay here, nursing your temper, instead of coming to help us. I have spoken to the Great Lady, and now you must come with me and see her. Keep your temper and try to look pleasant. Don't forget: Pleasant words and pretty phrases make the coldest day warm; but unkind hurtful words make it cold even in the sixth month. You have quarreled, but if you insist on being obstinate, where is it all going to end? People enjoy flattery, just as Buddha enjoys incense. Come and say you're sorry, and let us have an end to the business. It will be very awkward for our husband if you don't. He will not come to see you if he is afraid she will be angry."

"I can't make any show against her," Jinlian said. "She says she is the only duly married wife here. You and I are dewdrops. We are nobodies, not worthy to lick her boots."

"I told her she was killing several birds with one stone," Yulou said. "His Lordship is my second husband, I admit, but it wasn't I who made the advances. When we were married, I had a proper witness and a go-between. I did not come into the family by the back door. But don't cut off one branch and damage the whole tree. The Great Lady is angry with you, but some of us are not. And don't carry things to extremes. We have to keep our eyes open and see what we're about. We must make sure of our ground. It was a mistake to quarrel before the nuns and Miss Yu. Each of us has his reputation to think about, as every tree has its own bark. The Great Lady is not very well, and, if you don't go and see her, I can't tell what the consequences may be. We have to be together, like the lips on one's mouth. Dress your hair. We will go and see her."

Jinlian sat and thought for a long time. Then she swallowed her anger, went to her dressing table to brush her hair, and put on her net. She dressed and went to the upper room with Yulou. The Third Lady pulled aside the lattice.

"I have brought her," she said. "She did not dare refuse to come. Come, my child, and kowtow to your mother." Then she said to Yueniang: "My daughter is young. She hardly knows the difference between right and wrong. Otherwise she would not have offended you. Won't you forgive her this time? If she is ever rude to you again, you may punish her as much as you please. I will not raise a finger to stop you."

Jinlian kowtowed four times to Yueniang. Then she jumped up and slapped Yulou. "You little strumpet!" she cried, "do you think I would have you for a mother?"

The ladies laughed. Even Yueniang could not help smiling.

"You slave!" Yulou said, "your mistress gives you back her favor, then you jump up and beat your mother."

"It is splendid to see you sisters all merry together," Aunt Wu said. "The Great Lady sometimes says more than she means, but you must make allowances for her, and give way a little. Then everything will be well. The proverb says: The peony is beautiful, but it must have leaves for its beauty to appear."

"If she had not said anything, I should not have quarreled with her," Yueniang said.

"Mother," Jinlian said, "you are the Heaven and I the Earth. Forgive me. I am just a stupid creature."

Yulou patted her on the back. "Now you speak like my daughter. But we have no time to talk. We have been working a long time, and it is your turn to help us."

Jinlian climbed on to the bed beside Yulou and helped her to arrange the fruit in the boxes.

When Qintong came back with the medicine, Ximen looked at the note that came with it, and told the boy to take it to Yueniang.

"So there is some for you, too?" Yueniang said to Yulou.

"Yes," Yulou said, "I have my old trouble again, and I asked Father to get me some pills from Doctor Ren."

"It is because you didn't eat anything the other day," Yueniang said. "You must have caught a chill."

Song was the first to arrive. Ximen Qing took him to the arbor, and they sat down.

"Thank you for sending the tripod," Song said, "I must pay you for it."

"How can I accept money for it?" Ximen said. "I was afraid you would refuse it, even as a gift."

"You are really too kind," Song said. He bowed and thanked Ximen Qing.

When they had had tea, they talked about the official affairs of the district and the condition of the people. Song asked about the local dignitaries. "Prefect Hu is very well liked," Ximen Qing said, "and District Magistrate Li is most conscientious in his work. I have not had much to do with the others."

"You know Major Zhou," Censor Song said. "What do you think of him?"

"He is an experienced soldier," Ximen Qing said, "but I should hardly say that he is so efficient as Jing of Jizhou. Jing passed the military examination when he was still quite young, and he is as capable as he is brave. Perhaps your Excellency will keep an eye on him."

"Are you speaking of Jing Zhong? Do you know him?"

"He is a friend of mine," Ximen said. "Yesterday he brought a card and asked me to speak to your Excellency on his behalf."

"I have heard that he is a good officer," the Censor said. "Is there anyone else?"

"There is my wife's brother, Wu Kai. He is a Captain here and in charge of the alterations to the granary. He is due for promotion, and, if your Excellency helps him, I shall be involved in his honor."

"As he is your kinsman," Song said, "I will not only recommend him for promotion, but see that he gets an appointment worth having."

Ximen Qing bowed and thanked him. He gave the Censor the two men's records of service. Song handed them to one of his officers and said they were to be brought before him when he prepared his report. Ximen Qing quietly told a servant to give that officer three taels of silver.

Then they heard music, and a servant came to tell them that the Provincial Officers had arrived. Ximen Qing went to receive them while Song went to the garden gate to look on. When the officers had exchanged greetings, they looked around the great hall. There was a large table in the middle magnificently set out, and a smaller table only a little less splendid. They were very pleased. They thanked Ximen Qing and said that they must send him more money.

"We certainly have not sent him sufficient for all this," Censor Song said, "but, for my sake, Siquan, do not ask them for any more."

"I should not dream of accepting any more," Ximen Qing said.

They sat down in places according to their rank and tea was brought. A man was sent to invite Governor Hou. After some delay the messenger came riding on horseback and told them that the Governor was on his way. The musicians played together and all the officers went out to the gate to wait for him. Censor Song stood alone at the second door.

Cavalry with blue pennons trotted by. Then Governor Hou came wearing a scarlet robe with a peacock embroidered upon it, sable ear covers, and a girdle with a buckle of pure gold. He was in a sedan chair borne by four men. When he had got down from his carriage, the officers escorted him to the great hall. Censor Song was wearing a scarlet robe embroidered with gold clouds. The buckle on his girdle was of rhinoceros horn. Each invited the other to precede him, and at last they entered the hall together. When the two high officers had greeted one another, the others came to make their reverences. Ximen Qing was the last. The Governor remembered him from the day of the reception to Huang, and he told one of his officers to give Ximen a card, on which was written: "Your friend, Hou Meng." Ximen took the card with both hands and gave it to a servant.

They all took off their ceremonial robes, and the Governor sat down in the place of honor. The other officers ranged themselves on either hand. Censor Song took the place of the host. After tea had been served the musicians played and Song offered his guest wine, flowers and silk. He ordered food to be sent to the Governor's office. Then the banquet was served. The dishes were all garnished with flowers.

The dancers performed exceedingly well. Then the Haiyan actors came and kowtowed and presented their list. The Governor told them to play *The Duke of Jin Returned the Girdle*. The banquet proceeded. When two acts had been performed, Governor Hou ordered five taels of silver to be distributed among the cooks, waiters, musicians, and servants. Then he put on his ceremonial robes again and took leave of the company. All the officers went with him to the gate. When he had gone, Song and the rest thanked Ximen Qing again and went away.

Ximen Qing returned to the great hall and dismissed the musicians. It was still early and he said: "Don't take any of the things away." He sent boys for Uncle Wu, Ying Bojue, Fu, Gan, Ben the Fourth, and his son-in-law, Chen Jingji. He told the actors to have something to eat, and bade them, when his guests arrived, play *Han Xizai Entertained Scholar Tao by Night*. Then he sent for Chunmei to decorate the hall, that he might enjoy the beauty of the flowers while he was drinking.

The three clerks came first, then Scholar Wen, the two Wu brothers, and Ying Bojue made a reverence to Ximen and said: "I am sorry I was only able to offer your ladies such poor entertainment the other day. Thank you for the splendid presents you sent."

Ximen Qing laughed. "You dog!" he said. "What did you mean by peeping at my ladies through the window?"

"You don't believe that!" Bojue said. "I know who told you." He pointed to Wang Jing. "It was that dog. You wait and, one of these days, I'll bite you."

They sat down and had tea. Uncle Wu wished to go and see his sister in the inner court, and Ximen Qing took him there. On the way he told him what he had said to Censor Song. "His Excellency took your record of service," he said, "and I gave three taels of silver to the officer in whose charge he left it. He has your papers and Jing's. The Censor promised that there shall be something for you when he sends his report."

Uncle Wu was delighted. He bowed to Ximen and said: "This is very kind of you."

"I only had to say: 'This is my wife's brother,' and he said at once: 'Since he is a kinsman of yours, I must certainly do something for him.'"

They came to the upper room, and Wu Yueniang made a reverence to her brother.

"It is time you went home," Uncle Wu said to his wife. "There is nobody to see after the house, and you have been here too long already."

"She won't let me go away," Aunt Wu said. "She says I must stay until the third."

"Then you must be sure to come home on the fourth," Uncle Wu said.

He went back to the outer court and drank with the others. The actors played and then performed as Ximen had told them. When the excitement of the play was at its height, Daian came in. "Qiao Tong has come from Master Qiao and would like to speak to you," he said. Ximen Qing left his friends and went to see the boy.

"My father says he did not give you the money yesterday," Qiao Tong said, "so he has sent me with it now. There are thirty taels here and five more for the less important officers."

"I am going to see Prefect Hu about it tomorrow morning," Ximen said. "I think he will do what we wish, and there will be no need to give any money to anyone else. Take these five taels back." He told Daian to give food and wine to Qiao Tong.

Two acts of the play had now been performed, and it was about the first night watch. The guests took their leave, and Ximen Qing ordered everything to be cleared away. Then he went to Yueniang. She was sitting with her sister-in-law, but Aunt Wu withdrew at once.

"I have managed that business of your brother's with Censor Song," Ximen said to his wife. "His Excellency said that not only would he see that he got promotion, but that he would appoint him to some post worth having. So now he is sure of a military appointment. I have told your brother about it, and he is delighted."

"But he has no money," Yueniang said. "Where is he going to find two or three hundred taels?"

"There is no need for him to spend any money," Ximen Qing said. "I told the Censor that he was your brother, and his Excellency promised me that he would attend to the matter himself."

"Do what you think best," Yueniang said, "it is not my business."

"Yuxiao," Ximen said, "get that medicine ready for your mother. I want to see her take it."

"Go away and don't make a fuss," Yueniang said, "I will take the medicine when I go to bed."

Ximen Qing was on the point of going when Yueniang called him back.

"Where are you going?" she said. "If you are going to her, you had better think twice about it. She has just apologized to me, and if you go to her, it will look as if you go to make things right with her."

"I am not going to her," Ximen said.

"Where are you going, then?" Yueniang said. "I don't want you to go to that woman Ruyi'er either. Yesterday, in my sister-in-law's presence, the Fifth Lady said some very horrid things to me. She said I allowed Ruyi'er to take liberties, to please you."

"Surely you don't take seriously the things that little strumpet says?"

"Do what I tell you," Yueniang said. "I won't have you going to the front court, and I don't want you here. You must spend the night with Li Jiao'er. You may do what you like after that." Ximen was obliged to go and sleep with Li Jiao'er.

The next day was the eleventh of the twelfth month. Ximen Qing went early to the office and, with Captain He, busied himself with official papers. He was there all morning. When he came back, he got ready the presents, a pig, wine, and thirty taels of silver, and told Daian to take them to Hu, the Prefect of Dongpingfu. Hu accepted the presents and immediately sent the necessary papers.

Meanwhile, Ximen Qing sent for Xu, the Master of the Yin Yang, and set out pigs, lamb, wine and fruits in the great hall, and burned paper offerings as a sacrifice. When the ceremony was over, Xu went away.

The document that Daian brought back with him bore several seals. It referred to Qiao Hong as an officer in the District administration. Ximen told Daian to take two boxes of the food that had been offered at the sacrifice, to Qiao and to ask him to come and see the document. He also told a servant to take a box of food to Uncle Wu, Scholar Wen, Ying Bojue, Xie Xida, and the clerks. Then he sent invitation cards to Major Zhou, General Jing, Captain Zhang, Eunuchs Liu and Xue, Captain He and Captain Fan, Uncle Wu, Kinsman Qiao, and Wang the Third asking them to a celebration on the third of the month. He engaged musicians and four singers.

This day, Meng Yulou gave up the housekeeping accounts. She handed them over to Ximen Qing and told him to give them to Pan Jinlian. Then she went to see Wu Yueniang.

"Do you feel better, Mother, now you have taken the medicine?" she said.

"Yes," Yueniang said, "people say that women always get better when they have a man doctor to attend them, and it seems to be true. I am certainly better. My headache has gone, and my stomach feels much easier."

"Ah!" Yulou said, "it looks to me as if all you wanted was a man to hold your hand."

Even Aunt Wu laughed at this.

Then Ximen Qing came with the accounts. "You must attend to the matter yourself," Yueniang told him. "I don't know whose turn it is, and I can't imagine whom to give the accounts to. Nobody wants to be bothered with them."

Ximen took thirty taels of silver and thirty strings of coppers and gave them to Jinlian.

When Qiao came, Ximen took him to the great hall and showed him the document that Prefect Hu had sent. It said: "Honorary Lieutenant Qiao Hong has made a contribution of thirty measures of fine rice to the quartermaster's department, in accordance with regulations." Qiao was very pleased and bowed his thanks to Ximen Qing. He told Qiao Tong to take the paper home with the greatest care. "Now I can wear ceremonial dress," he said to Ximen, "and, when you have a party here, I shall be able to come."

"You must come early on the third," Ximen said to him.

When they had had tea, Ximen Qing told Qintong to set a table in the side room. "Kinsman," he said to Qiao, "let us go to the west room. It is warmer there." They went together to the study.

Then Ying Bojue came with a few presents. "The brothers have sent them," he said. Ximen looked at them. Abbot Wu's name was the first on the list: then came Ying Bojue, Xie Xida, Zhu Shinian, Sun Guazui, Chang Zhijie, Bai Laiguang, Li the Third, Huang the Fourth and Du the Third.

"I still have some more people to invite," Ximen said. "There are the younger Uncle Wu, Uncle Shen, Doctor Ren, Hua, Scholar Wen and the three clerks, more than twenty altogether. I must ask them all on the fourth." He gave the presents to a servant and told Qintong to go to Uncle Wu and tell him that Master Qiao was there. Then he asked if Scholar Wen was at home.

"No," Laian said, "he has gone out to see a friend.

After a while, Uncle Wu arrived and, with Chen Jingji they sat down to drink. While they were drinking, Ximen said to Uncle Wu: "We have to congratulate Kinsman Qiao here. He has got his papers today. We must buy some presents and give a party for him."

"It is a very insignificant matter," Qiao said. "You must not trouble to do anything of the sort."

Then a man came from the Town Hall with two hundred and fifty copies of the new calendar. Ximen gave the man a return card and sent him away.

"We haven't seen the new calendar yet," Ying Bojue said.

Ximen gave fifty copies to Uncle Wu, Qiao, and Ying Bojue. Bojue noticed that the new year was described as the first year of the reign of Chonghe, and that it would have an intercalary month.

They went on playing games, guessing fingers, and drinking until it was late. Qiao went away first, but Uncle Wu and Ying Bojue did not go until the first night watch. Ximen Qing told a servant to get a horse ready early the next morning and ask Captain He to come that they might go together to take leave of Governor Hou. Then he told Laian and Chunhong that they must accompany Yueniang when she went to Mistress Xia. Four soldiers were to go with them.

He went to Jinlian's room. She had taken off her headdress; her hair was disarranged; there was no powder on her face, and she was lying, with all her clothes on, on the bed. There was no light in the room and everything was very still. Ximen called Chunmei, but there was no answer. Then he saw Jinlian on the bed and spoke to her. There was no answer. He sat down on the bed.

"Little oily mouth, why are you treating me like this? Why don't you answer me?"

He lifted her in his arms and asked what was the matter. Jinlian turned her face away. Fragrant tears rolled down her cheeks, one after another. If Ximen Qing had been made of iron or stone, he would have melted. He put his arms around her neck.

"Funny little oily mouth. Why did you quarrel with her?"

For a long time, Jinlian did not answer. Then she said: "Who says I quarreled with her? It was she who began by finding fault with me, insulting me before a host of people. She said I was one of the husband-hunting devils, and that was how I got you. She said she was a real wife, properly married to you. Who told you to come here again? Go to her. If you go to her, perhaps I shall not be accused of monopolizing you. She said you always came to me. You know quite well you haven't been near the place these last few nights. And she tells lies. She said I asked you for the fur coat and never said anything to her about it. I am not her slave. Why should I go and kowtow to her and ask her to give me a fur coat? Chunmei scolded that scamp of a blind woman, and she said I didn't train her properly. She talked a lot of nonsense. If you were a real man, you would settle this sort of thing with your fist, and there wouldn't be all these rows and troubles. I suppose we must keep ourselves in our proper places. The proverb says: Things that are bought cheap are sold cheap; and things that are easily come by are easily forgotten. I came here as a second wife and now I am not to be allowed to breathe. Yesterday, she flew into a temper. Who was in her room all the time? Who sent for Doctor Ren? Who offered to do everything she wanted? Poor me! I was left in this miserable hole and nobody cared what happened to me. Oh, I know you! Then people come and ask me to go and apologize to her!"

Tears rolled down her flower-like face. She lay on Ximen Qing's breast and sobbed. She wiped her nose and dried her tears continually. Ximen kept his arms about her and comforted her.

"It is all right, my child," he said, "I have been very busy. You must forgive one another. I'm not going to say who is to blame. I was coming to see you yesterday but she said I was coming to apologize to you and would not let me come. So I went to Li Jiao'er, but all the time I was there, I was thinking of you."

"I know you now," the woman said. "You pretend to love me but, really, you love her. She is going to have a baby, and I am only a straw and cannot compare with her in any sort of way."

Ximen Qing hugged her. "Don't talk such nonsense, little oily mouth," he said.

Qiuju brought tea. "Ha!" said Ximen "here's a nice clean little slave! Who told her to bring the tea? Where is Chunmei?"

"You do well to ask for Chunmei?" Jinlian said "I shouldn't be surprised if she were dying by now. She has had nothing to eat for three or four days. She is in bed in the other room. She only wants to die. She thinks that's the best thing she can do now that your first wife has insulted her before everybody. She has done nothing but cry ever since."

"Is that true?" Ximen Qing said.

"Go and see for yourself."

Ximen got up and went to the other room. Chunmei was lying on the bed, her face unpowdered and her hair falling down.

"Get up, little oily mouth," he said. He called her by name, but she did not answer and pretended to be asleep. He tried to lift her in his arms but she struggled and stiffened herself till her back was like the backbone of a carp. She nearly knocked Ximen Qing onto the floor. Fortunately, he had firm hold of her and the bed prevented him from falling.

"Let me go," Chunmei cried. "Why do you come here to see a slave? You will soil your hands."

"Because the Great Lady scolded you a little," Ximen Qing said, "that's no reason why you should be so angry and refuse to eat anything."

"It doesn't matter to you whether I eat or not, Chunmei said. "I am a slave, and if I die, I die. But slave though I may be, I have done nothing wrong. Why should I be insulted because I told that blind vagabond what I thought about her? And the Great Lady found fault with my mother too, and said that she didn't keep me in order. Is it right that I should be punished because I cursed that blind scamp? Wait and see whether I don't point my finger at Han Daoguo's wife and insult her, when she comes here. She is responsible for all this trouble. It was she who introduced that blind creature."

"Yes, she introduced Miss Shen, it is true," Ximen said, "but there was no harm in that. How was she going to know that you would quarrel?"

"I should not have insulted her if she had been reasonable," Chunmei said, "but she was so obstinate."

"Well," Ximen said, "now that I'm here, won't you give me a cup of tea? I can't drink the tea Qiuju brought. Her hands are too dirty."

"You will have to drink it. When the butcher is dead, you must eat your pork with the bristles on it. I can't get up. How can I make tea for you?"

"Who told you to stop eating?" Ximen Qing said. "Come into the other room and let us eat and drink. Qiuju shall go for dishes and wine and cakes and fruit and soup."

He did not wait for further argument but took Chunmei's hand and went with her to Jinlian. He told Qiuju to take a box and go to the kitchen. When she came back, he bade Chunmei put slices of chicken with meat and fish, together with pickled bamboo shoots and radishes, and make a large bowl of soup. The dishes were set on the table with rice and warm buns.

Ximen Qing sat down beside Jinlian, and Chunmei sat facing them. They encouraged one another to drink and did not make an end for a long time. Then they went to bed.

Ximen rose early next morning. Captain He came in good time, and, after drinking a cup of wine, they set out beyond the walls to pay their respects to Governor Hou. Yueniang sent presents to Mistress Xia, then dressed and went in a large sedan chair to see her. Laian and Chunhong went with her, and four soldiers cleared the way. Daian and Wang Jing were left at home. About midday, old woman Wang, the tea seller, came with He the Ninth, and asked if Ximen Qing was at home.

"What wind has blown you here?" Daian said to them. "We don't see you very often."

"Old He wishes to see your master about a matter concerning his younger brother," old woman Wang said. "We should not have come otherwise."

"His Lordship has gone to say good-bye to Governor Hou," Daian said, "and the Great Lady has gone out too. But wait a moment, and I will tell the Fifth Lady."

When he came back, he said: "The Fifth Lady would like to see you."

"I will go and see her," old woman Wang said, "but you must take me in. I am afraid of the dogs."

Daian took the old woman to the garden, pulled aside the lattice and showed her into Jinlian's room. Jinlian was wearing a fur cap and silken clothes and looked very pretty. She was sitting on the bed with her feet on a footstool. Old woman Wang knelt down before her. Jinlian returned her greeting, and old woman Wang sat down beside her on the bed.

"It is a very long time since I saw you last," Jinlian said.

"I have wished to see you for a long time," the old woman said, "but I didn't venture to come. Have you any children?"

"I wish I had," Jinlian said, "but I have only had two miscarriages. Is your son married?"

"No," the old woman said, "I have not arranged a marriage for him yet. He has just come back from Huai. He made some money, and now he has bought a donkey and started a flour mill. I understand his Lordship is not at home."

"No, he has had to go outside the city today. The Great Lady is out, too. What did you want with him?"

"He the Ninth asked me to come and see his Lordship," old woman Wang said. "His brother, He the Tenth, has got mixed up in a case of theft. He has been taken to the courts and charged with being a receiver of stolen property. But he had nothing whatever to do with the matter, and we have come to ask his Lordship to get him off. He must not believe what the thieves say. When He the Tenth gets out of prison, he will come, with presents, to kowtow to his Lordship. Here is the paper."

Jinlian looked at it. "Give it to me," she said, "I will give it to my husband, with my own hands."

"He the Ninth is waiting outside," old woman Wang said. "I will tell him to come again tomorrow."

Qiuju brought the old woman a cup of tea. "Are you happy here, lady?" old woman Wang said. "Happy!" Jinlian said. "If there were not so many squabbles, I should be happy enough. But I have trouble of some sort every day."

"You have only to open your mouth when the food is brought to you, and to dip your hand when water is poured out for you. You have ornaments of gold and silver, and maids to wait upon you. What possible trouble can you have?"

"The proverb says, that where there is more than one wife, the first wife is the only one who counts for anything. The others do not matter. When you have more than one spoon in a bowl, they are bound to clash. What can one expect but difficulties of one sort or another?"

"My good Lady," old woman Wang said, "you are cleverer than anyone I know. Your husband is prosperous, and you must have a splendid life. Well, I will tell He the Ninth to come again tomorrow." She got up to go away.

"Don't be in such a hurry," Jinlian said. "Stay a while."

"I mustn't keep old He waiting too long," the old woman said, "I will come and see you some other day."

She went out. When she came to the gate, she spoke to Daian. The boy promised to speak to his master as soon as he came in. "Brother An," old He said, "I will come back tomorrow morning." Then he went off with old woman Wang.

In the evening, Ximen Qing returned. He went to Jinlian's room, and she gave him the paper. He handed it to a servant and said that it was to be given to him next day at the office.

When he had told Chen Jingji to send out the invitations, he gave Qintong a tael of silver and a box of cakes to take to Han Daoguo's house for Miss Shen. He was careful not to let Chunmei know what he was doing.

Wang Liu'er smiled and accepted the things. "Miss Shen will not be angry any more now," she said. "Tell your father and mother she is sorry if she annoyed Chunmei."

When Yueniang came back, she greeted Aunt Wu and the other ladies. Then Ximen Qing came and she made a reverence to him.

"Mistress Xia was very cordial indeed," she said. "There were a number of neighbors and relatives there, all ladies. Magistrate Xia has written to them and enclosed a letter for you that they are going to send tomorrow. They propose to start for the capital on the sixth or seventh of this month. Mistress Xia is very anxious that Ben the Fourth should go to the Capital with them. She will send him back immediately. By the way, Ben the Fourth's daughter is quite grown up now. I didn't know her. I thought she looked at me peculiarly when she gave me tea. Mistress Xia calls her Happy Cloud. She bade her kowtow to me, and the girl set down her tray and kowtowed four times. I gave her two gold flowers. Mistress Xia was pleased that I treated her maid so kindly. She is very fond of the girl and has regarded her rather as a daughter than as a maid."

"She is a lucky girl to have found such a comfortable place," Ximen Qing said. "In some places, she would have been more likely to be scolded."

Yueniang looked at him. "You mean I scold that beloved maid of yours, I suppose?"

Ximen Qing laughed. "If she takes Ben the Fourth, who is going to look after the shop?"

"Oh, close it for a few days," Yueniang said.

"No, I won't close it. This is the New Year season and there is a good deal of trade about. But we'll talk about that tomorrow."

Yueniang went to change her dress and then sat down with Aunt Wu. Her maids and women came to kowtow to her. That night, Ximen Qing slept with Sun Xue'e.

The next morning he went to the office. He the Ninth came again to the house and gave Daian a tael of silver. "I told my master about the matter," Daian said, "and I think there is no doubt your brother will be set free. You had better go to the office and see." He the Ninth went away at once.

When Ximen Qing reached his office, he had the thieves brought before him, put their legs in the press, and ordered each of them to be given twenty severe blows. He let He the Tenth go free and put a monk of the Temple of the Mighty Blossom in his place, on the score that the thieves had passed a night in that temple. It was as though Master Zhang drank the wine and Master Li got tipsy, and like people complaining of the willow, when the branches fall from the mulberry tree.

That day, when Ximen Qing was home again, he sent for the four singing girls, Wu Yin'er, Zheng Aiyue, Hong Si'er and Qi Xiang'er. They came about midday, and went at once to kowtow to Yueniang and Aunt Wu. Yueniang gave them tea, and they played and sang for the ladies. Then Ximen Qing came, and the four girls put down their instruments and kowtowed to him.

"You are late today," Yueniang said.

"Yes, I had several cases to deal with. There was the one old woman Wang came about yesterday. I let He the Ninth's brother go, though the thieves insisted that what they had said was true. Anyhow, I put them on the rack and ordered them twenty blows. I put a monk in He the Tenth's place, and, tomorrow, I shall send the documents in the case to Dongpingfu. Then there was another bad case, one of a woman carrying on with her daughter's husband. The man is only just over twenty and his name is Zong Deyuan. He was living with his wife's people. The mother died, and the father married again, a woman called Zhou. A year after this marriage, the father died too. Zhou was young and could not control herself and she began to carry on with the young man. They punished one of their maids, and the maid told everybody what was going on. The neighbors accused them and, today, I have extracted a confession from them and sent them to Dongpingfu. It is a very near relationship, and I'm afraid they will both be hanged."

"In my opinion," Jinlian said, "the maid who spread the scandal ought to be beaten to death. It was her duty as a maid to be loyal to her employers. Instead, her chattering will have caused the death of two human beings."

"I don't agree," Yueniang said, "the lower classes will never respect their betters when these do not behave properly. If a bitch will not have it, the dog cannot get his way. It was the woman's fault. If she had behaved with decorum, no one would have dared approach her."

"You are right, Mother," one of the singing girls said, smiling. "Even we singing girls do not receive our patrons' friends. And, in the family, one should be still more careful."

Ximen Qing had something to eat. Then music was heard in the front court. General Jing had arrived. Ximen hastily dressed and went out to welcome him. When they had drunk their tea, he said to Jing: "Censor Song accepted your record of service and promised to do what we asked. You will undoubtedly be promoted very soon."

"I am very grateful to you," Jing said. "I shall never forget how kind you have been in this matter."

"I mentioned Zhou to his Excellency," Ximen said. "It may be that something will come to him too."

The two eunuchs, Liu and Xue, came then. As they were escorted to the great hall, the musicians played. They both wore dark dragon gowns and gemmed girdles. When they had taken their places, Major Zhou arrived. They chatted together. "Yesterday," Jing said to Major Zhou, "Siquan was good enough to speak highly of you to Censor Song, who had a party here. Now Song will certainly remember you, and you cannot fail to receive promotion."

Major Zhou bowed and thanked Ximen Qing. Then Captain Zhang, Captain He, Captain Fan, Wang the Third, Uncle Wu and Kinsman Qiao came, one after the other. Qiao was wearing ceremonial dress, and four servants attended him. When he had greeted the others, he made a special reverence to Ximen Qing. People asked what appointment he held, and Ximen said: "My kinsman has just had honorary rank conferred upon him."

"Since he is your kinsman, we must congratulate him," Major Zhou said.

"I appreciate your kindness immensely," Qiao said, "but please do not trouble."

They all sat down according to their rank. After they had taken tea, wine was brought. The host offered it to his guests, and they all sat down again. Wang the Third refused to sit with them.

"You must sit down," Ximen said to him. "This is not a formal party and I wish you to help me to entertain my guests."

Then Wang the Third was compelled to sit down with them. When the soup course was finished, the musicians played different tunes and the four singing girls sang for them. Eunuch Liu, who sat in the place of honor, distributed money to the musicians and singers. It was a merry party and the guests did not leave until the first night watch. Then Ximen Qing paid the musicians and dismissed them, and the four singing girls went and played for a while to entertain the ladies. Yueniang asked Wu Yin'er to stay but let the others go. On their way, they went to the hall to say good-bye to Ximen Qing.

"I want you to come again tomorrow," Ximen said to Zheng Aiyue. "Bring Li Guijie with you."

"I know why you didn't send for Guijie today," the girl said. "It was because Wang the Third was here. It is rather late in the day for you to be taking precautions. What guests are you expecting tomorrow?"

"Nobody but relatives and friends," Ximen Qing said.

"I suppose Beggar Ying will be here," Zheng Aiyue said. "I won't come if that hateful fellow is here."

"No, he won't be here tomorrow."

"If I thought he was going to be here, I wouldn't come," Zheng Aiyue said. She kowtowed to Ximen and went away. He ordered the things to be cleared away, then went to Li Ping'er's room and slept with Ruyi'er.

The next day he went early to the office and sent the prisoners to Dongpingfu. Then he went home to the party. All the guests arrived. There were twelve tables. Three singing girls came, Li Guijie, Wu Yin'er, and Zheng Aiyue, and three boys, Li Ming, Wu Hui, and Zheng Feng.

While they were drinking, Ping'an came and said: "Uncle Yun has come to see you. He has inherited a title and has brought presents with him."

Ximen Qing told the boy to bring him in.

Yun Lishou was wearing a black silk ceremonial gown and a girdle with a gold buckle. Servants with presents followed him, and he handed the list to Ximen Qing. Upon it was written: 'Yun Lishou, who has recently inherited the rank of officer of the royal guard and subprefect of Qinghe in Shandong, presents his humble compliments and offers ten sable skins, a sea fish, a parcel of dried shrimps, four preserved geese, ten preserved ducks, and two blinds of oiled paper.'

Ximen Qing told his servants to take the gifts and thanked Yun Lishou.

"I only came back yesterday," Yun said, "and I have come at once to see you." He made a reverence to Ximen Qing. Then he said: "You have been very kind to me, and these things are intended as a slight token of my gratitude." He greeted the others.

Now that Yun Lishou had succeeded to a title, Ximen Qing treated him with more respect. He asked him to sit at the same table with the younger Uncle Wu. A cup and chopsticks were at once brought in for him, and Ximen Qing ordered food to be given to his servants. Then Ximen asked how he had come into the title.

"I am indebted to the kindness of his Excellency Yu of the Ministry of War," Yun Lishou said. "My elder brother, who was in his department, died, and his Excellency appointed me to carry on the ancestral title and take up his appointment. Now I am in the office of the writer to the signet."

Ximen Qing was pleased. "I congratulate you," he said, "and I must give a special party in your honor."

All the guests invited him to drink with them and the singers were bidden to offer him wine. Before long, Yun Lishou was tipsy. Ying Bojue might have been on the end of a string. He stood up and sat down again and joked and swore at the singing girls all the time. It was a very merry party; they all drank a great deal of wine, and nobody went away before the second night watch. Ximen Qing sent away the three singers and went to sleep in Yueniang's room.

The next day he was up late. He had his breakfast and was going to call on Yun Lishou when Daian came and told him that Ben the Fourth wished to speak to him. Ximen knew that he wished to speak about acting as an escort to Mistress Xia. He went to the great hall. Ben the Fourth gave Xia's letter to Ximen Qing. "His Lordship would like me to escort his family to the Eastern Capital, if you have no objection," he said.

Ximen Qing read the letter. It thanked him for looking after Xia's family and asked that Ben the Fourth might be allowed to take them to the Capital.

"Since he asks for you, I suppose you must go," Ximen Qing said. "When do they propose to start?"

"They sent for me this morning," Ben the Fourth said, "and told me they proposed to leave on the sixth. I hope to get back in about a fortnight." He gave the keys of the shop to Ximen Qing.

"Very well," Ximen said, "I will ask the younger Uncle Wu to look after the shop."

Ben the Fourth went home to see about his luggage, and Ximen Qing, in his ceremonial robes, went to call on Yun Lishou.

That day, Aunt Wu was going home, and a sedan chair came to fetch her. Yueniang filled two boxes with delicacies, and went with her sister-in-law to the gate. Huatong was standing there, sobbing bitterly. Ping'an was pulling him and shaking him, but the boy only cried the louder. When Aunt Wu had gone, Yueniang came back and said to Ping'an: "What is the matter? Why are you pulling him about like that? You have made him cry."

"Scholar Wen wants him, and he won't go," Ping'an said. "He stays here and answers me back all the time."

"Leave him alone," Yueniang said to Ping'an. She turned to the boy and asked him: "Why do you stand here crying? If Master Wen sends for you, you must go."

"It is not your business," Huatong cried to Ping'an, "and I won't go. Why do you keep bullying me?"

"Why won't you go?" Yueniang said.

The boy would not answer.

Then Jinlian came along. "You sly young rascal!" she said. "Why don't you answer the Great Lady?"

Ping'an boxed his ears, and the boy cried louder than ever.

"Don't hit him," Yueniang said, "let him explain himself quietly. Tell me, why won't you go?"

Then Daian came back with Ximen's horse.

"Is your father back?" Yueniang asked him.

"No," Daian said, "he is taking wine with Uncle Yun. I have brought back his ceremonial clothes and am going to take him his soft hat."

Then he saw the boy crying. "Hullo, my boy," he said, "what are you crying for? Is something hurting you?"

"Master Wen has called for him and he won't go," Ping'an said. "He stays there and is rude to me."

"Brother," Daian said, "when Master Wen sends for you, you must be on your guard. Scholar Wen is renowned for his fondness for hole-and-corner work. He can't live without it. But you have put up with it before, why can't you do so today?"

"You rascal!" Yueniang said to Daian. "What do you mean?"

"Ask him, Mother," Daian said.

Jinlian, who was one of those people who always want to know everything, drew the boy aside and said to him: "Boy, tell me the truth. What does he want you for? If you won't tell me, I shall ask the Great Lady to have you beaten."

"He keeps on coming up to me," said the boy, "and wants me to submit to him. He shoves his penis up my ass so roughly that today it's swollen and hurts. When I ask him to take it out, he refuses and presses it up and down."

"You thievish slave," Yueniang said, when she heard this. "Get away from me. I'm surprised at you, Sister, wanting to know things like that. I am ashamed of you. I was so ignorant I didn't realize what you were talking about and listened to every word you said. A splendid fellow that Scholar Wen must be. We let him have this boy, and this is the sort of thing he does."

"Oh, Mother," Jinlian said, "they all go in for this sort of thing. Even the beggars in their hovels."

"But this Southerner is a married man," Yulou said. "Why should he do it?"

"He has been here a long time, but we have never seen his wife," Jinlian said.

"No, ladies," Ping'an said, "and you are not likely to see her. He locks the door every time he goes out. I have only seen her once. She was going in a sedan chair to see her mother. She came back before the evening. She never goes out, but I have sometimes seen her in the evening emptying the chamber pots outside the door."

"She can't be a very respectable woman," Jinlian said, 'if she would marry a man like that. Why, she can never see the light of day. Her room must be as bad as a prison.'

The ladies went back to the inner court.

It was sunset when Ximen Qing came back.

"Have you been all this time at Yun's place?" Yueniang asked him.

"Yes," Ximen said. "He opened a jar of wine and insisted on my having something to eat. Now that Jing has been promoted, Yun will have charge of the seals. I and Qiao will get some presents ready and I will arrange for the officers to present him with a congratulatory scroll. I must ask Wen Guixuan to write it."

"Wen Guixuan or Wu Guixuan," Yueniang said. "The fellow is an atrocious scoundrel. If people get to hear of his goings on, we shall all be disgraced."

"What are you talking about?" Ximen Qing said, alarmed.

"Don't ask me. Ask the boy."

"What boy?" Ximen said.

Jinlian explained. "What boy!" she said. "Why! Huatong, of course. When we took Aunt Wu to the gate, we found him there, crying, and he told us what that Southerner had done to him."

Ximen Qing found it hard to believe. "Let us have the boy here," he said, "and I'll talk to him." He sent Daian for Huatong and threatened to put on the thumbscrews.

"What have you been doing with that man?" he said. "Tell me the truth."

"He gave me wine to drink and then misused me," Huatong said. "Today, he tried to do it again, but I got away and would not go back. He told Ping'an to make me go back, and Ping'an hit me. The ladies saw him. And he kept on asking me things about your ladies, but I wouldn't tell him. Yesterday, when you had a party, he told me to steal some of the silver for him. A short time ago, he went to see Scholar Ni and showed him your letters, and Scholar Ni told Magistrate Xia what was in them."

Ah!" Ximen Qing said. "It is easy enough to paint the tiger's skin, but who can paint the bones inside that skin? We may know people's faces but never their minds. I treated him as a man. How could I tell that he was a dog in human form? I won't have him here a moment longer."

"Get up!" he shouted to Huatong. "And never go near him again."

The boy kowtowed and went out.

"No wonder, the other day, when Kinsman Zhai scolded me for not being discreet, I couldn't imagine who had given away my secrets," Ximen said to Yueniang. "It was this dog bone. Why should I keep him here?"

"What is the use of asking me that?" Yueniang said. "You have no son for him to teach; why should you keep that fellow here to write your present lists for you? He lives at your expense and plays dirty tricks of this sort."

"Say no more about it," Ximen said. "Tomorrow he shall go."

He sent for Ping'an. "Go and tell Scholar Wen," he said, "that I need his house as a storehouse and he must go elsewhere. If he comes to see me, tell him I am out."

Ximen Qing told his wife that Ben the Fourth had called to see him and said that he was going to the Capital with the Xia family on the sixth. "I think I will ask your younger brother to look after the shop," he said. "What do you think?"

"I shall not express any opinion," Yueniang said. "If you want him, send for him. He is my brother, and somebody is sure to say I favor him."

Ximen Qing told Qitong to go and ask Uncle Wu the Second to come and see him. When the young man came, Ximen went with him to the great hall and took wine with him. Then he gave him the keys and asked him to go to the shop in Lion Street next morning.

Scholar Wen was very much upset, especially when he found that Huatong did not go near him. Then the next day, Ping'an came and said: "His Lordship says he is going to use this house as a storehouse, and I am to tell you to find somewhere else to live."

The scholar was greatly disturbed and changed color. He realized that Huatong must be the cause. He put on his scholar's gown and hat and went to see Ximen Qing.

"My master is at the office," Qintong told him.

When Ximen Qing came back from the office, Scholar Wen again dressed up and went across, with a long letter. He gave the letter to Qintong, but Qintong would not take it. "My master has just come back from the office," he said. "He is very tired and I dare not disturb him."

Scholar Wen understood what this meant. He went to Scholar Ni to ask his advice, and then went back to the house he had lived in before.

CHAPTER 77

Ximen Qing Visits Zheng Aiyue in the Snow

At the end of the year
The plums and the snow match themselves in beauty.
Under the moon they are white with the same whiteness.
When the wind blows, the tender petals half emerge
They have not the wildness of the willow catkins.

The shadow of a pair of sparrows
Seems like a snow-white parrot.
The snowflakes in the moonbeams
Glitter like a mass of crystal.
Above the flowers they know how to find sweetness
Like a pair of mandarin ducks.

Scholar Wen was not permitted to see Ximen Qing, so, greatly ashamed, he had to go back to live in his old house. Ximen turned the rooms he had left into additional reception rooms for his own use.

One day, Scholar Shang came to see him. He was going to the Eastern Capital to enter for an examination, and he wanted Ximen to lend him a leather trunk and a warm cloak. Ximen asked him to sit down, and they had tea.

"I am anxious to have two appropriate compositions written to congratulate my kinsman Qiao and my friend Yun Lishou," Ximen said. "Qiao has recently been granted honorary rank, and Yun has come into the family title. Perhaps one of your friends would not mind doing this for me. I should be glad to make it worth his while."

Shang smiled. "You need not speak of reward," he said. "My schoolfellow, Nie Lianghu, who is a graduate of the military academy and tutor to my son, is very learned. I will speak to him about it, and all you need do is to send the materials to him."

Ximen Qing thanked him and he went away. Then Ximen sent Qintong with the scrolls, enclosing two handkerchiefs and five *qian* of silver, and, at the same time, sent the leather trunk and the coat to Scholar

Shang. Two days later the scrolls were returned. Ximen Qing hung them on the wall and was very well satisfied with the composition and the writing of the golden characters.

Ying Bojue came to see him. "When are we going to have the feast in congratulation of Master Qiao and Brother Yun?" he said. "Are the scrolls ready? Why haven't I seen Scholar Wen lately?"

"Don't mention Scholar Wen to me," Ximen said. "He is a dirty dog." He told Bojue the whole story.

"Brother," Bojue said, "I told you the fellow could not be trusted. He is very sly. It is a good thing you have such sharp eyes, or he would certainly have ruined your boys. But who will write the scrolls for you?"

"Scholar Shang was here yesterday," Ximen told him. "He told me his friend Nie Lianghu was very well educated, and I asked him to write the scrolls. He has now finished them. Come and have a look." He took Bojue to the hall. Bojue thought they were admirable.

"Everything seems to be ready," he said. "Don't wait too long before you send them. We must let our friends have plenty of time to make preparations."

"Tomorrow is a good day," Ximen said. "I will send them then."

As they were talking, a servant came in to say that Xia's son had called to say good-bye. "He said," the man told them, "that they proposed to leave for the Capital on the sixth. I told him you were not at home, and he said, would you be good enough to ask Captain He to send someone to take charge of the house."

Ximen Qing looked at the card and said: "Now I must get ready two sets of presents, one for Xia and one for Shang." He told Qintong to go out and buy them and to tell Chen Jingji to send them with his compliments. Then he went to the study to have something to eat with Ying Bojue.

Ping'an came hurrying in with three cards. "Counselor Wang, General Li and Vice president An have come to see you," he said. Ximen Qing looked at the cards. They bore the names of Wang Boyan, Li Qiyuan, and An Shen. He hastily put on his ceremonial dress.

"Brother," Bojue said. "You seem to be very busy. I had better go."

"I will see you tomorrow," Ximen said, and went to receive his three visitors. He took them to the great hall. There they thanked Ximen Qing for the trouble he had taken, drank tea, and sat down to talk.

"Li, Wang, and I have come to trouble you again," An said. "Magistrate Zhao has been appointed to the Lord Chamberlain's office, and we should like to use your house for a reception. We have invited him on the ninth. Five tables will be needed and we will provide the actors. Will you be so kind as to allow us to do this?"

"The house shall be put in order for you, and I await your instructions," Ximen said.

An told his attendants to present three taels of silver, and Ximen Qing accepted them. Then the three officers went away. When they came to the gate, Li said to Ximen Qing: "The other day I had a letter from Qian Longye. He told me that a certain Sun Wenxiang was one of your underlings. I set him free. Did he tell you?"

"Yes, indeed," Ximen Qing said. "And I am very much obliged to you. One of these days I will come especially to thank you."

"You must not trouble," Li said, "we are very good friends." They got into their sedan chairs and were carried away.

Pan Jinlian had now taken charge of the housekeeping accounts. She began by buying a new pair of scales. Every day, when the boys brought vegetables, or things for the house, she insisted on having them shown to her, and would not hand over the money until she was satisfied. She did not count the money herself but made Chunmei do so. The maid measured the silver. Curses rained upon the boys' heads, and she was always saying she would tell Ximen Qing to beat them. The boys grumbled a great deal. "It was very much better in the Third Lady's time," they said.

The next day, when Ximen Qing had finished his work at the office, he said to Captain He: "Xia's family are now ready to start, and you should send somebody to take over their house."

"I have already sent one of my servants," Captain He said. "They sent word to me yesterday."

"Shall we go and look at it?" Ximen Qing said.

They left the office together and went on horseback to Xia's house. It was empty except for a few servants, and Ximen Qing showed Captain He how it was arranged. They went to the garden. It seemed very bare.

"When you move in," Ximen Qing said, "you will have to plant some flowers and trees here, and make a place where you can really enjoy yourself. These arbors need to be repaired."

"Yes," He said, "I shall set to work as soon as the Spring comes. I shall build a pavilion in the hope that you will often come and spend your leisure with me."

When they had finished their inspection of the house, He bade his servants clean the place and keep all the doors and windows shut. He made up his mind to write to his uncle and ask him to send his family before the New Year. He himself proposed to take up his quarters there the next day. The two officers took leave of one another. Ximen Qing went home and Captain He went back to the office.

When Ximen reached home, He the Ninth had come to thank him
with a roll of silk, four dishes of food and a jar of wine. Eunuch Liu's servant had brought a box of candles, twenty tablecloths, eighty packets of
official incense, a box of precious incense, a jar of homemade wine, and
a pig. When Ximen Qing came in, Eunuch Liu's servant kowtowed and
said: "My master presents his compliments and sends these trifles for you
to give to your servants."

"The other day," Ximen said, "I allowed your master to leave my table
hungry, yet still he sends me these delightful presents."

He told his servants to take the things and asked Liu's man to wait a
moment. Huatong brought the man a cup of tea and Ximen Qing gave
him a return card and five *qian* of silver. Then he ordered He the Ninth
to be shown in. When old He came, Ximen took his hand and went with
him to the hall. Old He knelt down. "Your Lordship," he said, "has shown
the generosity of Heaven in saving my younger brother's life. I shall never
forget your kindness."

He begged Ximen Qing to allow him to express his gratitude in the
humblest manner, but Ximen would not have this and dragged He the
Ninth to his feet. "Old Ninth," he said, "we are very good friends, and
you must not think of it. Please sit down."

"I am so contemptible a creature," He the Ninth said. "How shall I sit
in your presence?"

He remained on his feet, so Ximen Qing remained standing also and
drank a cup of tea with him. "Why did you bring me these presents?" he
said. "I will not take them. If anyone interferes with you in any way, let me
know, and I will see that you are protected. And, if you have any business
at the Town Hall, send me word, and I will write to Li on your behalf."

"It is very kind of you," He the Ninth said, "but I am an old man now
and I have handed over my office to my son He Qin."

"That was wise," Ximen Qing said, "you did well to retire. Since you
will not take all the presents away, I will accept the jar of wine, but you
must take away the rest. I won't detain you any longer."

He the Ninth thanked him repeatedly and went away. Ximen Qing
sat in the great hall watching his servants packing up presents, fruit boxes,
flowers, sheep, wine, scrolls, and money. He told Daian to take one set
to Qiao's place, and sent Wang Jing with the other to Yun Lishou. Daian
returned with five *qian* of silver that Qiao had given him, and then Wang
Jing came. Yun Lishou had given him tea, a roll of black cloth, and a pair
of shoes. He brought a return card. "Master Yun," he said, "sends his love.
He is going to send you an invitation later."

Ximen Qing was pleased. He went to the inner court for dinner.

"Ben the Fourth has gone," he said to Yueniang, "and Uncle Wu the Second is at the shop. I have nothing else to do today, so I will go and see him."

"Very well," Yueniang said, "tell him that, if he wants anything to eat or drink, he need only tell one of the boys to ask me for it."

Ximen Qing called for his horse, put on a felt hat, sable ear covers, a dark gown, and black boots with white soles, and went to Lion Street. Qintong and Daian followed him.

Uncle Wu and Laizhao were there. A sign was hanging outside the shop, and people came to buy silk, thread, and cotton wool. Trade was so flourishing that there were almost too many people to be served.

Ximen Qing dismounted, watched the people for a while, then went and sat down at the back of the shop. Uncle Wu the Second came to him. "We are doing twenty to thirty taels' worth of business a day," he said.

"I hope you are taking the greatest pains over Uncle Wu's food," Ximen Qing said to Laizhao's wife.

It was very cloudy, bitterly cold, and almost snowing. Ximen Qing decided to go and see Zheng Aiyue. "Go back and get my fur rug," he said to Qintong, "and ask the Great Lady to give you something for Uncle Wu to eat." Qintong went home. He was soon back with the fur rug, and a box of food and wine for Uncle Wu. Ximen Qing drank a few cups with his brother-in-law. "I suppose you will spend the night here," he said. "See that you enjoy yourself. I must be off now." He put on his eyeshades, mounted his horse, and, still followed by Daian and Qintong, went to Zheng Aiyue's house. When he came to East Street, it was already snowing.

Far and wide the bitter frost
Encompasses the earth.
The snow falls exquisitely
A flake and then another flake
Like the willow catkin and the cotton fluff
Each flake as big as a pussy willow.
The bamboos, the trees, the cottages
Slowly succumb beneath the weight of snow.
The rich say it will drive away calamity
And grumble that there is no more of it
Sit by their stoves with choice charcoal to warm them
Wearing coats of sable and embroidered mantles
Twirling a sprig of plum blossom
Between their fingers

And singing of good omen of prosperity
Heedless of the poor.
And poets lie at ease
And make a lot of verses.

The snow seemed like a mass of tiny fragments of jade. Ximen Qing walked over it and went into Zheng Aiyue's house. As soon as he had dismounted, a maid had rushed in and told her mistress that he was there. The old procuress came out to welcome him and took him to the hall. There she greeted him and thanked him for the presents he had sent and for his kindness to Zheng Aiyue. "Your Great Lady and the Third Lady gave her flowers," she said.

Ximen Qing answered politely and sat down. He told Daian to take the horse to the inner court.

"Please come to the upper room," the old woman said. "Zheng Aiyue has just got up. She is dressing her hair. We expected you yesterday, and she waited for you all day. Today she did not feel very well, so she did not get up till late."

Ximen Qing went in. The windows were partly open, and all the blinds were drawn. There was a bronze brazier on the floor with charcoal burning in it. He took the place of honor. Zheng Aixiang came in and offered him some tea. Then Zheng Aiyue, very daintily dressed, with plum-flower ornaments, gold pins, and a sealskin cap. Her hair seemed like the mist; her form as though it were carved from a block of jade. She smiled and made a reverence to Ximen Qing.

"Father," she said, "I was late the other day. Your party went on so long and, when I went to the ladies' court, the Great Lady kept me and insisted that I should have something to eat. I did not get home until the third night watch."

"Little oily mouth," Ximen said, "you and Li Guijie boxed Beggar Ying's ears very soundly."

"Yes," Zheng Aiyue said. "He is always saying such nasty things. Pock-marked Zhu was drunk too. He said he was going to see us safely home. I told him we had people with lanterns to take us home, and we didn't need him."

"Yesterday, I heard he had gone with Wang the Third to the house in the main street to see one of the girls," Ximen said.

"He only stayed one night and then he was done with her. Now he has taken up with Sesame."

They talked for a while, then Zheng Aiyue said: "Father, you must be cold here. Come into the inner room."

Ximen Qing went in. He took off his fur coat and sat down beside the fire with Zheng Aiyue. The air was deliciously scented. After a while, a maid brought food, and the two sisters and Ximen Qing ate it together. Zheng Aiyue offered him another half-bowlful, but he told her that he had had some cakes before he came out. "I meant to come and see you before," he said, "but the weather was so bad."

"You never sent me word, Father," Aiyue said, "and I waited for you all day. Today, when I didn't expect you, you came."

"Two friends came to see me yesterday, and I couldn't get away."

"I am going to ask a favor of you," Aiyue said. "Will you give me a sable fur? I want one to wear about my neck."

"That is easily done," Ximen said. "My friend Yun, who has just come back from the north, brought me some excellent specimens the other day. The ladies want some and, when they make up their own, I will ask them to make one for you."

"You don't say you will give me one," Aixiang said, "but I suppose you only think about Aiyue."

"You shall each have one," Ximen said.

The two girls stood up and made reverence to him.

"Don't tell Guijie or Wu Yin'er," Ximen said to them.

"The other day, when Guijie saw that Wu Yin'er was staying at your house," Aiyue said, "she asked me how long I thought she would stay. I told her. I told her, too, that when you invited Major Zhou, we four singing girls were there, but you didn't send for her because Wang the Third was there. Yesterday, when there were only relatives and friends, you did send for her. She didn't know what to say."

"You said exactly the right thing," Ximen Qing said. "I gave up sending for her brother Li Ming, but he persuaded Uncle Ying to come and speak for him. Then, on my third lady's birthday, Guijie herself came with presents and begged to be forgiven. The ladies pleaded for her. I didn't say anything but I deliberately asked Wu Yin'er to stay, just to show Guijie what 1 thought about things."

"I forgot the Third Lady's birthday," Zheng Aiyue said, "I didn't send her anything."

"Tomorrow my friend Yun will be giving a party," Ximen said. "Perhaps you and Wu Yin'er will come and sing for us."

"I shall be there," Aiyue said.

She got thirty-two ivory tablets and played with Ximen Qing. Aixiang sat with them and joined in the game. Wine was brought and the two girls offered it to him. Then they tuned their lutes and sang. When the song was done, they brought the dice box and threw dice with him.

They drank together and grew more and more gay. Suddenly, Ximen Qing saw a picture of the Moon Maiden over the bed and, underneath it, a poem.

> Here is a beauty, fair beyond all others
> The gentle breeze blows aside her crimson skirt.
> It is the third month of Spring and the flowers bloom
> In the golden valley.
> The moon shines and the shadows of the flowers move
> The night is at its best.
> The essences of jade and snow are combined in her
> Her learning and her beauty surpass those of Wen Jun.
> Love in youth should be kept as a precious thing
> And the lover should not wander with the white cloud.

Beneath the poem was written: "Sanquan, after drinking, wrote these words."

"I suppose Sanquan is Wang the Third," Ximen Qing said.

"Yes, but he wrote this a long time ago," Zheng Aiyue said, hastily. "He calls himself Xiaoxuan now. He has explained to everybody that your honorific name is Siquan and he has given up his old name to save you annoyance." She took a brush and crossed out the word "San."

Ximen Qing was pleased. "I didn't know he had changed his name," he said.

"I shouldn't have known if somebody or other hadn't told me," Zheng Aiyue said. "I understand his father's name was Yixuan, and that is why he calls himself Xiaoxuan."

By this time Aixiang had left them and Aiyue was alone with Ximen Qing. They sat side-by-side, drinking and throwing dice.

"Lady Lin is very fond of lovemaking," Ximen said. "The other day, I went and took wine with Wang the Third, and she invited me to go to the inner court to see her. She asked me to take the young man under my protection, and made him do reverence to me as to a father. She said I was to give him instruction and advice."

Zheng Aiyue clapped her hands in delight. "You have me to thank for that," she said, smiling. "One of these days you will have his wife."

"Yes, but I must burn a stick of incense to her first," Ximen said. "When the New Year comes, I am going to invite her to my house to see the lanterns and to drink wine with my ladies. Then we shall see what happens."

"Father," Aiyue said, "you have no idea how beautiful that young lady is. She is more exquisite and dainty than any figures painted on a lantern.

She is only nineteen, yet she has to live like a widow. Wang the Third never spends a night at home. If you devote a little time and attention to her, she will certainly be yours."

They drew closer and closer together. A maid brought fruit. Aiyue offered some to him. She passed honey lozenges from her own tongue to his. She unloosed his trousers with delicate fingers, took out his penis, and stroked it gently until it stood erect, proud and purple. He asked her to suck it; she bent her head, opened her red lips and took in half the penis, which moved this way and that with a pleasant sound. Before long, Ximen's passion was fully roused and he was ready for more serious things. Aiyue went to the back, and Ximen Qing also went out to change his clothes. It was snowing harder than ever.

When they were both back, Aiyue helped him to undress and he got into bed. Aiyue, when she had washed her cunt, closed the door and got into bed too.

It was the first night watch before they had done. Then they got up and put on their clothes, and Aiyue dressed her hair again. The maid came in and gave them something to eat. Ximen Qing drank some wine and asked Daian if umbrellas and lanterns were there. Daian told him that Qintong had just brought them. The old procuress and Zheng Aiyue went with Ximen to the gate and watched him mount his horse.

"Father," Aiyue said, "whenever you want me, let me know in good time."

Ximen Qing promised, then, holding an umbrella over his head, rode away over the snow. When he got home, he told Yueniang he had been drinking with Wu the Second.

The next day was the eighth. Ximen was told that Captain He had transferred his things to Xia's house, and sent him some presents. Then Ying Bojue came. It was very cold, and Ximen asked him to come to the study and sit by the fire. He told the boys to bring breakfast.

"I have sent all the things to my kinsman Qiao and Brother Yun," he said. "I gave them two *qian* of silver as a contribution from you, so you need not trouble to send them anything. Now you have only to wait until they send you an invitation."

Bojue thanked him. "What did his Excellency An want with you yesterday?" he said. "And who were the other visitors?"

"The others were General Li and Counselor Wang. They are both Zhejiiang men. They want me to give a party for a certain magistrate Zhao who has been appointed to the Lord Chamberlain's office. He was a prefect in their native place. I could not very well refuse them. They gave me three taels of silver towards the expenses."

"Civil officers are always stingy," Bojue said. "Their three taels will go no way at all. You will have to spend your own money."

"This Li," Ximen Qing said, "is the man who tried Sun Wenxiang, Huang the Fourth's brother-in-law. He reminded me that he had set the young man free."

"I see," Bojue said. "So naturally, he is careful not to forget it. You will have to give them the party if only for that reason." Then he said to Ying Bao: "Show the man in."

"Who is this?" Ximen asked.

"A young man," Bojue said. "He comes of a very decent family. His parents are dead, and he has been with the princely family of Wang since he was a child. He is married. He could not get on with the others and now he is out of work and finds it hard to get a job. He is a friend of Ying Bao, and asked Ying Bao to find him one. This morning Ying Bao asked me to recommend him to you, but I told him I didn't know whether you were in need of anybody."

"What is his name?" he said to Ying Bao. "Bring him in."

"His name is Laiyu," Ying Bao said.

Laiyu knelt down outside the lattice and kowtowed to Ximen Qing.

"He is a strong lad," Bojue said. "He looks as if he could carry a heavy load. How old are you?"

"I am twenty," Laiyu said.

"Have you any children?" Bojue asked him.

"No, I have only my wife."

"His wife is nineteen," Ying Bao said, "she is a good cook and she sews well."

Ximen Qing was impressed by Laiyu's appearance; he liked the way the young man bowed and stood upright again. He seemed an honest fellow.

"Since Uncle Ying has brought you to me, I will engage you," he said. "Mind that you serve me faithfully. Choose an auspicious day, then have the hiring contract made out and come with your wife."

Laiyu kowtowed. Ximen Qing sent him with Qintong to the inner court to kowtow to Wu Yueniang and the others. Yueniang gave him the apartment that Laiwang had had. Ying Bojue went away, and Laiyu and Ying Bao got the hiring contract written and gave it to Ximen Qing. Ximen called the young man Laijue.

We have now to speak of Mistress Ben the Fourth. After her young daughter had taken service with the Xia family, she had to depend upon Ping'an, Laian, or Huatong to run errands for her. Indeed, at one time or another, nearly all Ximen Qing's boys might have been found drinking wine in her place. She was a good-natured woman and used to cook food for them and give them tea or water whenever they asked for it. When Ben the Fourth came back from the shop, he often saw the boys about but did not give the matter a moment's thought. Now he was away, they all came to see what they could do for her. Daian and Ping'an, especially, were frequently about the place.

On the ninth, there was the reception that An, Li and Wang had asked Ximen Qing to give for Magistrate Zhao. Laijue and his wife came early in the morning. The wife went to the inner court to kowtow to Yueniang and the other ladies. She was wearing a purple coat, a black cape, and a green skirt. She was short and her face was shaped like a melon seed. She was carefully powdered, and her feet were very small. Yueniang inquired whether she could sew and asked a number of questions about housework. Her answers were perfectly satisfactory. Yueniang gave her the name Huiyuan and bade her take her turn in the kitchen every third day.

About this time, Aunt Yang died. Antong brought them the news. Ximen Qing sent an offering of food and five taels of silver, and Wu Yueniang, Li Jiao'er, Meng Yulou, and Pan Jinlian went to the funeral. Qintong, Qitong, Laijue and Laian went with them.

Ximen Qing, in the silk shop, watched the tailors making fur necklets for Yueniang. The first one they made he gave to Daian and told him to take it, with ten taels of silver, as a New Year gift to Zheng Aiyue. The people at the bawdy house made much of Daian and gave him five *qian* of silver. When he came back, he said to Ximen Qing: "Sister Zheng Aiyue is very grateful to you. She told me to say she was sorry she had entertained you so poorly the other day. She gave me three *qian* of silver."

"Keep it," Ximen Qing said. "By the way, now that Ben the Fourth is not at home, what are you doing at his house all the time?"

"When Mistress Ben's daughter went away," Daian said, "there was no one she could ask to do anything for her. So we are always ready to run an errand when it is necessary."

"That is right," Ximen said. "You must do all you can to help her now she has nobody else to do things for her."

He whispered to the boy: "Go and talk to her and say I should like to go and see her. See how she takes it. If she is well disposed, ask her to give you a handkerchief for me."

Daian went to see Mistress Ben the Fourth, and Ximen Qing went home.

Wang Jing had brought from the silversmith's a golden tiger and four pairs of pins with gold heads and silver stems. He gave them to Ximen Qing. Ximen put two pairs of pins away in his study and went with the others to Li Ping'er's room. He gave the tiger and one pair of pins to Ruyi'er and the other pair of pins to Yingchun. They kowtowed and thanked him. Ximen asked Yingchun to give him something to eat and afterwards went to the study and sat down. Daian came in quietly, but he said nothing, because Wang Jing was there. Ximen Qing told Wang Jing to go to the inner court for some tea.

"I told her what you said," Daian said. "She smiled. She said she would expect you this evening and gave me this handkerchief."

He handed to Ximen Qing a red embroidered silk handkerchief, wrapped in red paper. Ximen Qing put it to his nose and found it fragrant. He was delighted and put it into his sleeve. Wang Jing brought tea, and he drank it. Then he went back to the shop to watch the tailors at work.

He was told that Uncle Hua had come to see him, and gave orders that he should be brought in. They went into a small room and Huatong brought them tea.

"I have heard of a merchant with five hundred sacks of Wuxi rice," Hua Ziyu said. "Now that the river is frozen, he is anxious to sell it as soon as he can and get home again. I thought you might like to buy it, since it is so cheap."

"I don't need any rice now," Ximen said. "When the river is frozen, nobody buys rice. The price will go down again as soon as the ice melts. And, besides, I have no spare cash at the moment."

He told Daian to set a table and go for some food, and sent Huatong for Ying Bojue. When Ying Bojue came, the three men sat around the fire drinking. Ximen Qing called for some wheaten cakes. After a while, a novice from Abbot Wu's temple, Yingchun, came with presents and charms for the New Year. Ximen Qing asked him to sit down with them and have some wine. Then he asked him to arrange for a memorial service on the hundredth day after Li Ping'er's death, and gave him the necessary money.

At sunset, Hua Ziyu and Yingchun went away. Clerk Gan shut up the shop and joined Ximen and Bojue. They threw dice and guessed fingers. Lights were brought. Then Laian came and said that Yueniang and the other ladies had come back.

"Where have they been?" Ying Bojue asked.

"Aunt Yang is dead," Ximen said. "This is her third day. I sent an offering of food and money, and the ladies have been to offer their sympathy."

"How old was she?" Bojue asked.

"Seventy-five or seventy-six," Ximen said. "She had no children of her own and lived with her nephew. I gave her a coffin. I had it made for her several years ago."

"For an old lady to have a coffin is like having treasure in a chest," Bojue said. "It was very kind of you."

They drank more wine, and at last Ying Bojue and Clerk Gan went away. When Ximen himself left the shop, he told Wang Xian to be very careful about the fire and the candles. Wang Xian bolted the door after him.

Ximen Qing could see nobody about, and he went hurriedly to Ben the Fourth's place. The woman was standing at the door when she heard the door of the shop close and saw Ximen Qing coming out of the dark. She hastily opened her door and Ximen went quickly in. She shut the door again and said: "Please come in."

A door led to an inner room in which were a small bed and a bright fire. There was a lamp on the table. Mistress Ben was wearing a golden band about her hair, a purple silk coat, and a jade-colored skirt. She made reverence to Ximen Qing and offered him a cup of tea. "I hope my neighbor, Mistress Han, will not know anything about this," she said.

"You need not be afraid," Ximen Qing said. "It was quite dark when I came across. Nobody could have seen me." He kissed her and embraced her. Then he pulled aside the coverlet, laid her on the bed, twined her legs around his shoulders and went to work; for the clasp was already on. It was not long before the juices of love flowed from her so freely that they wet his trousers. Ximen extracted his penis and took some powder from his box; putting it in the usual place he returned to the attack. The powder held the fluid back, so things went more easily. She held his penis in her cunt and whispered words of endearment. Ximen, excited by the wine he had drunk, held her legs and pushed forward vigorously. He thrust with all his might almost three hundred times, until her disheveled hair covered his shoulders and her tongue was too cold to speak. Ximen was hardly breathing, but suddenly the sperm flowed forth and gave him an exquisite orgasm. After a long pause, he took out his penis and the juices of love flowed, but she wiped them away with her handkerchief. They both dressed, and she dried her face with balsam.

Ximen Qing gave her a few taels of silver and two pairs of gold-headed pins, and told her to buy flowers and ornaments for the New Year. She thanked him and quietly let him out. Daian was waiting for him in the shop. As soon as the boy heard Ben the Fourth's door open, he opened the gate and let Ximen Qing in. Ximen was sure that nobody had seen him, and afterwards went several times to see Mistress Ben and sported with her more than once. But, as the proverb says: If you would have no one discover your secret, never do anything that you do not wish to have known. Mistress Han found out what was going on, and she told Pan Jinlian. Jinlian did not say a word to Ximen Qing.

On the fifteenth, Qiao sent an invitation to Ximen, and he went with Ying Bojue and Uncle Wu. It was a large party and there were many people drinking and listening to the plays. The guests did not leave until the second night watch. The next day Qiao sent each of them a present of food.

At the beginning of this month, Cui Ben, who had bought silk and other merchandise to the value of two thousand taels of silver, loaded them upon a boat and started back. When the boat reached Linqiing, he left the boy Rong Hai in charge of the merchandise, hired a horse, and came to ask for money to pay the duty. When he came to the gate, Qintong cried: "What, are you back, Brother Cui? Come in. I will go and tell the master. He is in the shop."

But when Qintong came to the shop, Ximen Qing was not there. He asked Ping'an, and Ping'an said his master had gone to the inner court. Then Qintong went to Yueniang, but she said: "Your Father went out this morning and has not come back yet." The boy went to all the rooms, the garden, and the studies, but he could not find Ximen Qing. He went back to the gate.

"I'll be killed if I can tell you where he is," he said. "I can't find him anywhere. How he has managed to vanish in broad daylight is more than I can understand. And here is Brother Cui waiting for him."

Daian knew where his master was, but he said nothing.

Then Ximen appeared suddenly, and the boys were astonished. He had been amusing himself with Mistress Ben the Fourth. Ping'an made a face at Qintong. He and the other boys were worried for Qintong's sake. If Cui Ben, they thought, had gone away, there would be punishment in store for Qintong. Fortunately, Cui Ben had not gone away. He kowtowed to Ximen Qing and handed him the accounts.

"The boats are at the wharf," he said, "and I need money to pay both freight and duty. We set off together on the first day of the month and separated at Yangzhou. The others went on to Hangzhou. I stayed a couple of days at Miao Qing's. He has spent ten taels of silver on a Yangzhou girl for you. She is sixteen years old, the daughter of a captain there, and her name is Chuyun. I can't tell you how beautiful she is. I can only say that her face is like a flower, her skin like jade, her eyes like stars, her eyebrows like the new moon, her waist like the willow, and her feet hardly three inches long. She is so beautiful that the fish when they see her sink to the depths of the river, and geese fall stricken to the ground. She is pretty enough to make the moon retire in shame and the flowers hang their heads. She knows three thousand short songs and eight hundred long ones. At the moment she is at Miao Qing's house, and he is getting ready ornaments and clothes to send with her. He is going to send her with Laibao in the spring, in the hope that she will amuse you when you feel the need of amusement."

Ximen Qing was delighted. "You should have brought her with you," he said, "and there was no need for him to bother to buy clothes and ornaments for her. Do you think I couldn't provide her with things of that sort, myself?"

Ximen Qing loathed himself because he had no wings to fly to Yang-zhou, to bring back the girl and amuse himself with her.

He gave Cui Ben something to eat and five taels of silver to pay the duty and freight. He also gave him a letter to the officer at the wharf, asking him to be lenient. Cui Ben took it to Assistant Secretary Qian.

Ping'an noticed that Ximen Qing did not call for Qintong. "My boy," he said, "I could never have believed you'd be so lucky. His Lordship must be in a good temper today or you would have been tied up and beaten."

Qintong laughed. "You know his Lordship too well," he said.

It was the twentieth of the month when the merchandise arrived. It was stored in the house in Lion Street. Ximen Qing was busy preparing presents for the New Year, when a man came from General Jing. He was anxious to know whether the Imperial Rescript had come in response to the report that Censor Song had made. "My master says, perhaps you will send someone to the provincial office to find out." Ximen Qing sent a man with five *qian* of silver to the provincial office, and he found that the Imperial Rescript had arrived the day before. He made a copy and brought it back. It was a very long document, and, in the course of it, reference was made to Major Zhou, General Jing and Uncle Wu. They were all spoken of in terms of high praise and recommended for promotion.

Ximen Qing read the document with great satisfaction. He went to the inner court and said to Wu Yueniang: "Censor Song's recommendations have come. He has suggested your brother for promotion, and that he be given charge of the commissariat in this district. Zhou and Jing are commended too, and they will both be promoted. I am going to send a boy for your brother so that I can tell him."

"Yes, do," Yueniang said, "I will get the maids to prepare wine and food for you. But, if he takes up this new office, won't he need money?"

"Don't worry about that," Ximen said, "I will lend him anything he needs."

After a while, Uncle Wu came, and Ximen Qing showed him the Imperial Rescript. Uncle Wu thanked Ximen and Wu Yueniang. "I shall never be able to forget your kindness," he told them both.

"If there is anything you need, let me know," Ximen Qing said.

Uncle Wu thanked him again. They sat down with Yueniang in her room and had a meal there. Ximen asked Chen Jingji to make a copy of the document for Uncle Wu, and then sent it to Major Zhou and General Jing.

CHAPTER 78
Pan Jinlian and Her Mother

Uncle Wu went away in the evening. The next day, Jing came to thank Ximen Qing. "I read the Imperial Rescript yesterday," he said, "and was greatly pleased. It is all due to your kindness, and I can never forget the fact." He drank some tea and rose. "When is Master Yun going to invite us to take wine with him?" he asked.

"It is so close to the New Year that we are all busy," Ximen Qing said. "He will probably put it off until afterwards." Jing went away.

Ximen Qing killed a pig and sent it with two jars of wine, a roll of red silk, a roll of black silk, and a hundred fruit pastries to Censor Song. Chunhong took them with Ximen's card to the Censor's office. The officers took the boy in, and Song saw him in the hall at the back. While he was writing a note in return, he gave the boy some tea and three *qian* of silver. Then Chunhong came back and gave Ximen Qing the card. It said:

> To the most exalted and noble Ximen. Twice already I have enjoyed your magnificent hospitality, and I do not know how to thank you. Now, you send me presents that I feel I have no right to accept. You may, perhaps, have learned that I have recommended your kinsman and Jing. I am anxious to see you that we may talk about the matter. With most cordial thanks I now send back to you your servant. Your friend, Song Qiaonian.

The Censor sent a man with a hundred copies of the new calendar, forty thousand sheets of paper, and a pig.

One day a document arrived, confirming Uncle Wu in his new appointment. Ximen Qing went to call upon him, taking thirty taels of silver and four rolls of silk. On the twenty-fourth, Ximen Qing set seals upon his office and prepared a feast for his kinsmen and friends. When Uncle Wu returned from assuming office, Ximen invited him, and there was another celebration.

Now Captain He's family arrived. Ximen Qing sent tea to them in Wu Yueniang's name. On the twenty-sixth, Abbot Wu and twelve priests came to read the office for the hundredth day after the death of Li Ping'er. A host of relatives and friends came that day to offer tea to Ximen Qing. They, in turn, were asked to eat vegetarian food, and all went away the same evening. On the twenty-seventh, Ximen sent presents to his relatives and friends. He sent half a pig, half a sheep, a jar of wine, a sack of rice and a tael of silver to Ying Bojue, Xie Xida, Chang Zhijie, Clerk Fu, Clerk Gan, Han Daoguo, Ben the Fourth and Cui Ben. To Li Guijie, Wu Yin'er, and Zheng Aiyue, he sent a dress and three taels of silver each.

Yueniang wished Nun Xue to hold a service in her temple and sent Laian to her with oil, rice, flour and money.

The end of the year was drawing near. The moon lit up the plum blossom by the windows, and the wind howled through the snow-covered eaves. There was the noise of fireworks everywhere, and every household set up charms and spells for the Spring.

Ximen Qing burned paper offerings and went to Li Ping'er's room to make an offering to his dead wife. Then he assembled the whole household in the inner hall. The servants, boys, maids, and serving women came to kowtow to Ximen Qing and Wu Yueniang. Then husband and wife distributed kerchiefs, handkerchiefs, and money to all their household.

The next day was the first of the first month of the first year of the reign period Chonghe. Ximen Qing rose very early, dressed himself in his robes, and made sacrifice to Heaven and Earth. After breakfast, he got on his horse and went to the Censor's office to wish Song a happy New Year. The ladies rose early too. They dressed up and put on flowers and ornaments. They wore silken skirts and embroidered gowns, and looked very beautiful and charming. They came to kowtow to Yueniang.

Ping'an and one of the men from the office were at the gate to receive the New Year cards and write the names of the callers in a book. They were also ready to receive the officers and others who came to congratulate Ximen Qing at the New Year.

Daian and Wang Jing, wearing new clothes, new hats, and new boots, were outside the gate, playing shuttlecock, lighting bonfires, and chewing melon seeds. The clerks came and everybody connected with the houses. They were received by Chen Jingji.

About noon Ximen Qing returned from his calls upon the Censor and other officers. As soon as he had dismounted, Wang the Third came to offer his good wishes. Ximen Qing took him to the great hall, and there the young man kowtowed to him. Then Wang the Third asked to be allowed to see Yueniang, and Ximen took him to the inner court. When they returned to the hall, Ximen gave him wine.

They had drunk only one cup when Captain He was announced.

Ximen Qing told Chen Jingji to entertain Wang the Third, while he himself went to receive Captain He. Wang the Third went away when he had drunk a little more wine. Then Jing and Yun and Qiao came, one after the other. Ximen Qing was kept busy entertaining them until evening, and, by that time, he was almost tipsy. He spent the night with Yueniang.

The next day, he went out again making New Year calls and did not return until late. When he reached home, Uncle Han, Ying Bojue, Xie Xida, Chang Zhijie, and Hua Ziyu were there, and Jingji was talking to them. When Ximen came in, they greeted one another, and wine was brought. Uncle Han and Hua Ziyu lived outside the city gates and they left early. But Ying Bojue, Xie Xida, and Chang Zhijie lingered. Uncle Wu the Second came. He went to the inner court to greet his sister, then joined the others. After a while he went away.

By the time Ximen Qing took Bojue and the others to the gate, he was drunk. Daian was there, and Ximen squeezed his hand. The boy knew what this meant and said: "There is nobody there."

Ximen went at once to Mistress Ben the Fourth. She was waiting for him. Neither of them wasted any words: they undressed and set to work immediately. She was full of lust; she spread-eagled her thighs, opened her cunt with both hands, and let him reach her inmost recesses. Warm liquid oozed from her and wet the sheet. He put some powder on the head of his penis, gripped her body with both arms, and thrust so hard that the whole penis went in; not a hair's breadth stayed outside. The woman opened her eyes wide and called him Darling. Ximen asked her what her maiden name had been. "My mothers name was Ye," she said, "I was fifth child."

After that, Ximen Qing kept murmuring: "Ye the Fifth, Ye the Fifth."

Once, this woman had been a nurse. She had misbehaved with Ben the Fourth; then they had run away, and he had taken her to live with him as his wife. She was now thirty-two years old, and very well skilled in the arts of love. She called Ximen Qing by the sweetest names. He was delighted and yielded. He took his penis out of his trousers and was about to wipe it clean, but she interrupted him and said, "Don't wipe it; I'll suck it for you." Ximen wished for nothing more, so she bent down, took the penis with both hands and sucked it until it was quite clean. Then he pulled up his trousers.

"Why has my husband not come back yet?" Mistress Ben said.

"I expected him before this," Ximen said. "Possibly his Lordship Xia has kept him."

He gave her two or three taels of silver. "I should have liked to give you some clothes," he said, "but Ben the Fourth might find out, so I am giving you this money to buy some for yourself."

She opened the door for him and he went away. Daian was waiting in the shop and took his master into the house.

If the upper beams lean to one side, the lower ones also will give way. Mistress Ben the Fourth had misconducted herself with Daian even before she had dealings with Ximen Qing. Now, as soon as Daian had taken his master into the house, seeing that Clerk Fu was not in the shop, he took two jars of wine and went with Ping'an to see her. They drank until the second night watch. Ping'an went to the shop to sleep and Daian stayed with the woman.

"I have allowed your master to come to me," she said to him, "but I am very much afraid my neighbor, Mistress Han, will tell the ladies. Then they will treat me as they treat Clerk Han's wife, and I shall never be able to hold up my head again."

"The only two who count are the Great Lady and the Fifth Lady," Daian said. "There is nothing wrong with the Great Lady, but the Fifth is very sly. This is what I should do. Now that it is the New Year, buy something for the Great Lady. She is very fond of fruit pastries. Spend a *qian* or so on them and some fine melon seeds and take them to her. On the ninth, it will be the Fifth Lady's birthday. Take her some little presents and I will give her a box of melon seeds for you. That will stop their mouths."

The woman approved this plan, and the next day, when Ximen Qing was out, Daian took the boxes to Yueniang. When she asked where they came from, he told her Mistress Ben the Fourth had sent them.

"Why should she spend her money buying things for me?" Yueniang said, "especially when her husband is not at home." She accepted the presents and gave Daian two boxes of fruit and other things to take back, telling him to thank Mistress Ben the Fourth.

When Ximen Qing returned from his round of visits, Abbot Wu called to wish him the compliments of the season. They took wine in the hall and Abbot Wu went away. Ximen Qing told Daian to take a horse and go to see old woman Wen. "Tell her I want to go and see Lady Lin," he said. "What shall I do about it?"

"You need not bother, Father," the boy said, "I met old woman Wen riding past here on a donkey. She told me that Wang the Third is setting off tomorrow for the Eastern Capital to pay a visit to Marshal Huang, Lady Lin would like you to go and see her on the sixth. Old woman Wen will be there herself."

"Is this true?" Ximen Qing said.

"Should I dare to lie to you?" Daian replied.

Ximen Qing went to the inner court, but he had hardly reached his wife's room before Daian came to tell him that Uncle Wu had come. Wu was dressed in ceremonial robes, wearing a girdle with a gold buckle. He made reverence to Ximen Qing and said: "It is entirely due to your kindness that I find myself in this position today. Thank you for the presents you sent me. I am sorry I was not at home yesterday when you called. Today, I have come especially to pay my respects. Forgive me for being late." He knelt down and kowtowed.

Ximen Qing knelt down too. "Uncle," he said, "you have my heartiest congratulations. You must not worry about the question of money."

Wu Yueniang kowtowed to her brother. Uncle Wu hastily made a half-return to her, and asked her not to pay him the full honor. "That is quite enough for me," he said. "Your brother and sister-in-law are always coming here and troubling you. Now I am old, I depend upon your generosity."

Yueniang said: "Brother, I only trust you will forgive me when I fail to do things to your liking."

"Sister," Uncle Wu said, "you must not talk like that. Have we not troubled you enough already?"

"It is rather late, Uncle," Ximen Qing said. "You can't go anywhere else now. Take off your ceremonial clothes and come and sit down for a while."

They did not know that Meng Yulou and Pan Jinlian were there. When these two ladies found that Uncle Wu was going into the inner room, they came out hastily, kowtowed to Uncle Wu, and went away.

Ximen Qing and Uncle Wu went in and sat by the fire. The table was set, and the two maids, Yuxiao and Xiaoyu, came and kowtowed to Uncle Wu. Yueniang offered her brother a small gold cup of wine. Ximen Qing took the host's place, and Uncle Wu invited his sister to sit down. Yueniang asked to be excused for a moment and went into the other room for some fruit.

"Everything seems to be going well," Ximen Qing said to his brother-in-law as they drank their wine.

"It is all due to you," Uncle Wu said. "I have been to headquarters and I find that things are practically settled at the Capital. I haven't yet been to my own office of the commissariat. Tomorrow is an auspicious day, and I propose to break the seals and then go home to prepare some boxes and send them to the granary. Then I will see all the keepers of the granary and give them their orders. Ding, who used to be in charge, was reported upon adversely by Governor Hou and dismissed. I have taken his place. I have to go through all the books and give instructions to the keepers. I am making a thorough clearance of old records and reports so as to be ready for the new harvest when autumn comes.

"How many acres have you under your control?" Ximen Qing asked.

"The system of local supplies for the troops to avoid the trouble and expense of transport was established in the most remote times," Uncle Wu said. "Originally, contributions of grain were only made in autumn. Wang Anshi, when he was Minister, introduced the early grain system, which calculated for another contribution in the summer. In Jizhou, not counting barren land and marshes, we have twenty-seven thousand acres, and each acre must make a contribution of one tael and eight *qian*, so all together we have more than five hundred taels. At the end of the year we send the contribution to Dongpingfu. There, arrangements are made for buying grain and hay for the horses."

"Is there anything left over?" Ximen asked.

"There are some people not on the register," Uncle Wu said, "and people in general are very sly. If you treat them firmly and insist upon good measure, there is likely to be trouble."

"But I suppose there will be something to make it worth your while."

"To tell you the truth," Uncle Wu said, "if things are properly managed, I think I ought to make more than a hundred taels every year, besides chickens, pigs, geese and wine. Those things are presents, of course, and do not count. But I shall have to rely upon your assistance.

"I shall be very glad to do anything I can, if you can only make something out of it," Ximen said.

They drank until lights were brought, and then Uncle Wu went away. Ximen Qing went to Jinlian.

The next day he went to the office, removed the seals, and set to work again upon official business. An invitation came from Yun Lishou asking him to take wine with the other officers on the fifth. Captain He's wife invited Yueniang and the other ladies to visit her on the sixth.

Ximen Qing went with Ying Bojue and Uncle Wu to take wine with Yun Lishou. Yun had borrowed a house and engaged musicians to entertain his guests. The party did not break up until late. All the time, Ximen Qing was longing for the morrow.

The next day, Yueniang went to see Captain He's wife. Ximen Qing, dressed in his finest clothes, mounted a horse, put on his eyeshades, and went to Lady Lin's house. Daian and Qintong attended him. Wang the Third was not at home. Ximen sent in his card. Old woman Wen took it to Lady Lin. He was asked to go in, and taken through the great hall to the inner court, and into a room the floor of which was covered by rugs. The hangings and curtains were red. Lady Lin was wearing a scarlet straight-sleeved gown and her hair was piled up with pearls and ornaments. They greeted one another, then sat down and drank tea. The boys took the horse to the stable. After tea, Lady Lin begged Ximen to take off his ceremonial clothes and go to her room.

"My son," she said, "has gone to the Eastern Capital to wish his father-in-law the compliments of the season. He will be back after the festival."

Ximen Qing called Daian to take his long cloak. Beneath it he was wearing a white silk coat and a sky-blue gown embroidered with flying fish. It was very handsome.

The table was set and maids brought wine and dishes. Lady Lin offered him wine with her delicate hands; passionate glances flashed from her eyes. They guessed fingers, threw dice, and talked sweetly to one another. Spring was in the air. Then they began to glance sideways at one another and their heads whirled.

It was almost sunset. Silver candlesticks were brought. Daian and Qintong were being looked after by old woman Wen. Wang the Third's wife was in another apartment. She was served by her own maids and women and did not come to them. Lady Lin closed the door. After that, no servant would dare to come in. Then, stirred by the wine, they went to the inner room, pulled aside the embroidered curtains, and shut the windows. They turned up the lamps and closed the doors. Ximen Qing took off his clothes and got on to the bed; Lady Lin washed herself carefully, and then joined him. Ximen had come for this purpose; he had brought his instruments with him. He had taken some of his secret medicine, and the silver clasp was ready for action. He pulled up her legs and put his strong prick before her cunt, then reared up and thrust it in noisily. The woman called him her darling without ceasing.

Ximen burned grains of incense on her belly and by the hole of her cunt. He told her he was going to give a party and that he would like to invite her son's wife and herself to come and see the lanterns. The woman was so enraptured that she promised they would both go. Ximen Qing got up, drank with her until the second night watch, then mounted his horse and rode home. He went out by the back way.

When he got home, Ping'an said: "Eunuch Xue has sent a card to ask you to go to his country place to enjoy the signs of the approach of Spring. And Uncle Yun has sent five cards of invitation asking the ladies to a party."

Ximen went to Yueniang's room. Yulou and Jinlian were there. Yueniang had returned from Captain He's place and was talking to them. When Ximen came in, she rose and made a reverence to him.

"Where have you been all this time?" she said.

Ximen could think of no better excuse than that he had been drinking at Ying Bojue's house.

Yueniang told him about the party at Captain He's. "Mistress He," she said, "is very young. I don't believe she is more than eighteen. She is as beautiful and charming as a painted figure. She is well up in affairs of the day as well as those of the past. She was so sweet and pleasant to me she might have known me for a long time. It is two years since she married Captain He. She has four maids, two nurses, and two serving women."

"She is a niece of Eunuch Lan," Ximen Qing said. "When she married He, the eunuch gave her a very considerable dowry."

"Tomorrow," Yueniang said, "your friend Yun's wife has asked us to go and see her. There are five cards. Shall we go?"

"Yes, indeed," Ximen said. "All of you, if you are invited."

"I think Sun Xue'e ought to stay at home," Yueniang said. "It is the New Year, and, if anybody should call, there would be no one here."

"Very well. Xue'e shall stay at home and the rest of you can go. Eunuch Xue has asked me to go and see him, but I don't feel much like going. I don't know whether it is the Spring air or not, but the last few days I have had a good deal of pain in my legs and loins."

"There may be something wrong with your lungs," Yueniang said. "Don't waste any time but get Doctor Ren to give you some medicine."

"Oh, I don't think it is anything serious. If I leave it alone, it will get better of itself. If it doesn't, I will ask him for something later on. I think we might give a party for the Feast of Lanterns and invite some ladies, Mistress Ho, Mistress Zhou, Mistress Jing, Mistress Zhang, Mistress Yun, Lady Lin, Aunt Wu and Mistress Cui. What about the twelfth or the thirteenth? We can make a show of lanterns and have some of the actors from the royal household. Last year, we had a few large set pieces, and Ben the Fourth looked after them. This year he is at the Eastern Capital, and we shall have to find someone else."

"Since Ben the Fourth is not here, why not ask his wife?" Jinlian said. "She would do as well."

Ximen Qing looked at her. "You little strumpet!" he said. "You can't speak three sentences without making yourself objectionable."

Yueniang did not seem to be very interested, and the matter dropped.

"We have never seen Wang the Third's mother," Yueniang said. "What is the idea of asking her? I don't suppose she will come."

"Since Wang the Third is now my ward, we may as well send her an invitation," Ximen Qing said. "Whether she comes or not is her affair."

"I don't think I shall go to Yun's place tomorrow," Yueniang said. "I am getting near my time. If I get into a crowd, people may talk."

"You need not worry," Yulou said. "You are not very big. The baby is not due this month, and it is the New Year. Why not be merry and go?"

Ximen Qing drank a cup of tea and went to sleep with Xue'e. When Jinlian saw this, she went away with Ximen Dajie. Ximen asked Xue'e to pinch and rub his body for a long time.

The next day Ying Bojue came. "Mistress Yun," he said, "has sent a card to my wife to ask her to go and help her entertain your ladies. But my wife has only a few old dresses, and this is not a very suitable time to wear them. People would laugh at her. I have come to see if you would mind lending her some of your ladies' clothes and a few ornaments and things. Then she can wear them."

Ximen Qing said to Wang Jing: "Go and ask the Great Lady."

"Ying Bao is here with a box," Bojue said. "Take it, Brother, and bring something back in it."

Wang Jing took the box and went to the inner court. After a while he returned and handed the box to Ying Bao. "There are some silken clothes and a set of ornaments inside," he said. Ying Bao took them away and Bojue sat down to have tea with Ximen Qing.

"Eunuch Xue has asked me to go to his place outside the city to enjoy the coming of Spring," Ximen Qing said, "but I have too much to do. My kinsman, Wu, has invited me to go and take part in a service at his place on the ninth, but I can't go to that either. I must send my son-in-law instead. I don't know whether I have been drinking too much, but my back aches very badly and I feel too lazy to move."

"You have been drinking too much, Brother," Bojue said. "You must drink less."

"It is the New Year and I can't help myself," Ximen said. "Wherever I go, drink is pressed upon me."

Then Daian came in with a box. "Captain He," he said, "has sent you an invitation to a party on the ninth."

"There you are!" Ximen said. "Another invitation. And I can't refuse."

He opened the case. There were three cards inside it. One, a large red one, said: "To his Lordship, my colleague Siquan"; another: "To his Worship, Wu"; and the third, "To my good friend, the worthy Ying." They all ended with the words "your friend He Yingshou kowtows."

Daian said: "The messenger said he did not know the other addresses, so he brought all the cards here. He said he would be much obliged if we would forward them."

"What shall I do?" Ying Bojue said. "I have never sent the Captain any present. How can I accept his invitation?"

"I will give you something for Ying Bao to take to him. That will be all right."

Ximen told Wang Jing to wrap up two *qian* of silver and a handkerchief, and to write Bojue's name on a card. "Perhaps you will take this card with you. I will not send it," he said to Ying Bojue. He told Daian to take the other card to Uncle Wu. Wang Jing gave the packet to Ying Bojue. Bojue bowed to Ximen Qing and thanked him. Then he went away.

"I will come early, and we will start together," he said as he was leaving.

In the afternoon Yueniang and the others dressed and set out. They had one large sedan chair and three small ones. They took Laijue's wife to act as their maid, and she, too, had a small sedan chair. Four soldiers went before them to clear the way, and Qintong, Chunhong, Qitong, and Laian followed them. So they came to Yun Lishou's house.

When they had gone, Ximen Qing said to Ping'an, the gatekeeper: "No matter who comes to see me, you must say that I am not at home. Just accept any cards that may be brought."

Ping'an had had such instructions before, and he had learned his lesson. He did not dare to leave the gate. He sat down and, whenever a visitor came, said his master was not at home.

Ximen Qing's legs were still painful. He remembered that he had some long-lasting medicine that a doctor had once given him, to be taken with the milk of a woman. He went to Li Ping'er's room and asked Ruyi'er to give him some of hers. Ruyi'er was dressed in her holiday clothes. She at once gave him some milk and gave him what he needed for the medicine. Ximen sat by the fire and told Yingchun to bring him something to eat. Yingchun did so, then went to play chess with Chunmei. She knew that Ruyi'er would give him any water or tea he might want. When the maid had gone, Ximen lay down on the bed, pulled down his trousers, took out his prick, and asked her to take it in her mouth while he took some wine in his. "Suck it for me thoroughly," he said, "and I'll give you a decorated cloak to wear on holiday." "Certainly," she replied. "I want to suck it again and again." "My child," Ximen Qing said, "I should like to burn some incense on your body."

"Do what you like," the woman said.

Ximen Qing made fast the door, then took off his cloak and trousers. She lay on the bed, and Ximen took from his pocket three grains of incense, soaked in wine, which were left over from the time when he had his pleasure with Mistress Lin. He took off her clothes and put one grain of incense on her bosom, another on her belly, and the third in her cunt; then he burned them all. He put his prick in her cunt, bent down to look, and thrust vigorously; then he took a mirror to see better, and it was not long before the incense had burned down to her skin; she grimaced and ground her teeth in pain, and at last she said in a trembling voice, "Stop, I can't stand it any longer."

"Zhang the Fourth, you strumpet, whose woman are you?" Ximen Qing cried.

"I am yours."

"Say that you once belonged to Xiong Wang, but now you belong to me."

"This strumpet once was Xiong Wang's wife, but now she belongs to this darling."

"Do I know how to deal with a woman?"

"Yes, my darling, you know well how to treat a woman's cunt."

So they talked, in a manner we cannot describe. His penis was so long and thick that it filled her whole cunt. He traveled up and down, making the heart of her flower now red as a parrot's tongue, now black as a bat's wing. It was a delightful and wonderful sight. He held her legs; bodies squeezed together, and his prick went in right to its root. Her eyes opened wide, and love juices flowed from her. Ximen reached his orgasm, and his sperm flowed like a river.

After he had burned her in this way, he opened the cabinet and gave her a silk embroidered cape.

In the evening, Yueniang and the others came back. "Mistress Yun is going to have a baby," Yueniang told her husband. "Today, when we offered wine to one another, we agreed that, when the babies arrive, if one is a boy and the other a girl, we will arrange a marriage between them. If they are both boys, they shall go to the same school, and if girls, they shall be like sisters, do their needlework, and play together. Mistress Ying was our witness."

Ximen Qing smiled.

The next day was the day before Jinlian's birthday. Ximen Qing went to the office in the morning and told the boys to get out and clean all the lanterns and put them up. He told Laixing to buy fruits and to arrange with the singing boys to come in the evening.

Early that morning, Jinlian got up and dressed, putting on flowers and powdering her face till it was very white. Her lips were red; the sleeves of her coat green. She came to the great hall to watch Daian and Qintong putting up the lanterns. She smiled and said: "I see you are getting ready for the Feast of Lanterns."

"Yes," Qintong said, "today is the eve of your birthday, and Father said we were to get out the lanterns and have them up ready for your party tomorrow. This evening I am coming to kowtow to you. I'm sure you will have something for me."

"If it is a beating you want, yes, indeed; but if money, it is no use coming to me," Jinlian said.

"Mother," Qintong said, "you never speak without using the word 'beating.' We are your children and you ought to be kind to us instead of talking to us about beatings."

"Shut your mouth and get on with your lanterns," Jinlian said. "And don't set about your work in that offhand way. The lanterns will not stay up. The other day, when Cui Ben came and you said: 'How can the master have vanished in broad daylight?' you very nearly got a thrashing. If you don't put up these lanterns properly, you won't escape a thrashing this time."

"Mother," Qintong said, "you always use ill-omened words. My life is precarious enough as it is, and your words make it seem still less secure."

"You have a wonderful way of finding out things, Mother," Daian said. "How did you come to hear that?"

"Outside the palace there is a pine tree, and inside it, a great bell," Jinlian said. "The pine tree's shadow is easy to recognize, and the sound of the bell, easy to hear. So it is with things in this house. Yesterday, your master said to the Great Lady: 'Last year, Ben the Fourth was here to see about the big fireworks. Now he is away and there is nobody to see to them.' I said: 'Even if Ben the Fourth is not at home, his wife will do as well. Why don't you send for her?'"

"What are you suggesting now, Mother?" Daian said. "You surely can't think of such a thing. Ben the Fourth is one of our clerks."

"What am I suggesting now, indeed?" Jinlian said. "It is true, isn't it? A lovely state of affairs! He goes beyond all limits."

"Mother," Qintong said, "don't believe everything you hear. We must not let this reach Ben the Fourth's ears."

"That silly turtle!" Jinlian said. "What's the harm if that fellow does get to know? I say he is a turtle, and everybody knows that that is exactly what he is. He doesn't worry when he goes to the Eastern Capital. He knows that, when he leaves his wife behind, her cunt will not be unemployed. Don't argue with me, you scamp. You all help your father in these games. And when you arrange things of this sort for him, you get your own fingers in the pie. Isn't that so? You say I know too much. It is perfectly clear why that woman sent presents to the Great Lady the other day. I understand she is sending me some melon seeds to keep my mouth shut. She is very clever at these underhand games, but my first guess is that Daian devised the whole scheme."

"You must be fair, Mother," Daian said. "Why should I do anything of the sort? I have never been to her place unless there was something important to be done. Don't believe everything Mohammedan Han's wife tells you. She and Mistress Ben the Fourth have had quarrels over their children. As the proverb says: It is easy for people to pick a quarrel, but hard to keep on good terms. If the roof falls, it does not necessarily follow that somebody must be hurt; but an evil tongue, incessantly wagging, will be the death of anyone in time. In cases like this, if you believe a thing, it is true; if you do not believe it, it is false. Mistress Ben the Fourth is a very pleasant woman. She has been here some time and she is always kind. We all go to her for tea and things, and I can't believe we all have improper dealings with her. She hasn't a house big enough to hold us all."

"Oh, I know the bleary-eyed strumpet," Jinlian said. "She is no bigger than half a brick, but she blinks her watery eyes and seems to make people do what she wishes. She and that hashed-up, melon-faced Han Daoguo's wife! I know their tricks. I keep my eyes. How can I fail to see?"

At that moment, Xiaoyu came up and said: "The Great Lady is asking for you. Grandmother Pan has come, and she wants to pay the sedan chair men."

"I have been standing here all this time," Jinlian said. "How was it I didn't see her?"

"She went in by the passage," Qintong said. "She needs six *fen* of silver for the sedan chair."

"Where does she expect me to get the money?" Jinlian cried. "Why doesn't she bring her own money when she goes out to visit people?"

She went to the inner court to see her mother, but she would not give her any money.

"Give the old lady a *qian* of silver and put it down in the accounts," Yueniang said.

"No, I'm not going to upset our husband," Jinlian said. "He knows exactly how much money he gives me. He gave it to me to buy things with, not to pay for sedan chairs."

They all sat down and looked at one another. The sedan chair men kept pressing for their money. They wanted to go away. At last, Yulou could bear it no longer. She took a *qian* of silver from her sleeve and dismissed the men.

After a while, the two aunts Wu and the nun came. Yueniang gave them tea. Old woman Pan went to her daughter's room. Jinlian upbraided her harshly.

"Who told you to come, if you haven't money enough to pay for your chair? You come here, and people laugh at you. You have no shame at all."

"Daughter," old woman Pan said, "you never give me any money. Where am I to get it? Indeed, I found it very hard even to get presents to bring with me."

"It's no use looking to me for money," Jinlian said. "Money doesn't come my way. There are seven holes here and eight eyes trying to find them. In the future, come when you know you have money to pay for your chair and, if you haven't any, stay away. I'm sure nobody in this house is dying to see you, so you needn't make an exhibition of yourself. Though the god of war may have sold bean curd, it was the man himself who counted, not the stuff he sold. I can't put up with the insulting things people say. There was trouble the other day, after you had gone away. Did you know that? I am like the droppings that fall from a donkey. They look very fine and large, but there's nothing inside."

The old woman began to cry. "Mother," Chunmei said to Jinlian, "what is the matter with you today? Why are you scolding Grandmother so?" She did her best to console the old lady, took her to the inner room, and made her sit down on the bed. Then she gave her a cup of tea. The old woman was so upset that she went to sleep and did not wake up till she was called to dinner. Then she went to the inner court.

When Ximen Qing came back from the office, he had his meal in Yueniang's room. Daian brought him a card and said that Jing had called to see him. Upon the card was written: "The recently promoted Commander of the troops in the southeast and Superintendent of Communications, Jing Zhong, presents his humble respects." Ximen hastily put on his ceremonial clothes and went to welcome him. Jing was wearing a scarlet gown, with a unicorn embroidered upon it, and a girdle with a gold buckle. He was accompanied by a host of officials and soldiers. They greeted each other in the hall, then sat down, and tea was brought.

"The documents reached me the day before yesterday," Jing said. "I have not yet been to my new office, but I felt I must come especially to thank you."

"I must congratulate you, General," Ximen said. "It is only right and fitting that a man so capable as yourself should be appointed to a more responsible post. Your appointment sheds glory even upon myself. I must give a party in your honor."

He asked Jing to take off his ceremonial clothes and stay to dinner. At the same time he ordered a servant to set the table. Jing would not stay. "I came to thank you," he said, "before I went to anyone else, but I have a great deal to attend to. I will come and see you another day." He prepared to say good-bye, but Ximen Qing would not have it. He told a servant to take his guest's ceremonial robes and set the table at once. Charcoal was put into the brazier; the blinds were drawn. Jade-like wine was poured from a golden jar and food brought in a precious dish.

The wine had just been served when the two boys, Zheng Chun and

Wang Xiang, came in and kowtowed. "What makes you so late?" Ximen Qing asked Zheng Chun. "And who is this other boy?"

"He is Wang Xiang, a brother of Wang Gui," Zheng Chun said.

Ximen told them to bring their instruments and sing, and the two boys sang the song "This Delightful Weather." Servants brought two trays of food and two jars of wine for the people who had come with General Jing.

"This is really too much," Jing said. "I have troubled you enough. Why should you give food to all my people?" He ordered them to come and kowtow to Ximen Qing.

"Tomorrow or the day after," Ximen said, "my wife is going to invite your lady to come and enjoy the Feast of Lanterns. I hope you will persuade her to come. There will be your lady, Mistress Zhang, Captain He's wife, and the two ladies of my kinsman Wu, nobody else."

"If any invitation comes from your lady, my humble wife will be sure to come," Jing said.

"Why has Zhou not been given an appointment yet?" Ximen Qing asked.

"I am told he is to receive an appointment in the Capital in three months' time," Jing said.

"I am glad to hear it," Ximen said.

Jing stood up and said good-bye. Ximen Qing took him to the gate. Then, with the soldiers clearing the way for him, he went away.

That evening, they kept the eve of Jinlian's birthday. The two boys sang in the inner court. When the wine had been passed around, Ximen Qing went to her room. Aunt Wu, old woman Pan, Ximen Dajie, Miss Yu, and the two nuns stayed in Yueniang's room while Jinlian went to her own room to drink with Ximen Qing. She offered him wine and kowtowed to him. After a while old woman Pan came, and Jinlian sent her to sleep in the Sixth Lady's room, so that she herself could drink and sport with Ximen.

The old woman went to the Sixth Lady's room, and Ruyi'er and Yingchun helped her to get into the warm bed. But, before she did so, she looked at Li Ping'er's tablet in the outer room with many offerings set out before it. The portrait was hanging there. The old woman made a reverence to it. "Sister," she said, "you are safe in paradise now." Then she came and sat on the bed and said to Ruyi'er and Yingchun: "Your mistress is a happy woman. She is dead, but her husband has many prayers said for her and makes offerings to show he still remembers her."

"The other day we observed my mistress's hundredth day," Ruyi'er said. "Why didn't you come? Aunt Hua and Aunt Wu were here; there were twelve priests to read the prayers. They played instruments and waved banners about. It was really a splendid ceremony, and didn't come to an end before the evening."

"It was the New Year season," old woman Pan said. "I couldn't leave the boy at home alone. That is why I didn't come. But where is Aunt Yang today?"

"Didn't you hear that Aunt Yang had died?" Ruyi'er said. "On my mistress's hundredth day she didn't come, and, only a few days ago, all our ladies went to her funeral."

"What a sad thing!" old woman Pan said. "I believe she was even older than I am. I never knew she was dead. No wonder I missed her today."

"Grandmother," Ruyi'er said, "we have some sweet wine. Would you like some?" Then she said to Yingchun: "Sister, will you put a small table on the bed and warm some sweet wine for Grandmother?"

The wine was brought, and, while she was drinking it, the old woman said: "Your mistress was a very good woman. She was kind and sweet. When I came here, she never treated me as a stranger. She used to give me hot tea and hot water, and she would be angry if I wouldn't take them. And at night she would stay awake and talk to me. When I was going away she always gave me something. Why, Sisters, even this gown I am wearing now, she gave me. My own daughter never gives me so much as the half of a broken needle. That is the truth. If I were starving, she wouldn't give me a penny. She would see my eyes drop out on the ground first. When your lady was alive, my daughter used to scold me for a miser and say I was always trying to get things out of her. I know she has a lot of money, but, in spite of it, she would not give me even the few *fen* I needed to pay for my sedan chair. She bit her lips and said she had no money. In the end, the lady in the east room gave me a *qian* and paid off the chair men.

"When I went to her room, she gave me a fine dressing down. She said I was to come if I had money and to stay away if I hadn't. Let me tell you this: when I go away this time, I shall never come back. I won't come here to be insulted. I give her up entirely. There are many cruel people in the world but none so cruel as she is. Sisters, I tell you: if I die tomorrow, I don't know what the end of her will be. She will never take advice from anybody. You know, her father died when she was seven years old, and, from that day to this, I've never thought about anybody but her. When she was young, I taught her needlework and sent her to school. I dressed her carefully and took care that her hands and feet were well kept. She has been clever enough to rise to the position she holds now, and see how she treats her poor mother. Her eyes are never kind when they look on me."

"Did your daughter go to school?" Ruyi'er said. "Now I understand why she is able to read all the characters."

"Yes, she went to school when she was seven years old, and she spent three years there. She learned composition and how to read poems and songs and literature of all sorts."

As they were talking, there came a knock at the door. "Who is there?" Ruyi'er said. "Go and see, Xiuchun."

Xiuchun went to the door. When she came back, she said: "Sister Chunmei is here." Ruyi'er squeezed the old woman's hand.

"Don't say anything," she whispered. "Chunmei is here."

"She and my daughter walk with the same leg," the old woman said.

When Chunmei came in, she found them drinking wine with the old woman. "I have come to see how Grandmother is," she said. Ruyi'er asked her to sit down. Chunmei arranged her skirt and sat down on the bed, with an air of great self-importance.

Yingchun sat next to Chunmei, Ruyi'er on the left-hand side, and the old woman in the middle.

"Have your father and mother gone to bed?" the old woman said.

"Yes," Chunmei said, "I waited on them till they were in bed and then I came to see you. I have got some dishes and a cup of wine ready for you." She said to Xiuchun: "The dishes are all ready. Go and ask Qiuju for them." Xiuchun went out. She soon returned carrying a jar of wine. Qiuju brought a food box.

"Go back now," Chunmei said to Qiuju, "and, if they want me, come and tell me."

Qiuju went back. The dishes were put on the table. Xiuchun went to fasten the door, then came and joined them. When the wine was heated, Chunmei offered a cup to old woman Pan, then to Ruyi'er, Yingchun, and Xiuchun. She picked out all the tasty bits from the dishes and offered them to the old woman and the others. "Grandmother, do have some," she said. "I assure you it has been prepared especially for you."

"Sister," the old woman said, "your mistress never bothers about what I eat, but you take pity on a poor old widow. I foresee that you will make progress day by day. My daughter has not a human heart. I have always been miserable on her account. Whenever I offer her advice, she storms at me. Sister, you know I came today to see her, not to cadge a few bits of cold food. And you see how she has treated me."

"Grandmother," Chunmei said, "you don't understand. You only see one side: the other is hidden from you. My mistress is one of those people who are never satisfied so long as they are in a subordinate position. Compared with the Great Lady, who has money in plenty, she is in a most unfortunate position. My mistress is really poor, though you think she has a good deal and will not give you any. I know her better than anyone else does. My father leaves a great deal of money in her hands, but she will not touch a penny of it for her own purposes. If she wishes to buy flowers and things of that sort, she asks him straight out, instead of using his money and saying nothing about it. She will not allow the servants any handle against her. Grandmother, if you are angry with her, you are unjust. I am not standing up for her. I only want you to realize what the position is."

"Perhaps the old lady did not quite understand her daughter," Ruyi'er said. "After all, you are mother and daughter. If she had money, she would surely give it to you before anybody else. When you, old lady, come to your end, the Fifth Lady will have no one of her own to come and see her. She will be like the rest of us who have lost our mothers."

"I am old," the old woman said, "and I don't know whether I shall die today or tomorrow. I am not angry with her."

Chunmei saw that the old woman was becoming maudlin after her few cups of wine. She said to Yingchun: "Get the dice box and let us throw dice." They got a box with forty dice. Chunmei played with Ruyi'er, then with Yingchun. They drank great cups of wine, and, before long, their peach-flower cheeks were flushed. They finished the jar. Yingchun brought half a jar of Magu wine, and they finished that too. By the second night watch, old woman Pan could not stay awake any longer. Her body swayed backwards and forwards; her head began to nod. The party broke up.

When Chunmei went home, she opened the corner door and went through the courtyard. Qiuju was in the middle room, standing on a small bench and peeping through the partition. She was spying on the pair in the other room, and was very interested in the remarks they made to one another and the different sounds she heard. Just when she was most delighted, Chunmei came up and slapped her face. "You young rascal!" she said. "What do you mean by listening there?"

Qiuju was taken by surprise. She stared at Chunmei and said: "I was dozing. I wasn't listening at all. Why do you come and hit me?"

Jinlian overheard this. She called out to Chunmei: "Who is talking there?"

"I have told Qiuju to shut the door, but she won't move," Chunmei said.

Qiuju glared and went to shut the door. Chunmei took off the ornaments in her hair and went to bed.

The next day was Jinlian's birthday. Mistress Fu, Mistress Gan, Ben the Fourth's wife, Cui Ben's wife, Miss Duan, Miss Zheng, and the younger Wu's wife, came to congratulate her. Ximen Qing, with Uncle Wu and

Ying Bojue, dressed in their best clothes, went on horseback to Captain He's place. There were a great many guests, and four singing girls were there to entertain them. Major Zhou was present. In the evening, when the party broke up, Ximen Qing came back and spent the night with Ruyi'er.

On the tenth he sent out cards to invite the ladies.

"Why should we not invite Aunt Meng?" Yueniang said, "and my sister-in-law too? They will be very upset if they find we've left them out."

"You are quite right," Ximen said. He asked Jingji to write two more invitations and Qintong took them.

Jinlian overheard this and was annoyed. She went to her own room and urged old woman Pan to go away at once. As the old woman was leaving, Yueniang said to her: "Grandmother, why are you going away in such a hurry? You must stay another day at least."

"Great Sister," Jinlian said, "It is the New Year, and there is nobody to look after her boy. Please don't keep her."

Yueniang gave the old woman two boxes of cakes and a *qian* of silver for her sedan chair, and took her to the gate.

When the old woman had gone away, Jinlian said to Li Jiao'er: "The Great Lady is inviting her rich relations for the Feast of Lanterns, and my old mother would be out of place. I couldn't let her stay. When the guests come, I can't say she is a guest too, because her clothes make it quite obvious that she isn't. And I can't tell them she is one of the women from the kitchen, because she isn't that. It puts me in a very awkward position."

Ximen Qing told Daian to take two cards to Wang the Third's place, one for Lady Lin and one for the younger lady, whose family name was Huang. He also told Daian to go to the bawdy house to tell Li Guijie, Wu Yin'er, Zheng Aiyue, and another girl to come, as well as the three boys, Li Ming, Wu Hui and Zheng Chun.

That day, Ben the Fourth came back from the Eastern Capital. In his best clothes, he came to kowtow to Ximen Qing and gave him a letter from Xia.

"What has kept you so long at the Capital?" Ximen asked him.

"I caught a very bad cold," Ben the Fourth said, "and I wasn't well enough to leave before the second of this month. His Lordship Xia sends you his best wishes and thanks you for looking after his house."

Ximen Qing gave Ben the Fourth the keys of the thread shop again, but he set apart another room so that Uncle Wu the Second could sell silk there. He was going to let Uncle Wu the Second do business with Laibao when Laibao came back with merchandise from the South. He asked Ben the Fourth to get the firework makers to put up two set pieces ready for the party on the twelfth.

Then Ying Bojue came with Li the Third, who thanked Ximen Qing for all he had done for him in the past. They sat down and had tea. Ying Bojue began: "Brother Li knows of a piece of business, and he is anxious to find out if you would be interested in it."

"What is the business?" Ximen Qing said.

"A document has come from the Eastern Capital," Li the Third said "requiring the Thirteen Provinces each to send to the capital historic works of art to the value of tens of thousands of taels. Our Prefecture of Dongpingfu is to provide twenty thousand taels' worth. The order is still in the governor's hands and has not been sent down to the lower authorities. Zhang the Second, in the High Street, proposes to expend a hundred taels in getting the contract. There is about ten thousand taels profit to be made. I thought I would come with Uncle Ying to let you know about this so that, if you feel inclined, we can go into the business with Zhang the Second. It would mean five thousand taels from each of you. Brother Ying, Huang the Fourth, and I myself, would be your associates, and Zhang the Second would have two men in with him. We should share the profits in the proportion of two and eight. What do you think about it?"

"What kind of works of art do they want?" Ximen Qing said.

"Perhaps your Lordship has not heard," Li the Third said. "The work on North Mount has just been finished at the Imperial City, and its name has been changed to the 'Mountain of Long Life.' A number of buildings are to be constructed there, the Palace of the Pure and Precious Secret, the Hall of the Immortals, and the Sanctuary of the Jade Spirit. There is also to be a dressing chamber for the Lady An. All these buildings are to be adorned with rare beasts and birds, Zhou bronzes, and Shang tripods, Han seals, and Qin incense burners, stone drums of the Xuanwang period, bronzes and copper of the successive dynasties—antiquities, in fact, of every sort. It is a very great undertaking, and his Majesty is going to spend a great deal of money."

"I think it would be better if I managed the whole business myself," Ximen said. "I might as well provide the ten or twenty thousand taels and go in for the thing with my own people."

"It certainly would be better," Li the Third said. "We need say nothing about it, and Brother Ying, Brother Huang and I will give you our assistance. Then there will be no outsiders."

"Will you bring in one of your own people?" Bojue asked.

"When we have made all the arrangements, we will have Ben the Fourth to help us," Ximen said. He asked where the orders were.

"They are still at the Censor's office," Li the Third said. "They have not been sent on yet."

"That doesn't matter," Ximen said. "I will write to Song and send him some presents. That will be all right."

"But you must act at once," Li the Third said. "As the proverb says: Soldiers must always be on the alert, and he who cooks his rice first will be the first to eat. If we don't look out, somebody may get the job before us."

Ximen Qing laughed. "Don't worry about that," he said. "Even if the orders had been sent to the office of the Prefecture, Song would recall them for me. Besides, Hu, the Prefect, is a friend of mine."

He asked Li the Third and Ying Bojue to stay for a meal, and it was settled that Ximen Qing should send his letter the following day.

"I must tell you one thing," Li the Third said, "His Excellency is not at his office now. The day before yesterday, he set out for an inspection at Yanzhou."

"You shall go yourself with one of my boys tomorrow," Ximen said.

"Very well," Li the Third said, "I expect we shall manage it in five or six days. Whom will you send with me? Give him the letter and let him come and spend the night at my house so that we can start early in the morning."

"The only one of my servants whom his Excellency knows is Chunhong, and he likes him. I will send him and Laijue with you."

Ximen summoned the two boys and told them that they were to go on a journey with Li the Third and that they must spend the night at his house.

"You do well," Bojue said. "We must waste no time, for, in matters like this, the man with the fastest legs has the advantage."

When they had had something to eat, Ying Bojue and Li the Third went away. Ximen Qing told his son-in-law to write the letter, then measured about ten taels of gold leaf and gave it with the letter to Chunhong and Laijue.

"See that you go quickly and warily," he said to them, "and come back as soon as you have got the document. If it has been sent to the Prefecture before you get there, ask his Excellency to give you a letter to the Prefect, instructing him to let us have it."

"I understand," Laijue said, "I have been to Yanzhou before, on an errand for Counselor Xu."

They went to Li the Third's house and, the next day, hired horses and set out.

On the twelfth, Ximen Qing gave a party and did not go to the office. He invited Uncle Wu, Ying Bojue, Xie Xida, and Chang Zhijie to come in the evening. Early in the morning, the musicians of the princely household of Wang came and, when the ladies arrived, they sounded the bronze drums and gongs in their honor. A servant came from Major Zhou to say that Mistress Zhou had trouble with her eyes and would not be able to come. But Mistress Jing, Mistress Zhang, Mistress Yun, Mistress Qiao, Mistress Cui and Aunts Wu and Meng came early. Captain He's wife, Lady Lin, and Wang the Third's wife did not arrive so early, so Ximen Qing sent soldiers several times to urge them to come, and dispatched old woman Wen to Lady Lin.

About noon, Lady Lin came in a large sedan chair, with a smaller chair following. After he had greeted her, Ximen Qing asked why her daughter-in-law had not come.

"My son is not at home and she is obliged to stay there," Lady Lin said.

Sometime afterwards, Captain He's wife came. She was in a sedan chair carried by four men. Behind her came a smaller one with a serving woman. A number of soldiers followed with her dressing case, and servants walked beside the chair. The chair was brought to the second door; the lady got out, and the musicians played. Wu Yueniang and the others went to the second door to welcome her. Ximen Qing stood quietly in one of the side rooms, and looked at the young lady through the blind. She was not more than twenty years old, tall and slender, and she looked as pretty as a jade carving. There were masses of pearls and ornaments on her hair. She wore a red gown with long sleeves embroidered in five colors. Her girdle was set with gold and jade, and below it was a blue skirt. As she moved, the tinkle of jade could be heard, and she brought with her the fragrance of orchid and musk.

> Gracious and charming
> Dainty and alert
> Of manner fascinating
> And of figure perfect
> With eyebrows long and delicate, arching on the temples
> Eyes, like a phoenix's, delicately sloping.
> Her voice was as sweet
> As that of an oriole flying in the sunshine.
> Her tender waist like the willow
> Playing in the wind.
> From the host of the most elegant she came
> Without a trace of arrogance or common breeding
> As though one bred in a thicket of pearls.
> Her dress was chaste and dignified.
> She was like a cherry tree in full bloom
> Of whom no one knows how many flowers

Blossom in one night.
Like a willow slow in budding
So that no one can tell how far advanced
Is Spring.
Her lotus feet moved lightly
Gaily as the fairies.
With skirt raised just a little
Like the "Water-Moon" Guanyin.
A flower among flowers
But what the flowers do not know, she knows.
A precious jade among jades
But with a fragrance that no jade possesses.

Ximen Qing was entranced. Although he had not touched her, his heart was hers. Yueniang and the others took her to the inner hall and there they greeted one another. Then Ximen Qing was sent for. He hastily put straight his hat and clothes and rushed in. To him the young lady seemed like a tree of jade come to this world from paradise, an angel from the Wu Mountain. He bowed very low. His heart was beating fast and his eyes were dazzled. It was all he could do to control himself. When he had greeted her, he withdrew.

Yueniang entertained her guests in the arbor. They had tea. Then the musicians played and the guests took their places in the great hall. Lady Lin sat in the place of honor. The actors played two acts of *Little T'ien Hsiang Worshipping the Stars at Midnight*. Then the four singing girls came to sing the song of the lanterns.

Meanwhile, Ximen Qing and his friends were drinking wine elsewhere, and the three boys, Li Ming, Wu Hui, and Zheng Chun, sang for them. But, all the time, Ximen Qing was peeping through the window into the great hall.

Readers, the moon cannot always be at the full, and the most glorious clouds are soon dispersed. Happiness reaches its height, but sorrow follows after. So, too, when ill fortune reaches its climax, consolation is at hand. This is the will of Heaven. Ximen Qing thought of nothing but of gaining renown and increasing his riches: he spent himself in luxurious living and the pursuit of women, and never checked himself. He did not realize that Heaven abhors extremes. But the officers of Hell were coming to summon him. His days were nearly done.

That evening, the lanterns were lighted and the boys sang. Even before the first night watch, Ximen Qing was snoring as he sat with the others. Bojue, trying to rouse him, asked him to play games and guess fingers.

"What makes you so sleepy, Brother?" he said. "Are you not happy today?"

"I did not sleep very well last night," Ximen said. "Today, I don't seem to have any energy."

The four singing girls came to them. Bojue bade two of them sing and the other two serve the wine. They were drinking happily when Daian came and said: "Lady Lin and Mistress He are going." Ximen Qing hastily left the table and stood in the shadow beside the second door to watch them go. Yueniang and the others came with them and, when they reached the courtyard, they waited for a while to look at the fireworks. Mistress He had changed her clothes. She was wearing a scarlet cloak with sables. Lady Lin wore a white silk coat with sable cape, gold pins, and jade ornaments. Servants, with lanterns, took the ladies to their chairs.

Ximen Qing looked at them with starving eyes; his mouth watered so that he could hardly swallow. But they were beyond his reach. At that moment—it might have happened in a fairy tale—Laijue's wife, seeing that the ladies had gone, came from the inner court. So she met Ximen Qing and could not get away. She was a pretty young woman and Ximen had long desired to possess her. She was not so sprightly as Laiwang's wife had been, but she was not far behind her. Ximen was stirred by the wine he had drunk. He took the woman in his arms, carried her into her room, and kissed her.

This woman had once been a maid in a princely household, but she had carried on with her master and had been sent away through the jealousy of the other servants. Today the same fate overtook her, and she had to yield. She slipped her tongue into his mouth. They both undressed. Ximen put her on the edge of the bed and raised her legs. Then he took his pleasure of her.

CHAPTER 79

The End of Ximen Qing

Men born in the south and the north
Travel different roads.
There is no certainty in the life of man
Creation disposes of us as it chooses
Lifts us up and sets us down,
Makes us lie outstretched or stand upright.
It is the same wherever we go.

We sigh in vain, thinking of what is past,
For fame and wealth and dignity
Are not things to be sought.
Whatever the course of our life may be, whether misery or joy
We must follow it.

Whether we live in splendid palaces
Or ride on steeds caparisoned with gold
Or inhabit humble dwellings
Or live in small thatched cottages
All will still shed tears.

When Ximen Qing had finished with the woman, he went back to drink with Uncle Wu and the others. The ladies stayed for a while, ate some dumplings in celebration of the Lunar Festival, and then went away. Chen Jingji saw that the actors were given a meal, and dismissed them with two taels of silver. The four singing girls and the three men stayed on, singing and serving wine for the men.

"Tomorrow is Brother Hua's birthday," Bojue said to Ximen Qing. "Have you sent him a present?"

"Yes, I sent him something this morning."

"Uncle Hua has sent you a card of invitation," Daian said.

"Are you going, Brother?" Bojue said. "If so, I will come for you and we will go together."

"I can't tell you now," Ximen said. "I advise you to go alone."

After a while the four singing girls went to the inner court, leaving only the three boys to entertain the men. Ximen Qing was very sleepy and nodded all the time.

"Brother-in-law," Uncle Wu said, "you are tired. We had better go."

Ximen Qing would not let them go before the second night watch. Then he sent away the singing girls and gave the boys two large cups of wine each and six *qian* of silver. As they were going away, he said to Li Ming: "I shall want you here on the fifteenth. I am going to invite their Lordships Zhou, Jing, He, and some others on that day. Don't forget. And I want you to engage four singing girls for me."

Li Ming knelt down and asked whom he would like to have. "There is that girl from the Fans' house," Ximen said, "and Qin Yuzhi, and, at Captain He's the other day, I saw a girl called Feng Jinbao. Then there is Lü Sai'er. They will do."

When Li Ming had gone, Ximen Qing went to Wu Yueniang's room.

"Lady Lin and Mistress Jing seemed to enjoy themselves," Yueniang said to him. "They did not go until very late, and Mistress Jing thanked me repeatedly. She said you had been extraordinarily helpful to her husband, and they would never forget your kindness. General Jing is going next month to the Huai country to see about the transport of the grain. Mistress He drank plenty of wine. She seems to have taken a fancy to the Fifth Lady. I took her to the garden and showed her the artificial mound. She gave some very generous gifts to the servants."

Ximen Qing spent the night with Yueniang. During the night she dreamed, and when daybreak came, she told her dream to her husband. "It may have been because Lady Lin was wearing a red cloak," she said, "but I dreamed that Li Ping'er took a red cloak from her box and dressed me in it. Pan Jinlian snatched it away from me and put it on herself. That made me angry, and I said to her: 'You have her fur coat already. Why should you want this too?' Then Jinlian grew angry and tore the cloak. I began to shout. Then I woke and found it was a dream."

"Don't let the dream worry you," Ximen said. "I will give you a coat. When people dream about a thing, it is always because they would like to possess it."

He got up, but his head was heavy, and he did not feel like going to the office. When he had dressed, he went to the study and sat down. Yuxiao brought him some of Ruyi'er's milk in a little jar, and Ximen took it with his medicine. Then he lay on the bed, and Wang Jing softly tapped his master's legs. When Yuxiao came, the boy withdrew. Ximen Qing gave her a pair of gold pins and four silver rings, and asked her to take them to Laijue's wife. Yuxiao realized that he was again repeating the experience he had had with Laiwang's wife. When she came back, she said: "She has accepted your gifts and is coming to kowtow to you." Then she took the empty jar and went away.

Yueniang had ordered Xiaoyu to cook some gruel for Ximen Qing, but he would not come and take it. Wang Jing had brought a packet from his sister, Wang Liu'er, and told his master she was anxious to see him. Ximen Qing opened the packet. In it was a tress of glossy dark hair, tied with five-colored silk, with a lovers' knot of silken ribbon. There was also an embroidered purple bag with two openings, filled with melon seeds. Ximen Qing examined everything very carefully. He was pleased. He put the bag on the shelf and the hair in his sleeve.

Suddenly Yueniang came into the room. Ximen was still lying on the bed, with Wang Jing working on his legs. "Why don't you come to breakfast instead of staying here?" she said. "What is it that makes you so languid?"

"I don't know. But I feel wretched and my legs hurt."

"Perhaps it is the weather," Yueniang said. "But now you are taking the medicine, you will soon be well again." She took him to her room and they had breakfast there.

"It is the New Year," Yueniang said, "and you ought to be merry. Why don't you go and see Uncle Hua? It is his birthday today. Or send for Brother Ying to come and have a chat."

"Ying is not at home today," Ximen said. "He has gone to Hua's place. Make something for me to eat, and I will go to the shop and see Uncle Wu the Second."

"Very well," Yueniang said, "order your horse. I will tell the maids to prepare something."

Ximen Qing told Daian to saddle his horse, then he dressed and went to Lion Street. The Feast of Lanterns was in full swing, and the street was very busy. The sound of horses and carriages was like thunder, and the lanterns were as beautiful as embroidered silk. People swarmed like ants.

Ximen looked at the lanterns, then went to the shop. Uncle Wu and Ben the Fourth were doing a very brisk trade. Laizhao's wife made a fire in the parlor and brought tea. After a while, Yueniang sent Qintong and Laian with two boxes of food. There was some Southern bean wine in the shop, and they opened a jar of this and went upstairs. Ximen Qing drank with Uncle Wu and Ben the Fourth and looked out at the lanterns. People were pressing up and down the street below.

Ximen Qing sent Wang Jing with a message to Wang Liu'er. When she heard, he was coming she hastily made preparations. Ximen told Laizhao to let Uncle Wu and Ben the Fourth have the rest of the food, and bade Qintong take a jar of wine to Han Daoguo's house. Then he mounted his horse and rode there. Wang Liu'er, all dressed up, welcomed him and kowtowed four times.

"Thank you for your presents," Ximen Qing said. "But why haven't you been to my house? I have twice sent you an invitation."

"Though I didn't go, no one came to urge me," Wang Liu'er said. "And I have not been very well these last few days. I have no appetite and I don't feel able to do anything that requires the slightest exertion."

"You must be thinking of your husband," Ximen said.

"Thinking of my husband!" Wang Liu'er cried. "It is because you have not been to see me. I thought I must have done something to annoy you. You have been treating me like the ring on a hairnet, which is always put out of sight. But perhaps you have another woman now."

Ximen Qing laughed. "Another woman?" he said. "No, all through this festival there have been so many parties that I have been too busy to come."

"You had a number of ladies yesterday, I hear," the woman said.

"Yes, my wife has been visiting them, and we had to do something in return."

"How many ladies were there?"

Ximen told her about the party.

"So, when you have a party for the Feast of Lanterns, you invite everybody of any importance, but you don't ask me."

"Oh, you mustn't let that upset you," Ximen said. "There will be another party on the sixteenth, and the wives of those who work with me will all be invited. I shall not allow you to refuse."

"If your lady sends me a card, how dare I refuse?" Wang Liu'er said. "By the way, the other day, one of your maids insulted Miss Shen, and she complained to me most bitterly about it. As a matter of fact, she did not wish to go that day, and I persuaded her. After the trouble she came here and cried till I didn't know what to do. Then you were kind enough to send a box and a tael of silver, and that put matters right. Your maid seems to have been in a very bad temper. She ought to know that, before she beats a dog, it is well to look and see what the master thinks about the matter."

"That little oily mouth has a very sharp tongue," Ximen Qing said. "She even treats me like that sometimes. But Miss Shen herself was in the wrong. She was asked to sing and she should have sung. When she refused, of course people got angry. She said a few things to the maid, too."

"She told me she never opened her mouth," Wang Liu'er said. "She said the maid came and insulted her and shook her fist at her. When she came here, tears were rolling down her cheeks and she never stopped blowing her nose. I kept her here for the night and then took her home."

The maid brought tea and old woman Feng came and kowtowed to Ximen Qing. He gave her a piece of silver worth about three or four *qian*. "You have not been to my place since your mistress died," he said.

"Where should I go now that she is dead?" the old woman said. "But I often come here to talk to this lady."

They took Ximen Qing into the inner room and asked whether he had had anything to eat.

"I had some gruel this morning," he said, "and, just before I came here, I had some cakes with Uncle Wu the Second. I am not particularly hungry."

Still, the table was set. The woman asked Wang Jing to open the jar of bean wine, and heated some. They sat down to drink.

"Did you get the things I sent you?" Wang Liu'er said. "I cut off a lock of my own hair and arranged it with my own hands. I thought you would like it."

"It was very kind of you," Ximen said.

When they had drunk wine enough, and there was nobody in the room, Ximen Qing took the ribbon from his sleeve, put it around his penis and tied it around his waist. Then he drank some medicine mixed with wine. Wang Liu'er stroked the prick, which quickly became proud and erect. The veins stood out; it looked like a piece of purple liver. The silk ribbon had far more effect than the clasp. Ximen Qing lifted her onto his lap and pressed his prick into her cunt. They drank wine, each from the other's mouth, and their tongues played together.

In the evening, old woman Feng made some dumplings with pork and radishes for them. Wang Liu'er ate some with him and, when the maid had cleared away, they went to the bed. They pulled aside the silken curtains and took off their clothes. The woman knew that Ximen Qing liked to do things in the light, and she set the lamp on a small table near the bed. Then she made fast the door and went to wash her cunt. When she came back, she took off her trousers and went to bed. They lay down together and put their arms around one another. Ximen Qing was still thinking of Captain He's wife and his passion blazed like fire. His penis was very hard. He told her to get onto hands and knees like a horse, and he plunged to the flower in her bottom. He did this six hundred times, while her behind showed its noisy approbation. She felt down her body, played with the flower in her belly, and called him endearing names unceasingly.

Still Ximen was not content. He sat up, put on a white short coat and set a pillow beneath him. Then he bade the woman turn over and tied her feet with two ribbons to the bedposts. He began by playing the game of the golden dragon stretching its claws, and thrust this way and that, sometimes plunging deep, sometimes just a little way. He was afraid she might catch cold and wrapped a red silk coat about her body. He brought the light nearer and bent his head to watch the movements. Whenever he took out his penis, he put it in again right up to the hilt; he did this six hundred times. The woman, her voice trembling, called him every endearing word she could think of. Soon he withdrew completely and put some of the red powder on the tip of his penis; when it was set in motion again it so stimulated her cunt that she could hardly bear it. She climbed on top of him and begged him to go in deeper; but he deliberately played about the opening, touching the treasure inside only lightly and refusing to go in further. Love juices flowed from her like slime from a snail. In the candlelight Ximen beheld her white legs raised about his body on either side. He saw them quivering in response to his movements, which became still more violent.

"Do you love me, you strumpet?" he asked her.

"I have been thinking about you all the time," she said. "I can only hope that you will be like the pine tree and the cypress, evergreen. Do not weary of me and give me up. If you should do that, it would kill me. I dare not tell this to anyone else, and nobody knows it. And I shall not tell that turtle of mine. He is away and he has money. He has other women and need not bother about me."

"My child," Ximen said, "if you will give yourself entirely to me, I will find another wife for him when he comes back and then you can belong to me always."

"Darling," Wang Liu'er said, "do get him another wife. Whether you take me into your household or leave me outside does not matter. Do as you please. I give my worthless body to you utterly and entirely and I will do anything you wish."

"I know you," Ximen Qing said.

They went on for a very long time. Then Ximen unloosed the ribbons that tied her feet, and they went to sleep together. About the third night watch he got up, put on his clothes, and washed his hands. Wang Liu'er opened the door and bade the maid bring them wine and food. They drank again. After more than ten cups of wine, Ximen began to feel tipsy and asked for tea to rinse his mouth. He took a paper from his sleeve and gave it to Wang Liu'er. "Take this to clerk Gan, and ask him for a dress," he said. "You can choose your own pattern and design." She thanked him, and he went away. Wang Jing carried a lantern and Daian and Qintong led his horse, one on either side.

It was the third night watch. Dark clouds covered the sky, and the light of the moon could hardly pierce them. The street was deserted; only the barking of dogs could be heard in the distance. Ximen Qing went westwards. Suddenly, as he came near the stone bridge, a whirlwind swept before his horse. It was like a dark form advancing from the bridge to attack him. His horse was startled and reared. Ximen shuddered. He whipped his horse. It shook its mane. Daian and Qintong clung to the bridle with all their strength, but they could not hold it, and the horse galloped wildly till it came to Ximen's gateway. Then it stopped. Wang Jing, with the lantern, was left far behind. When Ximen Qing dismounted, his legs were almost useless, and servants came out to help him in. He went to Pan Jinlian's room.

Jinlian had come back from the inner court, but she had not gone to bed. She was lying upon her bed, dressed, waiting for Ximen Qing. When he came, she got up at once. She took his clothes and saw that he was drunk, but she asked no questions. Ximen put his hands on her shoulders and drew her towards him.

"You little strumpet!" he murmured, "your darling is drunk. Get the bed ready: I want to go to sleep."

She helped him to bed, and, as soon as he was on it, he began to snore like thunder. She could do nothing to wake him, so she took off her clothes and went to bed too. She played delicately with his weapon, but it was as limp as cotton wool and had not the slightest spirit. She tossed about on the bed, consumed with passionate desire, almost beside herself. She pressed his prick, rubbed it up and down, bent her head to suck it; it was in vain. This made her wild beyond description. She shook him for a long time and at last he awoke. She asked him where his medicine was. Ximen, still very drunk, cursed her.

"You little strumpet!" he cried, "what do you want that for? You would like me to play with you, I suppose, but today your darling is far too tired for anything of that sort. The medicine is in the little gold box in my sleeve. Give it to me. You will be in luck if you make my prick stand up."

Jinlian looked for the little gold box and, when she found it, opened it. There were only three or four pills left. She took a wine pot and poured out two cups of wine. She took one pill herself, leaving three. Then she made the terrible mistake of giving him all three. She was afraid anything less would have no effect. Ximen shut his eyes and swallowed them. Before he could have drunk a cup of tea, the medicine began to take effect. Jinlian tied the silken ribbon for him and his staff stood up. He was still asleep. She mounted upon his body, put some powder on the top of his penis, and put that in her cunt; immediately it penetrated right to the heart of her.

Her body seemed to melt away with delight. Then, with her two hands grasping his legs, she moved up and down about two hundred times. First it was difficult, because she was dry, but soon the juices of love flowed and moistened her cunt. Ximen Qing let her do everything she wished, but he himself was perfectly inert. She could bear it no longer. She put her tongue into his mouth. She held his neck and shook it. She writhed on his penis, which was entirely inside her cunt; only the two testicles remained outside. She caressed it with her hand, and it looked remarkably fine. The juices flowed; in no time she had used up five handkerchiefs. Still Ximen persevered, although the head of his prick was swollen and hotter than burning coal. The ribbon felt so tight that he asked her to remove it, but the penis stayed erect, and he asked her to suck it. She bent down and, taking it in her lips, sucked it and moved up and down. Suddenly the white sperm squirted out like living silver; she took it in her mouth and could not swallow it fast enough. At first it was sperm, and then it became an unceasing flow of blood. Ximen Qing had fainted and his limbs were stiff outstretched.

Jinlian was frightened. She hastily gave him some red dates. Blood followed sperm, cold air followed blood. Jinlian was terrified. She threw her arms around him and cried: "Darling, how do you feel?"

It was some time before Ximen came to himself. He said: "My head and eyes spin. I wonder what is the matter."

"What makes you yield so much today?" Jinlian said. "You must have taken too much medicine."

Readers, there is a limit to our energy, but none to our desires. A man who sets no bounds to his passion cannot live more than a short time. Ximen had given himself to the enjoyment of women, and he did not realize that he was like a lantern whose oil is exhausted and whose light is failing. Now his seed was used up, there was nothing in store for him but death. As we said at the beginning of this book:

> Beautiful is this maiden; her tender form gives promise of sweet
> womanhood,
> But a two-edged sword lurks between her thighs, whereby destruc-
> tion comes to foolish men.
> No head falls to that sword: its work is done in secret,
> Yet it drains the very marrow from men's bones.

The next morning, when Ximen Qing got up and went to dress, he suddenly felt dizzy and almost fell forward. Fortunately, Chunmei caught him and he did not actually fall. He sat down on a chair, and it was some time before he recovered. Jinlian was again frightened.

"You must be hungry," she said. "Stay here, and tell me what you would like to eat. I will not let you go until you have had something."

She told Qiuju to go to the kitchen for gruel.

"I want some gruel," Qiuju said to Sun Xue'e. "Father fainted and now he has asked for gruel."

Wu Yueniang heard this and came at once to ask Qiuju what was the matter. The maid told her how Ximen had nearly fallen when he was doing his hair. Yueniang was greatly upset. She urged Xue'e to hurry with the gruel and went at once to see her husband in Jinlian's room. He was still sitting on the chair.

"What is the matter?" Yueniang said.

"I don't know," Ximen said, "but my head feels very bad."

"It was fortunate Chunmei and I were there to catch him, or he would have hurt himself badly," Jinlian said. "He is so heavy."

"Perhaps his head is dizzy from drinking too much wine last night," Yueniang said.

"Yes," Jinlian said. "Where did you go drinking yesterday, that you came in so late?"

"He had something to eat in the shop with my brother," Yueniang said.

Chunmei brought the gruel. She gave some to Ximen Qing, but he ate only half a bowl and then set it aside.

"How does your head feel?" Yueniang asked him.

"It is not so bad now," he said, "but I don't seem to have any strength or energy at all."

"Don't go to the office today," Yueniang said.

"No, I won't. I'll go to the outer court and get Jingji to write some invitations. I am going to ask Zhou and Jing and Captain He to come on the fifteenth."

"You haven't had your medicine," Yueniang said. "Get some milk. You must take that. I think you must have been overdoing things the last few days."

She told Chunmei to get some milk from Ruyi'er, and the maid brought it in a bowl. Ximen took it with his medicine and went to the outer court. Chunmei helped him. When they came to the corner gate that led to the garden, his eyes clouded over; his body seemed to collapse, and he could not hold himself up. Chunmei took him back again.

"Listen to me," Yueniang said. "You must have a rest. We will postpone these invitations. There is no real need to write them now. Do absolutely nothing, and don't go out. And tell me anything you would like to eat. I'll make it for you."

"I don't want anything," Ximen said.

Yueniang went to the inner court and questioned Jinlian. She asked whether Ximen Qing had been drunk when he came in the previous night, whether he had had any more to drink, and if he had busied himself with her.

Jinlian was so full of denials that she hated herself because she had only one mouth to express them.

"Oh, no, Sister," she said. "He came back so late and he was so drunk that he never thought of such a thing. He asked me for more wine, but I gave him tea instead. I told him there was no wine and he must go to sleep. I have had nothing to do with him since you spoke to me the other day. I don't like to say anything, but I fancy he had been somewhere before he came home. But I'm not at all sure. I can only tell you that I had nothing to do with him in that way."

Wu Yueniang and Meng Yulou sent for Daian and Qintong and questioned them closely.

"Where did your father go drinking yesterday?" the Great Lady asked. "Tell me the truth. If you don't, and anything happens, I shall hold you two responsible."

Daian refused to say anything except that his master had gone to Lion Street and had taken wine there with Uncle Wu the Second and Ben the Fourth. Yueniang sent for her brother. "Do you know," she asked him, "if your brother-in-law went anywhere else after he took wine with you?"

"He stayed only a short time with us," Uncle Wu said. "Then he went away again."

This made Yueniang very angry. As soon as her brother had gone, she sent for the two boys again. She scolded them severely and threatened them with a beating. This frightened them, and they confessed that Ximen had been to see Han Daoguo's wife. Jinlian was waiting for this.

"Now, Sister," she said, "you see you have been blaming me, and I am innocent. The one who is really guilty is laughing at us. Just as every tree has its own bark, so each one of us has his own face to consider. How can you think that I exist only for things of that sort? You might perhaps ask these two slaves where our husband was the other day when you went to see Mistress He. It was very late when he came back and I don't believe he had been paying New Year calls."

Before Qintong had time to speak, Daian told them how his master had been carrying on with Lady Lin.

"No wonder he was so anxious we should send her an invitation," Yueniang said. "I said to him: 'We have never met her, and she certainly won't come.' Of course, we never dreamed of what was going on. No wonder that, in spite of her age, she paints her eyebrows and powders her face till it looks like the plaster on the wall. The old strumpet!"

"I have never heard of anybody like her," Yulou said, "and with a grown-up son too! It would be better for her to marry again than to carry on in this shameless way."

"The old whore doesn't know what shame is," Jinlian said.

"I didn't think she would come," Yueniang said, "yet she had the audacity to do so."

"Sister," Jinlian said, "now you see who is black and who is white. You scolded me when it was Han Daoguo's wife who was really to blame. It looks as though, in this household, almost everybody has a lover in secret. They are turtles openly and even send their young turtles here so that those young turtles can help them in their evil games."

"It is not for you to call Wang the Third's mother a whore," Yueniang said. "She told me that, when you were young, you were a maid at her place."

Jinlian's face became scarlet. "The old whore is mad," she said. "When was I ever at her place? My aunt was a neighbor of hers, and when I used to go and stay with my aunt, I occasionally went to the Lin woman's garden to play with other little girls. I come from her place, do I? Why, I know nothing whatever about her. She is just a blind old strumpet."

"You have too much to say," Yueniang said. "I only told you what she said, and there is no need for you to make such a fuss about it."

Jinlian was silent.

Yueniang told Xue'e to make some meat-stuffed dumplings for Ximen Qing. As she passed the second door, she saw Ping'an going to the garden. She stopped him and asked what he was about.

"Li Ming has engaged four singing girls for the party on the fifteenth and has come to know if everything is all right," Ping'an told her. "I told him the invitations had not been sent out yet, but he wouldn't be satisfied with that and asked me to go and see Father."

"Party?" Yueniang said. "What party, you rascal? What are you going to ask? Go and tell that young turtle to be off about his business? What is all the excitement about?"

Ping'an ran away in bewilderment.

Yueniang went back to Jinlian's room. She told Ximen Qing that Li Ming had come to inquire about the singing girls. "I told him we shouldn't need any as the party had been postponed," she said.

Ximen Qing nodded. He expected to be better in a day or two, but when one day had passed his warrior swelled up and there were red scrofulous spots on it. The testicles were swollen too, and as bright-colored as a tomato. When he pissed, it hurt like the cutting of a knife, and this pain he felt every time. The soldiers came to take him to the office, and were grieved to hear of his illness.

"You must do what I tell you," Yueniang said to him. "Send a card to Captain He and tell him that you must rest at home until you are stronger. And we must send at once for Doctor Ren, and get him to give you some medicine. This is serious, and we must not put off any longer. You can't go on in this state. You haven't had a proper meal for two or three days. Besides, you really are very much swollen."

But Ximen would not send for the doctor. He said: "Oh, it is nothing very serious. I shall be better in a few days and ready to go out."

He sent a card to the office excusing himself. He was very irritable and impatient at being in bed.

Ying Bojue heard he was not well and came to see him. Ximen asked him to come in. Bojue bowed and said: "I didn't know you were not well. So that is why you didn't go to Uncle Hua's place the other day."

"I should certainly have gone if I had been well," Ximen Qing said. "I don't know why, but I have not had energy enough even to move."

"What is the trouble, Brother?" Bojue asked him.

"Nothing very particular?" Ximen said. "My head feels heavy; my limbs seem to give way under me, and I can't seem to walk."

"Your face is flushed," Bojue said, "and judging by that, I think you must have some fever. Have you sent for a doctor?"

"No," Ximen said, "my wife talked about sending for Doctor Ren, but I told her not to bother because it wasn't serious enough."

"You are wrong, Brother," Bojue said. "You must send for him at once and let him have a look at you and give you some medicine to get rid of this fever. It is Spring now and a dangerous season for the lungs. I met Li Ming yesterday. He told me he had been bidden to engage some singing girls for a party you were giving today, but that you were not well and the party had been put off. That gave me quite a shock, and I came to see you at once."

"I haven't been to the office," Ximen said. "I sent a card of excuse."

"You certainly must not go out," Bojue said. "You need a rest."

After drinking tea, Bojue said he must go and that he would come again. "Li Guijie and Wu Yin'er will come and see you, I'm sure," he said. Ximen Qing asked him to stay and have something to eat, but he said he would rather not, and went away.

Then Ximen told Qintong to go for Dr. Ren. The doctor came and felt his pulse. "The fever is mounting," the doctor said, "and there is exhaustion of the fluid in your testicles. It is clearly a case of sexual exhaustion. I will give you something to supply the missing element."

He went away. Ximen Qing sent him five *qian* of silver, and a boy brought back the medicine. After taking it his head felt better, but his body was so weak that he could not get up. His prick swelled more and more and it was increasingly difficult for him to make water.

In the afternoon Li Guijie and Wu Yin'er came with presents. When they had kowtowed to Ximen Qing, they asked how he was.

"It is very good of you, Sisters, to come and see me, but why did you bother to buy presents?" he said. "For some reason I seem to have a little fever."

"Perhaps you have been drinking too much wine during the New Year celebrations," Guijie said. "You will be all right if you don't drink any more for a few days."

They went to the Sixth Lady's room. There they found Yueniang and the others, and were asked to go and take tea in the inner court. Afterwards they went back to Ximen Qing.

Then Ying Bojue, Xie Xida, and Chang Zhijie came. Ximen Qing told Yuxiao to prop him up in bed and asked the three men to stay for wine.

"Brother," Xie Xida said, "have you had any rice gruel?"

Yuxiao turned her head away and did not answer. Ximen Qing said: "No, I have not had any. I couldn't eat it."

"Well, send for some," Xie Xida said. "We will have some with you."

After a while, the rice gruel was brought. Ximen ate half a bowl and set it down again.

Guijie and Wu Yin'er had gone to join Yueniang in the Sixth Lady's room. Bojue asked where they were. Ximen Qing told him.

"Go and tell them to come and sing a song for your father," Bojue said to Laian.

But Yueniang would not let the girls go. She thought that Ximen Qing was in no condition to listen to songs, and told Laian to say to Ying Bojue that the girls were having something to eat with her.

When the three friends had drunk some wine, one of them said: "Brother, you will be tired if we keep you sitting up. We will go now and you must lie down for a while." Ximen thanked them for coming, and they went away.

When Ying Bojue came to the door of the smaller courtyard, he called Daian and said to him: "I don't like the look of your father's face at all. Go and tell the Great Lady she ought to send for a doctor at once. Hu, in the High Street, is very good in fever cases. I suggest you send for him, but you mustn't waste any time."

Daian went at once and told his mistress. She went to Ximen Qing. "Brother Ying says that Doctor Hu is very good in fever cases," she said to him. "Why shouldn't we send for him?"

"Why should we?" Ximen Qing replied. "He didn't do Li Ping'er the slightest good."

"Medicine will only cure cases that can be cured," Yueniang said, "and Buddha saves only those who merit salvation. You do not think he is any good, but, if he cures you, that is all we care about."

"Very well, send for him," Ximen Qing said.

In a short time, Qitong brought the doctor. Uncle Wu was there, and he was present while the doctor examined Ximen's pulse.

"The poison is concentrated in the lower parts," Dr. Hu said to Uncle Wu and Chen Jingji. "Something must be done at once, or he will begin to make blood all the time instead of water. This has been caused by his indulging in sexual intercourse without first making water."

They gave him five *qian* of silver for medicine and made Ximen Qing take it. But it was like throwing a piece of stone into the sea. He could not make water at all. Yueniang was very much alarmed. She sent away the two singing girls and sent a messenger for He Qixuan, the son of old He. He told them that there was an accumulation of poison in the male organ and that the bladder was very much inflamed. The fever was driving the poison downwards. Ximen's veins, the doctor said, were filled with poisonous matter, and his heart and kidneys were completely out of harmony.

They gave the doctor five *qian* of silver. Ximen drank the prescribed medicine, but the penis stayed erect, as if made of imperishable iron. Throughout the night, in her ignorance of the harm she was doing, she played with him, mounted his body, and put his candle into herself. He fainted several times.

The next day, Captain He came to see him. When a boy came in to announce him, Yueniang said: "Captain He has come to see you. This is not a fit place to receive anybody. Shall I take you to the inner court?"

Ximen Qing nodded. Yueniang put some clothes on him and she and Pan Jinlian helped him to go to the upper room. There they made a bed, cleaned out the place, and burned incense. Chen Jingji took in Captain He.

"Sir," the Captain said, "I will not exchange formal greetings with you today. How do you feel?"

"My head is better," Ximen said, "but I have still a great deal of pain down below."

"It looks like a case of poisoned urine," Captain He said. "Now it so happens that, yesterday, a friend of mine called to see me on his way to Dongchangfu to visit his people. He comes from Fenzhou in Shaanxi and his name is Liu Juzhai. He is very well versed in troubles of this kind. May I send him to see you?"

"It is very good of you," Ximen Qing said. "I will send someone to ask him to come."

Captain He drank his tea. "Sir," he said, "you must take great care of yourself. Don't bother about things at the office. I can manage quite well."

Ximen Qing raised his hand. "You are very kind," he said.

When Captain He had gone, Ximen told Daian to take a card and go with one of Ho's servants for Liu Juzhai. Liu felt his pulse, put some medicine upon the affected part, and gave him a dose of something to be taken with water. Ximen Qing gave him a roll of Hangzhou silk and a tael of silver. He took the first dose, but there was no improvement.

That day, Zheng Aiyue brought him a pair of young pigeons and a box of fruit pastries. She came in a sedan chair. When she had kowtowed to him, she said: "I did not know you were ill. That excellent pair, Li Guijie and Wu Yin'er, came before me, yet they never said a word to me about it. That is why I did not come before."

"Why have you troubled to bring these things for me?" Ximen said.

"They are not intended as proper presents," Zheng Aiyue said, smiling. "They are only something for you to taste."

"We are very anxious for him to take something, but he doesn't seem able to do so," Yueniang said. "This morning he has only had a mouthful of rice gruel. The doctor has just gone."

"Mother, will you ask one of your maids to cook these young pigeons? They are very tender, and perhaps he will try one of them with his gruel. You must eat something," she said to Ximen Qing. "You are a big man, like a mountain of gold, and you have a whole household dependent on you."

"He has no appetite," Yueniang said.

"Father," Zheng Aiyue said, "listen to me. You must eat something even if you don't feel like it. We are human beings. We have no roots such as plants have, and we must eat and drink to live. If you don't eat anything, you will waste away."

Before long, one of the young pigeons was cooked. Xiaoyu brought it with the rice gruel and some preserved fruits. Zheng Aiyue jumped on to the bed and sat down on her heels before Ximen Qing. She took the bowl in her hand and tried to make him eat. He did his best, but could only swallow a few spoonfuls of gruel and a little pigeon. Then he shook his head and would try no more.

"You need two things to make you better," Zheng Aiyue said, "medicine and food. I am glad to see you take even a little."

"He would not have eaten anything at all if you had not come," Yux-iao said.

Zheng Aiyue had some tea, then Yueniang entertained her and sent her away with five *qian* of silver. Before she left, the girl went and kow-towed to Ximen Qing. "Be patient," she said, "I will come again soon."

That evening, Ximen Qing took a second dose of Dr.. Liu's medi-cine. But his body began to ache all over and he groaned the whole night through. In the fifth night watch, his testicles swelled up and burst and blood poured upon the bedclothes. Sores came out on the end of his penis, and a yellow liquid came from them. The whole household rushed in a turmoil to his bedside. They realized that the medicine had done him no good and sent for old woman Liu to light a spirit lamp that they might know whether he would live or die. Then they sent a boy to Major Zhou's house to find out where the Immortal Wu was. They remembered how he had told them long ago that Ximen Qing would suffer as he was doing, and now his prophecy was fulfilled. Ben the Fourth told them that there was no need to send the boy to Major Zhou's place. The holy man was staying at the temple of the local god outside the walls. "He is spend-ing his time there," Ben the Fourth said, "telling fortunes, curing the sick, and practicing divination. He never cares what people pay him, but goes wherever he is wanted."

Yueniang sent Qintong to ask him to come.

When the Immortal came, he looked at Ximen Qing and found him entirely changed. His face was worn and thin, and his spirits low. He was lying on the bed with a kerchief tied about his head. The Immortal felt his pulse.

"Sir," he said, "you are ill because you have taken too much wine and had too much to do with women. Now your vital fluid is exhausted and a furious fever has taken hold upon the instrument of your passion. I fear I can do nothing for you. Your case is hopeless."

"If you can give him no medicine to make him well," Yueniang said, "perhaps you will tell us what the Fates say of him."

The Immortal made calculations upon his fingers and reckoned Ximen's eight characters. "His animal is the Tiger," he said, "he was born on the *renwu* day of the *wushen* month, of the *bingyin* year, and at the *bingchen* hour. The present year is *wuxu*, and he is thirty-three years old. But for calculating his fate we must take the year as *guihai*, and this is unfavorable, viewed in regard to the position of fire and earth. In this year, the *wu* earth is in conflict with the *ren* water. And this month hap-pens to be *wuyin*, so that there are three *wus*, all against him. He cannot withstand them."

Now he comes into conflict with the star of evil omen
His body is light and yet heavy. He is in desperate straits.
Beware the day and the hour of the planet Jupiter
For then the gods will knit their brows.

"Since the Fates are of such evil omen, is there nothing you can do for him?" Yueniang asked.

"The White Tiger is standing before him at this moment, and the Angel of Death is presiding over his destiny. Heaven itself can do nothing now, and even the Year Star Jupiter could not avert calamity. It is the will of Heaven, and neither god nor spirit can alter it."

Yueniang gave the Immortal a roll of cloth, and he went away. She sought diviners and soothsayers, but everywhere she was told that the omens were against her husband's life. That night, she burned incense in the courtyard and took an oath before Heaven. "If my husband recovers," she swore, "I will go every year for three years to the peak in Tai'an District to offer incense and a robe to the Goddess there." And Yulou took an oath to offer sacrifice to the stars every seventh day. Only Jinlian and Li Jiao'er did not take any oaths.

At one time, when Ximen was in a half-fainting state, he thought he saw Hua Zixu and Wu Da standing before him, come to demand payment of the debt he owed them. He would not speak of this but asked that he should not be left alone.

Once, when Yueniang was out of the room, he took Jinlian's hand, and cried. "My love," he said, "when I am dead, you sisters must keep my tablet and stay together."

Jinlian was very sorrowful. "I am afraid I shall not be wanted here any longer," she said.

"When the Great Lady comes, I will speak to her," Ximen said.

When Yueniang came back, she found them both with eyes red with crying. "Tell me what you want," she said. "We have been together as husband and wife so long now."

Ximen sobbed quietly. "I know I am going to die," he said, "and I want to say this. When your baby is born, I should like you all to stay here and bring him up together. You must not let the household go to pieces so that the neighbors come to look down upon it." He pointed to Jinlian. "Forgive her for all the things she has done wrong."

Yueniang could restrain herself no longer. Tears rolled down her cheeks like pearls. She sobbed aloud. Ximen asked her to summon Chen Jingji. When the young man came, Ximen said: "My son, if I had a son of my own, I could count on him. But, as yet, I have no son, and I must put all my trust in you. I look upon you as my own son and, if anything should happen to me, it will be for you to bury me. Afterwards, stay here and help your mother and keep up the good renown of this house. The silk shop is worth fifty thousand taels, but part of that belongs to our kinsman Qiao. Tell Fu to dispose of as much stock as is necessary, pay off our kinsman, then close the shop. The thread shop of which Ben the Fourth is in charge is worth six thousand five hundred taels, and the silk shop that Uncle Wu the Second looks after, five thousand taels. Both those shops should be closed as soon as the stuff can be sold. If Li the Third gets the contract we have spoken about, it will be better not to go further in the matter. Ask Uncle Ying to get somebody else to take it up. Li the Third and Huang the Fourth still owe me five hundred taels with interest amounting to another hundred and fifty. Ask them for payment. You and Clerk Fu can look after the household and the two shops that are here. The pawnshop is worth about twenty thousand taels and the medicine shop five thousand. Clerk Han and Laibao are still in Songjiang. When the river is free from ice, fetch them home again. They have about four thousand taels' worth of merchandise. Sell it and give the money to your mother. Liu, the Director of Studies, owes me three hundred taels. Hua owes me fifty. Xu the Fourth, outside the city, owes me, including interest due, about three hundred and forty. We have all the necessary documents, and you can ask them for payment at once. It will be best to sell the two houses, the one in Lion Street and the one opposite, because they will be too much for your mother to control."

Then he began to cry. Jingji promised to do all that Ximen had said. Clerk Fu, Clerk Gan, Uncle Wu the Second, Ben the Fourth and Cui Ben came to see him. He gave each of them his instructions, and each one in turn told him not to be alarmed because he was not really very ill. A great many people came to visit him and, when they saw how ill he was, went away sighing.

Yueniang still hoped that Ximen might get better, but Heaven had destined him for no more than thirty-three years of life. In the fifth night watch on the twenty-first day of the first month, the fever consumed him. He panted like an ox and so continued for a long time. He lingered on until mid morning, and then, alas and alack, his breathing ceased and he passed away.

Ximen Qing died before a coffin had been made ready for him. Yueniang hurriedly sent for Wu the Second and Ben the Fourth, opened a chest, and took out four bars of silver. These she gave to the two men and told them to buy a set of coffin boards. They had hardly left her when she felt a severe pain in her belly. She hurried to her room, lay down on the bed, and lost consciousness. Yulou, Jinlian and Xue'e were in the other room, dressing Ximen Qing in his robes. When Xiaoyu told them that the Great Lady was lying on the bed, Yulou and Li Jiao'er hurriedly went to her. They saw her with her hand pressed to her stomach, and knew that her time had come. Yulou left Li Jiao'er to look after Yueniang while she went to send a boy for old woman Cai. Li Jiao'er sent Yuxiao for Ruyi'er and, when Yulou returned, she had disappeared.

Yueniang was unconscious; the chest was lying open, and there was nobody about. Li Jiao'er took five bars of silver and went off with them to her own room. She came back with some paper.

"I could not find any paper here, so I went to my own room to get some," she said to Yulou.

Yulou suspected nothing. She looked after Yueniang and made everything ready. Yueniang's pains increased and the baby was born almost as soon as old woman Cai came.

Ximen Qing was laid out, stiff and cold, in the other room, and the whole household began to bemoan him.

Old woman Cai attended to the baby, cut the navel string, and they made a soothing drink for Yueniang and helped her to bed. Yueniang gave the old woman three taels of silver, but this did not satisfy her.

"When the other lady had a baby, you gave me more than this," she said. "I want now what I had then. Besides, this is your own baby."

"Things are different now," Yueniang said. "My husband is dead. Take this, and, when you come on the third day, I will give you another tael, no more."

"I would rather have a dress," the old woman said. She thanked the ladies and went away.

When Yueniang was a little better, she noticed that the chest was open. She scolded Yuxiao. "You should not have left the chest open with so many people about when I was unconscious. Hadn't you sense enough to lock it up?"

"I was sure you had locked it," Yuxiao said, "and I didn't give it a thought." She took the key and locked it.

When Yulou saw that Yueniang was in a suspicious mood, she did not stay very long. She said to Jinlian: "You see the sort of woman the Great Lady is. The moment her husband is dead, she begins to suspect people." She had no idea that Li Jiao'er had stolen five bars of silver.

Uncle Wu the Second and Ben the Fourth went to see Shang and bought from him a set of coffin boards. They engaged carpenters to make them up, and the boys carried Ximen Qing to the great hall. Then they sent for Xu, the Master of the Yin Yang, to write his certificate. Uncle

Wu came too, and he, his brother, and the clerks were all very busy in the outer hall. They took down the lanterns, rolled up the pictures, placed a sheet of paper over Ximen's body, and set lamps and incense on a table before it. Laian was left to strike the bell.

The Master of the Yin Yang looked at Ximen's hands and declared that he had died exactly at the hour of the Dragon, and that no harm would come to anyone in the household. After consulting Yueniang, he decided that Ximen should be put in his coffin on the third day. The grave was to be dug on the sixteenth of the second month, and the funeral held on the thirtieth. There would thus be more than four complete weeks between Ximen's death and his burial.

When Xu had gone away, they began to send out the sad news to all their friends and acquaintances. They sent the seal of his office to Captain He. Everyone in the household dressed in mourning, and a temporary building was set up.

On the third day Buddhist monks came to hold the first service and to burn paper money. Chen Jingji was dressed as Ximen's son, and stood before the body to receive those who came. Yueniang was not able to appear but was in a small room near by. Li Jiao'er and Yulou entertained the ladies. Jinlian, who was now in charge of the household funds, took in all the offerings that people sent. Xue'e stayed in the kitchen and superintended the preparation of tea and food for the visitors. Clerk Fu and Uncle Wu the Second kept the accounts. Ben the Fourth saw that mourning was distributed to the proper people. Laixing was responsible for the supply of provisions. Uncle Wu and Clerk Gan entertained the men who came.

When old woman Cai came to wash the baby, Yueniang gave her a silken dress and dismissed her. She called the baby Xiaoge.* The neighbors sent noodles as a token of congratulation. The news that Ximen Qing's first wife had borne a child immediately after his death had quickly spread. People said it was a very strange thing that a child should be born almost at the very moment of his father's death.

When Ying Bojue heard of Ximen's death, he came to bemoan his friend. The two uncles Wu were watching an artist paint a portrait of Ximen Qing.

"What a sad business!" Bojue said to them. "Even in my dreams I cannot bring myself to believe that our brother has gone." He asked to be allowed to pay his respects to Yueniang.

"My sister cannot appear," Uncle Wu said. "She gave birth to a son the very day of her husband's death."

---

*   Filial Devotion.

This was a surprise to Bojue. "Really?" he said. "That means that our brother has an heir to all his property."

Chen Jingji, in the deepest mourning, came and kowtowed to Ying Bojue.

"You have all my sympathy," Bojue said to him. "Your father is dead and your ladies are like stagnant water. You must be very careful. Do not do things as you yourself think they ought to be done. Consult your two uncles here. If you will forgive me for saying so, you are still very young and have hardly sufficient experience in business and affairs."

"No, Brother," Uncle Wu said, "I have too much other business to attend to. His mother is here."

"The Great Lady is here, it is true," Bojue said, "but she cannot attend to affairs outside the house. You will have to do what you can for her and you will remember the maxim that the uncle on the mother's side must always take a great part in the control of the family. You are not a stranger: you are the child's own uncle and the most important person in the household. Nobody here stands higher than you do." He asked when the funeral was to be.

"The grave will be dug on the sixteenth and the funeral will be on the thirtieth," he was told.

When the Master of the Yin Yang came again, Ximen Qing was put into his coffin and it was nailed up with longevity nails. The coffin was set in position, with a tablet bearing the words "General Ximen."

Captain He came and made reverence to the body. Uncle Wu and Ying Bojue gave him tea. Captain He asked about the funeral and gave orders that the soldiers who had been on duty at Ximen's house should remain there. Nobody was to go away before the day of the funeral. He appointed two sergeants to command the soldiers and declared that he would punish anyone who should dare to misbehave.

"If there is anyone who owes money, let me know," he said to Uncle Wu. "I will see what I can do to secure payment."

He went back to the office and sent a report of Ximen's death to the Eastern Capital.

When Laijue, Chunhong and Li the Third came to Yanzhou, they gave their letter and the present to the Censor. Song read it. It was a request that Ximen Qing might have the commission for the purchase of antiquities. "It is too late," he said to himself, "I have already given instructions about the matter to the Prefect." Then he saw that there were ten taels of gold leaf, and decided that it would be a pity to refuse. He told Chunhong, Laijue and Li the Third to wait and sent one of his officers in all haste to bring back the document from Dongpingfu. When it arrived, he gave it with a letter to Chunhong, together with a tael of silver for travel-ing money. The journey between the two places took about ten days, and when they reached Qinghe again they learned that Ximen Qing was dead. He had been dead three days, and, at that moment, service was being held for him.

Li the Third had an idea. He said to Laijue and Chunhong: "Let us keep this document and say his Excellency would not let us have it. Then we can take it to Chang. If you two don't care to come with me, I will give each of you ten taels and you can go home and keep your mouths shut."

Laijue did not object, but Chunhong would have nothing to do with the scheme. He would not promise anything.

When they came to the gate, paper money was hanging up and the monks were busy at their prayers. There were many people present. Li the Third went home, but Laijue and Chunhong came in and kowtowed to Uncle Wu and Chen Jingji. They were asked about the document and where Li the Third was, and, before Laijue could say anything, Chunhong handed the letter and the document to Uncle Wu. He told him that Li the Third had offered him ten taels to keep the letter and go to Chang's place with him. "I told him I would not do anything so shameful," the boy said, "and came straight to you.

Uncle Wu went to the inner court. "This young lad is really extraordi-narily honest," he said to Yueniang, "but what a dirty trick of that wicked fellow Li the Third, as soon as he heard of your husband's death!"

He went to Ying Bojue. "We have a note," he said, "showing that Li the Third and Huang the Fourth still owe us six hundred and fifty taels. As Captain He has advised, we will send the note to his office and ask him to make them pay. He will certainly not refuse, seeing that he was the dead man's colleague."

"Li the Third certainly ought not to have done such a thing, but do not make too much of it, Uncle," Bojue said. "I will go and speak to him about it."

He went to Li the Third's house, and they sent for Huang the Fourth. "You should not have offered the boys money," Bojue said. "That gave them a hold over you. Now you are like the man who was too slow to catch the fox and only came in for the smell. They are talking about going to the courts, and you know how those officials look after one another. These were in the same office, and you would have no chance at all. Listen to me. Send twenty taels quietly to Uncle Wu. Consider it as money you might have had to spend at Yanzhou. I understand that Ximen's people are not going on with the business, and all we have to do is to get the document and go and see Chang. You must scrape together two hundred taels and take some food to offer to the dead. Give them the two hundred taels and ask them to make a new arrangement with regard to the rest, telling them that you will pay the balance by degrees as your business progresses. That seems to me to be the best thing you can do and you will save your face at the same time."

"You are right, Brother," Huang the Fourth said. "Brother Li, you were in too much of a hurry."

That evening, Huang the Fourth and Ying Bojue went to see Uncle Wu, taking with them twenty taels of silver. They told him they wanted the document and asked his help. Uncle Wu knew that Yueniang did not propose to go any further in the matter, and, when he saw the silver before him, he promised to help them, and accepted it. Next day, Li the Third and Huang the Fourth came to Ximen's house with two hundred taels of silver and an offering of food. Uncle Wu told Yueniang. The old contract was torn up and a new one made in which it was stated that they owed four hundred taels, which they were to pay in installments. Yueniang forgave them the remaining fifty. The document was given to Ying Bojue and he went with Li the Third and Huang the Fourth to make a bargain with Chang.

CHAPTER 80

Li Jiao'er Goes Back to the Bawdy House

Like a woman in wine she swayed
And thought of the joys of past days.
The memory of them was beyond endurance.
There was silence in the high buildings
The Spring rain was falling.
At midnight, through the distant window, a dim light flickered.
She leaned against the pillar, and the breeze blew softly
She wandered through the passages, and her thoughts were troubled.
Through the window she could hear the sound of the snuffers,
But, when she beat upon the railing, no answer came.

On the seventh day after Ximen Qing's death, sixteen Buddhist monks came to hold a service. Ying Bojue brought together Xie Xida, Hua Tzu⁻-yu, Zhu Shinian, Sun Tianhua, Chang Zhijie, and Bai Laiguang, and they all sat down. Bojue said to them: "His Lordship is dead, and this is his first week's mind. We were his friends. He gave us food, money, things for our use, and now and again he lent us money. Now he is dead, and it is impossible for us to ignore the fact. If we throw a little dust, it will get into people's eyes. If we do nothing, he will certainly want to know why, when we come to meet him before the face of the god of Hell. I suggest that we all contribute one *qian* of silver. There are seven of us and that will make seven *qian*. With that, we can buy presents and a scroll and get Master Shui to write something appropriate upon it. Then we will go and make our offering to the dead and, in return, we shall get a mourning handkerchief that will cost them at least seven *fen*. What do you think?"

"It is an excellent idea, Brother," they all agreed. They gave their money to Ying Bojue to buy the things that had been agreed upon and left it to him to make the necessary arrangements. Shui was quite well aware that Ying Bojue had been one of Ximen's companions in evil doing, and the panegyric he composed was full of satire. In due course Bojue and the rest brought their presents and set them out before the body.

Chen Jingji, in mourning robes, received them. Bojue, as the leader, was the first to offer incense, and the others followed him. As none of them knew how to read, they had no idea what the panegyric said. So, when they made the offering of wine, they produced it and handed it over to someone else to read.

In the first year of the reign of Chonghe [it said], being the year *Wuxu,* in the second month, *Wuzi,* and the third day, *Gengyin,* we, Ying Bojue, Xie Xida, Hua Ziyu, Zhu Shinian, Sun Tianhua, Chang Zhijie, and Bai Laiguang reverently lay our offering of wine and food before the coffin of his Lordship Ximen, officer of the Royal Guard, and say:

He who is dead was a man of unimpeachable honor all his days. He never sacrificed the weak, nor did he surrender to the strong. He was a man of firmness and determination. He gave water to those who thirsted and distributed the essence of his glorious being to those in need of it. His chests and boxes were mighty: his appearance was elevated and proud. Whenever he came upon pleasant things, he rose to meet them; and when he came upon things that were dark, he withdrew. He lived in the company of silken trousers, and stored his wealth in the treasury of the loins. He had eight horns and needed not to scratch or dig; and when he came upon a flea or a louse, the itching was more than he could stand.

Now we humble fellows received many kindnesses at his hands. We were forever going with him to the chamber under the loins; we slept with him among the willows, and joyed with him among the flowers. We hoped that he might long lift his crest and fight valiantly. How could we foretell that he would suffer from this fatal sickness? Now his limbs are outstretched and he is gone; we are left behind trembling like doves upon our feet. We have no place to go; the camp of mist and flowers seems remote from us. No longer can we draw near to the red walls of the bawdy house. No longer can we go to battle with the tender jade. We cannot go hand in hand to warm and fragrant places. For him our heads are bent and our limbs weakened; he has made us lonely beyond all power to tell.

Now we have come to offer wine as milk and food. His spirit knows what we do, so we invite it to come here and partake of these our offerings.

After this, Chen Jingji came and made a reverence to express his thanks. Then he took them to the temporary building and entertained them to a substantial meal.

This day, the old procuress Li heard of Ximen's death and sent Li Guijie and Li Guiqing with offerings to lay before his body. Wu Yueniang could not come out, and they were entertained by Li Jiao'er and Meng Yulou.

"Mother says," the two girls told Li Jiao'er, "that now his Lordship is dead there is no sense in your staying here any longer. You are one of us. The proverb says: However large the arbor, no party can last forever. Mother says: Give your things to Li Ming and don't be silly about it. Yangzhou is a pleasant place, but one can't live there forever. Sooner or later, you will have to leave here." Li Jiao'er considered the matter.

The same day, Han Daoguo's wife, Wang Liu'er, came to burn some paper offerings for Ximen Qing. She was dressed in mourning. She set the things upon the table and stood waiting for a long time, but nobody came to greet her. The fact was that Wang Jing had already been dismissed, and the boys were all unwilling to tell their mistress that Wang Liu'er had come. Only Laian did not know this, and he went to Yueniang's room and said: "Aunt Han has come to burn paper offerings for my father. She has been standing there a long time, and Uncle Wu said I was to come and tell you."

Yueniang was still very angry with Wang Liu'er. She said to the boy: "Go away, slave! What do you mean by talking to me about Aunt Cunt or Aunt Devil? She is a husband-stealing whore, one of those creatures who bring families to destruction. She separates father from son, husband from wife, and then has the audacity to come here and offer her cuntish paper offerings!"

Laian did not know what to do. He went back to Uncle Wu, who asked him if he had spoken to the ladies. Laian made a face, and waited for a moment before he replied. Then he said: "All I got from the Great Lady was curses." Then Uncle Wu himself went to see his sister.

"What is this?" he said. "You ought not to use such language. It has always been conceded that though a man may himself be bad, the ceremonies he performs are none the worse for that. This woman's husband has a lot of your money and, if you behave like this to her, your good name will suffer. You must not do it. If you don't feel like going out to her yourself, tell the Second Lady or the Third to entertain her. Why make such a fuss about it? It may make people think very badly of you."

Wu Yueniang said nothing, but sometime later Meng Yulou went out to receive Wang Liu'er. They sat down and drank tea, but Wang Liu'er realized what was intended, and went away as soon as she could.

Guijie, Guiqing, and Wu Yin'er were in the upper room while Yueniang was calling Han Daoguo's wife every possible kind of whore, and they thought it likely that her remarks might be intended to apply to them also. Before sunset the two sisters prepared to go home, but Yueniang said: "There will be many people here tonight. Stay and watch the puppet plays and go home tomorrow."

Guijie and Wu Yin'er decided to stay, but Guiqing went home. In the evening, when the monks had done, more than twenty of Ximen's relatives and friends assembled. The puppet players came, and, while the party was proceeding in the temporary building, they played *How a Dog Was Killed to Teach a Lesson to the Husband*. The ladies sat in the hall in which the coffin lay. The lattice was drawn across, and their tables were placed near the screen.

Li Ming and Wu Hui were there, and did not go away that night. The guests, when they arrived, first made an offering to the dead. Then they sat around the tables, and candles were brought. It was the third night watch before the play was finished.

After Ximen Qing's death, Chen Jingji joked and trifled with Pan Jinlian every day. Sometimes, even before the coffin, they exchanged meaningful glances. Sometimes they made merry behind the screen. Now, when the guests were going away, and the ladies withdrawing to the inner court, Jinlian came close to Jingji and pinched him. "My son," she said, "tonight your mother will give you what you want. Your wife is here, so you must come to my place."

Jingji was delighted. He went to open the gate, and Jinlian ran through the darkness to her room. They did not utter a word, but undressed and lay down on the bed. Jingji did everything to her perfect satisfaction.

> For two years they had known each other
> And now today they come together
> And their eager love is satisfied at last.
> She gently moves her slender hips
> He hastens to extend the precious scepter.
> Then, ears pressed close to listen, they speak their love
> Pledging their troth eternally upon the pillow.
> She lets the butterfly possess her
> Most exquisitely giving proof of her delight.
> The rain is furious, the clouds submissive.
> She plays a thousand, nay ten thousand, loving tricks.
> "Darling," he whispers once and once again,
> "My own heart," she answers, with a warm embrace.

The willow now puts forth new foliage
And the blossom retains its brilliant redness.

When they had done, Jinlian was afraid someone might come, and hurried again to the inner court. Next morning, the young man came very early to her room. She was still in bed and he peeped through the window. The red bedclothes covered her like a crimson cloud, and her cheeks were like jade.

"Oh, what a splendid housekeeper you are," he cried. "Not out of bed yet! And today our kinsman Qiao is coming to make his reverence to the dead, and the Great Lady says we are to get rid of the food that Li the Third and Huang the Fourth offered yesterday. Get up and let me have the key."

Jinlian told Chunmei to go and open the door upstairs; she put her lips to the window and the young man kissed her.

They hate to hear the cuckoo through the lattice of pearl
For their hearts are sewn together as by a needle
And their love bound as things are bound by glue.
He looks upon her smiling face
Its dimples rival the dainty eyebrows.
How delicate those tender fingers.
The ornaments of jade release their hold
And the dark hair falls tumbling.
The languid air gives place to passion
And the paleness changes to a rosy flush.
He touches her sweet lips
And the fragrance of them stays upon his own.
Even the memory of that touch
Brings sweetness to his mouth.

Chunmei opened the door and Jingji went to the outer court to watch the table being properly cleared. Then the food came from Qiao. Both Qiao himself and his wife offered it to the dead man. The two uncles Wu and Clerk Gan took the guests to the temporary building and there entertained them. Li Ming and Wu Hui played and sang.

This day, Zheng Aiyue came to make her offering. Yueniang asked Yulou to give the girl a mourning dress. Then she went to join the ladies. When she saw Guijie and Wu Yin'er already there, she said: "Why didn't you tell me? If I had known, I should have been here before. A nice pair you are, not to say a word to me about it!"

When she found that Yueniang had a baby, she said: "Now, mother, you have both joy and pain together. It is indeed sad that my father should die so young, but at least you now have a son to support you, and you need not worry any more."

Yueniang gave the girls mourning, and kept them until the evening.

The next day was the third of the second month, the second week's mind for Ximen Qing. Sixteen monks came from the Temple of the Jade King. Captain He invited the two eunuchs, Liu and Xue, Major Zhou, General Jing, Captain Zhang, Yun Lishou, and other military officers, to go with him and offer food and a panegyric to their dead colleague. There was nobody to stop them and, dressed up like a lot of monkeys, they burned incense and kowtowed. Chen Jingji made a reverence to them in return. They were entertained and then went away.

Yueniang knew only too well that, of all the people who knew Ximen Qing, officers, friends, and servants alike, there were very few who were not seeking their own ends. She could trust none of them. But she believed Shutong to be honest and reliable, and appointed him to attend upon Li Jiao'er, giving him the keys of the Sixth Lady's rooms.

The water flows peacefully below the Xiang Wang Tai.
From the same love there spring two kinds of sadness.
The moon knows not the changes of mortal life
And in the depth of night
Still casts her beams upon the whitewashed walls.

Li Ming pretended to be helping Ximen's people, but secretly told Li Jiao'er to give him the things she was going to take away with her. He stayed for two or three days and did not go home. Yueniang knew nothing of this. The others were unwilling to mention the matter to her, for Li Jiao'er had not been guiltless in her dealings with the younger of Yueniang's brothers.

The ninth day of the month was the third week's mind, and again there was a religious service. There was none for the fourth week. On the sixteenth, Chen Jingji went to attend the digging of the grave. On the thirtieth, Ximen Qing was buried. There were many paper offerings, and a good number of people attended, but it was not such a magnificent occasion as when Li Ping'er was taken out to be buried. The Abbot of the Temple of Eternal Felicity officiated. He sat in a sedan chair and recited the scriptures in a loud voice. Then Chen Jingji broke a paper bowl and the coffin was taken out. The members of the household set up a wailing, and Yueniang, in her sedan chair, followed close behind the coffin. Then

came the chairs of the other ladies. The body was taken straight outside
the city and buried. Chen Jingji offered a roll of silk to Yun Lishou and
asked him to complete the tablet. Xu, the Master of the Yin Yang, directed
the funeral. It was sad to see how few people made offerings at the grave-
side. Uncle Wu, Qiao, Captain He, Uncle Shen and Uncle Han were the
only ones to do so, except for Ximen's clerks. Abbot Wu left twelve young
monks to perform the ceremony of the return; the tablet was set up in the
upper room, and Master Xu purified the house. Then the relatives and
friends went away.

Every day Yueniang and the others, dressed in their mourning, made
offerings before the tablet. After the first visit to the grave, the soldiers
went back to the office. For the fifth week's mind, Yueniang sent for the
nuns Xue and Wang, and the Abbess and twelve nuns came to speed
Ximen Qing on his way to paradise.

While the funeral party was being held, Guiqing and Guijie secretly
said to Li Jiao'er: "Mother says you have nothing much of great value, and
there is no reason why you should remain any longer in Ximen's house.
Think what it means. You have no child, and there is no sense in staying
on as a widow. Mother thinks the easiest plan is to start a quarrel and just
break with them. Yesterday, Ying Bojue came and said that Zhang who
lives in the High Street was minded to spend five hundred taels on getting you for his second wife. He will give you control of his household.
Mother thinks you would do well there. There is no point in staying at
Ximen's house all your life. We who come from the bawdy house have
always to work on the principle. Welcome the new and give up the old.
We must make up to those who are rich and powerful: we can't afford to
waste our time."

After Ximen Qing's fifth week's mind, Li Jiao'er remembered this. She
did not bother about the household but let things go as they would.

"The other day," Pan Jinlian said to Sun Xue'e, "I saw Li Jiao'er talking to Uncle Wu the Second in the small room at our family grave."

Chunmei saw her handing Li Ming a parcel behind the screen in the
great hall. He tucked it away underneath his clothes and went off with it.

Yueniang was told of these things. She scolded Uncle Wu the Second, and would not let him have any more to do with the shop. She told
Ping'an that Li Ming was not to be allowed to enter the house again. Li
Jiao'er was first ashamed and then angry. She had been waiting for an
opportunity to make trouble, and now she had it.

One day, when Yueniang was having tea with Aunt Wu, she asked
Yulou to join them, but did not ask Li Jiao'er. This made the woman
very angry. She shouted at Yueniang and thumped the table upon which

Ximen's tablet rested. At the third night watch, she said she was going to hang herself. Her maid went to tell Yueniang, who was very much upset. She consulted her brother, and they sent for old woman Li and told her to take Li Jiao'er away. The old woman feared that Yueniang would not allow her to take her clothes and ornaments.

"My girl has been here and suffered from ill usage and backbiting, and you are not going to get rid of her so easily. She must have some money to wash away her shame."

Uncle Wu, in view of his official standing, would not say anything either way, and, after much haggling, Yueniang let Li Jiao'er go with clothes, ornaments, boxes, bed, and furniture. She would not let the two maids go, though Li Jiao'er tried to insist.

"No," she said, "certainly not. If you do take them, I shall bring an accusation against you for procuring young maids to be whores."

This frightened the old procuress. She said no more, but smiled and thanked Yueniang. Li Jiao'er got into a sedan chair and was carried to her old home.

Readers, singing girls make their living by selling their charms. With them it is purely a business. In the morning, they receive Chang the dissolute, and in the evening Li the ne'er-do-well. At the front door they welcome the father, and by the back door they let in the son. They forget their old clients and love the new. It is their nature to keep their eyes open when there is any money about. Even if a man loves them with his whole heart and does everything in his power to make them true, their hearts can never be secured. They steal the very food from a man's mouth, and as soon as he is dead, they quarrel and go away, back to their old business.

I laugh at the flowers of the mist
Which no one can keep for long.
Every night they find a new bridegroom.
Their jade-like arms are the pillow for a thousand men
Their ruby lips are enjoyed by ten thousand guests.
Their seductions are many
And their hearts are false.
You may devise a host of schemes to hold them
But you can never keep them
From longing for their old haunts.

When Li Jiao'er had gone, Yueniang sobbed aloud and the other ladies tried to console her. "Sister," Jinlian said, "don't let it upset you so much.

The proverb says that when a man marries a whore, it is like trying to keep a seagull away from the water. When it cannot get to the water, it still thinks about the eastern ocean. All this was his fault."

While they were busied over this, Ping'an came and announced that his Excellency Cai, the Salt Commissioner, had come. "He is in the great hall," the boy said. "I told him that master had died. He asked when, and I said on the twenty-first day of the first month, and that we were now in the fifth week after his death. He asked me if the tablet had been set up, and I told him it was in the inner court. He wishes to pay reverence to it."

"Go and tell your brother-in-law to see him," Yueniang said.

Jingji put on mourning clothes and went to receive Cai. After a while, the inner court was made ready and Cai was invited to go there. He kowtowed before the tablet. Yueniang in return made reverence to him. He did not speak to her, except to invite her to retire. Then he said to Jingji: "Your father was very kind to me, and today, on my way to the Eastern Capital, I stayed especially to thank him. I never dreamed that I should find him dead. What was the cause of his death?"

"Inflammation of the lungs," Jingji told him.

"How very sad!" said Commissioner Cai.

He called his servants, and they brought him two rolls of Hangzhou silk, a pair of woolen socks, four fish, and four jars of preserved food. "These trifles," he said, "I offer to him who is dead." Then he gave Jingji fifty taels of silver. "Your father," he said, "was good enough to lend me this, and now that I have been paid myself, I return the money to set the seal upon our friendship." He asked Ping'an to take the money.

"Your Excellency is over-conscientious," Jingji said.

Yueniang told him to take Cai to the outer court, but the Commissioner said that he could not stay and would only drink a cup of tea. The servant brought the tea, and Cai went away.

Yueniang was half pleased, half sad when she received these fifty taels of silver. She reflected that if Ximen Qing had been alive he would never have allowed such a nobleman to go away without staying for something to eat. He would have remained, she thought, and enjoyed the pleasures of the table for many an hour. Now, he had stood up and gone. Though she still was rich, there was no man to entertain such guests.

When Ying Bojue heard that Li Jiao'er had gone back to the bawdy house, he went to tell Zhang the Second. Zhang took five taels of silver and went to spend the night with her. He was one year younger than Ximen Qing. His animal was the Hare, and he was thirty-two. Li Jiao'er was thirty-four, but the old procuress told him she was twenty-eight and warned Ying Bojue not to let him know the truth. So Zhang the Second paid three hundred taels and took Li Jiao'er for his second wife.

Zhu Shinian and Sun Guazui took Wang the Third to Li Guijie's house, and he attached himself to her again.

Then Ying Bojue, Li the Third, and Huang the Fourth borrowed five thousand taels from Eunuch Xu, and another five thousand from Zhang the Second, and began the business of purchasing antiquities for the authorities. Every day they went riding about on magnificent horses and calling at one bawdy house after another.

Zhang the Second, now that Ximen Qing was dead, spent five thousand taels in bribing Zheng, one of the royal family in the Eastern Capital, so as to secure the appointment that Ximen Qing had held. He did much work upon his garden and rebuilt his house, and Bojue was there nearly every day. Bojue told him everything he knew about Ximen's household.

"His Fifth Lady," he said, "is as beautiful as a painting. She knows poems, songs, literature, philosophy, games, backgammon and chess. She can write very beautifully and play the lute exquisitely. She is not more than thirty years old and much more charming than any singing girl."

Zhang the Second was greatly impressed and wondered what he could do to get her for himself.

"Is that the woman who was once the wife of Wu Da the cake seller?" he asked.

"Yes," Bojue said. "She has been in Ximen's household for five or six years. I don't know whether she would be inclined to consider another marriage."

"Please find out for me," Zhang the Second said. "If she has any such idea, let me know at once, and I will marry her."

"I have a man still in that household," Ying Bojue said. "His name is Laijue. I will tell him. And if he can do anything in the matter, I will certainly let you know. It would be much better for you to marry her than some singing girl. When Ximen Qing married her, he had considerable trouble, but things are never the same twice, and what will happen on this occasion, I cannot say. But anyone who gets hold of a beauty like this will be a lucky fellow. You are a man of position, and you certainly ought to have someone like her to enhance its splendor. Otherwise, all your wealth is wasted. I will tell Laijue to find out what he can for us. If there is the slightest whisper of the word marriage, I will see what my sweet words and honeyed phrases can do to inflame that amorous heart. It may cost you a few hundred taels, but it will be worth it."

Readers, all those who live upon others are men who seek for power and money. In their time, Ximen Qing and Ying Bojue had been like blood brothers. They might have been glued together, so close was their affection. Day after day, Bojue took his meals with Ximen, and was given clothes. Now, when his friend had only just died, almost before his body was cold, Bojue was planning to bring disgrace upon him. With friends, it is only too possible to know the face and to know nothing about the heart, just as an artist may paint the outside of a tiger, but must leave the bones unseen.

CHAPTER 81

Han Daoguo Defrauds Wu Yueniang

Han Daoguo and Laibao had taken four thousand taels of Ximen Qing's money and gone south of the river to buy goods. When they came to Yangzhou, they went at once to see Miao Qing, proposing to stay with him. Miao Qing remembered how Ximen had saved his life, and treated the two men with very great kindness. He bought a girl called Chuyun and took her to his house, intending to make a present of her to Ximen Qing in return for the favors he had received from him.

Han Daoguo and Laibao neglected their business and amused themselves with the young ladies of the town. But when winter came, they grew homesick and got busy buying silk and cloth, which they brought back to Miao Qing's place, proposing to start home again when they had bought enough.

Han Daoguo grew very attached to a girl called Wang Yuzhi, who lived at an old established bawdy house of Yangzhou, and Laibao to Xiaohong, the younger sister of a girl called Lin Caihong. One day, they asked Miao Qing and a salt merchant named Wang Haifeng, to go for a day's amusement on the Baoying lake. When they came back, they went to the bawdy house. It happened to be the birthday of Wang Yuzhi's mother, and Han Daoguo decided to invite a number of other men and have a party to celebrate the occasion. So he sent his boy Hu Xiu to ask two merchants, Wang Dongqiao and Qian Qingchuan, but before the boy himself came back, the two merchants arrived with Wang Haifeng. It was nearly sunset when the boy came.

"What has made you so late?" Han Daoguo, who had had a good deal of wine, said to him. "Where have you been drinking? I can smell the wine in your breath. My guests have been here some time already: they came long before you showed any signs of turning up. I will deal with you tomorrow."

Hu Xiu looked at Han Daoguo out of the corners of his eyes and went out. "It's all very well for you to scold me," he muttered, "when your own wife is in bed with another man. Here you are enjoying yourself, while in your house at home, your master is enjoying your wife. He only sent you here because he wanted her. You are happy here and you never think of the burden she has to bear."

The old procuress heard this and dragged the boy to the courtyard. "Master Hu," she said, "you are drunk. Go and sleep." But Hu Xiu shouted and struggled and would not go. Han Daoguo, who was entertaining his friends, heard the noise, and it made him very angry. He came out and kicked the boy.

"You slave," he cried, "I can hire anybody to take your place for five *fen* of silver a day. I don't need to keep you. Get out of here!"

Hu Xiu would not go. "You would dare to send me away, would you?" he shouted. "Have you found anything wrong in the way I've handled the money? Here you are, spending money on women, and you dare to drive me away. You will see whether I tell our master or not."

Laibao came out and took Han Daoguo away. Then he came back and said to Hu Xiu: "You rascal, this is just drunken brawling."

"Uncle," said Hu Xiu, "don't you meddle in this. I am not drunk, but I'll show him what I think of him."

Laibao hustled him into the house and made him lie down and go to sleep. Han Daoguo was very anxious that his friends should not lose their respect for him. He and Laibao entertained them; the three singing girls sang and danced for them, and they played all kinds of games. At the third night watch, the party broke up.

The next day, Han Daoguo would have punished Hu Xiu, but the boy swore he did not remember a word of what he had said, and Miao Qing intervened on his behalf. In due course, they finished their purchases. The goods were packed up and loaded upon the boat. But Chuyun, whom Miao Qing had bought to present to Ximen Qing, suddenly fell ill and could not go with them. "When she is better," Miao Qing said, "I will send her to your master."

He wrote a letter and prepared some presents, then saw the two men and Hu Xiu start back to Qinghe. The three singing girls also went to see them off.

It was the tenth day of the first month when they left Yangzhou. One day, they came to Linjiang lock. Han Daoguo was standing in the bows of the boat, when he saw his neighbor Yan the Fourth on a boat coming towards them. This Yan was coming to meet some official, and when he saw Han Daoguo, he bowed and shouted: "Han, your master died in the first month." The two boats passed so quickly that there was no chance for any further conversation. Han did not say a word to Laibao.

This was a very dry year in Henan and Shandong. There were no crops on the land; the cotton was a failure, and the fields were bare. The price of material went up and every roll of cloth fetched three-tenths more than its regular price. Merchants took their money with them and set out to buy goods even many miles away.

"We have four thousand taels' worth of goods," Han Daoguo said to Laibao. "Here we can get three-tenths more than the regular price and I think we should do well to sell half of what we have. We shall have less duty to pay and I don't believe we are at all likely to do any better at home. It would be a pity to let this opportunity slip."

"You are quite right," Laibao said, "but our master may be annoyed when we get home."

"If he is," Han Daoguo said, "I will take the blame."

Laibao said no more, and they sold a thousand taels' worth of cloth in that place.

"You and Hu Xiu stay here until the duty is paid," Han Daoguo said then, "and I will take the boy Wang Han, together with the thousand taels we have just got, overland to our master."

"When you get there," Laibao said, "ask him for a letter to Officer Qian so that we have not to pay so much duty and can get our boats through before the others."

Han Daoguo promised, and he and the boy packed some of their things, loaded them upon a mule, and started overland for Qinghe. At last, they reached the southern gate of the city about sunset and met Ximen's grave keeper, Zhang An, pushing a wheelbarrow in which were rice, wine, and boxes of food. He was taking them outside the city.

"What! Are you back, Uncle Han?" the grave keeper cried, when he saw Han Daoguo.

Han noted that the man was wearing mourning and asked the reason.

"Our master is dead," Zhang An said, "and tomorrow, the ninth day of the third month, will be his last week's mind. The Great Lady has sent me with these things to the grave because they are coming tomorrow to burn paper offerings for him."

"What a terrible business! What a terrible business!" Han Daoguo said.

He found, as he went home down the street, that everybody was talking about Ximen Qing's death. When he came to the crossroads, he thought for a while. "If I go to Ximen's place," he said to himself, "he is dead. Besides, it is very late and I had better go home and see what my wife has to say. It won't be too late if I go to my master's place tomorrow." So he and Wang Han drove the mules to Lion Street to his own house. When they reached there, they dismounted, knocked until the door was opened, then dismissed the porters, and Wang Han carried in the luggage. Han's wife welcomed him. He made reverence to the family god, then Wang Liu'er helped him to take off his outer clothes, and the maid brought tea. He told his wife all about his journey.

"I met Brother Yan and Zhang An," he said, "and so learned of our master's death. What did he die of? He was quite well when I went away."

"Heaven sends unexpected weather," Wang Liu'er said, "and human beings have many changes of fortune. Nobody dare prophesy about his own end."

Han Daoguo opened his luggage and brought out clothes and silk. He took out the thousand taels, one packet after another, and put them on the bed. His wife opened them and saw the shining silver.

"What is this?" she said.

"As soon as I heard of our master's death, I sold part of the merchandise for a thousand taels," Han Daoguo told her. He put down another hundred taels of his own.

"When I was away," he continued, "did he come to see how you were getting on?"

"Everything was all right so long as he was alive," the woman said. "Do you intend to give them all that silver?"

"I was going to see what you thought about it. I think if I gave them half, that would be quite enough."

"You silly fellow," Wang Liu'er said, "don't be such a fool. The master is dead now and we have really no more obligation to them. If you give them half, you may get into trouble because they may want to know where the rest is. Let us make up our minds, take the thousand taels, hire a mule or two, and go to the Eastern Capital. We will go to our daughter's place, and I don't imagine our own kinsfolk will turn us away."

"But we can't dispose of this house in such a short time," Han Daoguo said.

"What's to prevent us sending for your brother, you silly fellow?" Wang Liu'er said. "We can leave a few taels with him and he can look after the house. That's quite simple. If anybody from Ximen's family makes inquiries, they can be told we have gone to the Eastern Capital because our daughter was anxious to see us. We have no cause to be afraid."

"But I owe a great deal to my master's kindness," Han Daoguo said. "I don't like the idea of turning around on him and acting so deceitfully."

"If you are going to think about principles, you will starve," Wang Liu'er said. "He amused himself with your wife, and now you take his money. So you are quits. The other day, I bought presents and paper offerings and went to offer my sympathy. That whore, his first wife, kept me waiting for hours and insulted me most disagreeably. I did not know what to do with myself. At last, the Third Lady came out and sat down with me, but I came home as soon as I could. If that counts for anything, you certainly ought to take this money."

Han Daoguo said no more. They made their decision that very night. Before it was light, they sent for Han the Second, gave him twenty taels of silver to carry on with, and gave the house into his charge. Han the Second was quite agreeable. He told them to go their way and he would see after everything. So Han Daoguo and his wife, with the boy Wang Han and the two maids, set off for the Eastern Capital. They hired two large carts to carry their trunks and boxes, and left the city at daybreak.

That day, Wu Yueniang with her little son, Meng Yulou, Pan Jinlian, Ximen Dajie, and Ruyi'er, went with Chen Jingji to burn paper offerings at Ximen Qing's grave. While they were there, Zhang An told Yueniang that he had met Han Daoguo the night before.

"If he is back," Yueniang said, "why hasn't he been to see me? Perhaps he will come during the day."

She burned the paper offerings but did not stay very long at the grave. When she got home, she told Chen Jingji to go and see Han Daoguo and find out where the boats were. Jingji went and knocked at the door, but for a long time no one answered. At last Han the Second opened the door.

"My brother and his wife," he said, "have gone to the Eastern Capital to see their daughter. I know nothing at all about the boats."

Jingji went back and told Yueniang. She was greatly worried and told Chen Jingji to take a horse and go to the river to find out whether the boats had arrived. As soon as he came to the wharf, Jingji found Laibao and the boat there.

"Brother Han has already taken a thousand taels to you," Laibao said.

"We haven't seen anything of him," Jingji said. "Zhang An, the grave keeper, saw him and, when we went to the grave, we heard he had come back. The Great Lady sent me to his house, but they had taken all their belongings and gone to the Eastern Capital with the silver. Father is dead, and this is his last week's mind. The Great Lady was worried and sent me to see if the boats had arrived."

Laibao said nothing. He thought: "The fellow deceived me. Now I see why he suggested selling a thousand taels' worth of goods. He made up his mind that very moment. Really, even though men meet face to face, their minds might be a thousand miles apart."

So Laibao heard of his master's death. He decided to take Chen Jingji to the wine house and the bawdy house. Secretly, he removed eight hundred taels' worth of merchandise, sealed it up, and stored it at an inn. Then they went to the customs office, paid the duty, and their boat was allowed to proceed. They loaded their merchandise upon carts and so brought it to the city. The stuff was stored in one of the rooms in the eastern wing of Ximen's house.

After Ximen's death, the shop in Lion Street had been closed. Clerk Gan and Cui Ben got rid of all the goods in the other silk shop, paid over the money fairly, then gave up their jobs and went home. The house was sold. The medicine shop was still kept open, and Chen Jingji and Clerk Fu looked after it.

Laibao's wife had a son called Sengbao, now five years old. Han Daoguo's wife had a niece who was four years old. Their parents had arranged that these two children should some day marry. Yueniang did not know this.

When Laibao handed over the merchandise, he put all the blame on Han Daoguo. "He sold two thousand taels' worth of goods," he told Yueniang. She repeatedly urged him to go to the Eastern Capital to get the money out of Han Daoguo.

"It is better for me to keep away," Laibao said. "Their kinsman is a member of the Imperial Tutor's household, and nobody dare touch them. If I were to go, it would look as though I wished to make trouble. We have every reason to be satisfied that they don't come to us for something, and we must not stir up trouble."

"But it was my husband who arranged this marriage for Zhai," Yueniang said. "Surely he would remember that."

"Han's daughter is a favorite there," Laibao said, "and she would certainly take her parents' side. She will do nothing to help us. The best thing you can do is to keep quiet about the matter. Regard it as a dead loss, and say no more about it."

Yueniang could not think of anything else to say, so she said no more. She told him to try to find some customers to buy the merchandise he had brought. A number of people came, and Yueniang told Chen Jingji to deal with them. There was a long discussion, and in the end, they all said they did not want the stuff and took their money away.

"Your son-in-law is not sufficiently experienced," Laibao said to Yueniang. "I have been doing this sort of thing for years, and I know all there is to know about it. In business, the principle is: sell first and be sorry later. Don't let us be sorry first, and sell afterwards. The stuff is here, and if we can do even moderately well out of it, we ought to be content. If the price is set too high, so that customers won't make a deal, that is not good business. You must forgive me, but you are young and don't understand business. Don't think for a moment that I am ready to yield the advantage to others. I'm not; I simply want to sell the stuff and get it out of the way."

After this, Chen Jingji did no more in the matter. Laibao did not wait for Yueniang's instructions, but took over the abacus and brought the customers back again. They measured out two thousand taels, Jingji counted it, it was given to Yueniang, and they went off with the goods.

Yueniang offered Laibao twenty-three taels, but he put on an air of great dignity and refused to take it. "No, Lady," he said, "my master is dead, and your property is like stagnant water. Don't give me the money. You need it; I do not."

One evening, Laibao came in, very drunk. He went to Yueniang's room and put his hand on the bed. "Lady," he said, "you are very young. Your husband is dead, and you have only the baby. Don't you ever feel lonely?" Yueniang did not answer.

A letter came from Zhai at the Eastern Capital. It said that he had heard of Ximen Qing's death, and that Han Daoguo had told him there were still some very beautiful girls in the household. He would like to know the price put upon them, said that he would pay it, and asked for the girls to be sent to the Eastern Capital to amuse the old lady. Yueniang did not know what to do. She sent for Laibao. This time the man did not even address her as Lady. "Woman," he said, "if you do not send the girls, there will be serious trouble. It is all the fault of the dead old man. He was always trying to show off. Whenever he invited anyone here, he always had his own musicians. Everybody knew it. Now Han's daughter is at the palace; it is quite natural that she should tell the old lady. Now, perhaps, you realize the truth of what I was saying the other day. Here they are coming to ask us for something. If you don't do what he says, he will get someone from the local office to come and demand the girls. Then it will be too late, even if you give them up. I don't suggest you should send them all; a couple will probably satisfy him."

Yueniang wondered. She could not well spare Lanxiang, who was the Third Lady's maid, or Chunmei, who waited on the Fifth Lady. She wanted Xiuchun to look after the baby. She asked her own maid, Yuxiao, and Yingchun if they would go, and they both agreed. Then Yueniang told Laibao to hire suitable conveyances and take the two girls to the Eastern Capital. This he did and, on the way, enjoyed them both.

They reached the Capital, and Laibao went to see Han Daoguo and his wife. They talked over what had happened.

"If you hadn't prevented them," Han Daoguo said, "something disagreeable might have happened. Of course, I'm not in the least afraid of them."

Zhai was delighted with the two girls, both of whom were very beautiful. One could play the zither and the other the banjo. Neither was more than eighteen years old. He took them to the palace to wait upon the old lady, and she gave two bars of silver for them. Laibao took the silver home, but he only gave one of the bars to Yueniang. He tried to frighten her by saying: "If I hadn't gone, you would never have had this silver. The Hans are very rich and comfortable there. They have a house all to themselves and a host of maids and servants to wait on them. Master Zhai calls them Father and Mother. Their daughter goes to the palace to see the old lady every day. They are on such good terms that she is always going about with the old lady. When she asks for one thing, they give her ten. She chooses the kinds of food she likes best and clothes in the latest style. She has learned how to write and do sums. When luck is on one's side, cleverness always follows. She is tall and very pretty. When I saw her the other day, she was just as beautiful to look at as a tree of jade, and so charming and pleasant. She called me Uncle Bao. Those two girls of ours will have to ask her for their needles and thread."

Yueniang thanked him and gave him food and wine. When he refused to take her money, she gave him a roll of silk for his wife to make into clothes.

One day, Laibao and Liu Cang, his wife's brother, went to the river and brought away all the merchandise that had been left at the inn, and sold it for eight hundred taels of silver. Then he secretly bought a house, opened a store near Liu Cang's house, and gave parties to his friends every day. His wife used to tell Yueniang that she was going to see her mother, but really she went to the new house. There, she changed her ornaments, dressed up in pearls and gold and silver, and went to see Wang Liu'er's mother. This old lady was known as Old Sow Wang. They discussed the marriage between the young children. Whenever she went there, she went in a sedan chair and, when she came back, she dressed again in her ordinary clothes and returned to Ximen's house. Yueniang knew nothing of all this.

Laibao himself was always getting drunk and, on several occasions, came to Yueniang's room and made improper overtures to her. If Yueniang had not been a virtuous woman, she would have been caught by his bait and would assuredly have been seduced.

Then some of the other women told Wu Yueniang how Laibao's wife had arranged this marriage for her child, and how she was going about in gold and silver, showing every sign of great wealth. Pan Jinlian also told her several times, but she would not believe a word of it. Laibao's wife heard of this, and made a terrible to-do in the kitchen, abusing high and low alike.

Laibao himself began to swagger. He went about bragging. "You people are all very well at talking in bed, but that's about all you can do.

I went on the water and come back with the cash. If it hadn't been for me, Clerk Han would have walked off with all of it. His mouth was as wide open as a pair of the largest pincers. He would have gone off with all of it to the Eastern Capital, and it would have been just as if the whole lot had fallen into the water without so much as a splash. Yet nobody has a kind word for me. You talk about my getting money by robbing my master, and things of that sort. The one who cuts off the leg doesn't know, and the one whose leg is cut off doesn't know either. The proverb says: Don't believe scandalmongers or you will lose your calabash. Don't believe lies, or you will lose your net. Some backbiting women have been saying that we have suddenly got very rich and been fixing up a marriage. Why, she goes and borrows, as any poor priest might do, clothes and ornaments from her sister. People talk about our using our master's money because they want to get us kicked out. But don't worry. If we do leave here, Heaven will give no grass to the waterfowl. I shall wash my eyes and keep an eye on those strumpets who are shut up here."

Yueniang came to hear of this kind of talk and was anxious to find out what it meant. Laibao's wife quarreled with everybody and talked about killing herself. And the man treated her without any respect when he found her by herself. Yueniang was very angry, but she did not know what to do. Finally, she decided to send Laibao and his wife away. Then the man openly carried on business with his brother-in-law, and they did a roaring trade during the shortage of cloth.

CHAPTER 82

Pan Jinlian Makes Love with Chen Jingji

Now that Pan Jinlian had tasted the joys of love with Chen Jingji, never a day passed that did not witness some new proof of the passion that united them. Sometimes they would stand, close pressed together, and gaze into each other's laughing eyes; sometimes they sat, and so made love, giving each other gentle slaps and pinchings, with occasional ticklings, feeling themselves free of all restraint. If others were present and they could not speak the words they longed to speak, they would write short notes of love, and drop them on the floor, each picking up the other's. One day—it was about the fourth month—Jinlian took a silk handkerchief, and in it wrapped a powder satchel, in which she had placed a lock of hair and some fragrant pine leaves. She intended to give this to Jingji with her own hands, but, finding he was not in his room, she threw it through the window. When the young man returned, it lay there in its paper wrappings, and, when he opened it, he found the satchel and the handkerchief. There was a short poem with the gifts.

> This kerchief of silver silk and this perfume satchel
> Are for you.
> The lock of hair is a memory of our first mating.
> The pine leaves mark my trust
> That you will remember forever.
> I write my love with my tears.
> In the deep night I am alone with my shadow.
> Do not let the night pass in vain,
> But come quickly to the arbor of roses.

To the young man this seemed a clear sign that she wished him to go to the arbor. He took a piece of fancy paper and wrote a poem in reply. Then he went to the garden but found that Wu Yueniang was paying a visit to his loved one. At first, indeed, he did not know this, and when he reached the garden gate called: "Darling, are you there?" Fortunately, only

Jinlian heard him and, hurriedly lifting the lattice, she came out and made a warning sign to him with her hands.

"Oh, it is you!" she said. "I suppose you are looking for your wife. She was here a moment ago, but now she has gone to the garden to pick some flowers." The young man silently handed his poem to her, and she put it in her sleeve.

"What did he want?" Yueniang said. Jinlian said he was looking for his wife, and that she had told him he would find her in the garden. So Yueniang was deceived. Soon she went away, and Jinlian took from her sleeve the packet Chen Jingji had given her. It was a golden fan, with green rushes beside a flowing stream painted upon it. Accompanying it was a poem.

> On this white silk are painted dark bamboos
> And green rushes that seem to be alive
> With gold and silver to enhance their brightness.
> Will you not use this, darling, when the day is hot
> Not to bring cooling breezes, but to give you shade?
> When people throng around you, put it in your sleeve
> Let it refresh you when you are alone.
> I could not bear to think
> That vulgar hands might snatch it from your own.

When she had read this poem, Jinlian plied her maids, Chunmei and Qiuju, with wine, and when it grew late, sent them to another room to sleep. Then alone, she opened wide the green windows and lighted long tapering candles. She made ready the bed and perfumed it, then bathed and went out to stand beside the flower pleasance to await a fitting moment.

That night, Ximen's daughter had gone to Yueniang's room to hear the exhortations of Sister Wang, the nun. Only the maid, Yuanxiao, was left with Chen Jingji. He gave her a kerchief and said: "You stay where you are, I am going to play chess with the Fifth Lady. If your mistress should return, come and tell me at once." Then he went to the garden. The flowers in the moonlight cast their shadows, some long, some short. He found his way to the Rose Arbor but, long before he reached it, could see Jinlian, uncovered, standing there, her glorious tresses waving in the gentle breeze. He approached quietly, then suddenly dashed forward and took her in his arms. Jinlian was taken by surprise.

"Oh," she cried, "you young villain, what do you mean by rushing out and frightening me like that? It is a good thing it is I, with whom you know you can do what you like, but would you have dared to do it with anybody else?"

Jingji had taken more wine than usual that evening. "I don't think it would have mattered very much if it had been somebody else," he laughed. Then, hand in hand, they walked towards her room. It was brightly lighted by the candles on the table, and refreshments lay ready before them. They made fast the corner gate; then sat side by side and began to drink.

"Where is your wife?" Jinlian said.

"She has gone to hear the reading of the sacred texts," Jingji answered. "I told Yuanxiao that she must come and warn me at once if it became necessary. She thinks I have come to play chess with you."

They drank wine together in great content, for, as the proverb says: If the drinking of tea leads to frivolity, wine opens wide the floodgates of passion. As the olive-colored wine coursed through their veins, the ruddy hue of the peach flower mounted to their cheeks. One would seek a kiss; the other would not seem too shy. At last they snuffed out the candles and went to bed.

> When he came in,
> He took me in his arms and carried me
> And set me down upon his knee.
> I spread the silken coverlets, and that gay lover
> Well proved his valiance in the bed.
> He lifted up my feet, yes, lifted up my feet,
> Disordering my hair and putting out of place
> The knot that bound it.

Their passage at arms over, Yuanxiao came and knocked at the door, telling them that Jingji's wife had returned. He dressed hastily and went away.

> The bees that buzz so wildly and the merry butterflies
> We often see
> But, sometimes, they are hidden from our eyes
> When they plunge deep within the pear blossom.

The three rooms on the upper floor of Jinlian's apartments were arranged, with the middle one as the place for family worship, and the others as storerooms for drugs and incense.

One day the Fates decided that something should happen. Jinlian and Chen Jingji were so much in love with one another that nothing could keep them long apart. Every day they met at her place. One morning

Jinlian dressed and went upstairs to offer incense before the image of Guanyin. At the same time, Chen Jingji came to take some of the stores. So they met. There was nobody in sight, so Jinlian decided that she had burned incense enough. Instead, she threw her arms around her lover and kissed him, calling him her precious sweetheart, while he called her his own true darling. After a while they said to one another: "There seems to be no one here," took off their clothes, and found a convenient bench. Then they began a merry game. Over his shoulders two small feet were raised and all was going well. But were it not for the unexpected, there would never be any story to tell. Just at the moment when their happiness seemed about to reach its height, Chunmei came with a box to get some tea. The couple were disturbed, but it was too late for them to do anything. Chunmei discreetly but hastily withdrew. Jingji put on his clothes again, and Jinlian did likewise. It was she who took the situation in hand.

"Chunmei, my dear girl," she called, "come here a moment. I have something to say to you."

Chunmei came back. "My dear good sister," Jinlian said, "this gentleman, as you know, is not a stranger. I must tell you the plain truth. We are lovers, and we cannot do without each other. You must keep this to yourself and not breathe a word to a soul."

"Mother," Chunmei said, "why need you say that? I have served you all these years. Do you think I do not know you well enough? Of course, I shall tell no one."

"If you really mean to keep our secret," Jinlian said, "you must prove it to me. Here is the man, lie with him and I will believe you."

Chunmei flushed till her face was now pale, now red, but she could not refuse. Indeed she made the necessary preparations herself, lay down on the bench and yielded before the young man's impetuosity. So that day, Chen Jingji came into full possession of two priceless pearls. What could he do but thread them?

Afterwards, they went their ways. In the days that followed, the two women often brought the young man there, but they hid the matter from the maid Qiuju.

On the first day of the sixth month, old woman Pan died, and the news was brought to Ximen's household. Wu Yueniang prepared the prescribed offerings for the dead and told Pan Jinlian to take a sedan chair and attend the funeral outside the city. Two days later she came back and went to Yueniang's room, and talked there for a long time. Then she left Yueniang, but when she had passed through the great hall, she felt sorely pressed by Nature, pulled up her skirts and gave herself relief beside the wall. After Ximen Qing's death, few people came to see them, and the gate of honor and the doors that led to the great hall were kept shut. Chen Jingji lived in the rooms in the Eastern wing. He had just got up when suddenly he heard the sound of rushing water. Putting his head quietly out of the window, he saw that Jinlian was responsible for it. "What is this wild beast I see?" he laughed. "Mind you pull your skirts high enough. They might get wet." Jinlian hastily arranged her clothes and went over to the window.

"What!" she cried. "You still here! You are just getting up, I suppose. A nice life you lead. Is your wife about?"

"Yes," Jingji said. "It was very late when we came back from the Great Lady's rooms last night. I had to go too, for the Great Lady asked me to go and hear the Hong Luo Sutra read by the nuns. I stayed so long, I was ready to drop, and this morning I did not feel like getting up."

"What a liar you are, you rogue," Jinlian said. "I was not at home yesterday, but I swear you never went to hear any sutras read. The maids tell me you went to dine with Meng Yulou."

"Nothing of the sort," the young man retorted. "My wife will tell you that I went to see the Lady of the House. I never went near the Third Lady's room."

As he talked, he climbed onto the bed. His weapon was at the ready, and he thrust it through the window.

"Oh, you, who will meet an early end," Jinlian cried, "what do you mean by bringing out that old fellow. You gave me quite a fright. Take it back at once, or I will put a needle through it and hurt you."

Jingji laughed. "You don't seem very fond of him today, but you must be generous and treat him kindly."

"Jailbird!" Jinlian cried. She took a small brass mirror from her sleeve, and set it on the windowsill, pretending to powder her face, but in reality doing something quite different. The young man found her attentions most pleasurable, and they were feeling very pleased with one another when they heard footsteps. Jinlian hurriedly took up her mirror and the young man withdrew. It was Laian.

"Fu would like you to take a meal with him," the boy said.

"I am dressing my hair now," Jingji said." Tell him not to wait. I will be with him in a moment." The boy went away and Jinlian cautiously returned. "Tonight," she said, "don't go out. I want you, and will send Chunmei to give you warning. There is something I wish to say to you." Jingji promised to come and, when he had finished combing his hair, went off to attend to some business at the shop. Jinlian went to her own room.

That night was very dark, and the weather very sultry. Jinlian told Chunmei to heat some water for a bath, and dressed her nails. Then she had a light mattress set upon her bed, drove off the mosquitoes, and pulled down the net. She placed some incense in the small burner.

"Mother," Chunmei said, "do you know that this is the first day of the hottest season of the year? Would you like some 'Touch-me-not' to stain your fingers? If you would, I'll get some for you."

"Where?" Jinlian said.

"There is some in the great courtyard. I will get it for you at once."

"Tell Qiuju to get the pestle and mortar ready to pound some garlic," Jinlian said, adding softly: "Go to the East wing and tell your brother to come. I have something to say to him." Chunmei went out to do her bidding and, while she was away, the woman bathed her fragrant body. At last the maid returned with the flowers and told Qiuju what to do with them. Jinlian gave Chunmei a few cups of wine and told her to sleep that night in the kitchen. Then, by the light of the candles, she stained her delicate fingers, while the maid, at her direction, took a bench into the courtyard, with a mattress and some pillows. It was now the first night watch, and everything was silent as the stars moved slowly across the heavens. On either side of the Milky Way the stars of the Heavenly Lovers took up their station. The fragrance of flowers came over the wall, and a little band of glowworms gave their dainty light. Jinlian threw herself upon the mattress, fanned herself and waited. The maid closed the corner gate, but did not bolt it.

> Beneath the moon she stood and waited.
> The wind came and opened the gate
> And, on the walls, the shadows of the flowers moved.
> She thought her precious lover was come.

Chen Jingji had told her he would give warning of his coming by shaking the branches of a flowering shrub. So, when at last Jinlian saw them move, she knew he was there. She coughed gently, and the young man came in and sat beside her. She asked whom he had left at home. "My wife is not there," Jingji said, "but I told Yuanxiao that if anything should happen she must come and tell me at once." He asked if Qiuju had gone to bed, and the woman told him she was already fast asleep. They kissed each other and, there in the courtyard, enjoyed the pleasures of love without so much as a single garment to hinder them.

> Their two hearts beat as one
> They pressed together fragrant shoulders
> And touched each other's cheeks.

He grasped that perfumed breast, smooth as the softest down,
And found it perfect.
He raised those tiny feet, took off the embroidered shoes,
And jade met jade as precious as itself.
Each burning tongue sought sweetness from its mate.
Then like mad phoenixes they took their fill of love
And, when the storm was past,
She whispered to her lover, bidding him
To come again and not delay.

When they were done, Jinlian brought five taels of silver in small pieces and gave them to Chen Jingji.

"My mother has just died," she said. "My husband, when he was alive, provided a coffin for her. She was placed in it the third day after her death and, by our mistress's orders, I was present. I have only returned today. Tomorrow she is to be buried, but the Great Lady says that as we are still in mourning for your father, she cannot let me go. So here are five taels. I want you to go and see about things tomorrow. Pay the undertakers with this money and see the matter through. If you go, I shall be as satisfied as if I went myself."

"It will be no trouble," Jingji said, taking the money. "I will go early and, when all is over, I will come and tell you about it." Then it suddenly occurred to him that his wife might be returning, so he went away.

The next day, it was still morning when he came back. Indeed so early was it that Jinlian had not finished dressing. The young man gave her two branches of jasmine that he had plucked at the temple. "Did you actually see the coffin put in the earth?"

"That is what I went for," Jingji returned. "If I hadn't seen the old lady buried, should I have dared to come and tell you so? I did not spend all the money. There is still about a tael left, and I gave it to your sister. She told me to thank you."

Jinlian, now that her mother was buried, shed a few tears. Then she told Chunmei to put the flowers into a vase and bring the young man some tea. Jingji took some refreshment and then went away.

From that day, the pair seemed more closely drawn together than ever. One day—it was in the seventh month—Jinlian sent the young man a message asking him on no account to fail to visit her that evening. He promised, but unfortunately Cui Ben and a few other friends carried him off for a day in the country and, when he came back, he was so drunk that he could only throw himself on the bed and fall into a sound sleep. When night fell, Jinlian came to see where he was and found him lying on the bed in such a drunken sleep she could not waken him. By chance she thought to see what might be in his sleeve and there discovered a pin with a gold head shaped like a lotus. On it was engraved this legend:

> Horses with golden bridles neigh on the tender grass.
> The season of apricot blossom brings great joy
> To those who live in towers of jade.

She took the pin to the light and examined it. It belonged to Yulou. "Where has he got this?" she wondered. There must, she decided, be something between them or it could not have found its way into Jingji's hands. "No wonder that he has seemed somewhat lacking in manly vigor lately," she said to herself. "I must leave a few words behind me to show I have been here. I think I'll write a line or two on the wall and, next time I see him, I'll drag the truth out of him." Then with a brush she wrote:

> I came alone to visit you, and found you sleeping,
> Came like an angel from the skies.
> It was in vain. You are like Xiang Wang
> There is no spirit to you.
> Day and night I offer you my love
> And you reject it.

She went back to her room. Not long afterwards Jingji woke up, considerably more sober. He lighted a candle, suddenly remembering his tryst with Jinlian. Then he saw the poem written on the wall, the ink still wet, and knew she had been there. The young man felt extremely annoyed with himself. "It is about the first night watch," he said, remembering that his wife and the maid were still with Yueniang. "If I go, I shall find the corner gate closed." He went to the garden and shook the flowering shrub, but there was no response. Taking a large stone to step on, he climbed over the white wall. Jinlian, finding him drunk, had been very disappointed. She had gone back sadly and thrown herself on the bed fully dressed.

Jingji climbed over the wall. Nobody was to be seen in the courtyard: the two maids had gone to bed. He walked on tiptoe and found that the door had not been bolted, so he pushed it open and, by the moonlight that streamed upon the bed, saw Jinlian lying there. "Darling," he cried several times, but there was no reply. "Don't be angry with me," the young man went on. "Cui Ben asked me to go and practice archery outside the city, and I had too much to drink. I am very sorry I didn't come when I should have, and as for your visiting my room, I never knew it." There was still no answer. The young man was greatly upset. He knelt on the floor and kept repeating the same words over and over again.

"You deceitful scamp," Jinlian cried at last, slapping him in the face with the back of her hand, "be quiet. I don't want the maids to hear all about it. There is someone else now, and you care for me no longer. Where have you been today?"

"Really," Jingji assured her, "Cui Ben did take me outside the city. They gave me a lot of wine, and I got drunk and went to sleep. I beg your pardon for not coming. As soon as I saw the poem on the wall, I knew you were annoyed."

"Oh, you deceitful rascal!" Jinlian cried. "Be quiet and don't argue. Slippery as you are, you shan't escape me this time. If, as you say, you were drinking with those fellows and nowhere else, where did you get the pin in your sleeve?"

"I picked it up in the garden two or three days ago."

"In the garden, did you? Well, go to the garden and pick up another one like it and bring it to me. Then I may believe you. This belongs to Yulou, the little strumpet. It's hers beyond a doubt. Why, her name is on it, so what is the use of trying to deceive me? Of course, you and she are carrying on together. Once before I had to speak to you about her, and you swore you had never touched her. But, if that is so, how does this pin come into your possession? I suppose you've told her everything about me. That's why she was laughing at me the other day. Henceforth, my dear Sir, you are you and I am I. Kindly relieve me of your presence."

Jingji swore by all the gods and began to cry. "If I, Chen Jingji, have had the least little thing to do with her, may I die before my thirtieth year; may I have boils the size of bowls; when I want soup, may it turn to water, and when I want water, may there be no water." Still Jinlian refused to believe him.

"You deceitful rubbish," she scolded. "Oaths like that are the kind people take when they want to get rid of the toothache. I wonder you're not ashamed to say such things."

They went on squabbling till it was very late. The young man undressed and lay down beside her, but she turned away and would not answer him, though he kept repeating Lady this and Lady that. Indeed, she slapped his face. After that he did not dare to speak or even to move. When daybreak came, he feared the maids might be getting up, so he climbed over the wall and went back to his own place.

CHAPTER 83

Qiuju Spies on Pan Jinlian

Such love as this the world has seldom known
Alas, when things we treasure seem to be in our hands
We lose them.
Tears flow and the west wind carries them away
Like raindrops falling on Yangtai.

The moon has its mountains, its fullness, its waning
Mankind has happiness, sorrow, and parting.
When they whisper to each other before the fire
The gods know.
Do not say, then, this is the best time of all.

When, at dawn, Pan Jinlian saw Chen Jingji climb over the wall and
go away, her heart relented. It was the fifteenth day of the seventh month, the Festival of All Souls, and Wu Yueniang went in her sedan chair to the temple where Nun Xue lived, to burn some paper treasure chests for Ximen Qing. Jinlian and the others went to the outer gate to see Yueniang start, but when Meng Yulou, Sun Xue'e, and Ximen Dajie came back, Pan Jinlian waited. At the second door, she met Chen Jingji. He had been to the apartments that once belonged to Li Ping'er to get some clothes that were needed in the pawnshop.

"Yesterday I said a few words to you," she said, "and you flew into a rage, and dashed away ever so early. Does that mean you have finished with me?"

"Dear Lady," Jingji said, "how can you say such things? Last night, I never had a wink of sleep. You were so cruel that I nearly died. Look at the marks of your slaps on my face still."

"Scamp," Jinlian said, "if it is true that there is nothing between you, what gave you such a hangdog expression, and why did you run away?"

"The sun was rising," Jingji said, "and if I had not gone then, somebody might have seen me. I assure you, I have never even touched her."

"Then come and see me this evening, and you shall give an account of yourself again."

"You plagued me so much all night," Jingji said, "I never closed my eyes. Now, I shall have to try to get a little sleep in broad daylight."

"Come and see me again," Jinlian said, "and we will clear up this business."

She went to her room, and Jingji took the clothes to the pawnshop. He was busy for a long time, but at last was able to return to his own room. There he threw himself on the bed and went to sleep. It was almost sunset when he woke up. He was anxious to go to Jinlian when, suddenly, dark clouds gathered in the sky and it began to rain.

Jingji looked at the pouring rain. "Oh, what vile weather!" he said to himself. "She was all ready and waiting for me to go and explain things, and now it is raining. What wretched luck I have." He waited and waited, but the rain did not stop. At the first night watch, it was still coming down in torrents, and water was streaming from the roof. At last he could wait no longer. He took a red rug and wrapped it around himself. By this time Yueniang had come home and Jingji's wife and maid were both with her in the inner court. He locked the door, and went to the garden by the gate in the western corner. Still the drenching rain poured down. He pushed open the gate leading to Jinlian's rooms. She knew that he would come, and had told Chunmei to give Qiuju plenty of wine and send her to bed. None of the doors was locked, and Jingji was able to walk straight in.

The windows were partly open and candles were burning brightly. Fruits and refreshments were set out on a table, and golden cups for the wine. Jinlian and Jingji sat down side by side.

"Tell me," she said to him, "if you have had nothing to do with Yulou, how do you come to have her pin?"

"I picked it up by the white rose arbor in the garden. I swear it. May I die this very moment if I lie to you."

"If that is true," Jinlian said, "keep the thing. I don't want it. But remember this: whatever happens, you must not lose the little perfume satchel I gave you to keep your pins in. If anything happens to that, you will know what to expect."

They drank together and played chess. Before the first night watch was over they went to bed and there sported very merrily, spending half the night in transports of delight. In days gone by, Jinlian, by constant diligent practice, had acquired a most marvelous skill in all the arts of love, and this night it was made manifest to her young lover.

Qiuju woke. She could hear a man's voice in the other room, but could not be quite sure whose it was. Before dawn, she got up to make water, and heard the door of her mistress's room being softly opened. The rain had not stopped, but there was a glimmer of moonlight, and through the window she caught a glimpse of a figure wrapped in a red rug. It seemed very like Chen Jingji.

"So it is he who comes night after night to sleep with my lady," she said to herself. "She is always boasting about her virtue, yet here she is carrying on with her son-in-law."

The next morning she went to the kitchen and told her story to Xiaoyu. Xiaoyu was very friendly with Chunmei, and repeated the story to her. "Qiuju," she said, "says that your lady is carrying on with young master Chen. He spent last night with her and did not go away till this morning. You know his wife and her maid were not in their rooms last night."

Chunmei went back and told Jinlian what she had heard. "Mother," she said, "you will have to beat that slave. She can't be allowed to spread this tale all around the place. It might be disastrous for you."

Jinlian, furiously angry, summoned Qiuju. The girl knelt down. "I told you to go and make some gruel," the woman said, "and you have broken the pot. What is the matter with you? Is the hole in your bottom so large that all your brains have fallen out? I fancy your hide is beginning to tickle because it hasn't had a good drubbing for so long." She found a rod and with it gave Qiuju thirty hard blows. The maid squealed like a pig being killed, and her body was bruised.

"Mother," Chunmei said, "if you don't beat her harder than this, it will only allay that tickling. Why not take her clothes off and get one of the boys to give her twenty or thirty strokes with a good thick stick? Then she will begin to know what's what. If you give her gentle taps like this, you'll never make the water muddy. This is nothing more than play. Bold as she is, she seems to have no fear of you." Then she turned to Qiuju. "You are a slave," she said to Qiuju, "and you ought to know that you should never talk to outsiders about anything that happens in your own house. Why, if all maids were like you, people might as well keep a whistle."

"I never said anything," Qiuju cried.

"Still obstinate!" Jinlian said, "you master-murdering slave! Let's have no more from you."

Qiuju went to the kitchen.

One day, about the time of the Autumn Festival, Jinlian secretly arranged with Jingji to come and drink wine with her and enjoy the moonlight. They played Turtle Chess with Chunmei. It was very late when they went to bed, and they did not get up until it was time for morning tea. This was only asking for trouble. Again Qiuju discovered them, and she went at once to Yueniang's room to tell her. But Yueniang was dressing her hair and Xiaoyu was standing at the door. Qiuju took Xiaoyu aside and said:

"Brother-in-law has spent the night with my lady again, and they have not got up even yet. It is just as I told you the other day, yet I was beaten for my pains. Today I can prove what I say. This is no lie. I want the Great Lady to go and see for herself."

"Oh, you goggle-eyed slave!" Xiaoyu cried. "Here you are again with scandalous tales about your mistress. The Great Lady is doing her hair. Get off with you."

"What is she talking about?" Yueniang asked.

Xiaoyu was obliged to make some answer, so she said: "The Fifth Lady sent Qiuju to ask you to go and see her." Yueniang finished dressing and then hurried to the outer court to see what Jinlian wanted. Chunmei fortunately happened to see her coming. She rushed in and told Jinlian. The woman was still in bed with Jingji, and they were greatly alarmed when they heard that Yueniang was on her way. Jingji, rolled himself up in the coverlets and hid himself completely, and Jinlian made Chunmei set a table on the bed. She herself pretended to be making a pearl ornament.

Yueniang came in and sat down. "You are very late this morning," she said. "I wondered what you were doing. I see you are making an ornament." She took the work in her hands and examined it. "It is really very well made," she said. "There is the sesame flower in the middle, borders of squares on either side and, all around, bees resting on chrysanthemum flowers, and hearts interlaced. It is very pretty indeed. You must make one for me."

When Jinlian realized that Yueniang was speaking pleasantly, her heart began to beat more quietly. She told Chunmei to bring some tea. Yueniang drank it and shortly afterwards went away. "Sister," she said as she was going, "when you have dressed your hair, come and see me." Jinlian promised, and as soon as Yueniang had gone, she made Jingji get up and slip away. Both she and Chunmei had had such a terrible fright that they were bathed in sweat.

"The Great Lady has never been to see me before unless she had something definite to say. I wonder what made her come so early today."

"That slave has been at her tricks again," Chunmei said.

Before long, Xiaoyu came and told them what had happened. "Qiuju came," she said, "and talked about brother-in-law being here all day and all night. I scolded her for saying such things, but she still went on. Then the Great Lady asked what it was all about, and the only thing I could say was that you had sent to ask her to come and see you. Lady, you must be on your guard against such backbitings. And you must watch that slave."

Though Yueniang did not believe Qiuju, she was not quite easy in her mind because she realized that Jinlian was a young woman and easily carried away. Her husband was dead. If anything of the sort should happen, she was afraid the story would get out and there would be a scandal. Besides, she thought about Ximen Dajie. She would not allow her to go far away, and she gave the young couple the room that Li Jiao'er once had, so that henceforth they should live in the inner part of the house. Only when Clerk Fu went home did she allow Jingji to sleep at the shop. When the young man had to come for clothes or medicines or anything, Daian always came with him. The windows and doors were all securely fastened, and the maids and serving women were not permitted to go out without very good cause. The household, in fact, was governed much more strictly, and this made it practically impossible for Jinlian and Jingji to indulge their very warm affection for each other. They found, as we so often find, that the joys of this life seldom attain their fullest realization, and that fine weather never lasts very long.

For a month after Qiuju had told of the secret attachment between Jinlian and Chen Jingji, they never had an opportunity of meeting. At last Jinlian could bear the separation no longer. She was lonely behind her embroidered curtains and desolate in her painted chamber. She was afflicted by lovesickness, and became too languid to powder her face. She ate less food and drank less tea than was her custom. She grew thinner and thinner, and the girdle around her waist grew looser and looser. So languid was she that she would lie down on her bed and stay there for hours at a time.

"Mother," Chunmei said, "nothing can be done by worrying. The Great Lady has sent for the two nuns and I hear that tonight they are to stay and read the scriptures. This means that the door to the inner court will be closed early. I will pretend to go to the stable to get some straw to fill a mattress, but really I will go to the shop and ask young master Chen to come and see you. What do you think?"

"Good sister," Jinlian said, "do, for pity's sake, tell him to come. I will never forget how well and kindly you have served me."

"There is no need to say that, Mother," Chunmei said. "You and I are really but one. Father is dead, and whether you go up or down in the world, I shall always be ready to go with you and to stay wherever you may stay."

"If you feel like that, what more could I desire?" Jinlian said.

That evening, she went to Yueniang's room, but soon she excused herself, saying that she did not feel very well and went to her own place. She was like a cicada escaping from its chrysalis. Yueniang closed the door of the inner court very early and dismissed the maids and serving women. Then she settled down to listen to the nuns.

"Good sister," Jinlian said to Chunmei, "go at once and bring him to me."

"First I must give Qiuju some wine and get her comfortably out of the way. Then I will go." She heated two large cups of wine, gave them to Qiuju, and hustled her into the kitchen. Then she took a basket and went to the outer court. She filled the basket with straw and went stealthily to the pawnshop. She knocked softly at the door. Clerk Fu was not there and Jingji was alone. He had just gone to bed when he heard the knock. He recognized Chunmei's voice and, when he opened the door, found that it was indeed she.

"Come in," he said, smiling, "there is no one here but myself."

Chunmei went in. She asked where the boys were.

"Daian and Ping'an are both at the medicine shop," Jingji told her, "and I am left here to bear my loneliness as best I can."

"My mistress sends her love to you," Chunmei said, "and says what a fine person you must be to let all these days pass without coming near her. She says she supposes that, now you have Yulou, you don't care about her any more."

"Oh, what a thing to say!" Jingji said. "Ever since that last time I have been afraid, and the Great Lady keeps the doors and windows so tightly shut that I dare not move."

"For some days," Chunmei said, "my mistress has been miserable. She is restless all the time and never eats a thing. And when she has anything to do, she doesn't seem to know how to set about it. Today the Great Lady is busy listening to the nuns, but my mistress has gone back to her room and wants to see you there. She has sent me especially to ask you to go to her."

"I am grateful for her love," Jingji said. "You go first and I will follow in a few moments."

He opened the cabinet and took out a white silk kerchief and a pair of silver toothpicks. He gave these to Chunmei and embraced her. Then he lifted her on to the bed and kissed her. They were very well pleased with one another.

When they had amused themselves for a while, Chunmei went back with the straw. "Brother-in-law," she said to Jinlian, "was delighted to see me. He says he will come, and gave me this kerchief and these toothpicks."

"Keep a good lookout," Jinlian said. "He may come any moment."

It was the twelfth day of the ninth month, and the moon was very bright. Jingji went first to the medicine shop and ordered Ping'an to take his place at the pawnshop. He told the boy that the Great Lady had sent for him to listen to the exhortations of the two nuns. Then he went to Jinlian. He knew that the main garden gate would be shut, so he went in by the other and, when he came to Jinlian's apartments, shook the hibiscus tree as a signal. Chunmei came out to welcome him and took him into the room. Jinlian was standing at the door. "Oh, villain," she said to him with a smile, "how kind you are to stay away from me for so long."

"I wished to come ever so much," Jingji said, "but I was afraid I should get you into trouble." They held each other's hands and went into the room together. Chunmei closed the door in the corner and set food and wine on the table. Jinlian and Jingji sat down side by side and Chunmei opposite. They poured the wine and passed the cups to one another. When they had had wine enough, a sidelong look came into the woman's eyes and her cloudlike hair seemed to lose its tidiness. She brought out the love instruments that had once belonged to Ximen Qing. The Case for Mutual Enjoyment was there, the Trembling Voice and Lovely Eyes, the silver clasp and the Bell of Excitement. In the candlelight, Jinlian stripped herself of all her clothes and lay naked upon a "drunken old gentleman's chair." Jingji, too, took off his clothes. They found a set of twenty-four pictures representing the pleasures of love, and endeavored to reproduce in real life the joys depicted in the paintings.

"Go behind him and push," Jinlian said to Chunmei. "I'm afraid he must be exhausted."

Chunmei, indeed, gave the young man a push forward. So the warrior stood inside her cunt; he plunged up and down, and gave both of them a most delightful orgasm.

Qiuju, who was in the kitchen at the back, suddenly wished to make water and got up, but she found the door closed on the outer side, and could not open it at first. Finally, she put her hand around and succeeded in working back the bolt. It was quite light in the courtyard, and she went across on tiptoe to the other room. Peeping through the window, she could see candles shining brightly and three people in the room, all merrily drunk, and not a stitch of clothing on them. They seemed to be enjoying themselves immensely. Jinlian and Chen Jingji were plunging and rearing, and Chunmei, behind the young man, was rendering every assistance in her power, and in this way the three worked together.

"These are the people who make themselves out to be so good, while I am beaten," Qiuju said to herself. "But this time I have caught them in the act and tomorrow morning I will go and tell the Great Lady. She won't say I'm lying now."

She watched them until she was quite satisfied, and then went back to the kitchen and to bed.

The three others went merrily on until the third night watch. In the morning, Chunmei was the first to get out of bed. When she came to the kitchen, she found the door open. She questioned Qiuju, and the girl said: "Oh, yes! I had to get up in the night, and I pushed it open and went into the yard."

"You slave!" Chunmei said, "couldn't you see the chamber pot in the room here?"

"I didn't know it was there," Qiuju declared, and they squabbled for a long time. Jingji went away.

Then Jinlian asked Chunmei what all the noise was about, and Chunmei told her how Qiuju had opened the door. Jinlian was greatly annoyed and determined to beat the girl again, but Qiuju went to the inner court and told the whole story to Yueniang.

"You slave who would be the death of your mistress," Yueniang said. "Only the other day you came to me with a long cock-and-bull story. You said your mistress was carrying on with my son-in-law, and that he was with her all night and all day. So I went there: your mistress was in bed busy making an ornament, and my son-in-law was nowhere to be seen. When he did appear, he came from another part of the house altogether. You deceitful slave! My son-in-law is not a sugar figure that can be hidden away anywhere. Are you trying to throw dust in my eyes? If people knew the truth of this, they would know that you are a traitor to your mistress. But if they did not know, they would say: 'When Ximen Qing was alive, he had dealings with many women. And now, though he has been dead only a short time, his own wives are behaving in a most disorderly fashion.' They would even cast doubts upon my own child."

She was going to punish Qiuju, but the girl ran away in alarm and never dared to go to the Great Lady again. When Jinlian heard that Yueniang had refused to believe what Qiuju told her, she was even bolder than before. But Jingji's wife heard whispers, and asked her husband questions.

"Surely, you don't believe that story!" he said. "Why, I spent the whole time at the shop. How could I go to the garden? Besides, you know the garden door has been shut all the time."

"I won't argue with you," his wife said. "If I hear anything more and find that the Great Lady will not believe you, you can keep away from me."

"If I have done anything wrong," Jingji said, "sooner or later it will come out. You ought to refuse to listen to such scandal. You know the Great Lady doesn't believe it."

"I only hope you are telling the truth," his wife said.

CHAPTER 84

Wu Yueniang's Pilgrimage

One day, Wu Yueniang sent for Uncle Wu and told him she wished to go and offer incense at the temple at Taianzhou. When Ximen Qing was desperately ill, she had promised to make sacrifice there.

"If you go, I must go with you," Uncle Wu said. They got ready offerings, incense, candles, and paper things, and decided that Daian and Laian should go with them. They hired three horses, and a sedan chair for Yueniang. Before they left, Yueniang told Meng Yulou, Pan Jinlian, and Sun Xue'e to look well after the house, and Ruyi'er and the maids to take care of Xiaoge. They were to fasten the doors early and not to leave the house.

"You must stay at home," she said to Chen Jingji, "and keep the gate with Clerk Fu. I shall make my offerings on the morning of the fifteenth, which means that I shall be back here at the end of the month."

On the eve of her departure, she took leave of Ximen Qing's tablet, and drank wine with the ladies. She gave all the keys to Xiaoyu. They started before dawn and, leaving the city, set out on the high road. It was the end of autumn: the days were short and the weather cold. Though they only halted once during the day, they could not cover more than sixty or seventy *li,* and, when the sun set, they went to an inn or the house of some villager to spend the night and started again early the next day. It was almost wintry weather, and the wild geese seemed chill and full of sadness. The leaves had withered on the trees; the countryside was bare and melancholy, and there was a great air of mourning everywhere.

After some days, they reached Taianzhou. From there they could see Taishan, the most renowned of all the mountains in the world. It stood deep-rooted in the earth, and its summit pierced the heart of the sky. It is between the states of Qi and Lu, and the very air about it is holy. Uncle Wu saw that it was late, and they went to an inn. The next day they rose very early and went up the mountain to the Daiyo Temple built upon the mountainside. Dynasty after dynasty had venerated this temple, and generation after generation had worshipped there.

Uncle Wu took Yueniang there. She offered incense before the principal shrine and visited all the sacred images. A priest read her declaration. She burned paper money in all the chapels and partook of monastic food. Then she went with Uncle Wu to climb to the highest peak of the mountain. They went up the forty-nine winding paths, clinging to the ivy and scrambling past the vines, and at last caught sight of the Palace of Niangniang far above them in the sky. They had still forty or fifty *li* to go. Wind and cloud, thunder and rain, were all beneath them now. It had been the hour of the Dragon* when they left the Daiyo Temple. It was the hour of the Monkey† when they came to the Golden Palace of Niangniang. There was a red sign over the entrance with these words emblazoned in gold upon it: "The Palace of Radiant Sunset." They went inside and gazed upon the figure of Niangniang.

Wu Yueniang made obeisance. A Daoist priest came and stood beside her. He was a short man, about forty years of age, with three wisps of beard. His eyes were very light and his teeth white. He wore a hat with a pin, and a purple gown. His shoes were embroidered in a cloud design. He read Yueniang's declaration; then they burned incense in a golden burner, and gold and silver papers, and a boy was told to take away the offering.

This priest was really a very bad man. He was the principal disciple of the Abbot of the Daiyo Temple, and his name was Shi Bocai. He was immoderately fond of women and money, and a fellow completely absorbed in the affairs of this world and the pursuit of power. In this district there was an outrageous scoundrel called Yin Tianxi, a brother-in-law of Gao Lien, the local magistrate. This scoundrel was the leader of a band of villains who haunted the neighborhood of the two temples, armed with bows and arrows, and accompanied by hawks and dogs. They preyed especially on women pilgrims, and nobody had the courage to complain about them. The priest, Shi Bocai, allowed them to use his place for their evil purposes. He devised all manner of schemes for getting women to his rooms, and then handed them over to the scoundrel Yin to do what he liked with. He saw that Yueniang was beautiful and that she was in mourning. She must be, he decided, a lady of good family and wealthy. She had only a white-haired old gentleman and two boys to protect her. So he went up, made a reverence to her, thanked her for her offering, and asked her to take tea in his room.

Uncle Wu thanked him. "It is very kind of you," he said, "but we must go down at once."

---

* 5–7 a.m.

† 3–5 p.m.

"There is still plenty of time," the priest said, and took them to his apartments.

The room he led them into was very white and clean. In the place of honor was a couch with embroidery of sesame flowers upon it, and yellow hangings. Over a small table was a picture of Dongbin playing with white peony flowers. On either side was a scroll. One bore the words: "The Pure Wind made his sleeves dance like storks," and the other "In the Moonlight, he discussed the Holy Scriptures." The priest asked their names.

"My name is Wu," Uncle Wu said, "and this is my sister who has come to make sacrifice for her late husband. But we must not impose upon your kindness."

"Since you are so closely related," the priest said, "perhaps you would not mind both taking the place of honor." He himself sat down in the host's place and told one of the novices to bring tea. There were two novices, one called Guo Shouqing and the other Guo Shouli. They were about sixteen years old and very handsome. They wore black silk hats and long gowns, light shoes, and white socks, and used a great deal of perfume. They served the visitors who came to the temple with tea, water, and wine, and the guests who stayed the night there were accustomed to employ them for the basest uses. These two boys closed the door and brought in a number of delightful vegetarian dishes. They offered Uncle Wu and Yueniang excellent tea made of spring water. When the tea had been cleared away, they at once brought wine and a host of dishes, chicken, goose, duck, and fish. They poured the golden wine into amber cups.

When the wine appeared, Yueniang decided that it was time to go. She called Daian, and upon a red lacquer tray the boy offered the priest a roll of cloth and two taels of silver. Uncle Wu begged him to accept them. "Do not trouble to offer us wine and food," he said. "It is late and we must go back."

The priest thanked them. "Only by the grace of Niangniang," he said, "am I in charge of this temple. I live upon the charity of others and, if I may not spend what comes to me upon entertainment, upon what shall I spend it? I have offered you the very simplest of fare, yet you give me valuable presents. I really don't know whether I can accept them or not."

When they urged him to do so, he told the boys to take the presents. "But you must sit down," he said, "and have some wine, so that I may show how kindly I feel towards you."

Uncle Wu could not refuse, and they sat down again. Hot dishes were brought. The priest said to the boys: "This wine is not good enough. Go and open that jar of lotus wine that his Lordship Xu sent me, and offer some to this gentleman."

The boys brought another jar and warmed some of the wine. The priest filled a cup and offered it with both hands to Yueniang. She was unwilling to take it, and Uncle Wu explained that she never drank wine.

"Lady," the priest said, "after so trying a journey you must take some." He then offered half a cup and Yueniang took it. He filled another and offered it to Uncle Wu, saying: "My lord, try this wine and tell me what you think of it."

Uncle Wu tasted it. It was very sweet and well bodied. "It is excellent," he said.

"It was given to me by Xu, the Prefect of Qingzhou," the priest said. "His lady, and his son and daughter, come to offer sacrifice here every year, and he is one of my most intimate friends. His daughter's baby has been placed under the protection of Niangniang. They regard me as a hardworking, plain fellow, but they appreciate my sincerity and love and respect me. You see the government has cut down the revenue of these two temples by half, but, fortunately, this excellent prefect wrote and arranged that the whole of it should be left to us. So we have money enough to burn incense to Niangniang, and what is left we spend upon the entertainment of pilgrims."

While they were talking, the two boys and the porters were entertained elsewhere. There was as much as they could eat. Uncle Wu drank a few cups of wine and then again prepared to take his leave. It was getting late.

"The sun has gone down," the priest said. "It is too late for you to go down the mountain now. Will you not spend the night here and start tomorrow morning? That will be much pleasanter for you."

"I have left some luggage at the inn," Uncle Wu said, "and I am rather anxious about it."

The priest smiled. "Don't worry about that," he said. "I give you my word that it will be perfectly safe. When the people in the villages know you are at my place, they will be afraid of me. I could very quickly get hold of anybody who might steal your property and bring them before the local courts."

Uncle Wu said no more. The priest offered him another large cup of wine, but, realizing that it was very potent, he excused himself, saying he was tipsy enough already and that he must go and change his clothes. He went to the back part of the building and looked around. Yueniang was very tired. She went to lie down on the couch and the priest closed the door and went away.

Suddenly Yueniang heard a noise. It was a man creeping through a little door behind the bed. His face was red and bearded. He was about thirty years old, and wore a black hat and a purple gown. He took Yueniang in his two hands.

"I am Yin Tianxi, at your service," he said, "the brother-in-law of Magistrate Gao. I heard that you were a lady of good birth and very beautiful, and I was anxious to make your acquaintance. Now I have seen you, I realize my good fortune. If you are kind to me, I shall never forget it."

He pressed her down on the couch and would have forced her. Yueniang was frightened and cried aloud. "In this world of peace and brightness, would you dare to assault a woman of good birth?" she cried. She tried to escape, but the man prevented her. He knelt down.

"Lady," he said, "do not make such a noise. Take pity on me, and listen to my urging."

Yueniang only cried the louder: "Help! Help!" Laian and Daian recognized their mistress's voice and dashed to the back to call Uncle Wu. "Uncle," they cried, "come at once. Our lady is fighting with someone in the priest's room."

Uncle Wu hurried as fast as he could. He pushed the door but could not open it. He could hear Yueniang crying: "Why are you trying to keep me here?"

"Sister, don't be afraid," Uncle Wu shouted. "I am here." He picked up a piece of rock and forced open the door. When Yin Tianxi saw that someone was coming, he released Yueniang and slipped quickly away through the back. There were many ways of escape. Uncle Wu came in. "Sister," he cried, "has he done you any harm?"

"No," Yueniang said, "but he has got away."

Then Uncle Wu tried to find the priest, but the priest eluded him and sent his young novices to face the trouble. Uncle Wu was terribly angry. He bade Laian and Daian break all the windows and doors in the temple, and then took Yueniang away. She got into her sedan chair and they went down the mountain as fast as they could. It was about sunset when they left the temple and midnight when they came to their inn. Uncle Wu told the people of the inn what had happened. They were greatly disturbed. "You should not have challenged that evil star, Yin," they said. "He is the magistrate's brother-in-law, and everybody knows his goings-on. When you have gone, we shall suffer. He will not let you go for nothing."

Uncle Wu paid the reckoning and gave the innkeeper an extra tael. Then all the luggage was packed up; Yueniang got into her sedan chair, and they set off posthaste.

Yin Tianxi was angry. He gathered twenty or thirty of his men, all armed with swords and clubs, and they raced down the mountainside. Meanwhile, Uncle Wu and his people went straight on. About the fourth night watch, they came to a clearing and saw, afar off, a light shining through the forest. They went towards the light and came to a cave in which an old monk was reading the sacred scriptures by candlelight.

"Venerable Teacher," they said to him, "we have been to offer sacrifice at the temple, and now evil men are pursuing us. We have lost our way in the darkness. Will you tell us where we are, and how we can get from here to Qinghe?"

"You are on the eastern spur of Taishan," the old monk told them. "This cave is known as the Xuejian Cave, and I am called the Holy Man of Xuejian, though my real name is Pujing. I have been here for thirty years, mortifying the flesh. It is good fortune that has brought you to me. Do not go farther. There are many wild beasts on these mountain slopes, and it will be better for you to start tomorrow. The high road to Qinghe is not far from here."

"But I am afraid those evil men may find us," Uncle Wu said.

The old man looked about him. "Do not let that trouble you," he said. "The scoundrels have gone home already." He asked Yueniang's name.

"She is my sister," Uncle Wu said, "the widow of Ximen Qing. She came to offer sacrifice for her husband. Venerable Teacher, you have saved our lives, and we can never cease to be grateful to you."

They spent the night in the cave. Before dawn, Yueniang offered the old monk a roll of cloth. He would not accept it.

"I want one of your sons to be my disciple," he said.

"My sister has only one child," Uncle Wu said, "and she hopes to bring him up to continue the family. If she had another son, she would certainly give him to you."

"My baby is still very young," Yueniang said. "He is not a year old yet. He cannot come to you."

"I don't want him now," the old monk said, "I only ask for your promise that I shall have him in fifteen years' time."

Yueniang decided that she would settle that when the fifteen years were over. She made an indefinite kind of promise. Then they said good-bye to the old monk and set out along the high road to Qinghe.

CHAPTER 85

Chunmei Is Dismissed

The wheel of passion turns and never stops
And those who watch are oft bewildered.
The fortune of a man is subject to many vicissitudes
And when it is all but attained
It comes to naught.
Man finds it hard to hold his head aloft
While strangers look on coldly
And there is none to sympathize.

All through the day
Her brows were knit in sorrow.
She leaned on all the railings
Knowing not what to do.
She can only hope that the moon still shines
Over the five lakes
She must have patience, the time will come
When she will realize the debt of love.

Pan Jinlian and Chen Jingji followed one another about like a cock and a hen. One day, Jinlian felt a sudden pain and realized that her belly was growing bigger. She felt languid and tired and disinclined to eat anything. She sent for Chen Jingji.

"These last few days," she said, "I have been hardly able to keep my eyes open. My belly is getting big, and I can feel something moving inside it. I have no appetite and my body feels very heavy. When your father was alive, I got some medicine from Nun Xue to make me have a child, and nothing happened. Now he is dead, and I have been carrying on with you only a short time, yet I am with child. It was the third month, I think, when I was last unwell, and that would make the child about six months on the way. Now I, who have always laughed at other people, look like being laughed at myself. Pull yourself together. The Great Lady has not come back yet. Go and get some medicine to get rid of it. If I have the child, it will be the end of me, and I shall never be able to lift my head and look people in the face again."

"We have all sorts of medicines in the shop," Jingji said, "but I don't know which is the right one. And I haven't any sort of prescription for that purpose. Doctor Hu, in the High Street, is a specialist in women's troubles. I will go to him and ask him for something to put you right. He knows us quite well."

"Well, be quick about it, Brother," Jinlian said. "You must do something to save my life."

Jingji took three *qian* of silver and went at once to see Dr. Hu. The doctor was at home. He knew that Chen Jingji was Ximen Qing's son-in-law and took the young man in.

"It is a long time since I last saw you," he said. "What can I do for you?"

"I have come to trouble you for an abortive," Jingji said. "Here is the money. Thank you very much."

"The people of this world," Dr. Hu said, "regard the saving of life as a very noble thing. Everybody comes to ask for medicine to help them to get babies. Why do you come and ask for the very opposite? I have none."

Jingji gave the doctor another two *qian*. "Don't let us talk about nobility," he said. "If I am asking for it, it is because I want it. A young woman I know would find it very awkward if she should have a baby, and she wishes to make sure that she does not."

"I will give you some of the medicine that people call 'Clear all out,'" Dr. Hu said, taking the money. "Let her take it and, in the time it would take her to walk five *li*, the child will come away."

He gave Jingji two doses. The young man said goodbye and hurried back to give the medicine to Jinlian. In the evening she took it with some hot water. Immediately she began to feel pain. She lay down on the bed, and Chunmei pressed her belly. In a very short time, she called for the pail, and the child came away. She told Qiuju that she had been unwell and bade her throw everything into the privy. The next day, when the privy cleaners came, they found a white, well-nourished infant. As the proverb says: Good news is never heard outside the door, but bad news travels a thousand miles. In a very few days, nearly everyone in the household knew that Jinlian had been carrying on with Chen Jingji and had had a baby.

When Wu Yueniang came back, it was the tenth month and she had been absent for a fortnight. She was welcomed as though she had fallen from the skies. She made obeisance to the gods and burned incense, then went to visit Ximen Qing's tablet. Afterwards, she told Meng Yulou and the others of her adventures at the temple. She sobbed as she did so. Then the people of the house came to see her, and Ruyi'er brought Xiaoge. Mother and child came together again.

When she had burned some paper offerings, she gave her brother food and wine and he went home. In the evening, the ladies entertained Yueniang. She was weary after her long journey and the fright she had had, and for two or three days was not at all well. Qiuju, who had heard about the relations between her mistress and Chen Jingji, was very anxious to tell Yueniang all about them. She came to Yueniang's door, but Xiaoyu spat in her face and boxed her ears.

"Get off at once, you scandalmongering slave!" she cried. "My mistress is not well after her long journey, and she is still in bed. If you make her angry, it will be the worse for you."

Qiuju swallowed her anger and went away.

One day, Chen Jingji came for some clothes, and Jinlian and he again amused themselves upstairs. While they were enjoying themselves to the utmost, Qiuju again went to the inner court, and asked Yueniang to come and see for herself.

"Lady," she said, "I have warned you several times, but you would not listen. When you were away, they used to sleep together from morning till night and from night till morning. She even got in the family way. She and Chunmei have both been at the same tricks. Now they are upstairs doing wicked things together. If you do not believe me, come and see for yourself."

Yueniang hurried to the outer court. The couple upstairs were busily engaged, but Chunmei happened to see Yueniang coming and rushed upstairs to warn them. They were greatly alarmed and could think of no place in which to hide. Jingji could only pick up some clothes and run downstairs.

"My son," Yueniang said, "what are you doing here? You seem to have a very poor memory."

"Someone is waiting in the shop and there was no one else to come and get the clothes," Jingji said.

"Didn't I give definite orders always to send a boy for the clothes?" Yueniang said. "What right have you in the room of this woman who has lost her husband? You are utterly shameless."

Chen Jingji ran away as fast as his legs would carry him, and Jinlian stayed upstairs, not daring to come down. At last, however, she did come down, and Yueniang scolded her severely.

"Sister," she said, "you must give up this shameless way of behaving. You and I are widows, and things are very different now from when our husband was alive. Even vases and jars have ears. Why do you associate with this young man? The servants are all saying the most terrible things about you. The proverb says that a man without character is like iron without any strength, and that a woman without character is as soft as honey. When we behave with proper decorum, people will do what they are told without our having to go to extremes, but, if we do not so behave, they will not obey, however severe our orders. If you were straightforward and conducted yourself decently, nobody would dare to say a word about you. I have been told this several times before, but I would never believe it. Now I have seen with my own eyes, and there is no choice left to me. Make up your mind that you will so live as to maintain our dead husband's good name. Take my own case. If I had been a wicked woman, I should never have come back here when that bad man assaulted me."

Jinlian flushed and paled in turns. She was full of denials. "I was burning incense upstairs when he came for some clothes, and I had no conversation at all with him."

There was a good deal of argument, and then Yueniang went away.

In the evening, when Ximen Dajie and Jingji were in their own apartment together, Ximen Dajie said to him: "You villain! Will you still dare to say that I have no proofs? Will you argue with me now? What were you doing upstairs with her today? I can't find words bad enough for you. The best thing would be to put you and her together in a big jar. And that whore, who has stolen my husband, swaggers about in my presence! She is like a tile out of the privy, hard and stinking. She always thinks she is better than anybody else. Do you think you will continue to have your meals here with me?"

"You whore!" Jingji said, in a fury, "isn't my money kept here? I'm not begging for food in this place." He went away in a very bad temper.

After that time, he always stayed at the shop and never came to get anything. Daian and Ping'an were sent to bring anything that was needed. Even the midday meal was served at the shop. Clerk Fu used to take some money and go to the street for noodles, then take them back with him. It was one of those cases where, as when there is a fight between a dragon and a tiger, the little wolf suffers. All the doors and windows were kept shut, even before the sun went down. And so the lovemaking between Chen Jingji and Jinlian was interrupted again.

There was a house belonging to Chen Jingji, which was lived in by his mother's brother. This was a man named Chang, who had no work to do and spent all his time at home. To him Jingji went night and morning for his meals. Wu Yueniang asked no questions. Pan Jinlian and the young man were separated for about a month. She was desperately lonely. Each day seemed like a whole season, and each night was like half a summer. She could not bear the loneliness, and passion raged within her. There was no way she could see him. She could not send out a message, and he could not come near her.

One day, the young man saw old woman Xue going past the door and it occurred to him that she might be able to take a letter to tell Jinlian how much he loved her and how greatly he was distressed by their separation. As soon as he had an opportunity, he pretended to be going out to collect some money, but actually he took a donkey and went to see the old woman. When he came to her door, he tied up the donkey and asked if the old woman was at home. Her son, Xue Ji, and his wife were sitting on the bed nursing their baby. There were two girls in the room, waiting to be sold. When the young woman heard somebody asking for old woman Xue, she went out to see who it was.

"I should like to know if Madam Xue is at home," Jingji said.

The young woman asked him to go in. "Mother has gone to change some ornaments and to collect some money," she said. "If there is anything we can do for you, I will send for her." She made tea for Chen Jingji.

After a while, old woman Xue came back. She made a reverence to Jingji and said: "What wind has blown you here?" She bade her daughter-in-law make him a cup of tea, but the young woman told her she had already done so.

"I would not trouble you," Jingji said, "except on a matter of some importance. You know I have been on very close terms with the Fifth Lady for a long time. Now Qiuju has been blabbing, and we cannot get a chance to meet. The Great Lady and my wife, too, are treating me very badly. I can't live without that woman, yet we have been parted all this time and have no way even of sending a message one to the other. I have thought of sending a letter, but there is no one I can trust it with. So I have come to you. I am sure you can help me."

He took a tael of silver from his sleeve. "This," he said, "may serve to buy you a cup of tea."

The old woman laughed and clapped her hands. "I never heard of such a thing," she said, "a son-in-law carrying on with his mother. Tell me, however did you manage to get her?"

"Sister Xue," Jingji said, "this is not a joke. Here is my letter. You must take it to her for me."

The old woman took the note. "I have not been to see the Great Lady since she returned. I will go to pay her my respects."

"When shall I expect the answer?" Jingji said.

"I will come to your shop and tell you there," the old woman said.

Jingji mounted his donkey and went back to the shop. The next day, old woman Xue took her box and went to Ximen's house. First she went to see Yueniang, then Yulou, and finally Jinlian.

Jinlian was eating some rice gruel and talking to Chunmei, who was trying to make her more cheerful. "Mother," she said, "don't let yourself be so upset. Right or wrong, let people talk if they feel like it. After Father died, the Great Lady had a baby. Did anybody suggest there was anything wrong about that? She cannot control the things we do in secret. Cheer up. If the skies fall, there is always one who upholds them to put them back again. So long as we're alive let us be as merry as we can."

She heated some wine and gave a cup to her mistress. "Drink this," she said, "and drown your sorrow."

Then she looked out into the courtyard. Two small dogs were there, seemingly glued together.

"There!" she said, "even animals must have their enjoyment. Why not we human beings?"

Then old woman Xue came. She made a reverence to Jinlian and again to Chunmei. "I see you are having some fun," she said. Then she saw the two dogs.

"A good omen for this house," she said. "When one sees a thing like that, one ceases to feel lonely."

"You have not been here for a long time," Jinlian said. "What has brought you today?" She asked old woman Xue to sit down.

"I don't know what I have been doing all the time," old woman Xue said, "but I am never idle. I wasn't able to come and see your Great Lady when she came back from her pilgrimage. I have just come from her, and she was quite annoyed with me. The Third Lady was there too. She bought a pair of ornaments and some ribbon from me. She is a good lady, that. She just handed me eight *qian* of silver. But the lady Sun Xue'e, who bought two pairs of flowers in the eighth month and still owes me two *qian* for them, doesn't want to pay me. So mean she is! But why were you not in the inner court?"

"I have not been very well lately," Jinlian said. "I didn't feel like leaving my room."

Chunmei heated a cup of wine and gave it to the old woman. Old Xue made a reverence and thanked her. "Ought I to take it, when I have only just come in?" she said.

"It will bring you a good baby," Jinlian said.

"No more babies for me," old woman Xue said, "but my daughter-in-law had one a little while ago. He is two months old. I expect you have been very lonely since your husband's death, Lady?"

"Naturally," Jinlian said. "We have to suffer now in all kinds of ways. There are too many talkers in this household. The Great Lady herself, since her child has been born, has been quite a different woman. We are not so friendly as we used to be. As I told you, I have not been well lately, but we had a quarrel and that is one reason why I have not been near her."

"It was all Qiuju's fault," Chunmei said. "When the Great Lady was away, that slave told a pack of lies about my mistress, and even dragged me into it. It is most provoking."

"She is your maid," old woman Xue said. "How dare she say things about her mistress? One who wears a black gown should stand by a black pillar. She ought not to do things like that."

"Go and have a look," Jinlian said to Chunmei. "She may be listening to us again."

"No," Chunmei said, "she is in the kitchen, picking rice. She is like a torn sack or a leaking manger, going about and telling everybody our business."

"Since there is nobody here, I have something to tell you," the old woman said. "Yesterday, Master Chen came to my house. He told me your maid Qiuju had got you into this pickle. He said that the Great Lady had scolded him, and that she kept the doors and windows tightly closed. He said he was no longer allowed to come here for clothes and medicine, and that his wife had gone to live in a room in the east wing. Nobody sends him anything to eat, and he has to go to his Uncle Zhang's for his meals. It is not right that the Great Lady should not trust her own son-in-law but put all her confidence in the boys. He told me it was ever so long since he had seen you, and that he is dying to do so. He sends this letter and his love. Don't worry, he says. Now that the master is dead, you would perhaps be wise to come out into the open. There is nothing to fear. Sometimes, we are afraid of the incense making too much smoke, but now there is no reason why it should not."

She took Jingji's letter from her sleeve and gave it to Jinlian. It was in the form of a poem written to the meter of "The Embroidered Scarlet Shoe."

The fires of hell consume me
The waters beneath the dark blue bridge are almost to my neck.
What we have to do, let us do quickly
For scandal spreads over the districts of the south
And there is no avoiding it.
Let us then complete the work of joy
For if we do it not, it is as though we did.

When Jinlian read this, she put it into her sleeve.

"He would like you to give him some token, or write a few words to him," the old woman said. "Otherwise, he will not believe that I have given you the message."

Jinlian told Chunmei to drink with old woman Xue and herself went to the inner room. She came back with a white silk handkerchief and a gold ring. On the handkerchief, she wrote a poem to express her love. When she had finished, she wrapped the handkerchief and the ring up together and gave them to the old woman.

"Give him my love," she said, "and bid him be patient. Tell him if he keeps going to his uncle's for his meals, his uncle may get tired of him and say: 'You are doing your father-in-law's business, why do you come here to eat?' It looks as though our people have not food enough to feed themselves. So tell him not to go to his uncle, but to take some money from the shop and spend it on food and cakes and things to eat with Clerk Fu. And tell him to come to the house as usual. If he does not come, it will look as though he were afraid of somebody here."

The old woman promised to tell him all these things. Then Jinlian gave her five *qian* of silver, and she went to the shop to make her report to Chen Jingji.

They found a quiet place, and old woman Xue gave him the things that Jinlian had sent. "The Fifth Lady says you must be patient," she told him. "Don't allow yourself to be drawn into a quarrel. Come to the house as usual and don't go to your uncle's for your meals. It may displease him."

She showed him the five *qian* of silver Jinlian had given her. "You see there are no secrets between us," she said. "I am sure things will go well with you, and I tell you about this money because, if she told you about it herself sometime, it would look bad for me."

"I am very grateful to you, old lady," Jingji said, and bowed low to old woman Xue.

She had hardly taken two steps away from him when she came back. "I nearly forgot one very important thing," she said. "When I came away, the Great Lady sent Xiuchun after me. She told me to sell Chunmei. She said that the maid, as well as the mistress, had been carrying on with you."

"Take her to your house," Jingji said, "and I will come and see her there."

The old woman went home.

That evening, when the moon was shining, old woman Xue came to take Chunmei away. First she went to Yueniang's room.

"We paid sixteen taels of silver for her," Yueniang said, "and I will take sixteen taels now."

Then she said to Xiaoyu: "Go and tell Chunmei. She is to go without her clothes."

Old woman Xue went to Jinlian and broke the news to her. "The Great Lady," she said, "has told me to take Chunmei away because she helped you to receive your lover secretly. She is only asking the price for which she bought her."

Jinlian opened her eyes very wide, but she could not speak. Then she began to cry. "Oh, Sister Xue," she said, "you see the kind of treatment we receive now that my husband is dead. It is only a few months since he died, yet now they mean to rob me of my maid. How utterly heartless the Great Lady is. She thinks that, now she has a child of her own, she can drag us all through the mud. But Li Ping'er's child died when it was only eighteen months old. Children have been known to die of smallpox, and we never know what Heaven may have in store for us. She will do well not to raise her hopes too high."

"I suppose his Lordship, when he was alive, took his pleasure with Sister Chunmei," the old woman said.

"'Took his pleasure' indeed!" Jinlian cried. "He treated her like part of himself. She had only to say one word and he believed ten. When she asked for one thing, he gave her a dozen. Even his wives were less considered than she was. If she suggested that he should give one of the boys ten strokes of the rod, he would not dare to give them five."

"The Great Lady is in the wrong, then," old woman Xue said. "You say his Lordship had taken his pleasure of her, yet the Great Lady is sending her away without boxes and without any clothes. She is to go just as she came. The neighbors will think that very strange, I'm sure."

"Did she tell you Chunmei was not to be allowed to take away her clothes?" Jinlian cried.

"Yes, that was her order. Xiaoyu is coming to see about it."

Chunmei heard the whole of this conversation, but she did not shed a single tear. When she saw how her mistress was crying, she said: "Mother, why do you cry? You must not worry about me when I have gone away. It would make you ill and, if you are ill, there will be no one to look after you. Let me go. I don't want any clothes. A good man will not eat food that other people throw to him, and a good girl does not wear her wedding dress."

Then Xiaoyu came. "Mother," she said, "surely you are not going to pay any attention to what the Great Lady says now. She is obstinate at the moment. Sister Chunmei has served you well. Take some of the best clothes, and let Madam Xue take them away for Chunmei as a parting gift from you. She is going away now, and there is no reason why we should say anything to the Great Lady about it."

"You are very kind," Jinlian said.

"Lady," Xiaoyu said, "we never know what is coming to us. We are like frogs and crickets living here. A fox is sorrowful when it sees a dead rabbit; creatures are always sympathetic with their own kind."

They filled Chunmei's box with the things like kerchiefs and ornaments that had belonged to her. Jinlian gave her two of her own best dresses and some socks, making a large parcel of them. She gave her pins and rings and earrings. Xiaoyu took two pins from her hair and gave them to the girl. The pearls and headdresses and embroidered clothes she took back to Yueniang.

Chunmei said good-bye to Jinlian. Xiaoyu cried. When they were on their way to the gate, Jinlian wanted her to go and say good-bye to Yueniang and the others, but Xiaoyu advised them not to do so. Chunmei walked proudly behind old woman Xue and never turned her head. Jinlian and Xiaoyu went with her to the gate. Then Xiaoyu went back to Yueniang. "She has gone now," she said, "and she has left all her clothes behind." Jinlian returned to her room. She had been accustomed to talking to Chunmei, and now Chunmei was taken away from her. She was very lonely and cried bitterly.

CHAPTER 86

Pan Jinlian Leaves the House of Ximen

Chen Jingji, one morning after breakfast, pretended that he had money to collect, took a horse, and went to old woman Xue's house. The old woman was at home and asked him to come in. Jingji tethered his horse outside and went in. After he had taken tea, the old woman said: "What can I do for you, Brother-in-law?"

"I was out collecting some money," Jingji said, "and thought I would call to see you. I hear the maid came to you yesterday. Is she still here?"

"Yes, I have not found a master for her yet."

"I should like to see her. May I have a word with her?"

The old woman pretended to hesitate. "Good Brother-in-law," she said, "the Great Lady gave me very strict instructions. She said that this maid was being sent away because she and you had been misbehaving yourselves. I wasn't to let you see her. So go away, please. She might be sending some of her boys here. If they came and saw you, there would be trouble for me when they went back and told the Great Lady. I should never be able to go there again."

The young man smiled and took a tael of silver from his sleeve. "Buy yourself a cup of tea with this," he said, "I will give you more, later."

Then the old woman agreed. "I am not in any need of money at the moment," she said. "Perhaps you will keep it for me and give it me some other time. But one thing I do want. At the end of last year, I pawned two pairs of embroidered pillow ends at your pawnshop. That is about twelve months ago and, including the interest, I should probably have to pay eight *qian* of silver. Will you get them for me?"

"You shall have them tomorrow," Jingji said.

The old woman asked him to go to the inner room, and there he found Chunmei. She told her daughter-in-law to cook something for them, and went off herself to buy cakes, wine, and meat for Chen Jingji and Chunmei.

"Brother," Chunmei said, when she saw Jingji, "a fine fellow you are! Nobody but a murderer would have brought my mistress and me to such a pass that we can neither rise nor fall. Now the secret is out, and you see how people hate us."

"Sister, you have finished with that household now, and I don't see why I should bother about it any more. In this world, we have to go our own ways. See that Madam Xue finds a good home for you. When the fruit of the fields has been dug up and taken away, it can never return whence it came. That is how it is with me. I shall go to the Eastern Capital to see what my father has to say. Then I shall come back and divorce my wife, and claim the boxes and things that those people have of mine."

Old woman Xue soon came back with the refreshments. A table was set and the pair sat down and drank together. Old woman Xue joined them, and they chatted together.

"The Great Lady is very unfeeling," the old woman said. "To a beautiful girl like you, she might at least have given ornaments and clothes. It will be very awkward when you have to go to a new master's house. And she asked the same money for you as she paid. It is like pouring clean water from one cup to another. Some is bound to be spilled on the way. Yes, indeed, she is very, very mean. When you came away with me, Xiaoyu asked your mistress to give you two dresses. Without them, you wouldn't have had a rag to put on when you go to your new home."

When they had had wine enough, old woman Xue told her daughter-in-law to take the baby away, and left them alone to amuse themselves.

She was afraid that Yueniang might send someone to see what was happening, so she would not let Jingji stay very long. He mounted his horse and went home. In a day or two he gave Chunmei two kerchiefs and two pairs of drawers, and got the pillow ends for old woman Xue. He gave the old woman some money to buy wine for him to drink with Chunmei. Unfortunately, Yueniang sent Laian to the house to find out why the old woman had not found a master for Chunmei. Laian saw Jingji's horse outside, and went back at once and told his mistress.

Yueniang was very angry, and sent one boy after another to fetch the old woman. When she came, Yueniang scolded her severely.

"You have the maid, yet you keep putting off finding a master for her. You think you'll make a little extra money for yourself by keeping her to carry on with some young rascal. If you can't attend to this business, let me have the maid back again and I'll give the job to old woman Feng. You'll never be allowed near the place again."

Then old woman Xue plied her go-between's mouth. "Heaven! Heaven!" she cried. "Your ladyship really must not blame me. Do you think I would chase the god of wealth away with a stick? You were kind enough to give me this job, and I should never have the boldness not to get on with it. Yesterday, I took the maid to several places, but I didn't succeed in selling her. You ask sixteen taels for her, but I haven't got money enough to pay for her before I sell her."

"The boys tell me," Yueniang said, "that young Chen has been hanging about your place drinking with the maid."

"Ai ya!" the old woman cried. "What a lie! He certainly called to see me because he had to bring me two pillow ends that I left at your pawnshop twelve months ago. Since he had done me that favor, I asked him to have a cup of tea, but he would not and rode away on his horse at once. He did not drink wine at my place. What stories your boys have been telling you!"

Yueniang did not say anything for a long time. At last she said slowly: "I should not be surprised if that young man's passion put wrong ideas into his head."

"I am not a three-year-old child," old woman Xue said, "and it was easy to see what the position was. You gave me your orders, and I had to carry them out. He didn't stay a single minute at my house, just handed me the pillow ends, and went away without even a cup of tea. He hadn't time to see the maid. Really, Lady, you must make sure of the facts before you blame me. Now, his Lordship Zhou wants a girl to ensure the continuance of his family, but he does not want to pay more than twelve taels. I might get thirteen taels out of him. His Lordship has been here to parties and seen her. He liked her appearance: she is beautiful and can sing sweetly, or he would not have offered so much. You must remember that she is not a virgin, and we can hardly expect so high a price from anybody else."

Yueniang agreed to accept this sum and, the next day, old woman Xue took Chunmei to Major Zhou's house. The girl was beautifully painted and wore a headdress of pearls and ornaments. She was dressed in a red silk coat and blue silk skirt. Her shoes were small and pointed. Major Zhou thought her more beautiful than ever. He gave the old woman a piece of silver worth about fifty taels.

Old woman Xue took the silver back to her own place, cut off a piece amounting to thirteen taels, and gave it to Yueniang. She brought another tael with her, and told Yueniang that Major Zhou had given it to her as a reward for her services. She asked Yueniang for something more, and was given five *qian* of silver. So, all together, she made thirty-seven taels and five *qian* from this deal. Such is the way of go-betweens, nine out of ten of whom make their living in this way.

Chunmei was lost to Chen Jingji, and Jinlian was out of his reach. Yueniang was very careful about doors and windows. Every evening she took a lantern, went around the whole house, and made sure that all the doors were bolted before she went to bed. Jingji was powerless, and it made him very impatient. He quarreled with his wife.

"Strumpet!" he shouted. "Let me tell you straight out that I am the son-in-law in this family. I'm not a beggar. I'm sick of the place, and your people are keeping all my chests full of gold and silver. You are my wife, but do you take my part? No, you talk about my begging my food here. Do I ever eat a thing without rendering service in return?"

His wife cried.

It was the twenty-seventh day of the eleventh month, Meng Yulou's birthday. She got ready some dishes and wine and, out of the kindness of her heart, told Chunhong to take it to the shop for Clerk Fu and Chen Jingji. Yueniang tried to stop her. "That young man is a scoundrel," she said. "Don't have any dealings with him. If you would like to send something to Clerk Fu, well and good, but don't give that young man anything."

Yulou did not pay any heed. She told Chunhong to take the things to them. The boy put down the food on the counter of the shop. When Jingji had finished the jar of wine, he was still not satisfied and told the boy to go back and ask for more.

"I have had enough," Clerk Fu said. "I don't think we need ask for any more."

But Jingji insisted, and Laian was sent to ask for more wine. Sometime later he came back. "There is no more wine in the inner court," he told them. Jingji was already half tipsy. He again told the boy to go and fetch more wine, but the boy did not move. Then Jingji took some of his own money and bought wine. As he drank it, he cursed Laian.

"You wait, you thievish slave! Your mistress treats me badly, and you, you slave, think you can look down on me too. You won't go and do what I ask you. You know I am the son-in-law in this family. I am tired of eating and drinking in this haphazard way. You know how they treated me when my father-in-law was alive. Now he is dead, they sing a very different tune. Nobody bothers about me any more, and all they want is to get rid of me. My mother-in-law believes every little story the slaves carry to her. She entrusts her business to slaves and has no confidence in me. Let her do as she likes: I have patience enough to endure this injustice."

Clerk Fu tried to cheer the young man. "You mustn't talk like that," he said. "If they don't respect you, whom do they respect? I am sure they must be busy now. It is not that they don't want to give you the wine. Your scolding the boy doesn't matter, but the walls have ears. If anybody hears you, they will say: 'That young man is drunk again.' "

"Old friend," Jingji said, "you don't understand. I may have wine in my belly but I know what I'm talking about. My mother-in-law listens to every bit of tittle-tattle, and believes that everything about me is bad. She thinks that it is I who have made a fool of other people and not others who have made a fool of me. But if I amuse myself with every woman in that household, and she brings a case against me in the courts, it is no more than a case of carrying on with one's late father-in-law's women, and that is only a matter of imprudence. First, I shall divorce her daughter. Then I shall go to the courts myself, or else to the Eastern Capital, and I shall accuse her of detaining many chests full of gold and silver that ought either to belong to me or be given to the authorities, since they came from Yang Jian. If I do that, her house will be confiscated, and all the women will be sold. I am not hoping to catch any fish: all I wish is to stir up the mud. If she had any sense, she would treat me as her son-in-law as she used to do, then everything would be all right."

Clerk Fu did not care for the tone the young man was taking. "Brother-in-law," he said, "you are certainly drunk, and you are talking without thinking."

Chen Jingji opened his eyes wide and glared at Clerk Fu. "You thievish old dog!" he said haughtily. "Do you suggest that I am drunk, and don't know what I'm talking about? Well, it is not any wine of yours I'm drinking. Even if I am a scoundrel, I am still the honorable son-in-law of this household and you are a paid hireling. Will you dare to treat me badly too? You old dog! Wait! During the last few years, you have made money enough out of my father-in-law, and you have eaten his food. Now you have evil ideas in your head and you think, if you get rid of me as soon as you can, you will be able to make yourself the only man who can transact business here. If I send an accusation to the courts, you may be sure your name will be on it."

Clerk Fu was not a very brave man and, seeing that things did not seem to be taking a good turn, he put on his clothes and went home as fast as he could. The boy cleared the things away and took them to the inner court. Jingji lay down on the bed and went to sleep.

The next day, very early, Clerk Fu went to Yueniang and told her what had happened. There were tears in his eyes when he suggested that he should go away, give up the business, and hand over the accounts to her.

"Go on as usual," Yueniang said to him gently. "Treat that rogue as though he were some stinking offal, and don't pay the slightest attention to him. He came here because he was in trouble with the authorities, and only intended to spend a short time here. I should like to know where are all these treasures he spoke to you about. All I know of are my daughter's furniture and a few trunks. I remember how his father got away. We were terrified lest somebody should find out and spread the news about him.

We were worried day and night. When he came here, he was only six-teen or seventeen years old and like a hunted animal. He has lived on my husband's kindness ever since, and everything he knows about business he has learned here. Now that his wings have grown, he means to repay our kindness by hatred, and to pay no account to all the things we have done for him. What a young man! He seems to have no conscience and to disregard the principle of Heaven utterly. I am watching, and I shall see whether Heaven prospers him or not. My friend, go on as you always have done, and pay no heed to him. The time will come when that young man will feel ashamed of himself."

One day, something seemed destined to happen. There were a number of people in the pawnshop redeeming their things. Ruyi'er came with a pot of tea for Clerk Fu, carrying the baby Xiaoge in her arms. The baby howled, and she put the pot down on the table.

"Baby," Chen Jingji said, "don't cry." Then he turned to the people who were there and said, with a half-serious air: "Doesn't it seem clear that he is my own child? When I tell him to stop crying, he stops."

Nobody made any answer.

"Brother-in-law," Ruyi'er said, "I suppose you think that is a clever thing to say. You don't know your place. I shall tell my mistress about this."

Jingji went over and kicked her twice. He laughed and said: "You thievish creature! So I had no right to talk in that way, hadn't I? Well, now I am kicking your backside so as to make a sound that people should listen to."

The nurse picked up the baby and went to the inner court and told Yueniang all about it. She cried. "That is how he talked about the baby before all those people," she said.

Yueniang was dressing her hair before a mirror. When she heard this, she could not speak. Suddenly she fell forward on the floor in a faint. Xiaoyu was greatly alarmed. She called for nearly everybody in the house, and they picked up Yueniang and put her on the bed. Sun Xue'e jumped on the bed and lifted her up and down. After a while they were able to pour some ginger water down her throat. At last Yueniang came around, but her breath came with difficulty. She sobbed, but could not cry out. Ruyi'er repeated Jingji's remarks to Yulou and Xue'e. "I reproved him," she said, "and he came and kicked me. I nearly fainted on the spot."

When the others had gone away, Xue'e stayed to look after Yueniang. "Lady, it is no use being angry with him," she said. "It would be most seri-ous if you fell ill of anger. That fellow is annoyed because you sold Chun-mei and because he cannot get here to see that strumpet Jinlian. That is why he says things of this sort. Now let us make an end of this business once and for all. Your stepdaughter is married to him. We have to regard her as a piece of land that has been sold, and we cannot help her very much. As the proverb says: when once the frog gets into the water, it must take the consequences. But why should we keep that young man here any longer? Send for him. Let us give him a sound drubbing and drive him away. Then send for old woman Wang to take that strumpet away and sell her to anybody who will buy her. When we have got rid of these evil elements, we may have peace. I see no reason why we should deliberately keep them there. If we do, we may all suffer in the future."

"You are right," Yueniang said.

They decided upon a plan. The next day, Yueniang gave her maids and women clubs, seven or eight of them altogether, and hid them about the place. Then she sent Laian to summon Chen Jingji. The second door was closed when the young man went in.

"Kneel down," Yueniang said.

The young man refused, and turned his head impudently away, without speaking.

"You know what you have done?" Yueniang said.

Jingji paid no heed.

Yueniang was furious. With Xue'e, Laixing's wife, Laizhao's wife, Xiaoyu, Xiuchun and some others, she caught hold of him and threw him to the ground. Clubs, long and short, descended furiously upon him. Ximen Dajie went away and never spoke a word to save her husband.

In desperation, the young man pulled down his trousers and displayed his manhood. This startled the women; they all threw down their clubs and ran in every direction. Yueniang was annoyed, but she could not help being amused. She called him a turtle with nothing to boast of, but Jingji was pleased with himself. "If I had not thought of that," he said to himself, "I should never have got away alive." He got up and ran away, holding his trousers up with one hand. Yueniang told some of the boys to go after him and see that he cleared his accounts and handed them over to Clerk Fu.

It was now clear to Chen Jingji that he could stay there no longer. He packed his clothes and his belongings and, without saying good-bye to anyone, left Ximen Qing's house in a very bad temper. He went to stay at his Uncle Zhang's.

When Jinlian heard this, she was more melancholy and depressed than ever. Yueniang did what Xue'e had suggested, and sent Daian for old woman Wang.

The old woman had given up her tea business since she had come into some money. Her son, Wang Chao, who had been to the Huai country with some merchants, had come back with a hundred taels that he had stolen. Old woman Wang bought two donkeys, millstones and sieves, and had set herself up as a miller. When she heard that Ximen's people wished to see her, she hurriedly dressed and went with Daian.

"Brother," she said, as they went along, "it can't be very long since I saw you last, but I see, from your hair, that you have now reached man's estate. Are you married yet?"

"No," Daian said.

"Why have they sent for me?" the old woman said. "Your father is dead. Is the Fifth Lady going to have a baby and wants me to be the midwife?"

"The Fifth Lady is not going to have a son," Daian said. "She has had rather too much of a son-in-law. The Great Lady is going to ask you to take her away."

"Heavens!" old woman Wang cried. "I was sure she would not be able to hold herself in check after your master died. Dogs can never get out of their habit of sniffing about the filth. So she has been misbehaving herself. I know the young man. What is his name?"

"Chen Jingji," Daian said.

"Oh yes, now I remember. Last year I went to see your master with old He the Ninth. Your master was not at home, and that strumpet took me to her room. She didn't give me a thing, not even a needle. All she gave me was a cup of tea. I came away. I thought she was settled there for a thousand years, and now she is to be sent away. Oh, what a splendid whore! It was I who arranged her marriage, and really she ought not to have treated me like that, even if I had been somebody else."

"She and the young man made such a scandal they nearly killed the Great Lady," Daian said. "Now he has been kicked out, and my mistress wants you to take this one away."

"When she came, she came in a sedan chair," the old woman said, "and she will have to leave in one. And she will have some things to take. I suppose they will give her some boxes?"

"Of course," Daian said, "but the Great Lady will tell you all about that."

So they came to the house. The old woman went to see Yueniang, made a reverence, and sat down. The maid brought tea.

"Old woman Wang," Yueniang said, "I should not have asked you to come except for a matter of some importance." She told her all about the business of Jinlian. "When she came here," she said, "you brought her. I didn't wish to bring anyone else into the matter, so I sent for you to take her away. I don't care whether she marries again or not, I only wish to see the last of her. My husband is dead, and I can't control so many people.

I don't care how much my husband spent on her, but I think he must have spent enough to make a woman of silver. I leave the matter entirely in your hands. Give me whatever you get for her and I will spend the money on services for my dead husband. So perhaps some good will come of it."

"I see, Lady," the old woman said, "it isn't that you want the money. You are just anxious to get rid of the cause of so much trouble. I understand, and I will do what you desire. This is a good day, and I may as well take her with me now. But when she came, she had some property of her own and she came in a sedan chair. She must have a chair now."

"She may have her boxes, but she will get no sedan chair from me," Yueniang said.

"You say this because you are angry," old woman Wang said, "but you must let her have a chair, or, when the neighbors see it, they will laugh at you."

Yueniang said nothing. After a while she sent Xiuchun to fetch Jinlian.

When the woman saw old woman Wang there, she was excited. She made a reverence to Yueniang and sat down.

"Lady," old woman Wang said, "you must get your things together. The Great Lady has told me to take you away with me."

"My husband died only a short time ago," Jinlian said, "and I have done nothing wrong. Why should I be driven away like this without the slightest cause?"

"There is no use pretending you do not know what it is for," the old woman said. "When a snake goes through a hole in the wall, it knows what it's about. You know what you have done."

"Don't talk such nonsense," Jinlian said. "It is no use your using high-flown language with me. You are the very one who is always helping people to do things they should not."

There has never been a time when a feast did not come to an end. The beams that stand out are those that decay first. Trees cast their shadow, and each one of us has his own reputation to save. Flies cannot get into an egg if there is no crack in it.

Jinlian saw that things were in a bad way for her. She realized that now she must leave this house. "If you must beat a man," she said, "do not strike him on the face; and if you quarrel with anyone, do not talk about his faults. You have the upper hand now, but do not abuse your power. I have been here many years. Why should you drive me away without mercy, because you listen to the tittle-tattle of slaves and serving women? I will go. It is all the same to me. I warn you, though, that you and others will have to stay here to the ends of your lives. See that you don't bring scandal upon yourselves."

Yueniang went to her room. She got out two boxes, a small table, four dresses, a few ornaments, earrings and pins and a set of bedclothes. She filled up the boxes with shoes and socks. She told Qiuju to come to her, and Jinlian's room was locked up.

Jinlian dressed and said good-bye to Yueniang. Then she went to Ximen Qing's tablet and sobbed. Afterwards, she went to see Yulou. They had been sisters for a long time, and now, when they had to part, they both shed tears. Without saying anything to Yueniang, Yulou gave her a pair of gold pins, a light blue silk dress, and a red skirt.

"Sister," she said, "we shall have few chances to see each other in the future. Look for a good home and go forward. The proverb says: every banquet must come to an end, and now we must say good-bye. When you find a home, ask someone to let me know. When I go out, I may be able to come and see you. We love one another as sisters."

They left one another in tears. Xiaoyu went with Jinlian to the gate and quietly gave her two gold hairpins. "Sister," Jinlian said to her, "you are very kind." Old woman Wang had already found somebody to carry the things. Only Yulou and Xiaoyu saw Jinlian get into her sedan chair.

When the woman came to old woman Wang's house, she was taken to the inner room and they slept together during the night.

Wang Chao was now grown up and his hair was dressed as a man's. But he was not yet married, and slept in the other room. The day after her arrival, Jinlian dressed very daintily and stood looking out from behind the lattice. She had nothing to do and spent her time painting her eyebrows or playing the lute. When old woman Wang was not at home, she would play chess or dominoes with Wang Chao. The old woman busied herself feeding the donkeys and sifting the flour and did not pay much attention. So, in a few days, Jinlian was engaged in a love affair with Wang Chao. At night, when old woman Wang was asleep, Jinlian would pretend to get out of bed to make water, but really she went to the other room and sported with Wang Chao. Once the bed made such a noise that old woman Wang woke up.

"What is that noise?" she cried.

"The cat is catching a rat underneath the cabinet," Wang Chao answered.

Old woman Wang, half asleep, murmured: "Ever since I have had that wheat flour there, I have been worried about it. I can't even sleep at nights now."

After a while, the noise began once more, and the old woman again called out to know what was the matter.

"The cat has caught the rat and taken it under the bed."

The old woman listened attentively, and indeed the sound was like that of a cat worrying a rat. She said no more. Jinlian finished what she had begun, crept quietly into bed and went to sleep.

> The rat is small
> But bolder than it looks,
> Hungry and eager, ready for any prank.
> When anyone appears,
> It beats retreat and hides.
> Its scufflings in the depth of night
> Disturb good honest slumberers.
> Oblivious of the rules of good behavior
> It loves to find a hole in which to hide
> And always takes the most delight
> In stolen sweets.

When Chen Jingji heard that Jinlian had left Ximen's household and was now at old woman Wang's, he took two strings of coppers and went to call there. Old woman Wang was at the door sweeping up the donkey's droppings. Jingji bowed low.

"Brother, what can I do for you?" the old woman said.

"I should like a word with you," Jingji said.

The old woman took him into the house.

"I understand," Jingji said, "that the Fifth Lady of his late Lordship Ximen is here, looking for a husband. Is that so?"

"What is your relationship to her?" the old woman asked.

"I am her younger brother," Jingji said, smiling.

The old woman looked at him from head to foot. "I never knew she had a brother," she said. "Don't try to hoodwink me. Are you not Ximen's son-in-law? Your name is Chen, and you have come here to get her for yourself. You can't deceive me like that."

Jingji, still smiling, brought out the two strings of coppers and held them out to the old woman. "This may serve to buy you some tea," he said. "I only wish to see her for a moment. Later on, I will reward you more suitably."

When the old woman saw the money, she protested more strongly. "Don't talk about rewards to me," she said. "The Great Lady told me that nobody must be allowed to see her. If you really wish to speak to her, give me five taels of silver, and if you wish to speak to her a second time, that will be another five taels. If you wish to marry her, it will cost you a hundred taels with ten for myself. I shall not do this business for nothing.

These two strings of coppers won't even make a splash if you throw them into the water."

Jingji saw that the old woman had a good deal to say, and that she would not accept what he had brought. He took from his hair a pair of silver pins with gold heads, worth five *qian*. He knelt down.

"Old Mother Wang," he said, "take this. I will give you another tael another day. Just let me see her for a moment. There is something I must say to her."

The old woman took the pins and the money. "Go in," she said. "Speak to her and then come out again. I can't have you sitting there making faces at her. And I must have the other money tomorrow." She pulled aside the lattice and allowed Jingji to go in.

Jinlian was sitting on the bed. "You splendid fellow!" she said to Chen Jingji, "you have brought me to such a pass that, if I go forward, there is no village ahead of me, and, if I go back, no inn where I can rest. I don't know what to do, and everybody has heard this scandal about us. You never came to see me. I am a poor, helpless woman with nowhere to go. Whose fault is it?" She clung to Jingji and sobbed. This annoyed old woman Wang very much. She was afraid someone might hear.

"Sister," Jingji said, "I have sacrificed my skin and flesh and suffered from anger and shame on your account. I would have come to see you if I could. Yesterday, I went to old woman Xue's place, and they told me that Chunmei had been sold to some military gentleman. It was there I heard that you had left Ximen's house and were staying here to find a husband. I came at once to see you. I want to discuss matters with you. We love one another and we cannot bear to be parted. Now, I propose to divorce Ximen's daughter, and then I shall go to them for the money and things they have of mine. If they refuse, I will go to the Eastern Capital and accuse them before the courts. If that business is ever taken to law, they will be done for, even if they give up the stuff. When I get the money, I will marry you. I see no reason why we should not be happy together for ever and ever."

"Old woman Wang wants a hundred taels," Jinlian said. "Have you got so much?"

"Why does she ask so much?" Jingji said.

"Your mother-in-law told me," the old woman said, "that when Master Ximen got this woman, he spent more money than would have built a woman of silver. She insists upon a hundred taels and not a penny less."

"Old Mother," Jingji said, "I am crazy about this lady. We cannot live without one another. I see we are at your mercy. I will give you half the money, fifty or sixty taels. Then I will go to my uncle and arrange to have a small house and marry the lady. It is a beautiful idea, and you must soften your heart a little."

"Fifty or sixty taels, did you say?" the old woman cried. "Even if you offered eighty, you would not get her. Yesterday, a silk merchant from Huzhou, a man called He, offered seventy for her. Then Zhang the Second of the High Street, who is an officer, sent two of his men and offered eighty. They brought the money with them, but I would not take it and they had to go away. You are only a boy. You don't know what you're talking about. You come here and think you'll make a fool of me. You know I am not likely to be hard."

She set out for the street. "Whenever did anybody hear of a son-in-law wanting his mother-in-law?" she said loudly. "He thinks he'll come farting here, does he?"

Jingji was alarmed and dragged the old woman back. He knelt down before her. "Old Mother," he said, "don't say another word. You shall have your hundred taels. You know my father is at the Eastern Capital. I will go to him tomorrow and get the money."

"You must be quick or you'll be too late," Jinlian said. "Someone else will get me, and I can never belong to you."

"I will get a horse and start at once," Jingji promised.

"I shall be back in less than a fortnight."

"Let me tell you this," old woman Wang said. "If you are the first to cook the rice, you will be the first to eat it. Remember, that doesn't include the ten taels for myself."

"Do not mention it again," Jingji said. "If you will only help me, I shall never forget your kindness."

Jingji went away. He went home, packed his luggage, and the next day hired a horse and set off for the Eastern Capital to get the money.

CHAPTER 87

Wu Song Avenges His Brother

My home is far away. In this harassed world
We are dispersed, some to the east some to the west.
They who still live seek to have news of one another
But the dead are become dust,
And the poor are ruined.

At last the hero returns
He has walked for long.
The road was deserted and at sunset
The air was full of sadness.
Foxes he met, both large and small, which glared at him,
Their hair on end.
But a good sword have I, and I can deal with them.

Chen Jingji took a horse and set out with one of his uncle's servants. The day after Wu Yueniang had sent Pan Jinlian away, she sent Chunhong for old woman Xue. She had decided to sell Qiuju. When Chunhong came to the High Street, he met Ying Bojue. The man stopped him and asked him where he was going.

"The Great Lady has told me to go for old woman Xue," the boy said.

"Why?" Bojue asked.

"She is going to sell the Fifth Lady's maid Qiuju."

"Why did they send the Fifth Lady away?" Bojue said.

"She and my brother-in-law carried on together secretly, but the Great Lady found out about it," Chunhong said. "First, she dealt with Chunmei. Then, she gave the young man a beating and drove him away. And finally, she got rid of the Fifth Lady."

Ying Bojue nodded his head. "So there was something between the Fifth Lady and Master Chen," he said. "Really, there is no telling what people will do." Then he said to Chunhong: "My boy, now that your master is dead, why do you stay there? You will never do any good. I know you would prefer to be in the South. Why don't you go to your native place and get a job there?"

"You are right," Chunhong said. "Now that my master is dead, the Great Lady is very severe with us. Nearly all the businesses have been closed down, and several houses have been sold. Qintong and Huatong have gone, and, indeed, they don't need so many people about the place. I should have liked to go to the South, but I couldn't think of anyone who would take me there. And I don't know the people here very well, which makes it difficult for me to get a job in these parts."

"You silly boy!" Bojue said. "One who does not keep his eyes open will always be in difficulties. If you go to the South, you will have to cross ten thousand rivers and climb a thousand mountains. Why go there? You can sing, and there will be no difficulty in finding another master for you. I can tell you of one, straight off. There is his Lordship Zhang the Second of the High Street. He is very rich and now holds the office your master used to hold. Your Second Lady married him as his second wife. Let me introduce you to him. When he finds that you can sing the Southern tunes, I guarantee that he will take you on at once, and keep you as one of his most favored boys. He is very different from your old master, good-tempered and young. He is very generous and agreeable. You will certainly be in luck's way if you get him for a master."

Chunhong knelt down and kowtowed to Ying Bojue. "Uncle," he said, "I shall count upon your help. If I find a place with Master Zhang, I will buy you a present."

Bojue pulled the boy up. "Stand up, you silly boy," he said. "I am only too glad to be able to help people. I don't want any presents from you, for I know you haven't any money."

"If I go away, I expect the Great Lady will find out a number of things I have done wrong," the boy said.

"Don't worry about that," Bojue said. "I will go and see Master Zhang, and get a tael of silver and a card from him. If he sends them to your mistress, she will not dare to take any money. She will give you up for nothing."

The boy went on to old woman Xue's house. The old woman went to see Yueniang and took Qiuju away. She sold the girl for five taels of silver and paid the money to Yueniang.

Then Ying Bojue took Chunhong to Zhang the Second's house. When Zhang the Second found that the boy was intelligent and could sing the songs of the South, he told him to stay. He sent a tael and a card to Ximen's place and asked for the boy's luggage.

Yueniang was entertaining Yun Lishou's wife. Yun Lishou was now an assistant magistrate at Qinghe. After Ximen's death, knowing that Yueniang was a very rich widow, he struck up a friendship with her. That was why his wife had come to see Yueniang that day with eight presents. She wished to arrange a marriage between Yueniang's son and her own child who was two months old. They settled the matter as they were drinking together, and Mistress Yun gave Yueniang two gold rings as an engagement token.

Daian brought in Zhang the Second's card and the tael of silver. "Chunhong has gone to Zhang's place, and they have come to ask for his clothes."

Yueniang knew that Zhang the Second was now an officer, and she did not dare refuse to give up the boy. She would not take the money, and gave the boy's things to the messenger.

Sometime before all this, Ying Bojue had told Zhang the Second about Jinlian. "She is very beautiful," he said. "She plays the lute excellently, and she knows all about such things as poetry and games, and she can write. She is quite young and she won't like being a widow. Now I hear she has come out, after a quarrel with Ximen's first wife. She is at old woman Wang's place now."

One after another, Zhang the Second sent men to old woman Wang with money in their hands, but old woman Wang told them that Mistress Ximen would not take less than a hundred taels. They came again and offered eighty taels. Still old woman Wang would not agree. Then Chunhong came to Zhang's house and told his new master that Jinlian had been sent away because she had been carrying on an intrigue with her son-in-law. Zhang the Second gave up the idea of marrying Jinlian.

"I have a fifteen-year-old son," he said to Ying Bojue. "He is at school now. I couldn't do with a woman like that in the house."

Then Li Jiao'er told him that Jinlian had poisoned her first husband before she went to Ximen Qing, that she had misconducted herself with the boys, and murdered another lady and her child. Zhang the Second was even more determined not to marry Jinlian.

Major Zhou was delighted with Chunmei. He found her pretty, intelligent, and attractive. He gave her three rooms and a young maid, and stayed with her for three whole days. He had two dresses made for her. When old woman Xue went to see him, he gave her five *qian* of silver. He bought a maid for Chunmei and established her as his third wife. His first wife was blind. She ate vegetarian food, devoted herself to religion, and did not concern herself with household affairs at all. Chunmei lived in the western wing and Major Zhou, who was very fond of her, gave her all the keys.

One day, old woman Xue came and told Chunmei that Jinlian had left Ximen's house and was at old woman Wang's place. That night, Chunmei wept and said to Major Zhou: "My old mistress and I were together all those years and she never spoke a harsh word to me. I might have been her daughter. I believed that she and I would never see one another again, but now she too has left Ximen's house. If you marry her, we can live together most happily. She is very beautiful. She knows all about poetry and music, and she is clever and charming in every way. Her animal is the Dragon, so she is now thirty-two years old. If she comes, I will gladly take rank below her."

Major Zhou was impressed. He sent his servants, Zhang Sheng and Li An, with two handkerchiefs and two *qian* of silver, to old woman Wang's house to see Jinlian. They told him that she really was extraordinarily beautiful. The old woman still demanded a hundred taels, and Zhang Sheng and Li An discussed the matter with her for a long time. They offered eighty taels, but old woman Wang would not accept it. She declared that Mistress Ximen insisted upon a hundred taels. "You will have to pay the hundred," she said, "but you need not bother about my fee. Heaven will not allow me to go unrewarded for my pains."

Zhang Sheng and Li An took back the money to the Major, and he decided to let the matter rest for a day or two. But Chunmei cried every evening. "You must give a few more taels," she said. "If she comes here to live with me, I shall die happy."

So this time the Major sent his bailiff, Zhou Zhong, with Zhang Sheng and Li An. They offered the old woman ninety taels. This made her still more grasping.

"If ninety taels would have done, I could have sold her long ago," she said. "His Lordship Chang would have paid that."

This made Zhou Zhong angry. He told Li An to wrap up the money again. "Do you think that I, a three-legged frog, am not able to find a two-legged woman?" he said. "You old whore! You don't seem to realize whom you are dealing with. Would you talk about Zhang the Second to me? Do you imagine that my master cannot do what he likes with you? It is simply because his new wife has asked him to do this. He doesn't want the woman so much as all that."

"We have been here several times," Li An said, "and that seems to have made you get rather above yourself, you old whore."

He took Zhou Zhong's hand. "Come, let us go and tell our master," he said. "Let him get this old whore to his office and give her a beating."

But the old woman was still thinking of what Chen Jingji had promised and, in spite of all their abuse, she would not budge. The men went back to Major Zhou. "We offered her ninety taels," they said, "but she would not agree."

"Take a hundred taels and a sedan chair tomorrow," Major Zhou said, "and bring the woman here."

"Master," Zhou Chung said, "if you give her a hundred taels, she will certainly demand another five for herself. Leave her alone for a few days and we shall see if she is still so stupid. If she is, have her brought to your office and try the effect of the thumbscrews. Then she will be afraid of you."

> We know not what life has in store for us
> No one can tell what brings good fortune
> And what brings evil.
> But at last comes the reward alike of good and evil
> Sometimes at once and sometimes long delayed.

We have now to speak again of Wu Song. When he reached Mengzhou, the place to which he had been banished, he was fortunate enough to come under the charge of Shi En, the son of the Chief Jailer. On a certain occasion this Shi En and a man called Jiang Menshen had trouble at a drinking house. Shi En was hurt, but Wu Song came to his aid and Jiang Menshen was beaten. Later, Jiang's sister became a concubine of General Zhang, and, when Wu Song was working for the general, he was accused of stealing and sentenced to serve as a soldier. On his way into this further banishment, Wu Song killed two officials at Feiyunpu. Then he went back and killed all General Zhang's and Jiang Menshen's people, and afterwards took refuge at Shi En's house. Shi En gave him a letter and a leather trunk containing a hundred taels of silver and told him to go to Anping fortress, and see the officer in command there, a certain Liu Gao. On his way, he heard that the Emperor's successor had been proclaimed at the Imperial Palace, and that the Emperor, besides making sacrifice to Heaven, had declared a general amnesty. So Wu Song came home.

When he came to Qinghe, he gave the officers his papers and was reinstated in his old position at the Town Hall. He went to see his neighbor Yao, who had been looking after Ying'er. The girl was now about nineteen years old. Wu Song took her and settled down. He heard that Ximen Qing was dead and that Jinlian was no longer living in that household, but had gone to old woman Wang's house, and was trying to find a new husband. Then Wu Song determined upon revenge.

He put on a hat, and dressed himself well, and went to see what he could see at old woman Wang's house. Jinlian was standing behind the lattice and, when she saw Wu Song, went at once to the inner room. Wu Song pulled aside the lattice and said: "Is old woman Wang at home?"

The old woman was busy preparing dinner. "Who is there?" she said. But, as soon as she had spoken, she recognized Wu Song and made a reverence to him. Wu Song bowed low in return.

"Brother Wu, when did you get back?" the old woman said. "I am delighted to see you."

"My offense has been pardoned," Wu Song said, "so I was able to come home again. I got here yesterday. Thank you for having looked after my brother's house. I will reward you later."

The old woman smiled. "Brother," she said, "you are even better looking than you used to be. There is hair on your lip; you have become quite stout, and you have acquired most elegant manners." She took him into the house and offered him tea.

"There is something I want to talk to you about," Wu Song said.

"What is it?"

"I hear that Ximen Qing is dead and that my sister-in-law is back with you again. Will you let her know that I should like to marry her? Ying'er is grown up now and needs somebody to look after her and find her a husband. So we shall avoid people's rude remarks."

At first, old woman Wang decided she would not tell Wu Song the true story. "She is here," she said, "but I am not at all sure that she feels inclined to marry again." But when she found that Wu Song was ready enough to pay, she said: "I will broach the matter to her gradually."

On the other side of the lattice, Jinlian heard all that was said. She heard Wu Song say that he wanted to marry her in order to have someone to lock after Ying'er. She noticed that, after these years of absence, Wu Song seemed a more powerful man than ever. He spoke very agreeably. He seems to have given up his old ideas, she thought, and now is ready for marriage. So she did not wait for old woman Wang to call her, but came out of her own accord. She made a reverence to Wu Song.

"Am I right, Uncle, in understanding that you wish to take me to look after Ying'er and see about her marriage?"

"You must know," old woman Wang interrupted, "that Mistress Ximen wants a hundred taels."

"That seems a great deal," Wu Song suggested.

"Ximen spent so much money on her that he could have made a woman of silver with it," old woman Wang said.

"Well, we won't haggle," Wu Song said. "I want my sister-in-law, and I don't mind spending the money. And you shall have five taels for yourself."

This made the old woman so pleased that she farted and piddled with delight. "Brother Wu," she said, "I know no other man who has such intelligence as yours. You are a man, and you have been abroad a few years and seen the world."

Jinlian went to the inner room, made some strong tea, and offered it to Wu Song with both hands.

"Ximen's people are anxious to have the matter settled as soon as possible," the old woman said, "and there are four or five people falling over themselves to marry her. I refused them all because they would not pay the price. If you want her, you must let me have your money at once. As you know, the first man to cook the rice is the first to eat it. Heaven brings you together, so don't let anybody else do you out of such a good match."

"Yes," Jinlian said, "if you want me, you must not waste any time."

"I will bring the money tomorrow and take you away tomorrow night," Wu Song said.

Old woman Wang could not believe Wu Song had so much money. The next day he opened the leather trunk and took out the hundred taels that Shi En had given him. He added to it another five taels of his own and went to see old woman Wang. He asked for scales to measure the silver. When the old woman saw the table piled up with white silver, she said to herself: "That Chen Jingji promised me a hundred taels. But he has had to go to the Eastern Capital for it, and there is no telling when he will be back. Why should I not take the chance while I have it?" When the five taels for herself was produced, she accepted it and thanked Wu Song most profusely.

"Brother Wu," she said, "you know how to deal with me."

"Mother," Wu Song said, "take the money. I will take my sister-in-law today."

"Don't be in too much of a hurry, Brother," the old woman said. "You are like a man who lets off fireworks in some dark corner because he hasn't patience enough to wait for the evening. You must wait until I have paid the money to Ximen's people. Then you may take her. And what a fine bridegroom you are, with that smart hat!"

Wu Song grew impatient. Jinlian joked with him. When he had gone away, the old woman thought: "Mistress Ximen said I was to get rid of this woman and never said a word about the price. Now is my chance. I will give her twenty taels and keep the rest for myself."

She took twenty taels to Yueniang, who asked the name of the purchaser.

"Lady," old woman Wang said, "the hares scamper about over the hills but in the end they go back to their own holes. She is going back to the old food she used to eat: she is going to marry her husband's brother."

When Wu Yueniang heard this, she was sorry. She knew that when an enemy meets an enemy, they look closely one at the other. Afterwards, she said to Meng Yulou: "Jinlian will die at this man's hands. He is a man ready to kill for no reason whatever, and he will not spare her."

Old woman Wang went home and told her son Wang Chao to take Jinlian's belongings to Wu Song. The bridegroom had prepared a feast for them. In the evening, the old woman took Jinlian to him. She was no longer in mourning. She wore a new headdress, red clothes, and there was a veil on her head. When they came into the middle room, the candles were burning brightly.

Then they saw Wu Da's tablet on the table. This made them wonder. They felt as though someone were pulling out their hair and sticking knives into their flesh. When they had gone to the inner room, Wu Song told Ying'er to fasten all the doors.

"I must be going now," the old woman said. "There is nobody to look after my house."

"Stay and have something to drink, old Mother," Wu Song said. He told Ying'er to set the dishes on the table and heat some wine. Yet, when the wine was brought, he did not ask them to drink, but poured himself cup after cup and drank them all down.

"I have had quite enough to eat, Brother Wu," the old woman said, "I must go now and leave you two to enjoy yourselves."

"Old woman," Wu Song said, "don't be a fool. I, Wu the Second, have something to say to you." With a crash Wu Song drew out a knife, two feet long, with a very sharp blade. Grasping the knife in one hand, he seized the old woman with the other. His eyes were wide open and his hair stood on end.

"Old woman," he said, "you need not be surprised. Just as a debt finds out those who owe it, so hatred never fails to meet its object. Don't pretend to be a fool. It was your hand that ended my brother's life."

"Brother Wu," the old woman said, "it is getting late, and you are drunk. You shouldn't play with knives. It isn't funny."

"Be silent, old woman," Wu Song said. "I, Wu the Second, am not afraid of death. I will deal with that creature first, and with you, you old sow, later. Move a single inch, and you shall feel my knife."

Then he turned to Jinlian. "Listen, you whore," he said. "How did you murder my brother? Tell me the truth and I will forgive you."

"Uncle, don't be silly," Jinlian said. "How can you fry beans in a cold pan? Your brother died from heart trouble. I had nothing to do with it."

Almost before the words were out of her mouth, there was a crash. Wu Song banged the knife upon the table, seized the woman by her hair with his left hand, and grasped her breasts with his right. Then he kicked over the table. Dishes and cups crashed to the ground. Jinlian was not very strong. He lifted her like a feather from the other side of the table. Then he dragged her to the middle room, before the table on which Wu Da's tablet stood. Old woman Wang saw that he was in a mad rage and would have run away, but the door had been locked and Wu Song, striding after her, caught her. He threw her to the floor and, with his girdle, tied her up till she looked like a monkey offering a fruit. She could not get away.

"Oh, Sir," she cried, "don't be angry with me. This lady is responsible for the murder. It was all her doing. My hands are clean."

"You old bitch," Wu Song cried. "I know everything, and it is no use your lying to me. It was you who told Ximen Qing to have me banished. But I am here, and where is Ximen Qing?"

"I will kill you first," he said to Jinlian, "and then this old bitch."

He picked up the knife and brandished it twice before her face.

"Uncle, forgive me, and let me get up," she cried. "I promise I will tell you."

Wu Song picked her up. He stripped her of her clothes and made her kneel down before the tablet.

"Speak quickly, whore!" he shouted at her.

Now her spirit had left her. She told Wu Song everything; how, when she had been pulling up the lattice, the pole had struck Ximen Qing, how she had made clothes, and how the intrigue between them had begun. Then she said how Ximen Qing had kicked Wu Da in the chest, and old woman Wang had shown her how to poison him. Then, how they had burned his body, and Ximen Qing had married her. Meanwhile old woman Wang was sobbing. "Oh, you fool," she cried, "you have told him the truth. What can I do now?"

Wu Song, before the tablet, grasped the woman by the hair. With his other hand, he sprinkled wine upon the ground and set fire to some paper money.

"Brother," he said, "your spirit cannot be far away. This day Wu Song avenges you."

When Jinlian heard this, she was desperate and began to shriek. Wu Song took a handful of dust from the incense burner and threw it into her mouth so that she could not make any more noise. He tugged at her hair and threw her down upon the ground again. As she struggled with him, her hair was disordered and the pins and earrings fell out. Wu Song thought it possible that she might try to run away, and kicked her in the ribs. Then he stamped upon her arms with both his feet.

"You whore," he cried, "you make yourself out to be a very clever woman. I would like to know what sort of heart you have, and I will see."

He tore her arms apart, and thrust the knife deep into her soft white bosom. One slash, and there was a bleeding hole in her breast. Blood gushed forth. Now the woman's starry eyes were almost closed and her feet seemed to tremble. Wu Song took the knife in his teeth, tore open her breast with both hands, and dragged the heart and entrails from her body. The blood streamed from them as he set them on the table before the tablet. Then, with a single stroke, he cut off her head. The blood flowed over the floor.

Ying'er looked in, terrified, and covered her face with her hands.

A violent man, this Wu Song. And how sad, the case of this woman who, when the breath was still in her body, could use it in a thousand ways. Now she was powerless. She was only thirty-two years old. When his hand fell, her young life ended. The knife struck, and she was no more. Her spirit fled to the palace of the King of Hell, and her spirit vanished to the city of the dead. It was like the breaking of the golden branches of the willow by the snow in springtime, or the jade-like blossom rent and torn by the wild wind as the year goes out. We know not where her loveliness vanished that night, or where her sweet spirit went.

When Wu Song killed Jinlian, old woman Wang shouted, "Murder." Then he went to her, and struck off her head. He dragged away the body, then thrust his knife through the woman's heart, and pinned it to the eaves at the back of the house. It was the first night watch. He took Ying'er into the other room. "I am frightened, Uncle," she said. "My child," Wu Song said, "I can do nothing for you."

Then he jumped over the wall and went into old woman Wang's house. He wished to kill Wang Chao. But it seemed that Wang Chao's end was not to be yet. When he heard his mother's shrieks, he knew that Wu Song was killing her. He came to the front door but would not open it. He knocked at the back, but there was no answer. Then he rushed to the street to find a policeman. Meanwhile, the neighbors on either side knew that Wu Song was killing somebody, but none of them dared to interfere.

When Wu Song reached old woman Wang's room, he found a light burning, but there was nobody there. He opened her chest, took out the clothes and strewed them on the floor. Then he found the silver, about eighty-five taels, for the old woman had only given Yueniang twenty. But he took ornaments, pins and earrings. Then, taking his knife, he jumped over the wall at the back. About the fifth night watch, he left the city, and went to Shizipo, where Zhang Qing and his wife lived. Then he became a monk. Afterwards, he went to Liangshan and joined the bandits.

CHAPTER 88

Chunmei Mourns for Pan Jinlian

For a moment he beheld her in a dream
But, when he woke, he knew that there was no one.
He turned and tossed and could not sleep
Then threw his clothes about him and paced the floor.

The morning breeze is sharp
The moonbeams dim.
He lies alone, wakeful, till morning breaks
But she of whom he dreamed
Does not return.

When Wang Chao and the police came to Wu Song's place, the doors were still fastened. In old woman Wang's house, money and things were missing and clothes were strewn over the floor. They realized that Wu Song had murdered the woman and gone off with the money. They forced the door and found the two bodies on the floor, covered with blood. The entrails of Pan Jinlian were pinned to the eaves at the back of the house, and Ying'er was still shut up in the room. She could only cry when they questioned her. The next morning they brought the matter before the notice of the magistrate and produced such evidence as they could get.

This magistrate had been recently appointed, and his name was Li Changqi. He was a native of Zaoqiang in the prefecture of Chending. When he heard of the murder, he sent his runners to summon the neighbors and the members of both families. So Wang Chao and Ying'er came before the magistrate. The house and the bodies were examined. The magistrate declared that Wu Song, when drunk, had killed the women Pan and Wang. He ordered the bodies to be buried temporarily, and issued a warrant for Wu Song's arrest, offering a reward of fifty taels of silver for his apprehension.

Zhang Sheng and Li An took a hundred taels with them and went to old woman Wang's house again. But when they got there, they found that the two women had been killed and that the local officials were examining the bodies and taking steps to arrest the murderer. They went back and told their master. When Chunmei heard the news, she wept for three days and would neither eat nor drink. Major Zhou was much disturbed and sent for all kinds of different entertainers to amuse her, but they could not assuage her grief. Every day she sent Zhang Sheng and Li An to see if Wu Song had been arrested.

Meanwhile, Chen Jingji had gone to the Eastern Capital to get some money so that he could marry Jinlian. On the way, he met Chen Ding, a servant of his family, who was coming to tell him that his father was very ill and that his mother wanted him to take up the responsibilities of the household. Then Jingji traveled with even more haste than before. At last he came to the Eastern Capital and hurried to the house of his uncle, Zhang Shilian. But his uncle was dead, and his aunt told him that his father had died three days before. They were all wearing mourning clothes.

Jingji made a reverence before his father's tablet, and kowtowed to his mother and his aunt. His mother realized that he was now a grown man, cried with him, and talked about the matters that needed to be decided. "I am happy and sad at the same time," she said. When Jingji asked her what she meant, she said she was happy because the announcement of the Emperor's successor meant a general amnesty for all prisoners, and sad because of the death of Jingji's father and uncle. "Your aunt is now a widow," she said, "and we shall not be able to stay here any longer. You must take your father's body and bury it at our old home."

If I take the coffin and all the other things, Jingji thought, it will mean a long and slow journey, and I shall be too late to marry. I had better take the chests and valuables and go and marry Jinlian at once. Then I can come back for the coffin, and I shall not be too late.

When he had thought the matter over, he said to his mother: "The country is overridden by bandits and thieves and it is not at all safe to travel. If I take both the coffin and the boxes at the same time, they are likely to attract attention, and what can I do if anything happens? I suggest we do things more gradually. To begin with, I will get two carts and take all these trunks and things and go and see about a house for you. Then I will come back and take you, Chen Ding, and the coffin, at the beginning of next year. When we are settled, we will put the coffin into a monastery and offer sacrifice, then build a tomb and bury it."

His mother, being a woman, was deceived by these smooth-sounding words. She let him take everything away, two cartloads in all. They put banners on the carts to make it seem as though they were pilgrims and, on the first day of the twelfth month, Chen Jingji left the Capital.

When he reached Qinghe, he went to tell his Uncle Zhang that his father was dead, and that his mother and his father's body were coming shortly. "I have brought these things," he said, "so as to make everything ready for my mother."

"In that case," his uncle said, "I must go back to my own house." He bade his servants make preparations at once for the removal.

When his uncle had gone, Jingji was delighted. "Now I have got rid of that old fellow," he said to himself, "I can marry Jinlian straightaway and have a good time. My father is dead and my mother treats me with every indulgence. I will begin by divorcing my wife, and then send an accusation against my mother-in-law. She has no hold on me now since my family is no longer under the ban."

People decide upon courses of action like this, but Heaven often thinks otherwise. Jingji took a hundred taels for old woman Wang, and went to Amethyst Street. But when he got there, there were two rough graves outside the door, each with a spear and a large lantern upon it. On the door itself was pasted a notice that said: "Murder! The murderer Wu Song has killed Pan and Wang. Anyone who arrests him, or gives notice of his whereabouts, will receive a reward of fifty taels of silver."

Jingji looked at the notice. He was as if rooted to the ground. Two men came out of a tent.

"Who are you?" they cried. "Why are you looking at the notice? We haven't arrested anybody yet. Who are you?" They looked as though they would lay hands on Jingji. He ran away. When he came to a wine house, not far from the stone bridge, he saw a man dressed in black coming towards him.

"What are you doing here, Brother?" the man said. "You seem very brave."

Jingji saw that it was a great friend of his, a man called Yang the Second, who was nicknamed Iron Claw. They greeted one another, and Yang the Second asked Jingji where he had been. Jingji told him that he had been to the Eastern Capital, and that his father had died. Then he said: "This woman who has been killed was my father-in-law's wife. This is the first I have heard of it. I have only just read the notice."

"It was her brother, Wu Song, who came back from banishment and murdered her," Yang the Second said. "I don't know why he did it. He even killed old woman Wang. I know Wu Song had a niece, for she has been living with my uncle, Yao the Second, for the last three or four years. Wu Song ran away as soon as he had murdered the two women, and my aunt got the girl away from the authorities and found a husband for her. The two bodies, as you see, are still here. The police will have a very difficult task looking out for Wu Song all the time, and I doubt whether he will ever be caught."

Yang the Second asked Jingji to go and drink with him in the wine house. Now that the young man knew his lover was dead, he was very much upset and could not drink much. He drank three cups or so and then left Yang the Second and went home. That evening he bought some paper money. Then he went to the stone bridge not far from old woman Wang's door. "Sister Pan," he said, "your young brother, Chen Jingji, comes to offer you this paper money. It was because my coming back was so delayed that you met your death. Now you are dead, you will become a goddess. Use your spiritual power to help those who seek to arrest Wu Song. When he is found, I will go to the place of execution to see him cut to pieces. Only then shall I be satisfied."

He sobbed and set fire to the paper money. Then he went home, shut the gate, and went to his own room. He went to sleep. Jinlian appeared to him, wearing a simple dress, and covered with blood. She said to him, with tears: "Brother, I died such a bitter death. I longed to live with you, but, alas, before you came back, that fellow Wu Song murdered me. The underworld will not take me in, so all day I must wander about, and all night I seek for shelter everywhere and try to beg a little water to drink. I thank you for burning paper money for me. My murderer has not been found, and still my body lies in the street. If you think of our past love, buy a coffin and bury me properly, that I may not lie there exposed any longer."

"Sister," Jingji said, "you know that I would gladly bury you, but I am afraid of my mother-in-law, that cruel, heartless woman. If she hears of it, she will seek to do me some evil, and this would be an opportunity. Sister, go to Major Zhou's place. See Chunmei and ask her to have your body buried."

"I have been there," Jinlian cried, "and I could not get in. The god of the gate stopped me. But I will go again."

Jingji still cried and tried to hold her hand and talk to her, but the smell of the blood on her body came to him, and she escaped from him. He woke up and found it was a dream. The night watchman's drum was sounding the third night watch.

"How strange!" he said to himself. "Did I not see my sister? Did she not tell me all about this tragedy and ask me to bury her? But I do not know when Wu Song will be arrested. It is a sad business."

Search was kept up for Wu Song, but two months passed and there was no sign of him. At last there came news that he had gone to Liangshan and joined the bandits, and the policemen told the magistrate. Then the magistrate gave orders that the bodies might now be taken away and buried by their families. Wang Chao took away his mother's body, but there was no one to bury Jinlian.

Chunmei had been sending Zhang Sheng and Li An nearly every day to the Town Hall for news. Each time they could only report that the murderer had not been caught and that the bodies were still there. The police were keeping watch over them and nobody dared move them. At the beginning of the first month, Chunmei had a dream. Pan Jinlian came to her, covered with blood and her hair in disorder. "Sister," the woman said, "I had such a sad death. It was hard for me to come and see you because the god of the gate would not let me in. Now my enemy, Wu Song, has escaped. My body still lies in the street, blown by the wind and drenched by the rain. Dogs and fowls come and stand over me. I have no near relations, and there is no one to take me away. If you still remember the friendship there used to be between us, buy a coffin and bury me somewhere. Then, in Hades, I can close my eyes and mouth in peace." As she said this, she cried bitterly.

Chunmei wished to take her hand and ask her many things, but Jinlian slipped away from her. She woke up and knew it was a dream. She was still crying.

She did not know what the dream meant until the next day. Then she said to Zhang Sheng and Li An: "Go and see whether the bodies of those two women are still there."

When they came back, the men told her: "The murderer has escaped and the two bodies could not lie there forever with the police keeping watch over them, so the magistrate has ordered the relatives to take them away. The old woman's son has taken away his mother's body, but the other woman is still there."

"Now," Chunmei said, "I am going to ask you two to do something for me. If you do it, I will see you are well paid for it."

The two men knelt down. "Lady," they said, "you need not talk of payment. If you will speak kindly of us to our master, we shall be grateful and, if you tell us to go through fire or water, we are ready to do it."

Chunmei went into her room and got ten taels of silver and two rolls of cloth.

"The dead woman was really my sister," she said to them. "She married Ximen Qing and, after his death, left his household. Then she was murdered. Don't say anything to your master, but go and buy a coffin with this money, put her body into it, and take her outside the city. Find a suitable place and bury her there. I will pay you well."

"We will go and do so at once," the men said.

"I am afraid the magistrate will not let us take the body away," Li An said. "We ought to have a card from our master to give him."

"Oh, we will tell him that the dead woman is our lady's sister," Zhang

Sheng said. "I don't believe the magistrate will make any objection. We shan't need a card."

They took the money and went to the Town Hall.

"It is my belief that the dead woman must have been a friend of the master's young lady," Zhang Sheng said to Li An. "They probably lived together. That is why she is so concerned about this dead woman. Perhaps you remember that when the woman was killed, our lady cried for three or four days and wouldn't eat anything. The master sent for all sorts of people to come and amuse her, but they couldn't do anything. Now there is nobody to bury the woman and she wants to do it. If we manage this business, she will certainly say a kind word for us to our master. It is a stroke of luck for us, because he never refuses her anything. He considers her more than the other ladies."

They came to the Town Hall and sent in their petition. "The dead woman's sister is the Major's wife," they said. "It is by her orders that we have come to ask for leave to remove the body."

They paid six taels for a coffin. Then they dug up the body, put the woman's entrails back into it, and sewed up the gash with thread. Finally they wrapped her in a shroud and put her into the coffin.

"Our best plan," Zhang Sheng said, "will be to bury her at the Temple of Eternal Felicity, where our master worships. There is room there."

They hired two men to carry the coffin to the temple and said to the Abbot that they would like to bury the body there, since it was that of their young mistress's sister. The Abbot pointed out a place behind the temple, near a poplar tree, and there they buried her. Then they went back and told Chunmei all they had done. "We bought a coffin and buried her," they said, "and we have still four taels left."

"It is very kind of you," Chunmei said. "Will you take the four taels and give two to the Abbot and ask him to read a dirge to help her on her way to paradise?" She gave the two men each a tael and a present of food besides.

The two men knelt down. "We have done nothing," they said, "and we dare not take these gifts. We only ask that you should speak well of us to our master."

"I shall be angry if you do not," Chunmei said.

So the two men kowtowed and took the money. Then they went to drink, and said how kind their mistress was. The next day, Zhang Sheng took the silver and asked the Abbot to hold a service for the dead woman. Chunmei gave them five *qian* of silver to get paper money to burn for her.

*   *   *

Chen Ding reached Qinghe about this time. He brought with him Chen Jingji's family and his father's coffin. He set down the coffin at this same Temple of Eternal Felicity where, after a funeral service had been held, they proposed to bury it. When Jingji heard of their arrival, he brought in the luggage and kowtowed to his mother.

"Why did you not come to meet me?" she asked.

"I haven't been well, and there is no one to look after the house," he said.

"Where is your uncle?"

"When he found you were coming, he went back to his old house."

"You should not have allowed him to do so," Mistress Chen said. "He might just as well have stayed."

Then Zhang came to see his sister; they embraced each other and wept. Then they sat down together to talk.

The next day, Jingji's mother told him to take five taels of silver and some paper money and give them to the Abbot to hold a service for his father. Jingji set out on horseback. On the way, he met two of his friends, Lu and Yang. He dismounted, and greeted them. They asked him where he was going.

"My father's body is at the temple outside the city," Jingji told them. "Tomorrow will be the twentieth, and my father's last week's mind, so my mother has asked me to take some money to the Abbot for the ceremony."

"We are very sorry," the two men said. "We had no idea your father's coffin had arrived. When will the funeral be?"

"Not for a few days yet," Jingji said. "We shall not bury him until after this ceremony."

The two men bowed to him and were going on, but he called them back. "Yang," he said, "do you know who has taken away the body of that woman Pan?"

"About a fortnight ago," Yang said, "when it was clear that the police would not be able to lay hands on Wu Song, I told the magistrate, and the magistrate told the relatives they might remove the bodies. Old woman Wang's body was taken by her son, but the other remained for several days. Then somebody from Major Zhou's place brought a coffin and buried it at the Temple of Eternal Felicity outside the city."

Then Jingji guessed that Chunmei had taken it. "Are there many Temples of Eternal Felicity outside the city?" he asked.

"There is only one," Yang told him, "the one where Major Zhou worships. How many would you like?"

Jingji was delighted. It seemed to him that it was by a special dispensation of providence that Jinlian should be buried there. They went their ways. Jingji mounted his horse and rode on to the temple. Before he mentioned the service for his father, he said to the Abbot: "I hear that Major Zhou's people have buried a woman here recently. Can you tell me where the grave is?"

"Behind the temple, under the poplar tree," the Abbot told him. "The dead woman was the young lady's sister."

Jingji did not go to his father's coffin, but took the paper money and other offerings to Jinlian's grave. There he burned the paper money for her. "Sister," he cried, "this is your young brother, Chen Jingji, come to make an offering to you. Find a pleasant place in which to live, and spend the money when you are in need of it."

Then he went to the place where his father's coffin rested and burned paper money there. He gave the money to the monks and said: "May we have eight monks on the twentieth, to perform the service for the last week's mind?" The Abbot took the money and went to see about preparing the necessary things. Jingji went home and told his mother.

On the twentieth day, they all went to the temple for the service. When it was over, they selected a day of good omen and buried the dead gentleman in his ancestral tomb. After this they went home and mother and son settled down in their house.

At the beginning of the second month it was very warm. Wu Yueniang, Meng Yulou, Sun Xue'e, and Ximen Dajie, with Xiaoyu, went and stood at the gate to look down the street. Everything seemed lively and busy. They suddenly caught sight of a crowd of people following a monk. He was very fat and tall; there were three bronze figures on his head, and lamps all over his body. His robes were apricot colored and had broad sleeves. His feet were bare, and his ankles splashed with mud.

> He sits and gives himself to meditation
> Expounds the sacred scriptures, preaches the gospel.
> Broad shoulders, sunken eyes
> Themselves exemplify the manner of the Buddha.
> He begs his food and preaches
> According to the rule of his religion.
> By day he goes with staff and tinkling bell
> At night brings out the spear and club.
> Outside the door he beats his bald head to the ground
> On the street he strikes his lips.
> Reality is emptiness
> And emptiness reality.
> Who shall say what happens to this earthly life?
> Some go, some come
> Some come, some go.

But who has found a welcome
In the paradise of the west?

When he saw Yueniang and the other women standing at the gate, he came over to them and saluted them.

"Most charitable ladies," he said. "I see that you belong to an exalted family. This is a most opportune meeting. I have come from Mount Wu begging for alms, because I seek to build a temple for the ten Lords of Virtue and the Three Precious Ones. I rely entirely upon the charitable, who cultivate the field of generosity and give me alms. So this admirable work will be brought to a happy end, and a reward in the next life assured. I am but a wandering monk."

Yueniang told Xiaoyu to go and get a hat, a pair of shoes, a string of coppers, and a measure of white rice. She was always inclined to be generous to monks, and this one attracted her. She kept a store of hats and shoes especially for them. When Xiaoyu brought the things, Yueniang said: "Ask his Reverence to come and take them."

"You, monk, who will become a donkey in your next life," Xiaoyu said in her sweetest voice, "come here. My lady offers you these things. Why don't you kowtow to her?"

Yueniang scolded her. "You little scamp," she said. "He is a monk, a disciple of Buddha. You mustn't talk to him like that. It is his duty to ask for alms. You little strumpet, you will certainly be punished sooner or later."

Xiaoyu laughed. "That thievish monk!" she said. "What does he mean by letting his eyes roam over my body from head to feet?"

The monk accepted the gifts in both hands, made a reverence, and thanked them.

"Shaven rogue!" Xiaoyu said to him. "Where are your manners? There are several ladies here, as you see. Why do you content yourself with bowing twice to us, and why don't you make a reverence to me?"

"Do be quiet, you little rascal," Yueniang said. "He is a son of Buddha, and you have no right to expect a reverence from him."

"Lady," Xiaoyu said, "if he is a son of Buddha, who are Buddha's daughters?"

"The nuns are Buddha's daughters," Yueniang said.

"Oh, now I understand," Xiaoyu said. "Nun Xue and Nun Wang and the Abbess are all Buddha's daughters, are they? Well, I wonder who are Buddha's sons-in-law?"

Yueniang could not help laughing. "You little strumpet!" she said, "It is only lately you have learned to talk such nonsense. You are always being rude nowadays."

"You mustn't scold me only, Lady," Xiaoyu said. "That monk, with his thievish eyes, is looking at me all the time."

"If he looks at you," Yulou said, "I suppose it is because he wishes to make you give up the things of this world."

"Then I will go with him," Xiaoyu said.

They all laughed, but Yueniang said. "You are a little strumpet. You are always insulting monks and saying wicked things about Buddha."

The monk took the things and went away haughtily, the three images on his head. "Lady," Xiaoyu said, "that thievish monk had another look at me before he went away. Really, you shouldn't scold me."

As they were standing there, old woman Xue came to them, carrying her box of artificial flowers. She made a reverence to them.

"What have you been doing?" Yueniang asked. "It is a long time since I even saw your shadow."

"I hardly know myself what I have been doing," the old woman said. "A few days ago, his Lordship Zhang the Second, the new magistrate, was arranging a marriage with the Xu family. Xu's niece is going to marry Zhang's son. Old woman Wen arranged that. Yesterday was the third day and they had a splendid banquet. The young lady at the Major's place sent for me, but I was too busy to go."

"Where are you going now?" Yueniang said.

"I have come especially to see you," old woman Xue said. "There is something I want to talk to you about."

"Come in, then," Yueniang said, and took the old woman to her room. When she had had tea, the old woman said: "Lady, there is something you don't know. Last year, your kinsman Chen, at the Eastern Capital, died. His wife sent for your son-in-law to bring his father's body and the whole household here. They reached here in the first month, held a service, and buried the old gentleman. I thought that, if you had known, you would certainly have gone to burn some paper offerings for the old gentleman."

"But I would never have known, if you hadn't come to tell me," Yueniang said. "How was I to hear of it? I heard that Pan Jinlian had been killed by her first husband's brother, and that she and old woman Wang had been buried, but I have heard nothing of what happened since."

"If the Fifth Lady had not misbehaved herself and had stayed here, it would have been much better for her," the old woman said. "But she forgot her womanly virtue and behaved so badly that you had to send her away. If she had still been living with you, her brother-in-law would not have had a chance to kill her. Indeed, debts always demand that they who owe shall pay, and hatred never fails to find its victim. But Chunmei did not forget how she had loved that lady in the past. She bought a coffin and buried Jinlian, or the body would be lying there still. Wu Song has not been caught, and there was nobody else to care about her."

"Chunmei has only been at Major Zhou's house a short time," Xue'e said. "How comes she to be in such a position that she can afford to buy a coffin and bury the woman? Didn't the Major have anything to say in the matter? How does he treat her?"

"Ah! You can't imagine how fond he is of her," the old woman said. "He spends every night with her and obeys her slightest wish. As soon as she went there and he found how beautiful she was, he gave her three rooms and a maid. He spent three nights with her and had all the clothes she needed for a year made for her. On the third day he gave a feast and presented me with a tael of silver and a roll of silk. His first wife is now about fifty. She is blind, eats vegetarian food, and does not take any part in the management of the house. His second wife, Sun, has a little daughter and spends all her time looking after the child. Chunmei has all the keys. The Major does everything she suggests, and she never has any difficulty in getting money out of him."

Yueniang and Xue'e said nothing. When the old woman was preparing to go away, Yueniang said: "Come again tomorrow. I will get a food offering ready, a roll of silk, and some paper money, and you must go with my daughter to offer them to her dead father-in-law."

"Won't you go yourself, Lady?" the old woman said.

"Tell them I am not very well," Yueniang said. "I will go and see them another day."

"Then tell your daughter to have everything ready. I will be here about dinnertime."

"Where are you going now?" Yueniang asked. "Must you always be going to the Major's place?"

"If I don't go, they will be angry with me. They have sent for me several times."

"Why do they send for you?" Yueniang said.

"Lady, Chunmei is now four or five months gone with child and the Major is delighted. I shall certainly get a present when I get there."

The old woman went off with her box. "What a liar that old strumpet is!" Xue'e said. "Chunmei has only been there a short time. How can she be so far gone with child? The Captain has more than one wife already. Is it likely that he devotes himself entirely to her?"

"He has a first wife, and another lady who has a little girl " Yueniang said.

"These go-betweens," Xue'e said, "always talk about water a foot deep having waves ten feet high."

CHAPTER 89

Wu Yueniang Meets Chunmei Again

A beautiful woman's lot is grievous.
Alas, that one so exquisite
Should turn to a handful of yellow dust.
Is it that Heaven pays no heed,
That good and evil are but matters of chance?
It granted her beauty and intelligence
Then let her go as though she had been nothing.
It seems unjust.
And when we ask the Heavens why it happens,
No answer is vouchsafed us.

It is sad.
The beauty of the earth combined with Heaven's fragrance
Passes like the seasons.
They are many who lie buried.
May we not ask where there is gaiety?
Yet there are palaces where people dance and sing,
Where people walk in springtime on the purple path,
And, in the evening, sit beside green-painted windows,
Graceful and exquisite.
Surely the life of man seems purposeless,
Now as in the days long past.

Wu Yueniang prepared the food offering and paper things, and Ximen Dajie, in mourning dress, went in a sedan chair to her husband's house, with old woman Xue in attendance. When they came to the house, Chen Jingji was standing outside the door. He asked the old woman where the things had come from. She made a reverence.

"Your mother-in-law has sent them as an offering to your late father," she said, "and your wife has come too."

"Curses on my mother-in-law!" Jingji cried. "She is half a month too late. It is as if she set up the god of the door on the sixteenth day of the first month. My father has been buried a long time, and she comes now with her tribute of respect."

"Good Brother-in-law, as your wife's mother says, now she is a widow she is like a crab without legs. She knew nothing about your father's coffin coming, and you must forgive her if she is late."

As they were talking, Ximen Dajie's sedan chair came up.

"Who is this?" Jingji said.

"Whom do you expect? Your mother-in-law is not well and she has sent your wife to come and burn paper offerings for your father."

"Take the whore away," Jingji said scornfully. "Better people than she have died by thousands. What have I to do with her?"

"You should not talk like that. When a woman marries a man, she does so to live with him."

"I don't want anything to do with the whore. Be off at once."

The chair men were standing by, and Chen Jingji went up and kicked them. "Take her away," he cried, "or I will break your beggarly legs and pull that whore's hair out.

The sedan-chair men could only take the chair away. By the time old woman Xue was able to speak to Jingji's mother, it had been gone for some time. The old woman could do nothing, so she gave the things to Mistress Chen and came back to tell Yueniang what had happened.

Yueniang was so angry that she nearly fainted. "The rogue is utterly unprincipled!" she cried. "He came here to escape the law, and his father-in-law kept him all those years. This is how he repays us. What a pity that my dead husband kept such a rascal in the place and so gave us all this trouble today. It puts me in the position of a rotten rat, and he dares to insult me."

"Daughter," she said to Ximen Dajie, "you saw with your own eyes that neither my husband nor I ever treated him badly. So long as you live, you belong to the Chen family, and, when you die, you will be a Chen ghost. I can't keep you here. Go to him tomorrow. Don't be afraid. I don't think he will be quite so desperate as to push you into a well. He dare not kill you, because, fortunately, law still has some force in this world."

The next day Yueniang told Daian to go with her daughter. The young woman went in a sedan chair. When they came to the house, Jingji was out. He had gone to his father's grave to put earth on the mound. His mother was a lady of breeding and received her daughter-in-law.

"Go home and tell your mistress that I am very much obliged to her," she said to Daian. "Ask her not to be angry with the young man. He had taken too much to drink yesterday and that is why he behaved so strangely. I will bring him around by degrees." She gave Daian something to eat and dismissed him.

In the evening Chen Jingji came back. The moment he saw his wife he began to kick her and curse.

"You whore!" he cried, "why have you come back? You told me I begged my food from your family. The real truth is that your people have stolen a lot of my property, and that is how they got their wealth. If your people won't keep a son-in-law for nothing, why should I keep you now, you whore? Better people than you have died by thousands, yes, and by tens of thousands."

Then his wife cursed him in return. "You shameless rascal, you unprincipled scamp!" she cried. "Just because that strumpet was murdered, why do you vent your spite on me?"

Jingji pulled her hair and struck her violently with his fist. His mother came and tried to separate them, but he pushed her away and threw her on the floor. The old lady cried. "You rascal! Are your eyes so red that you do not even know your own mother?"

That same night Ximen Dajie was sent back again. Her husband said to her: "If you don't make them give me back my things, I will kill you." This frightened her so much that she stayed at home and never again tried to go and see her husband.

At the Festival of Pure Brightness in the third month, Yueniang prepared incense, candles, paper money, and other things and went outside the city to offer them at her dead husband's grave. She left Sun Xue'e, Ximen Dajie, and one or two maids to look after the house. She, with Meng Yulou, Xiaoyu, and the nurse Ruyi'er carrying the baby, went to the grave in sedan chairs. She asked Uncle Wu and Aunt Wu to go and join them there.

When they came outside the city, everything looked beautiful. The willows were green and the flowers fresh. Hosts of people were celebrating the coming of Spring, for there is no season more delightful. Then the sun is beautiful and the wind gentle, as the eyes of the willow open and the hearts of the flowers are unfolded. The very earth seems perfumed. A myriad flowers seem to compete with each other for the prize of beauty; the herbs put forth new shoots. They are the message of Spring. The light is soft and bright; the scenery warm and perfectly harmonious. The little peach flowers have painted their faces a deep red; the young willows bend their slender waists, tender and narrow as the palace gates. Orioles sing a hundred melodies, and wake people from their midday dreams. Purple swallows sing, and the melancholy of early spring is banished. The sun makes the days longer and warmer, and little yellow ducks splash in the pools. Through the green duckweed they dash. Beyond the river on some estate, we know not whose, the swing hangs high among the mist of green willows.

It is the festival of Spring
And mist is everywhere.
Outside the town the gentle breeze blows away the paper money
And hangs it in the trees.
People laugh and sing on the tender grass.
It is the season of apricot blossom
When the rain comes suddenly
And suddenly is gone again.
The gentle oriole chatters in the cherry trees,
Under the willows, guests who have drunk their fill
Sleep on the riverbank.
Charming women are busy to the strains of music
They bring a rope and make it fast, Swing to and fro
Like a flight of angels.

Yueniang and the others came to Wuliyuan, where the grave was. Daian took the food boxes to the kitchen; they made a fire and the cooks prepared the dishes. Meanwhile, Yueniang, Yulou, Xiaoyu, and Ruyi'er with the baby, went to the hall. There they had tea and waited for Aunt Wu. Daian set out the offerings before Ximen Qing's grave, and still they waited for Aunt Wu. She was delayed because she had not been able to get a sedan chair, and it was almost noon before she came along with Uncle Wu, both on donkeyback.

"I don't know how you manage to ride a donkey," Yueniang said to her.

Aunt Wu drank some tea, then she changed her clothes and they all went together to make their offering. Yueniang took five sticks of incense, kept one for herself, and gave the others, one to Yulou, one to Ruyi'er for the baby, and one each to her brother and his wife. She first put incense in the burner and bowed before the grave. "Brother," she said, "when you were alive, you were a man; now you are a spirit. Today is the Festival of Spring. Your dutiful wife Wu, sister Meng, and your son Xiaoge, who is now a year old, have come to your grave to burn paper money for you. Protect your son's life, that he may live long and come to do worship at your grave. Brother, you and I were once husband and wife. I treasure in my memory the remembrance of your features and your way of speaking, and I am sad."

She covered her face and sobbed. Then Yulou came forward, offered incense, made a reverence and cried with Yueniang. The nurse, Ruyi'er, with the baby in her arms, knelt down. Uncle Wu and Aunt Wu also offered incense and made reverence. Then they went to the arbor and there had food and wine. Yueniang asked Uncle Wu and Aunt Wu to take the places of honor. She and Yulou sat opposite, Xiaoyu and Ruyi'er and Aunt Wu's old maid sat at the side.

That day, Major Zhou also went to visit his ancestral tombs. Before the festival, Chunmei slept with him. She pretended to have a dream and cried during the night. Zhou asked her what was the matter.

"I had a dream," Chunmei said, "and in my dream, my mother came to me. She cried and said to me that she had brought me up, yet I was not going to burn paper offerings for her at the Festival of Spring. Then I cried and awoke."

"If she brought you up, you must do your duty as a daughter. But where is she buried?"

"At the Temple of Eternal Felicity outside the Southern Gate."

"Then you must not trouble any more," Major Zhou said. "That temple is my own place of worship. Tomorrow, I shall be going there to visit our family tombs and I will tell a servant to take something to the place where your mother is buried."

The next day, the Major told his servants to take food, wine, and fruit and go to his ancestral tombs outside the city. At the grave he had a large house with halls, rooms and a garden, a place for worship, and shrines. His two wives and Chunmei went with him each in a sedan chair carried by four men. Soldiers marched before them.

Yueniang drank wine with Uncle Wu and Aunt Wu. She was afraid it was getting late, and told Daian and Laian to clear everything away. They went to the village of Apricot Blossom. There was a hill near the village and a wineshop at the foot of the hill. Many people were strolling about, and she told the servants to take their food there. Aunt Wu had no sedan chair, so they all walked and the sedan chairs followed empty behind them. Uncle Wu came last, leading the two donkeys. They walked over the green grass for about three *li*, then came to the Peach Flower inn, and, when they had gone five *li*, saw the village of Apricot Blossom. The red and green dresses of the people seemed like masses of flowers and willows. They had all come to visit their graves. In the distance they could see a temple beneath the shade of a locust tree. It was a building of more than usual magnificence.

Yueniang asked what this building was called.

"It is the place where Major Zhou worships," Uncle Wu said, "and it is called the Temple of Eternal Felicity. Don't you remember how, when my brother-in-law was alive, he gave a great deal of money to repair the building? That is why it looks so new and beautiful."

"Let us go and have a look at it," Yueniang said.

Some of the novices saw them coming and went to tell the Abbot. When he saw a number of people coming, he came out to receive them. He made a reverence to Uncle Wu and then to Yueniang, and told one of the young monks to unlock all the shrines that they might see the different images of Buddha. When they had had tea, all the doors were opened. Yueniang and the others looked everywhere. Then they went back to the Abbot's apartments, and he offered them tea.

"May I ask your name in religion?" Uncle Wu said.

"My name is Daojian," the Abbot said, "and this monastery is the place of worship of his most generous lordship Major Zhou. Under my instruction are more than a hundred monks, and, at the back, is a place for the wandering monks who come here to meditate. They make intercession for the charitable." He asked them if they would not take something to eat.

"We must not put you to inconvenience," Yueniang said. She took five *qian* of silver and asked Uncle Wu to give them to the Abbot. "It is only a trifle to pay for incense to burn before the Buddhas," she said.

The Abbot made a reverence. "I have really nothing to offer you," he said, "but I should be glad if you would take a cup of tea. Thank you for this gift."

Novices set the table and brought vegetarian food and cakes. The Abbot sat down with them and took up his chopsticks to encourage them to eat something.

Suddenly two men in black clothes burst into the room and shouted in a voice like thunder. "Teacher, why don't you come out to welcome the young lady?"

The Abbot put on his robes and hat, told the young monks to clear everything away, and asked the ladies to go into a small room.

"I must go and see the young lady," he said. "When she has finished her worship, I will come back to you."

Uncle Wu suggested that they should leave, but the Abbot would not hear of it.

The monks, ringing bells and beating drums, went to the main gate to receive the visitor. A host of men in black clothes followed a large sedan chair, coming from the east like a flying cloud. The chair men's clothes were wet with sweat.

The Abbot bowed. "I did not know you were coming, Lady," he said. "I beg your pardon for not being ready to welcome you."

"Teacher," Chunmei said, who was sitting in the sedan chair, "I am sorry to put you to so much trouble."

The servants took the offerings and went to the back of the temple where Pan Jinlian was buried. They set out paper money and other offerings before the grave. Chunmei did not go into the temple but straight around to the back. There she left the sedan chair. The servants stood ready to do anything she might wish and, slowly and gracefully, she walked between them to the grave. There she offered incense and made reverence four times.

"Mother," she said, "I have come to offer paper money for you. I trust that you may rest in paradise and make use of this money when you are in need. If I had only known you would be killed, I would have made a plan to bring you to me. It is my fault that I was too late. Now I repent, but it is still too late."

She told the servants to burn the paper money, and sobbed loudly.

Yueniang, in the temple, only knew that some young lady had come and that the Abbot had gone to meet her. When he did not come back, she asked the young monk what was happening.

"A little while ago," the young monk said, "the young lady buried one of her sisters. It is the Festival of Spring today, and she has come to burn paper offerings."

"I should not be surprised if this were Chunmei," Yulou said.

"But she has no sister buried here," Yueniang said. "What is the young lady's name?" she asked the young monk.

"Her name is Pang," the young monk said. "A few days ago she gave the Abbot five taels of silver to hold a service for her sister."

"I remember our husband telling me that Chunmei's family name was Pang," Yulou said. "It must be she."

As they were talking, the Abbot returned and told the young monk to prepare tea. A sedan chair was brought to the second door and Yueniang and Yulou looked through the lattice to see what manner of young lady this might be. They recognized Chunmei. She was taller than before. Her face was like the full moon and she looked as exquisite as a figure of jade. Her head was covered with pearls and ornaments, and phoenix pins were thrust obliquely through her hair. She wore a crimson embroidered coat and a blue skirt with trimmings of gold, and little ornaments that tinkled as she walked. She was very different from the Chunmei they had known.

The Abbot set a large chair in the place of honor and asked Chunmei to sit down in it. The young monk made a reverence to her and brought tea. The Abbot offered it with his own hands. "Really," he said, "I did not expect you today. You must forgive me for not coming to meet you."

"I feel that I have been a great trouble to you," Chunmei said. "The other day I asked you to hold a service for me."

"That was nothing," the Abbot said. "I should have done it out of gratitude for the kindness you have shown. We had eight monks, and in the evening, when the ceremony was over, I burned paper offerings. Then I sent your servant away and bade him tell you all about it."

Chunmei drank tea, and the young monk took away the teacup. But the Abbot sat with her and talked, and Yueniang and the others could not come away. Yueniang was afraid because it was getting very late, and she bade the young monk go and tell the Abbot she would like to say good-bye to him. The Abbot would not hear of it.

"May I mention something to you?" he said to Chunmei.

"Say anything you like, Teacher," Chunmei said.

"There are a few ladies here who came to see the place. We did not know you were coming. Now they wish to go away."

"Teacher," Chunmei said, "why do you not ask them to come and see me?"

The Abbot went and told Yueniang what Chunmei had said, but Yueniang did not wish to go. "It is late and we must go home," she said. "We have not time to come and see her."

The Abbot was very much embarrassed. He felt that he had accepted Yueniang's money and had entertained her very inadequately. He implored them to go and see Chunmei. Then they could refuse no longer. Yueniang, Yulou, and Aunt Wu came out.

"Mothers and Aunt!" Chunmei cried. She made Aunt Wu take the place of honor, then, like a branch of blossoms, swaying in the wind, knelt down and kowtowed. Aunt Wu hastily greeted her in return.

"Sister," she said, "things are very different now. I dare now allow you to make such reverence to me."

"Good Aunt," Chunmei said, "you must not say that. I am not that sort of woman. I know the correct behavior of an inferior to a superior."

When she had kowtowed to Aunt Wu, she turned to Yueniang and Yulou. They wished to salute her, but she would have none of it. She kowtowed to them four times. They helped her to her feet.

"I did not know you were here," Chunmei said. "If I had known, I would have asked you to come before."

"Sister," Yueniang said, "since you left us, I have not been able to come and call on you. I am sorry."

"Lady," Chunmei said, "who am I that you should call on me? Why should you be sorry?"

Then she saw Ruyi'er with the baby Xiaoge. "The young master is quite big now," she said.

"Come here and make a reverence to your sister," Yueniang said to Xiaoyu. Then Xiaoyu and Ruyi'er, both smiling, came and made a reverence to Chunmei and she returned their greeting.

"Sister," Yueniang said, "you should accept their reverence."

Then Chunmei took a silver pin with a gold head from her hair and put it in Xiaoge's cap.

"You must thank your sister," Yueniang said. "Why don't you say something to your sister?"

Then, indeed, the baby did babble something. Yueniang was very pleased.

"Sister," Yulou said, "if you had not come here today, we might never have met."

"I came because my mother is buried behind this monastery," Chunmei said. "I lived with her for several years and she had no relatives of her own. The least I could do was to come and burn some papers for her."

"Now I remember," Yueniang said. "Some years ago your mother died, and you told us you did not know where she was buried."

"You don't understand, Sister," Yulou said. "She means our sister Pan. It is due to her kindness that Jinlian is buried here."

Yueniang said no more.

"Would anyone else have been as kind as you, Sister?" Aunt Wu said. "You did not forget one who had been your friend, and you gave her burial. And at this festival you have come to burn paper offerings for her."

"Lady," Chunmei said, "you know how well she treated me when she was alive. It was such a tragic end. Her body was lying there exposed. I could do no less for her than bury her."

The Abbot told the young monks to set the table again. They brought in two large tables with all kinds of vegetarian dishes and cakes. The tea was made with golden tea leaves as tiny as sparrows' tongues, and the purest of water. They enjoyed their food and, when they had finished, the things were taken away. Uncle Wu was entertained elsewhere by some of the monks.

Yulou rose and said she would like to see the grave of Jinlian. She wished to burn paper offerings too, for they had been as sisters. But seeing that Yueniang did not intend to go, Yulou took five fens of silver from her sleeve and asked one of the young monks to buy some paper money.

"Don't trouble to buy any, Lady," the Abbot said. "I have plenty. Take what you wish."

Then Yulou gave the money to the young monk and asked him to lead the way to the grave under the poplar tree. There she found a mound of yellow earth about three feet high and a few grasses growing on it. She offered incense and burned some paper money. Then she made a reverence, and said: "Sister, I did not know that you were buried here. By chance I came to this monastery, and now I offer you this paper money. May it be of use to you." She sobbed loudly.

When Ruyi'er saw that Yulou had gone to the back, she decided to go too. Yueniang, who was talking to Chunmei, said to the nurse: "Don't take the baby, you may frighten him."

"Don't be alarmed, Lady," Ruyi'er said. "I will see he comes to no harm."

Then she went to the grave, where Yulou was burning paper offerings and weeping as she did so.

The ladies changed their clothes and powdered their faces. Chunmei ordered one of her servants to bring a food box, and all kinds of dainties were set out on the table before them. Wine was heated. The cups were of silver; the chopsticks of ivory. She asked Aunt Wu, Yueniang, and Yulou to take the places of honor, and she took the hostess's seat. Ruyi'er and Xiaoyu sat at the side. Uncle Wu had wine in another room.

While they were drinking, two servants came in and knelt down. "Our master would like you to come and see some performers," they said. "The other ladies are there already, and he asks you to come at once."

Chunmei showed no sign of hurry. "Very well," she said, "you may go back to him."

The two men did not dare to go away, and waited outside the door. Aunt Wu and Yueniang rose. "Sister," they said, "we have troubled you long enough. It is late, and you have other matters to attend to. We must go."

Chunmei would not listen, and still told her servants to fill the cups with wine. "Ladies," she said, "it was not easy for us to meet, but now that we have chanced to come upon each other, I trust we may keep on good terms. I have no relatives of my own, and perhaps you will allow me to come and see you on your birthdays."

"Sister," Yueniang said, "it is extremely kind of you to suggest it, but I dare not put you to so much inconvenience. Will you not allow me to come to you first?"

Yueniang drank another cup of wine and then said she could drink no more. "Aunt Wu has no sedan chair," she said. "It will be very awkward if we are late."

"If she has no chair, I shall be glad to let her have one of my ponies," Chunmei said.

Aunt Wu thanked her and declined. They stood up again and made ready to go. Chunmei sent for the Abbot and gave him a roll of cloth and five *qian* of silver. He thanked her and went with all the ladies as far as the main gateway. There Yueniang said good-bye to Chunmei. The girl watched Yueniang and the others get into their sedan chairs, and then got into her own. The two parties went in different directions. Chunmei with her servants went to Xinzhuang.

CHAPTER 90
Sun Xue'e's Elopement

The dodder clings to the raspberry bush
Its tendrils are not very long.
To lose one's virtue at a rake's hands
Is worse than to be thrown out in the street.

In the night he is kind to me
But the mattress of my bed is not warm enough.
He comes in the evening and goes in the morning
Is this not too hasty of him?
I am going to my end
And the old pain stabs my heart.

Uncle Wu took Wu Yueniang and the others along the bank shaded by many great trees. Daian had already prepared for them at a small hill not far from the wineshop in the village of Apricot Blossom, where everything was busy and lively. He had been waiting for them a long time. Then the sedan chairs arrived with Yueniang and the other ladies, and the donkeys with Uncle Wu and Aunt Wu. He asked Yueniang why they were so late, and she told him of the meeting with Chunmei at the Temple of Eternal Felicity. Wine was served and they all sat down in the open air.

While they were drinking, they could watch the carriages with gaily decorated wheels, and people coming and going. From the hillock on which they were, the people in the street seemed like a sea or a mountain of human beings. Some were standing in a ring watching performing horses. Among them was the son of the magistrate, a young man called Li Gongbi. He was about thirty years old, and a student at the Imperial Academy of Learning. But he was a gay and dissolute young fellow, who cared more about hawks and dogs and horses than for the study of poetry and literature. He was always to be seen about the streets, and people called him Li the Wastrel. Today he was wearing a light silk gown, a palm hat with a gold button, and yellow boots. He was with a man named He Buwei, and they had with them a party of twenty or thirty lusty fellows with crossbows, blowpipes, balls, and quarterstaffs watching Li Gui putting the horses through their paces. Then they performed all sorts of tricks, fighting with spears and staves. The men and women standing by laughed and cheered.

This Li Gui was nicknamed the Demon of Shandong. He wore a hat with a swastika badge, a purple shirt, and an embroidered waistcoat, and was riding a silver-maned horse. He carried a shining spear with a red handle, and behind him were several streamers flying in the wind. He was displaying his skill for the benefit of the people in the street.

The young man Li was looking at this show when suddenly he raised his head and saw the ladies on the hill. One was rather taller than the others, and he could not take his eyes from her. He did not speak, but wondered to what family she belonged and whether she was married. Then he whispered to Little Zhang, one of the men with him: "Go and see who those three people in white are, standing on the hill. When you have made sure, come back and tell me."

Little Zhang hurried away. When he came back, he said: "They are members of Ximen Qing's family. The old man is Wu, the short woman is Yueniang, the first wife, and the tall one with pockmarks on her face, the third wife, Yulou. Of course, they are widows now."

Li felt particularly attracted to Yulou. He gave some money to Little Zhang.

When Yueniang and Uncle Wu had watched the show for some time, they told Daian to pack up the things, and the ladies went to their sedan chairs. Then they went home, as sunset was drawing near.

Sun Xue'e and Ximen Dajie had been left at home. They had nothing special to do, and about midday went to the gate and stood there. As Fate would have it, a mirror man came along. In those days, the people who sold powder, flowers and ornaments, and those who polished mirrors, all had a sign to show who they were.

"My mirror is very tarnished," Ximen Dajie said, and told Ping'an to fetch the man to polish it. He laid down his pack. "I am not a mirror polisher," he said, "I sell gold and silver ornaments and artificial flowers." He stood and looked hard at Xue'e.

"If you are not a mirror polisher," she said, "be off with you. What do you mean by staring at me like that?"

"Lady," the man said, "don't you remember me?"

"Your face seems familiar, but I can't quite remember you," Ximen Dajie said.

"I am Laiwang, who used to serve his Lordship," the man said.

"You have been away so many years you have grown fat," Xue'e said.

"When I left here, I went to my native place Xuzhou. But I could not get work there and took service with a nobleman who had an appointment at the Eastern Capital. I went there with him. On the way his father died and he had to go back again. Then I went to a silversmith and learned this trade. Business is very slack and my master told me to try and sell these things in the streets. I have seen you several times but felt shy about making myself known. If you had not stopped me today, I should not have dared to come to you."

"Now I know you," Xue'e said, "but I should not have known you if you had not told me. Why shouldn't you come? You are an old member of this household. What have you got there? Bring them in and let us see."

Laiwang took his boxes into the courtyard, opened them and, putting the gold and silver ornaments on a tray, showed them to the ladies. They were excellently made. When Ximen Dajie and Xue'e had looked at them, they said: "If you have any artificial flowers, we should like to see them too." Laiwang opened another box. He had all kinds of flowers, some to wear on the forehead, some large enough to make a complete headdress, others in the form of different insects. Ximen Dajie picked out two pairs of flowers for her hair, and Xue'e a pair of jade phoenixes and a pair of gold fish. Ximen Dajie paid for what she took, but Xue'e asked Laiwang to come another day for his money, one tael and two *qian*.

"The Great Lady and the others have gone to your master's grave to burn paper money," she told him.

"I heard last year that my master was dead," Laiwang said. "I suppose the Great Lady's baby is quite big now."

"He is eighteen months old, and the whole household treats him as though he were a pearl or some other jewel. The future of this house rests wholly upon him."

While they were talking, Laizhao's wife brought a cup of tea for Laiwang. He took the tea and made a reverence. Laizhao came out to talk to him. "Come tomorrow and see the Great Lady," he said. Then Laiwang picked up his boxes and went away.

In the evening Yueniang came back. Xue'e and Ximen Dajie and the maids kowtowed to her. Daian could not keep up with the men carrying the boxes, so he hired a donkey. When he reached home, the porters were dismissed.

"Today at the temple," Yueniang told her daughter and Xue'e, "we met Chunmei. Jinlian is buried at the back, and we never knew. Chunmei went to burn some paper money for her and we met her quite by accident. We were very friendly. The Abbot offered us vegetarian food, then Chunmei called for her servants, and they must have set out thirty or forty dishes. We could not drink all the wine she offered us. She looked at the baby and gave him some pins. She was most agreeable. And what a number of servants she had! She was in a large sedan chair with ever so many attendants following it. She is taller and stouter than she used to be, and her face seems whiter and fuller."

"She had not forgotten us," Aunt Wu said. "I remember when she was here, she was much more efficient and a much better talker than any of the other maids. She spoke so gently and quietly. Even then I knew she was a capable girl. Now she has been lucky her intelligence is more evident than ever."

"Sister," Yulou said, "she told me that she has not been unwell for six months. Her fortune is made. I understand she expects to have a baby in the eighth or the ninth month. The Major is delighted. So what old woman Xue said happens to be true."

"Today, while you were out," Xue'e said, "Ximen Dajie and I were standing at the gate and saw Laiwang. He is a silversmith now, and was selling gold and silver ornaments and flowers in the street. At first, I didn't recognize him. I bought a few things. He asked after you and I told him you had gone to the grave."

"Why didn't you ask him to wait for me?" Yueniang said.

"I told him to come again tomorrow." While they were talking, Ruyi'er came to them. "The baby has been asleep ever since we came in," she said, "and I can't get him to wake. His breath seems cold, but his body is as hot as fire."

Yueniang was frightened. She went to the bed and picked up the child. She kissed him and could feel a cold sweat on his body, though he seemed feverish.

"You wicked woman!" she said irritably to Ruyi'er. "He must have got cold in the chair."

"He could not," Ruyi'er said. "I had him well wrapped up in the bed-clothes."

"Well, perhaps when you took him to the grave he got a fright. I told you not to take him, but instead of listening to me you rushed off like a mad woman."

"Xiaoyu knows I had only had him there for a minute or two. How could he be frightened?"

"Don't argue," Yueniang cried. "Whether you had him there a short time or not, he is frightened now."

She called for Laian and sent him for old woman Liu. When the old woman came, she felt the baby's pulse and examined his body. "He has caught a chill," she said, "and would seem to have met an evil spirit." She gave them two red pills and asked them to give them to the child with ginger water. The nurse was told to put the baby to bed. During the night he began to sweat and his body became cooler. They gave the old woman some tea and three *qian* of silver and asked her to come the next day. The whole household was in a state of excitement. Some got up and some lay down, and they were running about half the night.

Next day, Laiwang came to the gate with his wares. Yesterday," he said to Laizhao, "Lady Xue'e bought something from me and told me to call today for the money. And I should like to see the Great Lady."

"Come another day," Laizhao said, "the young master is not well. They had to send for old woman Liu last night, and they were worried and busy all night. He is better today, but I don't think they will feel like seeing you."

As they were talking, Yueniang, Yulou and Xue'e came along with old woman Liu. Laiwang knelt down and kowtowed to Yueniang and Yulou.

"I haven't seen you for a long time," Yueniang said. "Why haven't you been to call on me?"

Laiwang told Yueniang of his adventures. "I felt shy about coming," he said.

"You are an old servant of ours," Yueniang said, "and your master is dead now. Your trouble was really due to that wicked woman Pan, who would carry fire to one place and water to another. Your good wife hanged herself and you were banished. But Heaven could not allow such a creature to live, and now she is dead too."

"I need not say anything, Mother," Laiwang said. "You understand so well."

When they had talked for a while, Yueniang asked what he had to sell. He showed her and she picked out ornaments to the value of three taels and two *qian* and paid him for them. Then she asked him to go to the second door, and told Xiaoyu to give him a pot of wine and some cakes. Xue'e went to the kitchen and herself gave him a large bowl of meat. When he had had a good meal, he kowtowed and prepared to go away. Yueniang and Yulou went to the inner court, but Xue'e stayed and talked to him.

"Come here as often as you like," she said to him. "There is nothing to fear. I will send you a message by Laizhao's wife. Tomorrow evening I will wait for you in the little room by the wall not far from this door." They exchanged glances, and Laiwang knew what the woman meant. He asked if the second door would be closed in the evening.

"Come to Laizhao's room," Xue'e said, "and, in the evening, take a ladder and climb over the wall. I will help you down on this side. I shall have something to tell you when we meet."

Laiwang was delighted. He said good-bye to Xue'e and took away his boxes.

The next day he did not bother to do any business. He came to Ximen's house and, when Laizhao came out, he bowed to him.

"I haven't seen you for a long time, Brother Laiwang," Laizhao said.

Laiwang smiled. "I would not have come except to ask Lady Xue'e for some money."

Laiwang took the man to his own rooms.

"Where is my sister-in-law?" Laiwang said.

"My wife is always in the kitchen during the day," Laizhao told him.

Laiwang gave him a tael of silver. "This is to buy a pot of wine for your wife and yourself."

"But a pot of wine doesn't cost so much as that," Laizhao said. He called his son, Little Iron Rod. The boy was now fifteen years old. He took a pot and went out to buy some wine. Then he went to the kitchen to see his mother.

Laizhao's wife came out with some hot rice and a large bowl of stew with two other dishes. "Oh, I see you are here, Brother Wang," she said.

Laizhao showed his wife the silver and said: "Our brother has given us this to buy some wine."

"I don't think we ought to take it," she said, smiling. "We have done nothing for you." She put a small table on the bed and asked Laiwang to sit down. Then she set out food and wine. Laiwang filled a cup and offered it to Laizhao, then he filled another and offered it to the woman.

"It is a very long time since we were last together," he said politely. "I fear this poor cup of wine is all I can offer you."

"I am not the sort of person who cares too much for wine and meat," Laizhao's wife said. "You are a friend, and you must tell me the truth. Yesterday, the lady told me that she and you still love one another. She has trusted my husband and myself to help you. There had better not be any pretence between us. As the proverb says: If a man wishes to find the track down the mountainside, he must ask a practiced guide. If you two meet here and you get anything out of it, don't keep everything for yourself, but let us have at least a taste of the gravy. We have to be responsible for you."

Laiwang knelt down. "Brother and Sister," he said, "if you help me, I will never forget." Then they had their meal. Laizhao's wife went to the inner court again and talked to Xue'e. Then she returned and told Laiwang to come to her rooms that evening. When the second door was closed and the people in the inner court had gone to bed, he would be able to get over the wall and join his beloved.

Laiwang went away. That night, he came again to Laizhao's rooms and bought wine for him and his wife. They drank until it was late, without anybody knowing that he was there. Then the gate was closed, the second door fastened, and everybody went to bed.

Xue'e and Laiwang had arranged a signal. When he heard a cough on the other side of the wall, he climbed up a ladder and got over the white wall in the dark. Xue'e had a bench waiting for him on the other side. They went to a small harness room near by. There they embraced and began to make love more earnestly. Neither had a mate, and their passion was ready to burst into flame. Laiwang's spear was hard and strong. They sported for a long time; then the moment of greatest happiness came to him, and he yielded to her.

Xue'e gave him some gold and silver ornaments, a few taels of silver, and two suits of clothes. "Come again tomorrow night," she said to him, "and I will have something more valuable for you. Take it and find a place for us to live. I know that this family can hardly prosper now. I will leave it, and we will get a house and marry. You are a silversmith and we shall not have to worry about a living."

"I have an aunt outside the East Gate," Laiwang said. "She is a famous midwife. Her place is out of the way, and I suggest that we go there. We will stay there a while until we know whether there is going to be trouble and, if not, I will take you to my native place. There I will buy a few acres of land, and we will work on that."

He climbed over the wall again and went back to Laizhao. There he stayed till dawn and slipped away as soon as the gate was opened.

The next evening he came again. He went as before to Laizhao's rooms, then over the wall, and they made merry again. So they went on for a long time. They stole a number of valuable things, gold, silver and clothes, and Laizhao and his wife had their share.

One day Yueniang was very depressed because the baby was ill again. She went to bed very early. Ximen Dajie's maid had been given to Xue'e, and Li Jiao'er's maid had been given to Ximen Dajie because Chen Jingji had wanted her. Today, Xue'e sent her maid to bed. She took a number of earrings, pins and ornaments and put them into a box. Then she covered her head with a kerchief. She had arranged with Laiwang that they should meet in Laizhao's place and run away.

"That is all very well," Laizhao said. "You can get away easily enough, but I am in charge of the gate, and how can I let you escape like a pair of wild ducks? The Great Lady is sure to find out, and what am I to say to her when she asks me about it? You had better get over the roof. Smash a few tiles, and then there will be something to show the way you went."

"That is a good idea, Brother," Laiwang said.

Xue'e gave Laizhao and his wife a silver cup, gold earrings, a black silk coat, and a yellow silk skirt. They waited until the fifth night watch, when it was very dark, and then climbed over to Laizhao's place. Laizhao heated two big cups of wine and gave one to each of them. "Drink this," he said. "It will strengthen you for what you are going to do."

At the fifth night watch, each of them took some incense, then they got a ladder and climbed out on to the roof. Step by step they climbed up, breaking a few tiles as they went. When they came to the other side, there seemed to be nobody about, no watchman in the street. Laiwang got down first, then helped Xue'e, who climbed down with her feet on his shoulders. When they came to the street a watchman stopped them and asked where they were going. Xue'e was alarmed, but Laiwang was cool enough. He held out the incense he had brought and said: "We are husband and wife going to offer incense at the temple outside the city. That is why we are up so early."

"What have you in those parcels? "the watchman asked them.

"Incense and paper money," Laiwang said.

"If you are husband and wife and are going to the temple, it is a good work and you may go," the watchman said.

At that, Laiwang took Xue'e's hand and they hurried off as fast as they could go. By the time they came to the city gate, it had just been opened. They went out, turned up one street and down another, and so came to the place where Laiwang's aunt lived. It was a very lonely place: there were only a few ramshackle houses. They came at last to the house of Midwife Qu. The door was shut, but they knocked and, after a while, the old woman, who had just got up, came and opened the door. There stood Laiwang with a woman.

Laiwang's real name was Zheng Wang. "This is my wife, whom I have lately married," he said. "Can you let us have a room? We should like to stay here for a few days while we look for a house."

He gave the old woman three taels of silver for expenses. When she saw the money, old woman Qu could not refuse to let them stay. But, one night, her son, Qu Dang, who had seen that Laiwang seemed to have a great deal of gold and silver, forced the door, stole the valuables, and went gambling. He was arrested and brought before the magistrate. The magistrate, Li, realized that the things must have been stolen and ordered runners to go with Qu Dang to the old woman's house. They arrested Laiwang and Xue'e. The woman was so frightened that her face became the color of wax. She put on plain clothes, covered her face with a veil, took off her rings, and gave them to the runners. Then they were taken before the magistrate, and people came to hear of the matter. Some recognized them and said: "Surely that is one of Ximen Qing's women. She has been carrying on with one of the servants, the fellow Laiwang, now called Zheng Wang. They stole some things and ran away. Then Qu Dang stole the stuff from them again and now they have to go before the magistrate."

One man told ten, and ten told a hundred, and so the news spread like wildfire.

When Xue'e had run away, her maid discovered that the most valuable ornaments had been taken away and that clothes were strewn about the floor. She went to tell Yueniang.

"You slept with her," Yueniang said, in astonishment: "how was it you didn't notice when she went away?"

"She said she wished to be alone," the maid said. "She went out quietly and then came back. I had no idea what she was doing."

Yueniang sent for Laizhao. "You are in charge of the gate," she said to him. "Why didn't you know that somebody was running away?"

"I have locked up the gate every night," Laizhao said. "She must have flown."

Then they discovered that some of the tiles were broken on the roof, and realized that Xue'e had escaped that way. They did not wish to send anybody to find out where she had gone, and made no fuss about the matter.

In his court, the magistrate tried the case. First, he had Qu Dang beaten, and that young man gave up four gold ornaments, three of silver, a pair of gold rings, a silver cup, five taels of silver, two suits of clothes, a handkerchief, and a box. From Laiwang the magistrate took thirty taels of silver, a pair of gold pins, a gold figurine, and four rings. From Xue'e, he took a gold ornament, a pair of silver bracelets, five pairs of gold buttons, four pairs of silver pins, and some silver. From old woman Qu, he took three taels of silver. His verdict was that Laiwang had stolen these things and abducted a woman, and Qu Dang had stolen the stuff from him. The two men were sentenced to imprisonment for five years and the property confiscated. Xue'e and old woman Qu were beaten and the old woman confessed. The magistrate sent to Ximen's house to ask them to take Xue'e away.

Yueniang sent for Uncle Wu and discussed the situation with him. They decided that, since everybody had heard about the matter, they would not take Xue'e back. She had disgraced the family and done injury to the reputation of her dead husband. So they gave something to the runners and asked them to get the magistrate to hand Xue'e over to the official go-between to sell.

Chunmei heard that Xue'e had been carried off by Laiwang and all that had happened afterwards. She made up her mind to buy the woman and set her to work in her kitchen. Thus she would have her revenge.

"This woman is a very good cook," she said to her husband. "She is clever at getting tea and meals ready, and I think we might buy her."

Major Zhou sent Zhang Sheng and Li An to the magistrate with a card. When Li learned who it was who wished to buy the woman, he asked for only eight taels of silver. The men paid the money and took Xue'e to Zhou's house. First they presented her to the first and second ladies, then they took her to Chunmei.

Chunmei was in her room, getting up from a gilded bed with silken curtains. The maids took in Xue'e. She recognized Chunmei, bowed her head, and kowtowed four times. Chunmei opened her eyes wide. Then she sent for the chief of the serving women. "Pull down this strumpet's hair," she cried, "and take off those clothes. Then let her serve in the kitchen, keeping up the fire, and cooking."

Xue'e could only swallow her resentment. It has always been possible for one who begins by sweeping up the rice to become the governor of a granary. Xue'e realized her position. How she was standing beneath low eaves and must perforce bow her head. She took off her headdress and changed her clothes, and went to the kitchen sadly and bitterly.

CHAPTER 91

Meng Yulou Marries Again

One day, Chen Jingji heard of this business of Sun Xue'e from old woman Xue. He sent the old woman with a message to Wu Yueniang.

"Your son-in-law says he does not mean to have anything more to do with your daughter. He is going to the Provincial Governor to say that, when your husband was alive, he had a number of chests of gold and silver left with him by old master Chen."

This was one more worry for Yueniang. Xue'e had run away with Laiwang; the boy Laian had run away; Laixing's wife had died and the funeral was only just over. When she heard the message old woman Xue had brought, she was alarmed, sent at once for a sedan chair, and told Ximen Dajie to go to Chen's house. Daian and other servants carried all the things belonging to her to Chen Jingji.

"These things were her dowry," Jingji said. "The things I am asking for are those I gave into their keeping."

"Your mother-in-law told me," old woman Xue said, "that in her husband's time these were the only things they had. She has never seen anything else."

Then Jingji claimed his wife's maid. Old woman Xue and Daian went back to Yueniang and told her. She refused to give up the girl. "She was Li Jiao'er's maid," she said, "and now she is looking after my baby. If he must have somebody, he may have Zhongqiu. She has been my daughter's maid."

Jingji refused to have Zhongqiu, and old woman Xue was kept going backwards and forwards between the two houses. At last Jingji's mother said to Daian: "Brother, go and tell your mistress that she has several maids. Why does she insist on keeping that particular one to look after her baby? And I don't see why she should keep Zhongqiu either, since Zhongqiu was my daughter-in-law's maid and was made a woman by my son."

Daian went and told Yueniang. Then she gave way and sent Yuanxiao. Jingji was very pleased with himself. "It is settled on my own terms after all," he said.

*   *   *

We now return to Magistrate Li's son. He had seen Wu Yueniang and Meng Yulou outside the city at the Festival of Spring. They were both beautiful and dressed alike, and he knew that they had been Ximen Qing's wives. He liked Yulou because she was tall. Her face was like a melon seed and she seemed charming and gay.

This young man's wife had died sometime before, and he had been looking about for a wife but could find no one who pleased him sufficiently. He was greatly taken with Yulou but did not know how to approach her. Besides, he did not know whether she wished to remarry.

Then he heard that Xue'e had been brought before his father's court. She was one of Ximen's wives also. He succeeded in persuading his father to return all the stolen property to Ximen's people. But Yueniang was afraid to have anything to do with the courts and would not send a man to claim the things. The young man was disappointed. The stolen goods were confiscated and Xue'e was sold. Then he talked over the situation with one of the officers called Yu.

"Why don't you send old Tao, the go-between, to Ximen's house to arrange the matter?" Yu said. "Tell the old woman that, if she brings the matter off, she shall have five taels of silver and be freed from her official work."

The young man spoke to old woman Tao, and the old woman was so delighted that she ran to Ximen's house as if she had had wings. Laizhao was at the door. The old woman made a reverence to him. "May I know if this is Ximen's house?" she said.

"Who are you?" Laizhao said. "What do you want? My master is dead."

"Will you kindly go and tell the lady that I am Tao, the official go-between. My young master tells me that one of the ladies is thinking of remarrying, and I have come to see about it."

"Old woman," Laizhao shouted, "you seem to have lost your manners. My master has been dead more than a year now. There are two ladies here, and neither of them wishes to remarry. You know the proverb: Howling wind and driving rain do not beat upon a widow's door. You are trifling and talking nonsense about marriage. Be off with you, and quickly. If the ladies hear of this, you may get a beating."

The old woman smiled. "The governor may be wrong," she said, "and his deputy too, but the messenger is always right. I should not have come if my young master had not sent me. Whether they wish to marry or not, kindly go and tell them. Then I will go back and let my young master know what they say."

"To do something for others is sometimes advantageous to oneself," Laizhao said. "Wait here, and I will go and tell them. One of the ladies has a baby. The other has not. I have no notion which it is you want."

"My young master told me that he saw her in the country at the Spring Festival. She has a few marks on her face."

Laizhao went and told Yueniang that the official go-between wished to see her. Yueniang was startled. "Nothing that is said here ever goes beyond these walls," she said. "What do they know of us?"

"The woman says they saw a lady with a few marks on her face, at the Festival of Spring."

"That is Sister Meng," Yueniang said. "I shall never remarry."

She went to Yulou. "Sister," she said, "I have something to tell you. A go-between has come, and she says Magistrate Li's son saw you at the Festival of Spring. She says you would like to remarry. Is that true?"

Now, as chance would have it, Yulou had noticed the young man that day and thought how gay and handsome he seemed. He was about the same age as herself, a good horseman, and skilled with the bow. When they looked at each other, they seemed to establish an understanding. But she had not known whether he was married or not. She had said to herself: "My husband is dead, and I have no child of my own. The Great Lady has a son, but, when he grows up, he will do his duty by his own mother and I shall be like a fallen tree that gives no shade, or as if I drew water in a bamboo basket. Since Yueniang has had this child, she does not behave to me as she used to do. It will be well for me to take a step forward and make sure of a home in which to spend my old age. Why should I be so foolish as to stay here? There is nothing here for me, and I am wasting my time."

She was thinking exactly this when Yueniang came and spoke to her. The man whom Yueniang mentioned was the very young man she had seen at the Festival of Spring. She was pleased but also a little ashamed. She said to Yueniang: "Don't believe a word of it. I have never even thought of remarrying." But she blushed.

"It is a matter entirely for you to decide," Yueniang said. "I have no authority over you." She told Laizhao to bring the go-between to the inner court.

Old woman Tao made a reverence to Yueniang and sat down. A maid brought tea, and Yueniang said: "What can I do for you?"

"I should not come to such a magnificent palace as this unless I had something of great importance to say," the old woman said. "I was ordered to come by his Lordship. It is said that there is a lady here who would like to marry again."

"It is possible that the lady may care to remarry," said Yueniang, "but she has never spoken of the matter to anyone. How did your young master come to know of it?"

"He only told me that he saw a lady at the festival. She was tall and had a face shaped like a melon seed, with a few white marks upon it. I think this must be the lady."

Then Yueniang understood that it must be Yulou. She took the woman to Yulou's room. There they sat down and, after a while, Yulou came out to them beautifully dressed. The old woman made a reverence to her.

"This is the lady," she said. "She is unusually beautiful and well worthy to be my young master's first wife."

Yulou smiled. "Don't be silly," she said. "Tell me how old the gentleman is. Has he been married before? Has he any women in his household? What is his name and what his position? Don't waste time. Tell me the truth."

"Heaven!" the old woman cried. "I am the official go-between. I'm not like the rest of them. I never tell lies. I say what I know and nothing else. The magistrate is over fifty, and this is his only son. The young gentleman's animal is the Horse, and he is now thirty-one. He was born at the hour of the Dragon on the twenty-third day of the first month. He is a student at the Imperial Academy of Learning and will shortly take his degree. He has a bellyful of literature, and is very skilled at archery and horsemanship. There is nothing about philosophy he doesn't know. His wife died two years ago, and now he has only a young girl to look after him. She is quite a common sort of girl, and he wants a wife to manage things. He has sent me here especially to ask you to marry him. If you are willing, my master says you shall be excused from paying taxes on your land, houses and property, and if anyone harms you in any way, you have only to point to him and he will be arrested and punished at once."

"Has the young gentleman any children?" Yulou asked. "And what is his native place? I ask this because when their term of office here expires, they will probably go away, and I do not wish to go very far. All my people live here."

"He has no children," old woman Tao said, "and his home is in the Zaoqiang district of Zhengdingfu. It is about six or seven hundred *li* on the other side of the river. They own miles and miles of land, have herds of mules and horses, and a host of people. The Imperial sign stands over all the arches. It is a splendid and glorious place. If you become his first wife, and he gets an official appointment, you will wear ceremonial dress and drive a carriage like a lady. Is that not good enough for you?"

Yulou made up her mind. She told Lanxiang to bring the old woman tea and cakes. "I must apologize for asking so many questions," she said, "but really go-betweens are such clever liars, and I did not wish to be deceived."

"Lady," the old woman said, "you should look carefully. Then you would see that the pure are pure and the foul, foul. Only too often the bad ones bring disrepute upon the good ones. I never lie, I have always set out to be an honest go-between. If you have made up your mind, please write a note and I will give it to the young master."

Yulou found a piece of scarlet silk and told Daian to take it to the shop and get Clerk Fu to write her eight characters upon it.

"When you came here," Yueniang said, "old woman Xue acted as your go-between. We will send for her, and then she and Madam Tao together can take your eight characters. That will look more dignified."

After a while, old woman Xue came. She made a reverence to old woman Tao. As they belonged to the same profession, it was arranged that they should take the note to the Town Hall together.

On the way, old woman Tao said to her companion: "Did you arrange this lady's marriage on the previous occasion?"

"I did," old woman Xue said.

"What family did she come from? Was she a virgin?"

"She is a Yang," old woman Xue said.

Then old woman Tao noticed that the characters on the silk showed that Yulou was born at the hour of the Rat on the twenty-seventh day of the eleventh month, so she was now thirty-seven years old.

"I am afraid my master will think she is rather old," she said. "He is only thirty-one, and she is six years older. Had we not better go to a fortune-teller and find out whether the parties are suited to one another? If the dates don't work out, we will make her a little younger. I shan't consider that anything wrong."

The two women went on, but they did not meet any fortune-tellers in the street. But from a distance they saw a black tent to the south of the road. Outside it were two signs. They bore the inscriptions: "I foretell good and evil fortune as Zi Ping. With an iron pen, I determine whether honor or ill-fame will come. To all who come to have their fortunes told, I tell the truth without fear and without favor." In the tent there was a table, and beside it sat a man who could write and tell fortunes. They went to him and he asked them to sit down.

"We have come to ask about the destiny of a woman," old woman Xue said, taking from her sleeve three *fen* of silver. "This is only a trifle, but please take it. I have very little money with me."

The man asked the eight characters. Tao gave him the card, on which the eight characters were written.

"I see this is a marriage," the man said. Then he began to calculate on his fingers and set out the counters on the abacus. "The woman is now thirty-seven years old," he said. "She was born at the hour of the Rat, on the twenty-seventh day of the eleventh month. The month is *Jiazi,* the day *Xinmao* and the hour *Gengzi.* She is an honorable woman. Working backwards, as one does with the life of a woman, we find that she is now at the period *Bingshen. Bing* comes in conjunction with *Xin,* which shows that she is destined to enjoy power and dignity and to be a lady. She has several husband stars, yet her influence is always happy for her husbands and they will love her. In these two years there seems to be an adverse influence. Has anything happened?"

"Two husbands have died already," old woman Xue said.

"That is good," the man said.

"Will she bear a child?" old woman Xue asked.

"Not yet. She will not have a child until she is forty-one. Then she will have a son who will comfort her declining days. Her fate seems to be excellent. She will be very rich and of high rank." He took a brush and wrote four lines.

Her charm is worthy to be compared with the beauty of the plum.
Three times the red silk is taken away, and twice she paints her brows.
We shall see the day when the horse's head is raised in victory
Then she will cast aside the covering of *Yin* and be free.

"Master," old woman Xue said, "what do you mean by those two last lines? We don't understand. Would you mind explaining?"

"I spoke of the 'horse's head' because the lady is going to marry a man whose animal is the Horse. Afterwards, she will live a life of ease. By 'the covering of Yin' I make reference to the man whose animal was the Tiger. That man is dead, and though he loved her, she was only a concubine in his household. From now onward, she will have a happy life. She will live to be sixty-eight and her son will close her eyes. Husband and wife will live together till they die."

"The man she is going to marry has indeed the horse for his animal," the old women cried, "but we are afraid he will think her too old. Can you make her a few years younger?"

"I will make her thirty-four," the man said.

"If you do that, will that fit in with the Horse?" old woman Xue said.

"Yes," the man said, "the *Ding* fire meets the *Geng* gold. From the gold melted in the fire, a precious jewel is made. It will be all right." He put down Yulou's age as thirty-four. The two old women went on to the Town Hall. There they were taken to the young man. He asked who old woman Xue was.

"She is the go-between of the other party," old woman Tao said. She told the young man the result of her visit. "The lady is very beautiful," she said, "but she is slightly older than you. I did not venture to settle the matter without your consent. Here is the card."

Li looked at it. "Born at the hour of the Rat, the twenty-seventh day of the eleventh month, thirty-four years of age," it said.

"That is all right," the young man said. "She is only two or three years older than I am."

"Yes, my lord," old woman Xue said hastily, "and doubtless you remember the proverb: When the wife is two years older than her husband, his wealth will be increased, and if she is three years older, she will be like a mountain of gold. The lady is very beautiful and has a perfect disposition. I need hardly say that she knows how to read and can manage a household very economically."

"You need say no more," the young man said. "I have seen her myself. We must select a day of good omen for the betrothal."

"When shall we come to receive your orders?" the old women said.

"We will not waste any time. Come two days from now."

He gave each of them a tael of silver for her pains, and they went off in high spirits.

Li was very pleased that his marriage was now so far advanced. He consulted with He Buwei and then told his father. Then he sent for the Master of the Yin Yang, who selected the eighth day of the fourth month for the betrothal and the fifteenth for the wedding. He made a handsome present to He Buwei and Little Zhang to buy tea and wine and other things. The two go-betweens went to Ximen's place and told Yueniang and Yulou the days that had been selected. On the eighth day of the fourth month, sixteen dishes of fruits and cakes, a gold headdress, a set of gold ornaments, a cornelian girdle, a set of little bells, gold bracelets and silver pins, two scarlet ceremonial cloaks, four embroidered dresses, thirty taels of silver, rolls of silk and cotton, were made into twenty separate parcels. He Buwei and the two women took them all to Ximen's house.

On the fifteenth, a number of servants from the Town Hall came to take Meng Yulou's things away. Yueniang made them take everything that had belonged to Yulou. Ximen Qing had given his daughter one of the lacquer beds, and now Yueniang gave Yulou the bed decorated with mother of pearl that had been in Jinlian's room. Yulou wished to take

Lanxiang with her and leave the younger of her maids to Yueniang. But Yueniang would not agree.

"No," she said, "I will not take your maid. I have Zhongqiu and Xiuchun and the nurse to look after the baby, and they are all I need."

Then Yulou sent all her things away, leaving two little silver pots as playthings for the baby. That evening there came for her a sedan chair carried by four men, with eight men from the Town Hall, and four pairs of red lanterns to attend her. Yulou put on her golden headdress, ornaments, and pearls. Then she dressed in a straight-sleeved scarlet gown. First she went to say farewell to Ximen Qing's tablet; then she kowtowed to Yueniang.

"Sister Meng," Yueniang said, "you are cruel. You are leaving me here alone, and I have no friend left." They held each other's hands and cried.

All the household went with her to the gate, and there an old woman put a veil of red silk on her head and gave her a golden vase to carry. As Yueniang was a widow, she did not go out, but asked Aunt Meng to take Yulou to her new husband.

"That is Master Ximen's third lady," the people in the street said to one another. "Now she is marrying the magistrate's son. This is the wedding day." Some said it was good, and some that it was bad. Those who considered it good said: "Ximen Qing was a very pleasant fellow. He is dead now, and his first wife lives on at his home as his widow. She could not possibly manage the household if it remained so big, so she lets the ladies go their own way, and all is as it should be."

Those who considered it bad said: "Now, even Ximen Qing's wives are remarrying. He was a most unprincipled fellow. He lived for money and to seduce other people's wives and daughters, and, now he is dead, his wives remarry and take his property with them. Some have married; some have run away; some have carried on intrigues with impossible people; some have even descended to theft. They are like the feathers of a chicken, all scattered to the winds. As the proverb says: we may have to wait thirty years for our reward, but, in this case, we see the reward today."

Aunt Meng came with the sedan chair to the Town Hall. The beds and furniture were all in their proper places. She was asked to take wine and then went home. Li gave the two old women Xue and Tao each five taels and a roll of silk, and they went home too. The young couple became husband and wife that same night and enjoyed each other as fishes enjoy water. Next day, Yueniang sent tea and food to Yulou, since Aunt Yang, who would have done it, was now dead. The three Aunt Mengs also sent tea. Then they received an invitation from the Town Hall asking them to go on the third day of the wedding. There was a very grand dinner; musicians and singing girls were present to perform plays and music. Yueniang dressed in pearls and put on a scarlet cloak, an embroidered skirt, and a girdle with a gold buckle, and went in a large sedan chair to the Town Hall. The ladies were entertained in the great hall and the magistrate's wife was there to receive them.

When Yueniang got home after this very lively feast, she went to the inner court. It was so quiet that not a sound could be heard. She remembered how busy all the ladies had been in Ximen Qing's lifetime, and how, when she had come back from a party, they had all come to welcome her home. Indeed, one long bench had not been enough for the ladies to sit on. Now they were all gone. She went to Ximen Qing's tablet and sobbed.

Young Master Li and Yulou, both very lively by nature, were delighted with each other. They were so much attracted one to the other that they found it hard to separate even for a moment. The young man looked closely at Yulou and, the more he looked at her, the more he loved her. And her two maids were very pretty too. Lanxiang was now eighteen. He was so delighted he did not know what to do with himself.

The young man's first wife, when she died, left an old maid called Yuzan. She was now about thirty years old. She painted her face till she looked like a demon. She used to dress her hair in a number of knots, then, around it, she put a handkerchief, and tied it with a gold ribbon as if it had been a hairnet. She wore the strangest green and red clothes and shoes like boats, with four eyes. Each of them was at least one foot two inches long. When she was in the presence of anyone, she shivered and shook, talked in a quavering voice, and behaved in the queerest manner. Before the young master had married again, it was she who served him every day with food and tea. She was very industrious, and smiled and talked even when she did not mean to. When Yulou came, and her young master attached himself so firmly to her, it was a very great trouble to Yuzan. She was furious.

One day, when the young man was reading in his study, she went to the kitchen and made a special cup of tea. She put the teacup on a tray and took it to the study. She put on a smiling face, pulled aside the lattice, and went to offer the tea. But the young man, after reading a while, had gone to sleep on the table.

"Master," she said, "nobody cares for you as I do. I have made you such a nice cup of tea. Your newly married wife is still comfortably asleep in bed. Why don't you order her maids to make some tea for you?"

The young man was half asleep and did not answer. "You old beggar," she said, "you have been so busy all night that you are tired out now. That's why you go to sleep in the daytime. Wake up and have this cup of tea."

Then the young man woke up and saw the maid.

"Put down that tea and go away, you dirty slave," he said.

Yuzan flushed, put down the tea, and went out in a bad temper. "You don't appreciate my kindness," she said. "I had the best of intentions when I made you this tea, and yet you shout at me. I may be ugly, but as the proverb says: an ugly person is a jewel in the household, but the beauty is a source of trouble. I may be ugly, but you used to like me well enough."

The young man kicked her. Yuzan pulled a face long enough to reach the ceiling. She never painted her face again, nor did she make any more tea. When she saw Yulou, she never addressed her as "Lady," but just said "You" and "I." She used to seat herself on Yulou's bed. Yulou said nothing.

Then she said, one day, to her mistress's two maids: "Don't call me Sister, call me Aunt. I am only slightly inferior to your mother and you must call me Aunt when your father is away. You must do what I tell you and work hard. If you don't obey me, you shall have a taste of my shovel."

She tried very hard to make up to the young man but he would have nothing to do with her. Then she was annoyed and would not get out of bed until noon. She refused to cook and would not scrub the floors.

"Don't bother about her," Yulou said to her maids. "Go yourselves to the kitchen and do the cooking and take the food to your master."

Yuzan was terribly jealous. She used to go to the kitchen, break the plates, and curse and beat the maids. "You thievish little whores!" she cried, "you must know that I was here before any of you. Your mother was not here before I was. Now you get hold of everything and don't exert yourselves in the least. The First Lady never used to call me Yuzan, but although you have been here only a few days, you have the audacity to call me by my name. I am not your servant. Before you came, I used to sleep with the young master. We slept together every night and did not get up till breakfasttime. We were like sugar and honey together, and I managed everything. Now you have come and smashed the honey jar and broken the relations between us. I am driven to a cold room where I have to put benches together to make a bed. I never enjoy my master's weapon any more. Indeed, I've forgotten what it is like. There is no place where I can say what I think. When she was in Ximen's family she was only the third lady, and I know she was called Yulou. I know it. And now that she comes here, she ought to control herself a little instead of boasting and ordering people about."

Yulou heard all this. It made her angry but she would not speak to her husband about it. One day, when it was very hot, the young man ordered them to heat some water and bring the bathtub so that he could take a bath with Yulou.

"Tell Lanxiang to go and do it," Yulou said. "Don't ask your own maid."

"No," the young man said, "it is her business to do it. I can't have her going on like this."

When Yuzan heard her master asking for water so that he could have a bath with his wife, she was very annoyed. She brought the tub and plumped it on the floor. Then she heated a great cauldron of water.

"I have never seen such a strumpet," she grumbled. "Always trying to harm me in some cunning way. What a strumpet she must be, washing herself nearly every day. Look at me! I slept with my master for months and months and never used a drop of water. But I didn't offend the eyes of Buddha. This whore has been trying to quarrel with me for a long time." She cursed all the way from the kitchen to the bedroom. Yulou heard her and said nothing, but the young man heard her too, and he was very angry. Though he had no clothes on, he picked up a stick and went out. Yulou tried to stop him.

"Don't be angry with her," she said. "It will be more trouble than it is worth if you go out now, when you are so hot, and catch a chill."

But the young man found it too much. "No," he said, "the ill-mannered slave!" He went out and seized her by the hair. Then he threw her to the ground, and blows fell from his stick like raindrops. Yulou tried to get him to stop, but she did not succeed until the maid had received thirty blows.

Then the maid knelt down before him. "Don't beat me any more, Master," she said. "I know you don't want me any more, and I will go away."

This made the young man angrier than ever and he struck her again.

"Since she is ready to go away," Yulou said, "don't beat her. And don't let yourself get into such a state."

The young man sent for old woman Tao to take the maid away. She was sold for eight taels of silver, and old Tao gave the money to the young man.

CHAPTER 92

Meng Yulou Outwits Chen Jingji

The savage tiger trusts to its own strength
But often is taken unawares.
It growls like thunder then, but that is all,
For the chains are set upon its legs.
When we see the tiger sleeping,
Its eyes have not the fierceness that we know.
The life of man is in worse case
Should evil men then not take heed?

Ximen Dajie came to Chen Jingji with all her belongings, but they were continually quarreling. He had asked his mother to give him some money to set him up in business. His Uncle Zhang borrowed fifty taels of silver from Mistress Chen and asked Jingji to find some work for him. One day, Jingji got drunk and quarreled with his uncle. This upset the uncle very much. He went elsewhere to borrow money and repaid the fifty taels he had had from his sister. This so distressed Mistress Chen that she fell ill. She had to go to bed; the doctors were sent for, and she took their medicine. Her son worried her so much about money that she gave him two hundred taels and Chen Ding was bidden to start a cloth shop at the front of the house. Jingji invited Lu the Third and Yang, and other foxy and doggish friends, to come to the shop, play the lute, gamble, and dice. This happened every day and, as they drank until midnight, the money was soon gone. Chen Ding told his mistress what was happening, and she placed her confidence in him. But Jingji accused Chen Ding and his wife of making money for themselves out of the dyeing of the cloth, and dismissed them. Then he asked Yang the Elder, whose name was Yang Guanyan, to be his manager.

This man's nickname was Iron Fingernails. He was a thorough-paced rascal, a magnificent liar, and skilled in the art of making something out of nothing. When he promised anything to anyone, they had as much chance of getting it as of catching a shadow, but when he made up his mind to get money out of anybody, it seemed as easy as if he took it from a sack.

Chen Jingji got another three hundred taels from his mother, so now his business had cost five hundred taels. First he had to go to buy cloth at Linqing. Yang went home, packed his baggage, then went back to Jingji and they started together for Linqing to buy what they needed. It was a place of considerable importance and a center of trade. People came to it from all sides. There were thirty-two flower and willow streets and seventy-two halls of music. Jingji was still young and only too glad to go with Yang to places of this sort instead of occupying himself with the purchases he had to make.

One day they went to a house where they saw a girl called Feng Jinbao. She was attractive and beautiful, and perfect from every point of view. They asked how old she was.

"She is my own daughter," the old procuress told them, "and my only source of livelihood. She is just sixteen years old."

Jingji was entranced. He gave the old woman five taels of silver and spent several nights with Feng Jinbao. When Yang saw how absorbed in the girl the young man was, so that he could not be persuaded to leave her, he suggested that Jingji should marry the girl and take her home with him. The old procuress demanded a hundred and twenty taels, but, after some discussion, she came down to a hundred. Jingji paid the money and took away the girl. She sat in a sedan chair; Yang and Jingji rode on horseback with the cloth they had bought. They cracked their whips, set their horses at the gallop, and were very pleased with themselves.

When they got home, Mistress Chen was so much upset to find that they had only bought a small supply of merchandise and that her son had married a singing girl that she died. Jingji bought a coffin, put his mother in it, called in some monks to hold a service and buried her in about a week's time. Her brother Zhang remembered how kind she had been to him and made no trouble with Jingji.

As soon as the young man came back from the grave, he set up his mother's tablet in the upper room and gave the other two rooms to Feng Jinbao, leaving only a little room for his wife. Then he bought a maid called Chongxi for Feng Jinbao. Yang looked after the shop and Jingji stayed at home and enjoyed the finest of food and drink. He spent every night with the singing girl and paid not the slightest attention to his wife.

One day he heard that Meng Yulou had married the magistrate's son and taken with her a considerable amount of property. Then the magistrate's term of office expired, and he was made Sub-Prefect at Yanzhou. He went to take up this new appointment. This reminded Jingji that he had once picked up one of Yulou's pins in the garden. He decided that he would take this pin with him to Yanzhou, and, with that as his evidence, claim that Yulou had had an intrigue with him and had given him the pin. He would say that everything she had brought with her from Ximen's household really belonged to Yang Jian and should have been confiscated. The magistrate Li, he thought, was only a civil officer and not one of very high rank, and a few sharp words would induce him to order his son to give up Yulou. "Then," the young man said to himself, "I will bring her back with me and, with Feng Jinbao, I shall have two women for my enjoyment." Unfortunately for him, the matter did not turn out as pleasantly as he expected.

He opened his mother's chests and took a thousand taels of silver. He gave a hundred to Feng Jinbao and re-engaged Chen Ding to look after the shop. Then he and Yang, with his servant Chen An, took the remaining nine hundred taels and set off for Huzhou at the time of the Autumn Festival. There they bought silk of various kinds enough to load half a boat. Then they came to the wharf of Qingjiang. They moored their boat and went to an inn kept by a man called Chen the Second. They ordered chickens to be killed and called for wine, and Jingji and Yang the Elder drank together.

While they were drinking, Jingji said to his friend: "You stay here a few days and keep an eye on the boat, and Chen An and I will go to visit my sister who is married to a nobleman at Yanzhou. We shall be back in three or four days."

"Yes, Brother, go by all means," Yang said. "I will wait for you and, when you come back, we will start for home."

So Jingji took his money and some presents and set out for Yanzhou. When he came to the city, he lodged at a temple. He heard that the new Sub-Prefect Li had entered upon his office a month before, but that his family had only arrived three days ago. Jingji wasted no time. He bought some food, put it with two rolls of silk and two jars of wine, and gave them to Chen An to carry. Then he dressed in his best clothes, and so, looking very handsome, came to the Prefecture. There he bowed to the gatekeeper.

"Excuse me," he said, "but I am a relative of your master's daughter-in-law."

The gatekeeper went at once to tell his master. The young man was in his study, reading. When he was told that his wife's brother had come, he ordered the servants to take the presents, and told the gatekeeper to introduce the visitor. He put on his ceremonial dress.

Jingji was taken to the hall, and there he and Master Li made reverence to one another.

"When I married," Master Li said, "I was not aware that my wife had a brother."

"I was away then," Jingji said, "buying goods in Sichuan and Guangdong. I was away about a year and did not know that my sister had married. I am sorry. But now I have brought a few trifles and have come in the hope of seeing my sister."

"I am only sorry I did not know you before," Master Li said.

When they had had tea, the young man ordered a servant to take the presents and the card to Yulou. She was in her room when the message came.

"It must be my brother, Meng Rui, who has come all this way to see me," she said. She looked at the card, and it bore Meng Rui's name. She gave instructions that the visitor should be taken in, told Lanxiang to see that the great hall was tidy, and, when she had dressed, went to see her brother. Through the lattice, she saw her husband with a young man. It was not her brother but Chen Jingji.

"What can this young man be doing here?" she said to herself. "I must go and see. Even if we are not relatives, we belong to the same part of the world, and whether the water tastes sweet or not, it is the water of my native place. Though he is not my brother, he is my son-in-law."

She went in and greeted Chen Jingji.

"Sister," he said, "I did not know that you were married and living here."

The words were hardly out of his mouth when a servant came and told Li that another guest had arrived. He asked his wife to entertain her brother and went to receive the other visitor.

"What wind blows you here?" Yulou said.

When they had exchanged greetings, Yulou asked him to sit down, and told Lanxiang to bring some tea. They talked about the affairs of the family. Yulou inquired after Ximen Dajie, and Jingji told her how his wife and all her belongings had been sent to him. Yulou told him that she had met Chunmei at the Temple of Eternal Felicity at the Festival of Spring, and that she had burned paper offerings there for Pan Jinlian.

"I often used to tell the Great Lady that she should love you as well as her daughter-in-law," she said. "After all, you are her son-in-law and not a stranger. But she would believe the gossip that came to her ears, and that is how you came to be sent away. I never heard anything about your property."

"It is true that I did have dealings with Jinlian," Jingji said. "The Great Lady believed what the slaves said and drove me away. Then Wu Song killed Jinlian. If she had still been in that house, Wu Song, however bold a man he may be, would never have dared to go and kill her. That is a fact I shall never forget. Now Jinlian is dead and in Hades, and she will never forgive."

"Well, it is all over and done with now," Yulou said; "as the proverb says: hatred should be forgotten and not made more intense."

The maids brought food and wine and set it on the table. Yulou poured out a cup of wine and offered it to Jingji with both hands. "Brother-in-law," she said, "you have come a long way and spent much money on me. Please accept this poor cup of wine." Jingji bowed to her and took it. Then he poured out a cup for her. He noticed that she always addressed him as Brother-in-law. "Why doesn't the strumpet take the hint?" he said to himself. "Now let us see what happens."

The wine was passed three times, and they had reached the fifth course. They seemed to be getting on very well. Jingji's face was flushed with wine and, as the proverb says: wine makes desire as deep as the sea and stirs up lust as high as the heavens. There was nobody about, and he began to make evil suggestions.

"I have thought of you," he said, "as a thirsty man thinks of water, as a man seeks refreshment from the blazing heat. You remember how, when my father-in-law was alive, we used to sit close together playing chess. We never thought we should have to separate, and that you would be in the east and I in the west."

"No, Brother-in-law," Yulou said, "but don't forget the difference between right and wrong."

Jingji smiled, took some fragrant tea from his sleeve and gave it to Yulou. "Sister," he said, "if you will have pity on me, take this tea." He knelt down before her.

Yulou flushed, and threw the tea on the floor. "Evidently, you have no idea how to behave in a proper manner," she said. "I was good enough to offer you wine, and now you think you can behave as you like with me." She got up from the table and prepared to go to her room.

When Jingji found that she would not do what he wished, he picked up the tea. "I came here to see you," he said, "but how you have changed. I suppose now you have married the son of a Sub-Prefect I'm not good enough for you any more. When you were the third lady in Ximen Qing's household, things were very different, weren't they?"

He took the silver pin from his sleeve and held it out. "Whose is this pin?" he cried. "If you never had anything to do with me, what am I doing with it? Your name is on it. You and that woman plotted together to share between you all the precious things I left there. They belonged to Yang Jian, and the authorities should have had them. Now you have brought them to this new husband of yours, but wait and see whether I don't bring you to the place where you belong."

Yulou heard this. She knew that the pin was really hers. It was a pin with a gold head shaped like a lotus. She remembered losing it in the garden, but had no idea how Jingji had got hold of it. She was afraid the servants might hear of it, so she smiled at him. She even went over to him and took his hand.

"Good Brother-in-law," she said, "why did you take me seriously? I was joking."

She looked around, saw that there was nobody about, and said quietly: "If you care for me, I care for you too." No more was said. They put their arms about one another and kissed. Jingji put out his tongue like a snake's and made her take it into her mouth.

"You must call me your dearest husband, or I will not believe you," he said.

"Hush!" Yulou said. "Somebody will hear us."

"On a boat in the river I have some goods that I have bought," Jingji said. "We will go to it together. This evening, you can disguise yourself as a servant and come with me. I don't see why we should not. He is only a civil official and will not make any trouble. He won't dare to come and arrest us."

"Very well," Yulou said. "I agree. Come for me this evening and wait at the back of the house. First of all, I will throw a parcel of valuables over the wall. Then I will dress as a servant and come to you by the door and we will go to your boat."

Readers, when a beautiful woman takes an idea firmly into her head, even if the walls are ten thousand feet high, she cannot be prevented from carrying it out. But if she rejects it, you may be sitting in the same room with her, yet it will be as though a thousand mountains kept you apart.

If Yulou had married a fool, a man who was not so attractive as Chen Jingji, Jingji would certainly have succeeded in seducing her, but she had married young Li, who not only had a future in store for him, but was a brisk and lively fellow. She loved him and was quite content with her marriage. There was no reason why she should yield to Jingji. The unfortunate young man told her all his plans, but she deceived him.

When Jingji had drunk more wine, he went away. Young Master Li took him to the gate, and he went away with Chen An.

"Where is your brother staying?" Master Li asked his wife. "I must call on him tomorrow and take some sort of a present."

"He is not my brother at all," Yulou said. "He is Ximen Qing's son-in-law, and he came here because he wanted me to run away with him. I told him I would wait for him this evening at the back of the house. I mean to cheat him so that he is arrested as a thief and got rid of finally."

"Really, the fellow goes beyond all bounds," Master Li said. "But without my going to see him, he will come of his own accord and meet his death at my hands." He went out and told a trusted servant.

Jingji suspected nothing. At the third night watch, he came to the back of the house with Chen An. He coughed and Yulou answered. Then, over the wall, some silver was lowered at the end of a rope. It was about two hundred taels and had been taken from the official treasury. Jingji had hardly told Chen An to take it, when the watchman's alarm sounded, and four or five tall fellows came running out, crying: "Thief! Thief!" They seized Jingji and Chen An. The matter was reported to the Sub-Prefect, and he gave orders that the men should be thrown into jail and brought up for examination the next day.

The Prefect of Yanzou was called Xu Feng. He came from Lintao in Shaanxi. He had taken his examination in *Gengxu*, and was a very just and honorable man. He came to the hall of justice, and all the officers attended him. Sub-Prefect Li came and signed his name in the register. Then an official came and told Xu about the case, and Jingji was brought in.

"Last night," the official said, "about the third night watch, these two men, whose names we now know to be Chen Jingji and Chen An, broke open the treasury door and stole about two hundred taels of silver that are the proceeds of other cases. Then they jumped over the wall, but were caught and arrested."

The Prefect ordered his men to bring forward the thieves, and Chen Jingji and Chen An were hustled towards him. They knelt down. The Prefect saw that Jingji was only a young man and very good-looking. "Young fellow," he said, "where do you come from? What do you mean by coming to a government building to steal money belonging to the treasury? Have you anything to say?"

Jingji kowtowed again and again and protested he was innocent.

"How can you be innocent?" the Prefect said. "You stole the money, didn't you?"

Then the Sub-Prefect, who was sitting beside Xu, bowed and said: "My lord, ask him no more. The silver was found upon him. Why do you hesitate to punish him?"

The Prefect ordered Jingji to be given twenty strokes.

"Men are hard creatures," the Sub-Prefect said. "They never confess without a good beating. This young man, you see, is no exception to the rule."

The attendants threw Jingji to the ground and beat him with a thick cane. He yelled and shrieked. "I never realized what that strumpet Meng was up to," he cried. "It is she who has done this. Oh dear! Oh dear!"

Now Xu was a man who had taken a degree and, when he heard this, he thought there must be something underneath. When the young man had had ten strokes, he gave orders that he should be taken back to prison and brought up again the next day.

"That, I suggest, is the wrong course," the Sub-Prefect said. "The proverb tells us that men's hearts are as hard as iron, but the law is heavy as a mountain. If you give him one night, he will take back his confession in the morning."

"I know what I am doing," the Prefect said, and again told the jailers to put Jingji into prison. He was somewhat suspicious as to what was behind this case, and sent a man he trusted to the prison to ask Jingji what it was all about. The man disguised himself as one of the prisoners and spent the night with Chen Jingji.

"Brother," he said, "you are a young man and you do not look like a thief. I believe you are innocent."

"It is a long story," Jingji said. "I am the son-in-law of Ximen Qing of Qinghe. The woman Meng, who married Sub-Prefect Li's son, was one of my father-in-law's wives. Once she had a love affair with me, and now she has brought ten chests of gold and silver and precious things to Li's son. Those things once belonged to Yang Chien, and he left them in my father-in-law's care. I came here to ask for them, but they laid this trap for me and I fell into it. They arrested me as a thief and made me confess. Oh dear! Oh dear! Now I can see the blue sky and the sun no more."

The Prefect's servant went back and told all this to his master.

"When he mentioned the woman Meng, I wondered what there was at the back of it," the Prefect said.

The next day, he came again to the hall, and Chen Jingji and Chen An were brought before him. The Prefect extracted the real truth from the young man and set him free. The Sub-Prefect, who did not know what had happened, said: "My lord, he stole the money. Why do you let him go?"

The Prefect rebuked his assistant before all the other officers. "I am the Prefect here," he said, "and I serve his Majesty faithfully. It is not my business to take up your private quarrels, and to brand this innocent young man as a thief. Your son married a woman named Meng, one of Ximen Qing's concubines, and she brought with her many things that ought to have been handed over to the government. This young man is Ximen Qing's son-in-law, and he came to claim them. You have no right whatever to make him out a thief and try to have him punished as such. I am not here to do your dirty work. You are an officer and you have children, and you are trying to forward your children's interests. If this is the way you do it, it is an offense against justice."

The Sub-Prefect was ashamed. He flushed and bowed his head. It was a great blow to his pride, and he dared not say a word. Chen Jingji and Chen An went away.

When the Prefect had retired, Li went home in a furious temper. "This is the son you have reared for me," he cried to his wife. "He has caused the Prefect to insult me in the presence of all the officers. It nearly killed me."

His wife was upset and asked what was the matter.

The Sub-Prefect sent for his son and told the servants to bring him a thick rod. "Now !" he cried. "That thief you said you caught is Ximen Qing's son-in-law. That woman of yours brought many things away from Ximen's house and the young man said in the court that they had belonged to the criminal Yang Chien. He came here to demand them. You told me that he stole silver from the treasury and got me to treat him as a thief. I knew nothing at all of the truth, and the result is that I have been disgraced by the Prefect before all the officers of the court. That is what my son does for me, and I have only been in this post a few months. What use is such a son to me?"

He ordered his servants to beat the young man, and the blows rained down upon him. His flesh and skin were torn and the blood gushed out. The old lady could not bear the sight, and sobbed and tried to make her husband stop. Yulou stood, weeping, at the corner door.

When the young man had been given thirty strokes, the Sub-Prefect bade his servants stop.

"Get rid of this woman at once," he said. "Let her marry whom she pleases. I am not going to have her here to ruin my family."

Young Master Li could not bear this. He knelt down before his parents and cried: "I would rather die than give up this woman."

Then the Sub-Prefect ordered his servants to shut up the young man in a room at the back of the house. He was put in chains, for his father meant him to die there.

"My lord," the Sub-Prefect's wife said to him, "you are of official rank, and you are more than fifty years of age. You have only this one son. It is not right that you should let him die for the sake of this woman. When you are old and retired, who will care for you?"

"No," the Sub-Prefect said, "so long as he is here, I shall have everybody insulting me."

"Then send them away to Zhengdingfu, where our home is, if you won't have them here," his wife said.

The Sub-Prefect agreed. The young man was brought out again and told that he would have to take his wife and leave for his native place within three days.

When Chen Jingji and Chen An left Yanzhou, they removed their luggage from the temple and went back to the inn where they had left Yang.

"Yang told me he had received a letter from you saying you were not coming back," the host said. "He has taken everything and gone."

Jingji could not believe this. He went to the river to look for the boat, but it was not to be seen. "What an outrageous scoundrel!" he said then. "Why did he go away without waiting for me?" He had just come out of prison and had no money. So he and Chen An got on a boat and pawned their clothes to pay the passage money. They looked like a pair of stray dogs, like fish wriggling out of the net. All the way along, they asked for news of Yang the Elder, but heard nothing. It was now the end of autumn. The leaves were withered in the woods, and the West wind drove fiercely. It was sad and cold.

> Sadly, the lotus withers
> Leaf after leaf, the *Wutong* fades
> The crickets chirp in the rotted grass
> The wild goose rests on the barren sand
> A fine rain drenches the dark forest
> A heavy frost chills the air.
> He who is not a wayfarer
> Will never know what Autumn is.

At last Chen Jingji reached home. Chen Ding was standing at the door. Jingji's face was as black as lacquer and his clothes were nothing but rags. The servant was shocked. He took his master in and asked him where the boat was.

For a long time the young man could not speak. Then he told the servant what had happened to him in Yanzhou. "Fortunately," he said, "the Prefect set me free or my life would have been in danger. Then that heaven-destroying rascal Yang stole my merchandise, and I have no idea where he has gone." He told Chen Ding to go to Yang's house to find out if he had returned. Chen Ding was told that Yang the Elder had not yet come home. Then Jingji himself went to Yang's house, but could get no information. He was very much upset and went to his wife's room. He found her quarreling with Feng Jinbao. Indeed the two women had spent all their time quarreling while he had been away.

His wife said that Feng Jinbao had given a great sum of money to the old procuress and that the old woman came every day, stole things away, and brought food and wine that she ate with her daughter. She herself could get nothing to eat. Feng Jinbao used to sleep until noon and would not give her a penny to buy anything with.

Feng Jinbao said that Ximen Dajie did not do a stroke of work. She would not even stoop down to pick up a piece of straw. She stole rice and changed it for buns. She stole the preserved meats and ate them with her maid.

Chen Jingji believed what Feng Jinbao said and cursed his wife. "You whore!" he cried. "Are you starving that you must steal rice and change it for buns? And you and your maid have been stealing meat."

He beat the maid and kicked his wife. This annoyed her so much that she went and beat her head against her enemy's. "You whore!" she cried. "It was you who stole the things and gave them to the old whore. Yet you lie to my husband and say I stole them. That is like the thief arresting the policeman. You told my husband to kick me. Well, I will live no longer and you shall die with me."

"How dare you, you little strumpet," Jingji cried. "You are not worth one of her little toes."

With one hand he seized his wife's hair and beat her with the other. He kicked her, too. She bled from nose and mouth and was unconscious for a long time. Jingji went to the other room with the singing girl.

Alone in her room, Ximen Dajie sobbed bitterly. Her maid went to sleep in another room. At midnight, Ximen Qing's daughter tied a rope around the beam and hanged herself. She was only twenty-four years old.

The next morning, when her maid got up and tried to open the door, she could not. Jingji and Feng Jinbao were still in bed. Feng Jinbao told her maid to go to Ximen Dajie and ask for a bowl so that she could wash her feet. But the maid could not open the door.

"What!" Jingji cried. "Is she still in bed? It is not early now. I will go and open the strumpet's door and pull her hair for her."

The maid looked through the window. "She is up there," she said; "I can see her swinging. She looks as if she were trying to be one of the dolls in a puppet play."

Then Ximen Dajie's maid looked through the window. "Father," she cried, "Mother has hanged herself."

Chen Jingji was much disturbed at this. He and Feng Jinbao got up. They forced open the door and cut Ximen Dajie down. But she had been dead a long time, and nobody knew the hour at which she had died.

When Chen Ding heard of his mistress's death, he was afraid he might be involved in the matter and went to tell Wu Yueniang. So she heard that her daughter had hanged herself and her son-in-law had taken up with a singing girl. The hatred between herself and Jingji was like ice three feet thick, not the result of one night's frost. She went with servants, maids, and women, seven or eight of them, and came to Jingji's door. There she roundly declared that her daughter had hanged herself, and made a great to-do. She seized Jingji and beat him and even stuck awls into him. The singing girl, Feng Jinbao, hid under a bed, but was dragged out and beaten until she was half dead. They smashed the doors and windows and took away the bed and curtains and furniture that had belonged to Ximen Dajie.

Then Yueniang went home and sent for Uncle Wu the Elder and Uncle Wu the Second.

"Sister," Uncle Wu the Elder said, "we must take this opportunity and bring him before the courts, or he will make things very unpleasant in the future. He is sure to come and demand his property, and, if we don't look a long way ahead, we shall have trouble. We had better go to law at once and have the thing settled once and for all."

"Brother, you are right," Yueniang said.

They drew up an accusation and, the next day, Yueniang herself went to the magistrate. When she went to the Town Hall, her accusation was sent in.

The new magistrate was called Huo Dali. He was a graduate and a native of Huanggang, an upright and conscientious man. When he was told about the suicide, he went to the hall and took the accusation. It said:

The accuser is the Lady Wu, thirty-four years of age, widow of the late Ximen Qing, Captain. She accuses her evil son-in-law as a deceiver and oppressor. He believed the words of a strumpet and forced his wife to hang herself. The Lady Wu implores you to investigate this matter and save her life.

This son-in-law is Chen Jingji. He came to her when he was in trouble and lived in her house for many years. He was fond of wine and caused trouble. He was undutiful and created disturbances within and without the household. Being a law-abiding woman, she got rid of him. Ever since that time he has hated her and treated his wife badly. He beat her and ill-used her, but she bore it for a long time.

Then he brought home a strumpet from Linqing, a certain Feng Jinbao. This woman occupied the room that should have been the Lady Wu's daughter's. He believed whatever she said to him, and ill-used his wife in every way. He pulled her hair and kicked her till her body was covered with bruises, and she could bear it no longer.

Then, at the third night watch on the twenty-third day of the eighth month of this year, she hanged herself.

This Chen Jingji obstinately seeks to oppress the Lady Wu, and threatens that he will kill her also. This is intolerable, and she implores your Lordship to arrest and try him for being the cause of her daughter's death.

So may evil doers know the law, and the good live in peace. So will the dead be avenged.

With this accusation, the Lady Wu accuses this man. To the Magistrate of the District, whose justice is that of the Blue Heavens.

The magistrate looked at Yueniang. She was wearing white. She was, he remembered, the widow of an officer of the fifth class. She was dignified in manner and refined in appearance. He rose and said: "Lady, stand up. I believe you are the widow of an officer. I understand. Go home and leave a servant to take your place here. I will have the man arrested at once."

Yueniang thanked him and went home in a sedan chair, leaving Laizhao behind. The magistrate ordered two runners to take the white badge to their office and arrest Chen Jingji and Feng Jinbao, and order the attendance of the watchman in that neighborhood.

Jingji was very busy making preparations for the funeral when he heard that runners had been sent to arrest him at the request of his mother-in-law. He was almost distracted. Feng Jinbao, who was in bed after the beating she had received at Yueniang's hands, was so terrified when she heard that she was under arrest, that she hardly knew whether she was alive or dead. Without stopping to think, Jingji tried to bribe the runners, but the runners bound them with one cord and hauled them to the Town Hall. The neighbors and the local watchman went to the Town Hall with them.

When the magistrate heard that they had come, he went again to the hall. Laizhao knelt down on the left, Chen Jingji, Feng Jinbao and the others on the steps.

"You wicked man," the magistrate said to Jingji, "why did you listen to this singing girl and cause your wife's death? Have you anything to say?"

"My lord," Jingji said, "I did not beat her. It is all because of a partner I had who went away with me to do business. He stole my money, and when I came home I was in a very bad temper. I asked her for some food and she would not listen to me. I did kick her that time. Then, in the night, she hanged herself and so died."

"You had that strumpet," the Magistrate said angrily. "Why should you ask your wife to get you food? It was unreasonable. According to the accusation that has been brought against you, you beat your wife and she killed herself. Is that true or not?"

"The Lady Wu hates me," Jingji said, "and she has made up the whole of this story. I implore you, my lord, to go most carefully into the matter."

"Her daughter is dead," the Magistrate said. "Do you imagine you are going to get out of it?" He told his attendants to give Jingji twenty strokes with the rod.

Then Feng Jinbao was called forward, and thumbscrews were put on her. The magistrate gave orders that they should be thrown into jail and told one of his underlings to go with the neighbors and police to examine the body. They found bruises all over the body and the mark of the rope around Ximen Dajie's neck. They wrote down this report: "After Chen Jingji had severely handled her, she hanged herself, unable to bear his ill usage any longer."

When this report was brought to the magistrate, he was very angry. He ordered ten more strokes to be given to Chen Jingji and ten to Feng Jinbao also. He declared that Jingji was guilty of his wife's death, and sentenced him to strangulation. Feng Jinbao was sentenced to a hundred strokes with a rod, and afterwards to serve as the public whore.

Jingji was in a terrible state. He sent a note to Chen Ding and told him to take every penny there was in the shop and his wife's ornaments, a hundred taels in all, and secretly take them to the magistrate. So, during the night, the magistrate altered the sentence and made it appear that he had been found guilty of having been the cause of his wife's death in the less criminal sense, imprisoning him for five years with permission to purchase his freedom.

Yueniang continually pressed the magistrate for justice.

At last he sent for her. "Lady," he said, "we have discovered the marks of the rope on your daughter's neck, so it is clear that she was not murdered. I do not wish to be unjust to anyone and, if you are afraid that he will make trouble with you in the future, I will arrange matters in such a way that he will never come near you again." He sent for Jingji and said to him: "I have been very lenient with you. You must amend your evil ways and begin to lead a new life. I forbid you ever to go and cause a disturbance at this lady's house. If you come before me again, I shall not forgive you. Go home and buy a coffin and bury your wife and then come back and report to me. I shall send an account of this matter to those in authority over me."

Jingji paid the fine that gave him back his freedom, and went home. He put his wife's body into a coffin, but kept it at home only seven days. Then the religious service was held and the body taken outside the city and buried. He returned to the Town Hall, and there spent much money. Feng Jinbao had gone; he had lost all his property; his things were sold and his house disposed of. Only his life was left to him. He dared not mention his mother-in-law's name.

CHAPTER 93
Chen Jingji Becomes a Monk

He stands on the steps and his tears fall silently
In the crowd his heart is full of discontent.
He breathes the air about him in a daze
And knows not his own feelings.

A warm breeze comes to the merry feast.
The sun shines brightly on the pollen of the flowers.
Yet even here his sorrow deepens.
He lives a life apart and only longs
To see the Springtide pass.

Chen Jingji had saved only his life. He sold his house and he had spent all his capital. His wife's ornaments were all gone, and there was no furniture left. He suspected that Chen Ding had made money at his expense, and dismissed him. Now he led a miserable existence without a penny to spend. He went several times to Yang's place to find out if Yang had come back with the goods.

One day, he went and shouted: "Is Yang the Elder at home?"

Now Yang had stolen Jingji's things and sold them. He hid himself in one place and another until he heard that Jingji's wife was dead and that the young man had been sent to prison for sometime on his mother-in-law's accusation. Then he came home. When he heard Chen Jingji's voice outside asking for the return of his property, he told his younger brother to go out and see him.

"You took my brother away on some of your business," Yang the Second said. "We have not heard a word from him for months, and, for all we know, you may have thrown him into the river and murdered him. Now, here you are, daring to come and ask about your merchandise. Do you think your merchandise is more important than my brother's life?"

This Yang the Second was a very bad man, a terrible fellow to meet in the gambling den. The purple muscles stood out on his arms and there was a mop of yellow hair on his chest. He was a villain pure and simple. He caught hold of Chen Jingji and demanded his brother. Jingji was frightened, struggled, and tried to get away. Yang the Second picked up a broken tile with three edges and deliberately gashed his own head so that the blood ran down. Then he ran after Jingji.

"I'll shove my spade in your mother's eye," he said. "What do we know about your money that you come farting around our house? Come here, and taste my fist."

Jingji ran for his life. When he got home, he fastened the door as tight as the lid of an iron pail. Outside it, Yang the Second cursed Chen Jingji, his father and his mother. Then he took some stones to smash open the door and Jingji held his breath. He had just come out of jail and had to put up with it. He was like a man who has once been bitten by a snake, afraid even of a piece of rope that he sees in a dream.

Some days later, he sold his house and got seventy taels of silver for it. He rented a small house in a very quiet road and went to live there. He sold the maid he had bought for Feng Jinbao and kept Ximen Dajie's maid to sleep with him. In less than a month, he sold the small house and went to live in a lodging house. Chen Ding no longer served him, and the maid died. He was alone in the world. He sold what furniture he had and was as poor as an old suit of clothes. Then he could not pay his rent and had to go and live at the Beggars' Rest.

The beggars knew he had been a rich man, and he was a good-looking fellow, so they gave him the stove bed to lie on and cakes to eat, and recommended him to the watchman as a bell ringer.

In the twelfth month, towards the end of winter, it was snowing heavily and the wind was very cold. Jingji came back from beating the alarm for the watchman. Then he went around the streets again with his bell. There were wind and snow together, and he had to tramp over the icy ground. It was so cold that he hunched his shoulders and bent his back and shivered all the time. About the fifth night watch, he saw a beggar ill and collapsed against a wall. The policeman thought the beggar was going to die and told Jingji to get some straw to warm him. Jingji went to sleep there, after doing all he could for the beggar. He had a dream. He dreamed he was back again in Ximen Qing's house, enjoying luxury and wealth, playing and joking with Pan Jinlian. Then he cried and woke up. Some of the other beggars came and asked him why he was crying. "Ah, Brothers," he said, "you do not know what I have had to bear." Every night, Jingji went to the Beggars' Rest, and every day went out to beg for food.

Long years he has suffered hardship
Bewailing his wife's death
Without clothes to cover his body
And food to put in his mouth.
His horse is dead
His servant run away
His house is sold.
Now, all alone, he wanders through the land
Standing, in the morning, outside the shops
To beg a scrap of bread
And, in the evening, lodges beside a ruined wall
Away from human habitation.
One hope alone is left to him
To go the watchman's round in the cold night.

In the city of Qinghe there lived an old man called Wang Xuan, whose other name was Ting Yong. He was more than sixty years old and very wealthy. He was a kind-hearted man who spent his money trying to help others. He always gave alms to the poor and assisted those in distress, and was very kind and very devout. His two sons were both married. One, Wang Qian, had inherited his grandfather's position at the royal mews and held the rank of Captain; the other, Wang Zhen, was a student at the Academy of Learning. The old gentleman had a small pawnshop. He had all the food he needed and all the clothes he could wear, and nothing to do but go to temples and monasteries to hear the preachings of the monks. He used to distribute medicine to the people, count his beads, and study the teachings of Buddha. He had two apricot trees in his garden, and took as his name in religion the Hermit of the Apricot Trees.

One day this old gentleman, wearing a monastic habit and a double-brimmed hat, was standing outside his door when Chen Jingji came along. The young man knelt down and kowtowed to him. The old man made a reverence in return.

"Brother," he said, "who are you? My sight is so bad I can't recognize you."

Jingji stood shivering. "Sir," he said, "I am Chen Hong's son."

The old man thought over this for a long time. "So you are Chen's son," he said at last. "My good nephew, how do you come to be in such a state? How are your father and mother?"

"My father died at the Eastern Capital," Jingji said, "and my mother is dead too."

"I believe you have been living with your father-in-law," the old man said.

"Yes," Jingji said, "but when he died, my mother-in-law would not have me any longer. Her daughter died, and we had a lawsuit. I had to sell my house, and I was cheated out of the little money I had. I have no work to do, and there is no way in which I can make a living."

"Where are you living now, my good nephew?" the old man said.

Jingji hesitated a long time, and at last said, "I will tell you the truth. It is like this. . . ."

"Dear, oh dear!" the old man said. "So you are now a beggar. And yet, if I remember rightly, you come of a very respectable stock. Your father was a great friend of mine. But you were a little boy then, and had your hair dressed in a knot, and were going to school. Can it be possible you have come down to this? I am very sorry for you. Have you no relative who can help you?"

"There is my Uncle Zhang," Jingji said, "but he has not come to me, and I don't feel I can go to him."

The old man took Jingji into his house. He told his boys to bring food and cakes and bade Jingji eat as much as he could. Then he saw how poor and thin the young man's clothes were, and found for him a long black cloth gown, a felt hat, and a pair of strong winter shoes and socks. He gave Jingji a tael of silver and five hundred coppers.

"Good nephew," he said, "these clothes and shoes are for you to wear and this money is for you to spend. Rent a little room and start yourself in business with this tael of silver. You will at least be able to make something to eat that way, and it seems to me better than staying at the Beggars' Rest, where you are bound to go downhill. When you have found a room, come and tell me what the rent is and I will pay it for you."

Jingji knelt down on the floor and thanked the old gentleman. He promised to do what he was told and went away with the money. But he did not go to look for a room, nor did he start a business. He spent the coppers in a wineshop, and changed the tael of silver into base money and spent it in the street. Then the police arrested him as a common thief and, when he was taken to the police station, he was well beaten. He came away with nothing but the torn flesh on his back.

In a couple of days he had gambled his clothes away, and even taken off his socks to change them for food. Then he went back to begging on the street.

One day he again went past old Wang's door, and the old gentleman was standing outside. Jingji came and kowtowed to him. The old man looked at him and saw that the clothes and socks had gone. He had only the hat on his head and the boots on his bare feet. He was shivering with cold.

"Master Chen," the old man said, "how is your business getting on? I suppose you have come for the rent for your room."

Jingji could not think what answer to make. At last, when the old gentleman pressed him, he said what had happened and how everything the old man had given him was gone.

"Ah, my good nephew," the old man said. "That is no way to make a living. You are no use for manual labor; you must get some sort of little business. It is much better than this begging. If you become a beggar, people will look down on you, and you will bring disgrace upon your father and grandfather. I wonder why you did not do what I told you."

Again the old man took Jingji into his house and ordered a boy to bring him food. When he had finished eating, the old man gave him a pair of trousers and a white cloth gown, a pair of socks, a string of coins, and some rice.

"Take this," he said, "and do start some business. Even if you sell firewood or charcoal or beans or melons, you can at least make a living, and it is surely better than begging."

Jingji promised and took the money and the rice away. In a few days he had spent all the money on food and meat and noodles that he shared with the beggars in the Beggars' Rest. Then he went gambling and sold the white cloth gown.

It was the beginning of the year, and, clasping his shoulders with his hands, he went wandering about the streets. He felt very shy about approaching the old man again, but nonetheless went to the old man's place and stood in the sun beside the wall. The old man saw him, but looked at him with cold eyes and said nothing. The young man came up hesitatingly, knelt down, and kowtowed. Then the old man found out again how Chen Jingji had spent his money.

"Good nephew," he said, "you are off the track altogether. Our bellies are as deep as the sea, and time flies as quickly as a weaver's shuttle. Nobody can help you to fill a bottomless pit. Come in. Now, let me tell you. I know of a quiet and peaceful place. It would be the very best place for you, but I fear you will not wish to go there."

Jingji, kneeling before him, wept and said: "Uncle, if you will only take pity on me once more, I will go, no matter where you send me, and stay in peace there."

"Not far from the Linqing wharf," the old man said, "there is a temple called the Yangong temple. It is a place that produces rice and fish, and much business is done there. The Abbot is a good friend of mine. He has only two or three novices at present and, if I take you to him with some presents, I think he may accept you. It will be very good for you to learn how to read the sacred books and perform sacred music. Then you will be able to offer divine worship for people."

"Uncle, I am very grateful to you. It is an excellent idea."

"If you are willing," the old man said, "come here early tomorrow morning. It is a good day, and I will go with you to the temple."

Jingji went away. The old man sent at once for the tailor and told him to make a religious habit, a hat, shoes, and socks for Chen Jingji.

The next day, Jingji came to the old man's house. He was sent into an empty room to take a bath. Then he combed his hair and put on the new hat, and dressed himself in a whole suit of new clothes. The old man took fruits, a jar of wine, a roll of silk, and five taels of silver. He mounted a horse and gave Jingji a donkey to ride. Two boys went with them and carried the presents. They went outside the city and came to the river, about seventy *li* away. The sun was setting when they came to the temple. Old Wang dismounted and went in. The pine trees were very luxuriant, and the dark cypress trees were massed closely together. The walls were shaped like the character *pa*. On the north side were three rooms. It was a very handsome temple.

The young monks at the gate saw them coming and went to tell the Abbot. He came out to receive them dressed in his robes. The old man told Jingji to stay with the presents outside, and went in with the Abbot. When they came to the Abbot's apartments, the priest said: "My lord Wang, why have you been so long without coming to see me? Why am I favored today?"

"I have been very busy, or I should have come to see you before," the old man said.

They sat down and young monks brought tea.

"It is late," the Abbot said, "and you will not be able to go away this evening." He gave orders that the old man's horse should be taken to the stable.

"I have come to this most venerable temple to ask a favor of you," old man Wang said. "I can only hope that you will grant it."

"Give me your orders," the Abbot said, "and I shall not fail to obey."

"I have brought with me a young man, the son of an old friend. His name is Chen Jingji, and he is twenty-four years old. He is very handsome and not lacking in intelligence. But his parents died while he was still young and his upbringing has been neglected. His family is a very estimable and noble one. At one time they were rich, but they were unfortunately compelled to go to law, and now the young man is homeless.

Because of the old friendship between his father and myself, I have suggested that he should come and become a monk in your temple."

"Since that is your wish, how dare I refuse?" the Abbot said. "Unhappily, though I have two or three novices here, none of them has any intelligence and they give me a great deal of trouble. All I should like to know is that this young man is honest."

"I can assure you, Sir, that he is most well-behaved. He is painstaking and clever in all things. I am sure he will make an excellent novice."

"When will you bring the young man?" the Abbot said.

"He is waiting outside at this moment. I have also brought a few humble presents that I ask you to accept with a smile."

"My lord," the Abbot said, "why did you not say so before?" He gave orders that the young man should be brought in. The servants carried in the presents. The Abbot looked at the card: 'Your humble disciple Wang Xuan respectfully offers a roll of coarse silk, a jar of wine, a pair of pig's trotters, two roast ducks, two boxes of fruits, and five taels of silver.'

The Abbot quickly made a reverence to the old man. "Why do you give me such a valuable present?" he said: "it would be rude for me to refuse, and it embarrasses me to accept."

He looked at Jingji, who was wearing a Daoist hat, gown, and shoes, and a girdle about his waist. He had beautiful eyebrows and bright eyes. His teeth were bright, his lips red, and his face as white as though it were powdered. He stepped forward and kowtowed four times to the Abbot.

The Abbot asked how old he was.

"My animal is the Horse," Jingji said, "and I am twenty-four."

The Abbot realized that Jingji was indeed intelligent. He gave him the name Chen Zongmei. The other novices were called, one Jin Zongming, and the other, Xu Zongshun. Old Wang asked the Abbot to introduce Jingji to the others. The Abbot accepted the presents; boys brought a light and the table was set. There was plenty of food on the table, and, needless to remark, chickens, ducks, fish and meat. Old man Wang could not drink very much and, though the Abbot tried to persuade him, he soon refused any more and, asking leave to retire, went to bed.

The next morning, boys brought him water and, when he had dressed, the Abbot came to offer him tea. Then they had breakfast and, after it, the old man drank two cups of wine. His horse was well fed, and the Abbot gave a present to each of the two boys.

Before the old man went away, he sent for Jingji. "Work hard," he said, "at learning the Sacred Scriptures, and obey the orders your Teacher gives you. I will come and see you again, and bring clothes, shoes and socks for you at every season."

"If he does not obey you," he said to the Abbot, "punish him. I shall not blame you."

Then he took Jingji aside. "You must cleanse your mind and change your ways," he said. "Learn. If you still remain as bad as you have been, I shall cease to trouble about you."

Jingji promised, and the old man went home. So Jingji was established at the temple, and became a novice.

The Abbot was elderly and red-nosed. He was tall and had a loud and resonant voice. His beard was long; he was a good talker and a good drinker. He spent all his time receiving visitors. The business of the temple was managed by the novice, Jin Zongming. At that time, the government had just completed the canal and built two sluices at Linqing to control the water. So all boats, whether those of officials or people, had to stop there, and it was customary for those who traveled upon them to visit the temple. Some said prayers, some offered gifts, some came in quest of miracles, some came to do works of charity. They gave cloth and money and rice, oil, paper and candles. Some gave poles and mats.

With the money that he could not spend, the Abbot had set up a money-changing shop and a rice store on the river, and put his novices in charge of them, taking the profit for himself.

Jin Zongming was not a good young man. He was about thirty years old, and spent much of his time in the bawdy house. He was a great fellow for wine and women. He had some younger novices of his own, very smart, good-looking boys, and spent the night with them. When Chen Jingji came, Zongming saw how handsome he was, how white his teeth and how red his lips. He seemed so intelligent that he could make his eyes speak for him in place of his mouth. So he asked the young man to come and sleep in his room. In the evening they drank and, when Jingji was drunk, they went to bed together. At first, one had his head at one end of the bed and the other at the other end. But Jin Zongming complained that Jingji's feet smelled, and asked him to come over the other way. Then he complained that Jingji's breath was bad, and asked him to turn his face around. Jingji pressed his back against the other monk's stomach and said nothing, feigning sleep. Then Jin Zongming's penis became firm and erect like a spear. He smeared it with spittle and plunged in. When Jingji had been living among the beggars, two of his companions had misused his bottom and stretched it, so the monk's path was now easy. Jingji still said nothing. "This fellow will fall into my hands," he thought. "He doesn't know who I am and he can't do me much harm. I will let him have a taste and then I will get hold of his money."

He suddenly cried out. Jin Zongming was afraid the Abbot might hear, and covered the young man's mouth with his hand.

"Brother," he said, "don't make a noise. Tell me anything you want and you shall have it."

"I will not tell anybody," Jingji said, "if you will promise me three things."

"Good Brother," Zongming said, "do you say three things? I am ready to promise ten."

"Very well," Jingji said. "If you want me, you must leave the other boys alone. You must let me have the keys of all the rooms. And, if I go anywhere, do not ask me where I have been. If you like to promise these three things, you can do whatever you wish."

"I will do everything you say," Zongming said. They spent half the night in their wild pursuits. Jingji had been a dissolute young wastrel and knew all the tricks of the trade. He used these tricks for the benefit of Jin Zongming, who was perfectly delighted. The next day, he gave all the keys to Chen Jingji. He kept his promise that he would sleep no more with the boys.

Days passed and Jin Zongming was always singing the praises of Jingji to the Abbot. The Abbot believed him and bought a priest's diploma for Jingji. He was not suspicious, and the young man frequently took money and went to the town. There, one day, he met a certain Chen the Third who told him that Feng Jinbao's mother was dead. The girl herself had been sold to Zheng's bawdy house and given a new name. She was now frequenting the wine houses in the street. Chen the Third asked Jingji if he would like to see her. Jingji had not forgotten his old love for the girl. He took his money and went to a large wineshop. He had been happy enough before, but now it was as though he met her whom he had loved for five hundred years.

> Do not spare your clothes of silk and gold
> Do not let your youth be wasted.
> When you see a flower that is ripe for gathering,
> Gather it.
> Wait not till all the flowers are faded
> For then only bare branches will remain
> For you to gather.

The wineshop to which they went was the finest in Linqing. It was known as Xie's wineshop, and had more than a hundred rooms. There were green balconies with, at the back, a little hill and, at the front, the river. It was in a very busy position, and all the boats called there.

The sun shines on the carven eaves
The painted columns shimmer in the air.
There are low green rails under the great windows
And long green curtains hanging there.
Young noblemen play the flute and the *sheng*
Singing girls and dancing maidens serve the wine
And bear the wine jars.
The drinkers feast their eyes on the blue sky
And the cloud-covered mountains.
Water and mist, like snow of good omen,
Take away the breath.
The wild birds sing in the green willows
And horses in gay trappings
Are tethered to the willow beside the door.

Chen the Third took Jingji in, and they went into a small room. He bade the waiter bring wine and food and send them a singing girl from downstairs. They heard footsteps coming up the stairs, and Feng Jinbao came into the room. She was carrying a little gong. She made a reverence to Chen Jingji. When the two lovers met, they could not prevent their tears from falling.

Jingji asked her to sit down with them. "Where have you been since I last saw you?" he asked her.

Feng Jinbao dried her tears. "After I came out of prison," she said, "my mother died. The shock had been too much for her. Then I was sold to Madam Zheng the Fifth. But lately, few people have come to see me, and I have had to go to the street to pick up business. Yesterday Master Chen told me that you had a money-changing shop here. I was anxious to see you, and at last my wish has been fulfilled. I have thought of you all the time." She began to weep again.

Jingji took out his handkerchief and dried her tears. "Sister," he said, "do not worry any more. I am all right again now. When I came out of prison, I had to spend all my money. Then I went to the Yangong monastery and became a priest. The Abbot trusts me absolutely, and I shall be able to come and see you as often as I like. Where are you living?"

"I am at Liu the Second's place," Feng Jinbao said. "It is west of the bridge. He has more than a hundred houses, all occupied by singing girls. Most of them come to the wine houses during the day."

They sat side by side and drank together. While the wine was being warmed, Chen the Third gave her a lute and she sang for them.

Tears fall in pairs
Tears fall in pairs
Three cups of wine at parting
Three cups of wine at parting
The phoenix and his mate are together no more
The phoenix and his mate are together no more.
Over the mountaintop
The slanting sun sinks gradually to rest.
Beyond the mountain the sun sets.
Now the sky is dark and the earth is gloomy
They do not wish to part
They do not wish to part.

When they had had wine enough, Jingji and Feng Jinbao went into a small room and did the work of love. It was a long time since Jingji had touched a woman, and he was very eager. Now that he had found Feng Jinbao, he put forth all his strength. They wished that they might never make an end, but at last they did so, and put on their clothes again.

It was late. Jingji left Feng Jinbao. He gave her a tael of silver, and three hundred coppers to Chen the Third. "Sister," he said to the girl, "we will meet here again. Whenever you want me, ask Chen the Third to tell me." He paid three *qian* of silver for the wine and then started back for the temple. Feng Jinbao went with him and left him at the bridge.

CHAPTER 94
Sun Xue'e Is Sold to a Brothel

Those of her kin are dead, and all is lost
Unwillingly she must become again
A light of love.
Her tears fall like great drops of jade
She leaves her home and with her dainty feet
Walks to the brothel.

Before the mirror she sighs
Laments the fate of her most perfect beauty
And before men begins to play the whore.
Rain and dew in springtime are like the waters of the sea.
She mates with Master Liu
Whom she finds better than Master Yuan.

Chen Jingji and Feng Jinbao met at the wine house every two or three days. If he failed to come, the girl would send him a message by Chen the Third. And every time he came he gave her a tael of silver or five *qian*. He also gave her rice and firewood, and paid her rent. When he went back to the temple, his face was always red. The Abbot would ask him where he had been drinking, and Jingji would say that he had drunk two or three cups with customers at the rice shop because he was so tired and worn out. Jin Zongming supported him in everything he said, to make sure of his companionship during the night. So things went on for a long time, and Jingji robbed the Abbot of nearly half his takings.

Liu the Second of the wine house was a famous tiger in this neighborhood. He was the younger brother of the wife of that Zhang Sheng who was the trusted servant of Major Zhou. He set up a number of houses for singing girls, foregathered with rich and powerful people, and oppressed the weak. He lent money to the singing girls, taking from them interest at three times the ordinary rate. If they did not pay, he altered the contracts, adding the interest to the loan and so making it more and more. He was fond of wine, and very quarrelsome in his cups; no one dared to cross him in any way. He was indeed a leader of those who beat singing girls and a captain of wineshop bullies.

He had observed Chen Jingji, a handsome young fellow and a novice of Abbot Ren, spending a great deal of time at the large wine house with the girl Feng Jinbao. One day, when he was drunk, he came to the wine house his two fists the size of rice bowls, and demanded Feng Jinbao. The host, Xie, bowed and said: "Uncle Liu, she is upstairs in Number Two." The man bounded upstairs with great strides. Jingji was drinking wine with Feng Jinbao behind a closed door with the lattice pulled down. Liu pulled aside the lattice and demanded that Feng Jinbao should come to him at once. Jingji was so terrified that he held his breath. Liu kicked open the door, and the girl had to come out.

"Uncle Liu," she said, "what can I do for you?"

"You whore!" Liu cried, "you haven't paid me any rent for three months and now you are trying to get away from me."

"Uncle," Feng Jinbao said, smiling, "go home and I will tell mother to send you the money."

Liu struck her in the chest and felled her to the ground with one blow. Her head hit the stairs, and blood streamed over the floor.

"You whore," Liu cried, "I'm not going to wait. I want my money now."

Then he saw Chen Jingji. He went forward, took hold of the table and smashed everything that was on it.

"Who are you," Jingji cried, "to come here and behave in this mad fashion?"

"I'll pound your mother's rice for her, you priest," Liu cried. He dragged Jingji by the hair, knocked him down, kicked him, and struck him. Meanwhile, the people in the wine house stood and watched him as if they were silly. The host could see that Liu was drunk and did not dare to interfere, but when he saw that matters were really getting serious he screwed up courage enough to come and say: "Uncle Liu, don't be annoyed with him. He doesn't know your honorable name, or he would never have done anything to upset you. Please forgive him and let him go, for my sake."

Liu paid no attention and went on beating Jingji until he was half dead. Then he sent for the police and told them to arrest both the girl and the young man and take them before the court. He had, in fact, a commission from Major Zhou to direct the police and keep watch for thieves and bandits on the river.

The Abbot did not know that Jingji had been arrested. He thought the young man had stayed at the rice shop for the night.

The next day the police took the young man to the court. They handed their charge to Zhang Sheng and Li An. This declared that Chen Zongmei, a priest of the Yangong monastery, had picked a quarrel with Liu the Second, and that the girl was a harlot.

The people at the court asked Jingji for money. "We are the executioners here," they said, "and there are twelve of us. We leave it to you. And there are the two officers who must not be overlooked."

"I had some money," Jingji said, "but it was stolen when I was having the trouble with Liu. He tore my clothes to rags. Now I have no money, only this silver pin, and that I must give to these two gentlemen."

The men took the pin to Zhang Sheng and Li An. "The fellow has no money," they said, "he only offers this pin, and it is of very inferior silver."

"Bring him in, and I'll see what he has to say," Zhang Sheng said.

They brought in the young man and he knelt down before Zhang Sheng.

"When did you become a disciple of Abbot Ren?" Zhang Sheng said. "What is your civil name? I don't remember having seen you before."

"My name is Chen Jingji," the young man said, "and I am of good family. I have only recently become a priest."

"Since you are a priest," Zhang Sheng said, "it is your duty to study the Sacred Scriptures; not to come out from your monastery, associate with whores, and make trouble with others. You seem to think my position here is not very important and that it is not necessary to give me anything. Why! if I throw this pin into the water, it won't even cause a ripple on the surface."

He ordered the attendants to take the man away to await the pleasure of his superior officer. "This doggish pair is very stingy," he said. "The only thing these priests care about is their money. Now this is an official matter, and when people come here to a dinner party, the least they can do is to bring a handsome handkerchief to wipe their mouths. When you beat him," he said to the others, "see you do it well."

Then he sent for the girl. She brought a man with her who gave three or four taels to the officers.

"You are a singing girl," Zhang Sheng said to her, "and of course you go to any place where it is busy to make a living. You did nothing wrong. It will all depend on whether my chief is in a good temper or not. If he is in a bad temper, you may get a beating; if not, he may let you go."

After a while they heard the signal, and Major Zhou entered the hall. The officers stood in ranks on either side.

In the eighth month of the year before this happened Chunmei had given birth to a son. The baby was now six months old. His face was like a piece of jade and his lips were as red as rouge. Zhou looked upon this child as the most precious thing in all the world. His first wife had died, and he had put Chunmei in her place. She lived in the upper rooms and had two nurses to look after the child, one called Yutang; the other, Jinkui. She also had two maids, Cuihua and Lanhua. She had two favorite singing girls, both sixteen years old, called Haitang and Yuegui. All these girls were devoted to the service of Chunmei alone. The Major's second wife had only one maid, Hehua.

Very often, Zhang Sheng would take the baby outside the court to amuse him and, when the magistrate was hearing a case, he would stand there with the baby in his arms and look on.

Today, when Zhou entered the court, a number of people were brought before him, but he decided to begin with Chen Jingji. So the young man and Feng Jinbao were brought forward. Zhou read the charge. "You are a priest," he said. "What do you mean by breaking your rule, frequenting whores, drinking, and disturbing the public peace? It is disgusting."

He ordered Jingji to be given twenty strokes of the rod, and canceled his priest's diploma. He put thumbscrews on Feng Jinbao, ordered her to be given a milder punishment, and sent back to the bawdy house. The attendants bound Jingji, took off his clothes, raised their rods and shouted. They were just about to begin their beating when the baby, who was with Zhang Sheng outside the hall, stretched out his arms to the young man and wanted to go to him. Zhang Sheng could hardly hold him. He was afraid that the Major might see the child and hurriedly took him away. The baby cried, and did not even stop crying when he was in his mother's arms again. Chunmei asked what was the matter with him.

"My master was in the hall trying cases," Zhang Sheng said, "and he was just about to have a priest beaten, a man named Chen, when the baby began to struggle and try to get to the man. I had to bring him away and then he began to cry."

When she heard the name Chen, Chunmei gathered up her skirts and went softly to the hall. There she peeped through a screen. She could hear the voice of the man who was being beaten and it sounded like that of Chen Jingji. But she could not understand how Jingji could have become a priest. She called Zhang Sheng to her.

"Do you know the man's name?" she asked him.

"He told me that his name as a layman was Chen Jingji," Zhang Sheng told her.

"It is he," Chunmei said to herself. Then she said to Zhang Sheng: "Go and ask my husband to come and see me."

Major Zhou was watching the punishment being administered to the young man. Jingji had had ten strokes when the Major was told that his wife wished to speak to him. He ordered the officials to stop, and left the hall.

"The priest you are punishing is my cousin," Chunmei said to him. "Please forgive him, for my sake."

"Why didn't you tell me before, my dear?" the Major said. "I have already given him ten strokes, and I can't take them back."

He went back to the hall and told the attendants to release both the man and the girl. Then he told Zhang Sheng to go after the priest and also to find out whether Chunmei wished to see him. This was just what Chunmei did wish, but she hesitated. After thinking for a long time, she said to Zhang Sheng: "Let him go. I will send for him another time."

So the Major allowed Jingji to go after no more than ten stripes. He went back to the temple.

The Abbot heard that his novice, Chen Zongmei, had been carrying on with a singing girl at the wine house, that he had got into trouble with Tiger Liu, and been beaten nearly to death. He heard, too, all that had happened afterwards. Now the Abbot was an old man and fat. He was very much upset. He opened his boxes only to find that many of his most treasured possessions had disappeared. Then he collapsed on the floor. The monks came and sent at once for the doctor. They poured medicine down his throat, but without effect. At midnight, the Abbot breathed his last. He was sixty-three years old.

The next day, as Jingji was approaching the temple, some of the people who lived near by said to him: "Do you still think of going to the temple? Because of you, your Teacher died last night!"

Jingji rushed back to Qinghe like a stray dog.

When Chunmei had told Zhang Sheng to let Jingji go away, she went back to her room. She took off her headdress and her long gown and went to bed. She groaned, pressed her hands to her bosom, and said she felt a pain. The whole house was upset. The Major's second wife came and said: "Lady, you have been very well until now, what is the matter?"

"Leave me alone and don't ask questions" was the only answer Chunmei would give to anybody.

Then the Major came from the hall. When he found his wife lying on the bed, groaning, he too became alarmed.

"How do you feel?" he said, taking her hand.

There was no answer.

"Has anyone been annoying you?"

There was still no answer.

"Perhaps it was I, when I punished your cousin."

Chunmei would not say a word.

The Major did not know what to do. He went out to Zhang Sheng and Li An. "You knew that man was your mistress's cousin," he said. "Why didn't you tell me instead of allowing me to punish him and upset my wife? I told you to stop him and let your mistress see him. Why did you let him go? You are a pair of fools."

"I told the mistress," Zhang Sheng said, "but she said she didn't wish to see him. That's why I let him go."

Zhang Sheng went weeping to Chunmei.

"Lady," he said, "please say a word to master for us, or we shall be beaten."

Chunmei opened her eyes wide and raised her eyebrows. She sent for the Major. "I am not well," she said, "but these two men are not to blame. As for that immoral priest, it is better he should suffer a little. I do not wish to see him now."

Zhou said no more to Zhang Sheng and Li An, but told Zhang Sheng to go and fetch a doctor for Chunmei. She was still in pain.

When the doctor had felt her pulse, he said: "It is anger that has upset this lady." He gave her some medicine, but she would not take it. The maids did not dare to try and persuade her, and they sent again for Major Zhou. He begged her to take the medicine. She took one mouthful and no more. Then he went away.

"Lady, do take some of it," the maid Yuegui said, taking up the cup. Chunmei took it and threw it in the maid's face. "You thievish slave," she cried angrily, "why do you try to make me drink this bitter stuff? What is there in my stomach now?" She told the maid to kneel down.

Then the Major's second wife came and asked why Yuegui was kneeling there. The other maid said: "Because she gave our mistress the medicine."

"But she had had nothing to eat," the Second Lady said. How could she take medicine?"

"Lady," said the second wife, "you have had nothing to eat today, but Yuegui did not know. Won't you forgive her?" She told Haitang to go to the kitchen and get some gruel for her mistress.

Chunmei told Yuegui to get up. Haitang went to the kitchen and very carefully prepared some gruel and four small dishes. She took them to Chunmei, all steaming hot. Chunmei lay on the bed, her face turned to the wall, so that the maid dared not disturb her, but had to wait until she turned over. Then she said: "I have brought you some gruel. Will you have a little?"

Chunmei did not open her eyes, and made no reply.

Haitang said: "Please, Lady, do get up and take some gruel. It will be cold soon."

"Lady, you have had nothing at all," the second wife said. "You must be better now you have had a sleep. Do get up and eat something."

Then Chunmei got up and told the nurse to give her a light. She took a mouthful of gruel and threw the bowl away. Fortunately, the nurse caught it and it did not break.

"You told me to have some porridge," Chunmei shouted to the second wife. "What sort of gruel do you call this? I am not having a baby. Why do you give me slops like this?"

Then she said to the nurse: "Box that slave's ears four times for me." The nurse did so.

Then the second wife said: "Lady, if you don't care for the gruel, have something else. You must not starve yourself."

"It is all very well for you to talk," Chunmei said. "My stomach is too weak." After a while, she said to Lanhua: "I will have some chicken soup. Go to the kitchen and tell that whore there to make me some chicken soup. She must be sure to wash her hands first, and put some pickled bamboo shoots into it. I want it very hot and very sour."

"Lady," the second wife said, "since you fancy it, it will be as good as medicine for you."

Lanhua went to the kitchen. "Mistress wants some chicken soup," she said to Sun Xue'e. "Make it at once: she wants it now."

Chicken soup is made of the wing, cut into very small pieces. Xue'e washed her hands, killed two chickens, plucked them, then cut the meat into very fine pieces with a sharp knife. She took onions and pepper, pickled bamboo shoots and sauce, and the soup was made. She filled two bowls, put them on a red lacquer tray, and Lanhua took them, very hot, to Chunmei.

Chunmei examined the soup under the lamp and tasted it. "Go and ask that whore what she calls this," she shouted. "It is nothing but plain water. It has no taste at all. You talk about my eating something and this is the sort of stuff you bring me."

Lanhua was afraid of being punished. She hurried to the kitchen and told Xue'e that her mistress complained that the soup had no taste. Xue'e did not say a word. She swallowed her anger and humiliation, washed out the pan, and made some more soup. This time she put more pepper into it. It had a delicious smell. Lanhua took it to her mistress.

Chunmei complained that it was too salty, took up the bowl and threw the soup on the floor. If Lanhua had not moved aside, the soup would have caught her.

"Go and tell that slave I know she hates cooking anything for me, but if she doesn't make good soup next time, she will know what to expect."

Then Xue'e made a great mistake. "You have not always been so high up in the world," she muttered, "but what airs you give yourself."

Lanhua heard this and told Chunmei. The woman opened her eyes wide and raised her eyebrows. She clenched her teeth, and her pale face flushed. "Bring that whore here," she cried.

Three or four women dragged Xue'e into the room. Chunmei tore at her hair and threw her headdress to the floor.

"You whore!" she cried, "how dare you say I have not long been so high up in the world? Well, I don't owe my position to Ximen Qing. I bought you so that you should do what I told you, but I find you are too proud. I told you to make some soup for me, and you make it either with no taste at all or with too much. Then you tell my maid that I nave not always been what I am now, and that I only wish to insult you. Why should I keep you here?"

She sent someone for her husband. Xue'e was taken to the courtyard and made to kneel down. Then Chunmei sent for Zhang Sheng and Li An and told them to strip the woman of her clothes and give her thirty strokes with a rod. The servants took lanterns and torches, and Zhang Sheng and Li An each had a big stick. Xue'e refused to take off her clothes. The Major, who was afraid of his wife, did not say a word.

"Lady," the second wife said. "Let her be beaten, but don't make her take off her clothes with all these men and servants about. I know she was in the wrong, but do forgive her this time."

Chunmei would not listen. She insisted that the woman's clothes should be stripped from her.

"Let anyone try to stop me, and I will kill my child first and then hang myself," she cried. "Then I shall be dead and you can have this strumpet in my place."

She did not give the word to beat Xue'e, but fell on the ground in a faint. Zhou was excited, picked her up, and said: "Tell them to beat her, and don't let yourself get upset like this."

Xue'e was thrown to the ground. Her clothes were stripped off and she was given thirty strokes, till the skin and flesh were torn from her bones. Then they sent for old woman Xue, who was to take her away immediately and sell her. Chunmei took old woman Xue aside. "I want eight taels of silver for her," she said, "and not a penny more. But I insist that she must be sold to a brothel. If you let her go anywhere else and I find out, you will never see me again. Otherwise, you can make what profit you like out of her."

"How can I do other than obey you?" old woman Xue said.

She took Xue'e away. The woman cried all night and Xue tried to console her. "Don't cry," she said. "It was your unhappy fate that brought you back to your old enemy. Your master was fair enough, but unfortunately there was an old hatred between you and her. She treated you badly, and the master could do nothing for you. Now she has borne him this son, he does absolutely everything she asks. Even his second wife must always give way. It is like an old bandit becoming governor of a granary; we have to put up with it. Don't cry."

Xue'e dried her tears and thanked old woman Xue. "I only hope," she said, "that I may come to some place where I shall get food enough to live."

"She told me repeatedly that I must sell you to a brothel," Xue said, "but I have children of my own, and I must think of what is right. I will find a husband for you, some merchant in a small way, and he will treat you as his wife and let you have all you need."

Xue'e thanked her gratefully.

A day or two later, one of the neighbors, Madam Zhang, came to see old woman Xue. "Sister Xue," she said, "who was it I heard crying so bitterly the other night?"

"Come in," old woman Xue said. "It was this lady. She comes from a very exalted family but she had a quarrel with her mistress and was sent away. Now she is here, hoping to find another husband. She doesn't want any more trouble and would like a single man."

"There is a guest from Shandong staying with me," Madam Zhang said, "a dealer in cotton wool. His name is Pan, and he is the fifth in his family. He has large stocks of cotton wool and keeps them at my place. He is thirty-seven years old. Only a day or two ago he told me that he has an old mother, an invalid of about seventy. His wife died six months ago, and he can't find anybody to look after his mother. He asked me, if I could, to find somebody for him to marry. I have looked about, but so far I haven't been able to find anybody suitable. This lady would do for him very well, I think."

"She has belonged to a very good family," old woman Xue said. "She can make clothes, both plain and fancy; she can sew well, and she is an excellent cook. She is thirty-five years old. There ought to be no difficulty, since they are only asking thirty taels of silver for her."

"Has she any boxes?" Madam Zhang said.

"No, she has only the clothes and ornaments she stands up in."

"I will go and tell him. Then he can come and see her for himself," Madam Zhang said. She had tea and went away. That night she told the man all about Xue'e and, the following afternoon, took him to see her. He thought her beautiful and still young, and immediately offered twenty-five taels for her with an extra one for the old woman herself. Old woman Xue did not attempt to bargain. She took what he offered and settled the matter. That evening, he took Xue'e away, saying that he was returning home next day.

Old woman Xue altered the contract and took eight taels to Chunmei, telling her that she had sold the woman to a brothel.

Pan slept that night with Xue'e at Madam Zhang's place. Before dawn next day, he thanked Madam Zhang and set off for Linqing. It was now the sixth month and the days were at their longest. When they came to the wharf, it was about the time when the sun turned to the west. They went to a wine house. There were many wine houses at Linqing, all occupied by singing girls from everywhere around. Xue'e was taken to a small one. She went into a little room with a bed in it. An old lady about sixty years old was sitting there. There was a maid too, about seventeen or eighteen. Her hair was dressed in several knots, her face powdered, and her lips red. She wore a silken dress, and played a lute as she sat on the bed. Then Xue'e cried out, for then she knew that this man, Pan the Fifth, was a woman-dealer, and he had bought her for a harlot.

The man proposed to send Xue'e to the wine houses to make herself agreeable to the customers and so make money. Without a word, he gave her a severe beating, then sent her to bed and kept her there for two days. In those two days, he gave her nothing but two bowls of rice to eat. Then he told her to learn a few songs and taught her how to play, and, when she did not succeed very well, he beat her again. When she was sufficiently trained, he dressed her up in pretty clothes and bade her stand outside the door and smile at the passersby.

Then Heaven took pity on her. One day, Zhang Sheng came to the river to buy ten measures of yeast for his master who wished to make some wine. When Tiger Liu saw his brother, he cleared a room in his wine house, and offered Zhang Sheng a feast. The waiter heated the wine and said: "Uncle, there are several singing girls here. Would you like one? Liu mentioned four names and the waiter went to fetch the girls. Soon laughing voices were heard and, one after the other, the four singing girls came into the room. They seemed as beautiful as flowers and were all dressed in light, soft silken clothes. They came and made reverences to the two men. Zhang Sheng looked at them. It seemed to him that one of them was very like Xue'e, whom his master had dismissed. But he could not understand how she could have become a singing girl. Xue'e recognized Zhang Sheng, but neither of them spoke.

"Brother-in-law," Zhang Sheng said, "who is this girl?"

The Tiger pointed them all out.

"This one, who you say is from Pan the Fifth's house, seems very familiar to me somehow," Zhang Sheng said. He called her forward. "Are you not Xue'e?" he whispered. "What are you doing here?"

Xue'e began to cry. "It is a long story," she told him. "Old woman Xue sold me for twenty-four taels, and here I am. I come to make myself pleasant to the guests, and sing for their entertainment."

Zhang Sheng had long been attracted by her beauty. Now, Xue'e entertained him so pleasantly and talked so agreeably that he was very pleased with her. She and one of the other girls took up their lutes and sang for him. Then they passed the wine and Zhang Sheng was more and more delighted. As the proverb says: Money, girls and wine houses are three things that no man can resist. That night, he asked Xue'e to stay with him. She let him appreciate her skill upon the bed, and he was perfectly satisfied.

The next day, when they got up and dressed, Tiger Liu had prepared an excellent breakfast for his brother-in-law. There was as much as they could eat. Zhang Sheng packed his luggage and fed his horses. When they were laden with the yeast, he started off with the other servants. He gave Xue'e three taels of silver and asked Tiger Liu to look after her and give her his special protection. Ever afterwards, when Zhang Sheng came to the river, he went to the wine house to meet Xue'e. They remained attached to one another, and, every month, he gave a few taels to Pan the Fifth so that he might reserve Xue'e for himself and she should not be forced to go out and receive all comers. Liu, who wished to please his brother-in-law, would not let him pay for the room. He took money from others and paid for the room with that. He also kept Xue'e supplied with rice and firewood.

CHAPTER 95

Ping'an Meets His Deserts

Only a few monks live in the ancient temple
Few travelers cross the ruined bridge.
When a house is poor, the slaves deceive their master
When one in authority is weak, his underlings will serve him ill.
Where the water is shallow, the fish will not stay
Where the wood has few trees, the birds will not sing.
So it is with the affairs of men.
We can only sigh and be sorry for it.

After the death of Ximen Dajie and the lawsuit with Chen Jingji, Wu Yueniang's servant, Laizhao, died. His wife took her son, Little Iron Rod, and married again. Laixing was given charge of the gate. Xiuchun became a nun with Nun Wang.

After the death of Laixing's wife, he did not marry again. The nurse, Ruyi'er, often used to take Xiaoge and play with him. Laixing gave her wine and, in course of time, their relations became very friendly. Yueniang noticed that Ruyi'er often came back to the inner court with a very red face, and so found out what was happening. She reproached Ruyi'er, but did not make very much fuss about the matter. She gave the nurse a dress and four pins, chose a day of good omen, and married her to Laixing. In the daytime the nurse came to the kitchen and looked after the baby, and at night she went to Laixing.

The fifteenth day of the eighth month was Yueniang's birthday. Her two sisters-in-law and the three nuns came to congratulate her, and she gave them wine in the inner court. In the evening they listened to the nuns reading their texts in the room that had once belonged to Yulou. About the second night watch, Zhongqiu was sent to the kitchen to make some tea. Yueniang called her several times but got no answer. Then she herself went to her room to try to find the maid. She did not find her, but discovered Daian and Xiaoyu on the bed amusing themselves to their own very great satisfaction. When Yueniang came in, they were so taken aback they did not know what to do with themselves.

"You young scamp, what are you doing here? Why don't you go and make tea?" was all Yueniang said.

"I told Zhongqiu to go," Xiaoyu said. She hung her head and went to the back. Daian went through the second door to the other part of the house. Two days later, when the nuns and the two Aunts Wu had gone, Yueniang told Laixing to go to the rooms that Laizhao had had, since he was now the gatekeeper, and gave Laixing's old rooms to Daian. She fitted out Daian with two sets of bedclothes, a new suit, a hat, shoes, and socks. To Xiaoyu she gave a hairnet, some gold and silver ornaments, four pins of silver with gold heads, rings, and two silk dresses. Then she selected an auspicious day and married Daian to Xiaoyu. Xiaoyu spent her days waiting upon Yueniang and at night went to Daian. The girl was always taking away dainties for her husband, but Yueniang pretended not to see. As the proverb says: If you are in love, you never see your lover's faults. Another proverb tells us: A greedy man will never be satisfied. When food and wine are distributed unequally, there will be trouble in the household, and when the mistress is unfair, maids and women will complain.

Ping'an saw that Yueniang had married Xiaoyu to Daian, and that he was given better clothes than the rest. He himself was two years older than Daian—he was twenty-two—but Yueniang had never thought of finding a wife for him.

One day he was in the pawnshop when somebody pawned a set of gold ornaments and two gilded hooks for thirty taels of silver. They were to redeem the things in a month with interest. Clerk Fu and Daian took them and put them in the large press in the shop. Ping'an stole them and took them to Long-footed Wu's place in Nanwazi. There were two receivers of stolen property there, one called Xue Cun and the other Pan Er.

Ping'an stayed there two nights. The man of the bawdy house noticed that he was spending money freely, and also saw that he had some gold ornaments in a box. He pretended to go out with a silver pot to buy some wine, but actually went to the police and told them what he had seen. The police came and found the young man there. They beat him about the head and then arrested him.

It happened that Wu Dian'en, who had recently been made an Inspector, rode down the street, with his tablet of office carried before him. He asked who this man was whom the police had arrested. The police knelt down and said: "This fellow stole some things and came here to spend the money in the bawdy house. We had reason to be suspicious and took him into custody."

"Take him to my court," the Inspector said. They all went to the Inspector's court. When Wu Dian'en had taken his seat, his underlings standing on either side, Ping'an was brought in. He recognized Wu Dian'en, who had once been one of Ximen Qing's friends, and thought he would certainly be set free.

"I am Ximen's servant," he said, "and my name is Ping'an."

"If you are a servant in Ximen's household," Wu Dian'en said, "why did you take these things and go to the brothel?"

"My mistress had lent them to one of her relatives and sent me to fetch them," Ping'an said. "I got back very late and the city gates were closed. I went to the brothel to pass the night. There, unfortunately, the police arrested me."

"Nonsense!" Wu Dian'en said angrily. "Have Ximen's people so much gold and silver that they even let you, a slave, look after gold ornaments like these and take them to the brothel? I believe you stole them. Tell me the truth and you shall not be beaten."

"Really," Ping'an said, "my Mistress's relative borrowed these things, and I was sent to bring them back. I am telling the truth."

Wu Dian'en was angry. "You slave," he cried, "you are a regular thief. I know you will never tell me the truth unless you are beaten. Give him a beating and put the thumbscrews on him."

The boy made a noise like a pig being killed. "Please stop," he cried, "and I will tell the truth."

"Tell me the truth and then I will stop," Wu Dian'en said.

"I stole the ornaments and the hooks from the pawnshop," Ping'an said.

"Why did you do it?"

"I am now twenty-three years old," Ping'an said, "and my mistress promised that she would see about getting a wife for me. She never did so. She has another servant, Daian, who is only twenty, but she has married him to one of her maids. I stole the things because I was jealous."

"Perhaps Daian has had some dealings with your mistress, and that is why she gave him her maid," Wu Dian'en said. "If that is what you say, I will forgive you."

"But I can't say that," Ping'an said.

"If you don't, I must put the rack on you again."

The attendants applied the rack again. Ping'an was so terrified that he cried: "Don't do it. I will tell you."

"Tell me and I will let you go," Wu Dian'en said. He told his attendants to put the rack away.

"Yes," Ping'an said, "my mistress secretly slept with Daian, and Daian also misconducted himself with Xiaoyu, the maid. My mistress found out what was going on between Daian and the maid, but she never said a word. She gave them clothes and ornaments and allowed them to marry."

Wu Dian'en ordered his clerk to write down what Ping'an had said. Then he kept the boy at his office and issued a warrant for the arrest of Yueniang, Daian, and Xiaoyu.

When Clerk Fu discovered the loss of the ornaments, he was very much upset. He asked Daian what he knew about the matter.

"I have been having my dinner in the medicine shop," Daian said. "I know nothing about it."

"I put the box into this cabinet, and it has disappeared," Clerk Fu said.

Then they looked for Ping'an. He had disappeared. Clerk Fu was in a terrible state. He swore all sorts of terrible oaths. When the owner of the things came to claim them, Fu could only say that he had not yet brought them from the house. The man came several times, but still the things were not forthcoming. Then the man stood outside the shop and shouted: "I pawned my things for a month only, I have paid for them and the interest too. Why don't you let me have them? They are worth seventy or eighty taels of silver."

In the evening, Clerk Fu could still see no sign of Ping'an, and realized that the young man had stolen the things. He sent people in every direction to try and find him. The owner of the things came again and kept shouting outside the door. Fu suggested that they should give the man fifty taels, but he would not accept it. He said the ornaments were worth sixty taels, and the hooks and jewels on the ornaments another ten, seventy in all. Clerk Fu offered ten taels more, but the man still refused. While they were disputing and arguing, a man came and said to Clerk Fu: "Your Ping'an has stolen the things and taken them to the bawdy house in Nanwazi. Now Inspector Wu has had him arrested. You had better send somebody to identify them."

Wu Yueniang knew that Wu Dian'en had once been a clerk in her husband's business. She sent for Uncle Wu. Together they made a statement and sent it by Clerk Fu to Wu Dian'en. She thought that the matter would be settled as soon as he received it. Fu took the paper to the office, quite sure that his old friend Wu Dian'en would give him the things at once. To his surprise, he was called an old dog. Indeed Wu Dian'en ordered his attendants to take off Fu's clothes and flog him.

Meanwhile, the Inspector said: "Your boy is here. He tells me that Mistress Ximen has been carrying on an intrigue with Daian. I am sending a report to the authorities, and later I shall send and examine Mistress Ximen herself. I am surprised that you, you old dog, dare to come here and claim these things."

Clerk Fu was sent away, with many shouts of "Old dog!" to pursue him. He hurried home as fast as he could and told Yueniang everything that had happened. She was so frightened that she felt as though her skull had been broken open and icy water poured into it. She was hardly able to move her feet and hands. Then the man who owned the ornaments came again and made a great to-do outside the door.

"You have lost my property," he shouted, "and now you will neither return it to me nor pay me what it is worth. You keep on telling me to come here and go there. Today, you say, you will go to the office and claim the things; and tomorrow, you will tell me to wait a little longer. Where are they? This won't do at all."

Clerk Fu went to the man and pacified him. "Give us one more day or perhaps two," he said, "and you shall have your things without fail. If we do not get them for you, you shall have double what they are worth."

"I will go and see what my master has to say," the man said, and went away.

Yueniang, what with one trouble and what with another, wore a continual frown. She sent a boy to ask her brother, Uncle Wu, to come and talk the matter over. "You must go to Wu Dian'en," she said, "and get this matter settled before things get any worse."

"I don't imagine he will do anything for us unless he gets well paid for it," Uncle Wu said.

"Remember that he owes his position entirely to us," Yueniang said. "And he still owes us a hundred taels of silver. My husband never asked him for any note, yet he repays our kindness by hatred."

"Ah, sister," Uncle Wu said, "there are only too many people who do that."

"Brother," Yueniang said, "I am counting on you to settle this. I will give you some money, and you can get back the ornaments and so end the wretched business."

When Uncle Wu had had something to eat, Yueniang took him to the gate. By chance, old woman Xue went past with a young maid. She was carrying her box.

"Where are you going, old woman?" Yueniang said. "I haven't seen you for a very long time."

"No, indeed, Lady," Xue said. "I have been very busy lately. Yesterday the young lady sent for me several times, but I could not go."

"Old woman, you are crazy," Yueniang said. "What do you mean by this young lady of yours?"

"Well, she is not a young lady any longer," old woman Xue said. "She is the mistress of the household now."

"How did she get into that position?" Yueniang said.

"It was just her good luck," the old woman said. "First, she had a baby. Then the Great Lady died, and the Major made her his first wife. His second wife has to do what she tells her. She has two nurses and four maids to wait on her, and two of them are very good singers. Though the Major has slept with both of them, if the lady takes it into her head to punish them, he never says a word to stop her. And still he is always anxious lest she should have something to complain about. The other day, for some reason or other, she punished Xue'e and pulled her hair out. She was sent away one night and sold for eight taels of silver. This morning, even before I was up, she sent for me twice. I was told to go at once and take two sets of green ornaments and one set of nine phoenix ornaments. They gave me five taels of silver. I have spent the silver, and they haven't seen the ornaments yet. Certainly I shall get a terrible scolding when she sees me."

"Come in and let me see what the ornaments are like," Yueniang said.

She took Madam Xue into the hall of the inner court. The old woman opened the box and took out the ornaments. They were indeed exquisitely made, with a beautiful blending of gold and green, and the backs gilded. Each ornament had a phoenix, and each phoenix held a string of little pearls in its beak.

"This set," the old woman said, "is worth three taels and five *qian*. The other, one tael and five *qian*. I have made no profit at all out of them."

As they were talking, Daian came and said: "The man has come again for those things that were pawned with us. He wants to know how much longer he will have to wait. He says if we don't get the things by tomorrow there will be trouble for Uncle Fu. He will go with Uncle Fu to a certain place. Uncle Fu is not well and has gone home. The man has gone too."

"What is it all about?" old woman Xue said.

Yueniang sighed. "Ping'an stole a set of gold ornaments and a pair or hooks from the pawnshop. He went to the bawdy house outside the city and there Inspector Wu arrested him. Now he is in jail and the man keeps coming for his things and shouts outside the door. Inspector Wu deliberately refuses to give the things up. He beat Clerk Fu. I don't know what to do. Ever since my husband died, I have had nothing but one trouble after another. It is very hard for me to have to put up with all these insults." She began to cry.

"My good lady," old woman Xue said, "there is one way out that you have not thought of. Let me go to the young lady, and ask her to send a card to the Inspector. Then you would get ten sets of ornaments if there were so many."

"Major Zhou is a military officer," Yueniang said. "What can he do with the Inspector?"

"Lady," the old woman said, "don't you know that he has special powers. He has many functions that a military officer usually does not have. He has something to do with the river and the taxes and the soldiers and all sorts of things. He seems to be able to settle any sort of question. And it is his business to see to the capture of robbers who go to the river. This is the very thing for him."

"Well," Yueniang said, "will you go to the young lady for me and ask her to speak to the Major on my behalf? If I get those ornaments back, you shall have five taels of silver."

"Money is not everything, my good lady," old woman Xue said. "I should not think of taking money for helping you out of such a sad predicament. Ask someone to write a note for you and I will take it to the young lady at once. If I do this business for you, just give me anything you think fit."

Yueniang asked Xiaoyu to give Madam Xue some tea.

"If you don't mind, I won't have any tea," the old woman said. "Tell a boy to write the note. I am rather busy."

"You must have something to eat. You have been out half a day."

Xiaoyu brought them tea and cakes, and the old woman ate something with Yueniang. She gave two cakes to the girl who was with her.

"How old is she?" Yueniang asked.

"She is twelve."

Daian finished the note and brought it in. Xue drank her tea and put the paper in her sleeve. She picked up her box and went away.

When she came to the Major's house, Chunmei was still in bed. Yuegui told her that Madam Xue had come. Chunmei told Haitang to open the windows and let in the bright sunshine.

"What, Lady," the old woman said, when she came in, "are you not up yet?" She set down her box and kowtowed to Chunmei.

"There is no need for ceremony between us," Chunmei said. "Stand up. I am not very well. That is why I didn't get up before this. Have you brought my ornaments?"

"Yes," the old woman said, "and I had a very hard business getting them. I did not get them, in fact, until last night. This morning, I was just going to bring them to you when your servant came for me."

She took the ornaments from the box and gave them to Chunmei. Chunmei did not care very much for one of the sets, but she put them in the box and gave the box to Yuegui. When the old woman had had some tea, she called forward the little girl who had come with her and told her to kowtow to Chunmei.

"Who is this?" Chunmei asked.

"The Second Lady has several times told me that her maid is only useful for cooking," old woman Xue said. "She wants a young girl to do needlework for her, and I have brought this one for her to see. She is a country girl and twelve years old. I think she will turn out well."

"You should have got her a town girl," Chunmei said. "Town girls are more intelligent. Indeed, I never think a country girl has any brains at all. How much does she cost?"

"Only four taels," old woman Xue said. "Her father is going to the army and needs the money."

"Take this girl to the Second Lady," Chunmei said to one of her maids. "We will pay for her tomorrow." Then she said to the other maid: "There is some Jinhua wine in the jar. Heat some for Madam Xue and bring her some cakes. If we don't give her cakes, she will say that we only give her wine to drink in the mornings and nothing to eat with it."

"Sister," the old woman said to the maid, "don't heat any wine for me. I have something to say to your mistress. I had some wine before I came."

"Where did you have some wine?" Chunmei asked her.

"I have just come from the Great Lady," old woman Xue said, "and she gave me something to eat. She is in great trouble and she cried to me. Her boy, Ping'an, stole a set of gold ornaments and a pair of gilt hooks from the pawnshop and went after some whore. Then he was arrested. Meanwhile, the owner of the things keeps coming and shouting and demanding his property. Inspector Wu was once a clerk in her family, and when Ximen Qing was alive he was very kind to Wu. But now the Inspector has forgotten all about that, and looks the other way. He had her servant beaten and refuses to give up the things. He insulted Clerk Fu and beat him. Fu got such a fright that he had to go home, ill. The Great Lady told me to bring you her love and ask you to take pity on her. She has no relatives of her own to help her, and she said I was to ask you if you would speak to the Major, so that she can get back the ornaments and give them to their owner. If you are good enough to do this for her, she will call to thank you.

"Have you brought any paper with you?" Chunmei said. "My husband is away on duty, but when he comes back this evening, I will tell him."

"I have the paper here," the old woman said. She took it from her sleeve. Chunmei read it and put it on the windowsill.

Then Yuegui brought four dishes on a tray. She filled a large silver cup with wine and offered it to the old woman.

"Lady," Xue said, "why do you give me so large a thing?"

Chunmei laughed. "It is not so large a thing as your husband's," she said. "If you can put up with that, you can drink this. If you won't drink it of your own accord, I shall tell Yuegui to hold your nose and pour it down your throat."

"Well, give me some cakes first so that I have something to make a foundation for it," the old woman said.

"You are an old liar," Chunmei said. "A moment ago you said you had just had something. Now you say you want something to make a foundation."

"I only had two cakes," old woman Xue said, "and they won't last forever."

"Mother Xue," Yuegui said, "drink the wine and then you shall have the cakes. If you won't, it will mean another beating for me. My mistress always says I am no use."

Old woman Xue could not help herself. She drank the wine and immediately felt as if a young deer were careering about inside her. Chunmei made a sign to Haitang, and the maid gave her another cup. The old woman put it aside.

"Mother," Haitang said, "you took the wine Yuegui offered you. You can't refuse mine. If you do, my mistress will give me a beating."

Old woman Xue knelt down.

"Well," Chunmei said, "give her some cakes to eat with it."

"Mother Xue," Yuegui said, "nobody is so kind to you as I am. I have kept these rose cakes especially for you."

She brought out a large plate of rose cakes, but the old woman ate only one.

"Take the others away and let your old turtle have them," Chunmei said.

When Madam Xue had had some wine, she wrapped up in paper some dried meat, buns and goose, and put the paper into her sleeves. Haitang pressed her to drink another half cup. Then she saw that the old woman was on the verge of being sick, so she cleared the table and urged her no more. Chunmei told her to come the following day and paid her for the ornaments. When Xue was going, she said: "Now, old woman, don't pretend to be deaf and dumb. One of these sets of ornaments is no good. I shall expect a better set tomorrow."

"Very well, Lady," the old woman said. "Will you send a maid out with me? I am afraid of the dog biting my leg."

"My dogs know what they're about," Chunmei said. "They will stop when they get to the bone." But she told Yuegui to take the old woman to the gate.

It was sunset when Major Zhou came back from his office. He went to the great hall. The maids took his hat and clothes. He went to see

Chunmei and his little son, and was very happy with them. When he had sat down, the maids brought tea to him and he told Chunmei about the work he had done that day. Then the table was set and they had dinner together. Afterwards, candles were brought and they drank wine. He asked if anything special had happened in the household, and Chunmei gave him the paper that old woman Xue had brought.

"Mistress Ximen's boy, Ping'an, stole some ornaments," she said. "Then he was arrested. Inspector Wu refused the people who went to claim the things and beat the boy severely to make him declare that Mistress Ximen had behaved improperly. He says he is going to send the case to a higher authority."

"But this is my business," Major Zhou said. "What does he mean by talking about sending the matter further? He is a most unreasonable fellow. I will send for him tomorrow and see how he likes a beating himself. I believe he used to be one of Ximen Qing's men. When Ximen went to the Eastern Capital with presents for the Imperial Tutor, it was he who got this appointment for Wu. Now he is trying to do all the harm he can to Ximen's family."

"That is just what I was going to say," Chunmei said. "You must look into the matter tomorrow."

The next day, Major Zhou told Yueniang to send an accusation to him. In his great hall, the Major wrote out an instruction and put it in an envelope. "The Major's office wishes to investigate a certain case of theft," it said. "The thief and the stolen property are to be sent to this office immediately. This instruction will be delivered by officers Zhang Sheng and Li An."

Zhang Sheng and Li An took the document. First they called to see Wu Yueniang. She entertained them with food and wine and gave each of them a tael of silver with which to buy shoes. Clerk Fu was still in bed, so Uncle Wu went with the two men to the Inspector's office.

Wu Dian'en remarked the fact that although Ping'an had been in prison for two days, nobody from Ximen's household had been to see him. He was preparing a document to send to his superiors. Then the two officers from Major Zhou's office came in and handed him an envelope. He read the superscription and opened it. Inside was an accusation from Yueniang. He was alarmed and made himself most agreeable. He gave two taels of silver each to Zhang Sheng and Li An. He wrote a document in reply, sent those concerned to the Major's office, and went with them himself.

After a long time, Zhou came to the great hall, and his underlings stood on either side. They went in and the Inspector handed his document to the Major. The Major read it. "This business belongs to my office," he said. "Why did you deliberately delay handing the matter over to me? You must have had some evil purpose."

"I was just preparing the document when your instructions arrived," Wu said.

"You doggish officer," Major Zhou shouted. "What is your rank that you should dare to go contrary to the law and disregard your superiors? By his Majesty's command, it is my duty to protect this district, control the soldiers here and the river too. You know what my duties are, yet you dare to arrest people, and do not send them to me. You abuse your authority and even punish people yourself. Then you accuse the innocent. Certainly you are actuated by some evil motive."

Inspector Wu took off his hat and kowtowed to the Major.

"I ought to punish you, you doggish officer," Zhou cried, "but this time I will forgive you. If anything of the sort happens again, I shall certainly deal with you as the law requires."

He called Ping'an before him. "You slave," he said, "you stole these things and lied most disgracefully about your mistress. If all servants were like you, no one would dare to employ one." He ordered that Ping'an should be given thirty severe stripes, and sealed up the stolen property until the owner should claim it. Then he called for Uncle Wu, who gave him a receipt for the things.

Then he sent Zhang Sheng with his card to Yueniang. Yueniang gave the man wine and another tael of silver. When he returned, he told the Major and Chunmei what she had said. So Inspector Wu gained nothing by arresting Ping'an, but lost a few taels of silver. Yueniang returned the ornaments and hooks to their owner, who examined them, recognized them as his own, and took them away without a word.

Clerk Fu was very ill and, after seven days, he died. He had taken medicine, but it did him no good. After this trouble in the pawnshop, Yueniang decided to let people redeem their pledges, but would not accept any new ones. She put her younger brother and Daian to look after the medicine shop, and this brought in sufficient to pay the household expenses.

When the business was settled, Yueniang sent for old woman Xue and gave her three taels of silver. The old woman refused to take the money, saying that if she did so, her young lady would be annoyed.

"But I am very much indebted to you," Yueniang said, "and Heaven does not employ people without assuring them of their reward. You need not say anything about it to her."

Then she got ready four dishes, a pig, a jar of wine and a roll of silk, and asked Xue to take them to Chunmei as a mark of her gratitude. Daian, dressed in black clothes, took the list of presents. The old woman took him to the hall in the inner court and there Chunmei came to see him. She was wearing a golden arched headdress, an embroidered coat and a silken skirt, and her women and maids came with her. Daian knelt down and kowtowed. Chunmei told the maids to give him something to eat.

"I have done nothing," she said. "Why does your mistress trouble to send me these presents? I don't think my husband will allow me to accept them."

"My mistress told me to say that she is very grateful for all the trouble you have taken over Ping'an," Daian said. "She has nothing worthy to offer you, but sends these trifles in the hope that you and his Lordship will condescend to give them to your servants."

"It embarrasses me to accept them," Chunmei said.

"If you do not take them, Lady," old woman Xue said, "I am sure the Lady Ximen will blame me."

Then Chunmei asked her husband to come, and asked him what he thought about it. They decided to accept the pig, the wine, and the pre-pared food, but not the roll of silk. Chunmei gave Daian a handkerchief and three *qian* of silver, and two *qian* of silver to the porter.

"How is your young master?" she asked Daian.

"He is very merry and plays all the time," Daian said.

"When did you first dress your hair as a man's, and when did you marry Xiaoyu?"

"I married her in the eighth month," Daian said.

"Thank your mistress for me and say how glad I should be if she would come and see me. The Major will be away on duty and, in the first month next year, when it is your young master's birthday, I will pay a visit to your mistress."

"Lady," Daian said, "I will tell my mistress as soon as I get home and say that she must expect you."

Then Daian was dismissed.

"Young man," old woman Xue said to him, "you go home. I have something to say to the lady and I will stay."

Daian took the empty boxes and went away. When he got home, he said to Yueniang: "Sister Chunmei took me to the hall in the inner court and entertained me with tea and cakes. She inquired after the young mas-ter and asked many questions about this household. She gave me a hand-kerchief and five *qian* of silver. She also gave two *qian* to the porter. She told me to thank you. For a long time she would not accept the present, but old woman Xue and I urged her, and at last she took the food, the pig and the wine, but made me bring back the roll of silk. She says she would like to send you an invitation, but she cannot do so now as her husband is going away on duty. She is going to come and see us on the young master's birthday. She occupies the upper apartments now, five rooms. She was wearing an embroidered gown and a silk skirt. Her headdress has a gold crown. She is taller and fatter than she used to be and has a great many maids and servants to wait upon her."

"Did she really say she was coming to see us?" the Moon Lady said.

"Yes," Daian said.

"We must certainly send someone to receive her," Yueniang said. "Why hasn't old woman Xue come back with you?"

"When I left, she was still talking to the lady," Daian said. "She told me to come back first."

After this, there was close friendship between the two households.

Chapter 96

Chunmei Revisits Her Old Home

It was the twenty-first day of the first month. Chunmei spoke to her husband and prepared a table of food, four kinds of fruits, and a jar of wine, and sent the servant Zhou Ren with them to Wu Yueniang. It was now two years since Ximen Qing had died, and this was the anniversary of his death; it was also Xiaoge's birthday.

Yueniang accepted the presents and gave the messenger a handkerchief and three *qian* of silver. Then she told Daian to put on his black gown and take a card to Chunmei. On the card was written this message: "To the most virtuous Lady Zhou. Heartfelt thanks for your most precious gifts. Now I have made ready wine and await the honor of your presence. I hope for the coming of your exalted carriage and shall be grateful for the honor of your visit. Wu, the widow of the late Ximen, kowtows."

It was about midday when Chunmei came to see Yueniang. She was wearing many pearls, and her ornaments were those of the golden phoenix. Her gown was broad-sleeved with a unicorn embroidered on it, and her skirt had the design of the hundred flowers. There was a golden buckle on her girdle. Her sedan chair was carried by four men. It had a black silk cover with golden ornaments. Before it soldiers with staves marched to clear the way, and servants carrying dressing cases came after it. There were two small sedan chairs immediately behind for her maids.

Yueniang had invited Aunt Wu. She had also sent for two singing girls. When Chunmei arrived, Yueniang, dressed in mourning, and Aunt Wu went to receive the guest in the outer hall. Yueniang was wearing a five-arched hat and very few ornaments. Her gown was of white silk, and her skirt of light blue. The sedan chair was carried to the second door, and there Chunmei got out and the crowd of servants followed her. When they went into the hall, Chunmei hastily knelt down and kowtowed to Yueniang. Yueniang made reverence in return.

"Lately," she said, "I have given you much trouble. Yet you would not accept the silk and, today, you have sent me valuable presents. I find it hard to express my gratitude."

"I am only sorry that my husband has nothing better than these trifles to offer," Chunmei said. "I have been intending to send you an invitation for some time, but I have not been able to do so because my husband is so often away on duty."

"Sister," Yueniang said, "when is your birthday? I hope to come and see you with a few presents."

"It is the twenty-fifth of the fourth month," Chunmei said.

"I will come to see you on that day," Yueniang said.

Then Chunmei made a reverence to Aunt Wu, and Aunt Wu returned it formally.

"Aunt Wu," Chunmei said, "you should not do that. You should stand and allow me to make reverence to you." But Aunt Wu would not agree, and finally they contented themselves with half the usual ceremonial. Then they sat down. Yueniang and Aunt Wu sat together in the host's place. Then the maids, the nurse, and the serving woman came to see Chunmei. Ruyi'er was carrying Xiaoge.

"My son," Yueniang said, "this is your sister. She has come to wish you many happy returns of the day."

Xiaoge seemed inclined to get down and bow to Chunmei. "You are a good boy!" Yueniang said to him, "bowing like that instead of kowtowing as you should."

Chunmei took a silk handkerchief and a set of gold ornaments from her sleeve and put them on the child's cap. "Sister," Yueniang said, "why should you give him such presents?"

Then Xiaoyu and the nurse kowtowed to Chunmei. She gave Xiaoyu a pair of pins with gold heads, and Ruyi'er a pair of silver flowers.

"Sister," Yueniang said, "I don't believe you know that Ruyi'er is now married to Laixing. His first wife died."

"She is a good woman," Chunmei said, "since she is ready to stay in this household always."

A maid brought tea. After it Yueniang said: "Sister, shall we go to the back room? It is cold here." Then Chunmei went to the room where Ximen Qing's tablet was. There were candles lighted before it. Food was set out, and Chunmei offered it. Then she burned paper offerings and shed a few tears. A screen was brought in and coal put on the fire. A large square table was set, and tea was brought with delicious cakes and rare fruits. The tea was of the scarcest kind. After tea, they asked Chunmei to go and change her clothes in the upper room. She took off her long cloak: her woman opened the box and put on her a dress of embroidered silk with a skirt the color of a purple clove. Then they all sat down in Yueniang's room.

"How is your baby?" Yueniang said. "Why didn't you bring him?"

"I should have brought him to kowtow to you," Chunmei said, "but his father said it was too cold and the boy might get a chill. He has gone to the great hall because he doesn't care for the rooms. I don't know what is the matter with him, but he has been crying a great deal the last few days."

"When you go out, does he often want you?"

"Yes, but there are two nurses to look after him."

"His Lordship is not a young man now, and he must be pleased you have borne him a son. He is your lucky star. I understand the Second Lady has a girl. How old is she?"

"The Second Lady's child is four years old," Chunmei said. "She is called Yujie, and my boy is called Jin'ge."

"I understand that his Lordship has two girls," Yueniang said.

"Two of our maids are learning music," Chunmei said. "They are both seventeen years old and very troublesome."

"Does his Lordship go to them very often?"

"He has hardly any time at home," Chunmei said. "He is nearly always on duty. There are so many thieves and bandits about nowadays. By his Majesty's command, he has to occupy himself with all sorts of matters. He is responsible for the charge of the district; he has to keep watch upon the river; to search out the bandits, and to keep the troops well disciplined. Yes, he has to spend a great deal of his time away."

Xiaoyu brought more tea. Chunmei said to Yueniang: "Lady, will you take me to the garden, where my mistress used to live?"

"Sister," Yueniang said, "you can hardly call it a garden now. Since my husband's death, nobody has bothered about it. It has gone to rack and ruin. The artificial mound has fallen in; the trees have died. I seldom go there now."

"Never mind," Chunmei said. "I only want to see the place where my mistress lived."

Yueniang could not refuse. She told Xiaoyu to find the garden key. Then she and Aunt Wu took Chunmei there. Chunmei went first to the Sixth Lady's room. There were a number of broken tables and chairs upstairs. Downstairs, all the rooms were locked. Grass was growing on the floors. Then she came to the place that had been Pan Jinlian's. The store for medicine and incense was still upstairs. In the room that Jinlian herself had occupied, there were only two cabinets, no bed.

"Where is my mother's bed?" Chunmei said. "I don't see it."

"The Third Lady took it away with her when she married," Xiaoyu said.

"When my husband was alive," Yueniang said, "he gave Meng Yulou's bed to my daughter, so when she remarried, I gave her your mistress's bed."

"But didn't you get the bed back when your daughter died?" Chunmei said.

"I sold it for eight taels of silver and gave the money to the officials at the Town Hall."

Chunmei nodded. Tears fell from her bright eyes. She remembered how, when Jinlian was alive, she always tried to have something that others did not have. "She asked my father to buy her that bed," she said to herself, "and I should have liked to have it to remember her by. Now somebody else has taken it." She was very sad.

"What has happened to the mother-of-pearl bed the Sixth Lady used to have?" she said to Yueniang.

"It is a long story. Ever since your master died, I have been spending money all the time, but no money comes in. As the proverb says: If we cannot make both ends meet, it is no good having gold lying about. I was pressed for money and I sold that bed."

"How much did you get for it?"

"I only got thirty-five taels," Yueniang said.

"What a pity. I remember Father saying it was worth sixty. If I had known you wished to sell it, I would have given forty myself."

"But it never occurred to me that you would like to have it," Yueniang said. They both sighed.

Then a servant came and said to Chunmei: "His Lordship asks you to go back early as the young master is crying for you."

Chunmei went back at once to the inner court, and Yueniang ordered Xiaoyu to lock the garden gate. When they returned to the upper room, they set the screen in position, pulled down the blinds, and wine and food were brought. The singing girls began to play the lute and sing. Yueniang offered wine and asked Chunmei to take the place of honor. Chunmei would only do so on condition that Aunt Wu sat with her. The two ladies sat down, and Yueniang took the host's place. After the wine had been offered, more food was brought in. Chunmei told her servant, Zhou Ren, to give the cook three *qian* of silver. It was an excellent meal, and they encouraged one another to drink.

About sunset, Major Zhou sent servants with lanterns to escort his wife home. Yueniang would not let her go but ordered the two singing girls to sing again. "You must sing your very best songs for Lady Zhou," she said. Then she ordered Xiaoyu to fill a large cup with wine and set it before Chunmei.

"Sister," she said, "bid the singers sing your favorite song and then drink this wine."

"Indeed, I cannot drink any more," Chunmei said, "and I am anxious about my baby."

"You have nurses to look after him, and it is still quite early," Yueniang said. "Besides, I know that you can drink."

Chunmei asked the singing girls their names and where they came from. They knelt down. One said she was Han Yuchuan, the younger sister of Han Jinchuan, and the other that she was Zheng Jiao'er, Zheng Aixiang's niece. Chunmei asked them if they could sing "Languidly I Paint My Brows." Yuchuan said they knew it. Yueniang offered wine to Chunmei before they began. Then the two singing girls, one with a lute, the other with a zither, sang.

> When shall I cease to love you?
> Spring is gone and Autumn is here
> Who knows my heart?
> Heaven sends me sadness. I grow thin.
> I wept when I had news of you
> The past is always in my mind
> I never thought you would so cruelly desert me.

Chunmei drank her wine, and Yueniang told Zheng Jiao'er to pour another cup for her.

"Lady," Chunmei said, "you must drink with me." Their cups were filled, and the singers began another song.

> For you, my lover, I cast happiness aside.
> Now the magpies chatter in the courtyard
> Their voice is sad, and yet they have no cause.
> It must be that Heaven
> Has made me love you always.
> You have gone away, but I never forget.
> I never thought you would so cruelly desert me.

"Lady," Chunmei said, "you must ask Aunt Wu to drink a cup."

"Aunt Wu is not a great drinker," Yueniang said. "I will give her a small cup." She told Xiaoyu to set a small cup before Aunt Wu. Then the two singers went on with their song.

> For you, my lover, I am become so sorrowful.
> I think of you by night and day,
> Sitting and walking.
> My dainty skin is wasted, my softness become hard.
> I am so lonely that my tears fall always.

Yet once we lived together and loved.
I never thought you would so cruelly desert me.

Xiaoyu was standing beside Chunmei, and Chunmei gave her a cup of wine.

"Sister," Yueniang said, "she cannot drink."

"Oh, she can drink one or two cups," Chunmei said. "When I lived here, I often drank with her." She gave the cup to the maid. The two singers continued their song.

> For you, my lover, I have suffered griefs
> I have been ill and lain for long upon my bed
> The sadness in my heart has knit my brows.
> You have forgotten me but I still think of you
> The thought makes tears stream down my cheeks.
> We said that we would be together forever.
> I never thought that, after but one year,
> You would so cruelly desert me.

Chunmei asked the singing girls to sing this song because she was thinking of Chen Jingji. She could not meet him, but he was always in her mind. For her, the songs expressed a secret sorrow. She was pleased that the singing girls addressed her as "Lady" and told Zhou Ren to give them each two *qian* of silver. The two girls put down their instruments and kowtowed to her.

Then she rose. Yueniang could not persuade her to stay longer and ordered a servant with a lantern to take her to the gate. Chunmei got into her sedan chair, and her maids into the smaller chairs. Before them and behind were four great lanterns, and an escort of soldiers followed.

Chunmei was anxious about Jingji. She did not know where he was. When she reached home, she went to bed at once in a bad mood. Her husband saw this, and decided she must be worrying because she did not know what had happened to her cousin. He sent for Zhang Sheng and Li An and said to them; "I have already told you to find my lady's cousin. Why haven't you done so?"

"We have looked," they said, "but we have not been able to find him. We told the lady so."

"I will give you five days," Major Zhou said. "If you have not found him by that time, you know what to expect."

The two men went all over the place, poking their noses everywhere, questioning people, and their faces became more and more gloomy.

When Jingji left the Major's court, he had intended to go back to the temple. But, when he was told of the Abbot's death, he did not dare. Neither did he dare to go and see old man Wang. So again he wandered about the streets by day and slept at night in the Beggars' Rest. One day when he was standing about the street, he saw Yang the Elder. Yang was wearing a new hat and a white silk gown. He rode on a donkey with a silver-mounted saddle, and a small boy followed him. They were coming down the middle of the street. Jingji recognized Yang at once. He went out and grasped the donkey's bridle.

"Brother Yang," he said, "I haven't seen you for a long time. After you stole my property at the river I went in quite a friendly way to ask at your place. But your brother, Yang the Second, broke his own head and ran after me all the way to my house. Now I am poor, and you are having a fine time."

Yang the Elder could see that Chen Jingji had become a beggar. He smiled haughtily. "This must be an unlucky day for me, that I should come to the street and meet a pestilential fellow like you. You are a beggar. Where could you get the money to buy goods? Do you say I stole your things? Keep your hands off my donkey, or I will use the whip on you."

"I am poor and you are rich," Jingji said. "I only ask you to give me something. If you don't, I shall take you to the proper place and the matter shall be thrashed out there."

Seeing that Jingji still held the donkey's bridle, Yang the Elder jumped off and thrashed Jingji with his whip. "Drive this beggar away," he cried to the small boy. The boy pushed at Jingji with all his might and the young man fell to the ground. Yang kicked him, and Jingji made as much noise as if he had been a devil. A crowd assembled. Among them was a man wearing a high black hat, a kerchief, a purple gown and a white vest. He had bare legs, and a pair of straw sandals on his feet. His eyes were sunken and his eyebrows broad and thick. His mouth seemed to curl upwards and he had three wisps of beard. His face was strong and red and the muscles stood out upon his arms. He had had wine to drink, and this had made his eyes seem fierce.

"Brother," he said to Yang the Elder, shaking his clenched fist, "you are unreasonable. Why should you beat a man so young and poor? You know the saying that a clenched fist should never smite a smiling face. This young man did nothing to provoke you. If you have any money, treat him as a friend and give him some. Why are you beating him? I don't think it is right, and I shall be on his side."

"You know nothing about it," Yang the Elder said. "He says I stole his property. How could a beggar like him have any property worth stealing?"

"I believe he was rich once," the man said. "He doesn't look to me as if he came from a poor family. And as for you, I very much doubt if you have been rich all your life. Now listen to me. If you have any money with you, let him have some."

Yang brought out a handkerchief in which was a piece of silver worth about four or five *qian*. He gave it to Jingji and raised his hand in salute to the man. Then he mounted his donkey again and rode proudly away. Jingji got up. He saw that his savior was no other than a man he had known in the Beggars' Rest, a fellow called Flying Ghost. He was now acting as foreman to a gang of fifty men who were working at a temple south of the city, building some new rooms. This man took Jingji by the hand. "Brother," he said, "if I had not used strong language to that man, you would not have that silver. He knows when it is time to give way. If he had not done so, I should have let him taste my fists. Come with me and have some wine."

They went to a small wine house, sat down, and ordered two pots of wine and four dishes. The waiter set out the dishes and two pots of olive wine that, at that time, was greatly liked. They drank this wine in large bowls instead of small cups.

"Brother," the man said, "which will you have, noodles or rice?"

"Our noodles are freshly washed and our rice the finest white rice," the waiter said.

"I will have noodles," Jingji said, and noodles were brought. Jingji had two bowls and his friend one.

"Brother," the man said, "come with me to my place today, and tomorrow I will take you to see the Abbot of the temple where I am working. We are building some rooms and cottages there, and I have fifty men working under me. I will give you a very light job. You will only have to carry earth, and for that you shall have five *fen* a day. Then I will get a room and we will sleep there together. We can cook our own food and lock our door, and I will let you have all you need. That will be better than the Beggars' Rest, and going around with the watchman. It will be much pleasanter for us to live together."

"You are very kind," Jingji said. "May I know if this work will last for long?"

"We only started a month ago, and I think we shall finish in the tenth month, but I am not sure."

They drank as they talked and finished two large pots of wine. The waiter brought them the bill. It was for one *qian* and three and a half *fen*. Jingji was going to pay, but Flying Ghost pushed his money aside.

"Do you think I would let you pay, you silly fellow?" he said. "I have money of my own." He brought out a handkerchief and gave the waiter

one *qian* and five *fen*, taking back the change. Then he put his arm around
Jingji and they went back to his place. That night they slept together. They
were both drunk and behaved in an unseemly manner. Indeed they did so
all night. Jingji called the man his brother, his sweetheart, his husband,
and other attractive names. In the morning they went together to the temple. Here Flying Ghost, whose name was Hou Lin, rented a room with a
fire and bought cups and bowls and other things that were necessary.

The workmen saw that Jingji was only about twenty-four or twenty-
five. They noticed his white face and handsome appearance and realized
that he was Hou's man. They made many jokes about him.

"Young man," one said, "what is your name?"

"I am called Chen Jingji."

"Well, Chen Jingji, you certainly live up to your name."*

And another said: "You are very young. How can you do such strenu-
ous work? Are you sure that pole isn't too much for you?"

Then Hou came up. "You beggars," he said, "what do you mean by
making fun of him?" He gave spades and shovels and baskets to the workmen, and they went to their tasks. Some carried earth, some mixed the
mortar, some worked on the foundations.

One of the monks in the temple was called Ye. The Abbot had given
him instructions to cook for all the workers. Ye was about fifty years old.
He had only one eye. He wore a long black gown, and his feet were bare.
There was a ragged girdle around his waist. He could not read the sacred
scriptures, but he was very attentive to his devotions. He was a skillful
fortune-teller.

One day, when the work was done and the workers had had their meal,
they were all gathered together, some lying down, some squatting on their
haunches. Ye looked hard at Chen Jingji.

"This young man is a newcomer," one of the men said to Ye, "why not
tell his fortune?"

"In my opinion, he is half one thing and half another," one of them
said.

The priest asked Jingji to go to him. "Too handsome and woman-
like," he said. "A charming voice and a tender body are unpardonable.
When an old man is like this, he will come upon hardship. When a young
man is like it, he will not be stout and strong. You suffer from that smooth
face of yours. All your life, you will be a woman's man. Eight, eighteen,
and twenty-eight. With eight years, eighteen, and twenty-eight, from the
root of your nose to the top of your hair, whether you have any means of

---

* There is a pun, of an ambiguous nature, on the word *ji*.

livelihood or not, you get less at both ends, and at thirty you cannot have a blackness between your brows. Your eyes are very handsome, and your mind is clever. Even if you cannot read, you have charm enough without. Whatever you do, people like you. When you play a trick, it is taken for the truth. Forgive me for saying so, but you are very cunning and get much sport from women. How old are you?"

"I am twenty-four," Jingji said.

"I am surprised that you got past the year before last," the monk said. "Your brows are narrow, and your son and your wife both die. The hanging jade is very dark, and your family will be ruined. Your lips do not cover your teeth and you will have many troubles in your life. Your nostrils are like the hob of a furnace, and you will not be able to keep your property. Have you experienced any such misfortunes?"

"I have had them all," Jingji said.

"One thing I must tell you," the monk said, "that your nose is detached is not a good sign. As the great teacher Ma says, he whose mountain root is broken will waste all his substance in his youth. He will bring ruin to the property he has inherited from his ancestors, and no matter how much his father left to him, he will spend it all. Your upper half is short and the lower half long. This is a sign that you are sometimes successful and sometimes fail. You spend your money, and money comes to you again. But, in the end, you will not leave a family behind you; you will be as when the hot sun shines on the hoar frost. But there is one sign of luck for you in the future. You are to be married three times. Have you ever been married and, if so, is your wife dead?"

"Yes, she is dead," Jingji said.

"Well, three marriages are indicated for you," the monk said. "But there is trouble also. "When you are about thirty, you will suffer from the machinations of others. You must not visit the flowers and the willows."

Then one of the workmen said: "Father Ye, you have made a mistake. He is a wife himself at this very time. How can you say that he will have three wives?"

All the workers laughed. Then the Abbot gave the signal, and they all took their tools and went to work again.

Jingji stayed for about a month and worked there. One day, in the middle of the third month, Jingji, who had been carrying earth, leaned against the temple wall and searched his body for vermin in the sun. A man who wore a swastika in his hat, a black gown with a purple lining, a girdle, and a pair of sandals, rode up on a brown horse. He was carrying a basket of fresh flowers. When he saw Jingji, he jumped off his horse at once and bowed low.

"Uncle Chen," he said, "I have been looking everywhere for you, and here you are."

Jingji, astonished, returned the greeting.

"Brother," he said, "who are you?"

"I am Zhang Sheng, the servant of Major Zhou," the man said. "Since you left the court, my mistress has been ill all the time. My master ordered me to find you, but it never occurred to me that you would be here. And even now I should not have seen you if my mistress had not told me to go to the country for these flowers. It is really a stroke of good luck for me. Don't waste a moment. Take my horse and go to my master's place."

The workmen stood and gazed. They did not speak. Jingji gave the keys to his friend Hou, mounted the horse, and rode quickly away.

CHAPTER 97

Chunmei Finds a Wife
for Chen Jingji

When they came to Major Zhou's place, Chen Jingji dismounted and Zhang Sheng went in to tell Chunmei. She ordered him to take Jingji to a room where he could have a bath, and told a woman to take him fresh clothes, boots and hat. The Major was still in the great hall, and Chunmei gave orders for the young man to be taken to the hall in the inner court. There she waited for him, beautifully dressed. Jingji came in and made a reverence to her as though she were his cousin. They sat down facing each other and talked of the things that had happened since they last met. Tears were in their eyes.

Chunmei expected the Major to come at any moment. She looked meaningfully at Jingji and said softly: "If he asks you any questions, say that you are my cousin and that I am a year older than you. I am twenty-five and was born at noon on the twenty-fifth day of the fourth month."

"I will remember," Jingji said.

The maid brought tea and Chunmei asked him how he became a priest. "My husband did not know that we had anything to do with one another," she said, "or he would not have punished you. He is sorry now. At that time I could not ask you to stay here, though I should have liked to, because Xue'e was here. That was why I let you go away. I got rid of her as soon as I could and told Zhang Sheng to look for you. I never imagined that things would come to such a pass that you would become a workman outside the city."

"It is a long story," Jingji said. "After we saw each other last, I made up my mind to marry Pan Jinlian. Then my father died at the Eastern Capital, and I came back too late. Wu Song had killed her. I heard that through your kindness she had been buried at the Temple of Eternal Felicity. I went there and burned paper offerings for her. Then my mother died. When I had buried her, my money was stolen. I came home and my wife died. That strumpet, my mother-in-law, took me to law and made off with all my wife's things. To settle the law case I had to sell my house and then I was as poor as if I had been cleaned completely out. Fortunately, I met an old friend of my father who took me to the Yangong temple to be a monk. Then some rascal gave me a beating. I was arrested and taken to the court. When I got away from there, I had no relative or friend to give me a helping hand, so I went to the temple and joined the workmen there. It was good of you, Sister, to tell Zhang Sheng to find me. I feel I am a new man now that I see you again." They both shed tears.

Major Zhou came from the hall. A servant pulled aside the lattice and he went into the room. Jingji stepped forward and knelt down before him. The Major hastily returned his greeting.

"I had no idea," he said, "that you were my good cousin. I was misled, or I should never have treated you so unbecomingly. I must apologize."

"It was my fault," Jingji said. "I have not been to see you. I trust you will forgive me." He again knelt down before the officer. Major Zhou helped him up and begged him to take the place of honor. Jingji was too clever to do this, and sat on a chair in the lower place. When they had all sat down together, tea was brought.

"Good cousin," Major Zhou said, "how old are you? I haven't seen you since we met that day. How did you come to go to the temple?"

"I am twenty-four years old," Jingji said, "a year younger than my cousin here. Her birthday is on the twenty-fifth of the fourth month. I went to the Yangong temple because my parents are dead and my family ruined. I did not know that my cousin had married you. If I had known, I should certainly have called to see you."

"Your cousin has been so worried about you all this time that she has never been at ease," Major Zhou said. "I sent out people to look for you, but they could never find you. It is a piece of good luck that I see you here today."

Major Zhou had been a friend of Ximen Qing. It was therefore to be expected that he would have made the acquaintance of Chen Jingji. But though Zhou was a friend of Ximen, he was an honest man and had never pried into his friend's domestic affairs. Always, when he had been at Ximen's house, Jing and Xia and other officers had been with him and he had never met Jingji. Besides, the young man had been a priest, and it never occurred to Zhou that he was Ximen Qing's son-in-law. So he was deceived by his wife and Jingji and believed that they were cousins.

Zhou ordered the servants to prepare dinner, and it was soon upon the table. The wine pots were of silver and the cups of jade. Wine was poured in a golden stream, and they feasted until the evening. Then the Major bade Zhou Ren prepare a room in the west court. Chunmei found two sets of bedclothes, and a boy called Xi'er was told to wait on him.

The time passed very quickly, the sun and moon racing like a weaver's shuttles.

When the old year drew near its end,
We saw the plum blossom.
Now, suddenly, New Year's Day is here
Dainty flowers appear upon the branches.
Fresh lotus leaves come out
Upon the surface of the water.

Jingji had been at Major Zhou's house for more than a month. It was Chunmei's birthday. Wu Yueniang sent Daian with a plate of longevity noodles, two geese, four chickens, two plates of fruit and a jar of wine. Major Zhou was sitting in the hall when a servant told him that Daian had come. He ordered the presents to be taken in. Daian brought the present list and came in and kowtowed.

"Tell your mistress it is very kind of her to send us these things," Zhou said to Daian. Then he handed the present list to a boy and told him to take it to his uncle. He said that Daian should be given a handkerchief and three *qian* of silver, and the porter a hundred coppers. Then he put on his ceremonial dress and went out. Daian stood at the door of the hall to wait for the return card. He saw a young man wearing a hat with a ribbed rim, a black gown, summer shoes, and light socks come through a corner door and give money to a boy. Then the man went back again. Daian thought he looked very like Chen Jingji, but he could not make out how Jingji could possibly be there. The boy gave Daian the handkerchief and the money, and he went home. He gave the return card to Yueniang.

"Did you see your sister?" Yueniang said.

"No, but I saw brother-in-law," Daian said.

"What do you mean, you young rascal?" Yueniang said, laughing. "What brother-in-law are you talking about? Do you have the audacity to speak of the Major as your brother-in-law, a man of his years?"

"I don't mean the Major," Daian said. "It was Chen Jingji I saw. When I got there, Major Zhou was in the great hall. I gave him my list and kowtowed. He said I was to thank you, and gave me some tea. Then he said to a boy: 'Take this card to your uncle and ask him for a handkerchief and three *qian* of silver for this man and a hundred coppers for the porter.' He dressed then and went out. I saw Master Chen coming by the corner door, and it was he who gave the return card to the boy. Then he went back, and I picked up my box and came away. I am sure it was he."

"I don't believe it, you scamp," Yueniang said. "I am sure that that young lamb must be wandering in other pastures now. He has probably died of starvation by this time. How could he be in that house? Would the Major have him there? Why, Chunmei herself would not have him."

"Lady, will you have a wager with me?" Daian said. "I am sure it was Master Chen I saw. I should know him even if he had been burned to ashes."

"What was he wearing?" Yueniang said.

"A new hat with a ribbed rim and a gold pin," Daian said. "He had a black gown, summer shoes, and white socks. He was looking very well."

"I can't believe you," Yueniang said.

Jingji went to the inner court where Chunmei was adorning herself in front of a mirror. He showed Yueniang's card to her. "Why is this woman sending you presents?" he said.

Chunmei told him that she had met Yueniang at the Temple of Eternal Felicity at the Festival of Spring, and that Ping'an had stolen ornaments from the pawnshop that Major Zhou had recovered for her. "She sent presents to thank my husband," Chunmei said, "and on the baby's birthday I went to see her. Now we are excellent friends, and she promised to send me birthday presents."

Jingji looked very hard at Chunmei. "Sister," he said, "you must have a very short memory. Have you forgotten how that whore treated you? She separated us and she is responsible for Jinlian's death. I only hope I may never set eyes on her again, and here you are actually befriending her. Why did you prevent Wu Dian'en from beating the boy? Then that woman would have been arrested and exposed. It was no business of ours. And, besides, if she has not been carrying on with Daian, why did she marry him to Xiaoyu? If I had been here then, I certainly would not have allowed you to do that. She is our enemy, and I can't understand why you let her come here. Friendship does not seem to mean anything to you."

Chunmei said nothing for a long time. Then she said: "Why not let bygones be bygones? I have a soft heart, and I do not like nursing a grievance."

"In these days," Jingji said, "if you have a soft heart you will suffer for it."

"Well, she has sent me these presents. I can't accept them without doing something in return. She is expecting me to send her an invitation."

"Have no more to do with her," Jingji said. "Why should you invite her again?"

"I shall feel very awkward if I don't," Chunmei said. "I will send her a card, and whether she comes or not will depend upon her. If she comes, you go to the other court and keep out of sight. Afterwards, I will break off relations with her."

Jingji was angry and went off without a word. He went to the front and wrote a card, and Chunmei sent a servant with it to Yueniang.

Yueniang dressed and, with Ruyi'er carrying Xiaoge, went to call upon
Chunmei. Daian went with them. Chunmei and the Second Lady both
came to welcome them. They went to the inner court and there greeted
one another. Ruyi'er, with the baby, made a reverence. Jingji, who was in
the other courtyard, kept out of the way.

Tea and wine were set out in the inner court and two singing girls
played and sang. Daian was entertained in a small room at the front. He
saw a boy, carrying a tray of food and cakes, going to the corner door on
the west side. Daian stopped him and asked him where he was taking
the tray.

"To my uncle," the boy said.

"What is your uncle's name?" Daian asked.

"Chen," the boy said.

Daian quietly followed the boy and went into the small courtyard on
the west side. The boy pulled aside a lattice and went in. Daian peeped
through the window. There was no doubt about it. Jingji was lying on
a bed, and, when the food was brought in, he got up and began to eat.
Daian went back to the front. In the evening people with lanterns came
to take Yueniang back. Daian told her what he had seen. From that time
onwards, Jingji dissuaded Chunmei from having any more to do with
Yueniang, and their relations were broken off.

Jingji, unknown to everyone in Major Zhou's house, associated secretly
with Chunmei. When Zhou was out, they had meals and drank wine
together, and sometimes played chess and other games. When he was at
home, Chunmei sent a maid with food to the young man and sometimes
went to him herself, even in the daytime. She used to stay in his rooms for
hours at a time. So they came and went one to the other and grew more
and more attached.

One day, when Major Zhou was out with some of his men upon a
tour of inspection, it was the Summer Festival. Chunmei arranged to have
a feast in a summerhouse in the west courtyard. She and the Second Lady
and Jingji drank together to celebrate the festival. Their maids and women
were all there to wait, and Chunmei bade Haitang and Yuegui sing for
them. They drank till the sun turned to the west and a very fine rain came
to bring coolness to the day. Chunmei took a great gold cup, shaped like
a lotus blossom, and urged the others to drink more. The Second Lady
could not, and went to her own room to sleep. Jingji and Chunmei were
left alone in the summerhouse. They guessed fingers, played games, and
drank together. After a while, the maid brought lanterns and the nurse
took away the baby to put him to bed. Jingji lost the game, went to the
study, and refused to come back. First, Chunmei sent Haitang for him,

but he would not come. Then she sent Yuegui. "You must drag him here, if necessary," she said. "If you fail, I shall box your ears ten times."

Yuegui went to the young man's room. When she opened the door, she saw him lying on the bed, snoring.

"My Lady says I must bring you back with me," she said. "If I do not, she promises to punish me."

"It doesn't matter to me whether you get punished or not," Jingji murmured. "I have had as much wine as I can drink, and I don't want any more."

Yuegui pulled him up. "I have to take you to my mistress," she said, "and if I can't drag you to her somehow, I shall own myself a feeble creature."

Jingji pretended to be more drunk than he was. He put his arms around Yuegui and kissed her. Yuegui made a fuss. "I came to take you away from here, not to behave like this," she said.

"My child," Jingji said, "do what I want of you and I will not treat you as a servant." He kissed her again, and they went together to the summerhouse.

"I have brought uncle," Yuegui said, "so you will not have to punish me."

Chunmei told Haitang to fill the large cups, and they played chess together. They played one game after another until the maids were sleepy and went away, all except Haitang and Yuegui, and Chunmei packed them off to get some tea. Then Chunmei and Jingji were alone together in the summerhouse. They kissed each other.

When they had been very happy together, Haitang returned with the tea. She asked Chunmei to go to the inner court because the baby was crying. Chunmei drank two more cups of wine with Jingji, then they rinsed their mouths with tea and she went to the inner court. The maid cleared the table and Jingji, with the assistance of his boy, went to his study and to sleep.

One day there came an Imperial Edict that instructed the Major to take his soldiers and join Zhang Shuye, magistrate of Jizhou, in an attack upon the bandits in Liangshan, who were led by Song Jiang. Before he set out on this expedition, he said to Chunmei: "Watch carefully over the baby, and send a go-between to arrange a marriage for your cousin. Then I will take him to the field with me. If he has good fortune and does his duty to his Emperor, he will get official rank, and that will be pleasant for you."

Chunmei promised to do this. In two or three months, Zhou joined his troops and went away. He took Zhou Ren with him and left Zhang Sheng and Li An at home.

One day Chunmei sent for old woman Xue. "When he went away," she said, "he told me to see about a marriage for my cousin. Go and see if you can find a suitable girl for him, someone about sixteen or seventeen. She must be beautiful and intelligent, because he has not the best of tempers."

"I know him," old woman Xue said. "You need not go into details. I remember that Ximen's daughter did not satisfy him."

"If you don't find a good girl for him, I shall box your ears," Chunmei said. "She must be pretty, because she and I will be living here as sisters. You must take the matter seriously."

She told a maid to give the old woman some tea. Then Jingji came in for something to eat. "Brother-in-law," the old woman said, "I haven't seen you for a very long time. Where have you been? I find I must congratulate you. I have just been told to find a pretty wife for you. What will you give me as a reward?

Jingji scowled and said nothing.

"Why don't you speak, you old beggar?" the old woman said.

"You mustn't call him brother-in-law," Chunmei said. "That is all over and done with. You must call him Uncle Chen now."

"I ought to be punished," old woman Xue said. "My doggish mouth gave him the wrong title. In the future, I will remember to call him Uncle."

Jingji could not help laughing. "I am glad to hear it," he said.

The old woman put on a great air of gaiety. She went up to him and gave him a little tap. "You old beggar," she said. "I am not your sweetheart. What do you mean by saying you are glad to hear it?"

Chunmei laughed. After a while, Yuegui brought cakes and tea for the old woman.

"I shall take the very greatest pains to find a suitable girl for you," Xue said, "and as soon as I find one I will come and tell you."

"We will see about clothes, ornaments, and all that sort of thing," Chunmei said. "All we care is that she should be a decent girl. This is not an ordinary family."

"I realize that," the old woman said, "and I am sure I shall be able to satisfy you."

Sometime later, Jingji finished his meal and went to the outer court.

"When did he come here?" old woman Xue asked.

Chunmei told her how he had become a priest. "I want to treat him as one of my relatives," she said.

"Excellent!" the old woman said. "You know your way about. I hear Mistress Ximen came here on your birthday."

"Yes," Chunmei said, "she sent me some presents, and I sent her an invitation in return. She was here quite a long time."

"I was very busy that day," the old woman said. "I very much wished to come, but I could not get away. Tell me, did Uncle Chen see Mistress Ximen?"

"He did not, indeed," Chunmei said. "He scolded me terribly because I invited her. He was very angry because I helped her and said I have no memory. Wu Dian'en, he says, should have punished the boy and dragged Mistress Ximen into the case. He says we ought to have left them alone and not bothered about them, because she treated us badly."

"I can understand his feelings," old woman Xue said, "but I don't think we ought to remember the things of the past forever."

"I had accepted her presents, and I could do no less than invite her," Chunmei said. "I have no wish to return evil for evil."

"No," old woman Xue said, "and that is why you have got on so well. You have a good heart."

They talked for some time, then old woman Xue picked up her box and went away. Two days later she came again. One of Master Zhu's daughters, a girl about fifteen, wished to marry as she had no mother. Chunmei considered the girl too young and would not agree. Then the old woman came again and suggested Ying Bojue's second daughter, who was twenty-two years old. But Chunmei would not have this either. Bojue was now dead; his daughter's marriage would have to be arranged by her uncle and she was not likely to have any dowry worth mentioning. So she returned their papers. A few days later, old woman Xue came again with some artificial flowers. She brought with her a proposal of marriage. On it was written: 'The eldest daughter of the silk merchant Ge Yuanwai. Her animal is the Cock. She was born at the hour of the Rat, on the fifteenth day of the eleventh month.'

"Her name is Ge Cuiping," the old woman said. "She is as beautiful as a picture. She is not tall, and her face is shaped like a watermelon seed. She is gentle, well-mannered and clever with her needle. Her parents are both alive and in good circumstances. Her father keeps a silk shop in the High Street and does business in Suzhou, Hangzhou, and Nanjing. We are not likely to find anyone more suitable. Besides, the furniture her father is sending with her is all of the Nanjing make."

"Let us settle this," Chunmei said. She told the old woman to take word to the other party at once. When she came to Ge's place, the silk merchant found that she came from Zhou's house and sent for another go-between, called Zhang, to go back with old woman Xue. Chunmei got ready two packets of tea leaves, dainties, and fruits, and asked the

Second Lady to go to Ge's place and see the girl. The Second Lady, when she came back, said that the girl was really very pretty. She looked like a flower, she said, and the family seemed to be a good one. Chunmei found a day of good omen for the betrothal. She sent the girl sixteen different kinds of fruit and food, two sets of ornaments, two sets of flowers and pearls, four wine sets, two sheep, a hairnet, and a complete outfit of gold and silver pins and rings. She sent two silk gowns and dresses for all the year round, with silk and cloth and twenty taels of silver. This was for the betrothal day.

The Master of the Yin Yang selected the eighth day of the sixth month for the wedding. Chunmei asked old woman Xue if the girl had a maid. "No," the old woman said, "her father will supply her with all her furniture, but no maid."

"Then we must buy a girl about thirteen or fourteen years old for her," Chunmei said.

The old woman promised to bring a girl the next day and did so. She was thirteen years old and came from the household of Huang the Fourth, the merchant. Huang and Li the Third had got into trouble over the official finances; they were arrested and thrown into prison and stayed there for more than a year. Li the Third died in jail, and his son was taken in his place. Their property was all sold. Laibao's son had run away and become a groom for some stranger. Laibao, Chunmei discovered, had changed his name to Tang Bao. He was mixed up in this affair.

"How much do they ask for the girl?" Chunmei said.

"Four taels and a half," the old woman said. "They want the money very badly so that they can pay off the authorities."

"Four and a half is too much," Chunmei said. "Give them three and a half, and I will have the girl." She gave the old woman the money and so the matter was settled. She called the girl Jinqian.

On the eighth day of the sixth month, Chunmei put on a pearl headdress, a crimson gown with broad sleeves, a girdle with gold ornaments and jade buckle, and went to meet the bride. She was carried by four men in a large sedan chair and a band of musicians and lantern bearers went with her. Chen Jingji rode on a white horse with a silver-mounted saddle. Soldiers marched before him. He wore a scholar's hat and a black silk gown, a pair of black boots with white soles and a pair of golden flowers in his hair. He seemed like the rain that visits the land after a long drought, or like a man who meets an old friend in a foreign land. Indeed, the happiest day in a man's life is that on which he marries, or passes his examination.

The bride's sedan chair came to Major Zhou's place. She was veiled in a veil of scarlet embroidery and carried a vase. When she had entered the great gateway, the Master of the Yin Yang took her to the hall. When the ceremonies were over, she was taken to her own room. Chunmei watched and then came away. When the Master of the Yin Yang had finished what he had to do, the bride and bridegroom sat together for a while. Then Jingji mounted a horse and paid a call upon his father-in-law to thank him for giving him his daughter. When he came back he was drunk. That night this very lively young man and the beautiful maiden enjoyed the first pleasures of their marriage. They were as happy as two lovebirds and as merry as fishes in the water.

On the third day after the wedding, Chunmei gave a feast in the hall of the inner court. Musicians were engaged and friends and kinsmen were invited.

Every day, Chunmei asked the young couple to take their meals with her. She called the bride her sister. They were so much together that the maids and serving women looked upon the new bride with respect. Chunmei gave them three rooms in the west courtyard and the rooms were papered till they looked like a cave of snow. New curtains and blinds were fitted. Jingji's study was outside the courtyard. There he kept a bed, tables, and some old books, and there he attended to Major Zhou's correspondence. There, too, Chunmei came to him, not always for conversation only.

CHAPTER 98

Wang Liu'er's Return

In the house of pleasure
The girls adorn themselves with powder and rouge.
When they are idle, they sit down
Looking at the flowers.
When they hear the old melody, they are sad,
But when they would go back to the old country
Where is now their home?

Before the mirror her cloudy hair is but half dressed;
Her tears flow and her silken gown is wet.
Today, once more, she met Pai Ssū-ma before the wine cups
And told her sorrow, playing the lute.

One day Major Zhou and Zhang Shuye, the magistrate of Jinan, took their forces and attacked the bandits of Liangshan. The thirty-six leaders of the bandits and more than ten thousand of their men were captured and order was restored. The victory was reported to his Majesty. The Emperor was pleased and promoted Zhang to be Censor and Commissioner in Shandong. Zhou was promoted to be general in Jinan to command all the forces there, guard the river, and pursue bandits and thieves wherever they might be. All Zhou's officers were advanced one degree in rank. Chen Jingji's name was put on the list, and he was appointed Counselor. Every month he was to draw two measures of rice. Now he was able to wear ceremonial hat and girdle, much to his delight.

In the middle of the tenth month, the new general was permitted by the Emperor to bring back his soldiers. He sent runners in advance to bring the news to Chunmei. She was delighted. She sent Jingji, Li An and Zhang Sheng to meet her husband outside the city. At the same time she prepared a banquet in the great hall to do honor to her husband. A number of officers came with presents.

When Zhou reached home, he went to the hall in the inner court and there his two wives welcomed him. Jingji, dressed in scarlet ceremonial

gown, with hat, boots, and girdle, came with his wife. Zhou admired the
bride and gave her a dress with ten taels of silver so that she might have
some ornaments made. In the evening, Chunmei and her husband talked
over the business of the household.

"My cousin's wedding, I am afraid, has cost you a great deal of money,"
Chunmei said.

"He is your cousin," Zhou said, "and since he has come to make his
home with us, we could hardly leave him without a wife. We have spent
some money, it is true, but he is not a stranger."

"Now you have secured this honor for him, it is indeed all that he can
ask," Chunmei said.

"His Majesty has commanded me to go to Jinanfu to take up my new
appointment," the General said, "but I shall not take you with me. We
will give your cousin some money to set him up in business with someone. He need only go to look at the accounts every three or five days. If he
makes any profit, it will be something for him to live on."

"That is an excellent idea," Chunmei said. They were very happy
together and went to bed.

The General only spent ten days at home. Then he started for Jinan
to take up his new appointment. It was the beginning of the eleventh
month. He took Zhang Sheng and Li An with him and left Zhou Ren
and Zhou Yi to look after his house. Jingji went as far as the Temple of
Eternal Felicity to speed the General on his way.

One day Chunmei said to the young man: "My husband thinks you
should go into business with a partner. If you make any money, it will be
yours."

Jingji was delighted. He went out to find a suitable partner and, by
chance, met his old friend Lu Bingyi on the street.

"Brother, I haven't seen you for a very long time," Lu said, bowing.

"My wife died, and I had a lawsuit," Jingji said. "Then Yang the Elder
stole all my property and I was completely cleaned out. Now things are
better again. My cousin married Major Zhou. I went to her, and she found
a wife for me. Now I am a counselor and have the right to wear ceremonial robes and hat. I am looking for someone to go into partnership with
me, but I haven't found anybody yet."

"After Yang the Elder stole your things," Lu told him, "he started a
wineshop at Linqing. He is a partner of Xie. Besides owning that wineshop, he is acting as a moneylender and doing very well. He lends to the
people of Linqing and especially the singing girls. He wears smart clothes
and eats good food. Every few days he gets on a donkey and goes to the
wine house to collect his share of the takings. He doesn't care for his old

friends any more. His younger brother has turned his place into a gambling den. He still keeps dogs and goes in for cock-fighting, and nobody dares to interfere with him."

"I saw him last year," Jingji said. "Instead of showing me the least kindness, he struck me. Fortunately a friend saved me from him. I hate that man as though my very marrow were imbued with hatred."

He took Lu to a wine house on the street, and they talked of finding a way by which Jingji could get his revenge.

"There is an old saying," Lu said, "that if a gentleman hates at all, he hates well. A great man must have a hand that can deal out ruin. When you come to deal with him, you must remember that unless you see a man's coffin, you do not weep for him. I have an idea. Brother, all you need do is to make out an accusation, send it to the court, and demand the money and goods that Yang stole from you. We can get his wine house. Then we need only add a little capital and carry on the place as a business ourselves. I will go and help Xie to manage it, and you can come every few days to go through the accounts. I am sure you would make more than a hundred taels a month. I can think of nothing else that would pay so well."

"Brother, you are right," Jingji said. "I will go and speak to my cousin and her husband about it. If we can get hold of that business, I will let you and Xie manage it."

They drank their wine, went downstairs and paid the reckoning. Jingji impressed upon his companion the necessity for keeping the matter secret, and they parted. When he got home, he mentioned the matter to Chunmei. "The General is not at home," he said. "What can we do about it?"

Zhang Sheng was there. He said: "Uncle, all you need do is to write out your accusation and say how much was stolen. Then seal it up with the General's card and I will send it to the magistrates. They will certainly order Yang's arrest, and, when he has been punished, we shall get the money."

Jingji wrote out an accusation at once. He put the General's card with it and gave it to Zhou Zhong to take to the courts. When Zhou Zhong came in, the two magistrates were in the hall hearing a case, but when they heard that Zhou had sent them a letter they called Zhou Zhong before them at once. They asked him about his master's new appointment, then opened the envelope and took out the card and the accusation. They were only too anxious to do anything for the General and issued a warrant for Yang's arrest at once. Then they gave Zhou Zhong a return card, and said: "Give our respects to your mistress and tell her that we will send you word when we get the money out of Yang." Zhou Zhong took the card and went home.

"The magistrates ordered Yang's arrest," he told Chunmei. "They say we have only to wait, and they will get the money back for us." Jingji looked at the card. It bore the words: "He Yongshou and Zhang Maode kowtow." He was very pleased. Two days later, the Yang brothers were arrested and the magistrates tried them upon the accusation Jingji had brought against them. They beat them and cast them into prison. Then the two Yangs gave up three hundred and fifty taels of silver, a hundred rolls of cloth, and the wineshop was valued at fifty taels. The total sum that Chen Jingji had mentioned was nine hundred taels, so they were still three hundred and fifty taels short. Yang sold his house for fifty, and was utterly ruined. Thus Jingji came into possession of the great wine house and went into partnership with Xie. Chunmei gave him five hundred taels more, so that he had a thousand taels in all. He made Lu Bingyi his manager. They redecorated the whole place, painted the walls, and brightened up the balconies. Everything was made to look new, even the tables.

It was about the middle of the first month when Jingji started this business, and every day they took thirty or fifty taels. Xie and Lu managed everything between them, and Jingji only came every few days. He used to ride there on horseback with a boy in attendance, and Lu and Xie always had an especially beautiful room prepared for him upstairs. They gave him wine and food and picked out the most beautiful singing girls for his benefit. Chen the Third was a waiter there.

One day in the third month, the Spring was bright and beautiful and everything sweet and fragrant. The willows and the locust trees on the banks of the river were wonderfully green, and the pink apricot and peach flowers seemed like embroidery. Jingji, leaning on the railing of his balcony, admired the exquisite scene.

The breeze blows softly
The mist enwraps the embroidered earth like a mantle.
In this season of peace the days grow longer
The hero's spirit grows lighter
And the beautiful maidens are gay once more.
The willows on the river's bank lengthen their branches
A pole is set beside the apricot tree.
The young man has not done all he would
Yet now he can enjoy the singing
And make his way into the world of dreams
To which wine leads.

As Jingji was looking down, he saw two small boats draw to the wharf. They were weighed down by boxes and furniture. Four or five men began to carry these things to the rooms downstairs. On the boat were two women, one middle-aged, tall, and dark-complexioned; the other young and very fair, her face powdered. She seemed about twenty years old. They entered the wine house.

"Who are they?" Jingji said to Xie. "Why did they walk in so haughtily instead of asking leave?"

"They have come from the Eastern Capital to visit a kinsman," Xie told him. "They cannot find a house, so they asked our neighbor Fan to give them a room. They are only going to stay two or three days. I was going to tell you about them when you asked me."

Jingji felt annoyed, but the younger of the two women came and made a reverence to him. "Sir," she said, "please do not be angry. It is not your manager's fault, but mine. We need a room so much that we came without giving you notice. I am very sorry. We shall stay only for a few days. Then we will pay for our rooms and go away."

Jingji listened to these soothing words and looked at the young woman from head to foot. She gazed at him with star-like eyes. Jingji thought: "I have seen this woman before." Then he looked at the other woman, and she looked hard at him.

"Are you not Ximen Qing's son-in-law?" she said to him.

Jingji was taken aback. "How did you know?" he said.

"I am Han Daoguo's wife," the older woman said, "and this is my daughter Han Aijie."

"But you and your husband live in the Eastern Capital," Jingji said. "What are you doing here? Where is your husband?"

"My husband is on the boat seeing to the furniture," the woman said.

Jingji ordered a waiter to go and bring Han. After a while he came. His hair was now white.

"Chen Dong," he said, "of the Imperial Academy, brought an accusation against six of the highest ministers of the Court. They were Cai, the Imperial Tutor; Tong, the Grand Marshal; Li, the Minister of the Right; Grand Marshal Zhu, Grand Marshal Gao, and Grand Chamberlain Li. The Censors supported this indictment, and the Emperor accepted it. They were all arrested, brought before the Supreme Court, and sentenced to banishment for life. Cai Yu, the Imperial Tutor's son, has been executed and his property confiscated. We three ran for our lives. We went first to Qinghe to find my brother, but he has sold my house and disappeared. Then we took a boat and came here. I am very glad to meet you. Are you still in Ximen's household?"

"No," Jingji said, "I left there. Now I am a counselor in General Zhou's department. I have two partners here and keep this wine house for a living. Now that I have met you, I shan't let you go. You must stay here and make this place your own."

Han Daoguo and the women kowtowed to Jingji. They went on moving their things into the wine house. Jingji found things going too slowly, and ordered Chen the Third and a boy to help them. Wang Liu'er thanked him again.

"You really must not thank me," Jingji said. "We belong, as it were, to the same family."

It was late and Jingji began to think of going home. He told his manager to give Han everything he needed to eat and drink. Then he mounted his horse and went home with his boy. All night through, he could do nothing but think of Han Aijie.

Two days later he again dressed himself in his best clothes and went to the wine house with his boy. He attended to his business and then Han Daoguo asked him to take tea. As a matter of fact, he was thinking of going to them when the invitation was brought to him. He went to them. Han Aijie came smiling towards him and made a reverence. Then she asked him to go into their room. Wang Liu'er and Han Daoguo were both there. After tea they talked over past days. Jingji looked at Han Aijie and Aijie looked at him. They soon came to an understanding.

Before very long, Han Daoguo went out. Aijie asked Jingji how old he was, and he asked her. "We are both the same age," she said, smiling. "And we were both members of Ximen's household. Now we meet again here. It would really seem as though Destiny had brought us together over so many miles."

Wang Liu'er saw that they seemed to be on very good terms with one another. She made some excuse and left them. They now sat face to face, alone. Aijie spoke to him with sweet words that he could not fail to understand, for he had been used to the society of women ever since he was a child. He smiled at her.

Both Han Aijie and her mother, on their journey from the Eastern Capital, had done some traffic in their bodies. Now that the girl met Jingji she felt that Heaven had sent him to her. They seemed to understand and love each other without need for words. She came closer and sat beside him.

"Will you show me that gold pin in your hair?" she said. "I should like to look at it." But before he could take it out for her she had taken it out for herself. "Come upstairs," she said, smiling, "and I will tell you something." She led the way and Jingji, who was only waiting for such an opportunity, followed her immediately.

"Sister, what is it you wish to say to me," he asked when they were upstairs.

"You and I have come together today," Aijie said, "and to me it seems that Heaven has ordained our meeting. I am ready to enjoy with you the pleasures of the bed."

"I am grateful to you, Sister," Jingji said, "but aren't you afraid some-one may find out?"

She put forth all her powers of fascination. She threw her arms around him and, with her dainty fingers, took down his trousers. Then they gave rein to their passion till they lost all control of themselves. She took off her clothes and gave herself to him.

Jingji asked what place she held in the family. "I was born on the Sum-mer Day," she told him, "and they called me the Fifth Maid, but my name is Aijie."

When they had taken their fill of pleasure, they sat down again together. She put the gold pin back into his hair. "My parents and I came from the Eastern Capital to visit our kinsman," she said. "We are very poor, and, if you have any money with you, I will ask you to give my father five taels and I will pay it back to you with interest."

"I will lend it to him without interest, since you ask," Jingji said.

He gave her the five taels and sat with her for a long time. But he did not wish anyone else to know what was happening, so he would only take a cup of tea with her, and when she asked him to stay and have something to eat, he declined. "I can't stay now," he said, "I have some business to attend to. I will bring you some more money."

"This afternoon, I shall prepare a poor cup of wine for you," the girl said. "That you cannot refuse. You must come." Jingji took his dinner in the wine house and then went to the street for a stroll. In the street he met Jin Zongming, the monk of Yangong Temple. They talked about the things that had happened there.

"I didn't know you had settled down in the General's household and had set up this wineshop, or I would have come to see you," the monk said. "Tomorrow I will send a boy with some tea. I hope you will come to the temple when you have leisure."

Then the monk went his way, and Jingji went back to the wine house.

"Our guest Han has been asking for you," Lu said. "He is anxious to offer you some wine. But we could not find you."

As they spoke, a messenger came from Han Daoguo asking them, the two managers and Jingji, to go. They went. Wine and food were set out on the table. Jingji took the place of honor and Han Daoguo the host's place. The two managers, Lu and Xie, sat facing Wang Liu'er and Han Aijie. Han's servant heated the wine for them. After it had been around several times, the two managers began to see light. "You stay," they said to Jingji, "we must go and attend to business."

Jingji had not a steady head, but, when the two managers had gone, he drank without restraint. After a few cups he began to feel tipsy.

"I suppose you won't go home today," Han Aijie said to him.

"No," Jingji said, "it is late. I will stay until tomorrow."

Wang Liu'er and Han Daoguo went downstairs. Jingji gave five taels of silver to Han Aijie, and she went to give the money to her mother. Then she came back, and they went on drinking. They did not stop before sunset. Aijie took off her long coat and asked Jingji to stay with her. They spoke hot words of love together, and her voice was as sweet as an oriole's. They enjoyed every manner of love's delight.

When Han Aijie had lived in the Eastern Capital as Zhai's concubine, she had often visited the Imperial Tutor's mother. She had learned how to read and write, how to play various instruments, and sing. She had become accomplished and attractive, and Jingji found her equal in charm to Pan Jinlian herself. He sported with her all the night. It was late the next day when he rose, and Wang Liu'er prepared a meal for him. Then he and the girl drank a few cups of warm wine.

The managers invited the young man to have dinner with them. He dressed and went. Afterwards, he came back to say good-bye to Han Aijie. She hated to see him go away, and shed tears.

"Never mind," he said, "I will come and see you again in a few days." Then he mounted his horse and, with his boy following, went back to the city. On the way, he warned the boy that he must not mention the Hans to anyone at home. The boy assured him that he did not need to be told.

When they reached home, Jingji told them that he had had so much to do that he had not been able to come back the night before and had spent the night at the wine house. He gave Chunmei the money he had brought back with him, about thirty taels. His wife, Cuiping, suspected that he had been with another woman and had left her alone at home. Now she clung to him for seven or eight days and would not allow him to go to the wine house. The boy was sent to fetch the week's money.

Han Daoguo was in such need of money that he had to tell his wife to get some other man, a merchant or one of those who came to take tea or to drink in the wine house. He had found before that he was well able to live upon his wife's earnings. It was true that she was growing older, but there was Han Aijie to take her place, and no reason why the business should come to an end. They even followed it openly.

When Chen Jingji did not come back, the waiter Chen the Third found them a merchant from Huzhou. His name was He. He was about fifty years old and had silk goods with him worth a thousand taels. He was very anxious to have Han Aijie, but she was thinking of Jingji and made the excuse that she was unwell. Several times she refused to come down and see the merchant. Han Daoguo was greatly annoyed.

This merchant He saw that Wang Liu'er was tall and dark. Her hair was dressed in long braids and her starlike eyes were extremely seductive. Her lips were painted very red. He thought it undoubtful that she must be skilled in the arts of love, so he gave her a tael of silver and spent the night with her. Han Daoguo went to sleep somewhere else. Han Aijie did not come down. He enjoyed himself immensely. He became so attracted to Wang Liu'er that they were almost inseparable. Every two or three days he came to her and spent the night, and Han Daoguo was very well paid for his self-denial.

Han Aijie missed Jingji. She thought of him so much that one day seemed like three autumns and one night as long as half a summer. She was, in fact, utterly lovesick. At last she sent their old servant to the city to try to get news of her lover. He went to the General's house and secretly questioned the boy.

"Why does your master not come to the wine house any more?" he said.

"My master has not been very well," the boy said. "He has not been out at all."

The old man came back and told Han Aijie. She spoke to her mother, and they decided to buy a pair of pig's trotters, two roast ducks, two live fish, and a box of cakes. Han Aijie made some ink and wrote a card. They gave the things to the old man and told him to take them to Jingji. "When you get to the city," Han Aijie told him, "you must take the things to Master Chen yourself and get a return card from him."

The old man tucked the card away and took the things to General Zhou's. He sat down on a large block of stone. After a while the boy came out.

"What are you doing here again?" the boy asked him.

The old man bowed to him and took him aside.

"I have come to see your master and brought him some presents. Go and tell him I am waiting here to see him."

The boy went into the house, and very soon Jingji came gaily out. It was the fifth month and very hot. He was wearing the lightest of clothes, a brimmed hat, summer shoes, and white socks. The old man bowed to him.

"Master," he said, "are you better? Han Aijie has sent me with these things. Here is her card."

Jingji took it. "How is she?" he said.

"She is not very well, now that you have been so long away from her," the old man said. "She told me to say that you must go."

Jingji looked at the card.

To my lover Chen [it said]. Ever since you left me, I have been thinking of you all the time. You promised me you would come back, and I have stood at the door and waited for you, yet you have never deigned to visit this poor place. Yesterday I sent our old servant for news of you, but he came back without seeing you. He heard only that you were not well. That word made me so sad that I cannot sit or lie down in peace. I wish I had wings that I might fly to you. You are at your own home, where you have a delightful lady to give you pleasure, and you think of me no more. I am like the kernel of a fruit that you have spat from your mouth. I send you some cakes and food to show my love for you. Please accept them with an indulgent smile, for my love knows no bounds. Your unworthy Han Aijie greets you.

Then came the words:

I am sending you an embroidered red bag with a lock of my hair to show how much I love you. The twentieth day of the second month of summer. Han Aijie again makes reverence to you.

Jingji read the letter and looked at the little bag. There was a lock of black hair in it, and, attached to it, a small label with the words "To my lover, Chen." He folded everything up as it had been before and put it in his sleeve.

Not far from the house there was a small wineshop. He told the boy to take the old man there and give him something to drink. "I am going to write a letter," he said. "Take in the presents and, if your mother asks whom they are from, tell her that my manager Xie at the wine house has sent them."

The boy took in the boxes. Jingji went to his study and secretly wrote a letter. Then he took five taels of silver and went to the wineshop.   .

"Have you had some wine?" he said to the old man.

"Yes, Master! Thank you very much. I can't drink any more because I must be going back."

Jingji gave the letter and the silver to the old man. "Tell Han Aijie," he said, "that she is to spend this money. I will come and see her in two or three days."

The old man took the letter and the silver and went away. When Jingji went home again, his wife asked him who had sent the presents.

"Xie, my manager at the wine house, heard that I was ill and he sent them."

His wife believed him. They gave one of the roast ducks, one fish, and one pig's trotter to Chunmei and told her that they had come from the manager of the wine house. Chunmei suspected nothing.

The sun had set when the old man came back to the wine house. He gave the silver and the letter to Han Aijie. She read it in the light of the lamp.

Younger Brother Jingji [it said] kowtows to his beloved Han the Fifth. I thank you for your letter and the delightful gifts that came with it. I, too, feel the desire for clouds and rain, and have not forgotten the joys of the bed I tasted with you. I have thought all the time of coming to you, but I have been ill and you have been disappointed. It was good of you to send someone to see me and to give me such charming dishes and that exquisitely made embroidered bag. I thank you with all my heart. I am offering you five taels of silver and a silk handkerchief, as a token of my love's sincerity. I trust you will appreciate my gift. Jingji kowtows.

There was a short poem written on the handkerchief.

Han Aijie read the poem and gave the silver to her mother. So both women were pleased. They waited eagerly for Jingji's coming.

CHAPTER 99

The Murder of Chen Jingji

There is a white cloud over the mountain
The leaves are red upon the trees.
They have seen the rise and fall of many things
Yet this world is as it has been always.
Many times the evening sun has passed over the fragrant grass
Many times the tide has ebbed and flowed
They have seen the generations come and go.

The way of Yuan
The road of Yang
They turn and twist like the guts of a sheep
And the wheels of the carriages go astray.
Where the horses neigh near the dreary bushes,
The strains of the recorder and the silver zither
Once were heard
And the sound of singing through the night.

Two days later, it was Chunmei's birthday, the twenty-fifth day of the fifth month. There was a feast in the hall of the inner court and the household kept holiday. The next morning, Jingji said: "I haven't been to the wine house for a very long time. Today I have nothing else to do, so I will go there. It will give me an opportunity to get away from this stifling heat, and I can go through the accounts with my managers,"

"You must take a sedan chair and not tire yourself," Chunmei said. She ordered two men to take him in a chair. He set off with his boy and came to the wine house about noon. When he got out of his chair, the two managers welcomed him and asked if he were better. He thanked them, but he was really thinking about Han Aijie. He had hardly sat down before he was up again.

"Get your accounts ready," he said to the managers, "and I will go through them with you when I come back."

He went to the back of the house. There the Hans' old man saw him and hurried in to tell his people. Han Aijie was upstairs on the balcony, composing a poem. Gathering up her skirts, she ran swiftly downstairs. Mother and daughter smiled. "Sir," they said, "it is seldom that we are allowed the pleasure of seeing you. What good wind has blown you here?"

Jingji bowed to them, and they went together into the room and sat down. Wang Liu'er made tea. When they had drunk it, Han Aijie took the young man to her room. They were so delighted in each other's company that they were as merry as the fishes in the water, and they spoke the tenderest words to one another.

Under the ink slab there was a piece of colored paper. Jingji took it and looked at it. "That is the poem I have been writing," Han Aijie told him. "I was thinking of you when I wrote it, but I fear you will find it very bad." Jingji read it.

> I rest upon the embroidered bed
> And am too weary to move.
> Alone, I pull down the silken curtain and bend my head.
> My treasure has gone
> And I have no message from him.
> I think of him throughout the day.

Jingji told her the poem was delightful. Then Wang Liu'er brought them wine and food. She took away the mirror and set out the food on the toilet table. They sat down together and Aijie offered him a cup of wine with both hands. She made a reverence and said: "Since you went away, I have been thinking of you all the time. The other day our old man brought the money you sent, and my parents and I are grateful to you."

Jingji took the cup and bowed to her in return. "It was only because I was ill that I did not come to see you," he said. "I am sorry." He drank the wine and gave the cup back to her. Then they sat down again and drank together. Wang Liu'er and Han Daoguo came up and had some wine with them, but they went away again almost at once. They knew that the young couple would rather get on with their lovemaking.

When they had drunk wine enough, their blood was stirred. They did not only what they had done before, but many things that were new, and their love seemed limitless. Then they dressed again, washed their hands and went on drinking. After a few more cups their eyes sparkled, and they felt that still they were unsatisfied.

The young man had been very ill-content at home. He had been thinking of Han Aijie all the time and had not touched his wife. Now that he again met the girl he loved, he could not be satisfied with one encounter. Their love seemed to have been maturing for five hundred years. He was fascinated by her. Soon his passions were roused again and he set to. Then he felt weary and could do no more. Indeed, he did not even take any food, but simply lay down on the bed and went to sleep.

That day the silk merchant He came to the house. Wang Liu'er drank with him, and her husband went to the street to buy fresh vegetables and fruit. While he was out, the merchant and Wang Liu'er took their pleasure together. When he came back, all three drank together.

About sunset, Tiger Liu rushed into the wine house. He was drunk and his unbuttoned clothes revealed his purple flesh. His hands were clenched. "Where is that Southerner He?" he cried.

The two managers were alarmed. They knew that Jingji was asleep upstairs and did not wish him to be disturbed. "Brother Liu," they said to the Tiger, "he is not here." Liu would not believe them. He strode to Han Daoguo's room, tore the lattice aside, and went in. The merchant was sitting beside Wang Liu'er, drinking.

"Ha, you doggish pair!" he cried. "I have been looking for you everywhere and at last I've found you. You had two girls in my wineshop and you haven't paid them. You haven't paid your rent either, and here you are with another woman."

He stood up at once. "Don't be angry, my friend," he said. "I am just going."

"Going, are you, you dog?" Tiger Liu said, in a furious temper. He drove his fist into the merchant's face, so that it swelled up immediately. He did not trouble about his face; he was only anxious to get to the door and run away. Liu kicked over the table and smashed all the plates. Wang Liu'er cursed him.

"Who are you, you thief? How dare you come farting here? You won't bully me."

Liu went to her and knocked her down. "Who are you, strumpet?" he said. "What do you mean by coming here and practicing your trade in secret without asking my leave? I do not permit you to stay here. Clear out at once, or you will taste my fist."

"Rogue, who are you?" Wang Liu'er said. "I suppose you think I have no one here to defend me. Well, I won't live any longer." She banged her head on the floor and sobbed loudly.

"Woman, you don't frighten me," the Tiger said. "I shall smash your belly in."

There was so much shouting and quarreling that all the neighbors came to look on. One of them said to her: "Mistress Han, you have only just come here, or you would know that this is the famous Tiger Liu, the brother-in-law of Master Zhang of the General's office. He lives at a wine house, and singing girls are his specialty. It is he who controls all the wine drinkers in these parts. You must let him have his way. You don't know how powerful he is. Nobody here ever dares to offend him."

"There must be somebody over him," Wang Liu'er said. "Why should I do what he tells me?"

Lu, seeing the Tiger in a fury, at last succeeded in getting him away. Jingji had heard the noise downstairs. He saw that the sun was setting and got up to ask what all the noise was about. Han Daoguo had disappeared, but Wang Liu'er, her hair in disorder and her face dirty, ran upstairs and told him.

"I don't know who he is," she said. "I only know they call him Tiger. They say he is the brother-in-law of Zhang at the General's office. He came here to see one of the guests and struck and insulted me. He upset the table and smashed all the plates." She cried loudly.

Jingji sent for the two managers and questioned them. They could only tell him the truth. Liu the Second, they said, had come to look for the merchant He. He saw the man he sought in Han Daoguo's room, went in, pulled up the lattice, and struck him. He ran away, and then Liu quarreled with Mistress Han. He knocked her down and people came out of the street to see.

Then Jingji remembered that this Liu was the man who had beaten him in the days when he was a priest. He knew that Liu was too much for him to deal with, so he said no more at that time, except to ask where Liu was then. "We got him out," the managers said. Jingji tried to console Wang Liu'er. "Don't worry," he said. "I am here, and I will protect you. You stay where you are. I am going home, and I shall know how to deal with him." He took the money from his managers, got into his sedan chair, and went home. It was quite dark when he arrived. He was very angry. He gave all the money to Chunmei and went to bed. The next day, he was several times on the point of telling her about Wang Liu'er, but, whenever he thought about it, he decided to say nothing. "I will wait and see if Zhang Sheng does not do something wrong," he said to himself. "Then I will tell Chunmei, and the General will put an end to him. I have never sought trouble with that fellow, but he has bullied me several times. It is his fault, not mine."

One day, Jingji went again to the wine house. He saw the mother and daughter, and they talked about the quarrel.

"Has Liu the Second been here again?" Jingji asked.

"No," Wang Liu'er said, "not since that day."

Then he asked Han Aijie if the merchant He had been to see them again, and she said he had not.

Jingji had his dinner, examined the accounts, and went upstairs to amuse himself with Han Aijie. Then he sent for the waiter, Chen the Third, and asked him if he knew anything that could be held against either Zhang Sheng or Tiger Liu. The waiter told him how Zhang Sheng was keeping Xue'e, who was now a singing girl at the wine house. He told him, too, how Liu lent money to people at a very high rate of interest, and indeed brought much discredit upon the General's administration. Jingji listened very carefully to all this. He got his money from the managers, gave Han Aijie three taels, and took the rest away. Then he rode home. He never forgot the trouble between Liu and himself, and the hatred between them was so strong that it seemed certain that, if they met, trouble was inevitable.

About this time, Huizong, the Son of Heaven, heard at the Eastern Capital that the army of Jin had attacked the frontier and even plundered places on this side. The situation was serious. The Emperor held a conference with his ministers, and it was decided that an envoy should be sent to them to declare that the Emperor was ready to pay several millions of money every year for the sake of peace. At the same time, he abdicated in favor of his son. Thus the seventh year of Xuanhe became the first year of Jinkang, and the new Emperor took the title of Qinzong. The old Emperor called himself the Supreme Daoist Emperor and retired to the Palace of Dragon Virtue. The new Emperor placed Li Gang, the Minister of War, in command of the whole imperial army, and Chong Shidao was appointed Marshal and Generalissimo.

One day an order came to Jinanfu appointing Zhou to the command of all the troops in Shandong, and instructing him to take ten thousand men to garrison Dongchangfu. There he was to join the Censor, Zhang Shuye, and check the advance of the Jin army.

When Zhou received this order, he sent at once for Zhang Sheng and Li An, placed them in charge of his treasure, and sent them home with it. He had been in Shandong for nearly a year and had amassed a considerable amount of wealth. Everything was carefully packed and the men were instructed to take the utmost care of the valuables entrusted to them. The General told them that he would set out for his new appointment from Qinghe.

When the two men reached home, they handed over the treasure to Chunmei. Jingji saw that Zhang Sheng was back again, and heard from him of the General's new appointment, and that he would be home very shortly. He decided to tell Chunmei about Zhang Sheng, so that they could both tell the same tale to Zhou when he arrived.

One day his wife, Cuiping, went to see her mother, and he was asleep in the study when Chunmei suddenly came in. There was nobody about, and they undressed and took their pleasure of one another. At that moment, Zhang Sheng was making the rounds of the house with a bell. When he came to the door in the courtyard by the study, he heard the sound of a woman's laughter. He stopped ringing his bell and went quietly to the window; so he discovered what Chunmei and Jingji were about. He heard Jingji say how he hated Zhang Sheng, and how badly Zhang Sheng had treated him. He heard him say that Zhang Sheng had ordered his brother-in-law, Tiger Liu, to go to the wine house and drive away his customers. The Tiger, with Zhang Sheng behind him, was lending money to people. Zhang Sheng was also sleeping with Xue'e, and keeping the matter dark. "I kept the matter to myself," he said, "because I didn't wish to worry you. But now the General is coming back, and so I tell you. If I don't, I shall never be able to go to the wine house to attend to my business."

"What a scoundrel the fellow is," Chunmei cried. "I sold Xue'e. How dare he sleep with her?"

"He ill-treats me and he has no respect for you," Jingji said.

"Wait till my husband comes," Chunmei said, "and we'll get rid of him for good and all."

The pair never suspected that Zhang Sheng was outside the window and could hear every word they said.

"If I don't finish them, they will finish me," Zhang Sheng said to himself. He put down his bell and went to his room. There he took a dagger and sharpened it on a whetstone. Then he went to the study.

Fortunately, Heaven saved Chunmei's life. One of her maids called her away. The baby had fallen, she said, and asked her mistress to go and see him. She had just left the room when Zhang Sheng, with his dagger, entered it. Jingji was still in bed.

"What do you want?" Jingji said.

"Uncle, I have come to kill you. I was not seeking trouble, but you dared to tell that strumpet that I must die. The proverb says: Black-headed vermin should not be spared; they eat human flesh. Don't try to escape. My knife is waiting for you. A year from today will be your year's mind."

Jingji had not a stitch of clothing on him. He could not get away, but he gripped the bedclothes tightly. Zhang Sheng pulled them off. He drove the dagger into Jingji's side and the blood gushed forth. As the young man still struggled, Zhang Sheng drove his dagger into his breast.

That was the end. Zhang Sheng grasped him by the hair and cut off his head. Jingji was only twenty-seven years old when he came to this miserable end.

Zhang Sheng, still grasping his dagger, went behind the bed to look for Chunmei, but she was not there. Then he rushed to the inner court. But when he came to the second door, Li An, who was also going the rounds, saw him coming like the god of wrath, dashing towards him with the dagger raised. He asked Zhang Sheng where he was going but got no answer. Then he stopped Zhang Sheng. Zhang Sheng pointed the dagger at him. Li An laughed. "My Uncle," he said, "is Li Gui the famous Demon of Shandong. You shall know what I can do." He lifted his right leg and kicked the dagger out of Zhang Sheng's hand. It fell with a clang on the floor. Zhang Sheng fought desperately, but Li An got him down and bound him with his girdle.

Chunmei heard the noise. Li An told her that he had secured Zhang Sheng. Chunmei, who had just finished seeing to the baby, was so frightened that she changed color. She rushed to the study and saw that Jingji had been killed. Blood was still running over the floor. She screamed. Then she told servants to go for Cuiping. The young wife came. When she saw that her husband had been murdered, she shrieked and then fainted. Chunmei helped her to her feet, sent to buy a coffin, and put the young man into it. Then she gave orders that Zhang Sheng should be thrown into prison for her husband to deal with.

When General Zhou returned, Chunmei told him of the murder of Jingji. Li An put the dagger before his master and told him what he knew of the story. The General was very angry. He went at once to the hall and called for Zhang Sheng to be brought before him. Without asking a single question, he ordered the attendants to give the man a hundred stripes. So Zhang Sheng was beaten to death. Then he sent to arrest the Tiger. When Liu was taken, Xue'e feared that she too might be arrested. She went to her own room and hanged herself. When Liu was brought before the General, he too was ordered a hundred stripes, and so he died. The news created a great stir in Qinghe and tremendous excitement in Linqing.

> Man should avoid deceit
> For above his head, God waits.
> If they who do all manner of evil
> Received not their reward
> Then all the ruffians in the world
> Would devour each other.

By this execution, the General rid the district of two devils. He bade Li An go to the wine house and give it back to its original owner, bringing back the things that belonged to him. He told Chunmei to hold a service for Jingji, and afterwards the young man was buried at the Temple of Eternal Felicity outside the city. Then he gave orders that Li An and Zhou Yi should remain at home to look after the place, while he took with him Zhou Ren and Zhou Zhong.

In the evening, Chunmei and the Second Lady offered him wine before he left. They shed tears and said: "You are going away and we have no notion when you will come back. You must take care of yourself when you are in the battle. The barbarians are very strong, and you must not regard them lightly."

And the General said to them: "You who stay at home must be always prudent. Take care of my son. Don't trouble about me. I take the Emperor's pay, and I must render loyal service to my country. Whether I live or die is on the knees of Heaven."

The next day the troops assembled outside the city. The General took his place at their head, and they marched off. When, one day, they came to Dongchangfu, he ordered a soldier carrying a blue flag to go first into the city. This was a notification to the Commissioner Zhang Shuye that General Zhou's army had arrived. He came out with the Prefect of the place to receive the General, and they went together to their headquarters. There they discussed the military situation and sent out scouts to get news of the enemy. The next day the army set forth to defend the city.

When Han Aijie heard of Jingji's death, she cried day and night and would not take anything to eat. The only thing she could think of was going to the General's place to see the young man's body. She thought that if she could only do that she would be content. Her parents tried to console her, but still she insisted that she must go. Han Daoguo sent his old servant to get what news he could. The old man came back and told them that Jingji had already been buried at the Temple of Eternal Felicity. Then Han Aijie determined to go to the temple to burn some paper offerings for her lover. She would bewail him at his grave.

Her parents could do nothing to dissuade her, so they hired a sedan chair and took her to the temple. There they asked a monk where Jingji was buried, and the monk sent a boy to take them to the grave, behind the temple. Han Aijie got out of her sedan chair and burned some paper money. She made a reverence before the grave and said: "Oh, dearest brother, I had hoped that I might live with you always. Never did I think that you would die so young." She gave a great cry and fell fainting to the ground. Her parents were frightened and came to help her up. They called her, but she made no answer and they became more frightened still.

It was the third day after Jingji's funeral. Chunmei and Cuiping, in two sedan chairs with their servants following, came to burn papers and offer food to the dead. When they came near the grave, they saw a young woman dressed in mourning, lying on the ground, and a man and woman of middle age trying to revive her. But when she got up, she collapsed again in a faint. They were astonished and asked the man who the girl was.

Han Daoguo and his wife made reverence to them, and told them how they had known Chen Jingji, and that the girl was their daughter Han Aijie. Then Chunmei remembered her from the days in Ximen's house and recognized Wang Liu'er also. Han Daoguo told her how they had come to leave the Eastern Capital.

"My daughter was a friend of Master Chen," he said. "Now he is dead, she came to burn paper money for him. But she cried so bitterly that she fainted."

They went back to their daughter and again tried to bring her around. After a while Han Aijie spat out a little water and revived. She still sobbed, but not so loud as before. She kowtowed four times to Chunmei and Cuiping.

"Though I was only his mistress," she said, "we loved each other truly. I had hoped that I might always belong to him, but Heaven would have it otherwise and decreed his death. Now I am all alone in the world. When he was alive, he gave me a handkerchief on which he had written a poem. I knew he was married, but I was willing to serve only for his amusement. If you doubt me, look at this handkerchief." She showed it to them and they both read the poem.

"I gave him a little embroidered bag too," Han Aijie said, "and he always carried it about with him. It had double lotus blossoms on both sides, and on each of the petals I wrote a word. 'I offer this to Chen my lover,' I wrote."

Chunmei asked Cuiping if she knew of this little bag. "It was under his clothes," Cuiping said, "and I put it into the coffin with him."

When they had made their offerings at the grave, they took Han Aijie and her mother into the temple to have tea with them. It was late and Wang Liu'er wished to go home. Her daughter would not hear of it. She knelt down before Chunmei and Cuiping and wept. "I do not wish to go back with my parents," she said to them. "I wish to live with you. Then I can see his tablet every day. We were lovers, and I should like people to say that I had been his wife." Her tears fell like the water from a spring.

"Sister," Chunmei said, "I am afraid you are very young to live such a life. You will be wasting the best of your years."

"No, Lady," Han Aijie said. "For his sake, I would cut out my eyes and break my nose. I shall never marry anyone else."

"You go home, old people," she said to her parents. "I am going with these ladies."

"We have been hoping that you would support us in our old age," Wang Liu'er said, with tears. "We have only just brought you from the Dragon's Pool and then you leave us."

"I will not go back with you," Han Aijie declared, "and if you try to make me, I will kill myself.

Then Han Daoguo saw that his daughter had made up her mind. He and Wang Liu'er cried and went back to the wine house. Han Aijie got into a sedan chair with Chunmei and Cuiping and went to the city with them. Wang Liu'er thought of her daughter and wept all the time. Han Daoguo saw that it was late, so he hired two animals to take them back.

> The horses are slow and the heart is eager
> It is a hard road that they travel
> They are like the weed that floats on the pond
> The climbing plant that creeps along the wall.
> The moon over the royal palace looks down
> Upon their parting
> The parting of those who go to the east
> From those who go to the west.

CHAPTER 100

The End of Ximen's House

The wealth and splendor of the past
Are now as nothing.
The silver screens and golden halls
Are now the stuff of dreams.
The setting sun shines on the ruined walls
And the withered rushes.
A cold mist shrouds the ancient palace
And the green moss.
In the passage below the ground
The lamp is nearly out.
The phoenix mirror in the tiring room
Is locked and sealed away.
To whom shall I speak of ruin or prosperity?
The slow moving cloud is a priest's gown
And the wind fills its sleeves.

Han Daoguo and Wang Liu'er went back to the wine house. Their daughter had left them and they had no way of making a living. They sent Chen the Third for the merchant He. Now that Tiger Liu was no more, He had nothing to be afraid of. He came back again to Wang Liu'er. He said to Han Daoguo: "Your daughter has gone and she will not come back. I suggest that, when I have sold all my merchandise and got the money, you had better come back to Huzhou with me. It is better than carrying on this business here."

Han Daoguo thanked him and agreed. That same day the merchant sold all his goods, collected the money, hired a boat and started back with Han Daoguo and Wang Liu'er for Huzhou.

At the General's house, Han Aijie wore mourning with Cuiping. They called each other "Sister" and were very great friends. They spent their days with Chunmei. The General's little son was now six years old, and his daughter ten. The women had nothing to do but look after these children.

But the General was away on duty, and Jingji was dead. Though Chunmei had the choicest food to eat and the finest clothes to wear, though she had golden ornaments and jewels and pearls, everything that she might desire, yet at night she was lonely and she could not bear it. The fires of passion consumed her. She saw that Li An was a man full of vigor. After Zhang Sheng's death, he kept watch over the house and did his duty faithfully.

One winter day, when Li An was on duty in the office, he heard a knocking at the door and asked who was there. Whoever it was, no answer was given: he was simply bidden to open the door. He opened the door. Somebody rushed in and turned with her back to the light. Li An looked closely and saw that it was the nurse.

"Nurse," he said, "what are you doing here so late?"

"I have not come on my own account," she told him. "My lady has sent me."

"Why did she send you?"

"Don't you understand?" the nurse said, smiling. "She told me to come and see if you had gone to sleep. I was to give you these." She took some clothes from over her shoulder. They were women's clothes. "They are for your mother. The other day you had much trouble, bringing back all our master's things. And you saved my lady's life. If you had not been there that day, Zhang Sheng would have killed her."

She put down the clothes and went to the door. But she had hardly taken two steps before she turned around again. "There is something else for you," she said. From her sleeve she took a piece of silver worth about fifty taels, threw it to him, and went off. Li An could not understand what all this meant.

The next morning he took the clothes to his mother. She asked him where he had got them, and he told her what had happened the night before. His mother cried bitterly.

"Zhang Sheng," she said, "did wrong and he was killed. Now she gives you these things. What does it mean? I am more than sixty years old. Your father is dead, and you are my only hope. If anything happens to you, what will become of me? Don't go to that place again."

"If I don't go back, they will only send for me," Li An said. "What shall I do?"

"I will tell them you have a bad cold," his mother said.

"We can't tell them that story always," Li An said. "And my master will be angry with me."

"Go and spend a few months with your Uncle Li Gui," his mother said, "and then we will think what we can do."

Li An was a dutiful son. He did what his mother told him, packed up his luggage and went to Qingzhou to his uncle's place. When Chunmei found that the man did not come to her, she sent a boy for him several times. At first the old woman said her son was ill. Then people came and demanded to search the house, so she told them that he had gone to his native place to get some money. Chunmei was very disappointed.

The days passed quickly. The cold season came to an end, and the days grew warmer. In the first ten days of the first month the General, who was with eleven thousand men in Dongchangfu, sent Zhou Zhong with a letter to Chunmei. It directed his two ladies and their two children to go to him. Zhou Zhong was to stay at home to look after the place and the General's younger brother would look after the estate. This brother, Zhou Xuan, lived on the estate. Zhou Zhong and Cuiping were to remain with him. Zhou Ren with an escort of soldiers took the ladies to Dongchangfu.

At last the party arrived safely. The General was very pleased. He found a place for them at the back of his headquarters. Zhou Ren told his master that Zhou Xuan had gone to live at the house and that he and Zhou Zhong were taking care of it. Zhou Zhong was Zhou Ren's father.

"Where is Li An?" the General asked.

"You do well to mention Li An," Chunmei said. "I was very kind to him. 1 gave him clothes for his mother, thinking how he had secured Zhang Sheng that night. But one night, when he was supposed to be on guard, he came to the inner court and stole fifty taels of silver. The money, which was on the table, had come from your brother. I sent several times for him and answer came back that he was ill. Then I sent for him again, but he had run off to Qingzhou, his native place."

"I would never have believed it of him," the General said. "Later, I will see about his arrest."

Chunmei said nothing to the General about Han Aijie.

The days passed. General Zhou devoted all his energies to the duties of his office. So careful and diligent was he that he hardly took a minute for dinner in the middle of the day. He had no time at all for lovemaking.

Chunmei came to the conclusion that Zhou Yi, the second son of Zhou Zhong, was a fine, handsome lad. He was nineteen. She made her eyes and eyebrows carry a message to him and soon began an intrigue. Morning and night, they sat together, playing chess and drinking wine. The only man who did not know what was going on was the General himself.

The King of the Jin country had conquered the kingdom of Liao in the north. Then he gathered a great force and invaded China from two directions, at the very time of the new Emperor's coronation. General Nian Muhe with a hundred thousand men came down by way of Taiyuanfu in

Shanxi to attack the Eastern Capital. The second general, Gan Libu, came down from Tanzhou and made a raid upon Gaoyangguan. The troops on the frontier gave way, and the Minister of War and the Commander-in-Chief sent desperate orders to the six generals of Shandong, Shanxi, Henan, Hebei, Guandong and Shaanxi, to place their troops in the road of the invading forces and protect the cities. These generals were Liu Tingqing of Shaanxi, who was in command of the Yan Sui army; Wang Bing of Guandong, who commanded the Fen Jiang army; Wang Huan of Hebei, in command of the Wei Bo army; Xin Xingzong of Ho-nan, of the Zhang De army; Yang Weizong of Shanxi with the Ze Lu army, and Zhou Xiu of Shandong with the armies of Qing and Yan.

When General Zhou realized that the barbarians were massing on the frontier in such strength, and when letters so urgent came from the Ministry of War, he at once marshaled the army and advanced with forced marches. But when his advance guard came to Gaoyangguan, the enemy had already captured that city and there had been a great slaughter there. It was the beginning of the fifth month, and the wind suddenly raised such a sandstorm that the men could not open their eyes. The General was still advancing, when suddenly the enemy attacked. An arrow struck him in the neck and pierced his throat. He fell from his horse dead. The barbarians with hooks and cords tried to secure the body, but the General's own men recovered it and brought it back on a horse. That day many soldiers were wounded. General Zhou was only forty-seven.

When Zhang Shuye, the Commissioner, saw that the general was killed on the field of battle, he immediately ordered the gongs to be sounded as a signal for retirement. The roll was called; he found how many soldiers had been killed or wounded, and took the remainder of his forces back to Dongchang. From there he sent a report to his Majesty.

The killed were brought back by the army. Chunmei and those of her household cried so loudly that the sound shook the skies. They put the general into a coffin and returned his seal of office. Then Chunmei and Zhou Ren took the coffin and went back to Qinghe.

After Chunmei had gone away, Cuiping and Han Aijie ate only the simplest of food. They kept their word and lived as widows. One day, at the beginning of summer, when everything was fresh and bright and the days were lengthening, they took a walk and came to the summerhouse in the west courtyard. There the flowers were blooming, the orioles singing, and the swallows chattering. The beauty of the scene saddened them. Cuiping was not so much depressed, but Aijie, who was thinking of Jingji, was greatly stirred. Frequently, a familiar scene will produce this effect. She wept.

While they were in this sad state, Zhou Xuan came to them. "Sisters," he said, "you must not be so melancholy. You must try to be cheerful. I myself have had several bad dreams these last few nights. I dreamed that a bow was hanging from a flagpole and that the flag was torn in half. I don't know whether the omen should be taken as good or evil."

"It may mean something about the master," Han Aijie said.

They were trying to make up their minds when Zhou Ren came to them in mourning dress. He was in a great hurry.

"Evil news," he said. "Our master died on the field of battle on the seventh day of the fifth month. The mistress and the Second Lady are bringing his coffin."

Zhou Xuan hastily made arrangements to clear the outer hall. The coffin was brought in and set down there. They made offerings to the dead general, and all the members of the household cried and lamented. Then vegetarian food was prepared, and Daoist and Buddhist priests were summoned to hold a funeral service. The two children were dressed in mourning. A host of people called to offer their condolences. Finally, a suitable day was chosen, and they buried the General in the tomb of his ancestors.

Zhou Xuan, acting for his little nephew, sent a memorial to the Emperor asking that royal homage might be offered to the dead general and that some title might be conferred upon the child. The Emperor sent a document to the Ministry of War, and the Minister of War sent it on.

> This dead General, Zhou Xiu, forgot his own life in the service of his country [the document said]. His loyalty and courage are worthy of the highest praise. His Majesty therefore appoints an officer to offer food to the dead and confers upon him the title of Marshal. His son shall receive a pension and, when he is of age, shall inherit his father's rank and position.

Chunmei had nothing to live for now but pleasure, and her passions seemed stronger than ever. She often made Zhou Yi spend the whole day with her. He came to her in the morning and did not go away till evening. They enjoyed themselves without the slightest restraint. Then Chunmei began to suffer from a wasting sickness. She took medicine, but her appetite fell off. Her spirits were depressed, and her body became very thin. Still, she never gave up the joys she most loved.

It was the sixth month, and her birthday was past. The weather was hot. She did not rise early but stayed in bed with Zhou Yi. They were doing the work of love, when suddenly, her breath grew cold. Water came from her cunt, and she died with Zhou Yi still upon her body. She was twenty-nine years old.

The young man was alarmed. He opened Chunmei's boxes and stole gold and silver and all the jewels he could lay his hands on. Then he fled. The maids went to tell Zhou Xuan. The old man, Zhou Zhong, was put in chains and they went to find his son, Zhou Yi. He was arrested as he was going to his aunt's house. Zhou Xuan knew this, but he was afraid that all the dirty business would come out and that, if it became public property, it would be very unpleasant for his young nephew when he came of age. So he asked Zhou Yi no questions but simply ordered him to be given forty stripes. So Zhou Yi died. Jin'ge and the Second Lady were both present.

Chunmei's funeral was hastily arranged, and she was buried with the General. Zhou Xuan dismissed the two nurses and sent away the two girls, Haitang and Yuegui. Only Cuiping and Han Aijie still remained. Han Aijie refused to go.

Then the army of the Jin people captured the Eastern Capital. Both the reigning emperor, and his father were taken and sent to the north. So China was without an emperor and the empire was completely disrupted. Soldiers and war were everywhere, and men and women wandered over the face of the land. The common people cried as though they were drowning in mud, as if they were hung up by their legs. Then the barbarians invaded Shandong, and the people ran away in such a flurry that husband and wife often went in different directions. Fathers and sons lost each other. Devils cried, and Gods screamed.

Cuiping's mother took her away, and they fled for their lives. Han Aijie was left alone. She dressed herself simply, packed a few things, and set off for Linqing to find her parents. But, when she got to the wine house, the place was closed and the managers had fled. Fortunately, she met Chen the Third. He told her that her parents had gone to Huzhou with the merchant He. She went on. She had taken a moon guitar with her, and on the way she sang songs for the people. Day and night she traveled, like a stray dog escaping from confinement or a fish slipping out of the net. Her feet were very small and the journey was hard for her. After several days she came to Xuzhou. It was very late when she came to a lonely village. There she went to an old lady about seventy years old who was standing before a fire cooking rice. Han Aijie went to her and made a reverence.

"I am a native of Qinghe," she said to the old woman, "and I am on my way to find my parents because the country in the north is in such a disturbed state. It is late and I should like to spend the night with you. I must set off again early tomorrow. I will pay you."

The old woman realized that this was no poor girl. Her manner was too gentle and her face too beautiful. She asked the girl to come in and sit down. "I must get on with the cooking of this rice because the men want it," she said.

The old woman put more fuel on the fire. She prepared rice and beans, chopped up some vegetables, and put them with salt on two plates. Then a few men came in, all barelegged and rough-haired. They were wearing short trousers covered with mud. As they came in, they set down their shovels.

"Now, Mother," they said, "is dinner ready?"

"Come in and help yourselves," the old woman said to them. Each took his own food and vegetables and ate it by himself.

There was one man who seemed about forty-five or forty-six. He had a very red face and his hair was light. "Who is that sitting on the bed?" he said to the old woman.

"It is a lady from Qinghe. She is going south of the river to find her parents. It is very late, and she came and asked me if she might spend the night here."

The man asked her name.

"My name is Han," the girl said. "My father is called Han Daoguo."

The man went over to her and took her hand. "Are you not my niece, Han Aijie?" he asked her.

"You must be my uncle," Han Aijie cried.

They threw their arms around each other and wept. He asked where her parents were and why they had come back from the Eastern Capital, and how she had come to be there. Han Aijie told her uncle the whole story. "I married a man at General Zhou's place," she said. "Then my husband died and I did not marry again. Father and mother went to Huzhou with a merchant called He, and I am going to them. But the country where I have come from is in such an unsettled state that I could find no one who would take me there. So I came alone, and I have been singing on my way to get the necessaries of life. Then I met you."

"After your parents went to the Eastern Capital," Han said, "my business went to bits, so I sold the house and came here as a worker on the river. Every day, I earn just about enough to keep me. I will go with you to Huzhou."

"That will be splendid," Han Aijie said.

Her uncle gave her a bowl of rice, but it was such coarse stuff she could only swallow a mouthful. Finally, she succeeded in finishing half a bowl.

The next day, when all the other men had gone to their work, Han the Second paid the old woman and set out with Han Aijie. She was delicate and her feet were very small. The only property she had was a few pins and ornaments, and she sold these to pay for things on the journey. When they got to Huai An, they took a boat and came to Huzhou by river.

So, after a very long journey, they found Han Daoguo and his wife at Merchant He's place. He had died and left no wife, so Wang Liu'er was looking after his daughter, who was now six years old. He had left a few acres of rice fields. A year after the merchant's death, Han Daoguo died too. Wang Liu'er had been intimate with her brother-in-law before. Now they married regularly and worked in the fields to keep themselves alive.

Several of the rich young men of Huzhou wished to marry Han Aijie, when they saw how beautiful and clever she was. Her uncle urged her to marry one of them, but she cut off her hair, went to a temple, and became a nun. In her thirty-first year she fell ill and died.

The Jin army plundered Dongchangfu and came on to Qinghe. When they came there, the officers had fled and the city gates were closed, even by day. The people fled in all directions and fathers and sons lost each other. There was dust and mist everywhere, and yellow sand obscured the sun. The wild pigs and the great snakes attacked and devoured one another. Dragons and tigers fought for supremacy. Black banners and red flags appeared in the outskirts: men cried, women sobbed. There was tumult in every house. Valiant soldiers and heroic generals swarmed like ants and bees. Short daggers and long spears were as a thick bamboo forest. Here were corpses; there, decaying bones scattered on the ground. Broken swords and broken daggers lay about. People gathered their babies in their arms, bolted their doors, and shuttered their windows. They fled like rats. Nowhere was any trace of Music or the Rites.

Wu Yueniang learned that the barbarians had arrived and that people were fleeing. She took such valuables as she could and set off to Jinan with Uncle Wu the Second, Daian, Xiaoyu, and Xiaoge, who was now fifteen years old. She proposed to take refuge with Yun Lishou. Uncle Wu was dead. She locked all the doors of the house. She went to Yun Lishou; not only to escape the barbarians, but because she wished Xiaoge to marry there. On the way everybody she saw seemed terribly excited and afraid. The poor Yueniang, dressed in her plainest clothes, followed with the crowd. There were five of them altogether. They struggled and got out of the city. Then they hastened onward. At last they came to a crossroads. There stood a monk wearing a purple gown, a staff with nine rings in his hand. He had straw sandals and, on his shoulders he carried a cloth bag that contained his sacred books. He strode up to Yueniang and made a reverence to her.

"Lady," he said, "'where are you going? You must give my disciple to me now."

Yueniang was frightened and changed color.

"Father," she said, "what disciple do you mean?"

"Lady, don't pretend you do not know," the monk said. "Many years ago, when you were being pursued by Ying Tianxi at Taishan, you came to my cave and spent the night there. I am the old monk of that snow cave and my name is Pujing. You promised that I should have your baby for my disciple. Why have you not given him to me?"

"Master," Uncle Wu the Second said, "you are a priest, and you must not be so unreasonable. These are troublous times, and we are fleeing for our lives. She wants her son to continue the family. How can she let you have him?"

"Are you sure you will not give him to me?" the monk said.

"Don't talk like this, Master," Uncle Wu said. "We must be going on our way. The soldiers are behind us. Time is precious."

"It is late," the monk said. "You can go no farther now. If you will not give me the boy, come to my temple and go on your way tomorrow. Even if the Jin soldiers are coming, they will not be here yet."

"Where is your temple, Master?" Yueniang said.

The monk pointed to the other side of the road. "There is my temple," he said, and showed them the Temple of Eternal Felicity.

Yueniang had been there before and recognized the place. When they reached it, they found that the superiors had gone and there were only a few monks sitting in the hall at the back. A great glass lamp was still burning before the image of Buddha, and incense was burning too. It was nearly sunset.

Yueniang, Uncle Wu, Daian, Xiaoyu and Xiaoge spent the night in the temple. One or two of the young monks knew them and set out food for them. The old monk sat down in the hall and began to beat a wooden fish and recite the sacred books.

Yueniang, Xiaoyu, and Xiaoge slept in the same bed. Uncle Wu and Daian slept together in some other room. They were all very tired and, except for Xiaoyu, went straight to sleep. She got up and went to the room where the old monk was. Through a crack in the door she peeped in. He was still reading there.

It was the third night watch. The west wind was melancholy and the moon very dim. It was quiet everywhere. There was not a sound to be heard. The light before the statue of Buddha was very low.

Seeing the disturbed state of the Empire and the pitiful condition of the people, of whom so many had perished, the old monk was sorry.

With all his heart he prayed to Buddha that their sad spirits might be purified and that hatred might cease among men. He wished to clear the path so that all might come to paradise. A hundred times he recited the same text, which was for bringing peace to the minds of men.

After a while, the cold wind came sadly. Several scores of ghosts appeared. Their heads were burned, their cheeks torn, their hair was tousled and their faces dirty. Some had broken arms and legs, some had their bellies ripped open so that their bowels protruded. Some had no heads and some no limbs. Some had died by hanging and some had chains and cangues about their necks. They all came to the old monk and stood on either side of him while he prayed for them.

"You are men who have always repaid evil by evil," the old man said to them. "You have never had a thought of reconciliation in your hearts. I ask you: when shall this hatred cease? Listen to me, and I will send you to the place of your desire."

> I exhort you
> Hate not one another
> For hate deep rooted in the heart
> Can never be done away.
> Hatred may arise in a single day
> But in ten thousand days it will still exist.
> If you use hate to combat hate
> It is as though you cast water upon snow.
> If you return hatred for hatred
> It is as though a wolf meets a scorpion.
> Of men that quarrel, none, I know
> Escapes the bitterness of hate.
> This is a year of gloom
> I wish to make you understand.
> Regard your own true nature
> Then hatred and ill will will melt away to nothing.
> I look deep into the sacred texts
> To find salvation for all evildoers.
> Go now to be born again
> And forgo hate forevermore.

The ghosts all bowed to the old monk and vanished.

Xiaoyu looked at them carefully but could not recognize any of them. After a time, there entered a tall man, seven feet high. There was an arrow in his breast. This was General Zhou. After his death on the field of battle against the barbarians, he came to the Teacher to receive his blessing. Then he went to the Eastern Capital to be born again there as Cheng Shoushan, the son of Cheng Zhen.

The General had only just gone when there came a man in beautiful clothes. He said he was a wealthy citizen of Qinghe and his name was Ximen Qing. He had died from a trouble of the blood. He received the Teacher's blessing and went to the Eastern Capital to be born again as Cheng Yue, the son of Cheng Dong.

When Xiaoyu recognized Ximen Qing, she was afraid, and dared not make a sound.

Then came a young man with his head in his hands and his body all covered with blood. He said he was Chen Jingji and that he had been killed by Zhang Sheng. He received the Teacher's blessing and went to the Eastern Capital to become the son of a certain Wang.

When he had gone, there came a woman. She, too, held her head in her hands and her bosom was covered with blood. She said she was the wife of Wu Da and Ximen Qing's concubine, Pan Jinlian. Wu Song, her enemy, had killed her. She received the Teacher's blessing and went to the Eastern Capital to be born as the daughter of a certain Li.

Then came a short man with a purple face. He said his name was Wu and that he had been poisoned by Jinlian with the connivance of old woman Wang. He thanked the Teacher for his blessing and went to Xuzhou to be born as the son of a countryman named Fan.

He was followed by a woman, whose face was pale and thin. Water and blood issued from her body. She said she was Li Ping'er, the wife of Hua Zixu and a concubine of Ximen Qing. She received the Teacher's blessing and went to the Eastern capital to be daughter of General Yuan.

Another man followed who said he was Hua Zixu. He had died, he said, as a result of his wife's misdeeds. He received the Teacher's blessing and went to the Eastern Capital as the son of Captain Zheng.

Then came a woman whose face was pale and thin. She said she was Chunmei, the wife of General Zhou, and that she had died from overindulgence in the pleasures of love. She received the Teacher's blessing and went to the Eastern Capital to be the daughter of a wealthy man.

Then a woman whose head was bound with the wrappings of a woman's foot. She said she was the wife of Ximen Qing's servant, Laiwang. She had hanged herself. The Teacher's blessing was granted to her, and she went to the Eastern Capital to become the child of a certain Zhu.

Then came a man, naked, and with his hair all in disorder. His body was covered with bruises. His name, he said, was Zhang Sheng and he had been beaten to death. He received the Teacher's blessing and went to the Eastern Capital to be the son of a poor man named Gao.

He was followed by another woman who had a long white cloth wound around her neck. She said she was Sun Xue'e, a concubine of Ximen Qing. She had hanged herself. Now she received the Teacher's blessing and went outside the Eastern Capital to be the daughter of a poor man called Yao.

Then came a young woman who said she was Ximen's daughter and Chen Jingji's wife. She had foot ribbons about her neck. She had hanged herself. Now she received the Teacher's blessing and went outside the Eastern Capital to be the daughter of Zhong Gui, who was servant to a foreigner.

She was followed by a young man who said he was Zhou Yi. He had been beaten to death. He received the Teacher's blessing and went to the Eastern Capital to be the son of a certain Gao. He was going to be called Gao Liuzhu. Then he vanished.

Xiaoyu was terrified and shivering. She realized that this monk could indeed speak to the ghosts. She wished to tell Yueniang what she had seen, but Yueniang was fast asleep and dreaming. She dreamed that she and those with her had with them a hundred large pearls and a ring of great value. They were going to Jinanfu to see Yun Lishou. They reached the city and asked for Yun's place. Then people told Yun, and he knew that she had come about their children's marriage. They greeted one another as old friends. Mistress Yun had recently died and Yun sent for his neighbor, old woman Wang, to entertain Yueniang. She was taken to the inner court and given a great feast. Uncle Wu the Second and Daian were entertained elsewhere.

Then Yueniang talked about the marriage of their children and the troubles in the country. She offered the hundred pearls and the precious ring. Yun Lishou took them but said nothing about the marriage. In the evening, he told old woman Wang to sleep with Yueniang. He wished her to talk to Yueniang and find out what she thought.

The old woman said to Yueniang that, although Yun Lishou was only a military officer, he was an educated gentleman. Since they had arranged the marriage between their children, he had taken a great fancy to her. Now his wife was dead and he had not remarried. Though his position was not very high, he rode on horseback and had soldiers under his command. When he dismounted, he attended to public business. He had powers of life and death.

"Lady," the old woman said, "unless you think he is too far beneath you, he would ask you to marry him and it will be to the advantage of you both. Your son can marry too and he can go home when peace returns."

When Yueniang heard this, she was amazed. For a long time she could not speak. Then the old woman went to Yun Lishou and told him. The next evening, Yun Lishou prepared a great feast in the hall and invited Yueniang. She believed it was to celebrate the wedding of their children and went gladly. When she sat down, he said: "Sister, this is but a poor city, but I have a number of soldiers under my command. I have gold, property, clothes, and jewels in plenty. But I have no wife to manage my home for me. I have been thinking of you all this time, and now I feel like a man dying of thirst who craves for water to drink, or as one who seeks coolness in the broiling heat. You have come here, Lady, for your son's marriage. It is surely the will of Heaven that we should arrange not one but two marriages. If we marry, we shall be happy all our lives here. And I see no reason why we should not."

Yueniang was very angry. "I did not realize," she said, "that beneath a human form you hid the carcass of a dog. My husband always treated you well, yet now you speak to me in the language of dogs and horses."

Yun Lishou smiled and went closer to her. He put his arms about her and pleaded.

"Lady," he said, "why did you come here? You came and, why I cannot tell, my spirit seemed to become wholly yours the moment I saw you. I cannot help it, and we must marry."

He offered wine to her.

"Send for my brother," Yueniang said.

"Your brother!" Yun Lishou said, laughing. "I have killed both him and Daian." He ordered a servant to bring proof of what he said. Two heads, blood still dripping from them, were brought in. Yueniang looked at them in the candlelight and her face became as pale as yellow earth. She cried and fell to the floor. Yun Lishou raised her up.

"Lady," he said, "you must not be sad. Your brother is dead, but I am asking you to marry me. I am not unworthy of you. I am a military officer of high rank."

"This man," Yueniang thought, "has murdered my brother and my servant. If I do not yield, he will kill me too." She began to smile.

"You must do what I wish," she said, "and then I will marry you."

"I will do anything you ask, no matter what it is," Yun Lishou said.

"First let your daughter marry my boy, and then I will marry you."

"Good!" Yun Lishou said. He sent for his daughter and pushed her over to Xiaoge. They drank wine together, exchanged the knotted heart, and so were married. Then Yun Lishou pulled Yueniang to him, and wished to make love to her, but she struggled with him. He was furious.

"You whore!" he cried, "you have deceived me. You got me to marry my daughter to your son. Do you think I am afraid to kill your son?" He drew his sword, and with one blow struck off the boy's head. The blood spurted for yards.

When her child was killed, Yueniang shrieked.

Then she woke up. It was a dream. She was so terrified that her body was drenched with sweat. "Strange! Strange!" she murmured.

"Lady, why are you crying?" Xiaoyu said to her.

"I have had a terrible nightmare," Yueniang said, and told her every-thing she had dreamed.

"A little while ago," Xiaoyu said, "I found I could not sleep. I went to watch the old monk. He was speaking to the ghosts. I saw him talking to my master, the Fifth Lady, Chen Jingji, Sun Xue'e, General Zhou, Lai-wang's wife and your daughter. Then they all disappeared.

"Some of them were buried outside this temple," Yueniang said, "but they died such miserable deaths that they come to the monk. It is so quiet too."

The two women talked until the fifth night watch. The cocks began to crow. Yueniang washed her face and dressed her hair. Then she went to the sanctuary and burned incense before the statue of Buddha. The old monk was there, sitting on a low stool. "Lady," he said in a loud voice, "I think you know now what I mean."

Yueniang knelt down. "Holy Master," she said, "with my fleshly eyes and human body, I did not know that you were Buddha himself. Now, since I have had that dream, I know everything."

"You understand," the old monk said, "so now there is no need for you to go to that man. If you do go, you will find that things happen exactly as they did in your dream. You will all die. It is fortunate for your son that you have met me. It is a reward for your good heart. Had it not been for this, you and your son must soon have parted. You remember what a bad man your husband Ximen Qing was. Your son is your husband. He would spend all your money, ruin your estate, and die by having his head cut off. Now I bless him, and take him as my disciple. You know the proverb that says when a son becomes a monk there is salvation for nine generations. If he becomes a monk, your husband's misdeeds will be forgiven. If you do not believe me, come and see."

He rose and went quickly to the other room where Xiaoge was asleep. The old monk lifted his staff and gently touched the boy's head. He turned around suddenly, and Yueniang saw that it was Ximen Qing. Upon his neck was a heavy cangue and there were chains about his waist.

The old monk touched him again with his staff, and again Xiaoge lay upon the bed.

Yueniang cried. She realized that Xiaoge was another incarnation of Ximen Qing. After a while the boy woke up.

"You are going to stay here," his mother said to him, "and become the disciple of this holy teacher. He will cut off your hair and give you orders in the name of Buddha."

Yueniang took the lad in her arms and cried bitterly. She felt that she had brought him up in vain. He was fifteen years old, and she had hoped that he would inherit the property and continue the family. Now the old monk was taking him. Uncle Wu the Second, Xiaoyu, and Daian were all sad. The old monk took the boy and called him Mingwu [Bright Enlightenment].

When Yueniang was going away, the old monk said to her: "You need go no farther. The Jin army is going to retreat. Then land will be divided between two dynasties and we shall have an Emperor again. In ten days all the soldiers will withdraw and peace will be restored. Go home then and spend the rest of your days in peace."

"Master," Yueniang said, "you have blessed my child. When shall I see him again?" She clasped the boy in her arms and cried aloud.

"Lady, don't cry," the old monk said. "Look, there is a Holy Master coming."

They all turned their heads to look, but when they turned around again, the old monk had vanished and become a pure vapor. He took Xiaoge with him.

Yueniang, her brother, and the others stayed ten days more at the temple. Then indeed the Jin people made Zhang Bangchang Emperor at the Eastern Capital, and set up a new administration, both civil and military. The two emperors, Huizong and Qinzong, were taken to the north. Then Prince Kang crossed the river on a clay horse and established himself as Emperor Gaozong at Jiankang. He appointed Zong Ze as his commander-in-chief and took back Shandong and Hebei. Thus the empire was divided into two parts. Soon peace was restored, and people returned to their old occupations. Yueniang went home. She opened all the doors and windows. Nothing had been disturbed.

She gave the name Ximen An to Daian who, in due course, came into the property. People called him Master Ximen. He lived with Yueniang. When she was seventy years old, Yueniang died. Her end was peaceful, a fitting reward for her kindness and virtue.

The record of this house must make us sad.
Who can deny that Heaven's principle
Goes on unceasingly?
Ximen was mighty and a lawless man
He could not maintain the issue of his house.
Jingji was wild and dissolute
And met a violent death in consequence.
Yueniang and Yulou lived long
And ended their days in peace.
Chunmei and Ping'er were wanton
And soon made their way to Hell.
It is not strange, therefore,
That Jinlian reaped the reward of evil,
Leaving a foul reputation to be spoken of
A thousand years.

THE END